# FORGE OF DARKNESS

# FORGE OF DARKNESS

Steven Erikson

A Tom Doherty Associates Book
New York

FORGE OF DARKNESS

Copyright © 2012 by Steven Erikson

Simultaneously published in Great Britain by Bantam Press, an imprint of Transworld Publishers

A Tor Book
Published by Tom Doherty Associates, LLC
175 Fifth Avenue
New York, NY 10010

www.tor-forge.com

Tor® is a registered trademark of Tom Doherty Associates, LLC.

Library of Congress Cataloging-in-Publication Data

Erikson, Steven.
   Forge of darkness / Steven Erikson. — 1st U.S. ed.
       p. cm.
   "A Tom Doherty Associates book."
   ISBN 978-0-7653-2356-9 (hardcover)
   ISBN 978-1-4668-1418-9 (e-book)
   I. Title.
   PR9199.4.E745F67 2012
   813'.6—dc23

                                                    2012024403

First U.S. Edition: September 2012

Printed in the United States of America

0  9  8  7  6  5  4  3  2  1

Clare Thomas, with love

# Contents

# Acknowledgements

Thank you to my advance readers: Aidan Paul Canavan, Sharon Sasaki, Darren Turpin, William and Hazel Hunter and Baria Ahmed.

# KHARKANAS
## (central)

**a**: Tailings and refuse heaps

**b**: Pits and sinkholes

**c**: Settling pools

**d**: Crypts

N

1. The Citadel
2. Hish Residence
3. Silann Residence
4. Purake Residence
5. River Market
6. Degalla House
7. Rend Residence
8. Durav Residence
9. Hust Sanctum
10. Skellor Village
11. Old Royal Vaults

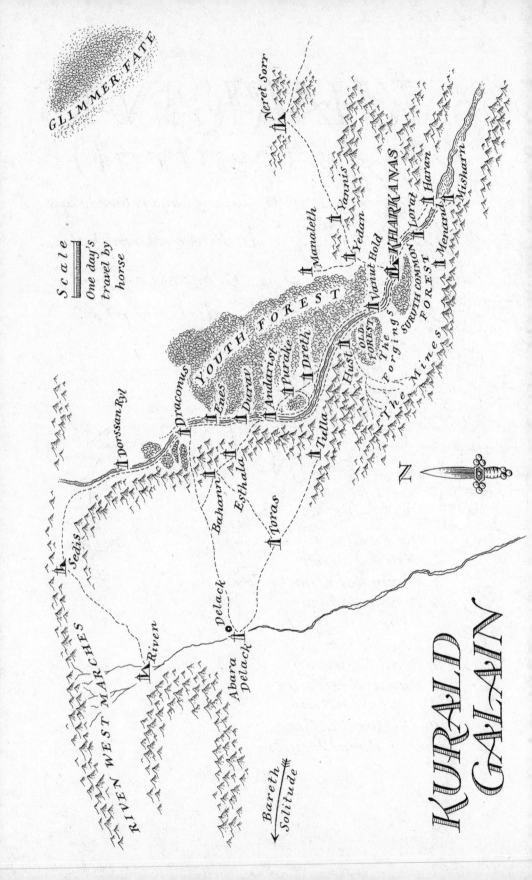

# THEL AKAI, JAGHUT, TISTE REALMS

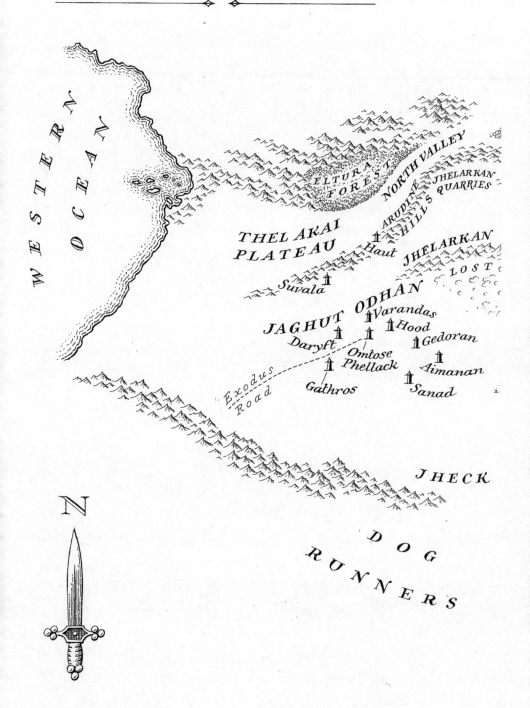

# DRAMATIS PERSONAE

*PURAKE HOLD*

Anomander
Andarist
Silchas Ruin
Kellaras
Prazek
Dathenar

*DRACONS HOLD*

Draconus
Ivis
Spite
Envy
Malice
Arathan
Raskan
Sagander

*TULLA HOLD*

Hish Tulla
Rancept
Sukul Ankhadu (hostage)

## HOUSE ENES

Jaen Enes
Enesdia
Kadaspala
Cryl Durav (hostage)

## HOUSE DURAV

Spinnock Durav
Faror Hend

## HUST HOLD (and Legion)

Hust Henarald
Calat Hustain
Finarra Stone
Toras Redone
Galar Baras

## ABARA DELACK

Korya Delath
Nerys Drukorlat
Sandalath Drukorlat
Orfantal
Wreneck

## NERET SORR

Vatha Urusander
Osserc
Hunn Raal
Risp
Sevegg
Serap
Renarr
Gurren

## URUSANDER'S LEGION OFFICERS

Scara Bandaris
Ilgast Rend
Hallyd Bahann

Esthala
Kagamandra Tulas
Sharenas Ankhadu
Tathe Lorat
Infayen Menand

## THE BORDERSWORDS

Rint
Ville
Feren
Galak
Lahanis
Traj

## THE CITADEL

Syntara
Emral Lanear
Endest Silann
Cedorpul
Rise Herat
Legyl Behust
Mother Dark

## THE SHAKE

Sheccanto Derran
Warlock Resh
Caplo Dreem
Skelenal
Witch Ruvera

## THE AZATHANAI

Grizzin Farl
Kilmandaros
Sechul Lath
Errastas
Caladan Brood
T'riss
Old Man

## THE JAGHUT

Hood
Gothos
Haut
Varandas
Korya Delath (hostage)

## OTHERS

Gripp Galas
Haral
Narad
Bursa
Olar Ethil

# The Tiste: Holds, Greater and Lesser Houses, Priesthood and Court

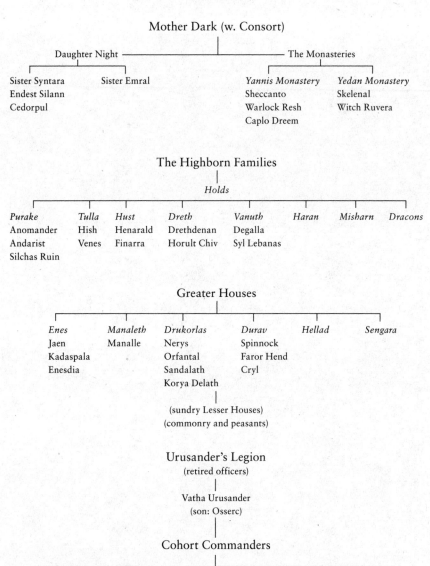

Mother Dark (w. Consort)

Daughter Night ——————————————— The Monasteries

| Sister Syntara | Sister Emral | | Yannis Monastery | Yedan Monastery |
|---|---|---|---|---|
| Endest Silann | | | Sheccanto | Skelenal |
| Cedorpul | | | Warlock Resh | Witch Ruvera |
| | | | Caplo Dreem | |

## The Highborn Families

*Holds*

| Purake | Tulla | Hust | Dreth | Vanuth | Haran | Misharn | Dracons |
|---|---|---|---|---|---|---|---|
| Anomander | Hish | Henarald | Drethdenan | Degalla | | | |
| Andarist | Venes | Finarra | Horult Chiv | Syl Lebanas | | | |
| Silchas Ruin | | | | | | | |

## Greater Houses

| Enes | Manaleth | Drukorlas | Durav | Hellad | Sengara |
|---|---|---|---|---|---|
| Jaen | Manalle | Nerys | Spinnock | | |
| Kadaspala | | Orfantal | Faror Hend | | |
| Enesdia | | Sandalath | Cryl | | |
| | | Korya Delath | | | |

(sundry Lesser Houses)
(commonry and peasants)

## Urusander's Legion
(retired officers)

Vatha Urusander
(son: Osserc)

## Cohort Commanders

Scara Bandaris   Ilgast Rend   Hallyd Bahann   Esthala   Tulas Shorn   Sharenas Ankhadu   Infayen   Tathe Lorat

# PRELUDE

---

*. . . so you have found me and would know the tale. When a poet speaks of truth to another poet, what hope has truth? Let me ask this, then. Does one find memory in invention? Or will you find invention in memory? Which bows in servitude before the other? Will the measure of greatness be weighed solely in the details? Perhaps so, if details make up the full weft of the world, if themes are nothing more than the composite of lists perfectly ordered and unerringly rendered; and if I should kneel before invention, as if it were memory made perfect.*

*Do I look like a man who would kneel?*

*There are no singular tales. Nothing that stands alone is worth looking at. You and me, we know this. We could fill a thousand scrolls recounting the lives of those who believe they are each both beginning and end, those who fit the totality of the universe into small wooden boxes which they then tuck under one arm – you have seen them marching past, I'm sure. They have somewhere to go, and wherever that place is, why, it needs them, and failing their dramatic arrival it would surely cease to exist.*

*Is my laughter cynical? Derisive? Do I sigh and remind myself yet again that truths are like seeds hidden in the ground, and should you tend to them who may say what wild life will spring into view? Prediction is folly, belligerent assertion pathetic. But all such arguments are past us now. If we ever spat them out it was long ago, in another age, when we both were younger than we thought we were.*

*This tale shall be like Tiam herself, a creature of many heads. It is in my nature to wear masks, and to speak in a multitude of voices through lips not my own. Even when I had sight, to see through a* single pair of eyes was a kind of torture, for I knew – I could feel in my soul – that we with our single visions miss most of the world. We cannot help it. It is our barrier to understanding. Perhaps it is only the poets who truly resent this way of being. No matter; what I do not recall I shall invent.

There are no singular tales. A life in solitude is a life rushing to death. But a blind man will never rush; he but feels his way, as befits an uncertain world. See me, then, as a metaphor made real.

I am the poet Gallan, and my words will live for ever. This is not a boast. It is a curse. My legacy is a carcass in waiting, and it will be picked over until dust devours all there is. And when my last breath is long gone, see how the flesh still moves, see how it flinches.

When I began, I did not imagine finding my final moments here upon an altar, beneath a hovering knife. I did not believe my life was a sacrifice; not to any greater cause, nor as payment into the hands of fame and respect. I did not think any sacrifice was necessary at all.

No one lets dead poets lie in peace. We are like old meat on a crowded dinner table. Now comes the next course to jostle what's left of us, and even the gods despair of ever cleaning up the mess. But there are truths between poets, and we both know well their worth. It is the gristle we chew without end.

Anomandaris. That is a brave title. But consider this: I was not always blind. It is not Anomander's tale alone. My story will not fit into a small box. Indeed, he is perhaps the least of it. A man pushed from behind by many hands will go in but one direction, no matter what he wills.

It may be that I do not credit him enough. I have my reasons.

You ask: where is my place in this? It is nowhere. Come to Kharkanas, here in my memory, in my creation. Walk the Hall of Portraits and you will not find my face. Is this what it is to be lost, in the very world that made you, that holds your flesh? Do you in your world share my plight? Do you wander and wonder? Do you start at your own shadow, or awaken to rattling disbelief that this is all you are, prospects bleak, bereft of the proof of your ambition?

Or do you march past sure of your frown and indeed that is a fine box you carry . . .

Am I the world's only lost soul?

Do not begrudge my smile at that. I too cannot be made to fit into that small box, though many will try. No, best discard me entire, if peace of mind is desired.

The table is crowded, the feast unending. Join me upon it, amidst *the wretched scatter and heaps. The audience is hungry and its hunger is endless. And for that, we are thankful. And if I spoke of sacrifices, I lied.*

*Remember well this tale I tell, Fisher kel Tath. Should you err, the list-makers will eat you alive.*

# PART ONE

---

*In these gifts the shapes of adoration*

# ONE

T*HERE WILL BE PEACE.*
The words were carved deep across the lintel stone's facing in the ancient language of the Azathanai. The cuts looked raw, untouched by wind or rain, and because of this, they might have seemed as youthful and as innocent as the sentiment itself. A witness lacking literacy would see only the violence of the mason's hand, but surely it is fair to say that the ignorant are not capable of irony. Yet like the house-hound who by scent alone will know a guest's true nature, the uncomprehending witness surrenders nothing when it comes to subtle truths. Accordingly, the savage wounding of the lintel stone's basalt face remained imposing and significant to the unversed, even as the freshness of the carved words gave pause to those who understood them.

*There will be peace.* Conviction is a fist of stone at the heart of all things. Its form is shaped by sure hands, the detritus quickly swept from view. It is built to withstand, built to defy challenge, and when cornered it fights without honour. There is nothing more terrible than conviction.

It was generally held that no one of Azathanai blood could be found within Dracons Hold. Indeed, few of those weary-eyed creatures from beyond Bareth Solitude ever visited the city-state of Kurald Galain, except as stone-cutters and builders of edifices, summoned to some task or venture. But the Hold's lord was not a man to welcome questions in matters of personal inclination. If by an Azathanai hand ambivalent words were carved above the threshold to the Hold's Great House – as if to announce a new age with either a promise or a threat – that was solely the business of Lord Draconus, Consort to Mother Dark.

In any case, it was not often of late that the Hold was home to its lord, now that he stood at her side in the Citadel of Kharkanas, making his sudden return after a night's hard ride both disquieting and the source of whispered rumours.

The thunder of horse hoofs approached through the faint light of the sun's rise – a light ever muted by the Hold's nearness to the heart of Mother Dark's power – and that sound grew until it rumbled through the arched gateway and pounded into the courtyard, scattering red clay from the road beyond. Neck arched by the reins held tight in his master's gloved hands, the warhorse Calaras drew up, breath billowing, lather streaming down its sleek black neck and chest. The sight gave the onrushing grooms pause.

The huge man commanding this formidable beast then dismounted, abandoning the reins to dangle, and strode without comment into the Great House. Household servants scrambled like hens from his path.

There was no hint of emotion upon the Lord's face, but this was a detail well known and not unexpected. Draconus gave nothing away, and perhaps it was the mystery in those so-dark eyes that had ever been the source of his power. His likeness, brushed by the brilliant artist Kadaspala of House Enes, now commanded pride of place in the Citadel's Hall of Portraits, and it was indeed a hand of genius that had managed to capture the unknowable in Draconus's visage, the hint of something beyond the perfection of his Tiste features, a deepening behind the proof of his pure blood. It was the image of a man who was king in all but name.

*     *     *

Arathan stood at the window of the Old Tower, having taken position there upon hearing the bell announcing his father's imminent return. He watched Draconus ride into the courtyard, eyes missing nothing, one hand up to his face as he bit skin and pieces of nail from his fingers – the tips were red nubs, swollen with endless spit, and on occasion they bled, staining the sheets of his bed at night. He studied the movements of Draconus as the huge man dismounted, carelessly abandoning Calaras to the grooms, to then stride towards the entrance.

The three-storey tower commanded the northwest corner of the Great House, with the house's main doors to the right and out of sight from the upper floor's window. At moments like these, Arathan would tense, breath held, straining with all his senses for the moment when his father crossed the threshold and set foot on the hard bared stones of the vestibule. He waited, for a change in the atmosphere, a trembling in the ancient walls of the edifice, the very thunder of the Lord's presence.

As ever, there was nothing. And Arathan never knew if the failing was his, or if his father's power was sealed away inside that imposing frame and behind those unerring eyes, contained by a will verging on perfection. He suspected the former – he saw how others reacted, the tightening of expressions among the highborn, the shying away of those of lesser rank, and how on occasion both reactions warred within the same individual. Draconus was feared for reasons Arathan could not comprehend.

In truth, he did not expect more of himself in this matter. He was a bastard son, after all, and a child born of a mother he never knew and had never heard named. In his seventeen years of life he had been in the same room with his father perhaps twenty times; surely no more than that, and not once had Draconus addressed him. He was not privileged to dine in the main hall; he was tutored in private and taught the use of weapons alongside the recruits of the Houseblades. Even in the days and nights immediately following his near-drowning, when in his ninth winter he'd fallen through ice, he'd been attended to by the guards' healer, and had received no visitors barring his three younger half-sisters, who had peered in through the doorway – a trio of round, wide-eyed faces – only to immediately flee down the corridor voicing squeals.

For years, their reaction upon seeing him had led Arathan to believe he was unaccountably ugly, a conviction that had first brought his hands to his face in a habit of hiding his features, and soon the kiss of his own fingertips served for all the tactile reassurance he required. He no longer believed himself to be ugly. Simply . . . plain, not worthy of notice by anyone.

Though no one ever spoke of his mother, Arathan knew that she had named him. His father's predilections on such matters were far crueller. He told himself that he remembered his half-sisters' mother, a brooding, heavy woman with a strange face, who had either died or departed shortly after weaning the triplets she had borne, but a later comment from Tutor Sagander suggested that the woman he'd remembered had been a wet-nurse, a witch of the Dog-Runners who dwelt beyond the Solitude. Still, he preferred to think of her as the girls' mother, too kind-hearted to give them the names they now possessed – names that, to Arathan's mind, shackled each sister like a curse.

*Envy. Spite. Malice.* They remained infrequent visitors to his company. Flighty as birds glimpsed from the corner of an eye. Whispering from around corners in the corridors and behind doors he walked past. Clearly, they found him a source of great amusement.

Now in the first years of adulthood, Arathan saw himself as a prisoner, or perhaps a hostage in the traditional manner of alliance-binding among the Greater Houses and Holds. He was not of the Dracons family; though there had been no efforts at hiding his bloodline, in fact the very indifference of this detail only emphasized its irrelevance. Seeds spill where they may, but a sire must look into the eyes to make the child his own. And this Draconus would not do. Besides, there was little of Tiste blood in him – he had not the fair skin or tall frame, and his eyes, while dark, lacked the mercurial ambivalence of the pure-born. In these details, he was the same as his sisters. Where, then, the blood of their father?

*It hides. Somehow, it hides deep within us.*

Draconus would not acknowledge him, but that was no cause for resentment in Arathan's mind. Man or woman, once childhood was past the world beyond must be met, and a place in it made, by a will entirely dependent upon its own resources. And the shaping of that world, its weight and weft, was a match to the strength of that will. In this way, Kurald Galain society was a true map of talent and capacity. Or so Sagander told him, almost daily.

Whether in the court of the Citadel or among the March villages, there could be no dissembling. The insipid and the incompetent had no place in which to hide their failings. *'This is natural justice, Arathan, and thus by every measure it is superior to the justice of, say, the Forulkan, or the Jaghut.'* Arathan had no good reason to believe otherwise. This world, so forcefully espoused by his tutor, was all he had ever known.

And yet he . . . doubted.

Sandalled feet slapped closer up the spiral stairs behind him, and Arathan turned in some surprise. He had long since claimed this tower for his own, made himself lord of its dusty webs, its shadows and echoes. Only here could he be himself, with no one batting his hand away from his mouth, or mocking his ruined fingertips. No one visited him here; the house-bells called him when lessons or meals were imminent; he measured his days and nights by those muted chimes.

The footsteps approached. His heart thumped in his chest. He snatched his hand away from his mouth, wiped the fingers on his tunic, and stood facing the gap of the stairs.

The figure that climbed into view startled him. One of his half-sisters, the shortest of the three – *last from the womb* – her face flushed with the effort of the climb, her breath coming in little gasps. Dark eyes found his. 'Arathan.'

She had never before addressed him. He did not know how to respond.

'It's me,' she said, eyes flaring as if in anger. 'Malice. Your sister, Malice.'

'Names shouldn't be curses,' Arathan said without thinking.

If his words shocked her, the only indication was a faint tilt of her head as she regarded him. 'So you're not the simpleton Envy says you are. Good. Father will be . . . relieved.'

'Father?'

'You are summoned, Arathan. Right now – I'm to bring you to him.'

'Father?'

She scowled. 'She knew you'd be hiding here, like a redge in a hole. Said you were just as thick. Are you? Is she right? Are you a redge? She's always right – or so she'll tell you.' She darted close and took Arathan's left wrist, tugged him along as she returned to the stairs.

He did not resist.

Father had summoned him. He could think of only one reason for that.

*I am about to be cast out.*

The dusty air of the Old Tower stairs swirled round them as they descended, and the peace of this place felt shattered. But soon it would settle again, and the emptiness would return, like an ousted king to his throne, and Arathan knew that he would never again challenge that domain. It had been a foolish conceit, a childish game.

*'In natural justice, Arathan, the weak cannot hide, unless we grant them the privilege. And understand, it is ever a privilege, for which the weak should be eternally grateful. At any given moment, should the strong will it, they can swing a sword and end the life of the weak. And that will be today's lesson. Forbearance.'*

A redge in a hole – the beast's life is tolerated, until its presence becomes a nuisance, and then the dogs are loosed down the earthen tunnel, into the warrens, and somewhere beneath the ground the redge is torn apart, ripped to pieces. Or driven into the open, where wait spears and swords eager to take its life.

Either way, the creature was clearly unmindful of the privileges granted to it.

All the lessons Sagander delivered to Arathan circled like wolves around weakness, and the proper place of those cursed with it. No, Arathan was not a simpleton. He understood well enough.

And, one day, he would hurt Draconus, in ways not yet imaginable. *Father, I believe I am your weakness.*

In the meantime, as he hurried along behind Malice, her grip tight on his wrist, he brought up his other hand, and chewed.

\*　　\*　　\*

Master-at-arms Ivis wiped sweat from his brow while he waited outside the door. The summons had come while he'd been in the smithy, instructing the iron-master on the proper honing of a folded edge. It was said that those with Hust blood knew iron as if they'd suckled its molten stream from their mother's tit, and Ivis had no doubt in this matter – the smith was a skilled man and a fine maker of weapons, but Ivis possessed Hust blood on his father's side, and though he counted himself a soldier through and through, he could hear a flawed edge even as a blade was being drawn from its scabbard.

Iron-master Gilal took it well enough, although of course there was no telling. He'd ducked his head and muttered his apologies as befitted his lesser rank, and as Ivis left he heard the huge man bellowing at his apprentices – none of whom was in any way responsible for the flawed edge, since the final stages of blade preparation were always by the iron-master's own hand. With that tirade Ivis knew that no venom would come back his way from the iron-master.

He told himself now, as he waited outside his lord's Chamber of Campaigns, that the sweat stinging his eyes was a legacy of the four forges in the smithy, the air wretched with heat and bitter metal, with coal dust and smoke, with the frantic efforts of the workers as they struggled with the day's demands.

Abyss knew, the smithy was no factory, and yet it had achieved an impressive rate of stock production in the past two months, and not one of the new recruits coming to the Great House was left unarmoured or weaponless for long. Making his task that much easier.

But now the Lord was back, unexpectedly, and Ivis scoured his mind for the possible cause. Draconus was a measured man, not prone to precipitous acts. He had the patience of stone, but all knew the risk of wronging him. Something had brought him back to the Great House, and a night's hard ride would not have left him in a good mood.

And now a summons, only to be left waiting here outside the door. No, none of this was normal.

A moment later he heard footsteps and the portal clicked open. Ivis found himself staring into the face of the House tutor, Sagander. The old scholar had the look of a man who had been frightened and was still fighting its aftermath. Meeting Ivis's eyes, he nodded. 'Captain, the Lord will see you now.'

That, and nothing more. Sagander edged past, made his way down the passageway, walking as if he'd aged a half-dozen years in the last few moments. At the notion, Ivis berated himself. He hardly ever saw the tutor, who overslept every morning and was often the last to make bed at night – there was no reason to imagine Sagander was anything more than disquieted by the early meeting, and perhaps an understandable stiffness as came with the elderly this early in the morning.

Drawing a steadying breath, Ivis strode into the chamber.

The old title of this room was acquiring new significance, but the campaigns of decades past had been conducted against foreign enemies; this time the only enemy was the mutually exclusive ambitions of the Holds and Greater Houses. The Lord's charnel house smithy was nothing more than reasonable caution these days. Besides, as Mother Dark's Consort, there was nothing unusual in Draconus bolstering the complement of his Houseblades until it was second only to that of Mother Dark herself. For some reason, other Holds were not as sanguine about the martial expansion of House Dracons.

The politics of the matter held no real interest for Ivis. His task was to train this modest army.

The round table dominating the centre of the room had been cut from the bole of a three-thousand-year-old blackwood. Its rings were bands of red and black beneath the thick, amber varnish. It had been placed in this chamber by the founder of the House half a thousand years ago, to mark her extraordinary rise from Lesser House to Greater House. Since her sudden death ten years past, her adopted son, Draconus, commanded the family holdings; and if Srela's ambitions had been impressive, they were nothing compared to those of her chosen son.

There were no portraits on the walls, and the heavy wool hangings, undyed and raw, were there for warmth alone, as was the thick rug underfoot.

Draconus was breaking his fast at the table: bread and watered wine. A scatter of scrolls surrounded the pewter plate before him.

When it seemed that Draconus had not noticed his arrival, Ivis said, 'Lord.'

'Report on his progress, captain.'

Ivis frowned, resisted wiping at his brow again. Upon reflection, he'd known this was coming. The boy was in his year, after all. 'He possesses natural skill, Lord, as befits his sire. But his hands are weak yet – that habit of gnawing on his nails has left the pads soft and easily torn.'

'Is he diligent?'

Still Draconus was yet to look up, intent on his meal.

'At his exercises, Lord? It is hard to say. There is an air of the effortless about him. For all that I work him, or set the best recruits against him on the sand, he remains . . . unpressed.'

Draconus grunted. 'And does that frustrate you, captain?'

'That I have yet to truly test him, yes, Lord, it does. I do not have as much time with him as I would like, though I understand the necessity for higher tutoring. Still, as a young swordsman, there is much to admire in his ease.'

Finally, the Lord glanced up. 'Is there, now?' He leaned back, pushing the plate away with its remnants of crust and drippings. 'Find him a decent sword, some light chain, gauntlets, vambraces and greaves. And a helm. Then instruct the stables to ready him a solid warhorse – I know, he has not yet learned to ride a charger, so be sure the beast is not wilful.'

Ivis blinked. 'Lord, every horse is wilful beneath an uncertain rider.'

As if he'd not heard, Draconus continued, 'A mare, I think, young, eager to fix eye and ear on Calaras.'

*Eager? More like terrified.*

Perhaps Ivis had given something of his thoughts away in his face, for his lord smiled. 'Think you I cannot control my mount? Oh, and a spare horse along with the charger. One of the walkers. Make it a gelding.'

*Ah, then not returning to Kharkanas.* 'Lord, shall this be a long journey?'

Draconus stood, and only now did Ivis note the shadows under the man's eyes. 'Yes,' and then as if answering a question Ivis had not voiced, 'and this time, I shall ride with my son.'

\* \* \*

Malice pulled him into the corridor leading to the Chamber of Campaigns. Arathan knew it only by name; not once had he ventured into his father's favoured room. He drew back, stretching the link between himself and his sister.

She twisted round, face darkening – and then she suddenly relaxed, loosening her grip on his wrist. 'Like a hare in the autumn, you are. Is that what you think he wants to see?'

'I don't know what he wants to see,' Arathan replied. 'How could I?'

'Did you see Clawface Ivis leaving? He was just ahead – took the courtyard passage. He'll have reported on you. He'll have talked about you. And now Father's waiting. To see for himself.'

'Clawface?'

'Because of his scars—'

'Those aren't scars,' Arathan said, 'it's just age. Ivis Yerrthust fought in the Forulkan War. They starved on the retreat – they all did. That's where those lines on his face came from.'

She was staring at him as if he'd lost his wits. 'What do you think will happen, Arathan?'

'About what?'

'If he doesn't like what he sees.'

Arathan shrugged. Even this close to his father – thirty paces down a broad corridor and then a door – still he could feel nothing. The air was unchanged, as if power was nothing but an illusion. The notion startled him, but he would not draw close to it, not yet. This was not the time to see where it led.

'He'll kill you,' said Malice.

He studied her face, caught the amused glint, the faintest hint of a smirk. 'Names shouldn't be curses,' he said.

She pointed up the corridor. 'He's waiting. We'll probably never see you again, unless we go behind the kitchen – below the chute where the carved-up bones and guts come out. Bits of you will be on the Crow Mound. I'll keep a lock of your hair. Knotted. I won't even wash out the blood.'

Pushing past him, she hurried away.

*Clawface is a cruel name. I wonder what name they've given me.*

He set his eyes on the distant door and set off, footfalls echoing. His father would not kill him. He could have done that long ago, and there was no reason to now. None of Arathan's own failings reflected a thing upon his father. Sagander told him so, over and over again. This was not a settling of shadows, because the sun's light, no matter how pale or dim, could never descry the binding lines of blood, and in place of light no words had been spoken to make it otherwise.

Reaching the door, he hesitated, wiped dry his fingers, and then rattled the iron loop beneath the latch. A muted voice bid him enter. Wondering at his lack of fear, Arathan opened the door and stepped into the chamber.

A heavy lanolin smell was the first thing to strike him, and then the light, sharp and bright from the east-facing window where the shutters had been thrown back. The air was still cool but rapidly warming as the day awakened. The sight of breakfast leavings on the enormous table reminded him that he'd not yet eaten. When his gaze finally lifted to his father, he found the man's dark eyes fixed on him.

'It may be,' said Draconus, 'that you believe she did not want you. You have lived a life with no answers to your questions – but for that I will not apologize. She knew that her choice would hurt you. I can tell you that it hurt her, as well. I hope that one day you will understand this, and that, indeed, you will find it in your heart to forgive her.'

Arathan said nothing because he could not think of anything to say. He watched as his father rose from the chair, and it was only now – now that he was so near – that Arathan finally felt the power emanating from Draconus. He was both tall and solid, with a warrior's build, and yet there was grace to the man that was, perhaps, more impressive than anything else.

'What we desire in our hearts, Arathan, and what must be . . . well, that is a rare embrace, so rare you're likely to never know it. You have lived that truth. I have no promises to make you. I cannot say what awaits you, but you are now in your year and the time has come for you to make your life.' He paused for a time, continuing to study Arathan, and the dark eyes flicked but once down to the hands – and Arathan struggled not to hide them further, leaving them at his sides, the thin fingers long and tipped in red. 'Sit down,' Draconus instructed.

Arathan looked round, found a high-backed chair against the wall to the left of the doorway, and walked over to it. It looked ancient, weakened with age. He'd made the wrong choice – but the only other chair had been the one his father had been sitting in at the table, and that would have set his back to Draconus. After a moment, he settled uneasily on the antique.

His father grunted. 'I'll grant you, they do better with stone,' he said. 'I have no intention of bringing you to the Citadel, Arathan – and no, it is not shame that guides that decision. There is growing tension in Kurald Galain. I shall do my utmost to placate the bereaved elements among the Greater Houses and Holds, but my position is far more precarious than you might think. Even among the Greater Houses I am still viewed as something of an outsider, and with more than a little mistrust.' He drew up then and shot Arathan a glance. 'But then, you know little of all this, do you?'

'You are Consort to Mother Dark,' Arathan said.

'Do you know what that means?'

'No, except that she has chosen you to stand at her side.'

There was a slight tightening round his father's eyes at that, but the man simply nodded. 'A decision which seems to have placed me between her and the highborn Holds – all of whom bear the titles of sons and daughters of Mother Dark.'

'Sons and daughters – but not by birth?'

Draconus nodded. 'An affectation? Or an assertion of unshakeable loyalty? By each claimant the scales shift.'

'Am I such a son to you, Lord?'

The question clearly caught Draconus off guard. His eyes searched Arathan's face. 'No,' he finally replied, but did not elaborate. 'I cannot guarantee your safety in Kurald Galain – even in the Citadel itself. Nor could you hope to expect any manner of loyalty from Mother Dark.'

'I understand that much, Lord.'

'I must journey to the west, and you will accompany me.'

'Yes, sir.'

'I must leave her side for a time – knowing well the risk – and so I shall have no patience if you falter on the trek.'

'Of course, Lord.'

Draconus was silent for a moment, as if considering Arathan's easy reply, and then he said, 'Sagander will accompany us, to continue your education. But in this detail I must charge you with his care – though he has longed to visit the Azathanai and the Jaghut for half his life, it seems that his opportunity has very nearly come too late. Now, I do not believe he is as feeble as he imagines himself to be. Nevertheless, you will attend to him.'

'I understand. Lord, will Master-at-arms Ivis—'

'No – he is needed elsewhere. Gate Sergeant Raskan and four

12

Borderswords will attend us. This is not a leisurely journey. We shall ride at pace, with spare mounts. The Bareth Solitude is inhospitable no matter the season.'

'Lord, when do we leave?'

'The day after tomorrow.'

'Lord, do you intend leaving me with the Azathanai?'

Draconus had walked to the open window. 'It may be,' he said, looking at something in the courtyard, 'that you will believe I do not want you, Arathan.'

'Lord, there is no need to apologize.'

'I am aware of that. Go to Sagander now, help him pack.'

'Yes, Lord.' Arathan stood, bowed to his father's back, and then strode from the chamber.

His legs felt weak as he made his way back down the corridor. He had not comported himself well, not in this, his first true meeting with his father. He had sounded foolish, naïve, disappointing the man who had sired him. Perhaps these were things all sons felt before their fathers. But time moved forward or not at all; and there was nothing he could do to change what had already taken place.

Sagander often spoke of building upon what has gone before, and that one must be mindful of that at every moment, with every choice made and about to be made. Even mistakes offered scraps, Arathan told himself. He could build from broken sticks and weathered bones if need be. Perhaps such constructs would prove weak, but then he had little weight for them to hold. He was a bastard son with an unknown mother, and his father was sending him away.

\*        \*        \*

*The ice is thin. Hard to find purchase. It is dangerous to walk here.*

Sagander well remembered the day the boy almost drowned. It haunted him, but in curious ways. When he was left with too many questions in his own life, when the mysteries of the world crowded close round him, he would think of that ice. Rotted from beneath by the foul gases rising up from the cattle sludge lying thick on the old quarry's lifeless rubble beneath thirty arm-spans of dark water, and after days of unseasonal warmth and then bitter cold, the ice had looked solid enough, but eyes were weak at distinguishing truth from lies. And though the boy had ventured alone on to its slick surface, Sagander could feel the treachery beneath his own feet – not those of Arathan on that chill, clear morning, but beneath the scholar himself; and he would hear the creaking, and then the dread cracking sound, and he was moments from tottering, from pitching down as the world gave way under him.

It was ridiculous. He should be excited. Before him, so late now in his life, he was about to journey among the Azathanai and beyond, to the Jaghut. Where his questions would find answers; where mysteries would come clear, all truths revealed, and peace would settle on his soul. And yet, each time his thoughts skated towards that imminent blessing of knowledge, he thought of ice, and fear took him then, as he waited for the cracking sounds.

Things should make sense. From one end to the other, no matter from which direction one elected to begin the journey, everything should fit. Fitting neatly was the gift of order, proof of control, and from control, mastery. He would not accept an unknowable world. Mysteries needed hunting down. Like the fierce wrashan that had once roamed the Blackwood: all their dark roosts were discovered until there were no places left for the beasts to hide, the slaughter was made complete, and now at last one could walk in safety in the great forest, and no howls ever broke the benign silence. Blackwood Forest had become knowable. Safe.

They would journey to the Azathanai, and to the Odhan of the Jaghut, perhaps even to Omtose Phellack itself, the Empty City. But best of all, he would finally see the First House of the Azath, and perhaps even speak with the Builders who served it. And he would return to Kurald Galain in crowning glory, with all he needed to fuel a blazing resurrection of his reputation as a scholar, and all those who had turned away from him, not even hiding their disdain, would now come flocking back, like puppies, and he would happily greet them – with his boot.

No, his life was not yet over.

*There is no ice. The world is sure and solid beneath me. Listen! There is nothing.*

A scratching knock at his door made Sagander close his eyes briefly. Arathan. How could a man such as Draconus sire such a child? Oh, Arathan was bright enough, and by all reports Ivis had run out of things he could teach the boy in matters of swordcraft. But such skills were of little real value. Weapons were the swift recourse among those who failed at reason or feared truth. Sagander had done his best with Arathan but it seemed likely that, despite the boy's cleverness, he was destined for mediocrity. What other future could be expected from an unwanted child?

The knock came again. Sighing, Sagander bid him enter. He heard the door open but did not turn from his examination of the many objects cluttering his table.

Arathan moved up alongside him, was silent as he studied the array on the ink-stained surface. Then he said, 'The Lord stated that we must travel light, sir.'

'I know very well what I shall need, and this is the barest minimum.

14

Now, what is it you want? As you can see, I am very busy – ideally, I need three days to prepare, but it is as Lord Draconus commands, and I shall make do.'

'I would help you pack, sir.'

'What of your own gear?'

'Done.'

Sagander snorted. 'You will rue your carelessness, Arathan. These matters demand deliberation.'

'Yes sir.'

Sagander waved a hand at the assemblage. 'As you can see, I have completed my preliminary selection, always bearing in mind that additions are likely to occur to me until the very last possible moment of departure, meaning it shall be necessary to ensure that the trunks each have room to spare. I expect I will be returning with many artefacts and writings, as well. Frankly, I don't see how you can assist me, apart from carrying the trunks downstairs, and you will need help for that. Best let the servants deal with it.'

Still the boy hesitated, and then he said, 'I can help you make more space in the trunks, sir.'

'Indeed? And how will you do that?'

'I see you have five bottles of ink, sir. As we will be riding hard throughout, there will be little time to write during the trip—'

'And what about once we arrive among the Azathanai?'

'Surely, they will have ink, sir, with which they will be generous, particularly when it comes to a visiting scholar of such high renown as yourself. Indeed, I imagine they will be equally generous with scrolls, lambskin and wax, as well as frames, gut and scribers.' Before Sagander could respond, he went on, 'And these maps – of Kurald Galain – I presume they are intended as gifts?'

'It is customary—'

'While there has been peace for some time between the Azathanai and the Tiste, no doubt other visitors among the Azathanai might value such maps, for all the wrong reasons. Sir, I believe Lord Draconus will forbid the gift of maps.'

'An exchange between scholars in the interests of knowledge has no relevant bearing on mundane political matters – whence comes this arrogance of yours?'

'I apologize, sir. Perhaps I could return to our lord and ask him?'

'Ask him what? Don't be a fool. Furthermore, do not presume a sudden rise in your status simply because you spent a few moments with our lord. In any case, I had already concluded that I would not bring the maps – too bulky; besides, these copies are the ones done by your hand, last year, and the rendition is suspect at best, deplorable in some instances. In fact, given that, they make most dubious gifts, rife

15

with errors as they no doubt are. You wish to assist me, student? Very well, give some thought to suitable gifts.'

'To one recipient or many, sir?'

Sagander considered the question, and then nodded. 'Four of respectable value and one of great worth.'

'Would the one of great worth be intended for the Lord of Hate, sir?'

'Of course it would! Now, be off with you, but be back before the evening meal's bell.'

As Arathan was leaving, Sagander turned. 'A moment. I have decided to reduce the number of trunks to two, with one only half filled. Bear that in mind with regard to these gifts.'

'I shall, sir.'

The door creaked when Arathan shut it behind him.

Irritated by the sound, Sagander fixed his attention once more on the gear on the worktable. He pushed the maps off the edge as they were cluttering his vision.

He did not think much of the boy's chances in finding a suitable gift for the Lord of Hate, but it would keep Arathan out from underfoot. Sagander had observed a new bad habit emerging from the boy, though the scholar was having difficulty defining it with any precision. It was in the way Arathan spoke, in the questions he asked and that mask of innocence on his face when he asked them. Not just innocence, but earnestness. Something about the whole thing was suspect, as if none of it was quite real.

There had to be a reason for Sagander to feel agitated following almost every conversation he'd had of late with Arathan.

No matter, this journey would put the boy back in his place – wide-eyed and frightened. The world beyond the house and its grounds was vast, overwhelming. Since the incident at the old quarry, Arathan had been forbidden from venturing into the countryside, and even his brief excursions down into the village had been supervised.

Arathan was in for a shock, and that would do him good.

* * *

Gate Sergeant Raskan tugged free his boot and held it up to examine its sole. He had a way of walking that wore down the heels from the back end, and it was there that the glued layers of leather started their fraying. Seeing the first signs of just that, he swore under his breath. 'Barely half a year old, these ones. They just don't make 'em like they used to.'

Rint, a Bordersword of seven hard years, stood across from Raskan, leaning against the keep wall. Arms folded, he had the bearing of a boar about to drive a sow into the woods. On the man's feet, Raskan

16

sourly observed, were worn moccasins of thick, tough henen hide. Commanding Rint and the other three Borderswords wasn't going to be easy, the gate sergeant reflected. Earning their respect was likely to be even harder. True, the two leaned one against t'other, but without respect, command faltered every time, whereas it wasn't always the same the other way round. Proof enough that titles and ranks which used to be earned were now coins on dirty scales, and even Raskan's lowly posting came from being cousin to Ivis, and he knew he might not be up to any of this.

''Sall those cobbles you're walking,' Ville said from where he sat at ease near the steps leading down to the sunken trench flanking the gate ramp. 'Soft ground don't wear you out the same. Seen plenty of road-marching soldiers back in the border wars, arriving with ruined knees and shin splints. If we was meant to walk on stone we'd have cloven hoofs like rock-goats.'

'But that's what hard-soled boots are,' Galak chimed in next to Ville. 'Hoofs for road-clompers. Just hobnail 'em or shoe 'em like a horse gets shoed.'

'Hobnails damage the pavestones,' Raskan countered, 'and plenty of times a day my tasks take me into the houses.'

'They should last the trip,' Rint said, his weathered face seaming into a faint smile.

Raskan studied the man for a moment. 'Been west then, have you?'

'Not far. None of us have. Nothing out there in the Solitude, not this side of the divide, anyway.'

The fourth and last of the Borderswords assigned to him now arrived. Feren was Rint's sister, maybe a few years older. Wiry where her brother was solid and if anything slightly taller, she had archer's wrists with a coiled copper string-guard on the left one that she never took off – or so went the rumour – and a way of walking somewhere between a cat and a wolf, as if the idea of hunting and stalking stayed close to the surface at all times. There was a tilt to her eyes that hinted of blood from somewhere east of the Blackwood, but it must have been thin since her brother showed little of that.

Raskan tried to imagine this woman walking into a High Hall any-where in the realm without offending the hosts, and could not do so. She belonged in the wilds; but then, so too did her companions. They were rough and uncultured, but ill-fitting as they seemed here on the House grounds, Raskan well knew how things would soon reverse, once they left civilization behind.

There were no ranks among the Borderswords. Instead, some arcane and mysterious hierarchy operated, and did so fluidly, as if circum-stances dictated who was in command at any given moment. For this journey, however, the circumstance was simple: Raskan was in charge of these four, and together they were responsible for the safety of not only Lord Draconus, but also the tutor and the boy.

The Borderswords would do the cooking, mending, hunting, setting up and breaking down camp, and caring for the horses. It was this range of skills among their sect that the Lord was exploiting, since he wanted to travel quickly and without a train. The only thing that concerned Raskan was the fact that these warriors were not fealty-sworn to House Dracons. If treachery were planned . . . but then, the Borderswords were famous for their loyalty. They stayed away from politics, and it was that neutrality that made them so reliable.

Still, the tensions within the realm had never been as high as they were now, and it seemed that his lord was at the very centre of it, whether Draconus wished it or not.

Thoughtful, eyes averted, Raskan pulled the boot back on, and then stood. 'I have horses to select,' he said.

'We will camp outside the grounds,' Rint said, straightening from the wall he had been leaning against. He glanced across at his sister, who gave a slight nod, as if replying to an unspoken question.

'Not on the training yard,' Raskan said. 'I need to get the boy on a warhorse this afternoon.'

'We'll take the far side?' Rint suggested, thick brows lifting.

'Very well, though Arathan's not at his best with too many eyes on him.'

Feren looked up sharply. 'Do you think we would mock the Lord's son, sergeant?'

'Bastard—'

'If the boy does not stand in his father's eyes,' she retorted, 'that is entirely the Lord's business.'

Raskan frowned, thinking through the meaning of the woman's statement, and then he scowled. 'Arathan is to be seen as no more than a recruit, as he has always been. If he deserves mockery, why spare him? No, my concern was that nervousness on his part could see him injured, and given that we depart on the morrow, I would prefer not to report to the Lord that the boy is incapable of travelling.'

Feren's uncanny eyes held on him for a moment longer, and then she turned away.

Raskan's tone hardened as he said, 'From now on, let it be understood by all of you that I am not obliged to explain myself to you. The boy is my charge, and how I manage that is not open for discussion. Am I understood?'

Rint smiled. 'Perfectly, sergeant.'

'My apologies, sergeant,' added his sister.

Raskan set off for the stables, his heels scuffing on the cobblestones.

*　　　*　　　*

It was late in the afternoon when the gate sergeant had the boy lead the warhorse by the reins out through the main gate and towards the training ground. The turf was chewed up beyond repair since the troop of lancers had taken to practising wheels-in-formation on a new season of chargers. The field was spring fed and beneath the turf there was clay, making footing treacherous – as it would be in battle. Every year they'd lose two or three beasts and as many soldiers, but many of the Greater Houses and Holds were, according to their lord, undertrained and ill-equipped when it came to mounted combat, and Draconus intended to be in a position to exploit that weakness if it came to civil war.

*Civil war.* The two words no one dared speak out loud, yet all prepared for. It was madness. There was nothing in the whole mess, in Raskan's eyes, that seemed insurmountable. What was this power that so many seemed determined to grasp? Unless it held a life in its hand, or the threat thereof, it was meaningless. And if it all reduced to that simple, raw truth, then what lust was being fed by all those who so hungered for it? Who, among all these fools buzzing round the courts of the realm, would be so bold and so honest as to say *yes, this is what I want. The power of life and death over as many of you as possible. Do I not deserve it? Have I not earned it? Will I not take it?*

But Raskan was a gate sergeant. He had not the subtle mind of Sagander, or of the lords, ladies and high servants of Kurald Galain. Clearly, he was missing something, and thinking only the thoughts of a fool. There was more to power than he comprehended. All he knew was that his life was indeed in someone else's hands, and perhaps there was some chance of choice in that, but if so, he had not the wisdom or cleverness to see it.

The boy was silent, as usual, as he guided the seemingly placid beast on to the soft, churned-up ground.

'Note the high saddle back, Arathan,' Raskan now said. 'Higher than you're used to seeing, but not so high as to snap your lower spine like a twig the moment you impact a line. No, better you are thrown off than that. At least then you have a chance if you survive the fall. Not much of one, but still. That's not of any concern to you for now, however. I'm just making it plain to you: this is a warhorse, and its tack is different. The cupped stirrups, the flanged horn. You'll not be wearing full armour in any case: the Lord has different ideas about that, and should we ever clash with mounted enemies among the Families, we'll ride circles round them. More than that, we're likely to survive dismounting, and not lie there broken and ready to be gutted like cattle.'

Arathan's eyes slid past Raskan during this speech, to where the four

Borderswords were seated in a row on one of the logs lining the field edge. The sergeant glanced over a shoulder at them and then returned his attention to the boy. 'Never mind them. I need and expect your attention.'

'Yes sir. But why have they pitched those tents? Are they not welcome in the House grounds?'

'It's what they choose, that's all. They're half wild. Probably haven't bathed in years. Now, eyes on me, Arathan. These chargers, they're bred special. Not just size, but temperament, too. Most horses will kill themselves rather than hurt one of us – oh, I don't mean bites and the occasional kick, or a panicked rearing and the like. That's just accidental, or bad moods. You've got to consider this. These animals are massive, compared to us. By weight alone they could crush us, trample us, pulp us into red meat and bone splinters. But they don't. They submit instead. An unbroken horse is a frightened horse, frightened of us, I mean. A broken one is gentled, and in place of fear there's trust. Blind trust, at times. Idiotic trust. That's just how it is.

'Now, a charger, well, it's different. Yes, you're still the master, but come battle, you both fight and you fight as partners. This beast is bred to hate the enemy, and that enemy looks just like you and me. So, in a melee, how does it tell the difference? Between friend and foe?' He waited, saw Arathan blink as the boy realized that the question had not been meant to be rhetorical.

'I don't know.'

Raskan grunted. 'A good honest answer. Thing is, nobody really knows. But the damned animals are unerring. Is it the tension in the muscles of their riders that tells them which direction the danger's coming from? Maybe. Some think so. Or maybe the Dog-Runners are right when they say there are words between souls – the soul of the rider and the soul of the mount. Bound by blood or whatever. It don't matter. The thing you need to understand is that you'll forge something together, until instinct is all you need. You'll know where the animal is going and it will know where you want it to go. It just happens.'

'How long does that take, sergeant?'

He'd seen flatness come to the boy's eyes. 'Well, that's the challenge here. For both of you. We can't take the time we rightly need for this. So, after today, well, we'll see how it's looking, just don't expect to be riding this animal for more than a league or two each day. But you will be guiding her and caring for her. Plenty of people say mares can't be good warhorses. The Lord thinks different. In fact, he's relying on the whole natural herd thing with these beasts, and it's Draconus who's riding the stallion, the master of the herd. Y'see his thinking?'

Arathan nodded.

'All right then, lengthen the lead. Time to get to work.'

Boy and beast worked hard that afternoon, with the lead and then without it, and even from where she and her fellow Borderswords sat on the log, Feren could see the sheen of sweat on the mare's black hide; and when at last the gate sergeant had the Lord's son turn his back on the charger, and the animal strode freely to come up alongside Arathan, Galak grunted and muttered, 'That was well done.'

'Grudging admission,' Ville commented. 'Thought I heard something split inside you, saying that, Galak.'

'Uniforms and hard-heeled boots. I admit I wasn't much impressed by these house-dwellers.'

'Just a different way,' said Rint. 'Not better, not worse, just different.'

'Back in the day, when there were still boars in the wood—'

'When there was still a wood,' Ville cut in.

Galak went on. 'The grand hunts had beaters and dogs. In a square of trees you'd need less than three bells to ride around. As if the boar had anywhere to go. As if it wasn't just minding its own business, tryin' to smell out a mate or whatever.'

'Your point?' Rint asked, laconic as ever.

'You're saying no better or worse just different. I'm saying you're being generous, maybe even false. You want to cut the carpet for them to walk on, you go ahead. I've watched a tereth come down to drink from a stream, in the steam of dawn, and the tears went silent down my face, because it was the last one for leagues round. No mate for it, just a lonely life and a lonelier death, even as the trees kept crashing down.'

Feren cleared her throat, still studying the boy who was now walking, the horse heeling like a faithful hound, and said, 'The ways of war leave a wasteland. We've seen it on the border, no different here. The heat sweeps in like a peat fire. No one notices. Not until it's too late. And then, why, there's nowhere to run.'

The gate sergeant was limping as he led his charges back towards the house.

'So she took a lover,' Galak said in a growl, not needing to add *so what?*

'The sorcery surrounding her is said to be impenetrable now,' Rint mused. 'Proof against all light. It surrounds her wherever she goes. We have a queen no one can see any more, except for Draconus, I suppose.'

'Why suppose that, even?' Galak demanded.

Feren snorted, and the others joined in with low, dry laughter, even Galak.

A moment later, Feren sobered. 'The boy is a ruin of anxiety, and is it any wonder? From what I heard, until this day, his own father was as invisible to his son as his new lover now chooses to be in her Citadel.'

'No sense to be made of that,' Galak said, shaking his head.

Feren glanced across at him, surprised. 'Perfect sense,' she replied. 'He's punishing the boy's mother.'

Brows lifting, her brother asked, 'Do you know who she is?'

'I know who she isn't, and that's more than enough.'

'Now you've lost me,' Ville said, his expression wry.

'Galak's tereth, Ville, lapping water at the stream as the day is born. But the day isn't born at all, not for her. You know she's doomed, you know it's finished for the sweet-eyed doe. Who killed her mate? With arrow or snare? Someone did.'

'And if that killer writhes in the arms of Chaos for all eternity,' Galak hissed, 'it'll only be what's deserved.'

Ville was now scowling. 'That's rich, Galak. We hunt every few days. We kill when we have to, to stay alive. No different from a hawk or a wolf.'

'But we're different from hawks and wolves, Ville. We can actually figure out the consequences of what we do, and that makes us . . . oh, I don't know the word . . .'

'Culpable?' Rint suggested.

'Yes, that's the word all right.'

'Rely not upon conscience,' Feren said, hearing the bitterness in her own voice and not caring. 'It ever kneels to necessity.'

'And necessity is often a lie,' Rint added, nodding.

Feren's eyes were now on the churned-up turf and mud of the practice field. Insects spun and danced over the small pools left by hoofs as the light slowly failed. From the coppiced stand behind them came evening birdsong, sounding strangely plaintive. She felt slightly sick.

'Impenetrable darkness, you said?' Ville said. He shook his head. ''Tis a strange thing to do.'

'Why not,' Feren heard herself say, 'when beauty is dead?'

*     *     *

Cut in half by the river Dorssan Ryl, the lands of the Greater House of Dracons consisted of a range of denuded hills, old mine shafts by the score, three woods that had once made up a small forest, a single village of indentured families, modest strip farms bordered by low stone walls, and a series of deep ponds filling abandoned quarry pits, where various breeds of fish were managed. Common land provided pasture for black-wool ahmryd and cattle, although forage was poor.

These lands marked the northwest border of Kurald Galain, fed by a single, poorly maintained rutted road and a single massive Azathanai bridge, since most traffic plied the Dorssan Ryl, where passage was facilitated by an extensive series of tow-lines and winches; although even these ox-powered machines were left idle during the spring flood, when even at a distance of a thousand paces the roar of the river could be heard from every room of the Great House.

The hills immediately to the west and north of the keep were mostly granite, of a highly valued dark, fine-grained variety, and this was the lone source of wealth for House Dracons. The Lord's greatest triumph, however – and perhaps the greatest source of envy and unease prior to his attaining the title of Consort to Mother Dark – was his mysterious ties with the Azathanai. Bold and impressive as was the native Galain architecture, with the Citadel its crowning glory, the masons of the Azathanai were without equals, and the new Grand Bridge in Kharkanas was proof enough of that, a bridge gifted to the city by Lord Draconus himself.

The thinkers in the court, those capable of subtle consideration, anyway, were not unmindful of the symbolic gesture the bridge represented. But even this proved sufficient cause for bitterness, resentment, and quiet denigration. The witnessing of an exchange of gifts will taste sour when one is neither giver nor recipient. By this measure station is defined, but no definition holds for long, and gratitude is thin as rain on the stones from a single cloud on a sunny day.

If words were carved upon the massive stones of the Grand Bridge, they were well hidden. Perhaps, if one were to moor a boat beneath the span, using one of the massive stone rings so cleverly fitted there, and shine a lantern's eye upward, one might find row upon row of Azathanai script. But in all truth this is probably a fancy and nothing more. Those who lived on and worked the river in Kharkanas did not mingle with the highborn, nor the artists, painters and poets of the time, and what they saw was their business.

Did they dream of peace, those grimy men and women with the strange accents, as they slipped past in their craft above depthless black waters? And where they walked, beyond the city, out where the banks were worn down and the silts were black along the shorelines, worshipping that kiss of water and land, did they fear the time to come?

And could we – oh gods, could we – have ever imagined the blood they would sacrifice in our name?

*There will be peace.*

# TWO

THE CANDLES PAINTED THE AIR GOLD, MADE SOFT THE PALE SUNLIGHT streaming in from the high, narrow windows. There was a score of them affixed to a disparate collection of holders – as many as could be spared from unused rooms of the keep – and more than half were melted down to stumps, their flames flickering and sending up tendrils of black smoke. A servant stood watchful nearby, ready to replace the next one to surrender its life.

'See the genius in his vision,' Hunn Raal said under his breath, a moment later catching young Osserc's cautious nod from the corner of his eye. There was risk in speaking at all. The man working the bristle brushes through pigments on the palette and then stabbing at the surface of the wooden board was notorious for his temperament, and the scene was already tense enough, but Hunn had judged his comment a sufficient compliment to assuage any possible irritation Kadaspala might feel at the distraction.

Clearly, Osserc was not prepared to risk even a muttered assent under the circumstances. This was what came of a young man yet to see his courage tested. Of course, that was through no fault of Osserc's own. No, the blame – and could there be any other word for it? – rested with the father, with the man who sat so stiffly in ornate regalia, one side bathed in the candlelight, the other in shadows brooding and grim, as befitted his darkening mood at the moment.

Kadaspala might well be the most sought-after painter of portraits in all Kurald Galain, famed for his brilliant talent and infamous for his impatience with subjects when composing, but even he was no match for the man seated in the high-backed blackwood chair, should Vatha

Urusander's frayed patience finally snap. The brocaded dress uniform was an invention, fit for official visits to the Citadel and other festive occasions, but in his day as commander of the legions, Urusander's attire had been virtually indistinguishable from the commonest cohort soldier's. The Kurald legions were now called Urusander's Legion, and with good reason. Though born of a Lesser House, Urusander had risen quickly through the ranks in the harrowing first months of the Forulkan War, when the high command had been decimated first by treacherous acts of assassination, then by successive defeats on the field of battle.

Urusander had saved the Tiste people. Without him, Hunn Raal well knew, Kurald Galain would have fallen.

The career that followed, through the entire campaign to drive back the Forulkan, and then the punitive pursuit of the Jhelarkan deep into the lands of the northwest, had elevated Urusander to legendary status, justifying this belated scene here in the upper chamber of the keep's newest tower, with the dust of the stone-cutters still riding the currents. The presence of Kadaspala of House Enes was in itself an impressive measure of Urusander's vaunted status. This portrait would be copied upon the wall of the Inner Avenue in the Citadel in Kharkanas, in place alongside images of highborn Tiste, both those still living and those long dead.

But the man sitting stiffly inside that garish uniform, with all its martial decorations, was moments from shattering this perfect image of resolute dignity. Hunn Raal fought back a smile. Neither he nor Osserc could fail to see the signs, even as Kadaspala worked on, unmindful, lost in his own world of frenzied haste. Urusander had gone very still – and no doubt the artist saw this, if he gave any mind to it at all, as a triumph of his own will over his recalcitrant subject.

Hunn wondered if Osserc would speak, to stem the dyke before it burst – or would he recoil, as he had done for most of his sheltered life, only to then stumble over himself in an effort to soothe any and all who might take offence at his father's tirade? Hunn was tempted to stand back and witness, but then, what good would be achieved? Even worse, Kadaspala might take such umbrage as to pack up his paints and brushes and march out, never to return.

There were reasons for Hunn Raal's presence in this chamber. Had he not nearly died taking an assassin's knife intended for Urusander? Well, he would step into the blade's path yet again. Clearing his throat, he said, 'Good artist, the day's light is fading—'

Kadaspala – not much older than Osserc – spun on the old soldier. 'You damned fool! The light is *perfect*! This very moment, can't you see that?'

'Even so, and in this, sir, I bow to your expertise. However, you must understand, Lord Urusander is a soldier who has taken many wounds in his career. Time and again he has bled in defence of Kurald Galain, winning for us all the peace we so take for granted. I know I could not sit still for as long as he has this day—'

'Of that,' Kadaspala snapped, 'I have no doubt. Not that your dog's face will ever grace a wall, unless as a mounted trophy.'

Hunn Raal snorted his laughter. 'Well said, sir. But it changes nothing. The Lord needs to stretch out his limbs, that is all.'

The artist's round face seemed to hover like a mask, as if moments from rushing, disembodied, straight for Hunn Raal; and then he turned away, flinging down his brushes. 'What's light, then, anyway? Isn't it enough that Mother Dark's stealing it all from us? What of the portraits in the Avenue? Useless!' He seemed to be speaking mostly to himself, and for a host of reasons the others in the chamber, Urusander included, were content to leave him to it.

The Lord straightened, sighing deeply.

'Tomorrow, Lord Urusander,' Kadaspala said, in a tone worthy of a beating. 'The very same time. And you, servant – more candles! Curse the darkness, curse it!'

Hunn watched his lord silently stride from the room, choosing the side passage leading to the steps that would take him down to his private chambers. The soldier then caught Osserc's eye and nodded, and with Urusander's son following he led the way out, using the main stairs. This wing of the keep still awaited furnishing, and they passed through empty rooms and echoing corridors before arriving at the main vestibule, where what had once seemed opulent now struck Hunn as tattered and worn, the walls, hangings and weapon-racks smoke-smeared and battered by a century of wear.

Little remained of the ancient fortress that had once commanded this hilltop, at the very heart of the town of Neret Sorr; most of its ruins had been dismantled and reused in the construction of the New Keep a hundred years ago, and of the bloodlines that had once laid claim to this settlement and its outlying territories, the last drop had long since vanished into the earth. The common belief was that Urusander's own family had been fealty-sworn to that vanished nobility, warriors from the very beginning, but Hunn Raal had been central in promulgating that legend. So much of history was nothing but gaping holes that needed filling with whatever was expedient, for now, and more significantly for the future, where the fruition of carefully planted inventions and half-truths would, if he had his way, yield a wealth of rewards.

They stepped outside into the courtyard, strode into the shadows cast by the thick, high walls. Off to one side, an ox-drawn cart had delivered ingots of raw iron outside the smithy and the smith's apprentices were busy unloading the stock. Unmindful of these efforts, the handler and the keep's cutter were digging a tick out from behind the ox's left ear, and the insect's stubbornness was attested by the blood running down the side of the ox's neck, while the animal lowed plaintively, hide rippling as its muscles flinched.

'Where are we going?' Osserc asked as they crossed the compound towards the High Gate.

'Down into town,' Hunn Raal replied. 'Your father will be in a dark mood at the table tonight, assuming he shows up at all. I've never seen a man so eager to put down his sword, and all for a trunkful of Forulkan cylinders – and half of those broken. If those white-faced fools had any thought worthy of admiration, it did them little good against Tiste vengeance.'

Osserc was silent for a moment, as they approached the gate, and then he said, 'It is his abiding fascination, Hunn. The laws of governance. The compact of society. We are in need of reformation, and proof of that is plain enough in all the troubles now coming home to roost.'

Hunn Raal grunted, feeling his face twisting. 'Draconus. The troubles you're talking about begin and end with that upstart.'

It had been a weighted comment on Hunn's part, and he made sure not to react to Osserc's sudden look, simply continuing on. 'There is no history, no precedent. The family of Dracons was ever a Lesser House. And now some dubious heir to its thin blood stands beside Mother Dark. This is the threat and it has nothing to do with reform. Ambition, Osserc, is a poison.'

'Well, my father has none of that.'

Inwardly, Hunn smiled, and it was a triumphant smile. 'Just so. Who better to govern, then? She doesn't need a damned Consort, she needs a husband.'

They emerged on to the first of the switchbacks leading down into the town. There was no traffic coming up this late in the day, but a cluster of carts heading down formed a logjam at the second turn, where the back end of a long-bedded wagon was being lifted by a dozen or so haulers to swing it clear.

'If Draconus is a commoner,' said Osserc, 'so too is my father.'

Hunn had been waiting for that observation. 'Not true. The earliest mentions of Neret Sorr note the ruling family's name as Vatha. And more important, retired or not, Urusander commands the legions. Tell me this: how well have we been treated? You've seen it for yourself, friend. We fought and so many of us died, and we won. We won the war for everyone in the realm. And now, well, they'd rather forget we ever existed. It's not right, how we're treated, and you know it.'

'We are no threat to the nobility,' Osserc retorted. 'That's not how it is, Hunn Raal. It's expensive maintaining the legions at full strength. The desire is to reduce active rosters—'

'And throw the rest of us out on the streets,' Hunn Raal said. 'Or worse, into the wood to grub alongside the Deniers. And when the Forulkan come back? We won't be ready, and not even your father could save us then.'

There were patterns to things, and Hunn Raal had his reasons for working them; in particular on this young man, this untried son of a hero who when speaking of the legions had said *we*, as if dreams were real. Hunn could see what was needed, but Urusander was not a man to be swayed by exhortations or arguments. He had done his service to the realm, and as far as he was concerned what remained of his life was now his own. He had earned it.

But the truth was, the realm needed a saviour, and the only way to the father was through the son. Hunn Raal went on, 'The future is not for someone else, though each of us might think so. It's for us. Your father understands that, at some deep level – beyond all the crazed Forulkan obsessions with justice and whatever – he knows that he fought for himself, and for you – for the world ahead of you. But instead he hides in his study. He needs drawing out, Osserc. You must see that.'

But there was an ugly cast to Osserc's face now, as they fell in behind the line of carts trundling down to the next turn. Hunn Raal could almost see the gnawing fangs inside Osserc's head. He edged closer, lowering his voice, 'He refused you a sword in your hands. I know. To keep you safe. But listen, in a cut-down army, what chance do you think you'll get to put all your training to good use? You say you want to march at my side, and I believe you. Abyss take me, but I'd be proud to be there, seeing that, too.'

'It will never happen,' Osserc growled.

'The legions want you. They see – and we who are here see every day – so much of the father in his son. We're all waiting. The day your father is made king, Osserc, is the day he will truly have to let go of the legions, with you taking his place. This is the future we want, all of us. And I tell you, I will work on Urusander. After all, he would never have had you trained to fight if he wanted you doing nothing but making lists of clay cylinders. You need a commission, and we'll see it done, and that's a promise.'

'So you keep saying,' Osserc muttered, but the strength had gone from his anger.

Hunn Raal slapped him on the back. 'I do. Now, friend, let's go drink, shall we?'

'You and your drinking.'

'Trust me; it's all down to what a soldier's seen. You'll find that out soon enough. I plan on getting drunk, and you'll need to drag me home.'

'Not if I get drunk first.'

'It's to be a race then, is it? Good!'

There was something pathetic, Hunn Raal reflected, when a young man longed for a good reason to drink, to sit silent and alone, staring at memories that would not go away. Remembering fallen friends, and the screams of the dying. In truth, Hunn would not wish that on anyone, but if something wasn't done to make the portrait of Urusander real, as real as it could be, there would be civil war.

With the legions trapped in the eye of the storm.

The true irony in all of this was the fact that Hunn Raal's own Issgin line had more claim to the throne than anyone, even Mother Dark herself. No matter. The past was more than just empty holes. Here and there, those holes had been filled long ago, every truth buried, down deep and out of sight. And it was just as well. What he sought wasn't for himself, was it? It was for the good of the realm. And even if it cost him his life, he would see Urusander on the Blackwood Throne.

His thoughts returned to Draconus, like a flash of sudden blood in the night, and he felt rage build hot in his chest. The common belief was that the legions would stand aside and take no part in the squabbles among the nobility. But the common belief was wrong. Hunn Raal would see to it. Should the tensions erupt into open warfare, Draconus would find himself facing not just the sons and daughters of Mother Dark, but Urusander's Legion as well.

*See you sweet-talk your way out of that mess, Draconus. See where your power-mad ambition finds you then.*

Night clothed the town below, but the inns glowed in the valley bed with soft lanternlight, yellow and gold like the flames of candles. Looking down upon them, Hunn Raal could feel his thirst awaken.

\*     \*     \*

Kadaspala wiped the last stubborn pigment stains from his hands using a cloth soaked in spirits, his eyes watering as the fumes reached his face. He'd sent the servant from his room. The idea of needing someone to help him dress for a meal was absurd. The secret of a great portrait was to meet the subject eye to eye, as equals, whether that subject was a commander of armies, or a shepherd boy who'd give up his own life to defend a flock of ahmryd. He despised the notion of betters. Station and wealth were flimsy props thrown up in front of people as flawed and as mortal as anyone else, and if it was their need to strut and prance behind them, it was proof of internal weakness and nothing else, and what could be more pathetic than that?

He would never have servants. He wanted no artificial prop to deference. Every life was a gift – he needed only look into the eyes opposite him, at any time on any given day, to know this. It did not matter to whom those eyes belonged. He would see true, and then make that truth plain to see for everyone else. His was a hand that would never lie.

The day's sitting had been ... adequate. The mood that took Kadaspala when rendering a portrait was a foul one, and he knew it. But most of his impatience was with himself. Each and every day was too short, the light too whimsical, his vision too sharp not to see the failings in his work – and no amount of praise from onlookers could change any of that. Hunn Raal had no doubt thought his comment soothing, even complimentary, but it had taken all of Kadaspala's will to keep him from stabbing the smirking soldier in the eye with his brush. The passion that stole his mind when composing was a dark, frightening thing. Murderous and vile. Such depths had once frightened him, but now he simply lived with them, like an unpleasant scar marring his face, or pockmarks on his cheeks from some past illness.

Yet it was the breadth of the contradiction that most disturbed him: that on the one hand he could adhere to the belief that every life was of equal value, a value that was immense, while at the same time despising everyone he knew.

Almost everyone. There were precious exceptions.

The reminder made him pause, vision blurring slightly. It did not take much, he knew. A flash of memory, a sudden rush of anticipation for when he would see her again. There was nothing untoward in his love for Enesdia, his sister. He was an artist, after all, who knew the truth of beauty, and she was his definition of that virtue, from the core of her gentle soul to the smooth perfection of her form.

He dreamed of painting her. It was an abiding dream, an obsessive dream, yet he had never done so and never would. No matter how consuming his effort, no matter how vast his talent, he knew he would fail to capture her, because what he saw wasn't necessarily there to be seen – though he could not be sure of that, as it was not something he discussed with anyone.

This battered old warrior, Urusander, offered him an appropriately stark contrast. Men like him were easy to paint. They might well have depths, but those depths were all of one colour, one tone. They were devoid of mystery, and this was what made them such powerful leaders. There was something frightening in that unrelieved monochrome, and yet it seemed to reassure others, as if it were a source of strength.

Some people suited their transformations, into paint on board, as dyed plaster on walls, or in the unrelieved purity of marble. They existed as both surface and opaque solidity, and it was this quality that Kadaspala found so cruel and monstrous, for it spoke of the will of the world. He knew he played his role. He gave the substance to their assertion of power.

Portraits were the weapons of tradition, and tradition was the invisible army laying siege to the present. And what was at stake? What victory did it seek? To make the future no different from the past. With every stroke of his brush, Kadaspala opened a wound, against all who would challenge the way things were. He fought that bitter knowledge, perversely setting his talents to the battlements as if he would refuse his own advance.

He wished he were less aware; he wished that his own talent could somehow blind him to its insipid appropriation. But this was not to be.

Thoughts churning, as they always did following a sitting, he dressed with haphazard indifference and made his way out, down to dine with the Lord of the House. Would it be this night, then, that Urusander or Hunn Raal finally broached the possibility of painting young Osserc? Kadaspala hoped not. He hoped that moment would never come.

Finish the portrait of the father, and then flee this place. *Return home, to see her again.*

He dreaded these formal suppers. They were filled with banal reminiscences of battle, mostly from Hunn Raal, warring with Urusander's daily discoveries when delving into the arcane idiocy of the Forulkan. With Osserc's head turning as if on a spike. There was nothing in the Lord's son that he wanted to paint, no depths to seek out. Behind Osserc's eyes there was bedrock, disfigured by Hunn Raal's incessant chipping away. The boy was destined for obscurity, unless he could be prised away from his father and his so-called friend. As it stood, the combination of Urusander's raising high unassailable walls around his son, and Hunn Raal's ceaseless undermining of those foundations, left Osserc in genuine danger. Should something lead to a collapse of his world he might well be utterly crushed. In the meantime the sheer oppression was visibly suffocating the young man.

No matter. None of this was Kadaspala's problem. He had plenty of his own to worry about. *Mother Dark's power grows, and with that power, she is stealing the light. From the world. What future has an artist, when all is in darkness?*

Mulling on these bleak thoughts, he strode into the dining room. And then paused. The chairs where he had expected to see Hunn Raal and Osserc seated were both vacant. Lord Urusander sat alone at his place at the table's head, and for once the surface before him was uncluttered – not a single fired-clay cylinder or unfurled scroll of notations weighted down at the corners and awaiting his studious perusal.

Urusander was leaning back, in one hand a goblet, cradled at his waist. His faded blue eyes were fixed on the artist with an acuity that was unprecedented in his recollection. 'Good Kadaspala Enes, please sit. No, here, upon my right. It seems that this evening it shall be you and me.'

31

'I see, my lord.' He made his way over. The moment he arrived and seated himself, a servant appeared with a goblet to match the Lord's. Taking it, he looked down. Blackvine, the rarest and most expensive wine in the realm.

'I was looking upon your day's work,' Urusander continued.

'Indeed, Lord?'

Urusander's eyes flickered slightly, the only detail to signal his mood, and that signal was obscure. 'You are not curious as to my opinion?'

'No.'

The Lord sipped, and it could have been stale water that passed his lips for all the change in his expression. 'One may presume, I hope, that the notion of an audience is relevant to you.'

'Relevant, Lord? Oh, it's relevant . . . to an extent. But if you imagine that I yearn for a heavenly chorus of opinion, then you must think me naïve. If I were to require such reward as if it were the blood of life, why, I would starve. As would virtually every other artist in Kurald Galain.'

'So opinions are without value?'

'I value only those that please me, Lord.'

'Then would you deny the potential worth of constructive criticism?'

'That depends,' Kadaspala replied, still to taste the wine.

'Upon what?' Urusander asked, as servants appeared once more, this time with the first course. Plates whispered down, the air was stirred by bodies in motion behind and around the two men, and the candles on the table flickered and dipped this way and that.

'How fare your studies, Lord?'

'You evade my question?'

'I choose my own path to answering it.'

Neither anger nor patronizing amusement touched Urusander's worn face. 'Very well. The issue I am struggling with is one of moral stance. Written law is in itself pure, at least in so far as language can make it. Ambiguity emerges only in its practical application upon society, and at this point hypocrisy seems to be the inevitable consequence. The law bends to those in power, like a willow or perhaps a cultured rosebush, or even a fruit-bearing tree trained against a wall. Where it grows depends upon the whims of those in power, and before too long, why, the law becomes a twisted thing indeed.'

Kadaspala set the goblet down, eyed the food on the plate before him. Smoked meat, some kind of glazed vegetable, positioned in a way as if to regard each other. 'But are not laws little more than formalized opinions, Lord?'

Urusander's brows lifted. 'I begin to see the direction of your thoughts, Kadaspala. To answer you, yes, they are. Opinions on the proper and peaceful governance of society—'

'Excuse me, but peaceful is not a word that comes to my mind when thinking of law. At its core is subjugation, after all.'

Urusander considered, and then said, 'Only in the matter of mitigating damaging or antisocial behaviour, and at this point I return you to my first comment. That is, of moral stance. It is the very matter with which I am struggling, with little forward progress, I admit. So,' he took another sip and then set the goblet down and picked up his knife, 'let us set aside the notion of "peaceful" for the moment. Consider the very foundation of the matter, namely, that law exists to impose rules of acceptable behaviour in social discourse, yes? Good, then let us add the notion of protecting one from harm, both physical and spiritual, and, well, you see the dilemma.'

Kadaspala considered that for a moment, and then he shook his head. 'Laws decide which forms of oppression are allowed, Lord. And because of that, those laws are servants to those in power, for whom oppression is given as a right over those who have little or no power. Now, shall we return to art, Lord? When stripped down to its bones, criticism is a form of oppression. Its intent is to manipulate both artist and audience, by imposing rules on aesthetic appreciation. Curiously, its first task is to belittle the views of those who appreciate a certain work but are unable or unwilling to articulate their reasons for doing so. On occasion, of course, one of those viewers rises to the bait, taking umbrage at being dismissed as being ignorant, at which point critics en masse descend to annihilate the fool. No more than defending one's own precious nest, one presumes. But on another level, it is the act of those in power in protecting their interests, those interests being nothing less than absolute oppression through the control of personal taste.'

Urusander had sat motionless through this, knife point thrust through a sliver of meat and suspended halfway to his mouth. When Kadaspala finished, he set the knife down and reached once more for his wine. 'But I am not a critic,' he said.

'Indeed not, Lord, which is why I said I wasn't curious about your opinion. I am curious about the opinions of critics. But about the opinions of those with no agenda beyond the aesthetic, I am *interested*.'

Urusander snorted. 'Take some wine, Kadaspala, you have just earned it.'

The mouthful he took was modest.

'Other nights when we sit here,' Urusander said, now frowning, 'you will finish off an entire carafe on your own.'

'Other nights, Lord, I am subjected to war stories.'

Urusander laughed, the sound startling the servants with its booming thunder. Somewhere in the kitchen something crashed down to the stone floor.

'The wine,' said Kadaspala, 'is exceptional, Lord.'

'It is, isn't it? And do you know why I have not served it before this night?'

'Every morning, Lord, I check my jugs of cleaning spirits, to ensure Hunn Raal has not plundered them.'

'Just so, artist, just so. Now, let us eat, but keep your wits about you. On this night, let us stretch our minds in dialogue.'

Kadaspala spoke with utter honesty. 'Lord, pray we talk these candles down as the only measure of the evening's passage.'

Urusander's eyes were narrow and thoughtful. 'I was warned to expect nothing but foul and bitter regard when in your company.'

'Only when I paint, Lord. Only when I paint. Now, if it pleases you, I am interested in hearing your thoughts on my work thus far.'

'My thoughts? I have but one, Kadaspala. I had no idea I was so transparent.'

He nearly dropped the goblet. Only the quick intercession of a servant saved him.

\*     \*     \*

Enesdia, daughter of Lord Jaen of House Enes, stood frowning at the silvered mirror. The dye in the dress was said to come from a tuberous vegetable, which when simmered produced a deep and pure scarlet. 'It's the colour of blood,' she said. 'This is what everyone in Kharkanas is going mad for?'

The seamstresses flanking her in the reflection looked pale and drab, almost lifeless.

Seated off to the left on a settee, Cryl of House Durav cleared his throat in a manner all too familiar to Enesdia, and she turned, brows lifting, and said, 'And what shall we argue about this morning, then? The cut of the dress? The style of the court? Or is it my hair that now dismays you? As it happens, I like it short. The shorter the better. Why should you complain about it, anyway? It's not as though *you've* let your hair go long as a horse tail just to fit in with the day's fashion. Oh, I don't know why I invited you in at all.'

Mild surprise played with his even features for the briefest of moments, and then he offered up a lopsided shrug. 'I was just thinking, it's more vermilion than scarlet, isn't it. Or is it our eyes that are changing?'

'Idiotic superstitions. Vermilion . . . well.'

'Dog-Runner wives call it the "Born of the Hearth", don't they?'

'That's because they boil the root, fool.'

'Oh, I would think the name more descriptive than that.'

'Would you now? Haven't you somewhere to be, Cryl? Some horse to train? Some sword to whet?'

'You invite me only to then send me away?' The young man rose smoothly. 'If I were a sensitive soul, I might be offended. As it is, I know this game – we have played it all our lives, haven't we?'

'Game? What game?'

He had been making for the door, but now he paused and glanced back, and there was something sad in his faint smile. 'I hope you'll excuse me, I have a horse to whet and a sword to train. Although, I should add, you look lovely in that dress, Enesdia.'

Even as she drew a breath, mind racing for something that made sense – that might even draw him snapping back on his leash – he slipped out and was gone.

One of the seamstresses sighed, and Enesdia rounded on her. 'Enough of that, Ephalla! He is a hostage in this house and is to be accorded the highest respect!'

'Sorry, mistress,' Ephalla whispered, ducking. 'But he spoke true – you look lovely!'

Enesdia returned her attention to the blurred image of herself in the mirror. 'But,' she murmured, 'do you think *he'll* like it?'

*    *    *

Cryl paused for a moment in the corridor outside Enesdia's door, near enough to hear the last exchange between her and her handmaid. The sad half-smile on his face remained, only fading as he set out towards the main hall.

He was nineteen years old, the last eleven of those spent here in the house of Jaen Enes as a hostage. He was old enough to understand the value of the tradition. For all that the word 'hostage' carried an implicit pejorative, caged in notions of imprisonment and the absence of personal freedom, the practice was more of an exchange than anything else. It was further bound by rules and proscriptions ensuring the rights of the hostage. The sanctity of their person was immutable, precious as a founding law. Accordingly, Cryl, born of House Durav, felt as much an Enes as Jaen, Kadaspala or, indeed, Jaen's daughter.

And this was . . . unfortunate. His childhood friend was a girl no longer, but a woman. And gone were his childish thoughts, his dreams of pretending she was in truth his own sister – although he now recognized the confusions swirling through such dreams. For a boy, the role of sister, wife and mother could – if one were careless – be so easily blended together into a heady brew of anguished longing. He'd not known what he'd wanted of her, but he had seen how their friendship had changed, and in that change a wall had grown between them, impassable, forbidding and patrolled by stern propriety. There had been moments of awkwardness, when either he or Enesdia stumbled too close to one another, only to be drawn up by freshly chiselled stone, the touch of which yielded embarrassment and shame.

They struggled now to find their places, shifting about in a search to discover the proper distance between them. Or perhaps the struggle was his alone. He could not be sure, and in that he saw the proof of how things had changed. Once, running at her side, he had known her well. Now, he wondered if he knew her at all.

In her room, only a short time ago, he'd spoken of the games now played between them. Not like the games of old, for these were not, strictly speaking, shared. Instead, these new ones held to personal, private rules, solitary in their gauging, and nothing was won but an abeyance of unease. And yet to this she had professed ignorance. No, ignorance was the wrong word. The word was *innocence*.

Should he believe her?

In truth, Cryl felt lost. Enesdia had outgrown him in every way, and at times he felt like a puppy at her heels, eager for play, but that sort of playing was behind her now. She thought him a fool. She mocked him at every turn, and a dozen times each day he silently vowed that he was done with it, all of it, only to once more find himself answering her summons – which seemed to be uttered ever more imperiously – and finding himself, yet again, the arrow-butt to her barbs.

It was clear to him, at last, that there were other meanings to the word 'hostage', ones not codified into the laws of tradition, and they bound him in chains, heavy and cruelly biting, and he spent his days, and nights, in tormented stricture.

But this was his twentieth year of life. He was only months away from being released, sent back to his own blood, where he would sit discomfited at the family table, trapped in his own strangeness in the midst of a family that had grown around the wound of his prolonged absence. All of this – Enesdia and her proud father, Enesdia and her frighteningly obsessed but brilliant brother, Enesdia and the man who would soon be her husband – all of it would be past, a thing of his history day by day losing its force, its power over him and his life.

And so, too sharply felt for irony, Cryl now longed for his freedom.

Striding into the Great Hall, he was brought up short at seeing Lord Jaen standing near the hearth. The old man's eyes were on the massive slab of stone laid into the tiled floor, marking the threshold of the hearth and bearing ancient words carved into its granite mien. The Tiste language struggled with notions of filial duty – or so Kadaspala's friend, the court poet Gallan, was fond of saying – as if hinting at some fundamental flaw in spirit, and so, as was often the case, the words were Azathanai. So many Azathanai gifts to the Tiste seemed to fill the dusty niches and gaps left gaping by flaws in Tiste character, and not one of those gifts was without symbolic meaning.

As a hostage, Cryl was forbidden from learning those arcane Azathanai words, given so long ago to the bloodline of Enes. It was

36

odd, he now reflected as he bowed before Jaen, this Tiste prohibition against learning the masons' script.

Jaen could well have been reading his mind, for he nodded and said, 'Gallan claims he can read Azathanai, granting him the blasphemous privilege of knowing the sacred words of each noble family. I admit,' he added, his thin, lined face twisting slightly, 'I find the notion displeasing.'

'Yet the poet asserts that such knowledge is for him alone, Lord.'

'Poets, young Cryl, cannot be trusted.'

The hostage considered that statement, and found he had no reasonable reply to it. 'Lord, I request permission to saddle a horse and ride on this day. It was my thought to seek sign of eckalla in the west hills.'

'Eckalla? None have been seen in years, Cryl. I fear your search will be wasted.'

'The ride will do me good, Lord, none the less.'

Jaen nodded, and it seemed he well understood the swirl of hidden emotions lying beneath Cryl's bland words. His gaze returned to the hearthstone. 'This year,' he said, 'I must give up a daughter. And,' he glanced back at Cryl, 'a most beloved hostage.'

'And I, in turn, feel as if I am about to be cast out from the only family I truly belong to. Lord, doors are closing behind us.'

'But not, I trust, for ever sealed?'

'Indeed not,' Cryl replied, although in his mind he saw a massive lock grinding tight. Some doors, once shut, were proof against every desire.

Jaen's gaze faltered slightly and he turned away. 'Even standing still, the world moves on around us. I well remember you when first you arrived, scrawny and wild-eyed – the Abyss knows you Duravs are a feral lot – and there you were, wild as a cat, yet barely tall enough to saddle a horse. At least it seems we fed you well.'

Cryl smiled. 'Lord, the Duravs are said to be slow to grow—'

'Slow in many things, Cryl. Slow to assume the trappings of civil comportment, in which I admit I find considerable charm. You have held to that despite our efforts, and so remain refreshing to our eyes. Yes,' he continued, 'slow in many things. Slow in judgement, slow to anger . . .' Jaen slowly swung round and fixed Cryl with a searching regard. 'Are you angry yet, Cryl Durav?'

The question shocked him, almost made him step back. 'Lord? I – I have no cause to be angry. I am saddened to leave this house, but there will be rejoicing this year. Your daughter is about to be wed.'

'Indeed.' He studied Cryl for a moment longer, and then, as if yielding some argument, he broke his gaze and faced the hearthstone, gesturing. 'And she will kneel before one such as this, in the great house that her betrothed even now builds for her.'

'Andarist is a fine man,' Cryl said, as evenly as he could manage. 'Honourable and loyal. This binding by marriage is a sure one, Lord, by every measure.'

'Does she love him, though?'

Such questions left him reeling. 'Lord? I am certain that she does.'

Jaen grunted, and then sighed. 'You see her truly, don't you – the years together, the friendship you have both held for each other. She loves him, then? I am pleased. Yes, most pleased to hear you say that.'

Cryl would leave here, soon, and when he did, he knew that he would not look back, not once. Nor, for all that he loved this old man, would he ever return. In his chest, he felt nothing but cold, a scattering of dead cinders, the grating promise of choking ashes should he draw too deep a breath.

She would have a hearthstone. She – and her new husband – would have words that only they would know; the first words of the private language that must ever exist between husband and wife. Azathanai gifts were not simple, were never simple. 'Lord, may I ride this day?'

'Of course, Cryl. Seek out the eckalla, and should you find one, bring it down and we shall feast well. As in the old days when the beasts were plentiful, yes?'

'I shall do my best, Lord.'

Bowing, Cryl strode from the Great Hall. He was looking forward to this expedition, away from this place, out into the hills. He would take his hunting spear but, in truth, he did not expect to sight such a noble creature as an eckalla. In the other times when he had ridden the west hills, all he had ever found was bones, from past hunts, past scenes of butchering.

The eckalla were gone, the last one slain decades ago.

And beneath him while he rode, if he so chose, Cryl could listen to the thunder of his horse's hoofs, and imagine each report as the slamming of another door. They seemed to go on without end, didn't they?

*The eckalla are gone. The hills are lifeless.*

*       *       *

Even bad habits offered pleasure. In her youth, Hish Tulla had given her heart away with what others had seen as careless ease, as if it were a thing without much worth, but it had not been like that at all. She'd simply wanted it in someone else's hands. The failing was that it was so easily won, and therefore became a thing of little worth for the recipient. Could no one see the hurt she felt, each and every time she was cast aside, sorely used, battered by rejection? Did they think she welcomed such feelings, the crushing despond of seeing the paucity of her worth? *'Oh, she will heal quickly enough, will our dear Hish. She always does . . .'*

38

A habit like a rose, and on the day of its blossoming, why, see how each petal revealed its own unique script, with smaller habits hiding within the larger one. Upon this petal, precise instructions on how to force out the smile, the elegant wave of the hand and the shrug. Upon another petal, lush and carmine, a host of words and impulses to resurrect her vivacious nature; to glide her across every room no matter how many or how gauging the eyes that tracked her. Oh and she held tight upon the stem of that rose, didn't she?

The horse was quiescent beneath her; she could feel the gelding's comforting heat against her thighs, her calves. Beneath the branches of the tree under which she had taken shelter, evading the sudden downpour, she could see, through the slanting streams, the three men standing now before the basalt gravestone, out in the clearing where crouched the crypts and tombs, as the rain poured down as if seeking to drown them all.

She had known the pleasures of two of the three brothers, and, though she was no longer inclined, the last one was now likely beyond her reach, for he was soon to be wed, and it seemed that for Andarist his love was rare enough, precious enough, that once set at the foot of one woman, never again would he look elsewhere, never again would he even so much as glance away. That flighty, vain daughter of Jaen Enes knew not her fortune; of that Hish was certain, for she saw too much of herself in Enesdia. New to womanhood, eager to love and drunk with its power, how soon before she chafed at her bridling?

Hish Tulla was mistress to her House. She had no husband and would now take no one into her life. At her side, these days, was the desiccated remnant of her old habit, the petals almost black; the thorny stem stained and thickly smeared with something like vermilion wax. It served the role of an old friend, confidante to her confessions, ever wise in its recognition, never spurred into judgement. And these days, when she crossed a room, the eyes that tracked her . . . well, she no longer cared what they thought they saw. The woman older than her years, the spinster of many scars, the wild slave to carnal excess now returned to the earth, wisely subdued, though still ready for a moment's bright vivacity, the flash of a smile.

The rain fell off; a curtain drifting down in sudden dissolution as the sun's light broke through once more. Water still ran from the leaves, slicking the black branches, dripping down upon her waxed cloak like old tears. Clucking, Hish Tulla edged her mount forward. Stones crunched wetly under hoofs, and the three brothers turned at the sound.

They had ridden up from the south track, ignoring the torrent from the sky, and she concluded that they'd not seen her as they reined in before the crypt, dismounted and walked to stand before the unmarked plinth sealing the tomb. The body of their father, Nimander, lay in eternal repose within that crypt, in the hollowed-out trunk of a blackwood tree, but two years dead, and it was clear that his three sons were not yet done with the memory of him.

Witnessing the scene, Hish had recognized its privacy, the lowering of guard, and in their expressions now she thought she could see their disapproval and, perhaps, faint dismay. Raising a gloved hand as she walked her horse closer, she said, 'I was sheltering from the rain, brothers, when you rode into sight. Forgive my intrusion, it was not intended.'

Silchas Ruin, to whom Hish had given ecstatic adoration for four months a few years ago, before he lost interest, was the first to speak. 'Lady Hish, we knew we had an audience, but the shadows beneath the tree hid from us your identity. As you say, it was but chance, but be assured, you are always welcome in our eyes.'

Her old lovers were consistently courteous, probably because she never fought to hold on to any of them. The heart thus broken had no strength and even less will, and but crawled away with a weak smile and welling eyes. In their courtesy, she suspected, there was pity.

'Thank you,' she replied. 'I thought only to identify myself, and now I shall ride on and leave you to your remembrance.'

To that, it was Anomander who said, 'Lady Hish Tulla, you misunderstand our purpose here. We require no gravestone to remember our beloved father. No, in truth, it was curiosity that brought us to this place.'

'Curiosity,' agreed Silchas Ruin, 'and determination.'

Hish frowned. 'Lords, I am afraid I do not understand.'

She saw Andarist look away, as if he would claim no part in any of this. She knew he meant her no disrespect, but then, he had no reason to pity her and so cared little for courtesy.

These three brothers had a way of standing apart, even when they stood together. All were tall, and each shared something both magnetic and vulnerable. They could pull entire worlds around their selves, yet not once yield to pride, or arrogance.

White-skinned, red-eyed, Silchas Ruin waved a long-fingered hand, directing her attention to the basalt plinth. 'By our father's own command,' he said, 'the words carved upon his gravestone hide on the other side, facing in. They were intended for him alone, though he has no eyes with which to see, and no thoughts left to consider.'

'That is . . . unusual.'

Anomander's sun-burnished face, the colour of pale gold, now smiled at her. 'Lady, your touch is no less soft for the years between us.'

Hish felt her eyes widen at those words, though, upon a moment's reflection, perhaps more at the open affection in his tone. She met his gaze, searchingly, but saw nothing ironic or cruel. Anomander had been the first man she had taken as a lover. They had been very young. She remembered times of laughter, and tenderness, and the innocence of the unsure. Why had it ended? *Oh, yes. He went to war.*

'We are of a mind to prise loose this stone,' said Silchas.

At that Andarist turned to his brother. 'You are, Silchas. Because of your need to know everything. But the words will be Azathanai. To you they will mean nothing, and that is as it should be. They were never meant for us, and to the bite of our eyes they will answer with bitter curse.'

Silchas Ruin's laughter was soft. 'These are your days of superstition, Andarist. Understandably.' So dismissing his brother, he said, 'Lady Hish, from here we ride on to the building site of Andarist's new house. And awaiting us there is a stone-carver of the Azathanai, who has arrived with the hearthstone Anomander has commissioned as a wedding gift.' He gestured again, in that careless way she remembered from years past. 'This was but a minor detour, an impulse, in fact. Perhaps we will force the stone, perhaps not.'

Impulsive was not a behaviour Hish would associate with Silchas Ruin; indeed, not with any of these brothers. If their father chose to gift those words to darkness, it was in honour of the woman he had served all his life. She met Anomander's eyes again. 'Upon opening a crypt, you will all draw the breath of a dead man's air, and that is truth, not superstition. What follows upon that, curse or ill, will be for seers to glean.' She gathered up her reins. 'Pray, withhold yourselves for a moment and grant me the time to depart this yard.'

'You are riding to Kharkanas?' Silchas asked.

'I am.' If he thought she would explain further, he was mistaken. She nudged her mount forward, directing it towards the track that cut over the hump of the hill. The crypts on all sides of this ancient burial ground seemed to crouch, as if awaiting the pounding of yet more rain, and the moss draped over many of them was so verdant it startled the eye.

Hish Tulla felt their regard following her as she rode on; wondered, briefly, at what words they might now pass among them, faintly amused perhaps, or derisive, as old recollections – at least from Anomander and Silchas – awakened, if not regret, then chagrin. But they would laugh, to break free of the discomfort, and shrug away their own impetuous years, now well behind them.

And then, in all likelihood, Silchas would exhort his muscles to prise loose the gravestone, to look well upon the hidden words etched into the black, dusty basalt. He would, of course, be unable to read them, but he might recognize a hieroglyph here, another there. He might glean something of his father's message to Mother Dark, like catching a fragment of conversation one was not meant to hear.

In the dead man's breath there would come guilt, bitter and stale, for the three men to taste, and Andarist would know fury – for that taste was not something to bring into a new home for himself and his wife to be, was it? He had every right to be superstitious – omens ever marked great changes in life.

A smell bitter and stale, a smell of guilt. Little different, in fact, from that of a dead rose.

*     *     *

'To this day,' Anomander muttered, 'my heart swells at the sight of her.'

'Just your heart then, brother?'

'Silchas, will you ever listen well to what I say? I choose my words with precision. Perhaps, in truth, you speak only of yourself.'

'It seems that I do, then. She remains lovely to my eyes, I admit, and if I find myself desiring her even now, there is no shame in admitting it. Even now, I think, we but spin in her wake, like leaves from a fallen tree.'

Andarist had listened in silence to this, unable to share in any tender memories of the beautiful woman who had ridden out from the shadows beneath the tree. Yet, in that moment, he saw an opportunity to draw out his brothers, in particular Silchas – and perhaps it would be enough to dissuade him from his intentions. So he faced Silchas and said, 'Brother, why did you end it with her?'

Silchas Ruin's white face bore droplets and streaks of rain as would a visage carved in alabaster. He preceded his reply with a sigh, and then said, 'Andarist, I wish I knew. No, I think I realized that she was . . . ephemeral. Like a wisp of fog, I could not grasp hold. For all that she lavished attention upon me, it seemed there was something missing.' He shook his head, shrugged helplessly. 'Elusive as a dream, is Hish Tulla.'

'And is this unchanged in her?' Andarist asked. 'She has taken no husband.'

'I imagine her suitors have all given up,' Silchas answered. 'Each draws near, only to see too sharply his own failings, and in shame pulls away, never to return.'

'You may well be right,' Anomander mused.

'She seems to have suffered nothing in her solitude,' Silchas observed, 'nor do I see any weakness in her attention to grace and perfection. In elegant remoteness, she arrives like a work of high art, and you may well desire to edge ever closer, seeking flaws in the maker's hand, but the closer you get, the more she blurs before your eyes.'

Andarist saw that Anomander was studying Silchas intently, yet

42

when he spoke it was clear that his thoughts had travelled tracks other than those consuming Silchas. 'Brother, do you see Hish Tulla as a potential ally?'

'In truth, I cannot say,' Silchas replied. 'She seems the definition of neutrality, does she not?'

'She does,' Anomander admitted. 'Well, let us consider it again, at a later time. For now, will you have at this gravestone?'

Eyes closing, Andarist awaited his brother's answer.

Silchas was a moment before replying. 'I see more rain, and we have another league before us. The valley floor promises mud and treacherous footing. I suggest we set this matter aside for now, as well. Be at ease, Andarist. I would do nothing to endanger your future, and though I have little time for omens and such, I do not await what awaits you. So, if you'll forgive my occasional amusement, let us not cross the lame dog's path.'

'I thank you,' Andarist replied, glancing over to meet Silchas's warm gaze. 'And will endeavour to think no ill of your amusement, irritating and patronizing as it may be.'

The smile on Silchas's face now split into a grin, and he laughed. 'Lead us on, then. Your brothers would meet this famous mason and look well upon his offering.'

'Famous,' muttered Anomander, 'and damned expensive.'

They returned to their horses and mounted up. Drawing their mounts round, they set off.

Andarist looked across at Anomander. 'One day I hope to answer your sacrifice, brother, with one as worthy and as noble as yours.'

'Where love is the coin, no sacrifice is too great, Andarist. And with that wealth, who among us would hesitate? No, I but teased with you, brother. I trust I will be well pleased with the giving of this gift, and I hope you and your bride find the same pleasure in its receiving.'

'I am minded,' Andarist said after a moment, 'of our father's gift to us. Mother Dark has rewarded his loyalty through the elevation of his sons, and you, Anomander, have been lifted the highest among us.'

'And the point you wish to make?'

'Would you have permitted Silchas the desecration of Father's tomb?'

'Desecration?' Silchas said in shocked disbelief. 'All I sought was—'

'The sundering of a seal,' Andarist finished. 'What else could it be called?'

'The moment is past,' Anomander said. 'There will be no more said on the matter. Brothers, we approach a precious time. Let us value it as it should be valued. The blood ever flows between us, and ever shall, and that is our father's greatest gift to us – would either of you argue against that?'

'Of course not,' Silchas replied in a growl.

'And though I am now elevated to First Son of Darkness, I will not stand alone. I see you both with me, at my side. Peace shall be our legacy – we will achieve it together. What must be done I cannot do alone.'

After a long moment of riding, Silchas seemed to shake himself, and then he said, 'Hish Tulla looks fondly upon you, Anomander. She will see the nobility in what you seek.'

'I hope so, Silchas.'

And Andarist said, 'Though I do not know her as well as either of you, by reputation alone she is known for affability and a certain . . . integrity, and not once have I heard a word of spite directed towards Hish Tulla, which is in itself remarkable.'

'Then shall I approach her?' Anomander asked, looking from one brother to the other.

And both nodded.

Anomander had done well, Andarist reflected, in reminding them of what awaited them in the time ahead. A struggle was coming, and in Mother Dark's name they would find themselves at the very centre of it. They could afford no divisiveness or contention between them.

Through the branches of the trees lining the track, the sky was clear, the glare of the sun like molten gold on the leaves.

'It seems,' said Silchas, 'the way ahead has seen no rain, Andarist. I imagine your builders are well pleased at that.'

Andarist nodded. 'It is said that the Azathanai have power over both earth and sky.'

'These are Tiste lands,' Anomander countered. 'Purake lands. I do not recall my invitation extending to the extravagant use of sorcery. Though,' he added with a half-smile, 'I find I cannot entirely object to a cloudless sky over us.'

'We shall arrive with steam rising from us,' Silchas observed, laughing, 'like children born of chaos.'

\*       \*       \*

Envy was an unwelcome emotion, and Sparo fought hard against it as the servants – the heavy burlap in their hands – slowly walked back from the wagon-bed, and the cloth slipped easily across the surface of the hearthstone, and gasps of wonder rose from his cadre of stone-workers and carpenters.

The massive foundation stones of the new house were behind the Tiste mason, and he did not need to turn and look at them to feel how their magnificence dwindled before the revelation of this Azathanai artefact. Destined to occupy the very centre of the Great Hall, the hearthstone would reside like a perfectly cut gem amidst a clutter of pebbles from the river. He felt diminished and offered no objection when the huge man standing at his side grunted and said, 'Withdraw your workers, good Sparo. In the transport of the stone, I shall awaken sorcery.'

Sweat trickled down Sparo's back beneath his rough tunic. 'That will do,' he barked to his crew. 'Retreat to a safe distance, all of you!' He watched his people hurry away, noted their uneasy glances back to the Azathanai High Mason.

'There is nothing to fear, good Sparo.'

'Earth magic is feral,' Sparo replied. 'It never sits well with us.'

Another grunt. 'And yet you Tiste invite its gifts time and again.'

That was true enough. He glanced at the High Mason, feeling once more the almost physical buffeting the man's presence delivered, as if the power the Azathanai held ever threatened to burst free; and saw once again the bestial wildness of a face that seemed moments from inviting such an eruption. 'A meal is made finer, Lord, when one can avoid bloodying one's own hands in the making of it.'

'Then you are not a hunter, Sparo? Is that not unusual among the Tiste?'

Shrugging, Sparo said, 'Less so of late, as most of the beasts are slain and shall never return to our lands. It seems that our days of glorious hunting will soon be at an end.'

'Then let us hope,' rumbled the mason, 'that the Tiste do not turn to the final prey left them.'

Sparo frowned. 'And what manner of creature might that be?'

'Why, each other, of course.'

With that, the Azathanai drew off his sheepskin cloak, letting it fall behind him, revealing the thick, scarred leather of his jerkin, the broad belt with its iron rings awaiting a stone-cutter's tools, and set out towards the wagon. Glaring at the foreigner's broad back, Sparo chewed on those last words, and found them displeasing to the palate. This Azathanai might well be a master of the shaping of stone, and in his blood the wild and raw sorcery of the earth, but such talents were no excuse for veiled insults.

Should he tell Lord Andarist of this exchange, however, it would no doubt be seen as trite, his own anger revealed as dishonest, little more than a reflection of his jealousy. It was one thing to be counted as among the finest masons when in the company of naught but his fellow Tiste, but these intrusions by the Azathanai arrived like salt to open wounds.

A febrile charge filled the air, rising like a breath from the ground. Muttering, the dozen or so workers backed further away, crowding against the heaps of rubble and wooden scaffolding on the other side of the main track. Fighting his own unease, Sparo watched the hearthstone lift from the wagon-bed. The oxen had already been unhitched and led away, to keep the beasts from panicking at the awakening of the Azathanai's power. As the enormous block of basalt slid clear of the bed, the High Mason began walking towards the house, and the stone drifted into his wake like a faithful hound. Where it passed, however, the earth sank down as if still buckling to its massive weight. Small rocks spun away as if snapped by the passing of a huge wheel, while others crumbled to dust. The crackling energy filling the air began radiating heat, shrivelling the nearby tufts of grass, and smoke threaded along the path as the Azathanai guided the hearthstone towards its destination.

Sparo heard the thump of horse hoofs from the tree-lined track that led to the road, and he turned in time to see Lord Andarist and his brothers ride out from the shade of the nearest trees. The riders drew up sharply upon taking in the scene before them. Ignoring them, the Azathanai continued on, the hearthstone gliding along behind him – across the semicircular clearing fronting the house, and then on to the broad ramp that marked the approach to the gap still awaiting stone framing. Beneath the floating stone the ramp buckled, fissures spreading out through the packed soil.

Andarist had dismounted and now approached Sparo, who bowed and said, 'My lord, I begged the Azathanai to await your arrival, but he is without patience.'

'No matter, Sparo,' Andarist replied, eyes fixed on the hearthstone as it slid over the threshold. The walls were not yet high enough to obscure their view as the High Mason guided his creation on to the earthen floor of what would be the Great Hall. The hearthstone left a depressed track as it approached the shallow pit awaiting it.

'It was discourteous—'

'The delay was ours – and the weather to the south.'

Lord Anomander had come up alongside his brother, while Silchas Ruin seemed content to remain seated on his mount a short distance back. Now, the First Son of Mother Dark spoke. 'It is said that earth sorcery finds its truest vein of power at certain times of the day – and night – and so I expect the High Mason saw no value in delay, if only to ease his strain.' He glanced over at Lord Andarist and said, 'This much, at least, I did ask for.'

Sparo knew that it had been by Anomander's instruction – and his coin – that this commission had occurred. Also, it was well known that this particular High Mason of the Azathanai was considered the lord among masters, his skill unequalled by any living mason, which set his status as, at the very least, equal to Anomander himself, whom Mother Dark had chosen to call her First Son.

Lord Andarist now turned to his brother, his eyes bright. 'I would

you accompany me, Anomander, to witness the placing of your gift.'
He turned then and waved Silchas forward. 'And you as well, Silchas!'

But Silchas simply shook his head. 'Anomander's gift, and you the
beneficiary, Andarist. I am well enough pleased to attend as I am. Go
on, both of you, and quickly now lest that impolite creature forget his
reason for being here, and for whom the stone was made.'

Andarist gestured that Sparo join them and the house-mason bowed
a second time. 'Lord, I am but—'

'—my mason, Sparo, whose love for his art is sufficient cause in my
eyes. Come, join us. Let us all look upon the majesty of this work.'

Trailing a step behind the two lords, Sparo followed along, feeling
the thump of his own heart. Of course he would see the High Mason's
creation often enough in the months to come, in its rightful place in
the Great Hall, but even hard basalt worked by an Azathanai was not
immune to wear and tear, the scratches, stains and battering that came
with a working hearth. And for all his envy, he was as Andarist had
said: a lover of stone and the art of its shaping.

Silent with privilege, he joined his lord and Anomander upon reaching the packed earthen floor of the Great Hall. The Azathanai now
stood to one side of the hearthstone, and the huge block hovered above
its waiting seat. The High Mason faced Andarist and spoke, his expression flat.

'The earth told of your approach. Are you the one soon to wed? Is
this to be your home, Lord?'

'Yes, I am Andarist.'

The High Mason's broad visage then shifted to Anomander. 'You,
then, must be the First Son of Mother Dark. The giver of this gift to
your brother and the woman he will take as wife.'

'I am,' Anomander replied.

'And in so doing,' the High Mason continued, 'you bind yourself
by blood and vow to what shall be made here, and to the secret words
carved upon this hearthstone. If your loyalty is uncertain, speak now,
First Son. Once this stone finds its place, the binding of the vow can
never be broken, and should you fail in your love, in your loyalty, then
even I cannot answer for the consequences.'

This sudden pronouncement stilled the two brothers, and Sparo felt
his chest tighten, as if his heart's beat was suddenly held, frozen. He
struggled to breathe.

Anomander then tilted his head, as if to counter his own tension or
affront. 'High Mason,' he said, 'you speak of my love for Andarist,
and my desire for the well-being of the new life awaiting him, as if they
were in question. You speak, too, of this gift as if it embodies a threat,
or indeed a curse.'

'Such potential exists in every gift, and in its giving, First Son.'

47

'The bargain made between myself and you,' Anomander said, 'involved the payment of coin for your services—'

'Not precisely,' the Azathanai replied. 'You have paid for the protection and transport of this hearthstone, and its extraction from the Jhelarkan quarry. Your coin has purchased wagons, draught animals, and the necessary escort across the Bareth Solitude. For my talents, I take no coin.'

Anomander was frowning. 'Forgive me, High Mason, but I surely paid for much more than what you have described.'

'The Jhelarkan quarries are contested, Lord. Lives were lost in the procurement of this stone. Aggrieved families required compensation.'

'This . . . distresses me,' Anomander replied, and now Sparo could see the warrior's taut fury.

'The stone selected is unequalled in its capacity to contain and, indeed, sustain the sorcery I invest in it. If you wished a lesser gift, then you should not have made an approach to me. There are many highly skilled masons among the Azathanai, any one of whom could have served you well in the making of this gift. Yet you sought the finest worker of stone, to reflect the measure of your fealty to your brother and his pending union.' The High Mason shrugged. 'I have done as you requested. This hearthstone is without equal in the realm of the Tiste.'

'And now you stand before us,' said Anomander, 'demanding my blood-vow.'

'I do not,' the High Mason replied, crossing his thickly muscled arms. 'The stone demands. The words carved upon its face demand. The honour you wish to do to your brother demands.'

Andarist made to speak, dismay heavy on his features, but a quick shake of his brother's head stilled him. Anomander said, 'I have only your claim that the glyphs you have carved upon it – for the understanding of Andarist and Enesdia alone – do indeed avow love, fidelity and fecundity. And yet you ask of me, here and now, to give by blood and vow my binding to those secret words. Words that shall remain for ever unknown to me.'

'I do,' the High Mason replied. 'On this, you have nothing but your faith. In my integrity, and, of course, in your own.'

Another moment, when it seemed nothing in the world could move, could break the stillness, and then Anomander drew a dagger from his belt and slid the edge across the palm of his left hand. Blood trickled down, dripped on to the ground. 'Upon the hearthstone?' he asked.

But the High Mason shook his head. 'Unnecessary, First Son of Mother Dark.'

The hearthstone slowly settled into its bed of earth.

Sparo drew a sudden breath, almost sagged as the world righted itself once more. Looking at his lord, he saw Andarist, pale and shaken, possibly even frightened.

Neither brother had expected a moment so fraught, so heady with portent. Something had left them both, like a child in flight, and Anomander's eyes were grave and older than they had been, as they held, steady as stone itself, upon the face of the Azathanai High Mason. 'Then it is done?'

'It is done,' the Azathanai replied.

Anomander's voice sharpened, 'Then I must voice this unexpected concern, for I have placed my faith in the integrity of an Azathanai whom I know solely by reputation – his talent in the shaping of stone, and the power he is said to possess. In the matter of faith, Lord, you have gone too far.'

The Azathanai's eyes thinned, and he slowly straightened. 'What do you now ask of me, First Son?'

'Binding of blood and vow,' Anomander replied. 'Be worthy of *my* faith. This and this alone.'

'My blood you already have,' the Azathanai replied, gesturing towards the hearthstone. 'As for my vow . . . what you ask of me is without precedent. Tiste affairs are no concern of mine, nor am I about to avow allegiance to a noble of Wise Kharkanas, when it seems that such an avowal might well engulf me in bloodshed.'

'There is peace in the Tiste realm,' Anomander answered, 'and so it shall remain.' After a moment, when it was clear that the Azathanai would not relent, he added, 'My faith in you shall not command your allegiance, High Mason. In your vow there shall be no demand for bloodshed in my name.'

Andarist turned to his brother. 'Anomander, please. This is not necessary—'

'This High Mason has won from the First Son of Mother Dark a blood-vow, brother. Does he imagine that a thing of little value? If there is no coin in this exchange, then is it not my right to demand the same of him in return?'

'He is Azathanai—'

'Are the Azathanai not bound by honour?'

'Anomander, it's not that. As you have said, binding by blood pulls both ways. As it now stands, all you have bound yourself to is this hearthstone. Your vow is to the upholding of your brother and the woman he loves, and the union thereof. If such was not your sentiment from the very first, then as the High Mason has said, best we not hear it now?'

Anomander stepped back as if rocked by a blow. He lifted his bloodied hand.

'I do not doubt you,' Andarist insisted. 'Rather, I implore you to reconsider your demand on this Azathanai. We know nothing of him, beyond his reputation – yet that reputation is unsullied by questions regarding his integrity.'

'Just so,' replied Anomander. 'And yet he hesitates.'

The High Mason's breath hissed sharply. 'First Son of Darkness, hear my words. Should you wrest this vow from me, I will hold you to it, and its truth shall be timeless for as long as both of us shall live. And you may have cause to regret it yet.'

Andarist stepped closer to his brother, eyes imploring. 'Anomander – can't you see? There is more to what you ask of him than either of us can comprehend!'

'I will have his vow,' Anomander said, eyes fixed on those of the High Mason.

'To what end?' Andarist demanded.

'High Mason,' Anomander said, 'tell us of those ramifications which we do not as yet comprehend.'

'I cannot. As I said, First Son, there is no precedent for this. Shall I be bound to your summons? Perhaps. Just as you may in turn be bound to mine. Shall we each know the other's mind? Shall all secrets vanish between us? Shall we for ever stand in opposition to one another, or shall we stand as one? Too much is unknown. Consider carefully then, for it seems you speak from wounded pride. I am not a creature who weighs value in coin, and in wealth I ever measure all that cannot be grasped.'

Anomander was silent.

The Azathanai then held up a hand, and Sparo was shocked to see blood streaming down from a deep gash in the palm. 'Then it is done.'

As he turned away, Anomander called out to him, 'A moment, please. You are known by title alone. I will have your name.'

The huge man half swung round, studied Anomander for a long moment, and then said, 'I am named Caladan Brood.'

'It is well,' said Anomander, nodding. 'If we are to be allies . . .'

'That,' replied the High Mason, 'still remains to be seen.'

'No blood shed in my name or cause—'

Caladan Brood then bared teeth, and those teeth were sharp and long as those of a wolf. 'That, too, Lord, remains to be seen.'

# THREE

N OT TOO MANY YEARS AGO, FEWER INDEED THAN SHE CARED TO
think about, Korya Delath had lived in another age. The sun
had been brighter, hotter, and when she had carried her dolls,
a dozen or more, up the narrow, treacherous stone steps to the Aerie's
platform, she had delivered them into that harsh light with breathless
excitement. For this was their world, cut clean with the low walls
enclosing the platform casting the barest of shadows, and the heat
rising from the stone was lifted up by the summer wind as if giving
voice to a promise.

Up here, in that lost age, it ever seemed she was moments from
unfolding wings, moments from sailing up into the endless sky. She
was a giant to her dolls, a goddess, and hers were the hands of creation,
and even without wings she could stand and look down upon them,
reaching to adjust their contented positions, tilting their faces upward
so that she could see their stitched smiles or surprised 'O' mouths,
and their bright knuckled eyes of semi-precious stones – garnet, agate,
amber – that gleamed and flashed as they drank in the fervent light.

The summers were longer then, and if there were days of rain she did
not remember them. From the Aerie she could look out and study the
vast world beyond her and her dolls, her little hostages. The Arudine
Hills girdled the north, barely a league distant from the keep, and
from the maps Haut had let her examine she knew that these hills
ran more or less west–east, only breaking up in the border reaches of
Tiste-held territory far to the east; while westward they curled slightly
northward, forming the southern end of a vast valley where dwelt the
Thel Akai. If she looked directly east she would see the rolling steppes

of the Jhelarkan Range, and the so-called Contested Territory, and in her memories she thought she caught glimpses of herds, smudged dark and spotting the land, but perhaps those images came from the ancient tapestries lining Haut's study, and in any case the huge creatures only wandered now through her mind, and nowhere else. To the south she could make out two raised roads, mostly overgrown even then; one angling southeastward, the other southwestward. One of them, she knew now, led to Omtose Phellack, the Empty City. The other reached for the eastern borderlands, and it had been upon that road that she had first journeyed, from the world she had known as a child of Lesser House Delack, in the Tiste settlement called Abara, to this, the northernmost Jaghut keep in the realm they no longer claimed yet continued to occupy.

For this reason Haut had often mocked the notion of contested territory, but he also cited Jhelarkan indifference or possibly, given their defeats at the hands of the Tiste, incapability in claiming new lands for their control. Besides, the land in question was now empty, of little worth except as pasture, and the Jhelarkan way of life did not include the maintenance of domestic animals. There was nothing to contest, and it seemed just one more of those pointless arguments neighbours fostered with each other, a stamping of feet and holding of breath, a fury that could end in the spilling of blood. Haut was right to mock such things.

In her memories she could find no hint that she had ever seen a Jheleck. The territory to the east seemed the demesne of conquering weeds and scrub, ruled by relentless winds polishing cracked bedrock. It had been a place she had been forbidden to explore, except from here, atop the Aerie, straining across blurring distances with her eyes and seeing only whatever her imagination could conjure to life. But then, this was how she explored everything beyond the keep. Haut had kept her inside ever since she had been delivered into his care, isolated, hostage to everything, and to nothing.

She knew now that the Jaghut had not quite understood the Tiste tradition of giving and receiving hostages; certainly they had never sent one of their own children eastward, and given how rare those children were, it was no wonder. In any case, Haut only spoke of her enforced imprisonment as one of education: he had taken upon himself the responsibility of teaching her, and if he was an unusually harsh master, well, he *was* Jaghut.

Her dolls remained in her room these days. It had been years since they last looked up at the sun in its sky, with their 'O' mouths and eternal smiles. Sometimes, surprise and pleasure just faded away. Sometimes, the world dwindled, down until it was no bigger than a small, shallow platform atop a tower, and goddesses ran out of games to play, gave up reaching down to adjust the posture of her insensate children. Sometimes, the hostages just died of neglect, and power over corpses was no power at all.

This day, however, she was a goddess gripped by something that might be fear, or perhaps alarm, and her heart was thumping fast in her thin chest as she stood alone on the platform, watching the score or so Jheleck drawing ever closer to the keep. There was no question that they were intent on accosting Haut, either with violence or threat – she could think of no other reason for defying the prohibitions, for crossing the border into Jaghut territory. Of course, it was a territory no longer held by anyone. Were these ancient enemies coming to claim it for themselves?

There had been no images of these creatures anywhere among the keep's tapestries, statuary and friezes, yet what else could they be? Arriving from the east, from the Jhelarkan Range, and no grass-eating beasts of old – she could see black leather harnesses on their long, lean forms; she could see the glint of iron blades strapped on to their forelimbs, and serrated discs flashing from their humped shoulders. They padded forward like swollen dogs, with hides of black or mottled tan, their long-snouted faces only hinted at beneath their boiled leather headgear – like hounds of the hunt, but they were their own masters.

It was said that this northern strain was kin to the Jheck of the far south, though purportedly much larger. Korya was relieved by that thought, since these Jheleck were nearly as big as warhorses. Though resembling dogs, they were said to be intelligent, possessors of a sorcery she knew only as *Soletaken*, though for her that was nothing more than a word, as meaningless as so many other words Haut had uttered over the years of her captivity.

She knew her master was not unaware of this intrusion. Nothing came on to his land without his knowing it, no matter how light the footfall or how thin the rush of air. Besides, he had sent her up here a short time past, his command harsh and snapping – she had at first imagined some transgression on her part, a chore not completed, a book left open, but she knew enough not to question him. In words he could wound deeply, and if he possessed humour she'd yet to find it. Yet still she was shocked when she heard the keep's massive iron gate thunder open, and when she saw Haut emerge, no longer wearing his ratty, moth-eaten woollen robe, but bedecked instead in ankle-length black chain, overlapping iron scales shielding his shins and booted feet, with more of the same stacked along the breadth of his shoulders. From the flared back rim of his helmet of blackened iron, chain hung down like braided hair. When he paused and twisted round, glancing up towards Korya, she saw more chain, webbing his face beneath the eye-holes, dangling in tatters around his massive, stained tusks.

A sword was belted at his hip, but he made no move towards its long, leather-wrapped grip, his gauntleted hands remaining down at his sides as he swung back to face the Jheleck.

Haut was a scholar. He complained endlessly of brittle bones and arthritic pangs; she believed he was ancient, though she had no proof of that. His contempt for warriors was matched only by his disgust for war and all its idiotic causes. She had never before seen the armour he was now clad in, nor the weapon he now bore. It did not seem possible he was able to move under the weight of his accoutrements, yet he did so with grace, an ease she had never before seen in him.

It was as if the Aerie shifted beneath her, the world slipping in its massive gears. Mouth dry, she watched as her master marched directly towards the Jheleck, who now positioned themselves in a ragged row facing the Jaghut.

Halting ten paces away, and then . . . nothing.

Surely the Jhelarkan could not form words, not from bestial throats such as they must have possessed. If they spoke, it was through other means, yet there was no doubt in her mind that a conversation was now under way. And then Haut reached up and drew off his helmet, his long black iron-streaked hair falling loose in greasy ropes, and she saw him tilt his head back, and she heard him laugh.

Deep, rolling, a sound that did not fit into Korya's world, a sound so unexpected it could stagger a goddess high upon her perch. Like thunder from the earth itself, that laughter rattled through her, climbed skyward like the beating of wings.

The Jheleck seemed to blur then, as if engulfed in black smoke, and moments later a score of warriors now stood in place of the beasts; and they began removing their long-snouted headgear, unstrapping the blades from their wrists and sliding the lengths down through iron loops in their harnesses; the serrated discs now jutted behind their heads like cowls.

What she could see of their faces was little more than the dark smudge of black beards and filthy skin. Apart from the now-loose leather armour, they appeared to be dressed in furs and hides. When they came forward, they shambled, as if unsteady on two legs.

Haut whirled round, looked up at her, and bellowed, 'Guests!'

\*     \*     \*

A solitary Jaghut and a young Tiste hostage: in this household there were no servants, no cooks, no butchers, no handmaids or footmen. The keep's vast storerooms were virtually empty, and though Haut was quite capable of conjuring food and drink through sorcery, he rarely did so, relying almost exclusively on regular visits by the Azathanai

54

traders who plied on seasonal rounds the tracks linking all the still-occupied keeps.

In the absence of staff, Korya had learned to bake bread; she had learned to make stews and broths; she had learned to chop wood and mend her own threadbare clothes. Haut had proclaimed these tasks to be essential elements of her education, but she had begun to believe such chores were the product of less sanguine factors, beginning and ending with Haut's own indolence, and his general dislike of company. It was, she often reflected, a wonder that he had ever accepted her presence, and the responsibility of taking her in.

As a people, the Jaghut rarely had anything to say to each other; they seemed perversely divisive and indifferent to such concepts as society or community. But this rejection was a conscious one; they had once dwelt in a city, after all. They had once built an edifice to civilization unequalled anywhere in all the realms, only to then conclude that it was all some kind of mistake, a misapprehension of purpose, or, as Haut described it, a belated recognition of economic suicide. The world was not infinite, and yet a population could aspire to become so; it could (and would) expand well beyond its own limits of sustainability, and would continue to do so until it collapsed. There was, he said, nothing so deadly as success.

Wisdom did not belong to mortals, and those whom others called wise were only those who, through grim experience, had touched the very edges of unwelcome truths. For the wise, even joy was tinged with sorrow. No, the world made its demands upon mortals and they were immediate ones, pressingly, ferociously so, and even knowing a reasonable course was not enough to alter a mad plunge into disaster.

Words were no gift, said Haut. They were tangled nets snaring all who ventured into their midst, until an entire people could hang helpless, choking on their own arguments, even as dissolution closed in on all sides.

The Jaghut had rejected that path. Defying the eternal plea for communication among peoples, in the name of understanding, peace or whatever, they had stopped talking, even with each other. And their city was abandoned, home now to a single soul, the Lord of Hate, the one who had laid bare the brutal truth of the future awaiting them all.

This was the history Korya had learned, but that had been another age, when she was a child, and it was the child who made answer to the bewildering tale told her by Haut, with her dolls, a family, perhaps even a society, and in that society there were no wars, and no arguments and no feuds. Everyone smiled. Everyone looked on in surprise and wonder at the perfect world their goddess had created for them, and the sun was always bright and always warm. There was, she knew, no end to the dreams of children.

The Jheleck had brought food: meat still dripping blood, jugs of thick, dark wine, leather bags holding sharp stones of crystallized sugar. At Haut's command she brought forth salty bread from the stone cupboard forming the back wall of the kitchen, and dried fruit from the cellar; and the fire was lit in the main hall and the high-backed chairs drawn in from the walls, their legs making furrows in the dust closing in on the long table from all sides. Tapers were dipped and awakened to smoky flame, and as the twenty-one Jheleck crowded in, flinging off pungent furs, barking in their sharp tongue, the vast room grew steamy and redolent with old sweat and worse. Rushing back and forth from back rooms and storage cupboards, Korya almost gagged again and again upon plunging into the fug; and only when at last she could sit down, upon Haut's left, drinking deep from the flagon of bitter wine pushed her way, was she able to settle into this new, heady world.

When the Jheleck spoke the Jaghut language, their accent was hard, all edges, yet clear enough to Korya's ears, even if it carried with it a snide tone of contempt. The visitors ate the meat raw, and before long Haut himself joined in, his long-fingered hands slick with gore as he tore at the flesh, his inner teeth seeming to disengage from the flanking tusks when he chewed – something she had never seen before. Most of the animal products consumed in this house were of the smoked or dried variety, old and tough until soaked in wine or broth. Her master was regressing before her very eyes; she felt off-balanced, as if Haut had become a stranger.

Through it all, however, even as the wine softened the scene, she took in every word, every gesture, desperate to make sense of this gathering.

*Guests.*

They never had guests. Traders simply visited, and those that stayed overnight camped outside the walls. On much rarer occasions, another Jaghut arrived, to pick up on some obscure argument with Haut – a reluctant, pained exchange of words – and then was gone again, often leaving in the dead of night, and Haut's mood would be foul for days thereafter.

The Jheleck had ignored her upon seating themselves and settling into their feast. Wine was guzzled like water from the well. Comments in two languages were flung back and forth. Belches and grunts accompanied every mouthful. There were no women among the warriors, leading Korya to wonder if this was some sect, a gaggle of priests or a brotherhood. Among the Thel Akai could be found monks sworn to weapons they themselves had fashioned from raw ore; perhaps these Jheleck were similarly avowed – they had not discarded their blades, after all, whereas Haut had divested himself of his martial gear as soon as he strode into the chamber.

The warrior seated on her left crowded against her, his heavily muscled shoulder and arm jostling her again and again. The Jheleck opposite seemed amused by her discomfort when he finally took notice. 'Sagral,' he suddenly barked, 'ware your lumpy self, lest you end up in her lap.'

Raucous laughter greeted this comment, while Haut simply grunted, reaching for a jug of wine. Pouring himself another cup, he then said, 'Careful you do not awaken her temper.'

The one who'd spoken lifted shaggy eyebrows. 'You've suffered it, then, captain?'

*Captain?*

'I have not, but she is Tiste and she is a young woman. I have waited for its coming since she first arrived, and still I wait. I am certain that it exists, although no amount of abuse I hurl at her has managed to sting it awake.'

Sagral leaned hard against her, thrusting close his broad, scarred face. 'Anger is a sign of sharp wits, nay, of intelligence itself.' His black eyes fixed on her. 'Is it so?' he asked. 'Have years of Jaghut nonsense obliterated every spark? Assuming you had any to begin with?'

She studied him, making no effort to recoil, and said nothing.

Sagral's eyes widened, and then he looked to Haut. 'Is she a mute?'

'She's never said as much,' Haut replied.

The brutes laughed again, and already she longed to be ignored as she had been earlier, but it seemed that now she was to be the butt of every jest. She turned to Haut. 'Master, I wish to be excused.'

'Impossible,' Haut replied. 'After all, they're here for you.'

*    *    *

Typically, Haut was in no hurry to explain and she was left with a tumble of pointless questions filling her mind. They had given him a title; they had called him a captain. That was a military rank in the manner of Urusander's Legion, or the Forulkan. But hostages were never given to soldiers: no army could be said to hold noble title, after all. Had her people erred in sending her here? Had they sent her into the keeping of a commoner?

No, that made no sense. If she—

'Captain,' said the warrior opposite her, his sharp tone snapping her out of her confused thoughts, 'without trust there can be no peace. You, among all of us, know this as truth. In this gift, we shall find a name, and it shall be a name of honour.'

Haut slowly nodded – all at the table were now silent, listening. 'And you wish to twine your gesture with that which I have the power to give to you. In return for what?'

'Peace.'

'I have peace, Rusk.'

The spokesman grinned, showing filed teeth. 'Nothing lasts for ever.'

Haut grunted, reaching again for his cup. 'Did your defeat at the hands of the Tiste teach you hounds nothing?'

Rusk's grin vanished, and it was Sagral who answered, 'You have no Borderswords. You have no Urusander's Legion. You have no House-blades of the High Families. What have we learned, captain? Your army is gone. This is what we have learned.'

'We never had an army, Sagral,' Haut replied, the vertical slits of his pupils narrowing as if in bright light. 'We are Jaghut. Armies are anathema, and we have no taste for war. When facing fools who proclaim themselves our enemy, we simply destroy them. And we are thorough. For centuries you have tested us, and each time we have flung you back.'

'We came in small packs,' Sagral said in a growl. 'This time, we shall come in our thousands.'

'And when you came to raid, in your small packs, Sagral, we were content to drive you off, killing only a few of you. Should you now come in your thousands, our restraint is at an end.'

Rusk had been sucking on crystals of sugar, one after another, his small eyes fixed on Korya, and now he said, 'We will return her home unharmed, captain.'

'This is not how the hostage system works,' Haut answered, slowly shaking his head. 'Your treaty with the Tiste demands from you hostages – of your own blood. You cannot borrow one from someone else in lieu of the sacrifice you must make. The Tiste will accept only Jheleck hostages.'

'But they offer none to us!' Sagral snapped.

'Because you lost the war, Sagral. You were faced with a simple choice: concessions or annihilation. By your presence we see which choice you made; now you must live with it or plunge once more into war.'

'The Jheleck are not slaves!'

Haut glanced at Korya. 'Hostage, do you consider yourself a slave?'

She knew the answer he expected from her, but it was the thought of travelling in the company of these beasts that motivated her reply. 'Of course not. I am Tiste, born of House Delack. I am hostage to the Jaghut; the only hostage to ever have come to the Jaghut, and now the only one who ever will. In two years I will be returned to my family: the Jaghut tell us they are no longer a people. They tell us they have surrendered all claims.'

Sagral thumped the table, startling her. 'Even their claim to you, child! It is only Haut's selfishness that keeps you in his clutches! We will deliver you home, and we can leave with the dawn! Do you not wish this, or has Haut crushed the life from you? Made you a slave in all but name?' He reared back, on his feet. 'Even the Tiste know to disregard the Jaghut now – these tusked fools are nothing. They have abandoned the future and are doomed to die out. Their city lies in a bed of dust, ruled over by a mad man! You, hostage! You waste your life away here – two more years! For nothing!'

Korya had twisted in her chair to look up at him. She studied his rage-darkened face, the gleam of his bared teeth and their sharpened tips, the challenge in his eyes. Then she faced Rusk and asked, 'Does this one need a leash?'

The sudden laughter stole the tension from the room, and all down the length of the table Jheleck warriors reached once more for the wine jugs. Sagral thumped back down, silent with shame. Bested by a Tiste female barely a woman – if that boyish frame was any indication – and made a pup once more was dour Sagral, kicked cowering into the cold – and all these biting comments were spoken in Jaghut, for her benefit, no doubt. When Korya glanced at Haut, she saw his pale eyes fixed upon her. She could never read them – neither approval nor disgust could alter that look; it was steady and unrelenting.

*Captain.* There had never been a Jaghut army. He had never been a captain of anything. The honorific made no sense at all.

Some unseen signal quelled the raucousness once more, and then Rusk spoke. 'Captain, the Tiste have asked for fifty hostages. Fifty of our young ones. We will not surrender the lives of fifty Jheleck, young or old.'

'It is hardly surrendering their lives, Rusk—'

'The Tiste are heading into civil war.'

'That fear has been uttered before,' Haut replied. 'It is meaningless. And even then, should civil war erupt, the lives of hostages will remain sacrosanct; indeed, I expect each family would immediately return your children to you, even at the risk of the preservation of their own Houses.'

Rusk snorted. 'If you believe so, captain, then you understand nothing of civil war. And why should you? It is unthinkable to the Jaghut; but it is not so with us.'

A third Jheleck, silver-haired and scarred, said, 'Our kin to the south were once united with us; in all ways they were identical – we were all Jheleck.'

'I well recall your civil war,' Haut said, nodding slowly. 'And I have seen how it has made of you two people now. Varandas has written at length on the birth of the Jheck culture, and its myriad distinctions from your own.'

Rusk growled deep in his throat. 'Varandas had no right.'

Shrugging, Haut said, 'No matter, Rusk. The fool burned all his writings on the Night of the Dissension. What value history when no one heeds it anyway? My point remains none the less. Through your own experience, you now predict a similar fate to engulf the Tiste. But the Tiste are not Jheleck, nor are they Jheck, and the power at the heart of Kharkanas is not the wild force of your Vitr-born Soletaken, and Mother Darkness made no bargain with beast gods. No, Wise Kharkanas is a black diamond at the heart of the Tiste people, and so long as its inner fires burn, no sword can shatter it.'

'We will not yield up fifty of our young.'

'Then, Rusk, you will have war again. Although, if that occurs, you can find reason for relief, in that such an external conflict will unite the Tiste once more, thus ensuring no civil war.'

'We do not fear their civil war, captain. We would welcome it, for when it closes, all Tiste lands will be ripe for conquest. But we will not risk the lives of our young.'

'Korya is not your solution,' Haut said.

'Send her home then! Free her! She is of no value to you!'

'When it is time I shall do precisely that. Education, Rusk, is a long-term investment. Expect no fruit in the first season. Expect none in the next, nor the one that follows. No, the reward is years away, and so it has been and so it remains with Korya. I have prepared the way for her life, and in that I am almost done. But not quite.'

'You can do nothing more for her,' said Rusk. 'We can feel the essence of her soul. It is dark, empty. It has no power. She is not a child of Mother Dark, not in her soul, for the darkness that dwells there is not Kurald Galain. It is simply *absence*.'

'Yes, perfectly so.'

'Then what awaits it?' Rusk demanded.

'In the language of the Dog-Runners, Rusk, I have fashioned a mahybe. A vessel. Protected, sealed and, as you say, empty. What remains to be done? Why, its filling, of course.'

*Hostage.*

Stunned, frightened, Korya thought of the dolls in her room, each one awaiting life, each one awaiting the destiny that only a goddess could grant. They'd not moved in years. They crowded the darkness inside a stone chest.

'With the dawn,' said Haut to the Jheleck, 'you leave. Alone.'

'You will regret this,' Rusk vowed.

'One more threat from you,' Haut replied, 'and your host will feel ire. He might well cast you out to sleep under the stars, as befitting rude hounds that know nothing of honour. Or, if he judges you beyond salvage, he might simply kill you all.'

Korya saw Rusk pale beneath the grime. He rose, gestured, and all the other warriors pushed back their chairs, reaching for their discarded gear. 'For the repast,' Rusk said, voice heavy, 'we thank you, captain. When next we dine in this hall, it shall be upon your snapped bones.'

Haut also rose. 'So you twitch in your dreams, Jheleck. Now begone. I am done with you.'

*　　　*　　　*

Once they had trooped out, and Korya prepared to clear away the leavings, Haut gestured distractedly and said, 'I shall awaken the sorcery of Omtose Phellack this night, Korya. Return to your room.'

'But—'

'Sorcery has value,' he said. 'It will aid me in de-lousing this chamber at the very least. Now, to your room. You have nothing to fear from those Soletaken.'

'I know,' she replied. 'Master, if you have made me into a vessel . . . well, I do not feel it. I am not empty inside. I am not at peace.'

The word seemed to startle him. 'Peace? I spoke not of peace. In absence, Korya, there is *yearning*.' His strange eyes focused on her. 'Do you not so yearn?'

She did. She knew the truth of it, as soon as he had spoken of what was inside her. She was the goddess who had tired of her children, who had seen the summers grow ever shorter, tinged with impatience, yet had not known what might arrive in place of the lost age.

'Sleep this night,' Haut said, in a tone she had never before heard from him. It was almost . . . gentle. 'On the morrow, Korya, the lessons begin in earnest.' He turned away, 'My last task awaits us both, and we shall be worthy of it. This I promise.' He gestured again, and she hurried from the room, her mind awhirl.

*　　　*　　　*

The carriage had been drawn up in front of the once-palatial entrance to the House of Delack. A single horse stood forlorn in the harness, head nodding as it chewed on its bit. The journey awaiting it would be arduous, for the carriage was heavy and in years past would have been drawn by a team of four. Beyond it, just visible from where stood Lady Nerys Drukorlat on the steps, the small boy was playing along the edge of the charred ruin of the stables, and she could see that his hands were black with soot, and he'd already stained his knees.

Here, in this failing estate, this was a battle that Nerys had no hope of winning. But childhood was short, and in these troubled times she would do all she could to make it even shorter. The boy needed guidance. He needed to be shaken free of his imaginary fancies. Nobility was born in the rigid stricture of proper attitude, and the sooner her grandson was bound to the necessities of adulthood, the sooner would he find his place as heir to the ancient House; and with

61

proper guidance he would one day return the bloodline to the glory and power it had once possessed.

And she would hear nothing of that dreadful word, that cruel title that hung now over Orfantal like a crow's mocking wing.

*Bastard.*

No child could choose. The venal stupidity of his mother, the lowborn pathos of his drunken father – these were not the boy's crimes, and his innocence was not for others to denigrate. People could be vicious. Eager with hard judgement, eager with contempt.

'*The wounded will wound.*' So said the poet Gallan, and no truer words were spoken. '*The wounded will wound / and every hurt is remembered.*' These lines came from his latest collection, his ominously titled *Days of Skinning*, which had been published at the beginning of the season and continued to foment outrage and heated condemnations. Of course, the truly cultured among the Houses could look upon unpleasant truths without blinking, and if Gallan in his courage had set blade to the Tiste culture and peeled back the skin, was not all that fury proof that he had seen true?

There was much to despise about one's own kind, and the banality of fading glory was indeed bitter to bear. One day, there would be a rebirth. And if one saw clearly, and planned well enough in advance, then in the rising of a new age of fervour the bloodline could burst into new life, at the very heart of unimagined power. The opportunity would come, but not in her time. All that she did now was meant to serve the future, and one day they would see that; one day, they would understand her own sacrifices.

Orfantal had found a splintered shaft of wood, from one of the fence rails, and was now waving it over his head, shouting and running. She watched as he clambered atop a low heap of rubble, his expression one of triumph. He jammed one end of the shaft between two chunks of masonry, as if planting a standard, only to suddenly stiffen, as if speared through by some invisible weapon. Back arching, he stared skyward, his expression shocked, filling with imagined agony, and then he staggered down from the mound, stumbling to his knees, one hand clutching his stomach. A moment later he fell over and lay like one dead.

Silly games. And always ones of war and battle, heroic yet ending in tragedy. She'd yet to see the boy pretend to die while facing his imagined enemy. Again and again, it seemed he was enacting betrayal, the knife thrust from behind, the surprise and hurt filling his eyes. The hint of indignation. Boys were foolish at this age. In their ridiculous games they martyred themselves to their own belief in the injustice of the world, the chores that cut into their play time, the lessons that stole the daylight and summer's endless dreaming, the shout from the kitchen that ended the day.

It all needed expunging. From young Orfantal's mind. The great wars were over. Victory had won this peace, and young men and young women must now turn to other things – the sword-wielders' time was past, and all these veterans, wandering through the settlements like abandoned dogs, getting drunk and spinning wild tales of bravery and then weeping over lost comrades – it was a poison to everyone, especially the young, who were so easily seduced by such tales and those crushing, wretched scenes of grief.

Soldiers lived in ways no others had, or could hope to, unless they too found the truths of war. Veterans returned home with all illusions scoured from their eyes, their minds. They looked out from a different place, but there was nothing healthy in that, nothing worthy. They had lived their days of skinning, and now all that they looked upon was duly exposed: gristle and sinew, bone and meat and the trembling frailty of organs.

Her husband had confessed as much to her, the night before he took his own life, the night before he abandoned them all, leaving only a legacy of shame. The hero who returned – what cause had he to kill himself? Returned to his beloved wife – the woman he had talked about, and longed for, each and every day while on the march – returned, rewarded, honoured, invited into a well-earned retirement far from strife and rigour. Home for less than a month, and then he drives a dagger into his own heart.

When the shock passed; when the horror faded; when eyes settled upon Nerys, the veiled widow . . . then came the first whispers.

*What did she do to him?*

She had done nothing. He had arrived home already dead. No, that was not it. When he had come home, it was she who was dead. To him. Out on those marches, on those fields of battle, on those miserable, cold nights under indifferent stars, he had fallen in love with the idea of her: that ageless, perfect idea, and against that she could not compete. No mortal woman could.

Her husband had been a fool, susceptible to delusion.

The truth was, the bloodline was already weak, almost fatally so. And things would only get worse. It had been some other soldier, a youth who'd lost an arm to a horse bite long before he drew blade against an enemy, who'd come to Abara drunk and bitter – oh, he'd told his share of lies, but after it had happened, Nerys had made inquiries, had discovered the truth. No, he had not lost his arm defending a Son of Darkness. No, he had not been recognized for his bravery. But it was too late. He had found Nerys's daughter. He had found Sandalath, just a young girl still, too young to regard him with proper scepticism, and his slurred words seduced her easily, his calloused hand found the parts of her just awakened, and he stole from them all their future.

*Bastard son.*

Nerys kept him – that pathetic father – in coin, in the village. Enough to ensure that he stayed drunk, drunk and useless. She had made him the offer, made clear the only bargain available to him, and of course he accepted. He would never see his son, never see Sandalath, never come up to the house, nor walk the estate's grounds. He had his corner of the root cellar in Abara Tavern, and all the wine he could pour down his numb throat. She even arranged to send him whores, not that he could manage much with them any more, according to their reports. The wine had stolen everything; he had the face of an old man and eyes that belonged to the condemned.

The door behind her opened and Nerys waited, without turning, until her daughter came up alongside her.

'Do not say goodbye to him,' Lady Nerys told Sandalath.

'But he's—'

'No. There will be a scene and we won't have that. Not today. We have had word. Your escort is taking a meal at the inn and will be with us soon. The journey awaiting you is long, daughter.'

'I am too old to be a hostage again,' said Sandalath.

'The first time was four years,' Nerys replied, repeating her part in this exchange almost word for word with the dozens of other times they had argued the matter. 'It was drawn short. The House of Purake no longer exists as such – besides, Mother Dark has taken Nimander's sons for her own.'

'But they will take me back – at least let me go back to them, Mother.'

Nerys shook her head. 'There is no political gain in that direction. Remember your duty, daughter. Our bloodline is damaged, weakened.' She held on that last word, to ensure that it cut in the manner that it should – after all, who was to blame for this last wounding? 'We do not choose such things.'

'I will say goodbye to him, Mother. He is my son.'

'And my grandson, and in this matter his welfare is of greater concern to me than is yours. Save your tears for the inside of the carriage, where none can see your shame. Leave him to his play.'

'And when he looks for me? What will you say then?'

Nerys sighed. How many times did she have to say these things? *Just this last time – I see the rider on the road.* 'Children are resilient, and you well know his education is about to begin in earnest. His life will be consumed by scholars and teachers and studies, and each night after dinner he will sleep and sleep deeply. Do not be selfish, Sandalath.' She did not have to add *again.* 'It is time.'

'I am too old to be a hostage once more. It is unseemly.'

'Consider yourself fortunate,' Nerys replied. 'You have served the

House of Drukorlas twice, first among House Purake, and now, in the House of its rival.'

'But House Dracons is so far away, Mother!'

'Keep your voice down,' Nerys hissed. She couldn't see Orfantal any more – perhaps he had run behind the stables, which was just as well. Leave him to his adventures and his stained hands. In a very short time, a new life would take hold of him; and if Sandalath believed that the house behind them would soon be crowded with tutors, well, it did no harm to let her hold some comforting beliefs.

Orfantal was destined for Kharkanas. Where the whispers of *bastard* would never reach him. Nerys had prepared the way for that arrival: the boy was a cousin from an outland holding, south of the Hust Forges. He was being given to the House of Purake, not as a hostage, but to serve the palace and Mother Dark herself. He would be schooled by the Sons of Darkness, as one in their retinue. Of course, the boy had been raised from a very young age by Sandalath, and often called her his mother, but that affectation would wear off in time.

The horseman from House Dracons rode up, reining in behind the carriage. Remaining in the saddle, he bowed towards Lady Nerys and Sandalath. 'Greetings and felicitations from the Consort,' the man said. 'I am named Ivis.'

Nerys turned to her daughter. 'Into the carriage.'

But Sandalath was looking past the carriage, stretching to catch a last glimpse of her son. He was nowhere to be seen.

'Daughter, obey your mother. Go.'

Holding herself as would someone with diseased lungs – shoulders hunched, caving in round the infection – Sandalath made her way down the stone steps. She had a way of seeming both old and impossibly young, and both states filled Nerys with contempt.

Nerys tilted her head towards the escort. 'Ivis, we thank you for your courtesy. We know you have ridden far this day.'

Atop the bench at the front of the carriage the coachman was eyeing Lady Nerys, awaiting the signal. In the pale sky behind him a flock of birds winged towards the tree-line.

'Lady Nerys,' said Ivis, drawing her attention around, 'we shall ride through the night and arrive at the house of my lord shortly after dawn.'

'Excellent. Are you alone in this task?'

He shook his head. 'A troop awaits us east of Abara, milady. Of course, we respect the traditional possessions of your bloodline, and so would do nothing to displease you.'

'You are most kind, Ivis. Please convey my compliments to Lord Draconus, for selecting such an honourable captain for this task.' She then nodded to the coachman, who snapped the traces, startling the horse into motion.

The carriage rumbled forward, bouncing over the uneven cobble-stones, swinging on to the track that led round the back of the house. Halfway down the hill it would join the road into Abara, and from there it would take the north track, alongside the river, for a short distance before finding the branch leading northeast.

Drawing her heavy cloak about her shoulders, faintly chilled in the shadow of the entranceway, Nerys watched until the rider and the carriage disappeared round the side of the house, and then she looked once more to catch sight of Orfantal. But still he was out of sight.

This pleased her.

Some other battle in the ruins. Another triumphant stand. Another knife in the back.

Children dreamed the silliest dreams.

*　　*　　*

Standing in the shadow of the burnt-out stables, hidden from the steps of the house, the boy stared after the carriage. He thought he had seen her face, there in the small, smudged window, pale and red-eyed, as she strained to find him, but then the carriage trundled past, turning so that all he could see was its high back and strongbox, the tall wheels leaning and wobbling on old axles. And then, the strange rider in the soldier's garb rode by, his horse kicking up puffs of dust once past the cobbles.

Soldiers came to Abara. Some had missing limbs or only one eye. Others bore no wounds but died with knives in their chests, as if the weapon had followed them all the way from those distant battles they'd fought in. Darting silver, barely seen in the night, following, finding, at last catching up. To kill the man who'd been meant to die weeks, even months, earlier.

But this soldier, who called himself Ivis, had come to take away his mother.

He didn't like to see people cry. He'd do anything to keep them from crying, and in his mind, in the imaginary world of strife and heroism that he lived in, he often voiced vows over the tears of a broken woman. And then fought his way across half the world in the name of that vow. Until it killed him, like a knife creeping up from the distant past.

The boy watched the carriage until it was lost from sight. And his mouth then moved, voicing a silent word.

*Mother?*

There were wars far away, where hate locked weapons and blood sprayed like rain. And there were wars in a single house, or a single room, where love died the death of heroes, and weeping filled the sky. There were wars everywhere. He knew this. There were wars and that's all there was, and every day he died, taken by that knife that followed him across the whole world, just as it had done to his grandfather.

But for now, he would hide in the shadows, in the stables that had caught fire, killing all but one of the horses. And maybe slink into the wood beyond the corral, to fight ever more battles, losing every time because the real heroes always did, didn't they? Death always caught up, to everyone. And the day would rush past, as it always did.

Until the call came from the kitchen, ending the world for another night.

*       *       *

Sandalath thought she had seen him, there in the gloom, ghostly against one of the last still-standing walls of the burnt-out stable, but probably had only imagined it. The footing of her mind was uncertain, or so her mother always said; and imagination, such as she'd bequeathed to her son, in abundance, was no virtue in these stressful times. The air inside the carriage was stifling, smelling of mould, but the hinges on the side windows had seized with rust and grime, and the only draught to reach her came from the speak-box leading up to a tube of wood that rose beside the bench where sat the coachman. She barely knew him – he had been hired from the village for this one task – and should she call up to him, to beg his help opening a window, well, that tale would soon fill the taverns – the fallen House and its cursed, useless family. There would be laughter, mockery and contempt. No, she would not ask anything of him.

Sweat trickled beneath her heavy clothes. She sat as still as she could manage, hoping that would help, but there was nothing to do, nothing to occupy her hands, her mind. Too much rocking and jostling to resume her embroidery; besides, dust was already drifting in, sliced bright by thin spears of sunlight. She could feel it coating her face, and had there been tears on her cheeks – which she knew there were supposed to be – then the streaks would darken with dirt. Unsightly, shameful.

She remembered her first time as a hostage; she remembered her time in the Citadel, the breathless excitement of all those people moving through countless sumptuous rooms, the tall highborn warriors who never seemed to mind the tiny girl underfoot. She remembered the wealth – so much wealth – and she had come to believe that this was her world, the one to which she had been born.

She had been given a room, up a winding flight of stairs; there she would often sit waiting, flushed and excited, for the high bell announcing meals, when she'd rush down, round and round those ever-turning steps, to lunge into the dining room – and they would laugh in delight upon seeing her.

For most of that first year it seemed that she had been the centre of attention in the entire Citadel, feted like a young queen, and always nearby were the three warrior sons of Lord Nimander, to take her hand whenever she reached up, whenever she needed to feel safe. She remembered her fascination with Silchas Ruin's white hair, the glint of red in his eyes, and his long fingers; and the warmth of Andarist's smile – Andarist, whom she dreamed she would one day marry. Yet the one she truly worshipped was Anomander. He seemed solid as stone, sun-warmed and smoothed by winds and rain. She felt him like a vast wing, protective, curled round her, and she saw how the others deferred to him, even his brothers. Anomander: most beloved by Mother Dark, and most beloved by the child hostage in the Citadel.

The wars stole them away from her, father and sons all, and when Lord Nimander returned early on, crippled and broken, Sandalath had huddled in her room, frozen with terror at the thought of any of her guardians dying on some distant field of battle. They had become the walls of her own house, her own palace, and she was their queen, for ever and always. How could such things ever end?

Outside the carriage window the single-storey buildings of the village rolled past, and before them fleeting figures moved here and there, many stopping to stare. She heard a few muted calls flung up to the driver, heard a muffled bark of laughter, a drunken shout. Breath catching suddenly, Sandalath leaned back to keep her face from the dust-streaked window. She waited for her heart to slow. The carriage bounced across deep ruts, pitching her from side to side. She folded her hands together, gripping hard, watching the blood leave her knuckles until she could see the bones.

Her imagination was fraught. This was a difficult day.

Abara had been a settlement known for its growth, its wealth, before the wars took all the young men and women; in the time when House Drukorlas was on the verge of becoming a Greater House. When Sandalath had finally been sent back, like a gift that had lost its beauty, its purpose, she had been shocked by the poverty of her home – the village, the grand family house and its tired, tattered grounds.

Her father had just died, before her return, a wound brought back from the war gone suddenly septic – striking him down before any healer could attend; a tragic, shocking death, and for her, a new emptiness to replace an old emptiness. Her mother had always kept her husband – Sandalath's father – for herself. She spoke of her selfishness as her reason for sending her daughter from the room, or keeping closed a door. There was talk of another child, but no child had come, and then her father was gone. Sandalath remembered him as a tall, faceless figure, and most of her memories of him were the sound of his boots on the wooden floor in the chamber above her bedroom, pacing through the night.

Now her mother never spoke of him. She was a widow and this title seemed to carry with it all the wealth it would ever hold, but it was the solitary kind; it embraced no one but Nerys herself. Meanwhile, poverty gnawed inward on all sides, like undercut riverbanks in a spring flood.

The young warrior who came to Abara, one-armed and soft-eyed, had changed her world, in ways she only now understood. It was not simply the child he gave her, or the nights and afternoons out under the sky, in meadows and glens on the estate, when he taught her to open herself up and draw him inside. He had been a messenger from another world, an outside world. Not the Citadel, not the house where dwelt her mother, for ever awaiting her husband. Galdan's world was a hard place of violence, of adventure, where every detail glowed as if painted in gold and silver, where even the stones underfoot were one and all gems, cut by a god's hand. She understood it now as a world of romance, where the brave stood firm in the face of villainy, and honour held vigilance over tender hearts. And there was love in the fields, in a riot of flowers and hot, bright summer days.

This was the world she whispered about to her son, when she told him old tales, to show him who his father was, and where he had lived, the great man he had been, before she snuffed out the candle and left Orfantal to sleep and dreams.

She was forbidden from speaking the truth, the ignominy of the discoveries about Galdan's real past, or the fact that Nerys had sent the young man away, exiled into the lands of the Jaghut, and that word had come back that he had died, the circumstances unknown. No, such truths were not for her son, not for his image of his father – Sandalath would not be so cruel, could not. The boy needed his heroes. Everyone did. And for Orfantal, his father would be a man impervious to infamy, unsullied by visible flaws, the obvious weaknesses that every child eventually saw in their living parents.

In her creations, as she spoke at her son's bedside, she remade Galdan, building him from pieces of Andarist, Silchas Ruin, and, of course, Anomander. Mostly Anomander, in fact. Down to his very features, his way of standing, the warmth of his hand closing upon that of a child – and when Orfantal awoke in the night, when all was dark and quiet and he might become frightened, why, he need only imagine that hand, closing firm about his own.

Her son asked her, where had he gone? What had happened to his father?

A great battle against the Soletaken Jheleck, an old feud with a man he'd once thought his friend. A betrayal, even as Galdan gave his life defending his wounded lord. His betrayer? Dead as well, stalked by his treachery – they said he took his own life, in fact – but no one ever speaks the tale, not a word of it. All the Tiste grieved over the sad events, and then vowed that they would speak of it no more, to mark their honour, their grief.

There were things a child needed to believe, sewn like clothes, or even armour; that he could then wear until the end of his days. So believed Sandalath, and if Galdan had stolen her own clothes, with his sweet lies, only to leave her shivering and alone . . . no, Orfantal would not suffer the same. Would *never* suffer the same.

The carriage was a cauldron. She felt fevered with the heat, wondering who would tell her son stories at night. There was no one. But he could reach out in the darkness, couldn't he, to take his father's hand. She need not worry any more on that matter – she had done what she could, and her mother's rage – Nerys's bitter accusation that Sandalath was too young to raise a child – well, she had proved otherwise, had she not? The heat was suffocating her. She felt ill. She thought she had seen Galdan, in the village – she thought she had seen him, stumbling as if to chase down the carriage, and then he'd fallen, and there had been more laughter.

Her imagination was unfettered, the heat driving it wild, and the world outside her window had transformed into something blinding white, the sky itself on fire. She coughed in the dust of that destruction, and horse hoofs were pounding now on all sides, voices raised, hoofs stuttering like drums.

The carriage rocked to a halt, edged down into a ditch, tilting her to one side so that she slipped down from the seat.

The sweat was gone from her face. It felt dry and cool.

Someone was calling to her, but she could not reach the shout-box, not from down here.

The latch rattled, and then the door swung open, and the fire outside poured in, engulfing her.

\*     \*     \*

'Vitr's blood!' Ivis swore, clambering into the carriage to take the unconscious woman in his arms. 'It's hot as a forge in here! Sillen! Raise a tarp – she needs shade, cooling down. Corporal Yalad, stop gawking! Help me with her, damn you!'

Panic thundered through the master-at-arms. The hostage was as white as Ruin himself, clammy to the touch and limp as a trampled doll. She seemed to be wearing almost all her clothes, layer upon layer. Bewildered as he laid her out on the ground beneath the tarp Sillen was now stretching out from the carriage side, he began unbuttoning the clasps. 'Corporal Yalad, a wet cloth for her brow, quickly!'

If she died – if she died, there would be repercussions. Not just for himself, but for Lord Draconus. The Drukorlas family was old, venerated. There had been only the one child, this one here, and if cousins existed elsewhere they remained lost in obscurity. His lord's enemies would be eager to see blood on Draconus's hands for this tragic end, when instead his lord had been seeking to make a gesture, taking into his care the last child of this faded bloodline. A recognition of tradition, an honouring of the old families – the Consort had no desire to isolate himself in a mad grasp for power.

He stripped off yet more clothes, rich brocades heavy as leather armour, quilted linens, hessian and wool, and then paused, swearing again. 'Sillen, take down that strongbox – see what's in that damned thing. This must be her entire wardrobe!'

The coachman had climbed from the carriage and stood looking down on the unconscious woman. Ivis scowled. 'We were about to leave the road anyway, driver – this one can ride, surely?'

'Don't look like it at the moment, sir.'

'Once she's recovered, you fool. Can she ride?'

The man shrugged. 'Can't say, sir. I ain't a regular on the house-staff, right?'

'You're not?'

'They let go most of the staff, sir, must be two years ago now. It's all the fallow land, y'see, with nobody left to work it. People just died off, or wandered off, or wandered off and died.' He rubbed at his neck. 'There was talk of turning it to pasture, but that don't take many people to work, does it? Mostly,' he concluded, still staring down at the woman, 'people just gave up.'

Sillen and two others had got the strongbox down, straining and cursing at its weight. 'Locked, captain.'

'Key's right here,' Ivis replied, lifting free an ornate key looped through a thong of leather round the young woman's flushed neck. He tossed it over, then glared up at the coachman. 'Take a walk – back to the village.'

'What? I got to return the carriage! And the horse!'

'One of my men will do that. Go, get out of here. Wait!' Ivis plucked a small leather pouch from his belt and tossed it over to the coachman. 'You didn't see any of this – not her passing out, nothing at all. Am I clear?'

Wide-eyed, the man nodded.

'If word reaches me,' Ivis continued, 'that what's happened here has gone through Abara, I will hunt you down and silence your flapping tongue once and for all.'

The coachman backed up a step. 'No need to threaten me, sir. I heard you. I understand what you're saying.'

Hearing the lock on the strongbox click, Ivis waved the coachman back on to the road. The man hurried off, his head bent over as he peered into the leather pouch. The glance he threw back at the captain was a surprised one, and he quickly picked up his pace.

Ivis turned to Sillen. 'Open it.'

The lid creaked, and then Sillen frowned. Reaching in, he lifted clear a well-wrapped clay jar, the kind used to hold cider. When he shook it even Ivis could hear the strange rustling sound the contents made. *Not cider.* Meeting Sillen's questioning eyes, the captain nodded.

The soldier worked free the heavy stopper, peered in. 'Stones, captain. Polished stones.' He nodded towards the strongbox. 'It's full of these jars.'

'From the shores of Dorssan Ryl,' Ivis muttered, nodding to himself. He took from Corporal Yalad the wet cloth and leaned over to brush Sandalath's forehead. Stones of avowed love – they all carried a few, mostly from family and mates. *But whole jars filled with them? An entire damned strongbox of stones?*

'More than a few suitors, I guess,' Sillen said, returning the stopper and slapping it tight with one palm.

Ivis stared across at the soldier. 'If that was meant as a jest, Sillen, I'll—'

'No sir!' Sillen said quickly, looking back down as he replaced the jar and closed the lid. 'Begging your pardon, sir. What do I know of pretty daughters from noble houses?'

'Not much, it seems,' Ivis allowed. 'Lock it up, damn you. And give me back that key.'

'She's coming round, sir,' said Corporal Yalad.

'Mother's blessing,' Ivis whispered in relief, watching her eyelids fluttering open.

She stared up at him without comprehension. He waited for some recognition as she studied him, but it did not seem forthcoming.

'Hostage Sandalath Drukorlat, I am Captain Ivis. I am leading your escort to House Dracons.'

'The – the carriage . . .'

'We have to leave the road now, mistress – the track before us is good only for riding. Can you sit a horse?'

Frowning, she slowly nodded.

'We'll stay here for a while longer,' Ivis said, helping her to sit up. Seeing her notice her half-undressed state, Ivis took up her outer cloak and draped it about her. 'You were overheating in that carriage,' he explained. 'You fainted. Mistress, we could well have lost you – you've given us all a serious fright.'

'I am weak with imagination, captain.'

He studied her, trying to make sense of that confession.

'I am better now,' she said, managing a faint smile. 'Thirsty.'

Ivis gestured and a soldier closed in with a canteen. 'Not too much all at once,' he advised.

'You're holding my key, captain.'

'It was constricting your throat, mistress.' When she looked across at the strongbox, he added, 'We'll rig a harness between two horsemen.' He smiled. 'No idea what's in that thing, but it's damned heavy. Young women and their toiletry – it seems there's no end to paints and perfumes and such. I know – got me a daughter, you see.'

Sandalath's gaze dropped away and she seemed to concentrate solely on sipping from the canteen. Then she looked up in alarm. 'The coachman—'

'Sent him away, mistress.'

'Oh. Did he—'

'No. On my honour.'

It seemed she was about to press him on this, but lacked the strength, sagging back down as if moments from collapsing once more.

Ivis took her weight. 'Mistress? Are you all right?'

'I will be,' she assured him. 'So, how old is she?'

'Who?'

'Your daughter.'

'Only a few years younger than you, mistress.'

'Pretty?'

'Well, I'm her father . . .' And then he ventured a wry grin. 'But she'll need more wits about her than most, I'd wager.'

Sandalath reached out and touched his upper arm, a gesture that a princess might make upon a kneeling subject. 'I am sure,' she said, 'she is very pretty.'

'Yes, mistress,' he replied. He straightened. 'If you will excuse us for a time – I need to see to my troop, and see to the strongbox. Gather your strength, mistress, and when you feel able we will resume our journey to House Dracons.'

When he moved round to the other side of the carriage, Sillen edged close and said, 'Mother help her if she looks like you, sir. That daughter of yours, I mean.'

Ivis scowled. 'You've got a mouth on you, soldier, that's going to see you looking up at us from the bottom of a latrine.'

'Yes, sir. Didn't know you had a daughter, that's all. It's, uh, hard to work my way round, sir.'

Behind them, Corporal Yalad snorted. 'You really that thick, Sillen?'

'See to that harness, Sillen,' Ivis said.

'Yes sir.'

*　　*　　*

Proper men had two arms for good reason. One to reach for things, the other to keep things away. Galdan had lost the arm that kept things away, and now, when every temptation edged into his reach, he snatched it close to be hungrily devoured.

He'd discovered this grim curse in the depths of cheap wine, and then in a young, innocent woman who lived only to dream of a better life. Well, he'd promised it, hadn't he? That better life. But the hand that touched belonged to the wrong arm – the only arm he had left – and the touch did nothing but stain and leave bruises, marring all the perfect flesh that he should never have taken in the first place.

Love had no limbs at all. It could neither run nor grasp, couldn't even push away though it tried and tried. Left lying on the ground, unable to move, crying like an abandoned baby – people could steal it; people could kick it until it bled, or nudge it down a hillside or over a cliff. They could smother it, drown it, set it on fire until it was ashes and charred bone. They could teach it how to want and want for ever, no matter how much it was fed. And sometimes, all love was, was something to be dragged behind on a chain, growing heavier with each step, and when the ground opened up under it, why, it pulled a person backwards and down, down to a place where the pain never ended.

If he'd had two arms, he could have stabbed it through the heart.

But nobody around here understood any of that. They couldn't figure the reasons why he drank all the time, when in truth there weren't any. Not real ones. And he didn't need to do much to throw out excuses – the empty sleeve was good enough, and the beautiful woman stolen away from him – not that he'd ever deserved her, of course, but those who reached too high always fell the furthest, didn't they? *Forulkan justice*, they called it. He'd had his fill of that, more than most people. He'd been singled out; he was certain of it. Touched by a malign god, and now its grisly servants stalked him, there in the shadows at his back.

One of them squatted close now, in this narrow, rubbish-choked alley beside the tavern, crouching low in the pit below the four steps leading down to the cellar. It was softly laughing at all the excuses he had for being what he was, for doing what he did. Reasons and excuses weren't the same thing. Reasons explained; excuses justified, but badly.

They'd sent her away – he'd seen the carriage, rolling down the centre street – and he'd caught a flash of her face behind the dirty window. He'd even shouted her name.

Galdan dragged closer the day's jug of wine. He'd drunk more from it than he should have, and Gras didn't like it when he had to give up another one too soon. One a day was the rule. But Galdan couldn't help it. Sand was gone now, for ever gone, and all those nights when he weaved his way to the edge of the estate, like a reaver haunting a border, and fought against his desire to find her, take her away from this useless life – he would never make that journey again.

Of course, it hadn't been her life that was useless, and that journey in the dark had been a sham, despite all the river stones he left in the hidden place only they knew about. She found them; he knew that much. Found them and took them somewhere, probably to the refuse heap behind the kitchen.

Galdan stared at the jug, at the filthy hand and the fingers twisted down into the ceramic ear. It was all like this wine – he would grasp it, only to have it disappear – the hand that only took could hold nothing for very long.

Proper men had two arms. With two arms they could do anything. They could keep the world just far enough away, and take only what they needed and it didn't matter if it then vanished, because that's how it was for everybody.

He'd been such a man once.

From the deep shadows at the bottom of the stairs, his stalker laughed on, and on. But then, everyone in the village laughed when they saw him, and in their faces he saw all his excuses, the ones he liked to call *reasons*, and those were good enough for him. And, it seemed, for everyone else, too.

*          *          *

Galar Baras knew that the Forulkan had believed themselves pure in their enmity towards disorder and chaos. Generations of their priests, their Assail, had devoted entire lives to the creation of rules of law and civil conduct, to the imposition of peace in the name of order. But to Galar's mind they had taken hold of the sword from the wrong end. Peace did not serve order; order served peace, and when order became godlike, sacrosanct and inviolate, then the peace thus won became a prison, and those who sought their freedom became enemies to order, and in the elimination of such enemies, peace was lost.

He saw the logic to this, but it was a form of reasoning that surrendered its power when forced; as was the case with so many lines of reasoning. And arrayed against its simplicity was a virulent storm of emotional extremity, an array of vehemence, with fear wearing the crown.

The Forulkan Assail solution was order born of fear, a peace deemed for ever under assault, for ever threatened by malicious forces, many of which wore the face of strangers. There was, he had to acknowledge, a kind of perfection to their stance. Dissent could find no purchase, so quickly was it cut down, annihilated in a welter of violence. And being unknown, strangers always posed a threat to those serving fear.

75

Theirs was a civilization tempered on a cold anvil, and the Tiste had revealed the flaw in its forging. Galar Baras found it ironic that the great commander who had defeated the Forulkan was such an admirer of their civilization. For Galar himself, he could well see its seductive elements, but where Urusander had been drawn closer by them, Galar had recoiled in unease. What worth peace when it was maintained by threat?

It was only the fearful who knelt in worship before order, and Galar refused to live in fear.

Before the war, the south Borderswords had been a loosely organized, under-equipped force. Still, it had been the first to respond to the Forulkan invasion, the first to stagger the enemy. The cost had been horrendous, and yet Galar could still appreciate that the birth of what would come to be called the Hust Legion was found in the chaos and discord of battle. There had been no peace in that creation, and the first years of its life had been cruel and harsh.

Among the weaponsmiths of the Hust forges, there was a belief that every length of blade had a thread of fear in its heart. It could not be removed; indeed, it was bound to the life of the iron. They called it the Heartline of the Blade. Cut it and the weapon lost its fear of shattering. The forging of a weapon was devoted to strengthening that Heartline: every folding of metal twisted that thread, wound it tighter, until the thread knuckled, again and again – there were secret arts in this tempering, known only to the Hust weaponsmiths. Galar knew that they claimed to have discovered the essence of that thread of fear, the vein of chaos that gave a sword its strength. He could not doubt such claims, for the Hust had given that Heartline a voice, taut with madness or overflowing glee, a sound both wondrous and terrible, crying out through the quenched iron, and no two voices were the same, and those that sang loudest were known to be the most formidable of all weapons.

The Hust Forge began supplying the south Borderswords towards the end of the Forulkan War, but the enemy was already in disarray, broken in retreat and fleeing the relentless advance of Urusander's Legion. Their numbers reduced by attrition, the Borderswords had been serving as veteran auxiliaries, and had participated in all the major engagements over the last two years of the war. They had been exhausted, on the verge of dissolution.

Galar still remembered the now-legendary day of the Hust Resupply, the huge wagons lumbering out of the dust clouds and the moaning and lowing that filled the air – sounds the battered troop of Borderswords believed were coming from the burdened oxen, only to discover that the terrible cries came not from beasts, but from the weapons nestled in their wooden crates. He recalled his own horror when he was summoned to exchange his blade, when he set down his worn, scarred sword and took in hand the new Hust weapon. It had shrieked at his touch, a deafening peal that seemed to drag talons down all the bones of his body.

It had been a son of Hust Henarald himself who had given him the weapon, and as the cry abruptly fell off, its echo a ringing clangour in Galar's skull, the young weaponsmith had nodded and said, 'Well pleased by your touch, captain, but be warned, this is a jealous sword – the most powerful ones are, we have found.'

Galar was unsure whether to thank the weaponsmith or not. Some gifts proved curses. Yet the weapon's weight suited the strength of his arm, and in his grip it felt like an extension of his own bones, his own muscles.

'There is no such thing,' the weaponsmith went on, 'as an unbreakable sword, though Abyss knows we have tried. Captain, listen well, for the words I now speak are known to only a few. We struggled in the wrong battle against the wrong enemy. All iron has limits to its flexibility, its endurance: these are true laws. I cannot guarantee that your new sword will not break, though it is of such power that no mortal blade is likely ever to shatter it edge to edge; nor could any swing or thrust you manage make the weapon fail you. Yet, should it ever break, captain, abandon not the sword. There are many knuckles in the Heartline, you see. *Many.*'

At the time he had known nothing about 'knuckles' or 'Heartlines'. Such knowledge came later, when the secrets of the Hust swords became his obsession. He thought now that he understood the significance of these knuckles, and though he had yet to witness, or even hear of, a Hust sword breaking, he believed that a miracle was buried in each blade, an expression of sorcery unlike any other.

Hust swords were alive. Galar Baras was convinced of this, and he was hardly alone in that opinion. Not one soldier in the Hust Legion believed otherwise. Urusander's soldiers were welcome to mock and make their snide remarks. It had been the Hust mines that had been a Forulkan primary target in their invasion, and it had been a stand by the south Borderswords that had preserved them. Hust Henarald had shown his gratitude in the only way he could.

Even the highborn warriors of the Houseblades were made uneasy by the Hust Legion and their haunted weapons. Not all, of course, and something was about to come of that, and it was for this reason that Galar Baras found himself riding in the company of Kellaras, commander of the Houseblades of Purake.

There had been changes to that House. Upon the blessing of Nimander, for his service to Mother Dark, all land holdings had been relinquished to Mother Dark, and all those Tiste born to the bloodline, and their attendant staff, warriors, mendicants and scholars, now served her, taking the name of *Andii*, Children of Night.

The First Son of Darkness, Lord Anomander, whom Kellaras served, had shown no reluctance in his praise for the Hust Legion, and was open in his admiration for the House of Hustain. His forces had been the first to arrive in relief of the south Borderswords following the Stand at the Mines, and Galar remembered seeing Lord Anomander crossing the bloodied ground to speak with Toras Redone, the seniormost warrior who had assumed command of the Borderswords and in the days following would be officially granted the title of commander. That march itself was a measure of respect: the Lord could have as easily summoned Toras; instead, it was he who reached out to clasp her forearm, astonishing all the Borderswords present.

On that day, in the minds of the warriors who would soon become soldiers of the Hust Legion, they became Andiian; they too became Sons and Daughters of Night.

None of them could have imagined the political divisiveness that would result from that fateful moment: the schism that would rupture the relationship between Urusander's Legion and that of the Hust. From months fighting side by side, suddenly Galar Baras and his fellow Hustain – with their dread weapons – were no longer welcome among Urusander's ranks.

It was absurd and it was hurtful, and every effort to bridge that schism had failed; if anything, it was growing ever wider. Most of Urusander's Legion had been disbanded, sent into the limbo of the reserve ranks, while the Hust Legion remained intact, standing continued vigilance over the precious mines. As Toras Redone had muttered, on a drunken night in her headquarters, when all the other staff had departed leaving only Galar and his commander, peace had become a disaster. Recalling that night, Galar allowed himself a private smile. He hadn't been drunk – he couldn't stomach alcohol – while she'd finished off most of a bottle of wine, but there'd been no recriminations afterwards. For both him and Toras, it had been their first lovemaking since the war. They'd needed each other, and though thereafter they rarely spoke of that night – the only one they had shared – she had once commented, in a private moment, that she'd drunk so much to find the courage to invite him to lie with her. When he'd laughed, she'd turned away, as if mortified. He'd hastened to explain that his laughter had been of disbelief, for in courage he too had failed until that instant.

They should have held to that moment of confession, he knew now. They should have found each other's eyes and forged into a single blade their desires. Galar's smile faded in the thinking of such thoughts, as they did every time he succumbed to reminiscence.

She had sent him away only a few months later, to serve in Kharkanas as the liaison officer of the Hust Legion. For a man and a woman who had fought a war, it seemed that their bravery ended at the edge of the battlefield. Still, it was no doubt all for the best. Toras Redone was married, after all, and her husband was none other than Calat Hustain, the son of Henarald – the man who had given him his Hust sword.

Now that Galar spent most of his time in the Citadel, he could at any time find comfort in the arms of a priestess, though he'd yet to do so. Instead, he seemed to be spending his days under siege, blind to half the weapons being thrust at him, and each night he slumped, exhausted, in his modest quarters. Wishing he could stomach alcohol.

He had since heard that Calat Hustain had accepted the commission of commander of the Wardens of the Outer Reach, far to the north on the Plain of Glimmer Fate. Was Toras now alone? Did she drink herself into other arms? He did not know and, perhaps, did not want to know.

Still, he was unable to fight off his anticipation, twisted as it was with anxiety, as they rode into the vastly thinned Old Forest. Once they emerged from its patchwork, silent stillness, they would come within sight of Hust Forge, the Great House itself. He told himself to expect nothing – it was likely she was not even in attendance, since the mines, where the Legion was stationed, were well to the south. Indeed, it would be better if she wasn't. He had enough discord in his life these days.

Since settling into the city, Galar Baras had realized that the schism between Urusander's Legion and the Hust Legion was but one of many; that even the beloved adoption of the title Andii had become a source of contention. To make matters worse, there was a growing power at the side of Mother Dark, and none could predict the fullest extent of Lord Draconus's ambitions – though his most vociferous detractors never hesitated to imagine all manner of diabolical intent. For himself, Galar saw Draconus as a man in a precarious position, especially now that there was talk of a marriage – a union explicitly political, of course, seeking to mend old wounds; seeking, in fact, to head off civil war. If Draconus had ambitions, surely they did not extend further than solidifying whatever status he had attained, and even then the Consort must understand that he could fall from grace at any moment.

Unless, as his enemies boldly proclaimed, Draconus was forging secret alliances among all the noble families – the least absurd of the rumours to date – seeking to make the marriage impossible. The flaw in that possibility was, of course, the power possessed by Mother Dark herself. She might well love Draconus – and Galar suspected she did – but she was not a submissive creature. Her will was its own Heartline of the Blade. No lover could sway her, just as no argument could batter her down by sheer force of exhortation.

In many ways, she embodied the Forulkan ideal of justice and order

79

– not that, in their myopic bigotry, they were even capable of recognizing that truth.

Her greatest gift to her children – to all of her children – was just that, Galar believed. So long as she remained, there would be no disorder, no chaos. And in that there was immeasurable comfort. Should the marriage occur, should Urusander of Neret Sorr find himself sharing Mother Dark's rule as her husband, perhaps then the enmity would end, every schism healed, and no longer would the Hust Legion struggle in this seething atmosphere of malice and spite.

What would Draconus do then? He would have no place in the Citadel; indeed, no place in all of Kharkanas. Would he simply bow with grace and then retire to his north Hold on the banks of Young Dorssan Ryl? Galar believed Draconus was an honourable man. He believed that the Lord would yield to the will of the woman he loved.

No one could escape sadness in their lives. No one could evade the pain of loss. Draconus was wise enough to know this.

Peace could be forged. Only a fool would invite civil strife. Sons and daughters of the Tiste had given their lives defending the realm; the blood of every House and Hold, no matter how powerful or how minor, had been spilled. Who would dare turn their backs on that?

*         *         *

Commander Kellaras held to his silence as he rode alongside the Hust captain. He could hear muttering from the blackwood scabbard strapped to Galar's side, and the sound chilled him like the touch of a corpse. He had heard many tales about this grim legion with its haunted weapons, but this was the first time he had been in extended company with a Hust soldier.

The journey out from Kharkanas, pacing the Dorssan Ryl with the plain called the Forging stretching out upon his left, and now this denatured scattering of trees, the old name of which could now not be spoken without the drip of irony, had been conducted with but the briefest exchanges; nothing approaching a conversation, and Kellaras had begun to believe the tales he'd heard from the Citadel Wardens, who were one and all veterans of Urusander's Legion. The Hust swords were cursed, bleeding poison into their wielders. There was a darkness about such men and women now, but not pure as among those who served Mother Dark; this was murky, shot through with something sickly, as if infected with the chaos of Vitr.

Kellaras's hands were damp with sweat inside his riding gloves. He felt buffeted by the power beside him – this officer of the Hust Legion with his never-silent sword, who seemed the heart of some swirling malevolence. Outwardly, Captain Galar Baras had the look of a man too young to bear the weight of a past war; his features were boyish in the way that never seemed to surrender to age – he would, Kellaras suspected, look much as he did now in three hundred years, or even five hundred. Yet, that sort of face usually belonged to someone irrepressible in their humour, in their optimism. It was a face that should be quick to smile, and smile often, alight with laughter at every turn.

Instead, Galar looked like a man who had lost sight of joy, and now stumbled in shadows. Ill-chosen as liaison, as the Hust Legion's representative and ranking officer in Kharkanas – he was unliked in the city, rarely invited to events. As far as Kellaras knew, Captain Galar Baras spent his unofficial time alone. What were his interests? No one could say. What brought him pleasure? As Gallan once wrote, *Closed doors do not sweat*. There was nothing garrulous here, and he could not imagine ever approaching the captain's private quarters, seeking his company. As far as he knew, no one did.

There were as many stumps in this wood as living trees, and the ones still standing looked unwell, the leaves more dull grey than polished black. He had seen no small mammals flittering through the dried leaves of the forest floor, and the rare birdsong he caught sounded querulous and plaintive, as if ever unanswered. Despite the sunlight finding its way down through the gaping holes in the canopy overhead, Kellaras could feel his spirits struggling.

He carried in his messenger's satchel, strapped to his mount's saddle, a missive from his master, Lord Anomander. He had been instructed to deliver it into the hands of Hust Henarald himself, and to await a reply. None of this required an escort, and it seemed to Kellaras that Galar's insistence on this matter marked a kind of mistrust, even suspicion. It was, in fact, offensive.

Yet the First Son of Darkness was not ill-disposed towards the Hust Legion; in fact, the very opposite, and so Kellaras was not prepared to challenge his companion on this or any other matter. They could ride in silence then – it was not much farther, as he could now see the way open ahead – and pretend to amity.

Galar Baras startled him with a question. 'Sir, have you any notion of your lord's message to Lord Henarald?'

Kellaras stared across at the man as they cantered into the light. 'Even if I knew the details, captain, it is not for us to discuss them, is it?'

'Forgive me, sir. I did not mean to ask for details. But Lord Hust Henarald is well known for his personal involvement in the workings among his forges, and I fear he will not be in residence at his house. Therefore, I sought to ascertain if there was some urgency to the missive.'

'I see.' Kellaras thought for a moment, and then said, 'I am to wait for the Lord's response.'

'Then it may well be sensitive to any delay.'

'What do you propose, captain?'

'The Great House to begin with, of course. If, however, Lord Henarald has travelled south to the mines, then I am afraid I must pass you on to a household escort, as I cannot be away from the Citadel for that length of time.'

Ahead of them waited the massive stone walls surrounding the Hust Forge. Kellaras said nothing, forcing himself to admit to having been knocked askew by the captain's words. He cleared his throat and said, 'You lead me to wonder, captain, why you insisted on escorting me in the first place. Do you doubt the reception I might receive at the house?'

Brows lifted. 'Sir? Of course not.' He then hesitated for a moment, before adding, 'Very well, sir. I elected to ride with you in order to stretch my legs. I was a Bordersword since I first came of age, yet now I find myself trapped inside stone walls, in a palace where darkness bleeds so thick one cannot stand on a balcony and see a single star in the night sky. I thought, sir, that I might go mad if so confined for much longer.' He was slowly reining in, eyes suddenly averted. 'I apologize, sir. Hear the chimes? They have identified you and now prepare your welcome. I need go no further—'

'But you shall, captain,' Kellaras said, only now realizing that the young face belonged to a young man. 'Your horse needs the rest and watering – if indeed I must ride onward, then I expect you to accompany me, for I shall be riding into holdings under the command of the Hust Legion. You will accord me the proper honour of an officer's escort.'

It was a gamble. Strictly speaking, Kellaras's rank could not be imposed upon an officer of the Hust Legion. But if this man was wilting inside what he viewed as a prison, chained there by duty, then only a countermand could keep him from returning to his office of misery.

He caught a moment of bright relief on the captain's flushed visage, only to see it overwhelmed with sudden dread.

*What now?*

But Galar Baras kicked his horse forward again, resuming the pace alongside Kellaras. 'As you command, sir, I am at your disposal.'

The enormous bronze gates were swinging open ahead, in a slithering rattle of heavy chains. Kellaras cleared his throat a second time, and said, 'Besides, captain, have you no interest in seeing Lord Henarald's expression when he learns that my master seeks to commission a sword?'

Galar Baras's head snapped round in shock.

And then they were through the gates.

# FOUR

THE PLAIN OF GLIMMER FATE HAD NOT SEEN RAIN IN DECADES, YET the black grasses were thick as fur on the gently rolling land, rising as high as a horse's shoulder on the level flats. The thin, spiky blades gathered close the heat of the sun, and to pass through them was akin to plunging into the cauldron of a furnace. Iron accoutrements – buckles, clasps, weapons and armour – burned to the touch. Leather slowly shrivelled and cracked in the course of a day's travel. Cloth suffocated skin, making it red, hot and irritated.

The Wardens of the Outer Reach, that northernmost region of the plain verging on the silver, mercurial sea of Vitr, wore silks and little else, and even then more than a few days out from their outlier posts they suffered terribly, as did their horses, which were burdened with thick wooden leaves of armour protecting their legs and lower quarters from both the heat and the sharp, serrated blades of the grass. Patrols out to the Vitr Sea were an ordeal, and there were few among the Tiste willing to serve as Wardens.

Which was just as well, Faror Hend reflected: if there were yet more people as mad as they were, then the Tiste would be in trouble. Close to the edge of the Vitr the grasses died away, leaving bare ground studded with rotting stones and brittle boulders. The air sliding in from the tranquil silver sea stung in the lungs, burned raw the inside of the nose, made bitter every tear.

She sat astride her horse, watching her younger cousin draw out his sword and set one edge into a groove in a boulder near the Vitr's edge. Some poison from the strange liquid dissolved even the hardest rock, and Wardens had taken to fashioning whetstones from select boulders.

Her companion's sword had been forged by the Hust, but long ago and thus mercifully silent. Still, it was new to Spinnock Durav's hand, a blade the length of which crossed generations in the family. She could see his pride and was pleased.

The third and last rider in this patrol, Finarra Stone, had ridden along the shoreline, westward, and Faror had lost sight of her some time back. It was not unusual to set off unaccompanied when so near to the Vitr – the naked wolves of the plain never ventured this close, and of other beasts only bones remained. Finarra had nothing to fear and would eventually return. They would camp for the night in the shelter of the high crags where past storms had gnawed deep into the shoreline, far enough from the Vitr to escape its more toxic effects, yet still some distance from the verge of the grasses.

With the reassuring sound of Spinnock's blade rasping as he honed it, Faror twisted in her saddle and stared out over the silver expanse of the sea. Its promise was dissolution, devouring flesh and bone upon contact. But for the moment the surface was calm, yet mottled, as if reflecting an overcast sky. The terrible forces that dwelt in its depths, or somewhere in its distant heart, remained quiescent. Of late, this was unusual. The last three times a patrol had arrived here, they had been driven back by the ferocity of storms, and in the aftermath of each one, more land was lost.

If the mystery of the Vitr could not be solved; if its power could not be blunted, forced back, or destroyed, then there would come a time, perhaps less than a dozen centuries away, when the poison sea devoured all of the Glimmer Fate, and so reached the very borders of Kurald Galain.

None knew with any certainty the source of the Vitr – at least, none among the Tiste. Faror believed that answers might be found among the Azathanai, but then, she had no proof of that and she was but a Warden of middling rank. And the scholars and philosophers of Kharkanas were an inward-looking, xenophobic lot, dismissive of foreigners and their foreign ways. It seemed that they valued ignorance, finding it a virtue when it was their own.

Perhaps among the war-spoils of the Forulkan, now in the possession of Lord Urusander, some revelations might be found; although it seemed that Urusander's particular obsession, upon laws and justice, made the discovery of such revelations unlikely. Still, in his manic studies he might well stumble upon some ancient musings on the Vitr . . . *but would he even notice?*

The threat posed by the Vitr was acknowledged. Its imminence was well recognized. A few millennia were a short span indeed, and there were truths in the world that took centuries to truly understand. This led to a simple fact: they were running out of time.

'It is said,' Spinnock spoke, straightening and setting an eye down the length of his sword, 'that some quality of the Vitr infuses the edge, strengthening it against notching and, indeed, shattering.'

She smiled to herself. 'So it is said, cousin.'

He glanced up at her, and once more a strange kind of envy rushed through her. What woman would not lie prone before Spinnock Durav? Yet *she* could not, dared not. It was not that he was barely into manhood whilst she had eleven years on him and was betrothed besides. She would have discarded both obstacles in an instant; no, their bloodline was too close. The Hend – her own family – was but once removed from that of House Durav. The prohibitions were strict and immutable: neither the children of brothers nor those of sisters could mate.

Still, out here, so close to the Vitr, so distant from the lands of the Tiste, a voice whispered inside her, rising gleeful and urgent in moments like these: who would know? Finarra Stone had ridden off and would probably not return before dusk. *The ground is bare and hard / and will hold all secrets / and the sky cares not / for the games of those beneath it.* So many breathtaking truths in Gallan's poetry, as if he had plied her own mind, and could at will reach into countless others. These were the truths that found their own flavours and made personal the taste, until it seemed that Gallan spoke directly to each and every listener, each and every reader. The sorceries of the delvers into the secrets of Night seemed clumsy compared to the magic of Gallan's poems.

His words fed her innermost desires, and this made them dangerous. She forced silence upon the whispering in her mind, pushed down delicious but forbidden thoughts.

'I have heard rumours,' Spinnock went on, sheathing his sword, 'that there are Azathanai vessels capable of holding Vitr. Made of strange and rare stone, they must be.'

She had heard the same, and it was details like that which convinced her that the Azathanai understood the nature of this terrible poison. 'If there are such vessels,' she now said, 'one wonders what purpose might be served by collecting Vitr.'

She caught his shrug before he strode back to his horse. 'Which camp is near, Faror?'

'The one we call the Cup. You've not yet seen it. I will lead.'

His answering smile – so impossibly innocent – brushed her awake between the legs and she looked away, taking up the reins and silently cursing her own weakness. She heard him climb into the saddle of his own mount. Drawing her horse round, she guided the animal forward, back on to the trail leading away from the shoreline.

'Mother Dark is the answer to this,' Spinnock said behind her.

*So we pray.* 'The poet Gallan has written of that,' she said.

'Why is that no surprise?' Spinnock said, clearly amused. 'Go on then, oh beautiful cousin, let's hear it.'

She did not reply at once, struggling to slow the sudden leap of her heart. He had joined the Wardens a year past, yet this was the first time he had included her in his easy flirtations. 'Very well, since you are so eager. Gallan wrote: *In unrelieved darkness waits every answer.*'

After a moment, as their horses scrabbled over uneven footing, Spinnock grunted. 'As I thought.'

'What thought is that, Spinnock?'

He laughed. 'Even a bare handful of words from a poet, and I lose all sense of meaning. Such arts are not for me.'

'One learns subtlety,' she replied.

'Indeed?' She could hear his smile in the word. Then he went on, 'And now, in your grey-haired wisdom, you will, perchance, pat my hand?'

She glanced back at him. 'Have I offended you, cousin?'

He gave a careless shake of his head. 'Never that, Faror Hend. But the years between us are not so vast, are they?'

She searched his eyes for a long moment, and then faced forward once more. 'It will be dark soon, and Finarra will be most upset if we fail to have a meal awaiting her when she returns. And the tents raised, as well, with all bedding prepared.'

'Finarra upset? I have yet to see that, cousin.'

'Nor shall we this night.'

'Will she find us in the dark?'

'Of course, by the light of our fire, Spinnock.'

'In a place called the Cup?'

'Ah, well, there is that. Still, she well knows the camp, since it was she who first discovered it.'

'Then she will not wander lost.'

'No,' Faror replied.

'And so,' Spinnock added, amused once more, 'this night shall see no revelations. By the fire's light no answers will be found.'

'It seems you understood Gallan well enough, Spinnock Durav.'

'I grow older with every moment.'

She sighed. 'As do we all.'

\*　　　\*　　　\*

Captain Finarra Stone reined in, her eyes fixed upon the carcass thrown up on to the ragged shoreline of the sea. The bitter air had sweetened with the heavy stench of rotting meat. She had spent years patrolling Glimmer Fate, and the Outer Reach that was the verge of the Vitr Sea. Never before had a creature washed ashore, living or dead.

She had ridden far from her companions and it would be dark well before she managed to return to them. This time, however, she regretted her solitude.

The beast was enormous, yet so much of it had been devoured by the acidic Vitr that it was difficult to determine what manner of creature it might be. Here and there, along the back of the massive torso, ragged sheaths of scaled hide remained, bleached of all colour. Lower down, closer to the ground, the thick slabs of muscled flesh gave way to a curved fence-line of red-stained ribs. The pale sack encased by these ribs had ruptured, spilling rotting organs on to the ground, close to where the Vitr slowly lifted and fell on the quartzite sand.

The nearest hind limb, bent like that of a cat, reached up to a jutting hip bone, level with Finarra's eyes as she sat astride her horse. There were remnants of a thick, tapering tail. The forelimbs seemed to be reaching for the shore, the hand of one stretched out with thick claws buried deep in the sands, as if the beast had been trying to climb free of the Vitr, but this seemed impossible.

Its head and neck were missing, and the stump between the shoulders looked chewed, torn by fangs.

She could not tell if the creature belonged to land or sea, and as far as she knew the mythical dragons were winged, and there was no evidence of wings behind the humped shoulders. Was this some earth-bound kin to the legendary Eleint? She had no way of knowing, and among all the Tiste, only a few had ever claimed to have seen a dragon. Until this moment, Finarra had half believed those tales to be exaggerations – no beast in all the world could be as large as they had made them out to be.

Her horse shifting nervously beneath her, Finarra studied the stump of the neck, trying to imagine the weight of the head that those huge muscles had held aloft. She could see a large blood vessel, possibly the carotid, the severed end forming a mouth big enough to swallow a grown man's fist.

Some vagary of air current carried the heavy stench towards them and her horse backed a step, hoofs thudding the sand.

At the sound, the stump lifted.

The breath froze in her lungs. She stared, motionless, as the nearest hand dug deeper into the glittering sands. The hind limbs bunched, pushed. The torso rose and then lurched further up the beach, thumping back down heavily enough to make the shoreline shiver. The reverberation awakened in Finarra a sudden sense of danger. She backed her horse away, watching that ghastly torn stump wavering about, blindly groping. The second arm twisted round, coming up beside its companion, to sink talons long as hunting knives into the sand.

'You are dead,' she told it. 'Your head has been torn away. The Vitr dissolves your flesh. It is time to end your struggles.'

A moment of stillness, as if somehow the beast heard and understood her words, and then the creature heaved forward, straight for her, crossing the distance between them impossibly fast, one hand scything through the air.

Her horse reared, screamed. The bludgeoning, raking hand caught its forelimbs, shattering the wooden leaves of armour, twisting the animal round in the air. Finarra felt herself pitched downward to her left, felt the immense weight of her horse suddenly above her. Disbelieving, overwhelmed by the impossibility of her death, she sensed one booted foot slipping free of the stirrup – but it would not be enough; already they were falling together.

The second hand came from the other side. She caught a flash of talons scything close, filling her vision, and then there was an impact and the horse's scream cut off abruptly, and Finarra was spinning through the air.

She landed hard on her left shoulder, facing back the way she had come, and saw the carcass of her horse, its head and most of its neck torn away. The beast had lunged again, savaging the horse with its hands. Bones splintered to drumming concussions, blood pouring out on to the sand.

Then the demon fell still once more.

Pain was filling Finarra's shoulder. A bone had broken and fire was lancing down her arm, numbing the hand. She fought to control her breathing, lest the creature hear her – she did not believe it was dead, and indeed wondered if death was even possible for a beast such as this one. Sorcery held its life-force, she suspected, an elemental defiance against all reason, and if the Vitr had worked its absolute dissolution, devouring even its bones, something shapeless yet white-hot would now reside on this shore, washed up from the depths, as virulent as ever.

Teeth clenched against the waves of pain, Finarra began pushing herself away, heels digging into the sand. She froze when she saw the beast flinch, the severed neck trembling. Then a shudder took the entire body, violent enough to tear flesh, and the demon seemed to sag, sinking down until a swath of hide on its flank facing her began to show bulges, and then split, the broken ends of ribs pushing through.

She waited a dozen heartbeats, and then resumed her slow, tortured retreat up the slope of sand. At one point her boot dislodged a fist-sized rock that broke under her heel, but the crunching snap elicited no response from the beast. Emboldened, she drew her legs under her and regained her feet, her left arm hanging useless and swollen at her side. Turning, she mapped out her avenue of retreat between boulders, and then cautiously set out.

Reaching the high ground she turned about and looked down on the now distant creature. She'd lost her saddle and all the gear bound to it. She could make out her lance, a weapon she'd possessed since her Day of Blood, half its length pinned under the carcass of her horse. And her mount had been a loyal companion. Sighing, she faced east and set out.

As the day's light faded, Finarra was faced with a decision: she had been walking along the boulder-strewn ridgeline above the beach, but her pace was slow, made more difficult by her useless arm. If she set off down to the beach . . . she had to admit to herself a new fear of that shoreline. There was no telling if the beast that had dragged itself ashore marked a solitary intrusion. There could well be others, and what she might in the gloom imagine to be a boulder could prove to be another such creature, that had crawled up higher on the strand. Her other choice was to cut inland, on to the flatter verge of Glimmer Fate, where the grasses had died, leaving nothing but gravel and dusty earth. The risk in that, with night fast approaching, would come from the high grasses – the naked wolves were not averse to pursuing prey into the lifeless area.

Still, she could pick up her pace on the level ground, and so reach her companions that much sooner. Finarra drew out the long-bladed sword that had once belonged to her father, Hust Henarald. It was a silent weapon, predating the Awakening, water-etched and a known breaker. Serpentine patterns flowed up the length of the blade, coiling at the hilt. Off to her left the Vitr Sea was an ethereal glow and she could see its play on the polished iron of the sword.

Finarra swung inland, threading past the rotted boulders until she reached the verge of the plain. She eyed the wall of black grasses off to her right. There were darker gaps in it, marking some of the hidden paths forged by the beasts dwelling in Glimmer Fate. Many were small, used by deer-like animals the Wardens saw but rarely, and even then as little more than a flash of scaled hide, a blur of a serrated back and a high, slithering tail. Other gaps could easily accommodate a horse, and these belonged to the tusked heghest, a kind of reptilian boar, massive and ill-tempered; but the passage of these beasts through the high grasses eschewed stealth and she would hear any approach from some distance. Nor could a heghest outrun a mounted Warden: the animals were quick to tire, or perhaps lose interest. Their only enemy was the wolves, evinced by the occasional carcass found on the plain, in trampled clearings drenched in blood and torn pieces of hide.

She recalled once hearing such a battle in the distance, the keening, ear-hurting cries of the wolves and the heavy, enraged bellowing of the heghest brought to bay. Such memories were unwelcome and she kept her eyes upon that uneven wall of grasses as she padded along.

Overhead, the swirling pattern of the stars slowly appeared, like a spray of Vitr. Legends spoke of a time before such stars; when the vault of night was absolute and not even the sun dared open its lone eye. Stone and earth were, in that time, nothing more than solid manifestations of Darkness, the elemental force transformed into something that could be grasped, held cupped in the palm, sifting down through the fingers. If earth and stone held life back then, they were little more than promises of potential.

Those promises had but awaited the kiss of Chaos, as a spark of enlivening, and as a force in opposition. Entwined with the imposition of order that was implicit in Darkness, Chaos began the war that was life. The sun opened its eye and so slashed in two all existence, dividing the worldly realm into Light and Dark – and they too warred with one another, reflecting the struggle of life itself.

In such wars was carved the face of time. *Birth is born and death ends*. So wrote the ancients, in the ashes of the First Days.

She could not comprehend the existence they described. If there was neither a time before nor a time after, then was not the moment of creation eternal and yet for ever instantaneous? Was it not still in its birth and at the same time forever dying?

It was said that in the first darkness there was no light, and in the heart of light there was no darkness. But without one the other could not be known to exist – they needed each other in the very utterance of defining their states, for such states existed only in comparison – no, all of this snarled mortal thoughts, left a mind trapped inside concepts hidden in shadows. Instinctively, she shied from extremes of any sort, in attitude and in nature both. She had tasted the bitter poisons of the Vitr; and she had known the frightening emptiness of unrelieved darkness; she had flinched from the heart of fire and blinding light. For Finarra, it seemed that life could only cling to a place much like this thin verge, between two deadly forces, and so exist in uncertainty – in these cool, indifferent shadows.

Light now warred in the sky's deepest night – the stars were proof of that.

She remembered kneeling, in the time of her avowal to serve as a Warden, and cringing in that sorcerous absence, the deathly cold of the sphere of power surrounding Mother Dark. And by that chilling touch, there upon her brow, she had been invited into a kind of seductive comfort, a whisper of surrender – the fears had only come later, in that shivering, breathless aftermath. After all, Mother Dark had, before embracing Darkness, been a mortal Tiste woman – little different from Finarra herself.

*Yet now they call her goddess. Now, we are to kneel before her, and know her face as Dark's own, her presence as the elemental force itself. What has become of us that we should so descend into superstition?*

Treasonous thoughts – she knew that. The philosopher's game of separating governance from faith was a lie. Beliefs ran the gamut, from worshipping vast spirits in the sky down to professing love for a man. From listening to the voice of a god's will to accepting an officer's right to command. The only distinction was one of scale.

In her head she had run through her arguments in this assertion countless times. The proof, as far as she was concerned, was found in the currency used, because it was always the same. From the Forulkan commander ordering her soldiers into battle, to the paying of a fine for baring a weapon on the streets of Kharkanas: *disobey at peril to your life. If not your life then your freedom, and if not your freedom then your will, and if not your will, then your desire. What are these? They are coins of varying measure, a gradient of worth and value.*

*Rule my flesh, rule my soul. The currency is the same.*

She had no time for scholars and their sophist games. And no time for poets, either, who seemed obsessed with obscuring hard truths inside seductive language. Their collective gifts were ones of distraction, a tripping dance of entertainment along the cliff's edge.

A sudden blur in the grainy gloom. A high-pitched scream intended to freeze the prey. Iron blade, serpent-twined, rippling out beneath the swirling stars, like a tongue of Vitr. Piercing scream, the thrashing on the ground of a mortally wounded body. A hissing growl, paws scrabbling behind her. Lunging motion—

*     *     *

Faror Hend straightened, holding up a hand to keep Spinnock silent. Another eerie cry sounded in the night, distant and to the west. She saw Spinnock draw his sword, watched him slowly rise to his feet. Finarra Stone was late – half the night was gone. 'I hear no other voice,' Faror said. 'No heghest or tramil.'

'Nor that of a horse,' Spinnock said.

That was true. She hesitated, breath slowly hissing out from her nostrils.

'Still,' Spinnock went on, 'I am made uneasy. Is it common that Finarra remain out so late?'

Faror shook her head, and then reached a decision. 'Stay here, Spinnock. I will ride out in search of her.'

'You ride to where those wolves do battle, cousin.'

She would not lie to him. 'If only to ascertain that their quarry is not our captain.'

'Good,' he grunted. 'Because I fear for her now.'

'Build up the fire again,' she said to him, collecting her saddle and hurrying over to her mount.

'Faror.'

She turned. His eyes glittered above the first lick of flames from the embers. The light made his face seem flushed.

'Be careful,' he said. 'I do not want to lose you.'

She thought to say something to ease him, to push him away from things lying beneath his words. To push herself away. 'Spinnock,' she said, 'you have many cousins.'

He looked startled.

She turned back to her horse, not wanting to see more. Her tone had been dismissive. She'd not meant it to be, and its harshness seemed to echo in the silence between them now, cruel as a cut. She quickly saddled her horse, mounted up and lifted her lance from its sheath. Heel-nudging her mount out from the shelter of high, craggy boulders, she guided it towards the verge.

More wolves were keening to the night. Against small prey, the packs amounted to but three or four. But this sounded like a dozen, perhaps more. Too many even for a heghest. But she could hear no other cries – and a tramil's bellow could knock down a stone wall.

*It's her. Her horse is dead. She fights alone.*

Beneath the swirl of starlight, Faror urged her mount into a canter.

The memory of Spinnock's face, above those newborn flames, hovered in her mind. Cursing under her breath, she sought to dispel it. When that did not work, she forced upon it a transformation, into the visage of her betrothed. Few would claim that Kagamandra Tulas was handsome: his face was too thin, accentuating the gauntness that was his legacy from the wars – the years of deprivation and hunger – and in his eyes there was something hollow, like emptied shells, haunted by cruel memories that shied from the light. She knew he did not love her; she believed he was no longer capable of love.

Born in a Lesser House, he had been an officer in Urusander's Legion, commanding a cohort. If nothing else had ever overtaken Tulas in the wars, his station would have been of little value to House Durav. A lowborn of the Legion was no prize for any bride. Yet if love were possible – if this bitter, damaged man could earn such a thing, and learn to reciprocate in kind – then few would have opposed the union. But glory had found Tulas, and in that moment – when he saved the life of Silchas Ruin – the cohort commander had won the blessing of Mother Dark herself. A new High House would be the reward of this marriage, the elevation of Kagamandra's extended family.

For the sake of her own bloodline, she would have to find a way to love Kagamandra Tulas.

Yet, as she rode through the night, she could not find his face – it remained blurred, formless. And in those dark smudges where his eyes belonged, she saw glittering firelight.

Obsessions were harmless, so long as they remained trapped inside,

imprisoned and left pacing the cage of firm conscience; and if temptation was a key, well, she had buried it deep.

The lance's weight had drawn her arm down, and she decided to seat
the weapon in the socket riveted to the saddle. The wolf cries had not
sounded for some time, and there was nothing on the bleak, silvered
landscape before her to mark their presence. But she knew how far
those cries could carry.

Faror willed her mind blank, opening her senses to the verge. She
rode on for a time, until some instinct made her slow her mount. Hoofs
thumped a succession of double beats as the beast dropped out of its
canter, jostling her as she settled her weight into the trot. She now
listened for the sound she dreaded: the muted snarls of wolves bickering
over their kill.

Instead, a fierce shriek sliced through the night, startling her. Un-
seating the lance, she half rose in her stirrups. Drawing tight the reins
she forced her frightened horse into a walk. The cry had been close.
Still, before her she could see nothing untoward.

*There.*

A humped form, a trail of blood and gore, black in the grey dust.
Beyond it, another.

Faror brought her mount up alongside the first dead wolf. A sword
thrust had impaled the soft tissues of the belly, ripping open its gut.
Fleeing, the savage creature had dragged its entrails behind it, until
stumbling in them. Now the wolf huddled in a tangle, like a thing
pulled inside out. Blood sheathed its scaly hide and the lambent eyes
were ebbing.

The second beast lying a dozen paces further on had been hacked
almost in half, a downward chop through the spine and down between
ribs. The ground around it was scuffed, criss-crossed with ragged
furrows. Wary, she guided her horse closer.

No boot prints in the dirt, but the gouges of claws and kicking limbs
could well have obscured such signs.

Blood still poured down from the deep wound, and, leaning over, she
could see the beast's labouring heart. Alarmed, Faror pulled back. The
wolf's baleful eyes tracked her and the head tried to lift.

She set the point of the lance into the soft sack of the creature's
throat, and then punched the blade deep into the neck. The wolf tried
biting at the long blade for a moment, and then fell back, jaws gaping,
eyes fading. Straightening, tugging her weapon free, Faror looked
around.

The edge of the grasses was a broken wall off to her left, perhaps
sixteen paces away. Most of that barrier had been battered down,
chewed by the passage of many beasts. Random sprays of blood made
dark sweeps in the grey dust. Her searching gaze fixed on one path,

93

where it seemed the passage had been at its most violent. The root bundles flanking the gap were thick with gore. She saw stalks sliced clean, blade-cut.

Halting her mount, she listened, but the dark night was again silent. Faror eyed the mouth of the trail. If she set out upon it, she suspected, she would come upon a grisly scene – the wolves feeding on a corpse. She would have to drive them off, if she could, if only to recover Finarra Stone's body. It was clear to her that the fighting was over.

She hesitated, and not without some fear. It was not a given that she'd succeed in defeating the naked wolves; more packs would have been drawn to the kill site by the scent, and the eerie howls she had heard earlier. Somewhere in the high grasses there was a clearing, trampled down and bloody, and around it circled rival packs. There could be as many as fifty of the animals by now, and they would be hungry.

Thoughts of marriage, life in Kharkanas, and illicit desires, all fell away, as she realized that Spinnock might well find himself alone, facing the peril of returning to the fort with unguarded flanks: alone and abandoned; and Kagamandra Tulas would be left to mourn, or at least give the appearance of mourning – but that too would sink into those hollow eyes, one more cruel memory joining countless others, and he would know the guilt of not feeling enough, carving out still more emptiness in the husk of his soul.

She adjusted her grip on the lance, leaned forward to whisper in her horse's ear, and prepared to urge it into the trail.

A faint sound behind her – she twisted round.

Finarra Stone was edging out from between the boulders forming the ridge above the shoreline. Her sword was sheathed and she gestured.

Heart pounding, Faror backed her horse from the trail mouth and then swung the beast round. She rode at a walk towards Finarra.

A second gesture told her to dismount. Moments later she was facing her captain.

Finarra was splashed in drying blood. Her left arm appeared to be broken, the shoulder possibly dislocated. Wolf fangs had torn into the muscle of her left thigh, but the wound was roughly bound.

'I thought—'

Finarra pulled her close. 'Softly,' she whispered. 'Something has walked out of the sea.'

*What?* Confused, Faror pointed back at the trail mouth. 'A blade passed through the grasses. A weapon-wielder. I thought it you, captain.'

'And you were about to set off after me – Warden, I would have been dead. You would have given up your life for no reason. Have I taught you nothing?'

94

Chastened, Faror was silent, only now realizing that she had begun to welcome that end, even though the grief others might feel at it still pained her. Her future felt hopeless – was it not simpler to surrender her life now? She had been about to do so, and a calm had come over her, an ecstasy of peace.

'A small pack found me,' Finarra resumed after a moment in which she searched Faror's face intently. 'Swiftly dealt with. But the danger was too great, so I returned to the broken path between the rocks. It was there that I found a trail – emerging from the Vitr.'

'But that is impossible.'

Finarra grimaced. 'I would have agreed with you . . . yesterday. But now . . .' She shook her head. 'Small footprints, puddles of Vitr pooled in them. I was following their trail when I came upon you.'

Faror faced the high grasses once more. 'It went in through there,' she said, pointing. 'I heard a wolf cry.'

'As did I,' the captain said, nodding. 'But tell me, Faror Hend, if you believe a creature from the Vitr need fear wolves?'

'What do we do, sir?'

Finarra sighed. 'I wonder if I have not caught your madness. We need to discover more about this stranger. We need to gauge threat – is that not our purpose here in the Outer Reach?'

'Then we follow?'

'Not tonight. We will return to Spinnock – I need to rest, and my wounds need purging, lest infection take hold. For the moment, however, lead your horse by the reins. Once we are well clear of this place, we will ride double.'

'Did the wolves kill your mount, captain?'

Finarra grimaced. 'No.' She straightened. 'Keep your lance at the ready, and 'ware the grasses.'

They set off.

\*       \*       \*

Her wounded leg slowed them down, and Finarra longed to climb into the saddle behind Faror. The numbness of her arm had faded and in its place was a throbbing agony that lit the world red, and she could feel bone grinding on bone in her shoulder. Yet none of these concerns could scour away the look she had seen in Faror Hend's eyes.

There was a lust for death, flowering black and fierce. She had seen it before, had come to believe it was a flaw among the Tiste, emerging in each and every generation, like poisonous weeds in a field of grain. The mind backed into a corner, only to then turn its back upon the outer world. Seeing nothing but walls – no way through, no hope of escape – it then longed for turmoil's end, the sudden absence of self found in some heroic but doomed deed, some gesture intended to distract others, offering false motivations. Burying the secret desire was the goal, and death precluded all argument.

She thought she knew what haunted Faror Hend. An unwelcome betrothal, the prospect of a life bound to a broken man. And here, in this wilderness where all proscriptions fell away, there was at her side a young man she had known most of her life. He was young, bold in innocence, mindful of his own innate charm and the treasures it might win. Spinnock Durav had been pursued by women and men since he had first come of age. He had learned to not give up too much of himself, since those hands reaching for him desired little more than conquest and possession. He knew enough to guard himself.

Yet for all that, he was still a young warrior, and the adoration he clearly held for his elder cousin was growing into something else. Finarra had caught the flicker of earnestness amidst Spinnock's subtle flirtations with Faror Hend. The two cousins were now engaged in exquisite torture, seemingly unaware of the damage it promised, the lives it might ruin.

In the darker times in the Legion, truths had been discovered about the nature of torture. As an act of cruelty, seeking to break the victim, it only worked with the promise of its end: all torture found efficacy in the bliss of *release*. This game of exquisite pain, between Faror Hend and Spinnock Durav, was at its heart the same. If no release were found, their lives would sour, and love itself – if ever it came – could not but taste bitter.

Faror Hend understood this. Finarra had seen as much in the woman's eyes – a sudden revelation roiling in the storm of her own imminent death. The two had fused together into a web of impossibilities, and so the lust to die was born.

Finarra Stone was shaken, but there was little she could do – not yet. They would have to return to the outpost first. If they managed that, it would be a simple thing to reassign one of them – as far away from the other as possible. Of course, the captain well knew that it might not work. Torture could stretch vast distances, and indeed often strengthened under the strain.

There was another option. It had begun as an idle thought, a moment of honest admiration, but now a spark had found it – she remained wise enough to fear that her own motivations might have become suspect, and even here there would be repercussions. She could anticipate some but not all of them. No matter. Selfishness was not yet a crime.

It would be an abuse of her rank, true, but if she accepted all responsibility she could mitigate the damage, and whatever she herself lost, well, she would live with it.

'Now,' she said, then watched as Faror pulled herself astride the horse, kicked one foot free of the stirrup and reached down.

Finarra took hold of that grip with her good arm, cursing at the awkwardness, as she would have to use the wrong hand. Balancing on one leg, she lifted the other and set her boot into the stirrup, and then pulled herself upward. She worked her free leg over the rump of the horse before shifting her weight across the back of the saddle, and only then released her grip on Faror's hand.

'That looked . . . painful,' Faror Hend said in a murmur as she took up the reins.

Finarra slipped her boot from the stirrup, her breaths harsh. 'I'm here now,' she said, her good arm sliding round Faror's midriff. 'Ride to Spinnock, Warden. He will be beside himself with worry.'

'I know,' Faror Hend replied, kicking the horse into motion.

'The sooner he knows we are safe, the better.'

The woman's head nodded.

Finarra continued, 'After all, you are his favourite cousin, Faror Hend.'

'We know each other well, captain, that is true.'

Finarra closed her eyes, wanting to sink her face against Faror's shoulder, nestling into the thick black hair coming out from beneath the helmet's flaring rim. She was exhausted. The events of this night had left her fraught. She wasn't thinking clearly. 'There are responsibilities,' she muttered.

'Captain?'

'He's too young, I think. This Vitr – it is like the kiss of Chaos. We must . . . we must guard against such things.'

'Yes sir.'

The silks were slick between them, sliding with the roll of the horse's slow canter. The motion rushed waves of pain through her wounded thigh. Her left arm felt impossibly swollen, monstrous as a demon's.

*They might have to cut it off. Infection is the greatest risk. Vapours of the silver sea are inimical, or so it is believed. Am I already infected?*

'Captain?'

'What is it?'

'Tighten your clasp upon me – I can feel you slipping. It would not do for you to fall.'

Finarra nodded against Faror's shoulder. The horse was labouring under them, its breaths harsh and hot. *Only dumb beasts are capable of carrying such burdens. Why is that?*

\*　　　\*　　　\*

The captain's weight upon her back was a shifting thing, ever on the edge of sliding away entirely, and Faror Hend was forced to take the reins into one hand and fold her other arm alongside Finarra's, grasping the wrist to keep it in place.

The body against her was hard and wiry, almost a man's. Finarra Stone had fought in the defence of the Hust mines, as a Houseblade under her father's command. She was only a few years older than Faror, and yet it was clear to the younger woman that in that modest gap there had been a lifetime of experience. In the years they had patrolled together on the Glimmer Fate, Faror had begun to think of her captain as old, professionally remote as befitted all veterans. Physically, the daughter of Hust Henarald was stretched and twisted like rope. Her face was hard angles, and yet perfectly proportioned, and her eyes only rarely met those of another; they were ever quick to shy away.

She recalled how Finarra had stared at her earlier, and how it had seemed almost physical, as if pushing Faror up against a wall. The moment had left her rattled. She had hardly been prepared for the other revelation. *Someone has come from the sea.* She thought back to those wolves, hacked and huddled in their own blood, the gore-spattered trail mouth cutting into the wall of grasses.

*Someone has come from the sea.*

Ahead, she could make out the faint glow of the campfire. Spinnock must have used up their entire supply of wood to create this beacon. The captain would not be pleased.

She guided her horse on to the trail wending between misshapen boulders and crags. It was, she saw, close to dawn.

Spinnock had heard their approach and he appeared ahead, weapon drawn. She gestured him back into the camp, and rode in behind him.

'The captain is injured – help her down, Spinnock. Careful – her left arm and shoulder.'

She felt him take Finarra's weight in his arms – the woman was barely conscious – and gently pull her down from the horse's back. Faror then dismounted, feeling cool air slide along the length of her back as the sodden silks drew away from her skin.

Spinnock carried the captain to the bedroll that had been laid out. 'She took a fall from her horse?'

Faror could see the half-disbelieving look he threw her. It was rumoured that Finarra Stone had once ridden a horse up a tower's spiralling staircase. 'She was attacked.'

'I did not think the wolves would risk such a thing.'

Saying nothing, Faror went to her kit and began rummaging for the collection of bandages, scour-blades and unguents that made up their healing supplies. She joined Spinnock and knelt beside the captain. 'The bite on her leg first,' she said. 'Help me remove the dressing.'

The wound revealed was severe and already the flesh around it was swollen and red. 'Spinnock,' she said, 'heat up a scour-blade.'

*   *   *

The sun was high overhead and the captain had yet to regain consciousness. Faror Hend had told Spinnock all she knew of the night's events, and Spinnock had grown quiet in the time since. They had used up most of the healing salves and the gut thread treating the leg wound after burning away what they could of torn, dead flesh. The scarring would be fierce and they were not yet certain they had expunged the infection. Finarra Stone remained fevered, and had not even awakened when they reinserted her dislocated shoulder and then set, splinted, and bound the broken humerus. The prospect of setting off in pursuit of the stranger seemed remote.

Finally, Spinnock turned to her. 'Cousin, I have been thinking. It seems we are destined to spend another night here, unless we rig up a harness between our horses to carry the captain. If we are to do that, it should be now. This will give us enough time to ride to the outpost before night arrives.'

'The captain desires that we track the stranger.'

He glanced away. 'It is difficult to believe, I admit. From the Vitr Sea?'

'I believe her. I saw the dead wolves.'

'Might they not have been the ones that attacked Finarra? If fevered by infection, she might have become lost, doubling back on her own trail. Those footprints might well have been her very own.'

'She seemed clear of mind when I found her.'

'Then we are to wait?'

Faror Hend sighed. 'I have another idea.' She glanced across at the recumbent form of Finarra Stone. 'I agree with you – the captain must be brought back to the outlier post as soon as possible. She is in no condition to lead us on to the trail of the stranger, and without a proper healer she might well die.'

'Go on,' Spinnock said, his eyes grave.

'She will sit behind on your horse – bound to you. And you will take her to the outpost. I will track the stranger.'

'Faror—'

'You have the stronger horse, and it's rested. There are times when we must ride alone when on these patrols. You know that, Spinnock.'

'If she awakens—'

'She will be furious, yes. But the responsibility is mine. She can save her ire for me.' She rose. 'As you say, we must hurry.'

*     *     *

Faror had held to cold professionalism throughout the preparations, and had said nothing as she watched her cousin ride off, plunging into the furnace-hot path through the grasses and vanishing from sight in a bare half-dozen heartbeats. There could be no ease, no warmth shared between them. They were two Wardens of the Outer Reach and they had tasks before them. The Glimmer Fate was rife with dangers. Wardens died. These were simple truths. It was time he learned them.

She set out at a trot westward, back along the track she had ridden the night past. In the harsh sunlight the verge seemed even more forbidding, even more inimical. It was a conceit to imagine that they knew the world; that they knew its every detail. Forces ever worked unseen, in elusive patterns no mortal mind could comprehend. She saw life as little more than the crossing of unknown trails, one after another. What made them could only be known by following one, but this meant surrendering one's own path: that blazing charge to the place of endings. Instead, a person pushed on, wondering, often frightened. If she glanced to her left she could see the wall of black grasses, shivering and rippling and blurry in the heat; and she knew there were countless paths through Glimmer Fate. Perhaps, if she could become winged as a bird, she might fly high overhead and see each and every trail, and perhaps even discern something of a pattern, a map of answers. Would this offer relief? Directly ahead, the verge stretched on like a beaten road.

She came at last to the first of the dead wolves. Small scaled rats had ventured out from the grasses to scavenge the carcass. They fled at her approach, slithering snake-like back into shelter among the thick stalks. She trotted her mount past and came opposite the gap in the grasses. The spilled gore was black, swarming with beetles, and in the heat Faror could smell the rot of fast-decaying flesh.

She reined in, eyed the gap for a moment, and then nudged her horse into it.

Once among the tall stalks, the heat swirled round her, cloying and fierce. Her mount snorted heavily, agitated, ears flattening. Faror murmured to calm the beast. The stench of spilled blood and ichor felt thick in her throat with every breath she took.

A short distance in, she came upon two more dead wolves, and crushed-down dents in the grasses to either side. Halting her horse and leaning forward to peer down one such side-trail, she could just make out the hind legs of a third wolf carcass. Straightening, she did a quick count of the breaks to either side.

Five. Surely there wasn't a dead beast at the end of each of them? But the dried blood was everywhere.

Faror continued on.

Fifty heartbeats later, the path opened into a clearing, and here she found another slain pack, four creatures flung by savage blows to either side of a worn deer-trail that cut directly across the centre of the glade and vanished opposite. There was something almost dismissive about

100

the way the wolves had been cut down and left dying from terrible wounds.

Shivering despite the heat, Faror Hend crossed the clearing. The resumption of the trail upon the other side narrowed markedly, and her horse was forced to push aside the thick, serrated stalks, the edges rasping against the wooden sheaths of armour protecting its legs and flanks. The heavy blades wavered and threatened to fold over both rider and mount. Faror drew her sword and used the weapon to keep the grasses from her face and neck.

Before too long she concluded that this was not a game-trail, for it ran too straight, passing near streams and springs but giving no sign of digression. The direction was south. If it remained true, it would lead to Kharkanas.

The stranger had travelled through the night; Faror saw no signs of a camp or even a place where rest had been taken. It was closing on late afternoon, the sky cloudless overhead, the light assuming a molten quality, as of fires raging beneath a thickening crust; and this light bled down through the black grasses with lurid tongues. She had never experienced such light before and the world around her seemed suddenly ethereal, uncanny. *Changes are coming to this world.* Sweat streamed beneath her silks.

Somewhere to the east, Spinnock Durav would be approaching the outlier post, but probably not arriving until well after dusk. She knew that he – and Finarra – should be safe enough while astride the horse. The wolves did not like the beasts and besides, the Warden mounts were trained for battle. And yet she feared for them none the less. If the captain's infection had worsened—

Her horse broke through into a clearing, and at its far end stood a woman, facing them. Fair-skinned, her blonde hair dishevelled and roughly hacked at shoulder length. She was naked but for the scaled hide of a wolf draped over her shoulders. Faror could see fierce sunburn virtually everywhere else.

Reining in, Faror sheathed her sword and then raised a hand. 'I mean you no harm,' she called out.

Faror could see no weapons, not even a knife. Yet that made no sense – the wolves had been slain with a blade, and the woman's golden tresses were cut with, it seemed, the same absence of subtlety.

*She is very young. Slim as a boy. She is not Tiste.* 'Do you understand me? Are you an Azathanai?'

At that word the woman's head lifted, eyes suddenly sharp. Then she spoke. 'I know your language. But it is not mine. Azathanai. I know that word. *Azat drevlid naratarh Azathanai.* The people who were never born.'

Faror Hend shook her head. She had never heard the language the

101

woman had spoken. It was not Azathanai, nor Forulkan. 'You have been tracked from the Vitr Sea. I am of the Tiste, a Warden of the Outer Reach. My name is Faror Hend, blood-bound to House Durav. You are approaching the borders of Kurald Galain, the home of my people.'

'A sea?'

'Can you tell me your name?' Faror asked.

After a moment the woman shook her head.

'You refuse to, or you cannot remember?'

'I recall . . . nothing. A sea?'

Faror Hend sighed. 'You travel south – why?'

Again the woman shook her head. 'The air is so very hot.' She then looked round and added, 'I think I did not expect this.'

'Then I shall give you a Tiste name. For now, until your memory returns. And I shall escort you to Kharkanas, where rules Mother Dark. Is this acceptable?'

The woman nodded.

'I name you T'riss.'

Cocking her head, the woman smiled. 'I am "born of the sea".'

'Will you walk, or ride with me?'

'The beast you are on seems useful. I shall have one too.' She turned then and seemed to fix her attention on the high grasses off to her left.

Sudden motion from there, and Faror made to unseat her lance as the black blades of grass buckled and twisted, drawing into vast knots. She heard roots being torn loose from the hard ground, heard thick snapping and something like the twisting of ropes. A creature was taking form before her eyes.

A horse of bound grass. It clambered upright as if pushed from the earth, shedding dust, massive as a destrier. The sockets of its eyes were gaping holes; the maw of its mouth was a mass of spiked blades. Its own weight seemed to be vast, far greater than it should have been for a conjuration of grasses.

Faror's own horse backed away in alarm and she struggled to control it.

T'riss had now turned to creating clothing from the grasses, the style seeking to mimic Faror's own silks. She made no gestures as the black blades snaked up around her body, revealed no hint of power beyond her own will. This was god-like sorcery and it frightened Faror to the core. Now clothed in grasses woven sleek and strangely flowing, the woman conjured into being a lance of the same material, and then a belted sword, and finally faced Faror once more. 'I am born of the sea. I travel with Warden of the Outer Reach Faror Hend blood-bound to House Durav, and we ride to Kharkanas, where rules Mother Dark.' She waited a moment, brows slowly lifting.

Faror nodded.

Seemingly satisfied with that, T'riss strode to her strange mount and lithely leapt astride its back. She took hold of reins that seemed to grow out from the creature's cheeks, just behind the tuck of the mouth, and slipped her now-booted feet into twisted-rope stirrups. She looked across to Faror. 'Shall I break the path, Warden Faror Hend?'

'If you would, thank you.'

'The same direction?'

'Yes.'

'Mother Dark.' T'riss smiled. 'That is a nice title.'

\*     \*     \*

The sun was settling on the western horizon as if melting into a pool of fire, and Sharenas Ankhadu knew she was probably alone among her companions in not welcoming its demise. Her skin was of a quality that deepened most becomingly, rather than burned, and she could feel its glow on her face, neck and the backs of her hands where they rested on the saddle horn.

True, the heat had been savage, but Sharenas delighted in that as well. She was not inured to cold as many of her kin seemed to be, and her memories of the northern campaigns against the Jheleck were one and all unpleasant. Her cohort had on occasion mocked her with extra furs and hoarded firewood when they camped, and more than a few had offered to share her bed, out of duty, they insisted.

There were rules in the Legion, of course, prohibiting such dalliance with the enlisted soldiers, and that was but one of many such rules that Sharenas had occasion to curse – even if only to herself. She had been young to take command of a cohort, but it was hardly surprising given the renown of her two elder kin. There had been legacies to live with, not all of them reputable.

As she rode now, in the company of other officers of the Legion – including those since stripped of their rank and made inactive – she spared a thought for regret. Neither Infayen Menand nor Tathe Lorat had elected to accompany this party; and Sharenas knew that the others were left wondering what their absence signified. Should they look to Sharenas for answers – and she'd caught the occasional glance sent her way – they would be disappointed. That said, Sharenas loved and admired both her sister and her cousin, and held them in great esteem, in which faith was strong. If sides must be chosen in the days to come, Sharenas was certain that they would not hesitate in answering the summons.

For all that, she had to admit that she could not be fully confident of some of her companions on this venture, and with that thought her eyes tracked once more to the huge ex-soldier riding behind the vanguard of

Hunn Raal and Osserc. Ilgast Rend had accepted this invitation with reluctance, or so it was purported, and without question his mood was sour, unrelieved since their departure from Neret Sorr three days past. Indeed, upon arriving on the outskirts of the settlement, his first words to Hunn Raal had been a pointed question: *'Does Urusander know of this?'* Smiling, Hunn Raal had evaded the question. Ilgast would have pressed if not for Osserc's sudden claim that his father was not only aware of the pending journey, but approved of it.

That, Sharenas suspected, had been a lie. For a moment she'd thought that Ilgast would actually challenge Urusander's son, but then he had turned away, his silence both dismissive and – in Osserc's eyes – insulting. Hunn Raal's sudden laughter and a heavy slap upon Osserc's back had mollified the threat. For the time being, Sharenas had caught the glowering look Osserc had thrown at Ilgast's back a few moments later.

Well, allies need not be friends. Ilgast Rend was master of a Greater House. In many ways, he had more to lose, potentially, than any other person present, should things go wrong.

*But they won't. Hunn Raal is honourable. He knows what he is doing, and he knows, as do we all, that what he is doing is the right thing to do.* To crush the birth of any doubts in her mind, she needed only think of Urusander. And so long as her old commander remained as the singular focus of all their ambitions – the source of the reasoning voice through which their claims for recognition and justice would be heard, *must* be heard – then she need not worry overmuch about young Osserc and his thin skin, or his childishness and irritating diffidence. In any case, Hunn Raal was ever at the boy's side, serving to mitigate Osserc's tirades and impulsive reactions.

Four others accompanied them, although only one earned serious regard in her eyes. Hunn Raal's three cousins, Serap, Risp and Sevegg, were soldiers, true enough, but followers of Hunn; and if there was any truth to the rumours, then Hunn's assurance of their alliance was at least in part forged beneath the furs, even though all three were second cousins – not close enough to be a crime, but close enough to raise eyebrows and, perhaps, earn a few murmurs of disapproval. In any case, it was clear that the three young women worshipped their older cousin, and it amused Sharenas to imagine that sexual prowess lay at the heart of that worship. Alternatively, shared pity could on occasion resemble loyalty, and since she had never shared Hunn Raal's furs she couldn't be certain either way. After all, the man drank too much.

She suspected she would straddle him sooner or later, but only when a clear political advantage served to motivate her. He was not highborn enough though his bloodline was, and she could well see his untoward arrogance, ever warring with his duty to Lord Urusander. There would come a time when someone would need to take him down a few notches – for his own sake – and what he might initially believe a triumphant conquest on his part would quickly reveal a different nature. There was nothing easier than belittling a man when he lay between a woman's legs. The effect was very nearly instantaneous and always unmistakable.

It was easy then to dismiss Raal's three wet-lipped cousins. Not so easy to dismiss the last soldier in their party, who somehow managed to seem to be riding alone though he was in truth in their midst – indeed, at Sharenas's side, upon her left. Straight in the saddle, welded together like iron blades into a man both forbidding and dangerous, Kagamandra Tulas had not spoken since leaving Neret Sorr.

Of course he well knew that the outpost of the Wardens that they now rode towards was also the station of his betrothed, Faror Hend, and that before this night was done he would find himself standing before her – the first time since the announcement.

Sharenas so wanted to witness that moment. It would be . . . delicious.

Kagamandra Tulas was dead inside. Every woman could see it, with but a single glance into his lightless eyes. His wounded soul had been left behind, discarded on some field of battle. He was a husk, the animation of his being grinding like worn teeth in an iron gear; it seemed Tulas did not welcome his own aliveness, as if he but longed for death, for the stillness that lay within him to seep out, poison the rest of his being, his flesh, his skin, his face, whereupon he could in his last breath thank the generosity of those who were about to inter him inside his silent tomb.

Poor Faror Hend. In the new way of things, upon the ascension of Urusander, political expediency would work none of its cruelty upon such things as marriage and love. The power of the Greater Houses, with all its guarded gates and patrolled walls, its outer pitfalls and deadly traps, would be struck aside. Service to the realm would be the only standard of value, of worth. In that future, drawing ever closer, Faror Hend would be free to wed whomever she chose, although in the irony of that future world, Kagamandra Tulas, who had given virtually all of himself to the defence of the realm, might well prove a most valuable prize.

Indeed, who else was likely to find himself standing at Lord Urusander's side, like the ghost of a brother, warding the clasping of hands that would join Mother Dark with the commander of the Legion? Who but Urusander would be brave and humble enough to so honour Kagamandra Tulas? And did not Mother Dark herself make a grand gesture of solemn recognition to the saviour of Silchas Ruin's life? No, Sharenas had no doubt, Tulas would soon find himself standing next to the throne, one gauntleted hand resting on the worn pommel of his sword, his empty eyes scanning the throne room, seeking a challenge none would dare.

For all that, he would be a wretched husband to any woman, making bitter any political advantage.

Would he have as his wife Faror Hend? So it seemed, a decision already carved deep in stone, firm as a mason's will. Idly, Sharenas wondered if she might contrive to save Faror that lifetime of sorrow and loneliness. Kagamandra could not be reached, could not be sullied – nor would she even consider such a thing, no matter how sweet that triumph would be. This left Faror Hend herself. Sharenas did not know her well, barring that she was among the Durav bloodline. An unranked Warden – and that was hardly a posting one would eagerly choose. *Unless . . . think on what she did, coming out here . . . she is betrothed, and days later she chooses her own exile from Kharkanas.*

*Ha! I see it now. She fled him. Out here, as far from Tulas as she could manage. Oh, how wonderful. Faror Hend – your betrothed has tracked you down! Are you not thrilled? Do you not swoon at the romance of the gesture?*

The outpost ahead promised a lively evening. She had thought to stay close to Hunn Raal when he spoke with the commander of the Wardens; when he sought to forge an alliance with Calat Hustain. But, fascinating as that exchange might prove to be, her interest had now shifted to the drama, or even melodrama, of this fated meeting of the intended.

Poor Faror Hend. She would be left reeling. Made to feel . . . vulnerable.

Sharenas would be quick, then, to offer comfort. Wise, understanding, ready to listen without judgement – and in that lonely outpost, to whom else could Faror dare turn? *Tell me your secrets, sister, and together we will find a way out of this nightmare. Even if it means ruining your reputation – you will thank me for it in a century or two, I am sure.*

*Show me the path of your longing, and I will take your hand and guide you down it. As true friends do.*

\*     \*     \*

Directly ahead of Ilgast Rend rode Captain Hunn Raal and Osserc, the son of Lord Urusander. Neither man inspired Ilgast. The captain was vain and arrogant. The would-be prince was the palest reflection of his father, thin-skinned and prone to malice. It was, frankly, astonishing that Lord Urusander had produced such an heir to the House. But then, Ilgast well remembered Osserc's mother and her grasping ways. If not for the physical similarities between father and son, he could well have believed that Osserc was the spawn of some other man's seed.

Abyss knew, this was an age of frenzied spilling among the Tiste. Wives cheated, husbands wandered, and now even Mother Dark had taken for herself a lover.

Whelps were falling to the floor like sour fruit these days. Ilgast was not impressed with who his Tiste had become. The peace they had won was now stained with indolence and a distinct withering of probity.

His thoughts led to Urusander. The Lord had proved a fine leader of soldiers, but an end to the wars had not served the man well. He too had stumbled off the trail, losing himself in arcane indulgences better suited to wizened clerics with ink-smeared hands.

Urusander would make an indifferent king, and his disinclination to grant favour – his unassailable belief in justice – would soon turn his supporters. Men like Hunn Raal would find themselves no better off. No gifts of wealth, no grants of land or power, and no tipped scales of court influence. How long before they began plotting against their beloved lord? Ilgast understood these fools all too well. Their only true ambition was the elevation of their own station.

His greatest worry was that the ascension of Urusander would spill blood. Even the immensely satisfying ousting of Draconus and his outlander ilk was not enough to salve Ilgast's fear. The Houseblades of the majority of the Greater Houses would resist the elevation of Lord Urusander and his followers. There was more to that position than simply protecting the power they possessed. He knew his own people. The political machinations by soldiers such as Hunn Raal would offend them to the core: they would see all too clearly the brutal ambition behind such efforts. They would be affronted, and then indignant, and then furious. Decorum was a fragile thing. It would not take much to see it shattered. *In a world of blood, everyone drowns.*

Yet here he rode in the company of these soldiers, sickened by the pathetic air of mischief surrounding Hunn Raal and his three vapid cousins; the febrile self-importance of Osserc as he continued to delude himself that he was leading this party; and behind Ilgast there was Kagamandra Tulas, who still faced the past war and would likely continue to do so until his dying day; and Sharenas Ankhadu – granted, the least objectionable of the trio of Legion captains who proclaimed themselves sisters of the spirit – yet he was disappointed that she was here. He'd thought her wiser, too sharp to fall into this wake of fools and be swept along like so much detritus. What then of *his* purpose in such dire company?

He knew that Hunn Raal counted his presence as a conquest of sorts, and no doubt the captain envisaged Ilgast's alliance in persuading Calat Hustain and the Wardens to their cause. But the truth was, Ilgast knew he had isolated himself, too content with his retirement. Yet the world did not stand still for his seeming indifference. Though none had sought his counsel, he now saw himself as firmly between the two sides. With the blood of a Greater House in his veins, and his history as a cohort commander in Urusander's Legion, he stood astride the chasm. Neither side had yet pulled with a force he could not resist, so he remained standing firm – a position that invited righteousness in his more careless moments.

Only slowly did he come to comprehend his solitude, and the other risks entailed in his stance. He had been fending off the occasional pull, particularly from the side of Legion, but events were progressing at an ever swifter pace, and now he no longer feared being pulled. He feared being pushed.

There were many others like him, he knew. There was, in his mind, no truer measure of stupidity than to imagine that the world could be reduced to two sides, one facing the other with fangs bared, brandishing weapons and hurling hate at the enemy. Things were never so simple. Ilgast disliked the immorality of a Consort to Mother Dark – if indeed she loved Draconus, she should damned well marry him. In the growing power of Mother Dark's cult, there was a burgeoning strain of sexual excess. He did not lack his own appetites but he sensed a hedonistic undercurrent swirling beneath the extravagant displays, a rot at the core.

If religious ecstasy were no different from a cock in a cunt, then make a temple of every whorehouse and be done with it. If the bliss of salvation were a mindless shudder, well, who was left to clean up the mess? Yet Mother Dark seemed to be inviting this sordid surrender. Any faith that encouraged the mind to set aside its greatest gifts – of reason, of scepticism – in favour of empty platitudes and the glory of an end to thinking . . . well, he would have none of it. He would not blind himself, would not stop up his ears, would not close his mouth nor cut off his hands. He was not a beast to be yoked to someone else's idea of truth. He would find his own or die trying.

The Consort needed to go. Mother Dark needed a proper marriage or none at all. The licentiousness of the court had to end. But these statements did not drag him into Urusander's shadow, just as they did not insist he stand with his nobleborn kin. They were opinions, not fortifications.

He knew Calat Hustain. The man's loyalty was absolute – to his own House. Hunn Raal would fail, and in failing, carve into his list of enemies the name of Calat Hustain.

Ilgast Rend meant to speak with his old friend. Late in the night, at the Rising of the Watch, long after the fools had drunk themselves into a belligerent stupor down in the main hall. They would discuss the new, deadly currents, and perhaps, before dawn, they would find a way of navigating these savage waters.

Such was his hope.

One night, someone might well slit Hunn Raal's throat, and he'd not be missed. Leave Urusander to his intellectual masturbations – he did no harm and besides, he had earned his last years of pleasure, no matter how dubious that pleasure might seem. Mother Dark would tire of Draconus eventually. Indeed, she might travel so far inside the sorcery of Endless Night – or whatever it was that the cult worshipped – that such physical desires were left behind. Was it not already said that she was enwreathed in bitter cold darkness day and night now?

When the Consort vanished into that darkness, what did he find?

Ilgast remembered when Mother Dark was known by her birth name; when she was simply a woman: beautiful, vivacious, possessor of unimaginable strengths and unexpected frailties – a woman like any other, then. Until the day she found the Gate. Darkness was many things; most of all, it was selfish.

Dusk was fast closing, and directly ahead Ilgast Rend could see the midnight line of the grasses of Glimmer Fate, and there, crouching at its edge, stood a stone gate that marked the North Road. Down that road, in a short time, they would come to the outpost where Calat had established his headquarters this season.

The Wardens were an odd lot, a loose rabble of misfits. This was what made them so important. In a decent society, there must be a place for misfits, a place free of prejudice and torment. In a decent society, such people were not left to the alleys, the shadows beneath bridges, the gutters and the slums. They were not thrown out into the wilderness, and not throat-cut either.

Misfits had a place in the world, and must be cherished, for one day, they might be needed.

Torches flared at the gate. Guards were at their post.

Ahead, Hunn Raal twisted in his saddle and glanced back, though it was too dark to see where his eyes fixed. Facing forward again, he muttered something, to which Osserc shot a look over a shoulder. Then, turning back, he laughed.

Overhead, the stars appeared, a swirling whirlpool spanning the entire sky.

# FIVE

ARETH SOLITUDE WAS A VAST PLAIN CROSSED BY ANCIENT BEACH ridges of water-worn limestone cobbles; these ridges ran for leagues but they were relatively shallow, evidence, explained Tutor Sagander months ago, of an inland sea that had taken thousands of years to die. If he let his mind wander, Arathan could imagine that they were now riding through the thinnest water, the water of the past, the water of dim memory, and the seabed under the horses' hoofs, with its ribbons of wild-blown sand and its blooms of yellow grasses, was far beneath the surface of another world.

If he let his mind wander, he could almost feel himself rising up, lifting clear of this hard, brutal saddle; he could ride his thoughts instead, as they floated out of his battered, weary body, ever upward. Thoughts alone, thoughts unfettered, could find a thousand worlds in which to wander. And none here, riding with him across the plain, would know; his body would give nothing away. There were many kinds of freedom, and the most precious ones were secret.

Sagander would not have understood such musings. Just as there were many kinds of freedom, so too were there many kinds of prison. It came as something of a shock when Arathan first comprehended this truth. The stone walls were everywhere, and no hard grey tower was needed as proof of their existence. They could hide behind eyes, or form barriers in the throat leaving no escape for words. They could rise suddenly around thoughts in the skull, suffocating them. They could block the arrival of other thoughts – foreign thoughts, frightening thoughts, challenging thoughts. And in each case, there was one thing they all shared – all these vicious walls: they were enemies to freedom.

Arathan had known hard grey walls all his life.

Yet now he rode, under an open sky, a sky too vast and too empty. His skull throbbed; his back was sore; he was blistered along the inside of his thighs. The helm he had been made to wear made his neck ache with its clunky weight. The supposedly light armour, banded bronze strips sewn on to leather, dragged at his shoulders. The vambraces covering his wrists and the thick metal-strapped gauntlets on his hands were hot and heavy. Even the plain sword belted at his side pulled at his hip.

He rode in the company of exhaustion, but still the air felt sweet as water on his face, and even the huge figure of his father, riding ahead at the side of Sergeant Raskan, seemed to hold no power over him. There were, he told himself again, many kinds of freedom.

On the day of leaving he had been filled with fear, and it had shamed him. Dawn had broken cold and sleep was still grainy in his eyes when he stood shivering in the courtyard, watching the frenzied activity as mounts were readied and various supplies were strapped on the saddles. Servants rushed about, mostly in response to the shrill demands of Sagander. The tutor's two travel chests, packed with precision, had been flung open, the contents frantically rummaged through – there would be no packhorses for this journey, and this left Sagander in a state of such agitation that he had begun shouting abuse at all the servants, the stable-boys and anyone else who ventured near.

Excepting Raskan, of course, and the four Borderswords who looked on with flat expressions from where they stood near the gate.

Lord Draconus had yet to appear, although his two horses stood ready, a lone groom clutching the reins of Calaras; the huge warhorse seemed immune to the panic surrounding him, standing virtually motionless beside the mounting block. The other horses looked nervous to Arathan's eye; his gaze caught another groom who was leading out from the stables his own mounts. The mare, Hellar, tossed her head as she emerged from the shade, and behind her was Besra, the gelding on which Arathan decided he would begin this ride – a solid-looking roan with a scarred neck. Both animals seemed enormous, as if they had grown overnight, and Arathan struggled to recall the confidence he had found by the end of the riding lessons.

'Arathan! Come here, quickly!'

Startled by the command, he looked over to see Sagander on his knees beside one of the trunks. The old man gestured frantically, his visage darkening.

'Come here, I said! Student you were and student you remain! Attend to me!'

Longing to be in his room, warm beneath the heavy furs, with a day ahead no different from all the other days, Arathan forced himself forward. His limbs felt stiff from cold and his mind was sluggish with lack of sleep, and the dread of leaving the world he had known all of his life left him feeling sick.

'There shall be no trunks on this journey! I wasted half the night packing them. I was foolish listening to you, and see how I am now beset! You must make room among your own kit.' He pointed at a heap of materials. 'For those, do you understand?'

'Yes, sir.'

'Be quick about it then, before your father appears!'

Arathan went over to the objects. He studied them for a moment, considering how he might fit into his bedroll the assayer's scales and the weights and measures. If there had been a small bag to hold the weights, it no longer accompanied them. He counted a dozen gradations of the pure metal, the heaviest feeling solid and filling the palm of his hand when he picked it up. The lightest one was barely the size of a pebble, like a thick coin. He tucked that one into his belt pouch.

At a snapping insult from Sagander, he quickly gathered up the rest of the equipment and made his way over to his horse.

The groom, a boy of about the same age as Arathan, had already strapped the kit to the gelding's saddle, and upon seeing Arathan's approach he made an expression of annoyance and turned to drag it free.

'Set it down,' said Arathan. 'I need to fit these in.'

The groom did so, and then backed off, as if unwilling to draw too close to the strange instruments.

'You can go,' Arathan said to him. 'I will do this.'

With a quick nod the boy hurried away, vanishing into the gloom of the stables.

Arathan loosened the careful knots he had tied to secure the bedroll. He'd already packed his change of clothes inside, including a new pair of henen hide boots. As the boots were heavy he had been careful with the balance, since Raskan had told him that horses were easily irritated by such things, especially over a long trek. Pulling the tie-strings clear, he unfurled the bedroll. He laid out the measures and the weights, but the scales were too large to fit. As he knelt, contemplating what to do with the awkward instrument, he became aware of a general silence in the courtyard, apart from the heavy approach of boots. A shadow fell over him and Arathan looked up.

'Why are you not ready?' Lord Draconus demanded.

At the question, Arathan felt his throat tightening, choking the words from him. He continued peering upward, silent.

He saw his father's eyes shift to the scales on the ground beside Arathan, and then he reached down and picked them up. He held them out to one side. A servant appeared to take the instrument from him and hurry off, back towards the house. 'There is no time for this,' Draconus said, turning away.

Arathan watched his father walk back to Calaras. The servants in the courtyard all stood with bowed heads. Tutor Sagander was already beside his own mount, glaring across the distance at Arathan.

He quickly rolled up the bedding, leaving the weights and measures in place. He tied rough knots to bind the kit and lifted it to the back of the saddle. He struggled for a time with the straps; his hands felt clumsy, almost useless, the tips of his fingers too soft and yielding since they lacked most of their nails. Finally, he fumbled his way through and stepped back. Facing round he saw that his father was now astride Calaras, reins in gloved hands. Raskan was pulling himself on to his own mount, while two servants helped Sagander do the same. By the gate, the Borderswords had vanished and no doubt now waited outside.

Arathan took up Besra's reins, which had been left to dangle. He had to grope to slide his boot into the stirrup, almost losing his balance, and then he pulled himself up and on to the saddle.

Draconus led them out through the gate, followed by Raskan and then Sagander, who curtly waved Arathan into his wake.

Glancing back, a moment before the gate's shadow fell over him, Arathan saw his half-sisters, atop the steps before the door of the house. They were in their nightclothes: loose and flowing and black as ink. Above this filmy darkness their faces seemed deathly pale. A faint shiver ran through him at the sight, and then he faced forward once more and, trailed by his charger on a long lead, rode out from the courtyard.

The Borderswords were mounted on dun-coloured horses, the beasts lighter-boned yet longer-legged than the stable horses being ridden by those of the Lord's household. In addition to their riders, the animals carried bundled tents and cookware, as well as packs bulging with dry foods and casks of water.

Feeling uncomfortable, burdened by the armour and the heavy helm on his head, Arathan guided his horse after Sagander – until without warning the tutor reined in. Besra edged deftly around the sudden obstacle, only to draw up when Sagander reached out and took hold of the bridle. 'Look back, student. Go on, do as I say.'

The Borderswords were falling in behind Draconus and Raskan as they set out on the curving track that would lead them westward.

Arathan twisted in his saddle and studied the gate and the wall of the estate.

'Tell me what you see,' Sagander demanded, his voice oddly rough.

'The Great House of Lord Draconus,' Arathan replied.

'Your entire world, student. Until this day.'

'Yes sir.'

'Over with now.'

Arathan nodded.

'Your sisters didn't want to see you off. But your father commanded. Those girls despise you, Arathan.'

'I know.'

'Do you know why?'

He thought for a moment, and then he nodded. 'I was born to the wrong mother.'

Sagander snorted. 'Your life as you knew it is now over. You must look to yourself and none other, for all that awaits you. Even my own teaching is mostly done. Your half-sisters – they do not expect to ever see you again.'

'They wore black, yes.'

'Foolish boy, they always wear black. But yes, they wanted you to see.' He released Besra's bridle. 'Come, let us catch up. You ride at my side, but I should tell you, your father was disappointed this morning – he did not expect to have to wait for you.'

'I know, sir.'

'Even more disappointing in his eyes, Arathan, was that you chose the gelding over the mare.'

'But – I was told that I should not ride Hellar too much—'

'When you leave the Great House, you ride your charger. Bastard son you may be, but in the eyes of the staff, you are still the Lord's son. Do you understand me?'

'I was not so instructed—'

'Such instruction should not have been necessary! You have not just shamed your father, you have shamed me as well! I am your tutor who clearly has failed to teach you anything!'

'I am sorry, sir.'

'And you left behind the scales. What use the weights and measures without the scales?'

Ahead, the track opened out, winding and dipping through low hills. Beyond that, according to the maps Arathan had perused, the path angled slightly south, leading to the settlement of Abara Delack. Past Abara Delack was the Bareth Solitude, and at the far end of that vast plain there waited the lands of the Azathanai and the Jaghut.

'I trust you brought with you my gifts, including the special one for the Lord of Hate?'

'I have, sir.'

'Tell me what it is – no, do not bother. After all, it is too late to change it, isn't it? I expect it is worthy.'

'That is for the Lord of Hate to decide.'

Sagander shot him a look. 'I remain your tutor,' he snapped. 'You will speak to me with proper respect.'

'Always, sir. My apologies.'

'You are not particularly likeable, Arathan. That is your problem. No – both hands on the reins! Would you have your father look back to see you chewing your nails again? Sit straight in that saddle.'

The day would be hot, and the way ahead promised no hope of shade. Arathan could feel sweat trickling down beneath his heavy clothing. It was hard to believe that only a short time ago he had been shivering, feeling lost in a courtyard he had known all his life. Now, the sky was lightening, unrelieved by any cloud, and it was the blue of ice and steel, and the new sun felt hot on his back.

They continued on at a steady trot, suddenly amongst the denuded hills. A track cutting to the right looked vaguely familiar to Arathan. He pointed. 'Where does that one lead, sir?'

Sagander seemed to flinch. 'The quarries. I am not surprised you remember it.'

'I don't, really.'

'Just as well.'

'It's where I almost drowned, isn't it? Down at the end of that trail, where the cattle are driven to slaughter.'

'You are better to forget all that, Arathan.'

'Yes, sir.'

Arathan fixed his attention on the back of his father – the shoulders wider than Sergeant Raskan's, wider than those of any other man Arathan could recall seeing. A heavy cloak of tanned hide hung down to drape across the rump of Calaras. It had been dyed black but that was years past and now it was bleached with salty sweat and years in the sun, giving it a mottled, shadowy hue.

Raskan kept his horse a step behind his lord, positioned on the left. Arathan did not think they were speaking. It suddenly struck Arathan that Ivis had not made it back in time to see them all off. His father had sent the master-at-arms away the day before, along with a troop of Houseblades. Arathan regretted that: he would have liked to say goodbye.

By mid-morning they had ridden clear of the hills and before them stretched land that had once been forested, perhaps a hundred or more years ago. Now it was covered in gorse and bracken, deceptively deep in places where uprooted trees had left pits. The track that crossed it was narrow, forcing the riders into single file. The land sweeping out to either side swarmed with butterflies, bees and tinier insects, all feeding on the small yellow, purple and white flowers studding every bush. Birds dipped and dived low overhead.

They met no one else and the horizons seemed too far away. The forest that had once stood here must have been vast. An entire city could have been built of the wood harvested here. Where had it gone?

Sagander had begun complaining of aches, groaning with every jolt in the saddle as the pace quickened slightly. He'd fallen silent shortly after passing the quarries and now that he rode ahead, the prospect of twisting round in his saddle to address Arathan was clearly too much, though once or twice he did glance back, if only to confirm that his student remained behind him.

Arathan welcomed the relative silence, although he too felt worn out. He hoped that for the rest of this journey he would be ignored by everyone. Life was easier that way. With attention came expectation, and with expectation there was pressure, and he did not do well with pressure. If he could slide through the rest of his life, unnoticed, unremarkable in any way, he would be content enough.

The sun was directly overhead when they reached an area roughly cleared of bracken, where the ground had been pounded level and two long stone troughs flanked the trail's resumption at the far end. One contained burlap sacks of feed for the horses and the other was brimming with water. This was the nominal edge of the Lord's land, and riders had been out the day before to supply the station. A halt was called, and at last Arathan was able to dismount, his legs weak as he stepped away from the gelding. He stood for a moment, watching the others, until a faint tug from his mount's reins awakened him to the fact that he needed to lead his horses to the troughs.

Draconus had already done so, but the others had all waited – *oh, they're waiting for me.*

Sagander's savage hiss was unnecessary but it stung him like a switch to the back as he hurried forward, both horses thumping after him.

His father had leaned forward to splash water into his face beside Calaras's muzzle as the warhorse drank, and then he drew the animal over to the second trough. Raskan held his lord's second mount off to one side, making it clear that Arathan should precede him, but as Arathan made to guide Besra to the water he caught a sudden shake of the head from the gate sergeant.

The boy hesitated. He had ridden Besra all morning; surely it was right to let the beast drink before the warhorse. After a moment, he decided to ignore Raskan, and drew Besra up to the trough. If his father even took note of this, he made no sign.

When Arathan reached down to cup some water, however, the gate sergeant said, 'No, Arathan. You share with your warhorse and none other. That will have to wait.'

'I will share with the beast on whose back I have ridden, sergeant.'

Sudden quiet, and Arathan could feel himself wilting, yet he managed to hold Raskan's hard gaze for a moment longer, before bending down to dip his hand into the cool water.

Standing near the other trough, Draconus spoke. 'Sergeant Raskan,

116

Hellar is now in your care, until such time as the boy awakens to his responsibilities.'

'Yes, milord,' Raskan replied. 'I would that he still ride the charger this afternoon, for a time.'

'Very well.' Draconus led Calaras from the second trough, and beckoned the Bordersword, Feren. 'I will speak with you,' he said to her, 'in private.'

'Of course, Lord.'

Her brother took the reins from her, and she set off after Draconus as he strode to the far end of the clearing.

Raskan's tone was rough and low as he moved up alongside Arathan. 'I warned you clear enough on this.'

'My error was in choosing the wrong horse this morning, sergeant.'

'That's true enough. You showed your fear of Hellar – to everyone. I feel a fool and I tell you, I do not appreciate that.'

'Should we not honour each and every beast that serves us?'

Raskan scowled. 'Who put such nonsense into your skull? That damned tutor? Look at him – it'll be a miracle if he survives the trek.'

'The thought was my own, sergeant.'

'Be rid of it. And if you come up with any more of your own thoughts, Arathan, keep them to yourself. Better yet, crush them. You are not the one to challenge Tiste ways.'

Arathan almost heard the added words: *leave that to men like your father.*

But he would be free of all this soon enough. He had seen the last of the High House, and the way to the west stretched before him. Leading Besra to the second trough, he glanced over at the remaining Borderswords. If he had expected to meet their hard eyes, he was spared that, as Rint, Ville and Galak were all busy preparing the midday meal. Their mounts stood motionless, reins looped over the saddle horns – not ten paces from the long trough of water, and yet not one animal moved. Arathan looked for hobbles about their ankles but found none.

*I think I understand. Before there can be disdain, there must be pride.*

*One day I will find something to be proud of, and then I will find this taste of disdain, and see if it suits me. Should I not think this, being my father's son?*

*And yet, I do not. Pride needs no claws, no scaled armour about itself. Not every virtue must be a weapon.*

*These thoughts are my own. I will not crush them.*

Sagander hissed behind him, 'When next you turn to me, student, I will see the face of my own humiliation. I wish he had left you behind. You're useless. Hands from the mouth!'

Rint hunched down over the embers, watching as the first flames licked the tinder alight. He fed in a few sticks and then nodded over to Galak, who began breaking up a brick of dried dung. Grunting, Rint straightened.

'What do you think?' Ville asked, standing close.

Rint shrugged, forcing himself from looking over to where Lord Draconus stood speaking with his sister. 'She's her own mind, as if you don't know that.'

'He wants a soft body for the cold nights, is my guess.'

'We'll see,' muttered Rint in reply, and it was all he could do to keep his teeth from cracking at the thought. 'He is a High Lord, after all.'

'But he ain't *our* High Lord, Rint.'

He glared across at Ville. 'This ain't none of your business. None of mine, neither. Feren decides and whatever she decides, we stand behind it.'

Galak grunted from where he crouched over the small fire. 'Goes without saying, Rint.'

Ville scowled. 'Still don't like it. Consorts – what are they, anyway? Crotch-boys. Even worse than the damned priestesses in Kharkanas. Y'think he knows a damned thing about being honourable?'

Rint stepped close. 'Keep it down, Ville. Any more of that and we'll do without you, understand?'

In the tense silence following the low exchange, Galak rose. 'Back in the courtyard,' he said under his breath, 'when I saw him standing there, holding out those scales. A shiver took my spine, that's all. A shiver like the breath of the Abyss.'

Ville grinned at Galak. 'You and your damned omens.'

'Get the pot out,' Rint said to Ville. 'All this jabbering is wasting time.'

Leaving his two companions, he walked over to Sergeant Raskan and the old man, Sagander. Beyond them, the boy was sitting on the ground at the edge of the clearing, his back to them all. Both men were looking that way and if they'd been talking, it had been under their breaths and they ceased at Rint's approach.

'Sergeant,' said Rint when he joined them. 'This is the first meal of the journey. In the days that follow, our midday repast will of course make use of food that requires no cooking.'

Raskan nodded. 'The Lord is well aware of your traditions, Bordersword.'

'I assumed as much,' Rint replied, 'but I just wanted to make certain.'

'Seems a ridiculous tradition,' Sagander said, his expression sour. 'Barely half a day out and we halt to gorge ourselves, when we should be hastening onwards.'

Rint regarded Sagander. 'The first day of any overland journey, tutor, is always a difficult one, even for hardened travellers. Rhythms need finding, bones need shaking out, and not just for us but for our mounts as well. More injuries take horses on the first day than on any other. The early morning start, the cold muscles . . . these things pose risks.'

In response, Sagander shrugged and looked away.

Rint returned his attention to Raskan. 'Sergeant. Two days to Abara Delack. When we are a few leagues out from the village, I will send Galak ahead—'

'Forgive me,' Raskan interrupted. 'My lord has instructed me that we shall be riding around Abara Delack. We shall not be staying in the village, nor will we be guests of any of the resident highborn families.'

Rint considered that for a moment, and then he said, 'None are to know of this journey.'

'That is correct.'

'Such secrets, sergeant, are very difficult to keep.'

'That is understood, Rint, but we shall try nevertheless.'

'Very well, I will inform the others.'

'One other thing,' Raskan said as Rint turned away.

'Sergeant?'

'It would be best if you Borderswords did not keep to yourselves so much. This is a small party, after all, and we have many days ahead of us. We saw some disagreement among you at the campfire. If there are matters that need discussing, bring them to me.'

'Of course, sergeant.'

Rint walked back to where he'd left Ville and Galak, and saw that his sister had returned from her meeting with Lord Draconus. Oddly enough, it seemed that no one was speaking. Feren looked over as Rint arrived and shook her head.

Suspicion flooded through Rint, and from it swirled fury, thick and vile. He struggled to give nothing away, and said, 'The sergeant wants us to be sociable.'

Ville grunted. 'We take orders from two of 'em and the other two amount to an old man of letters and a rabbit in a boy's skin. What kind of socializing is he expecting?'

'How the fuck should I know?' Rint said under his breath.

To his relief all three laughed, although Rint saw a glint of something in his sister's eyes, something walled off from any pleasure. But then, he reminded himself, there was nothing new in that.

'Rabbit in a boy's skin,' said Galak to Ville. 'I like that one.'

'Now forget you ever heard it,' Rint warned.

'Sure, but still, it fits—'

'And how do you know that?' demanded Feren, startling the others. 'I like what he did with the horses. Traditions are all very well, but they started for good reasons. These days, it seems everybody's so caught up in the forms they forget those reasons. The boy was right – you share with the beast that served you. That's how you give thanks.'

'You give thanks to the beast you ride into battle with,' Ville retorted.

'Give thanks to them all. That's how it started, Ville. Back when it meant something.'

Rint studied his sister. He'd not seen such fire from her in years. He should have welcomed it; he should have found hope from it. Instead, he felt vaguely disturbed, as if he was missing some hidden significance to this outburst.

'Meat's soft enough for chewing,' said Galak.

'I'll call the others,' Rint said.

*       *       *

Arathan sat on the ground, studying the gorse and the clouds of busy insects. The heat was making him sleepy. His spirits sank when he heard the scrape of feet behind him.

'Arathan, my name is Feren.'

Startled, he clambered to his feet and faced the Bordersword. Wiping wet fingers on his thigh, he stood uncertainly.

'We have a ritual,' she said. Her eyes were level with his, and their steadiness unnerved him as she continued, 'The first meal of the journey. Meat is shared. With everyone.'

He nodded.

She moved slightly closer and suddenly Arathan felt cornered. She smelled of tanned leather and something like blossoms, but spicier. She was twice his age, but the lines in the corners of her dark eyes made him think of passion, and then she gave him a half-smile. 'In my eyes,' she said, 'you did right with your horse. There are ways that people think must be followed, and then there are ways of the heart. If two paths await you, one cold and the other warm, which would you choose?'

He thought about this for a moment, and then asked, 'And if there are no paths?'

'Then make your own, Arathan.' She gestured. 'Come along, the first taste must be your father's. The next must be yours.' She set out and he fell in behind her.

'I am a bastard son.'

She halted and turned. 'You are about to come of age,' she said in a low tone. 'From that day forward, you are your own man. We all had fathers and mothers, but when we come of age we stand in our own shadow and none other's. If you are called a bastard then the failing is your father's, not yours.'

This woman was nothing like his sisters. Her attention confused him; her interest frightened him. He suspected that she had been given this task – of escorting him – because no one else wanted it. Yet even pity felt like a caress.

When she resumed walking, he followed.

The others were all waiting by the fire.

As they arrived, one of the other Borderswords grunted and said, 'Relax, lad, it ain't rabbit.'

The one whose name Arathan knew was Rint seemed to scowl, before saying, 'My sister offers you the gift, Arathan. Your father has already shared the meat.'

Feren went over to the pot and speared a grey sliver of flesh with a dagger. Straightening, she offered it to Arathan.

When he took the dagger from her hand there was some chance contact, and the roughness of her palm shocked him. Regretting that the instant had been so brief, he bit into the meat and tugged it from the iron point.

It was tough and tasteless.

Feren then handed her dagger to one of her comrades and he repeated the ritual with Gate Sergeant Raskan. The fourth Bordersword did the same with Sagander. Once this was done, hard bread was provided, along with bowls of melted lard in which herbs had been mixed. Arathan watched Rint dipping the bread into the lard and biting into it, and so followed suit.

Unlike the meat, this was delicious.

'In the cold season,' one of the other Borderswords said, 'it is lard that will save your life. Burning like an oil lamp in your stomach. Bread alone will kill you, as will lean meat.'

Raskan said, 'There was a pursuit of the Jheleck, I recall, in the dead of winter. It did not seem to matter how many furs we wore, we could not stop shivering.'

'Wrong food in your packs, sergeant,' said the Bordersword.

'Well, Galak, none of your kin were accompanying us.'

'Did you track them down in the end?' Rint asked.

Raskan shook his head. 'We gave up after one bitter night out in the cold, and with a storm coming down from the north we knew we would lose the trail. So we returned to the fort. A warm fire and mulled wine enticed me back from death's ledge, but it was most of a day and a night before the chill left my bones.'

'It was well you turned back,' observed Galak, nodding as he chewed. He swallowed before adding, 'Jheleck like to use storms to ambush. I'd wager my best sword they were tracking back to you, hiding in that storm.'

'That was an unpleasant war,' Rint said.

'Never knew a pleasant one,' Feren replied.

Arathan had noticed his father's retreat from this easy conversation, and he wondered at what force or quality of character Draconus possessed, to ensure loyalty, when camaraderie was so clearly absent. Was it enough that Mother Dark had chosen him to be her Consort?

Draconus had fought well in the Forulkan War. This much was known, meaning his courage and valour were above reproach. He had led Houseblades into battle, and he wore his heavy armour as if it were light as silk, and the sword at his belt looked worn and plain as a common soldier's. These details, Arathan suspected, meant something. There was a code among soldiers – how could there not be?

The meal was suddenly over and everyone was preparing to resume the trek. Arathan hurried over to Besra – and saw that Raskan had instead readied Hellar. His steps slowed slightly, and then Feren was walking beside him, her eyes on the warhorse.

'A formidable beast,' she said. 'But see her eyes – she knows you as her master, her protector.'

'There is nothing that I can protect her from.'

'But there is, at least in her mind.'

He glanced across at her. 'What?'

'Your father's stallion. Oh, true enough, it is by the Lord's hand that Calaras is held in check. But this mare looks to you. Such are the ways of beasts. Faith defies logic, and for that we are fortunate. But I see the animal is tall – here, I will give you a boot up.'

'Why are you doing this?' he asked suddenly, the words out before he could stop them.

She drew up at the question.

'My father called you over – I saw that, you know. Did he tell you to be kindly towards me?'

Feren sighed, looked away. 'None of this is by his command.'

'Then what did he say to you?'

'That shall remain between me and him.'

'Has it do with me?'

A flash of anger lit her eyes. 'Give me your boot, lad, or will we all have to wait on you again?'

Lifting him into the saddle seemed effortless to her, and once she'd done so she turned away, returning to where her comrades waited on their mounts.

Arathan wanted to call her back. He could hear his own tone echoing in his mind, the words sounding plaintive and thin as a child's. A petulant child at that. But his suspicions had taken hold of him, and with them he had felt a deep, turgid humiliation, hot and suffocating. Did his father believe a woman's attention was still required for his son? Was he to be mothered until his very last day in the man's company?

'*It may be that you will believe I do not want you.*' Such had been his words in the Chamber of Campaigns.

122

*But you don't. Instead, you pass me off on whomever you choose.*
'Student! To my side!'

Gathering the reins, Arathan nudged Hellar into a trot. The beast lumbered, her stride very different from Besra's loping gait. Apart from Sagander, no one else remained in the clearing.

*I would have liked her better without your meddling, Father. Not every woman should be made to be my mother. Why do you bother interfering in my life at all? Cast me away; I will welcome it. In the meantime, leave me alone.*

'She means you no good, Arathan. Are you listening to me? Ignore her. Turn your back on her.'

He frowned across at the tutor, wondering at the man's vehemence.

'They carry lice. Diseases.'

'Yes, sir.'

'I am your company on this journey, is that understood?'

'How soon before we arrive at Abara Delack?'

'Never. We're going around.'

'Why?'

'Because Lord Draconus wills it. Now, enough of your questions! It is time for a lesson. Our subject shall be weakness and desire.'

*   *   *

By mid-afternoon they were riding through old logging camps, broad swaths of level ground fringed on all sides by uprooted, burnt stumps. They were still some leagues from Abara Delack, but all tracks that remained led towards that settlement. Here they were able to ride side by side and Sagander insisted that Arathan do so.

In a way it was something of a relief. He could see that Rint had been just ahead of Sagander when they'd been in single file, and the Bordersword could not help but have heard the tutor's loud, harsh proclamations that passed for a lesson, though Arathan had made certain that his infrequent replies to the tutor's questions were muted.

Once on the wider path Rint kicked his mount up alongside his sister's and the two fell into quiet conversation.

'Weakness,' Sagander now said, his tone both exhausted and relentless, 'is a disease of the spirit. Among the noblest of our people, it simply does not exist, and it is this innate health, this natural vibrancy, that justifies their station in life. The poor worker in the fields – he is weak and his miserable poverty is but a symptom of the disease. But this alone is insufficient to earn your sympathy, student. You must be made to understand that weakness begins outside the body, and it must be reached for, grasped and then taken inside. It is a choice.

'In all society there exists a hierarchy and it is measured by strength of will. That and nothing else. In this manner, the observation of society reveals a natural form of justice. Those possessing power and wealth are superior in every way to those who serve them. Are you paying attention? I will not accept a wandering mind, Arathan.'

'I am listening, sir.'

'There are some – misguided philosophers and bitter agitators – who argue that social hierarchy is an unnatural imposition, and indeed, that it must be made fluid. This is wilful ignorance, because the truth is, mobility does exist. The disease of weakness can be purged from the self. Often, such transformative events occur in times of great stress, in battle and the like, but there are other paths available for those of us for whom soldiering is not in our nature. Principal among these, of course, is education and the rigours of enlightenment.

'Discipline is the weapon against weakness, Arathan. See it as sword and armour both, capable at once of attack and defence. It stands in stalwart opposition to the forces of weakness, and the middle ground, upon which this battle is waged, is *desire*.

'Each of us, in our lives, must fight that battle. Indeed, every struggle that you may perceive is but a facet of that one conflict. There are pure desires and there are impure desires. The pure desires give strength to discipline. The impure desires give strength to weakness. Have I made this plain and simple enough for you?'

'Yes sir. May I ask a question?'

'Very well.'

Arathan gestured to the wasteland surrounding them. 'This forest was cut down because people desired the wood. To build, and for warmth. They appear to have been very disciplined, as not a single tree remains standing. This leaves me confused. Were their desires not pure? Were their needs not honest needs? And yet, if the entire forest is destroyed, do we not therefore see a strength revealed as a weakness?'

Sagander's watery eyes fixed on Arathan, and then he shook his head. 'You have not understood a word of what I have said. Strength is always strength and weakness is always weakness. No!' His face twisted. 'You think confused thoughts and then you voice them – and the confusion infects others. No more questions from you!'

'Yes sir.'

'With discipline comes certainty, an end to confusion.'

'I understand, sir.'

'I don't think you do, but I have done all that I could – who would dare claim otherwise? But you are drawn to impurity, and it grows like an illness in your spirit, Arathan. This is what comes of an improper union.'

'My father's weakness?'

The back of Sagander's hand, when it cracked into Arathan's face, was a thing of knotted bones hard as rock. His head snapped back and he almost pitched from his horse – there was hot blood filling his mouth – and then Hellar shifted beneath him, and a sudden surge of muscles jolted Arathan to the right. There followed a solid, loud impact, and a horse's scream.

Sagander's cry rang through the air, but it seemed far away. Stunned, Arathan lolled on the saddle, blood pouring down from his nose. As Hellar tensed beneath him once more, front hoofs stamping fiercely at the ground, making stones snap, Arathan tugged the reins taut, drawing in his mount's head. The beast back-stepped once, and then settled, muscles trembling.

Arathan could hear riders coming back down the trail. He heard shouted questions but it seemed they were in another language. He spat out more blood, struggled to clear the blurriness from his eyes. It was hard to see, to make sense of things. Sagander was on the ground and so was the man's horse – thrashing, and there was something wrong with its flank, just behind its shoulder. The ribs looked caved in, and the horse was coughing blood.

Rint was beside him, on foot, reaching up to help him down from Hellar. He saw Feren as well, her visage dark with fury.

*Sagander was right. It's hard to like me. Even when following a lord's orders.*

The tutor was still shrieking. One of his thighs was bent in half, Arathan saw as he was made to sit down on the dusty trail. There was a massive hoof imprint impressed down on to where the leg was broken, and blood was everywhere, leaking out to puddle under the crushed leg. Against the white dust it looked black as pitch. Arathan stared at it, even as Feren used a cloth to wipe the blood from his own face.

'Rint saw,' she said.

*Saw what?*

'Hard enough to break your neck,' she added, 'that blow. So he said and Rint is not one to exaggerate.'

Behind him, he heard her brother's affirming grunt. 'That horse is finished,' he then said. 'Lord?'

'End its misery,' Draconus replied from somewhere, his tone even and cool. 'Sergeant Raskan, attend to the tutor's leg before he bleeds out.'

Galak and Ville were already with the tutor, and Galak looked up and said, distinctly – the first clear words Arathan heard – 'It's a bad break, Lord Draconus. We need to cut off the leg, and even then he might die of blood loss before we can cauterize the major vessels.'

'Tie it off,' Draconus said to Raskan, and Arathan saw the sergeant nod, white-faced and sickly, and then pull free his leather belt.

The tutor was now unconscious, his expression slack and patchy.

125

Galak had drawn a dagger and was hacking at the torn flesh around the break. The thigh bone was shattered, splinters jutting through puffy flesh.

Raskan looped the belt round high on the old man's thigh and cinched it tight as he could.

'Rint,' said Draconus, 'I understand you witnessed what happened.'

'Yes, Lord. By chance I glanced back at the moment the tutor struck your son.'

'I wish the fullest details – walk at my side, away from here.'

Feren was pushing steadily against Arathan's chest – finally noticing this pressure he looked up and met her eyes.

'Lie down,' she said. 'You are concussed.'

'What happened?'

'Hellar attacked the tutor, knocked down his horse, and stamped on his leg. She was about to do the same to Sagander's head, but you pulled her back in time – you showed good instincts, Arathan. You may have saved your tutor's life.' As she spoke, she fumbled at the buckle under his sodden chin, and finally pulled away his helmet, and then the deerskin skullcap.

Arathan felt cool air reaching through sweat-matted hair to prickle his scalp. That touch felt blessedly tender.

A moment later he was shivering, and she managed to roll him on to his side an instant before he vomited.

'It's all right,' she whispered, using her blood-stained cloth to wipe sick from his mouth and chin.

He smelled woodsmoke, and moments later burnt flesh. Feren left his side for a moment and then returned to drape a woollen blanket over him. 'They're taking the leg off,' she said. 'Closing off the bleeding. Cutting the bone end as even as possible. Sagander still breathes, but he lost a lot of blood. His fate is uncertain.'

'It's my fault—'

'No, it isn't.'

But he nodded. 'I said the wrong thing.'

'Listen to me. You are the son of a lord—'

'Bastard son.'

'He laid a hand upon you, Arathan. Even if Sagander survives the loss of his leg, your father might well kill him. Some things are just not permitted.'

'I will speak in his defence,' Arathan said, forcing himself to sit up. The world spun round him and she had to steady him lest he topple over. 'I am the cause of this. I said the wrong thing. It's my fault.'

'Arathan.'

He looked up at her, fighting back tears. 'I was weak.'

For a moment he studied her face, the widening eyes and then the

126

scowl, before blackness rushed in from all sides, and everything fell away.

*     *     *

Brush had been hacked down to clear space for the tents, the horses unsaddled and hobbled well away from the carcass of their slain companion. Ville had butchered as much horse flesh as they could carry and now crouched by the fire, over which sat an iron grille bearing vermilion meat that sizzled and spat.

When Rint returned from his long meeting with Draconus, he walked to the fire and settled down beside Ville.

Galak was still attending to Sagander, who'd yet to regain consciousness, whilst Feren hovered over the bastard son, who was as lost to the world as was his tutor. Raskan had joined his lord where a second fire had been lit, on which sat a blackened pot of steaming blood-broth.

Ville poked at the steaks. 'First day out,' he muttered. 'This bodes ill, Rint.'

Rint rubbed at the bristle lining his jaw and then sighed. 'Change of plans,' he said. 'You and Galak are to take the tutor to Abara Delack and leave him in the care of the monks, and then catch us up.'

'And the boy? Coma's a bad thing, Rint. Might never wake up.'

'He'll wake up,' Rint said. 'With an aching skull. It was that damned helmet, that lump of heavy iron, when his head was snapped back. It's a mild concussion, Ville. The real risk was breaking his neck, but thankfully he was spared that.'

Ville squinted across at him. 'That must've been some blow – didn't know the old man was that strong.'

'The boy wasn't expecting it at all – Abyss knows, no reason to. Anyway, we'll take it slow on the morrow, Feren keeping a close eye.'

'And the Lord's judgement?'

Rint was silent for a moment, and then he shrugged. 'He didn't share that with me, Ville. But you know how they look on such things.'

'Bad luck for Sagander. Makes me wonder why me and Galak got to take him to Abara Delack. Why not just slit the fool's throat and stick his head on a pole?'

'You worked on him hard – the Lord saw that.'

Ville grunted. 'Don't want to insult us, then?'

'If you like. Thing is, there's proper forms, I suppose. Making a point about something ain't no use if there's no way of people seeing it.'

'What about Abara Delack, then? What do we tell the monks, since this whole trip was supposed to be a secret?'

'You were escorting the tutor to the monastery – they make the finest paper, after all.'

'Used to, you mean.'

127

'You tried explaining that to the tutor, but the old man was fixed on it.'

'So, if he comes round we'd best be there – to tell him how it is.'

'No. If he survives the night we're to wake him tomorrow morning, and Draconus himself will tell the tutor what needs telling.'

'Then we catch you up.'

Rint nodded, drawing a knife to stab at a steak.

Ville snorted. 'Why'd I bother? Might as well take bites out the carcass itself.'

'But then you don't get the smoky flavour, Ville.'

Feren joined them. 'It's normal sleep now,' she said, sitting down. 'He's tossing and turning, but not so much – no fever. Breathing's deep and steady.'

Ville was studying Feren with narrow eyes, and then he grinned. 'Never saw you being a mother before, Feren.'

'Nor will you, if you value your life, Ville.' She set a hand on Rint's arm. 'Brother, what I told you earlier.'

When he shot her a look, she simply nodded.

Rint studied the half-raw meat in his hands, and then resumed chewing.

'You two can be so damned irritating,' Ville muttered, reaching to turn the remaining steaks again.

*     *     *

Sergeant Raskan dipped a knife blade into the blood-broth. The soup was thickening nicely. Sagander might retch at the taste, at least at first, but this rich broth might well save his life.

Draconus stood beside him, eyeing the horses. 'I was wrong to take Hellar from him, I think.'

'Lord?'

'They are truly bound now.'

'Yes, Lord, that they are. She acted fast – no hesitation at all. That mare will give her life defending Arathan, you can be sure of that.'

'I am . . . now.'

'Not like the tutor, was it, Lord?'

'There can be deep bitterness, sergeant, when youth dwindles into the distant past. When the ache of bones and muscles is joined by the ache of longing, and regrets haunt a soul day and night.'

Raskan considered this, as respectfully as he could, and then he shook his head. 'Your capacity for forgiveness is greater than mine would be, Lord—'

'I have not spoken of forgiveness, sergeant.'

Raskan nodded. 'That is true. But, Lord, were a man to so strike my son—'

128

'Enough of that,' Draconus cut in, his tone deepening. 'There are matters beyond you here, sergeant. Still, no need for you to apologize – you spoke from your heart and I will respect that. Indeed, I begin to believe it is the only thing worth respecting, no matter our station, or our fate.'

Stirring the blood-broth again, Raskan said nothing. For a moment there, he had forgotten the vast divide between him and Lord Draconus. He had indeed spoken from his heart, but in an unguarded, unmindful fashion. Among other highborn, his comment might well have earned a beating; even a stripping of his rank.

But Draconus did not work that way, and he met the eye of every soldier and every servant under his care. *Ah, now if only he would do that for his only son.*

'I see by the firelight that your boots are sadly worn, sergeant.'

'It's the way I walk, Lord.'

'Out here, moccasins are far better suited.'

'Yes, Lord, but I have none.'

'I have an old pair, sergeant – they might prove somewhat too large, but if you do as do the Borderswords – filling them out as needed with fragrant grasses – then you will find them serviceable.'

'Lord, I—'

'You would refuse my generosity, sergeant?'

'No, Lord. Thank you.'

There was a long time of silence. Raskan glanced over to where the Borderswords were crouched round the second cookfire. Ville had called out that the steaks were ready but neither the sergeant nor his lord moved. Hungry though he was, the cloying reek of the blood-broth had drowned Raskan's appetite. Besides, he could not abandon Draconus without leave to do so.

'This swirl of stars,' Draconus suddenly said, 'marks the plunge of light into darkness. These stars, they are distant suns, shining their light down upon distant, unknown worlds. Worlds, perhaps, little different from this one. Or vastly different. It hardly matters. Each star swirls its path towards the centre, and at that centre there is death – the death of light, the death of time itself.'

Shaken, Raskan said nothing. He had never heard such notions before – was this what the scholars in Kharkanas believed?

'Tiste are comforted by their own ignorance,' Draconus said. 'Do not imagine, sergeant, that such matters are discussed at court. No. Instead, imagine the lofty realm of scholars and philosophers as little different from a garrison of soldiers, cooped up too long and too close in each other's company. Squalid, venal, pernicious, poisoned with ambitions, a community of betrayal and jealously guarded prejudices. Titles are like splashes of thin paint upon ugly stone – the colour may look pretty, but what lies behind it does not change. Of itself, knowledge holds no virtue – it is armour and sword, and while armour protects it also isolates, and while a sword can swing true, so too can it wound its wielder.'

Raskan stirred the soup, feeling strangely frightened. He had no thoughts he could give voice to, no opinions that could not but display his own stupidity.

'Forgive me, sergeant. I have embarrassed you.'

'No, Lord, but I fear I am easily confused by such notions.'

'Was I not clear enough in my point? Do not let the title of scholar, or poet, or lord, intimidate you overmuch. More importantly, do not delude yourself into imagining that such men and women are loftier, or somehow cleverer or purer of integrity or ideal than you or any other commoner. We live in a world of facades, but the grins behind them are all equally wretched.'

'Grins, Lord?'

'As a dog grins, sergeant.'

'A dog grins in fear, Lord.'

'Just so.'

'Then, does everyone live in fear?'

The firelight barely reached the huge man standing beside Raskan, and the deep voice that came from that vague shape sounded loose, unguarded. 'I would say, most of the time, yes. Fear that our opinions might be challenged. Fear that our way of seeing things might be called ignorant, self-serving, or indeed evil. Fear for our persons. Fear for our future, our fate. Our moment of death. Fear of failing in all that we set out to achieve. Fear of being forgotten.'

'My lord, you describe a grim world.'

'Oh, there are balances on occasion. Faint, momentary. Reasons for joy. Pride. But then fear comes clawing back. It always does. Tell me, sergeant, when you were a child, did you fear the darkness?'

'I imagine we all did, Lord, when we were little more than pups.'

'And what was it about darkness that we feared?'

Raskan shrugged. His eyes held on the flickering flames. It was a small fire, struggling to stay alive. When the last of the sticks had burned down, the coals would flare and ebb and finally grow cool. 'The unknown, I suppose, Lord. Where things might hide.'

'Yet Mother Dark chooses it like raiment.'

Raskan's breath stilled, frozen in his chest. 'I am a child no longer, Lord. I have no cause to fear that.'

'I wonder, at times, if she has forgotten her own childhood. You need say nothing on that matter, sergeant. It's late. My thoughts wander. As you say, we are no longer children. Darkness holds no terrors; we are past the time when the unknown threatens us.'

'Lord, we can now let this cool,' said Raskan, using his knife to lift the pot clear of the flames and setting it down.

'Best join the others then,' said Draconus, 'before that meat turns to black leather.'

'And you, Lord?'

'In a few moments, sergeant. I will look some more upon these distant suns, and ponder unknown lives beneath their light.'

Raskan straightened, his knees clicking, his saddle-sore muscles protesting. He bowed to his lord and then made his way over to the other fire.

*　　*　　*

It was dark when Arathan opened his eyes. He found that he was pressed against a warm body, both soft and firm, solid as a promise, and he could smell faint spices on the still night air. The blanket was now shared, and the person sleeping beside him was Feren.

All at once he could hear his heart pounding.

From the camp there was no other sound; even the horses were quiescent. Blinking, he stared up at the stars, finding the brightest ones all in their rightful places. He struggled to think mundane thoughts, fought to ignore the warm body slumbering at his side.

Sagander said that the stars were but holes in the fabric of night, a thinning of blessed darkness; and that in ages long past there had been no stars at all – the dark was complete, absolute. This was in the time of the first Tiste, in the Age of Gifts, when harmony commanded all and peace stilled every restless heart. The great thinkers were all agreed on this interpretation, his tutor had insisted, in that forceful, belligerent way he had whenever Arathan asked the wrong questions.

*But where is the light coming from? What lies behind the veil of night and how could it not exist in the Age of Gifts? Surely it must have been there from the very beginning?*

Light was an invading fire, waging an eternal war to break through the veil. It was born when discord first came to the heart of the Tiste.

*But in a world of peace and harmony, where did the discord come from?*

'The soul harbours chaos, Arathan. The spark of life knows not its own self, knows only need. If that spark is not controlled through the discipline of higher thoughts, then it bursts into flame. The first Tiste grew complacent, careless of the Gift. And those who succumbed, well, it is their souls you see burning through the Veil of Night.'

She shifted against him. She then rolled over so that she faced him, and drew closer, one arm crossing his chest. He felt her breath on his neck, felt her hair brushing his collarbone. The scent of spices seemed

131

to come from all of her, from her breath and her skin, her hair and her heat.

Her breathing paused for a long moment, and then she sighed, drew closer still until he felt one of her breasts pressing against his arm, and then the other one, sliding down to rest on the same arm.

And then her hand was reaching down to his crotch.

She found him hard and already slick, but if that amounted to failure she seemed unperturbed, using her palm to slide what he had spilled out over his belly, and then taking hold of him once again.

With that grip she pulled him on to his side, and her leg, lifting to settle over him, felt astonishingly heavy. Her other hand reached down, forced itself under his hip, and pulled him over her lower leg until he was clenched between her thighs.

She made a sound when she guided him inside her.

He did not know what was happening. He did not know where she'd put him in, down there between her legs. Was it the hole where she pushed out her wastes? It could not be – it was too far forward, unless women were different in ways he had not imagined.

He'd seen dogs in the yard. He'd seen Calaras savagely mount a mare, stabbing with his red sword, but there was no way to tell where that sword went.

She was moving against him now, and the sensation, of burgeoning heat, was ecstatic. Then she grasped his wrists and set his hands round her hips – they were fuller than he'd imagined they would be, and his fingers sank into deep flesh.

'Pull,' she whispered. 'Back and forth. Faster and faster.'

Confusion vanished, bewilderment burned away.

He shuddered as he emptied himself into her, felt exhaustion take him – a deep, warm exhaustion. When she let him slide back out, he rolled to lie on his back.

But she said, 'Not so fast. Give me your hand . . . no, that one. Back down, wet the fingers, yes, like that. Now, rub here, slow to start, but faster when you hear my breathing quicken. Arathan, there are two sides to lovemaking. You've had yours and yes, I enjoyed it. Now give me mine. In the years ahead, you and every woman you lie with will thank me for this.'

He wanted to thank her now, and so he did.

∗    ∗    ∗

The boy had done his best to be quiet, but Rint was a light sleeper. Though he could not make out what his sister was saying to Arathan, the sounds that followed told him all he needed to know.

So she was ensuring that she'd get some pleasure from this. He could not begrudge her that.

She'd told him that Draconus had not commanded her. He had but requested, and no repercussions would attend her refusal. She had replied that she would give the matter some thought, and had said the same to Rint, pointedly ignoring his disapproval.

*Leave the teaching in the hands of some court whore. Play it out like the cliché it's come to be. There are ways of learning and they repeat generation after generation. Of all the games of learning, surely this is the most sordid one.* Feren was a Bordersword. Did Draconus understand nothing but his own needs, and would he trample everyone on his way to answering them? So it seemed. His son was about to become a man. *Show him what that means, Feren.*

No, it wouldn't be a whore for Arathan. Nor a maid, nor some farm girl from one of the outlying hamlets. After all, any one of these could come back to haunt House Dracons, seeking coin for a bastard child.

Feren would do no such thing, and Draconus well knew it. The father need not worry about his son spilling seed into her womb. If she took with child she would simply disappear and make no claim upon Arathan, and she would raise that child well. Until, perhaps, the day when Arathan came for it.

And so the pattern would be repeated, from father to son and ever onward. And of women with broken hearts and empty homes, well, they were nothing worthy of concern – *but this is Feren. This is my sister. If you get with child, Feren, I will escape with you, and not even the kin and will of House Dracons will ever find us. And should Arathan somehow do so, I swear I will kill him with my own hands.*

High overhead, the stars blurred and spun, as if swimming a river of rage.

\*     \*     \*

Sagander regained consciousness just before dawn and after a moment he gasped. Before the tutor could make another sound, a gloved hand pressed down upon his mouth, and he looked up to see Lord Draconus crouched over him.

'Be silent,' Draconus commanded in a low tone.

Sagander managed a nod and the hand left his mouth. 'My lord!' he whispered. 'I cannot feel my leg!'

'It is gone, tutor. It was that or your death.'

Sagander stared up in disbelief. He pulled one hand free from the blankets and reached down, only to find his hand flailing where his thigh should have been. A mass of sodden bandages met his groping fingers halfway down from his hip.

'You struck the face of my son, tutor.'

Sagander blinked. 'My lord, he spoke ill of you. I was – I was defending your honour.'

133

'What did he say?'

Sagander licked dry lips. His throat felt swollen, hot. He had never before felt as weak as he did at this moment. 'He suggested that *he* was your weakness, Lord.'

'And how did this statement come about, tutor?'

In fragmented, stuttering phrases, Sagander explained the gist of the lesson, and the conversation that had followed it. 'I defended your honour, Lord,' he said upon finishing. 'As your servant—'

'Tutor, hear me well. I do not need you to defend my honour. Furthermore, the boy was correct. If anything, he was to be commended for his acuity. Finally, Arathan has shown me something I can respect.'

Sagander gaped, his breaths coming in short, frantic gasps.

Remorselessly, Draconus went on. 'The boy has wits. Furthermore, he saw through to the venality underlying your assertions. The poor have taken weakness into themselves? By some dubious temptation of desire? Old man, you are a fool, and would that I had seen that long ago.

'Arathan was right – is right. He is indeed my weakness – why do you imagine I am now taking him as far away from Kurald Galain as I can?'

'My lord . . . I did not understand—'

'Listen well. For giving me this one thing to respect in my son, you have my gratitude. It is this gratitude that now saves your life, tutor. For striking my son, you will not be gutted and skinned, your hide spiked to the wall of my estate. Instead, you will be taken to Abara Delack to recover from your injury, and I shall have some further instructions on that matter before we part ways. You are to remain in the village's chapter of the Yedan Monastery until my return this way, whereupon you will accompany me back to the estate. Once there, you will gather such belongings as you cherish and then depart, never to return. Is all of this within your understanding, tutor?'

Mute, Sagander nodded.

Draconus straightened and spoke in a louder voice, 'The sergeant has prepared some blood-broth. You have lost too much of your own blood and it needs replenishing. Now that you are awake, I will have Raskan feed you.'

Sagander had to turn his head to watch Draconus walk away. His thoughts were a black storm. The man whose honour he had defended would now destroy him. Execution would have been a far better fate. Now, it was his reputation and standing that the Lord had murdered, all in the name of an ancient prohibition against striking a highborn. *But Arathan is no highborn. He is a bastard son.*

*I have struck him countless times, as befits a wayward, useless student. He is no highborn!*

134

*I shall challenge this. In Kharkanas, I shall make challenge before the law!*

But he knew he wouldn't. Instead, he would be kept in isolation for months, perhaps even longer, in a monastery cell in Abara Delack. And he would lose the fire of his indignation, and even should he hold on to it, flaring it anew each time he found himself struggling to move a leg that no longer existed, by the time he finally made it back to Kharkanas, the tale of his disgrace would have long preceded him. He would be mocked, his righteous claims laughed at, and he would see the glee in the eyes of his rivals upon every side.

Draconus had indeed destroyed him.

*But I have other paths. A thousand steps to vengeance, or ten thousand, it does not matter. I will have it in the end. Arathan. You will be the first to pay for what you have done to me. And then, when you are cold as clay, I will stalk your father. I will see him humiliated, broken. I will see his skinned hide spiked above the gates of Kharkanas itself!*

They had taken his leg. He would in turn take their lives.

*The ice has cracked beneath me. I have fallen through and I feel such cold. But it is the cold of hatred and I am no longer afraid.*

A sleepy-eyed Raskan arrived, setting down a smoke-blackened pot. 'Breakfast, tutor.'

'You are kind, sergeant. Tell me, was the boy terribly injured?'

'Not so bad, tutor. Rint, who saw, was quick to point out the great weight of the helmet was equally responsible.'

'Ah. I had not considered that.'

'No more conversation for the moment, tutor. You must partake of this broth – your pallor is far too white for my liking.'

'Of course, sergeant. Thank you.'

*I should have swung harder.*

\*     \*     \*

When Arathan awoke again she was gone from his side. His head ached, a throbbing pain behind his forehead that made both eyes hurt as he blinked the sleep away. He listened to people moving about in the camp, heard the snort of Calaras, a heavy sound that seemed to thud into the hard ground and stay there, trembling earth and stones. There was the smell of smoke and cooking. Though the morning sun was warm, still he shivered beneath his blankets.

The events of the day before and of the night past were confused in his mind. He remembered blood, and the crowding round of people. Faces, looking down on him, had the appearance of masks, blank of expression but ready for cruelty. Recalling the blood on his face, he felt a return of the shame that had dogged him since leaving House Dracons.

135

Yet seeping through such emotions there was ecstasy, and for Feren there was no mask, only darkness filled with warmth and then heat, a spicy realm of quick breaths and soft flesh. He had known nothing like it before; oh, he had been spilling into his sheets for a few years now, and there had been pleasure in reaching such release, but he had imagined this to be a private indulgence, until such time as he was old enough and ready to make a child, although that concept was vague in its details.

Vague no longer. He wondered if her belly would now swell, making her movements ponderous and her moods mercurial – soldiers' talk among his sparring partners suggested as much. *'They become impossible, don't they? A woman with child has armour in her eyes and triumph in her soul. Abyss help us all.'*

He heard the thump of boots drawing closer and turned his head to see Sergeant Raskan arrive.

'Arathan, you have your wits about you?'

He nodded.

'It was decided to let you sleep – we shall be riding today, though not as hard as perhaps your father would like. In any case, if you are able, we intend to reach the river this day. Now, a meal awaits you.'

Arathan sat up and looked across to where the Borderswords had their cookfire. He could see only Rint and Feren. Ville and Galak were nowhere in evidence. A quick search of the camp revealed that Sagander too had gone missing. Sudden dread filled him. 'Sergeant – the tutor – did he die?' *Are they off raising a cairn?*

'No,' Raskan replied. 'He is being taken to Abara Delack, where he will remain until our return. They left early this morning.'

Once more, bitter shame flooded through him. Unable to meet Raskan's gaze, he stood, drawing the blankets round him. The scene spun momentarily and then steadied before his eyes, the pain in his skull fierce enough to make him gasp.

Raskan stepped closer to lend a supporting arm, but Arathan stepped away. 'I am fine, thank you, sergeant. Where is the latrine trench?'

'Over there. Beware the pit's edge – it was hastily dug.'

'I will,' Arathan replied, setting off.

His father was tending to Calaras and had not yet looked over, nor did Arathan expect him to. His son had ruined the life of a loyal tutor, a man long in his employ. Sagander's excitement upon discovering he would be making this journey now returned to Arathan with a bitter sting. It was no wonder Draconus was furious.

The latrine pit was behind some bracken and as he edged round the spiny bushes he halted in his tracks. The pit was shallow and indeed rough.

Sagander's leg was lying in it like an offering, in a nest of blood-soaked cloths. Others had been here since and their wastes smeared the pallid, lifeless flesh.

Arathan stared at the mangled limb, the bared foot white as snow, motionless as the day's first flies crawled upon it, the hard, misshapen nails yellow as the petals of the gorse flowers, the deflated tracks of veins and arteries grey beneath the thin skin. At the other end jutted splintered bone, surrounded in hacked flesh. Bruises had spread down around the knee.

Pulling his gaze away, he stepped round the edge of the pit, and continued on through gaps in the bracken for a few more paces.

Of course they would bury it, as the camp was packed up. But scavengers would find it none the less. Foxes, crows, wild dogs. As soon as the wind picked up and carried off the smell of blood and death, long after he and his companions had left, the creatures would draw close, to begin digging.

He listened to his stream splash through spiny twigs and sharp leaves, and he thought back to the last hand that had touched him down there. The stream dwindled quickly. Cursing under his breath, Arathan closed his eyes and concentrated on the pain rocking back and forth inside his skull. Moments later he was able to resume.

As he made his way back to the camp he saw Rint standing nearby, a short-handled spade resting on one shoulder. The huge man nodded, his eyes thinning as he studied Arathan for a long moment, before setting off to fill in the latrine pit.

At the cookfire, Feren was scraping food on to a tin plate. Raskan had joined Lord Draconus with the horses. Pulling the blanket tighter Arathan made his way to the woman.

She glanced up, but only briefly, as she handed him the plate.

He wanted to say something, so that she would look at him, meet his eyes, but it was clear, after a moment, that she had no desire to acknowledge him. *I wasn't very good. I did it all wrong. She is disappointed. Embarrassed by me.* He carried his plate off a little distance to break his fast.

Raskan strode over, leading Besra. 'This one today, Arathan.'

'I understand.'

The sergeant frowned. And then shook his head. 'I don't think you do. Hellar is returned to your care. You have found your warhorse, a true destrier. But she needs to walk some on her own, to work out the violence that your touch might well incite all over again. She is to wonder – by your inattention – if she has failed you. Later this day you will go to her and take the saddle, and she will be relieved.

'Speak to her then, Arathan, words of comfort and satisfaction. She will know their meaning by the breaths upon which those words reach her. To communicate with a horse, think of truth as a river – never fight the current. Ride it into the beast's heart.'

Uncertain as to the sergeant's meaning, Arathan nevertheless nodded.

Raskan handed him the reins. 'Now, give me that empty plate – it is good to see that you are with appetite – and go to your father. He wishes to speak with you.'

He had known that this moment was coming. As he set out, pulling Besra after him, Raskan said, 'Hold, Arathan . . .' and he took the blanket from the boy's shoulders. 'I will tie this up.' He half smiled. 'You had the look of a peasant.'

*A peasant. Yes. About to stand shamefaced before his lord.*

'Mount up,' said his father when he reached him. 'To begin this day, you ride at my side, Arathan.'

'Yes sir.'

He felt weak pulling himself into the saddle, and as he settled his feet into the stirrups a clammy sweat broke out, and he realized that he was not wearing his armour or his helmet. 'Sir, I am unarmoured—'

'For now, yes. Rint has your gear. We shall take the lead on the trail. Come.'

The sensation was strange – to be riding at his father's side – and he felt hopelessly awkward, displaying none of the ease that seemed so much a part of Draconus.

'Sagander owes you his life,' his father said.

'Sir?'

'Twice, in fact. Though stunned by his blow, you still had the wits to pull Hellar away. Your horse would have crushed the fool's skull with a single stamp, shattering it like an urthen egg. That was well done. But it is the second time you saved his life of which I will speak.'

'Sir, I misspoke—'

'You wondered if you were my weakness, Arathan. There is no dishonour in that question. How could there be? The matter concerns your life, after all. Is it not your right to wonder at your place in the world? Furthermore, it was perceptive – and this encourages me.'

Arathan was silent.

After a long moment, Draconus continued. 'Until now, there is little that has impressed me about you – tell me, do you imagine your gnawing upon your fingers well suits the man you have become? This habit has even damaged your ability with the sword, and should it continue, Arathan, it may well see you killed. The hand holding the sword must be firm, lest what you will is failed by what you achieve.'

'Yes sir. I am sorry.'

'That said,' Draconus grunted, 'women will appreciate your touch in tender places.'

Something slammed down inside Arathan, and he knew then that

Feren had reported to his father. In detail. She had done as her lord commanded. She belonged to Draconus, just as did Rint and Sergeant Raskan – everyone here, except for Arathan himself, was but an extension of his father's will. *Like weapons, and my father's hand is surely firm. Will is bound to deed and no room for failure.* 'I am sorry that Sagander was injured,' he said in a dull tone.

'You have outgrown him, Arathan. Hellar was right in dismissing him – she knew your mind before you did. Remember that, and in the future trust in it.'

'Yes sir.'

'Have you pain in your head, Arathan? I believe Rint has some willow bark.'

'No, sir. No pain at all.'

'You are quick to recover, then. Perhaps that is yet another of your gifts, so well hidden until now.'

'Yes sir.'

'Understand, Arathan. If you were to have remained at my keep, you would have been vulnerable. I have enemies. Your half-sisters, however, are protected. Though their mother is no longer with us, her family is powerful. The same cannot be said for your mother. To get to me, my enemies could well look to you. Especially now, as you come of age.'

'Sir, would it not have been easier to kill me when I was a child, un-skilled with the blade, too trusting in adults?'

Draconus glanced across at him. 'I was not speaking of direct violence, Arathan. Your being dead would remove the vulnerability that you pose to me and my interests.'

'They would kidnap me?'

'No. You are a bastard son. You are meaningless and worthless as a hostage.'

'Then I do not understand, sir. What would they want of me?'

'Arathan, you will be a young man with grievances. Against your father, who refuses to acknowledge you as his rightful son. Being young, you possess ambitions. My enemies will approach you, feeding both your anger and your desires. They will guide you into betrayal.'

*You send me away to protect yourself. I am indeed your weakness. Because you do not trust me.* 'I have no ambitions,' he said.

'I might well believe that – no, I do not think you are lying. But time twists every path. You cannot claim to know your mind in the future. And we must be honest here – you have no cause to love me, or feel any manner of loyalty towards me.'

'I did not know, sir.'

'You did not know what?'

'That love needs a cause.'

139

The conversation ended then, and did not resume. And Arathan had no idea why.

*    *    *

They reached the river at dusk, some two leagues south of Abara Delack. There was an old trader ford here, spanning the fast-moving water, marked by standing stones on either bank, along with the stumps of huge trees left in place in case winching was needed. Old campsites on either bank showed signs that they had fallen into disuse, the grasses high and the tracks leading down to the water treacherous with run-off and exposed stones. There was a smell of rotted fish in the still air.

Rint worked alongside his sister to raise the tents, unsaddle the horses, and begin the evening meal, neither of them speaking. The Bordersword saw that Arathan was alone once more – he had been sent back by his father some time earlier, as if the Lord needed to reject the image he and his son had presented in riding side by side on the trail, and Arathan had been ordered to change mounts, returning to Hellar with obvious trepidation – a detail earning a snap from Sergeant Raskan; and thereafter the boy had ridden behind the sergeant and Draconus, with Rint and Feren taking up the rear. Arathan had drawn his armour from the back of Besra and was laying it out on the ground, an air of loss about him.

Feren had not said much since the morning, leaving Rint to fill his own mind with imaginings, hard exchanges, accusations, and judgements so deadly and final they seemed to drip blood as if from a knife tip. Through it all he could feel the sweet lure of his own righteousness, as if he stood at the centre of a storm, untouched by doubt.

The violence of his thoughts made him taciturn and edgy. He missed the company of Ville and Galak, and feared that any conversation with his sister could well erupt.

With Raskan feeding the horses and Feren at the cookfire, Rint walked down to the water's edge, a leather bucket in one hand. Draconus had walked across the stream and was now striding up the stony slope, as if eager to look out upon Bareth Solitude.

There were hidden purposes to this journey, and the secrecy drawn tight around it was proof enough of that. There was risk here, danger born of ignorance, and Rint did not like that. To make matters worse, he knew little of Bareth Solitude; and of the lands and peoples beyond the plain he knew even less. The Azathanai were enigmatic in the way of all strangers – they came among the Tiste singly, naturally remote and seemingly uninterested in forging friendships. In truth, Rint did not see much use in them at all. He would rather Jaghut than Azathanai; at least the Jaghut had seen fit to deny the Jheleck their

140

belligerent expansion into the lands of the south. The Azathanai had done nothing, even as their villages were raided.

*But the Jheleck never attacked a single Azathanai. They stole no children, raped no women. They merely burned down houses and ran off with loot, and to all of that the Azathanai simply laughed, as if possessions were meaningless.*

'Wealth,' they said, 'is a false measure. Honour cannot be hoarded. Integrity cannot adorn a room. There is no courage in gold. Only fools build a fortress of wealth. Only fools would live in it and imagine themselves safe.'

These words had been repeated, although Rint knew not which Azathanai had first uttered them; they had rushed through the soldier camps during the war, told like a tale of heroism, yet in tones of confusion, incomprehension and disbelief. But it was not the complexity of the thoughts that so confounded Rint and the others; in truth, there was nothing particularly complicated about them. Instead, the source of the unease engendered was that the Azathanai had given proof to that indifference.

*The man decrying the starvation of peasants eats well every night. This is how convictions are revealed as hypocrisy, as empty words.* But the Azathanai had spoken truth, and had watched, unperturbed, as the Jhelarkan raiders stole or destroyed all they had.

Such people frightened Rint. Were they even capable of anger? Did they not feel indignation? Did they not take offence?

He tossed the bucket out to the end of the rope knotted about its handles, watched as it settled and filled. The pull on his arms was solid as he drew against the weight.

Draconus had reached the rise and was staring out to the west, where the sun had lost all its shape in a welter of red upon the horizon. Moments later he raised one gauntleted hand.

Rint pulled the bucket up in a slosh of water and set it down on the bank, his heart suddenly thudding heavy as a drum. He watched as Draconus turned about and made his way back down to the river. He waded across and was met by Raskan. A few words were exchanged and then the Lord moved on, leaving the sergeant to stare after him.

*Someone is coming. From the west. Someone . . . expected.*

Feren came down to his side, her moccasin-clad feet crunching on the rounded pebbles of the bank. 'You saw?'

He nodded.

'Who might it be, I wonder?'

'I would not think a Jaghut,' Rint replied. 'Who then? Azathanai?' He saw her glance back at the camp, followed her gaze. 'Do you fear for the boy now? What is he to all of this?'

'I don't know.'

141

'You did what was asked of you, Feren. He will have expectations.'

She shot him a hard look. 'And is he nothing more than a damned pup to be brought to heel?'

'You are the only one who can answer that,' he retorted.

'You are a man. Of this, you understand nothing.'

'I don't? How old would the boy have been by now? Same as Arathan, or close enough.' He saw the effect of his words, like blades crossing her face, and it sickened him. 'Sister, I am sorry.'

But her eyes had gone flat. 'Children die. A mother gets over it, as she must.'

'Feren—'

'The failure was his father's, not mine.'

'I know. I did not mean—'

'Grief led his hand to the knife. Selfishness sank it into his own heart.'

'Feren.'

'He abandoned me when I needed him the most. I learned from that, brother. I learned well.'

'Arathan is not—'

'I know that! Is it me who's been chewing dead meat all afternoon? Am I the one worked into a black rage? I had a son. He died. I had a husband. He is dead, too. And I have a brother, who thinks he knows me, but all he knows is a sister he has invented – go to her again, Rint. She's easy to find. Bound to the chains inside your head.' She lifted a hand as if to strike him and he steeled himself against the blow, but it never came, and moments later she was walking back to the fire.

He wanted to weep. Instead, he cursed himself for being a fool.

A figure appeared at the rise on the other side of the river. Massive, towering, clad in thick plates of leather armour, a clutch of spears balanced over one shoulder, a heavy sack held in one hand. His head was bare, his hair unbound and lit like fiery blood in the glare of the setting sun. He paused for a moment and then lumbered his way down to the ford.

And Rint knew this Azathanai, though he had never seen him before.

*The lone warrior among the Azathanai. The one known as Protector. Though whom he has fought is a question I cannot answer. Thel Akai halfblood, mate to Kilmandaros.*

*This is Grizzin Farl.*

The water barely breached his heavy boots.

'Draconus!' he bellowed. 'Is this how you hide from all the world? Ha, I had not believed the tales – now see me for the fat fool I am! But look, I have ale!'

\*　　\*　　\*

142

He came among them like a man with nothing to fear and nothing to lose, and only much later – years later – did Arathan come to understand how each fed the other and could in turn fashion sentiments of both admiration and great pity. But with his arrival in the camp, it was as if a giant had descended from some lofty mountain crag, down from some wind-whipped keep with echoing halls and frost at the foot of wooden doors. Its master had grown weary of the solitude and now sought company.

There are those from whom pleasure exudes, heady as ale fumes, inviting as the warmth of a fire on a cold night. They encourage amusement with but a glance, as if jests fill the world and the company they share cannot help but fall into that welcoming embrace.

The Azathanai named himself Grizzin Farl, and he did not wait for Draconus to introduce him to the others; instead walking to each in turn. Raskan, Rint, and then Arathan, and when his hand clasped Arathan's wrist the nest of wrinkles bracketing the giant's eyes sharpened and he said, 'A sword-wielder's forearm, that. Your father has not been careless in preparing you for the life ahead. You are Arathan, inconvenient son of Draconus, lost child to a grieving mother. Will it be this hand I now hold that sends the knife into your father's back? So he fears, and what father wouldn't?'

Arathan stared up into those grey eyes. 'I have no ambitions,' he said.

'Well you may not, but others have.'

'They will never find me.'

Gnarled eyebrows lifted at that. 'Will you live a life in hiding, then?'

Arathan nodded. The others were standing close, listening, but he could not pull his gaze from that of Grizzin Farl.

'That is not much of a life,' the giant said.

'I am not much of a life, sir. Therefore it well suits me.'

Grizzin Farl finally released his grip on Arathan's arm and turned to Draconus. 'It is said Darkness has become a weapon. Against whom is it intended to strike? This is the question, and I go to hear its answer. Tell me, Draconus, will Kharkanas reel to my fated arrival?'

'Towers will topple,' Draconus replied. 'Women will swoon.'

'Ha! As well they should!' But then he frowned. 'Those observations, old friend, do not sit well together.' And with that he turned to Feren and lowered himself to one knee. 'Who could expect such beauty here on the very edge of Bareth Solitude? It is ever in my nature to save the best for last. I am Grizzin Farl, known among the Azathanai as the Protector, known among the Jheleck as the warrior who misses every fight, sleeps through every battle, and but smiles at every challenge. Known, too, by those Jaghut who remain as the Stone that Sleeps, which is their poetic way of describing my infamous lethargy. Now, I would have you speak your own name, so that I may cherish it and hold the memory of your voice for ever in my heart.'

Through all of this, Feren seemed unimpressed, though the colour was high on her cheeks. 'I am Feren,' she said. 'A Bordersword and sister to Rint.'

'Too young,' Grizzin Farl said after a moment, 'to lose hope. Your voice has told me a tragic tale, though the details remain obscured, but in loss there is pain, and pain will become a sting that ever reminds of that loss.'

She backed away at his words. 'I reveal no such thing!' she said in a rasp.

Grizzin Farl slowly straightened, then spread his arms out as if to encompass them all. 'Tonight we will drink ourselves into wild joy, until the fire has dimmed and the stars flee the dawn, whereupon we will all grow maudlin and each swear everlasting fealty to one another, before passing out.' He lifted his sack. 'Ale from the Thel Akai, who are masters, if not of brewing, most certainly of drinking.' He paused, and then added, 'I trust you have food. In my haste to meet you, I fear I left home without any.'

Arathan was startled to hear his father's sigh.

Then Grizzin Farl smiled, and once more all was right in the world.

*   *   *

The ale was strong and went immediately to Arathan's head. Shortly after the evening meal, and in the midst of a bawdy song about a Thel Akai maiden and an old Jaghut with an aching tusk, sung with great melodrama by the Azathanai, Arathan fell asleep. Raskan awoke him the next morning with a cup of strong herbs and willow bark, and it was while he sat, sipping the hot drink, that he saw that Grizzin Farl was no longer among them.

Even now it seemed like a dream, blurred and raucous, almost fevered. Head aching, Arathan kept his eyes on the ground before him, as the others began breaking camp. He wondered what other matters were spoken of in the night just past, and he felt his own absence as if it mocked whatever claims he might make to having become a man. He had fallen unconscious like a boy at his first cups, a tankard stolen from the table and hastily gulped down behind a chair.

He had wanted to hear more about Darkness as a sword, a weapon. And it was clear that Grizzin Farl knew Arathan's father – in ways no one else did, perhaps not even Mother Dark herself. What strange history did they share? What mysterious tales bound their past? A few covert glances to Raskan, Rint and Feren suggested that nothing momentous had been revealed; if anything, everyone seemed at greater ease than they had shown in the time before Grizzin Farl's arrival, as if barriers had been pushed down after a night of ale and laughter.

After a moment of consideration, Arathan looked again at Feren, and saw that *something* had changed. There was a looseness about her, and then he caught a smile she sent her brother's way at some muttered comment, and suddenly it seemed as if *everything* had changed. Tensions had vanished. The oppressive weight that had been Sagander's accident had disappeared. *Grizzin Farl came among us, and then he left, but when he left, he took something with him.*

He saw his father watching him, and after a moment Draconus strode over. 'I should have warned you about Thel Akai ale.'

Arathan shrugged.

'And you barely recovered from a concussion,' his father continued. 'It must have hit you like a sleeping draught. I am sorry, Arathan, that you missed most of an enjoyable evening.' He hesitated, and then said, 'You have had too few of those.'

'He called you his friend,' Arathan said, his tone painfully accusing.

A flatness came to his father's eyes. 'He calls everyone "friend", Arathan. Give it no further thought.'

Arathan glared after him as he walked away.

From a lone, diseased tree upriver drifted the morning cry of a bird and he looked over but could not see the creature among the crooked branches and sullen leaves.

*It hides, and it is free.*

*Free to fly away from all of this.*

*     *     *

A short time later they ascended the slope and came out upon the Bareth Solitude, and the way ahead stretched on in ribboned rows beneath a clear sky, and Arathan was reminded of Sagander's lessons recounting the death of a great inland sea.

As he rode, he thought of water, and freedom.

And prisons.

To the west was the land of the Azathanai, where dwelt protectors who protected nothing, and wise sages who never spoke, and Thel Akai came down from the mountains to share drunken nights no one remembered the next day. It was a world of mysteries, and he would soon see it for himself. With the thought, he felt light in the saddle, as if moments from transforming into a bird, from taking wing in search of a diseased tree.

But the thin sea ahead was bereft of trees, and the beach ridges with their bleached cobbles edged basins of grass and little else.

He wasn't interested in stabbing his father in the back – that broad back just ahead, beneath that worn cloak. No one would ever wield him like a knife.

Grizzin Farl had told him: his mother still lived. She lived, tormented by grief, which meant that she loved him still. He would find her and steal her away.

In a world of mysteries, there were plenty of places in which to hide.
*For both of us.*

*And we will love each other, and from that love, there will be peace.*

# PART TWO

*The solitude of this fire*

# S I X

UST HENARALD'S EYES WERE LEVEL AND DARK, AS IF TO TEST THE
weight of the words he was about to speak, to see if they sank
claws deep into the man seated opposite him, or merely slipped
past. The low light sculpted out the hollows of his cheeks, and above
the prominent bones flaring out from his narrow, hooked nose those
sharp eyes seemed to have retreated far in their shadowy recesses, yet
remained piercing and intent. 'One day,' he said, voice rough from years
at the forge, in the midst of bitter smoke and acrid steam, 'I will be a
child again.' He slowly leaned back, withdrawing from the oil lamp's
light on the table, until he seemed to Kellaras more a ghostly apparition
than a mortal man.

From outside this overheated chamber, the great machines of the
bellows thundered like an incessant heart, the reverberations rolling
through every stone of the Great House. The sound never fell away –
in all the days and nights Kellaras had been guest to the Lord of Hust
Forge, he had felt this drum of industry, beating the pulse of earth and
stone, of fire and smoke.

This was, he had begun to believe, a place of elemental secrets, where
truths roiled in the swirling heat, the miasmic tempest of creation and
destruction clamouring without surcease on all sides; and this man,
who had finally granted him audience, now sat across from him, in a
high-backed chair shrouded in shadows, both lord and arbiter, ruler
and sage, and yet his first words uttered had been . . . nonsense.

Henarald might have smiled then, but it was difficult to see in the
gloom. 'One day, I will be a child again. Carved toys will caper and
dance from my mind, out across rock I will raise as mountains. Through

grasses I will proclaim forests. For too long I have been trapped in this world of measures, proportions and scale. For too long I have known and understood the limits of what is possible, so cruel in rejecting all that can be imagined. In this way, friend, we are each of us not one but two lives, for ever locked in mortal combat, and from all things at hand, we make weapons.'

Kellaras slowly reached for the goblet of riktal on the tabletop before him. The spirit was fire in the throat and the only alcohol the Lord was purported to drink, but Kellaras's first mouthful still rocked through his brain.

'You hide your sudden acuity well, captain, but I well noted your intensity when I spoke the word "weapons". To this you cleave, for among the words I have spoken, this alone you understand. I was speaking of all that we lose as the years crawl over us and the past – our youth – falls away.' He closed both hands round his goblet, and those hands were massive, scarred and blunted, shiny in places from deep burns acquired over a lifetime at his forge. 'Your lord wishes from me a sword. As a gift? Or does he seek to join the Hust Legion, perhaps. I cannot imagine Urusander's supporters would be much pleased by a proclamation so overt.'

Kellaras struggled for a reply. Henarald's easy shift from the poetic to the pragmatic left him feeling wrong-footed. His thoughts felt clumsy, like a child's when confounded by a puzzle box.

But the Hust lord was of no mind to await a reply. 'When I am a child again, the grown-ups will retreat from my eye. Drifting away into their own worlds and leaving me to mine. In their absence I am filled with trust and I reorder the scale of things to suit my modest command. Time yields its grip and I play until it is time to sleep.' Henarald paused to drink. 'And should I dream, it will be of surrender.'

After a long moment, Kellaras cleared his throat. 'Lord, my master well understands that such a commission is, at this time, unusual.'

'There was a time when it was anything but unusual. But to call it so now is too coy for my liking. A commission for a sword from the First Son of Darkness cannot help but be seen as political. Will my acquiescence unleash rumours of secret allegiance and conspiracy? What snare does Anomander set in my path?'

'None, Lord. His desire reaches back to the honour of tradition.'

Brows slowly lifted. 'His words, or your own?'

'Such was my understanding, Lord, with respect to the First Son's motivations.'

'In choosing you, he chose well. One day I will be a child again.' Then he leaned forward. 'But not yet.' The sharpness of Henarald's gaze glittered like diamond shards. 'Captain Kellaras, has your master specific instructions as to this blade of his desire?'

'Lord, he would it be a silent weapon.'

'Ha! Does the cry of the sword's supple spine unnerve him, then?'

'No, Lord, it does not.'

'Yet he would prefer a gagged weapon, cut mute, a weapon cursed to howl and weep unheard by any.'

'Lord,' said Kellaras, 'the weapon you describe leads me to wonder which is the greatest torment, silence or a voice for its pain?'

'Captain, the weapon I describe does not exist. Yet those fools in Urusander's Legion would tell you otherwise. Tell me, will your master hide the origin of his blade?'

'Of course not, Lord.'

'Yet he would have it muted.'

'Must all truths be spoken, Lord?'

'Does the riktal un-man you, captain? I can call for wine if you prefer.'

'In truth, Lord, I had forgotten that I had goblet in hand. I beg your pardon.' Kellaras swallowed down another mouthful.

'He wishes a blade of truth, then.'

'One that demands the same in its wielder, yes. In concord, then, but a *silent* concord.'

Abruptly Henarald rose to his feet. He was tall, gaunt, yet he stood straight, as if the iron of his world was in his bones, his flesh. In the pits of his eyes now, nothing was visible from the low angle at which sat Kellaras. 'Captain, there is chaos in every weapon. We who forge iron, indeed, all metal, we lock hands with that chaos. We fight it, seeking control and order, and it fights back, with open defiance and, when that fails, with hidden treachery. Your master seeks a blade devoid of chaos. Such a thing cannot be achieved, and the life I have spent is proof of that.'

Kellaras hesitated, and then said, 'Lord, First Son Anomander is aware of the secret of the Hust swords. He knows what lies at the core of every weapon you now make. This is not the path he seeks in the making of his chosen sword. He requests that the spine of the blade be quenched in sorcery, in the purity of Darkness itself.'

The Lord of Hust Forge was motionless, the lines of his face seeming to deepen the longer he stared down at Kellaras. Then he spoke, in flat tones. 'It is said that the sceptre I made for Mother Dark now possesses something of the soul of Kurald Galain. She has imbued it with sorcery. She has taken pure but plain iron and made it . . . unnatural.'

'Lord, I know little of that.'

'It now embodies Darkness, in some manner few of us understand. Indeed, I wonder if even Mother Dark is fully aware of what she has done.'

The direction of this conversation was making Kellaras uneasy.

Henarald grunted. 'Do I speak blasphemy?'

'I would hope not, Lord.'

'But now we must take care in what we say. It seems, captain, that as her power grows, her tolerance diminishes. They are like lodestones, pushing each other away. Does power not grant immunity? Does power not strengthen the armour; does power not find assurance in itself? Can it be that those who hold the most power also know the greatest fear?'

'Lord, I cannot say.'

'And yet, do not those who are most powerless also suffer from the same fear? What does power grant its wielder, then? Presumably, the means with which to challenge that fear. And yet, it would seem that it does not work, not for long, in any case. By this we must conclude that power is both meaningless and delusional.'

'Lord, the Forulkan sought to extend their power over the Tiste. Had they succeeded, we would be either enslaved now, or dead. There is nothing delusional about power, and through the strength of our legions, including the Hust, we prevailed.'

'If the Forulkan had won, what would they have achieved? Mastery over slaves? But let us be truthful here, captain. Not one Tiste would kneel in slavery. The Forulkan would have had no choice but to kill us all. I ask again, what would that have achieved? A triumph in solitude makes a hollow sound, and to every glory proclaimed the heavens make no answer.'

'My master requests a sword.'

'Pure and plain iron.'

'Just so.'

'To take the blood of Darkness.'

The captain's brows rose. 'Lord, her sorcery is not Azathanai.'

'Isn't it? She feeds her power, but how?'

'Not by blood!'

Henarald studied Kellaras for a moment longer, and then he sat once more in his heavy, high-backed chair. He drained the goblet in his hand and set it down on the table. 'I have breathed poison for so long, only riktal can burn through the scars on my throat. Age numbs us to feeling. We are dulled as black bedrock on a crag. Waiting for yet one more season of frost. Now that the First Son has discovered the secret of the Hust, will he barter his knowledge to suit his political ambitions?'

'My master states as his sole ambition the desire never to yield to ignorance, Lord. Knowledge is all the reward he seeks, and its possession is the measure of his own wealth.'

'Does he hoard it then?'

'He understands that others would use such knowledge, in unseemly ways. I have known my master since we were both children, Lord, and I can tell you, no secrets pass through his hands.'

Henarald's shrug was loose, careless, his eyes fixed on the floor somewhere to his right. 'The secret of the Hust swords is in itself a thing without power. I held it close for . . . other reasons.'

'To protect those who wield such weapons, yes, Lord. My master well understands that.'

The hooded gaze flicked over at Kellaras for a moment, and then away again. 'I will make Anomander a sword,' Henarald said. 'But in the moment of its final quenching, I will attend. I will see for myself this sorcery. And if it is blood, then,' he sighed, 'then I will know.'

'She dwells in Darkness,' said Kellaras.

'Then I shall see nothing?'

'I believe, Lord, you shall see nothing.'

'I think,' said Henarald, 'I begin to understand the nature of her power.'

*     *     *

Outside the chamber, Kellaras found that he was trembling. In the fraught exchange just past, it had been Henarald's promise of a return to childhood that most disturbed the captain. He could make no sense of it, and yet he suspected some dreadful secret hid within that confession.

Muttering under his breath he pushed the unease away, and set out for the main hall at the corridor's far end, where a hundred or more residents and guests of the house now dined, in a riotous clamour of voices and laughter, and the heat from the great hearth roiled in the chamber, filling the air with the heady smells of roasting pork. He would lose himself in that festive atmosphere, and should moments of doubt stir awake, he need only remind himself that he had won Henarald's promise to forge a sword for his master, and then reach for another tankard of ale.

Striding into the main hall, Kellaras paused for a moment. New, unfamiliar faces swirled on all sides, dust-grimed and weary. A troop of Hust soldiers had arrived, returned from some patrol, and voices were loud as kin called greetings across the room. He scanned the crowd, seeking out Galar Baras, and moments later found the man, standing close to a side passage and leaning against the smoke-stained stone wall. Kellaras began making his way over, and then drew up when he finally noted his friend's intent gaze, which was fixed upon one of the newcomers, a woman of rank who seemed to be the centre of much of the attention. She was smiling, listening to a bent old man too drunk to stay upright without the aid of a high-backed chair. When her gaze finally slipped past him, Kellaras saw her stiffen slightly upon meeting Galar's eyes.

An instant later she was looking away again, and with one hand affectionately settling on the drunk's shoulder, she eased past the old man and made her way towards another table, where her fellow soldiers were now settling in.

A harried servant was edging through the crowd, drawing close to where Kellaras stood, and the captain accosted the young man. 'A word, please. Who is that woman? The officer?'

The servant's brows lifted. 'Toras Redone, sir, commander of the Hust Legion.'

'Ah, of course. Thank you.'

He was certain he had seen her before, but always from a distance – upon a field of battle – and of course helmed and girded for war. She was not one for attending formal events in the Citadel, preferring instead to remain with her legion. It was said that she had arrived to kneel before Mother Dark in sweat-stained leathers, with dust upon her face – he'd thought that tale apocryphal, but now he was not so sure.

She sat now amongst her soldiers, a tankard in one hand, and for all the grime of hard travel upon her, he could see that she was beautiful, yet in a dissolute way, and when Kellaras watched her drain the flagon of ale and then reach for another, he was not surprised.

He considered paying his respects, then decided that this was not the time, and so he continued making his way towards Galar Baras.

'You look rattled, captain,' Galar said when he drew close.

*Not half as much as you, friend.* 'I have just come from my audience with your lord.'

'And did he speak to you of childhood?'

'He did, though I admit to my failing to make sense of it.'

'And the other matter?'

'My master will be most pleased. I see you have no drink in hand – I feel bold enough to assail the ale bench—'

'Not on my account, captain. I cannot stomach it, I'm afraid. I see your surprise – what veteran cannot drink, you wonder? Why, I will answer you: a sober one.'

'Does this prevent you from sharing in the festivities? I see you standing apart, as if outcast. Come, let us find somewhere to sit.'

Galar's smile was faint, with a hint of sadness in his eyes. 'If you insist.'

They made their way to a table, Kellaras choosing one close to the servants' entrance where a score of used flagons crowded the surface. As they sat he said, 'Can you explain, then, your lord's obsession with becoming a child once more?'

Galar Baras seemed to hesitate, and then he leaned close, one forearm pushing the flagons to one side. 'It is troubling to us all, captain—'

'Please, call me Kellaras.'

'Very well. Kellaras. Something afflicts Henarald, at least in his own mind. He claims he is losing his memories, not of distant times, but of the day just past, or indeed the morning just done. Yet we do not see it, not yet in any case. There is an illness that takes smiths. Some believe it resides in the fumes from the forge, in the steam from quenching, or the molten drops of ore that burn the skin. It is called the Loss of Iron—'

'I have indeed heard of this,' Kellaras replied. 'Yet I tell you, after my audience with your lord, I saw nothing afflicting his intellect. Rather, he speaks in abstractions, in the language of poets. When the subject demands precision, his wit sharpens quickly. This requires a facility, a definite acuity of the mind.'

Galar Baras shrugged. 'I reveal no secrets here, Kellaras. The rumour is long out – our lord feels afflicted, and the keenness of his intelligence, that you so surely describe, is to him evidence of the war he wages with himself, with the failings he senses besieging him. He strikes out with precision to battle the blunting of memories.'

'I had first thought that he feared this return to childhood,' Kellaras said, frowning. 'But I began to suspect that he will welcome it, should it come to him. A release from all the fraught things of the adult world.'

'You may well be right,' Galar admitted. 'Will you report to your master on this matter?'

'He has promised Anomander a sword – do his skills fail him?'

'No, we have seen nothing like that.'

'Then Lord Henarald's fears for his own health have no bearing on the commission.'

'I thank you, Kellaras.'

Kellaras waved the gratitude away. 'Besides, I could tell you my master's likely response should he hear of your lord's assertions.'

'Oh, and what would he say?'

'I imagine he would nod most thoughtfully, and then say: "There is much to be said for a return to childhood."'

After a moment, Galar smiled, and this time there was no sadness to be found in it.

*       *       *

Kellaras drank his fair share of ale and offered up easy company that did much to ease the turmoil in Galar Baras's soul, and when at last the captain rose, slurring his words of departure, and made his way unsteadily from the chamber, Galar was left alone once more, helpless to fend off the pain caused by the sight of Toras Redone.

The room was quieter now; the candles little more than stumps, as weary servants cleared plates and tankards, with only a few tables still occupied. She still held command of one of those tables, although her compatriots were drifting off where they slumped in their chairs, and when she at last rose, wavering for but a moment, and made her way over to Galar, only then did he realize that he had been waiting for her. And that she had known it.

'How fares your courage, Galar Baras?' Alcohol had rounded her words in a way he well recalled.

He watched as she took the chair Kellaras had been sitting in earlier. Stretching her legs out, the mud-caked boots edging towards his own leg upon the right, she folded her hands on her lap and regarded him with red-shot eyes.

'You have come from the south?' he asked.

'Where else? Patrolling the Forulkan border.'

'Any trouble?'

She shook her head. 'Quiet. Not like the old days. But then, nothing is, is it?'

'We must all move on, yes.'

'Oh, people do that, don't they. Consider my husband – could he have gone any further away than he has? Glimmer Fate, seasonal forts, a handful of the lost and broken to command. This would be true service to the realm; you'd have to say that, wouldn't you?'

He studied her. 'It is a great responsibility.'

Abruptly she laughed, broke his gaze to look away. Her right hand drummed a rattle of taps on the tabletop and then fell still once more. 'We all skirt the borderlands, as if to test our limits.'

'Not all of us,' he replied.

She glanced at him, then away again. 'You are a pariah in the Citadel. They think you arrogant and dismissive, but that's not you, Galar. It never was.'

'It seems I have little in common with the Citadel's denizens.'

'We chose you for that very reason.'

He considered that, and then sighed.

She leaned forward. 'It wasn't punishment, Galar. It was never that.'

But it was, and he knew it.

'You could at least take a priestess to your bed, you know. Leave the celibates staring at walls in their monasteries; that's not the way for people like us. We're soldiers and we have the appetites to match.'

'And are you well fed these days, Toras?'

As usual, his barb had no effect upon her. 'Well enough,' she replied, leaning back once more. 'You probably would not understand this, but it is my very certainty that my husband has remained true that drives me to do as I do.'

'You are right – I do not understand that at all.'

'I am not his equal. I had no hope of becoming that, not from the very start. I walked the trench at his side, always. That's not an easy thing to live with, not day after day.'

'There was no trench, Toras. None saw you as his lesser – you command the Hust Legion, for Abyss' sake.'

'This has nothing to do with military rank, or achievements.'

'Then what?'

But she shook her head. 'I have missed you, Galar.'

All of this without once meeting his gaze. He had no idea if others were watching, or even striving to listen in on this conversation. He did not think it likely. Servants had brought rushes into the room to set out upon the floor. Someone was singing drunkenly, forgetting lines, and laughter echoed. Woodsmoke hung heavy, stinging his eyes. He shrugged. 'What is to be done, then?'

She rose, slapped him on the shoulder. 'Go to your room. It's late.'

'And you?'

Smiling, she wheeled away. 'That's the thing about courage, isn't it?'

He watched her return to her original seat, watched her pour full the tankard in front of her, and he knew that he would not spend this night alone. As he stood and made his way out of the chamber, he thought of his quarters in the Citadel, and the narrow bed he would not share with any priestesses; and then he thought of Calat Hustain, lying on a cot in some northern fort. Two men dwelling in solitude, because it was in their nature to choose it: to remain alone in the absence of love.

And the woman these two men shared, why, she understood nothing.

\*　　　\*　　　\*

Over the past three days, Kadaspala had been spared the company of Hunn Raal and Osserc. He'd not even seen them ride out, and Urusander had made no mention of where they had gone, or to what purpose. This was satisfying, as it left him to work on the portrait without suffering the assault of ignorant commentary, unsolicited advice, or inane conversations at the evening meal. Unshackled from the expectations of his cadre, Urusander was a different man, and their arguments over a host of subjects had proved mildly entertaining, almost enlivening, so much so that Kadaspala had begun looking forward to the meals they took at day's end.

Still, the situation galled him. Work left him impatient, irritated and dissatisfied. At each sitting's conclusion he fought to keep from slumping in exhaustion, instead applying himself with diligence to the cleaning of his brushes, his mind tracking the lines of the charcoal studies he referred to again and again when gauging the image on the board – he did not have to actually look at the vellum sheets, so fiercely were they burned into his mind's eye. Urusander's face haunted him, as did each subject he painted, but this time it felt different.

There was political intent to all works of art, but this one was too brazen, too bold, as far as he was concerned, and so he found his hand

and eye fighting that overt crudity, with a shifting of tones, a deepening of certain lines, with a symbolic language only he understood.

*Painting is war. Art is war.*

His colleagues would recoil in horror at such notions. But then, they were mostly fools. Only Gallan would understand. Only Gallan would nod and perhaps even smile. There were so many ways to wage a battle. Weapons of beauty, weapons of discord. Fields of engagement across a landscape, or in the folds of a hanging curtain. Lines of resistance, knots of ambush, the assault of colour, the retreat of perspective. So many ways to fight, and yet every victory felt like surrender – he had no power over a stranger's eyes, after all, and if art could lay siege to a stranger's soul, it was a blind advance against unseen walls.

This portrait of Urusander – which he now sat facing, as the last of the night's candles flickered and wavered – bore all of Kadaspala's wounds, yet who might see that? No one, not even Gallan. One learns to hide the damage taken, and an eye pleased is an eye seduced.

And Urusander was well pleased indeed.

He was done. He would leave with the dawn. *I have painted a man worthy of being her husband. They will see his strength, his resolute integrity, because these lie on the surface. They will not see the underside of such things – the cruelty beneath strength, the cold pride behind that stern resolution. The blade of judgement grasped firm in integrity's hand.*

*They will see in his stance his soldier's discipline, and the burdens assumed without complaint. Yet see nothing of withered empathy or unreasonable expectation.*

*In the tones they will find warmth with but a hint of the underlying metal, and in so seeing they will understand nothing of that melding of fire and iron and all that it promises.*

*My power is vast, the talent undeniable, the vision sure and true. Yet all it leaves me is torment. There is but one god, and its name is beauty. There is but one kind of worship, and that is love. There is for us but one world, and we have scarred it beyond recognition.*

*Art is the language of the tormented, but the world is blind to that, for ever blind.*

*Urusander, I see you – I face you now – in the failing light, and you frighten me to the core.*

'You will not dine with me on this last night?'

Startled, it was a moment before Kadaspala turned in his chair to face Lord Urusander. 'For an instant, Lord, as you spoke, I thought I saw the mouth of your portrait shaping your words. Most . . . disconcerting.'

'I imagine it would be, yes. You have fashioned a true likeness.'

Kadaspala nodded.

'Will you copy it yourself in the Hall?'

'No, Lord. The Citadel's artists will do that. They are chosen especially for their skills at imitation. When they are done, this painting will be returned to you here – or wherever you end up residing.'

To that Urusander said nothing for a time. He walked slowly closer to where sat Kadaspala, his hooded gaze on the portrait. Then he sighed. 'Where I reside. Do I appear so displeased with my present abode?'

'I saw nothing of that, Lord.'

'No, you wouldn't. Yet,' and he gestured, 'you would have me . . . elsewhere.'

Faint bells chimed to announce dinner, but neither man moved. 'Lord, it is a portrait of you, by the hand of Kadaspala, who has turned down a hundred commissions.'

'That many?'

'Those denied do not announce their failure, Lord.'

'No, I suppose they wouldn't. Very well, then, why did you accept this one?'

'I had a thought.'

'Indeed, and will you tell me that thought, Kadaspala?'

'If anyone can prevent civil war' – and he nodded towards the portrait – 'it is that man.'

Breath hissed from Urusander and his words were harsh with frustration. 'This is all madness! If the nobility so resent the Consort, then they should challenge Mother Dark herself!'

'They dare not, but this does not dull their disapproval – they cut and stab elsewhere, as befits their bold courage.'

'You reveal little admiration for your kind, Kadaspala.'

'I have painted the faces of too many of them, Lord, and so invite you to view that rogue's gallery of venality, malice, and self-regard. My finest works, one and all, the very proof of my genius.'

'Do you always paint what you see, Kadaspala?'

'Not always,' he admitted. 'Sometimes I paint what I fear. All these faces – all these greats among the Tiste, you here included – you may think they are about each of you. Alas, they are just as much about me.'

'I would not challenge that,' Urusander replied. 'It must be so with all artists.'

Kadaspala shrugged. 'The artist is usually poorly disguised in his works, revealed in each and every flaw of execution. The self-confession is one of incompetence. But this is not my failing. What I reveal of myself in these works is less easily discerned. And before you enquire, Lord, no, I have no interest in elaborating on that.'

'I imagine that those imitators in the Citadel will fail in repeating what you have captured here.'

'I believe you are right, Lord.'

Urusander grunted. 'Just as well. Come then, join me in one final meal. I believe you are soon to attend a wedding?'

Kadaspala rose from the chair. 'Yes, Lord, my sister.'

They made their way out of the sitting room.

'Andarist is a good man, Kadaspala.'

'None would deny that,' he replied, pleased at the ease with which those words flowed from his lips.

'Your sister has become a most beautiful woman, or so I am told.'

'She is that, Lord . . .'

*       *       *

There were people who feared solitude, but Cryl did not count himself among them. He sat astride his horse, the barren hills stretching out on all sides, a warm wind brushing across the grasses like the breath of a contented god. Near a jumble of half-buried stones there was a scatter of white bones, and set upon one of those boulders was the multi-tined rack of a bull eckalla. Slain by a hunter years past, the perched antlers pronounced the triumph of the kill.

It seemed a poignantly hollow triumph in Cryl's eyes. The ancient tradition of hunting had been held aloft as a standard of virtue, emblazoned with the colours of courage, patience and skill. It was also a hand upon the beating heart of the earth, even if that hand was slick with blood. Challenges and contests of wits between Tiste and beast – when the truth was, it was rarely any contest at all. Unquestionably hunting for food was a sure and necessary instinct, but forms were born of pragmatic needs until such endeavours came to mean more than they once did. Now, hunting was seen as a rite of passage, when necessity had long since ceased.

It was a curiosity to Cryl that so many men and women, well along in their years, still found need to repeat those rites of passages, as if emotionally trapped in the transition from child to adult. He well understood the excitement of the chase, the sweet tension of the stalk, but for him these were not the reasons to hunt, while for many he knew that they had become just that.

*Do we hunt to practise for war? The blood, the dying eyes of the slain . . . our terrible fascination with suffering? What vile core do we dip into in such moments? Why is the taste not too bitter to bear?*

He had seen no sign of living eckalla, and he had ridden far from House Enes, far from sad Jaen and his excited daughter, far from the world of weddings, hostages and the ever growing tensions among the highborn, and yet even out here, among these hills beneath this vast sky, his kind found him, with trophies of death.

Years past, when he was still young enough to dream, he imagined setting out to discover a new world, a place without Tiste, without

160

civilization, where he could live alone and unencumbered – no, perhaps not alone: he also saw her at his side, a companion in his great adventure. That world had the feel of the past, but a past no Tiste eye had witnessed, which made it innocent. And he would think of himself as prey, not predator, as if shedding the skin of brazen killer, and with this would come a thrill of fear.

In his weaker moments, Cryl still longed for that place, where freedom's risks were plain to understand, and when he rode out from the estate, as he had done this time, vanishing into as much of the wild as remained, he found himself searching – not for eckalla, or their sign; not for wolves on the horizon or in the valleys; not for the hares and the hawks – but for a past he knew was for ever lost. Worse yet, it was a past he and his people did not belong in, and so could never know.

He had been trained for war just as he had been taught how to hunt and how to slay, and these were deemed necessary skills in preparation for adulthood. How sad was that?

His horse's ears flicked and then tilted. Cryl rose to stand in his stirrups, scanned the horizon in the direction of the horse's sudden attention.

A troop of riders coming down from the north. Their appearance startled him. He could see that they were Tiste, wearing armour but bareheaded, helms strapped to the saddles.

The only settlement remotely close was Sedis Hold, at least three days to the northwest, and these riders would have had to cross Young Dorssan Ryl, a difficult task at any time of year, when it would have been simpler to remain on the road on the river's other side, which would take them down past House Dracons and thence onward to Kharkanas. There was no reason for such a risky crossing when solid bridges beckoned to the south.

Cryl's mind raced, trying to recall who was stationed in Sedis Hold. The keep had been raised at the close of the war against the Jheleck. A garrison was ensconced there permanently, ever since the defeated Jheleck had thought to resume their raiding – as if the war had never happened.

The riders were drawing closer, but not in any haste; indeed, they seemed to be leading a score of individuals on foot.

Nudging his horse round to face the newcomers, Cryl hesitated a moment, and then rode towards them. As he approached, he saw that those figures on foot, trailing the riders, were all children, and, even more astonishing, they were Jheleck.

He could see no chains linking the captives, and each child appeared to be burdened under hide sacks of, presumably, possessions.

The Tiste riders amounted to a score of regular soldiers, a sergeant and, at the forefront of the troop, a captain. This man's eyes were intent, studying Cryl as if looking for something in particular. Evidently failing to find it, he visibly relaxed, and then held up a hand to halt those behind him.

'You journey far,' the captain said. 'Do you seek to deliver a message to Sedis Hold?'

Cryl shook his head. 'No sir. To do that, I would be upon the other side of the river.'

'Then what brings a young highborn out wandering these hills?'

It seemed, then, that this captain was determined to ignore the matter of their all being on the wrong side of the river. Cryl shrugged. 'I am Cryl Durav, hostage to—'

'House Enes.' The captain's lean, weathered face broke into a smile. 'Is it a rude guess that you fled the frenzied preparations for marriage?'

'Excuse me?'

The man laughed. 'I am Captain Scara Bandaris, Cryl. My journey into the south is twofold.' He gestured at the Jheleck children. 'One, to find out what to do with this first gaggle of hostages. And here we thought we'd face another war before the Jheleck ever surrendered a single child of theirs. Imagine our surprise.'

'And the other reason, sir?'

'Why, to attend the ceremony, of course. It so pleases me to know that Andarist is upon the very cusp of wedded bliss. Now, will you escort us to House Enes? I would hear of Jaen's lovely daughter, whom you have grown alongside all these years.'

Cryl knew the name of Scara Bandaris, an officer who had fought with distinction in the wars. What he had not known was that he had been posted in Sedis. 'As hostage to House Enes, sir, it would be my honour to escort you. I have tarried in these wilds long enough, I suppose.' He brought his mount round as the captain waved his troop forward once more.

Scara Bandaris rode up alongside him. 'If I were in your place, Cryl Durav, I might well be seeking an empty cave among the hermits of the north crags. A young woman about to be wed – whom you have known for so long now – well, have I guessed wrong as to your motives?'

'My motives, sir?'

'Out into the wilds, alone and blissfully at peace – you have been gone some days, I wager.'

Cryl sighed. 'You see the truth of it, sir.'

'Then we'll speak no more of wounded hearts. Nor will I torture you with questions about Enesdia. Tell me, have you seen any eckalla?'

'None living, sir,' Cryl replied. He glanced back at the Jheleck children.

Scara Bandaris grunted. 'Better on two feet than four, I tell you.'

'Sir?'

'Twenty-five whelps, Cryl, that no leash can hold. We shall raise wolves in our midst with these ones.'

'I have heard, not quite wolves . . .'

'True enough. Hounds, then. This tradition of hostage taking, so venerated and inviolate, may well come back to bite us.'

Cryl shot the man a look.

Scara Bandaris burst out laughing, forcing up a smile from Cryl.

Perhaps, Cryl reconsidered after a moment, with jests erupting from the soldiers behind them, followed by yet more laughter, his need for solitude was at an end.

\*　　\*　　\*

'*Where is he?*'

The cry made the handmaids flinch back, a detail that savagely pleased Enesdia, if only momentarily. 'How dare he run away? And Father does nothing! Have we ceased to respect the ancient tradition of hostages, to so let him vanish into the wilds like some half-wild dog?' The array of blank faces regarding her only frustrated Enesdia the more. Hissing under her breath, she marched from the room, leaving the handmaids to scurry after her. A gesture halted them all. 'Leave me, all of you.'

After a lengthy, increasingly irritating search, she found her father out behind the stables, observing the breaking of a horse in the corral. 'Father, are we to lead the way in the rejection of all valued traditions among our people?'

Jaen regarded her with raised brows. 'That strikes me as somewhat . . . ambitious, daughter. Best I leave such things to the next generation, yes?'

'Then why have we abandoned our responsibilities with respect to our hostage?'

'I was unaware that we had, Enesdia.'

'Cryl has vanished – for days! For all you know he could be lying at the bottom of a well, legs shattered and dying of thirst.'

'Dying of thirst in a well?'

She glared at him until he relented and said, 'I sent him in search of eckalla in the hills.'

'A hopeless quest!'

'No doubt, but I imagine he is familiar with those.'

'What do you mean?'

Jaen shrugged, eyes once more on the horse as it fast-trotted round its handler, hoofs kicking up dust. 'This is your time, not his. In fact, his sojourn with our family is coming to an end. It well suits him to stretch his lead, as it does every young man at his age.'

She disliked hearing such things. Cryl was her companion, a brother in every way but blood. She struggled to imagine life without him at her side, and she felt a tremor of rising shock as it suddenly struck her that, once she was married, her time with Cryl would be truly at an end. After all, had she really been expecting him to join them in the new house? Absurd.

So much had been happening, devouring her every thought; only now was she thinking things through. 'But I miss him,' she said. Hearing the weakness of her own voice misted her eyes.

Her father faced her. 'Darling,' he said, taking her arm and leading her away from the railing. 'A changing world is a most frightening thing—'

'I'm not frightened.'

'Well, perhaps "bewildering" is a better description.'

'He's just . . . grown past me. That's all.'

'I doubt he sees it that way. You have made your choice, Enesdia, and the path before you is now certain, and the man who will walk at your side awaits you. It is time for Cryl to find his own future.'

'What will he do? Has he spoken to you? He's said nothing to me – he doesn't say anything to me any more. It's as if he doesn't even like me.'

They were returning to the Great House, Jaen electing to use a side entrance, a narrow passageway leading into an enclosed garden. 'His feelings for you are unchanged, but just as you set off into your new direction – away from this house – so too must Cryl. He will return to his own family, and it is there that his future will be decided.'

'The Duravs – they are all soldiers. Cryl has only one brother left alive. The wars almost destroyed that family. He'll take up the sword. He'll follow in Spinnock's footsteps. Such a waste!'

'We are no longer at war, Enesdia. The risks are not what they once were, and for that we can all be thankful. In any case, the youngest born among the nobility have few recourses these days.'

They stood in the garden, in still air made cool by the raised pond commanding the centre. The fruit trees trained up two of the inner walls were laden with heavy, lush fruit, the purple globes looking like dusty glass. She thought, if one should fall in the next moment, it might shatter. 'I have been unmindful, Father. Selfish. We are parting, and it will be difficult for both of us.'

'Indeed.'

She looked up at him. 'And even worse for you – is not Cryl the son you never had? This house will seem so . . . empty.'

Jaen smiled. 'An old man treasures his peace and quiet.'

'Oh? So you cannot wait to be rid of us?'

'Now you have the truth of it.'

'Well, then I'll not spare your feelings another thought.'

'Better. Now, return to your maids, lest they make mischief.'

'They can wait a while longer – I wish to stay here for a time. I need to think.'

Still smiling, her father departed the garden.

*I could ask Andarist to offer Cryl a commission. In the Citadel Wards. Somewhere safe. It will be my gift to Cryl. A gift that he will never know about. He will have Andarist as his commander – or will it be Anomander? No matter. He could advance far.*

She walked to the nearest tree, reached out and took hold of a globe of fruit. Soft, ripe. She twisted it loose. *See? No risk of shattering. Nothing like that at all.* She felt something wet trickling down her hand. Gentle as she had been, the skin had split.

*Oh, now I am stained!*

Annoyed, Enesdia flung the fruit into the pond, the splash loud as a retort.

A commission for Cryl. She would have to work hard at hiding her intentions – he seemed to see right through her.

*It's good that he's gone away.*

*　　*　　*

The estate road joined the track leading east, and it was there that Orfantal waited, standing beside a slope-backed nag purchased in Abara Delack, at his side the stable boy, Wreneck, a sour dog-faced boy with greasy hair and a constellation of acne on his broad, flat brow. There had been a time, not so long ago, when Wreneck played with Orfantal, and for those few months – shortly after the fire when the responsibilities of a stable boy more or less ceased to exist – Orfantal had discovered the pleasures of friendship, and in the shambling stable boy an agreeable companion in his imagined wars and battles. But then something had happened and Wreneck grew taciturn and, on occasion, cruel.

Now the boy stood stroking the nag's neck, impatient with the wait as the day's heat built and the sun's glare sharpened. There was no shade to be found barring that cast by the horse. They had stood in this place since shortly after dawn, circled by three feral dogs from town drawn by the smell of the fresh bread and egg pie the servants had made up for Orfantal's lunch, which filled the small hessian bag he clutched in one hand.

There had been no conversation. At ten years, Wreneck was twice Orfantal's age and it seemed that this span of years had become vast, over which no bridge of words could cross. Orfantal thought long and hard on what he might have done to offend Wreneck, but he could think of no way to broach the subject. The stable boy's expression was closed, almost hostile, all his interest seemingly consumed by the somnolent horse at his side.

His legs growing tired, Orfantal went to sit down on the travel trunk containing his clothes, wooden swords and the dozen lead toy soldiers he owned – four Tiste and three Jheleck and five Forulkan, none painted, as his grandmother had concluded that if given paints he would make a mess of the tabletop. He had been astonished to discover that all of his possessions fit into the single, small trunk that had once held his grandfather's war gear – with room to spare. Indeed, he thought he could fit himself into that trunk, and make of his entire life a thing to be carried about, passed from hand to hand, or flung into the ditch and left behind and forgotten by the whole world.

Wreneck wouldn't mind. His mother wouldn't mind; and his grand-mother, who was sending him away, might well be pleased to see the last of him. He wasn't sure, in truth, where he was going, only that it was away, to a place where he would be taught things and be made into a grown-up. Eyeing Wreneck askance, he tried to imagine himself as old as the stable boy, finding the year that unhappiness came to every boy's life, and feeling his own features sag into that angry, helpless expression. And ten years later, his face would find a new set, to match the sadness of his mother.

Hundreds of years after that, he saw himself with his grandmother's face, bearing the look that always reminded him of a hawk eyeing a field mouse speared to the ground by its talons. This was the path to adulthood, he supposed, and Grandmother was sending him off to learn how to live with what everyone had to live with, the steps of growing up, all the faces to find in his own.

A rumble in the road lifted him to his feet, looking west to see a troop of riders and two heavily burdened wagons appear from the dusty haze. The wagons were stacked high in sheep and goat skins, from the culled herds outside Abara Delack, destined for somewhere to the south. This was to be his escort.

Wreneck spoke behind him. 'That's them.'

Orfantal nodded. He fought the urge to take Wreneck's hand, know-ing the boy would sneer and bat his away. When he'd left the Great House this morning, his grandmother's only touch had been a bony hand upon his back, pushing him forward and into Wreneck's care.

'You can go,' Orfantal said as the stable boy came round to stand beside him.

But Wreneck shook his head. 'I'm to make sure you're on the horse, and that the trunk's properly loaded. And that they know where to leave you.'

'But didn't Grandmother arrange all that?'

Wreneck nodded. 'Still, I'm to make sure.'

'All right.' Though he would not say it, Orfantal was glad of the company. He did not recognize any of the riders, after all; they looked dusty and in bad moods as they rode up and reined in, their hooded gazes fixed upon Orfantal.

One gestured to the trunk as the wagons trundled up, and another rider, old and scar-faced, dismounted to collect it. When he crouched to lift it he had been clearly expecting something heavier, and almost tipped on to his backside when he straightened. He shot Orfantal a quizzical look before carrying the trunk to the first wagon, where the driver reached down and heaved it up to position it behind the back-board of his bench.

Wreneck's voice was strangely timid as he said, 'The Citadel. He is nobleborn.'

The lead rider simply nodded.

Turning to Orfantal, Wreneck said, 'Let me help you on to the horse. Her left eye is bad, so she angles to the right. Keep her head tight and stay on the left side of the track – no horse on her left, I mean, as that spooks her.'

'I understand.'

Wreneck's scowl deepened. 'You've never ridden this far all at once. You'll be sore, but her back's broad enough and you got a wide saddle here, so if you need to, you can sit cross-legged on her for a break.'

'All right.'

The stable boy almost threw Orfantal up astride the nag, checked the stirrups once again, and then stepped back. 'That's it,' he said.

Orfantal hesitated, and then said, 'Goodbye, Wreneck.'

The boy turned away, flinging a wave behind him as he set off up the hill back towards the estate.

'We ain't going so fast,' the lead rider now said. 'She'll walk, won't she?'

'Yes sir.'

'Sir?' The man snorted. He took his reins and nudged his mount forward.

Orfantal waited until his mounted companions were past and then kicked his horse into their wake, keeping the beast on the left side of the track. Behind him the oxen jolted into motion at a switch from the driver.

The three wild dogs ran off, as if fearing stones or arrows.

\*     \*     \*

Wreneck paused on the slope and turned to watch them leave. The tears ran down cool on his cheeks and flies buzzed close.

Back to that evil hag now, and no Orfantal to make life easier, to make it better than it was. She'd forbidden him to play with the little boy, and that was mean. She'd told him if she saw him even so much as talking to Orfantal, he'd lose what was left of his job, and then his ma and da would starve and so too his little sisters.

He'd liked playing with the boy. It had reminded him of happier times, when the war was over and things seemed to be getting better for everyone. But then the stables burned down and they'd all heard that Sandalath was being sent away, and then Orfantal too, and the food in the kitchen wasn't as good as it used to be and half the staff was sent off.

And this was a miserable day, and Orfantal had looked so . . . lost.

He should have defied her. He should have wrapped the runt in a big hug. They could have played together all morning while they waited. But he had been afraid. Of her. Of what she might do. But maybe this was better – if he'd showed any kindness then this parting would have been worse for Orfantal. A part of him railed at the thought, but he held to it. To ease his mind.

The dogs returned, and, heads slung low, trailed him all the way back to the estate.

\*　　\*　　\*

It was dusk by the time the caravan arrived outside Toras Keep, setting up camp in the clearing on the other side of the track opposite the keep's gate. Blistered and sore from the ride, Orfantal clambered down from the horse. The scarred old man who'd loaded the trunk now came up to take the reins from his hands.

'Likely her last journey,' he said, pulling the mount away.

Orfantal stared after them. Riding the animal for so long, he had almost forgotten that it was a living creature, the way it had plodded without surcease. He thought about its life, wondered what things it had witnessed in its long journey through the years. The eyes looked sad – Wreneck hadn't even told him the mare's name. He was sure it had one. All living things did, at least those living things that worked for people.

He decided that the mare had once served a warrior in the wars, and had saved that Tiste countless times, yet had looked on helpless when betrayal came to strike down that brave warrior. This was why its eyes were so sad, and now all it longed to do was die, and in so dying re-join its master to haunt old battle grounds and ride through the mist on moonless nights so that villagers heard the heavy hoofs yet saw nothing, and no tracks were left in the mud come the morning. Still, villagers would know that a bold spirit had passed them in the darkness, and they would take up small stones from the path to ease its nightly travels. He'd seen such stones even on this track, in small heaps left to one side, because everyone knew that death was a restless place.

The leader of the troop now approached Orfantal. 'My name is Haral. You don't call me "sir" because I ain't one. I guard merchants and that's all I do.'

'Are there bandits?' Orfantal asked.

'In the hills round Tulas Hold, sometimes. Deniers. Now, you'll be sharing Gripp's tent – that's the man taking care of your horse. You can trust him, when maybe some of these here you can't, not with a little boy in the night. Even with you nobleborn and all. Some hurts people keep secret and that's what bad ones rely on, you see?'

Orfantal didn't, but he nodded anyway.

'They're happy for the work, though, so they know if they cross me it'll be misery for them. Still, I lost most of my regulars. Went to join Dracons' Houseblades. I'm doing the same,' he added, his weathered eyes narrowing as he looked across to the high blackstone walls of Toras Keep. A lone guard was seated on a bench beside the high gate, seemingly watching them all. 'This is my last trip.'

'Were you a soldier once, Haral?'

The man glanced down. 'In my generation, few weren't.'

'My name is Orfantal.'

A scowl twisted his rough features. 'Why'd she do that?'

'Who, what?'

'Your mother. That's Yedan dialect – the monks' holy language. Shake, it's called.'

Orfantal shrugged.

One of the guards, who was crouching to build the cookfire nearby and clearly had been listening in, snorted a laugh and said, 'Means "unwanted", lad. If that don't say it all and you off to Kharkanas.'

Haral turned on the man. 'I'll be glad to see the end of you in my company, Narad. From now on, this trip, keep your damned mouth shut.'

'Fine, as I'm still taking orders from you, but like you say, Haral, that won't last much longer.'

'He's got the meaning wrong,' Haral said to Orfantal. 'The meaning's more obscure, if you like. More like "unexpected".'

Narad snorted again.

The toe of Haral's heavy boot snapped Narad's head to one side in a spray of blood. Dark-faced but silent, Haral then walked up to where the man writhed on the ground. He grasped hold of the long greasy hair and yanked the head up so that he could look into Narad's face. He drove his fist into it, shattering the nose. A second punch slammed the mouth so hard against the teeth that Orfantal saw – through all the blood – the glint of white stitching a line beneath the man's lower lip. Haral then threw the unconscious man back on to the ground and walked away without a backward glance.

169

The others stood motionless for a half-dozen heartbeats, and then one walked over to drag Narad away from the smouldering fire.

Orfantal could barely draw a breath. A fist was hammering inside his chest. He found that he was trembling, as if caught with fever.

Gripp was at his side. 'Easy there,' he muttered. 'It's discipline, that's all it is. Narad's been pushing for weeks. We all knew it was coming and Abyss knows, we warned the fool enough. But he's the dog that ain't got brains enough to know its place. Sooner or later, y'got to kick 'im, and kick hard.'

'Is he dead?'

'I doubt it. If he ain't come around by the morning, we'll just leave him here. He lives or dies by his own straw. He just spat in the face of all the rest – me, I woulda left him toasting on the damned fire. Now, let me show you how to raise a tent. Skills like that might come in handy one day.'

In Orfantal's mind, the faceless betrayer in all his battles now found a face, and a name. Narad, whom nobody wanted, who lived with a stuttered line of scars between chin and mouth, like a cruel smile he could never hide.

\*     \*     \*

Emerging out from the hills, Master-at-arms Ivis and his company came within sight of Dracons Hold, its heavy bulk like a gnarled fist resting on the hard ground. He glanced over at the woman riding at his side. 'We have arrived, milady, but as you can see, Lord Draconus is not in residence. I imagine his journey to the west will see him gone for some weeks yet.'

The hostage nodded. She rode well, yet frailty surrounded her, as it had done since her collapse.

Ivis had convinced her to remove all but the most necessary layers of clothing, and she was revealed as both shapely and thinner than he had at first thought. By his eye he might judge that she'd known childbirth, in the weight of her breasts and in her manner of moving, and of course such things were known to occur, with the illegitimate children quickly whisked away, given up or sent to be raised in ignorance by distant, remote family members. In truth, however, it was none of his business. She was now a hostage in the House of Dracons, twice-used by the desperate matriarch of House Drukorlas, and Ivis was determined to see her treated well.

'Your rooms are awaiting you,' he said as they rode towards the gate. 'If they are not to your liking, be sure to inform me at once and we will see it put aright.'

'Thank you, captain. That is most kind. It is a most imposing house, rising so above the walls.'

'The Lord brought wealth with him when he took up residence.'

'Whence did he come?'

Ivis shook his head. 'Even we who serve in his household are not certain of that. Chosen as heir by Lady Dracons, a cousin she said. In any case,' he added, 'he served well in the wars – no one can deny that. Well enough to earn the regard of Mother Dark.'

'A most loving regard, I have heard.'

'As to that I cannot say, milady. But it suits us well to think so, does it not?'

She studied him briefly, as if uncertain as to his meaning, and then smiled.

Ahead, the gates had been opened and they rode up the track and then into the shadow beneath the heavy lintel stone. Ivis saw Sandalath frowning up at the unknown words carved into the stone, but she ventured no query, and then they were through, riding into the courtyard, where servants and grooms clustered in waiting and voices rose in greeting from a half-dozen Houseblades arrayed in a line. Ivis frowned at the presentation – in his absence, discipline had slackened and he reminded himself to plug the ears of this sorry lot once the hostage was inside.

Dismounting, he passed over the reins to a groom and moved up to help Sandalath down. It seemed her frailty had come upon her again, sudden as a chill, and the relaxed ease she had revealed on occasion during the long ride vanished. Once she was on her feet, servants drew up to fuss over her.

'Milady,' said Ivis. 'The head of the house-servants now serves you in the absence of Lord Draconus. Hilith, present yourself.'

The elderly woman so named had been standing back, close to the stone steps fronting the house, and now she stepped forward with a stiff bow and said, 'Hostage, we welcome you to this house. I see the journey has wearied you. A bath is ready.'

'That is most kind,' Sandalath said.

'If you will follow me?' Hilith asked.

'Of course.' Sandalath stepped forward, and then paused and turned back to Ivis. 'Captain, you have been a most courteous escort. Thank you.'

'My pleasure, milady.'

Hilith instructed two maids to lead Sandalath inside, and then quickly stepped close to Ivis. 'Captain,' she hissed, 'her title is hostage and nothing else. You accord her a title that does not belong to her, not yet in her own house, and never in this one!'

Ivis leaned closer, as if to hint at a formal bow of acquiescence. Instead, he said, in a low tone, 'Old woman, you are no queen to so command me. I will choose the honorific our guest deserves. She rode well and without complaint. If *you* have complaint, await the pleasure of our lord upon his return. In the meantime, spit out that sour grape you so love to suck on, and be dutiful.'

'We shall return to this,' she said in a rasp. 'As you said, I am in charge of the house in our lord's absence—'

'The servants, maids and cooks, yes. Not me.'

'It is unseemly, this twice-used hostage—'

'For which the hostage is not to blame. Now, be gone from this courtyard, where my command holds reign, and if any rumours return to me of your gnawing misery set upon the hostage of this house, we shall indeed return to this.'

He watched her stalk off, and then he glanced across to see a row of grinning Houseblades. 'Smiling, are you? Now isn't that a pleasing sight? Comportment so slovenly I nearly choked in shame to see you. Let us see, shall we, how fare those smiles in the course of double drills. Straighten up, you dogs! Eyes forward!'

*     *     *

The servants struggled with the travel chest as they carried it into the room. Looking round, marvelling at the vastness of the chamber that was to be her quarters, Sandalath gestured to one wall. 'Set that over there. No, do not open it – the only clothing I will use is in those saddle bags – terribly creased by now, I should imagine. They will need cleaning.' This last detail she addressed to the two maids standing before her. Both women, younger than Sandalath by a few years, quickly bowed and set to unpacking the saddle bags. The other servants retreated from the room.

A moment later Hilith entered, glanced once at the rumpled clothing now appearing from the dusty leather bags, and then faced Sandalath. 'Hostage, if you will accompany me, we shall see to your bath.'

'Is the water hot? I prefer it hot.'

The old woman blinked and then nodded. 'It is indeed, hostage. Or it was when we last left it. I imagine it is cooling even as we speak.'

'I trust the fire is close, Hilith, should more heat be required. Now, please do lead on. Afterwards, I wish a tour of this house I now call my own.'

Hilith tilted her head and then marched from the room.

Sandalath followed.

'Upon the Lord's return,' the matron said over her shoulder, 'the two maids attending you shall be at your call. I, however, have other responsibilities that will demand my attention.'

'Day and night, I am sure.'

Hilith shot a glance back at her and then continued on. 'Just so.'

'In the meantime,' Sandalath said, 'you will attend to me, as if the house were my own.'

'Just so,' Hilith snapped without turning this time.

'If the bath is insufficiently heated, I will wait for the remedy.'

'Of course, hostage.'

'I am curious, Hilith. Were you in charge of the household staff in the time of Lady Dracons?'

'I was.'

'Then you have indeed given your life to this service.'

'Without regret, hostage.'

'Indeed? That is very well, then, isn't it?'

She made no reply to that. Their swift passage down the hallway came to an end at a landing leading down. Hilith led Sandalath down the stairs, into a steamy laundry room dominated by a huge basin. Two maids – laundry-beaters by their chafed hands – stood in waiting beside the basin.

'These will attend to you now,' Hilith said, turning to leave.

The smell of lye was overwhelming, and Sandalath felt her eyes beginning to water. 'A moment,' she said.

'Hostage?' Hilith's expression was innocent.

'Tell me, does the Lord bathe in this chamber?'

'Of course not!'

'Then neither shall I. I stand in his stead in his absence, and I will bathe accordingly. Have freshly boiled, clean water brought to the appropriate chamber. I wish this done in haste, so I will entrust the task's overseeing to you, Hilith.' Sandalath gestured to one of the maids. 'This one will lead me to the proper bathing room.'

Hilith's narrow face was pale despite the heat. 'As you wish, hostage.'

In her first time as a hostage, in the Citadel, there had been a frightening hag still tottering in the service of Lord Nimander's household, and she had been most cruel – until by chance Andarist was made aware of the endless torment. That hag had disappeared. If Hilith were to prove a similar harridan, then Sandalath would speak to Draconus, and see the woman deposed and sent away.

She was not a child any more, to cower before such creatures.

As she walked with the young laundress, she said, 'If I have made an enemy, I trust I will in turn have many allies?'

Wide eyes lifted to her, and then the girl's round face split into a broad smile. 'Hundreds, mistress! Thousands!'

'My father was a hero in the wars,' Sandalath said, 'and I am his daughter.'

'In the wars! Like Ivis!'

'Like Ivis,' she agreed. 'Is Ivis well liked?'

'He never looks happy, mistress, and is known to be harsh with his soldiers. But to us he is ever kind.'

'As he was to me. Will you tell me more of him?'

'All I know!'

'Do you think him handsome? Soldiers have a way about them, I think.'

'But he is old, mistress!'

'Perhaps in your eyes, he is. But I see a man still in his years of strength, younger than my father, and sure of command. No doubt Lord Draconus values him most highly.'

They came to a heavy wooden door, artfully carved in intricate geometric patterns. The girl pushed it open to reveal a narrow room tiled from floor to ceiling, and at the far end a wash basin and then a tub of copper, large enough to accommodate a man. As Sandalath entered the chamber, she felt waves of heat rising from the floor. Crouching, she set a palm flat upon the tiles. 'There is fire beneath?'

The girl nodded. 'I think so, yes. I am rarely here, mistress. But there are flues from the Great Hearth, leading everywhere.'

'Then this is not a cold house in the winter.'

'No, mistress, it is blessedly warm!'

Sandalath looked round. 'I feel welcomed by this house, most welcomed.'

The girl smiled again. 'You are very pretty, mistress. We'd thought—'

'What did you all think? Tell me.'

'We thought you'd be a child, mistress.'

'As are most new hostages, yes. But you see, I have done this before. And truth be told, in some ways I feel a child again. Every day, the world is born anew.'

The girl sighed.

'Born anew,' Sandalath repeated, breathing deep the warm, scented air.

# SEVEN

THERE WERE MOMENTS OF LUCIDITY, WHEN FINARRA STONE BECAME aware of strange, discordant details. She was bound to Spinnock Durav, a horse labouring under them both. Black blades of Glimmer Fate's savage grasses rasped against the mount's wooden armour, rustled past like swirling waves. It was night and she could smell Spinnock's sweat, could feel his heat against her chilled body.

She slipped away, only to awaken again, and this time she saw before them a wavering blur of yellow light, swimming in a penumbra that seethed with moths and bats. The frenzied motion of the creatures hurt her eyes and she looked away, to where the high grasses had been chopped down, forming a killing field surrounding the fort; and then the walls, stretched out beneath the lantern suspended above the gate – the 'logs' of bound grass, patchy with sun-fired black clay – the gate opening and sudden voices – she felt Spinnock sag as ropes were cut and she was gently drawn away from him.

Firm hands carried her quickly into the fort, crossing the compound, a flare of harsher light, the gust of heat from a fire, and then she was inside the main room. They set her down on a bench. A dog brushed close, wet nose smearing the back of her swollen hand, and was then sent scurrying with a slap.

Finarra blinked her vision clear and found she was staring up at her commander's face, the man's features grave, his eyes firelit from a blazing hearth. 'We have guests, captain,' he said to her. 'Serendipitous guests. Ilgast Rend is with us, well versed in the healing arts. The poison will be expunged – he wagers your leg will be saved. Do you understand my words?'

175

She nodded.

'Spinnock tells us of Faror Hend's mission – she has not yet returned. Tracking a stranger from the Vitr – this was not wise.'

'The decision,' Finarra said, startled at finding her voice sounding so thin, so cracked, 'was hers.'

'Her betrothed is with us. He even now prepares a troop to set out in search of her.'

*Kagamandra Tulas? Has he come for her, then?* She stumbled in the confusion of her own thoughts. Where was Spinnock? What had driven Faror Hend into such a foolhardy venture? She suddenly recalled the look in Faror's eyes, at the moment when she was about to ride into the high grasses. *The lust for death, the curse of the Tiste.* Had Faror known that her betrothed was coming for her? But Finarra had heard nothing of that before they'd departed, and she most certainly would have done.

'She is in great danger,' she said to Calat Hustain.

'You know more of this stranger, then?'

'Inimical. Defiant of death. They may be . . . Soletaken.'

'From the Vitr? You speak of more than one – have invaders come among us?'

'They come,' she said. 'Eager to slay. The one Faror tracks, it took a human form. A child or woman. No less dangerous. Upon the shore . . . my horse, slain.'

'I will send a troop back upon your trail, captain.'

'Tell them . . . do not assume death in what they find, no matter the evidence before their eyes.'

'Ilgast Rend will attend to you now, captain. He will make you sleep.'

She struggled to sit up. 'I have slept too long as it is—'

'You are fevered. Infection has set in – the bite of a naked wolf. He will scour it from your blood. If you refuse to sleep, there will be great pain. There is no virtue in knowing it.'

'I was careless—'

'If this proves a matter for disciplining, that is for me to decide, captain. Lie back, the Lord insists.'

She relented, caught site of Ilgast Rend's broad, battered face, the softness in his eyes. He set a calloused hand upon her brow, and darkness flooded up to take her.

*      *      *

Watching from a distance, Hunn Raal stood with his arms crossed, his back resting against a smoke-stained wall of cracked clay. He was drunk, but in the way of old, in that few could tell, and his thoughts, while loose, were clear enough. Beside him was Osserc, his young face high with colour from the unexpected excitement of this broken troop's

176

return. The Vitr was a mystery, to be sure, but until now it had been indifferent in its destruction, no more malicious than a winter storm or spring flood. The thought of that vast sea bearing ships or some such thing, followed by the heavy footfalls of invaders, was indeed alarming.

They did not need another war, and yet in that possibility Hunn Raal could see certain advantages, though he could not but view them with unease. The resurrection of Urusander's Legion. An invasion would give cause to take up arms once more, in a flurry of veterans reinstated, and so set the stage for undeniable clout should internal matters turn sour and threats were needed. Of course, this assumed that the invaders could be quickly dealt with, and Hunn Raal was reluctant to walk that path. He well understood the risks of being dismissive, and was not unaware of how sweet self-serving beliefs could taste in these heady times.

He could see Calat Hustain's sudden sharpness on the matter. The commander had a quick and sure cause now to dismiss the turgid debate that had threatened to bog them all down in this fort for days, if not weeks. Ilgast Rend had spoken in private with Calat, and there had been betrayal in that, Hunn suspected. The firstborn son of Hust Henarald was now adamant in his neutrality, and in the immediate aftermath of that decision this had amounted to a defeat in Hunn Raal's eyes.

But in truth he had no cause to be shocked by it. And in some ways, now that he'd time to mull on the matter, he might even consider it a kind of victory. Calat was married to the commander of the Hust Legion, after all, and everyone knew that the Hust Legion belonged to Mother Dark, and were one and all her children.

There would be highborn who were determined to oppose the ascension of Urusander, but without the Hust Legion behind them, they could hardly pose a credible threat to Urusander's forces. Houseblades were all very well, impressive in battle, but they numbered too few. The will of seven thousand soldiers, all loyal to the cause, would drive Urusander into Mother Dark's arms, and if they needed to roll over a few hundred Houseblades on the march, well, that would suffice as clear warning to the other noble families.

*Power will shift to us. But we seek no tyranny. Only justice. We fought and many of us fell, and those that remain must not be forgotten or cast aside.*

'This is disturbing,' Osserc said under his breath. 'Hunn Raal, have you seen this Vitr for yourself?'

Hunn Raal shook his head. 'A devouring sea, I am told.'

'What manner of invaders might come from there? Soletaken – might they be kin to the Jheleck, then, taking the form of giant wolves?'

'We shall find out soon enough.'

Osserc leaned close. 'Ill-timed, this. We must set aside—'

'Not at all,' Hunn Raal cut in. 'If anything, this has potential to serve us well. Our disbanded kin will have their commissions returned to them – indeed, I envisage our new mission to be riding to Kharkanas with word of this new threat. Or, rather, I will do so. You had best return to your father, to apprise him of what may be, by Mother Dark's own command, his necessary return to service.'

Osserc frowned. 'He may well refuse.'

'He will not,' Hunn Raal replied. 'Your father knows his duty.'

'Perhaps he will charge me with taking his place.'

The obvious answer to that served no value, so Hunn Raal instead assumed a thoughtful expression, but one bearing a glint of amusement. 'Why do you think I invite you to bring the news to your father? The two of you will speak, and decisions of the blood will be made. Stand tall before him, friend, and be resolute in your regard. Show nothing of eagerness or avid desire. Assume a troubled mien, but not too troubled, obviously. Sober and stern shall serve our cause well, in both your imminent aspiration and indeed in ours as well.'

Osserc slowly nodded. 'Well said. I shall leave at once—'

'I would think morning will do. Perhaps even later. It will do us well to hear Calat Hustain's thoughts on the matter of this threat, and his course of action beyond sending a troop out to investigate. We are now here as representatives of the Legion, and we must be direct in our offers to assist.'

But Osserc scowled. 'Well enough for you, Hunn, but I am representative of nothing—'

'Untrue. Here, and in the morning, you will stand in your father's stead, and I will be certain to make the others aware of that.'

'But what will I say to them?'

'Nothing. Just listen and, if a sharp question pricks you awake, voice it. But be spare in your queries – let others ask the bulk of them, and heed well the conversations to follow.'

Osserc nodded, although he remained nervous.

'See Sharenas over there?' Hunn Raal asked. 'She watches and listens – not to my cousins so eager to adopt her, but to Ilgast and Calat. Heed her methods, Osserc. She plays well these political scenes.'

'We must learn more of this Vitr.'

'We shall,' Hunn Raal assured him. *And probably have little say in the matter, for I feel events quickening.*

*     *     *

Sharenas had watched Tulas leave the room, had observed with interest the man's sudden acuity. Dead in spirit he might be, but in the matter of salvation of others – in this case his betrothed – he was first to the fore. In fact, she could almost see the lurid flames ignited in him, this potential opportunity to die in defence of the woman he was to take as wife, and so live pure in noble grief for ever, rather than descend into the squalid truths of an unhappy marriage, where old ashes would begin settling on glory before the last stone was set on the threshold of their new home.

There was something almost pathetic in Kagamandra's energy as he prepared to set out into the night in search of Faror Hend. This was a man who would wither without hands and feet, without the promise of sure motion and actions to undertake with verve and will. But those brave expostulations were all short-lived, the echoes of deeds quickly falling away, and what was the poor man left with, but a renewed silence or, worse, the unheard howl inside his own skull? No, far better these hands in motion, these feet to carry him; better all these things that need doing, and indeed could be done with.

To bind a broken man, by word or thread or chain, was ever a lost cause. Worse yet, how likely was the broken man to in turn break all that was given to him, including young Faror Hend? Was it not Gallan who wrote '*On trembling floor / ashes will flow*', and would not Faror's world tremble so in the company of Kagamandra Tulas? *He will dust her, coat her from head to toe, and she will become the hue of stone, a statue blind to every garden. Gallan, you should write about this betrothal, and set it well upon a stage. I see knives in the wings.*

Serap leaned close, ale-soured breath hot on Sharenas's cheek, 'Join us tonight, will you? See how heated it's all become? Blood rushes close under the skin at times like these.'

'What times would those be?' Sharenas asked drily.

On Serap's other side, Sevegg giggled behind her hand.

*Hunn Raal's whores. That's all they are. He brings them and casts them out among those he would make into allies or, Abyss forbid, friends. But I'm not interested in that, dear captain. I fall in on your cause, as will my sister and cousin. Be content with that, lest you sour my regard.* She stepped away from the cousins, evading a drunken paw from Risp, and strode from the main room.

In the small compound, she found Tulas saddling a horse. Six Wardens were doing the same with their own mounts, while a dozen of their comrades checked over the kits of those soon to leave the fort. Lanternlight played out yellow and filled with night insects. Sharenas found a groom standing nearby and gestured him over. 'Ready my horse,' she told him. 'I will ride with them.'

The boy hurried away.

Looking up, she saw Tulas staring across at her.

Sharenas walked to him. 'You know my skill with a spear,' she said.

He continued studying her for a moment longer, and then turned back to his horse. 'You are most welcome, Sharenas Ankhadu, and I thank you.'

'There is too little love in the world to see it so endangered.'

She saw how her words made him stiffen – but slightly, as he was a man used to self-control. 'Have you spoken to Spinnock Durav?' she asked.

'I did, before exhaustion took him.'

'Then we have a trail awaiting us.'

'Yes.'

The groom returned with her horse. She resigned herself to a long, wearying ride. But she was determined to witness this pursuit. *Anyway, better the horse than the whore. If that Durav had eyes open this night, well, I might have stayed in the fort. A most handsome young warrior.*

*I wonder if Finarra and Faror shared him out there in the wilds?*

Amused by the thought, she climbed into the saddle and took up the reins.

The others were ready. The gate was opened once more this night, and they all rode out.

*     *     *

Ensconced in the commander's private room, modest as it was, Ilgast Rend settled in the rickety chair, wincing as it creaked beneath him. Opposite him, in a matching chair, Calat Hustain asked, 'Your thoughts on what she had to say, Lord?'

Ilgast rubbed hard at his eyes, blinked away swimming blots of colour, and then scratched down through his beard, considering. 'I spared them no room, commander.'

'Ah, of course. The efforts at healing must try you, Lord. I admit to a sense of wonder, at this rare skill with earth and heat, moulds and roots. Upon battle's field, I have seen miracles performed with sharp knife and gut and thorn, but this mysterious sorcery you have found in such mundane things, it is most astonishing.'

'There is power in nature,' Ilgast replied, 'and what is often forgotten is that nature lies within us as much as it does out there, amidst high grasses or shoreline. To heal is to draw across the divide; that and nothing more.'

'It is said that such power grows.'

Ilgast frowned at the suggestion, not because he would deny it, but because the notion – which he himself sensed – disturbed him. 'It was ever my belief, commander, that we who blinked the mist clear from our eyes, and so saw truly the flow of life, were but privileged, by quirk of temper or gift of vision. We beheld a power in constancy, yet one

180

unaware of itself. Of no mind, if you will. Neither living nor dead; rather, like the wind.' He paused, chewing on those thoughts, and then sighed and shook his head. 'But now, I grow to sense . . . something. A hint of deliberation. Purpose. As if, in taking from the power, it shifts a shoulder and sets regard upon the taker.'

'That is . . . strange, Lord.'

'As if in looking down into the river,' Ilgast continued, his frown deepening, 'one discovers the river looking back up at you. Or a stone returning stern attention. A glance catching the eye of earth, or sand.' He rubbed vigorously at his face again. 'It leaves one startled, I tell you, as if in an instant the world is unmade, and all its comforts are revealed as false, and the solitude we'd thought private was in truth played out before a silent audience; and the minds that gave thought to all we did, why, they think nothing like us.'

He saw Calat Hustain look away, into the fire.

'Forgive me, commander,' Ilgast said, with a gruff laugh. 'Healing wearies me. There is a Shake word to describe that sense, as of the myriad things in nature giving sudden and most fixed attention upon a person, and the uncanny shiver that comes of it.'

Calat nodded, eyes still on the fire. '*Denul.*'

'Just so.'

'But the monks speak of it as a kind of ecstasy. A moment of spiritual revelation.'

'And if the revelation diminishes the self? What ecstasy is found in that?'

'That of helplessness, I should imagine.'

'Commander, I dislike helplessness.'

'And so you wage battle with *Denul.*'

*Perhaps. Yes, it could be seen that way.* 'Her wounds will mend. The poison is gone. She will lose no limbs, and even now the last of the fever rides out on her breath. Your captain will return to you, sound of mind and body, in a few days hence.'

'I thank you, Lord.'

Ilgast studied the commander for a moment and then asked, 'This Vitr – you have taken its challenge upon yourself. What can be made of the captain's claim that strangers have crossed this inimical sea?'

Calat smiled. 'So you gave heed after all.' He shook his head. 'I admit, I am inclined to disbelieve. Stone is devoured by the liquid. Wood crumbles after a few moments in contact with it. Flesh burns and the air upon the sea is itself caustic. What vessel could survive those alien waters?'

'She spoke of no vessels, no ships. She said the strangers have come *from* the sea. She spoke, with little coherence it is true, of a demon lying on the beach, a thing that appeared to be dead.'

'This night,' Calat said, 'I have only questions.'

'Have you theories on the origin of this Vitr?'

'You well know I am firm in my opinion that it poses a grave threat to Kurald Galain. It is destroying land. With each surge of wave more of our world is taken away, never to reappear. Storms open like jaws and teeth descend to tear away stone and clay. Cliffs weaken and crumble, slide down into oblivion. We map these inroads—'

'Commander, I would hear your theories instead.'

Calat scowled. 'Forgive me, Lord, but in that I am frustrated. Where are the legends of the Vitr? Not among us. Perhaps among the Azathanai there are old tales referring to it, but I know nothing of them. The Jaghut, in all their written histories, might well have made note of the Vitr; indeed, the entirety of its reason might have been plainly writ in their works—'

'But those works have all been destroyed, by their own hands—'

'By the Lord of Hate, you mean. It was his arguments that mined unto crumbling the foundations of the Jaghut, until they could not trust all they stood upon. The losses to us all, of that vast knowledge, are immeasurable.'

Ilgast Rend grunted. 'I never shared your respect for the Jaghut, commander. They remind me of the Deniers in the manner in which they turned away from the future – as if to wash their hands of it. But we must all face our days and nights, for they are what await us. Not even a Jaghut can walk back into his or her past. No matter how directionless a step seems when taken, it is always forward.'

'The Lord of Hate would not disagree with you, Lord. Which is why he has chosen to stand still. To take no step at all.'

'Yet time bends not to his deep root,' Ilgast retorted in a growl. 'It but flows around and past. He vows to forget and so is forgotten.'

'He has slain their civilization,' Calat Hustain said, 'and in so doing, proclaimed all knowledge to be dust. And so I am made to feel, Lord, gaping pits awaiting us ahead, that need not have been, if not for the Lord of Hate.'

'The loss is only in what was written, commander. Might it serve us, in the matter of the Vitr, to seek out the counsel of a Jaghut? All have not dispersed, I understand. Some still reside in their old keeps and holds. I am of a mind to seek one out.'

'Yet now the Jheleck have laid claim to the abandoned lands.'

Ilgast shrugged. 'They could claim the heavens, for all it matters. A Jaghut choosing to remain in a tower cannot be moved, and those Soletaken fools should know better.' He snorted. 'Like any dog that's been whipped, it is never humble for long. Stupidity returns triumphant.'

'Hunn Raal carries word to Kharkanas in the morning,' Calat Hustain said.

Ilgast regarded the commander with level eyes.

*     *     *

Trailing the woman she had named T'riss, Faror Hend saw the last of the high grasses dwindle a short distance ahead, and beyond it, worn and rotted, the range of denuded hills lying to the west of Neret Sorr. The sun was past zenith and heat shimmered in the still air. They rode clear and Faror called out to halt.

Their journey through Glimmer Fate had been uneventful, and in her exhaustion Faror had begun to believe that they wandered lost, despite her reading of the night sky, and that they might never find a way through the endless cobwebs and rustling blades. But now, at last, the Fate was behind them. She dismounted, legs weak beneath her. 'We must rest for a time,' she said. 'I wager your horse is tireless, but mine is not.'

The woman slipped down from the grass-bound beast, stepped away. The simulacrum stood motionless, a woven sculpture too robust, too raw to be elegant. The faint wind against its angular form made a soft chorus of whistles. Red and black ants swarmed its neck, emerging from some hidden root-nest.

Faror Hend drew free the heavy water bag for her horse, loosened the leather mouth and set it down for the beast to drink. She drank from her own waterskin and then offered it to T'riss.

The woman approached. 'Vitr?'

Startled, Faror Hend shook her head. 'Water. Against the thirst.'

'I will try it, then.'

Faror watched the woman drink, tentatively at first, and then eagerly. 'Not too much too quickly, else you sicken.'

T'riss lowered the skin, her eyes suddenly bright. 'The ache in my throat is eased.'

'I imagine Vitr did not manage the same.'

The woman frowned, glanced back at the forest of high grass. 'An excess of vitality,' she said, 'can burn the soul.' She looked again to Faror. 'But this water, it pleases me. I imagine it in full coolness, about my limbs. Tell me, is there water in abundance?'

'In places, yes. In others, no. The hills to the south were once green, but when the last of the trees were cut down the soil died. There remains a single spring, which we must now ride to. It is, however, a risk. There are outlaws – they first became a problem during the wars. Men and women who refused to join the legions and saw opportunity once the soldiers departed. Such militias as a town or village mustered were too small to extend patrols beyond the settlement's outskirts.'

183

'These outlaws command the spring?'

'Like us, they depend upon it. When a troop of Wardens or a well-armed caravan arrive to make use of the water, they hide. We are but two, and they will see in that an invitation to make trouble.'

'Do they wish to rob us, Faror Hend?'

The Warden looked back at the grass horse. 'They may have cause to hesitate. Otherwise, we must fight to protect ourselves.'

'I will see this spring, this place of abundant water. Are you rested, Faror Hend?'

'No. Feed for the horse, and then for us.'

'Very well.'

Faror Hend regarded her. 'T'riss, you seem new to your . . . your form. This body you wear and its needs. Water. Food. Do you know what you were before?'

'Tonight,' T'riss said, 'I will dream of water.'

'Do you not understand my meaning?'

'Dreams in the Vitr are . . . unpleasant. Faror Hend, I begin to understand this world. To make, one must first destroy. The grasses I made use of are even now losing their life, in this my mount, and in these my clothes. We dwell in the midst of destruction. This is the nature of this world.'

'You are indeed a stranger,' Faror observed. 'A visitor. Do you come with a purpose?'

'Do you?' T'riss asked. 'Have you its knowing upon your birth? This purpose you speak of?'

'One comes to discover the things that one must do in a life,' Faror replied.

'Then what you do is your purpose for being, Faror Hend?'

'No,' she admitted. 'Not always. Forgive me, but I saw you as a harbinger. Created by someone or something unknown, for a cause – and come among us for a reason. But your challenge shames me. None of us knows our own purpose – why we were born, the reason that sets us here. There are many meanings to each life, but none serve to ease the coldest question of all, which is *why?* We ask it of the Abyss, and no answer arrives but the echo of our own cry.'

'I meant no challenge, Faror Hend. Your words give me much to think about. I have no memories of the time before.'

'Yet you recognize *Azathanai*.'

But T'riss frowned. 'What is Azathanai?'

Faror Hend blinked, and then her eyes narrowed. 'There is knowledge hidden within you, T'riss. Hidden with intent. It pushes your thoughts away. It needs you unknowing.'

'Why would it do that?'

*I can think of but one reason. You are dangerous.* 'I don't know,

T'riss. For now, I am taking you to Kharkanas. The problem you pose is well beyond me.'

'The Vitr is your enemy.'

Faror had turned to feed her horse; now she shot T'riss a sharp look over a shoulder. 'Is it?'

But the strange woman's face was blank, her eyes wide and innocent. 'I believe I am hungry.'

'We will eat, and then ride on.'

T'riss was as enamoured of food as she had been of water, and would have devoured all that remained of their supplies if not for a word from Faror Hend. The Warden thought to question her guest further, but did not know where to start. The child-like innocence in her seemed to exist like islands, and the seas surrounding them were deep, fathomless. And each island proved barren once reached, while between them, amidst dark tumultuous waves, Faror floundered. But one thing seemed clear: T'riss was losing knowledge, as if afflicted by a disease of the mind, a Loss of Iron; or perhaps the new body she had taken – this woman's form with its boyish proportions – was imposing its own youthful ignorance. And in the absence of what she had been, something new was emerging, something avid in its appetites.

They mounted up and resumed the journey. The landscape around them was level, dotted here and there by thorny brush, the soil cracked and shrivelled by drought – as it had been since Faror had first joined the Wardens. She sometimes wondered if Glimmer Fate was feeding on the lands surrounding it, drawing away its sustenance as would a river-leech snuggling warm flesh; and indeed, might not this sea of black grasses mark the shallows of the Vitr itself, evidence of the poison seeping out?

Faror Hend's gaze fell upon her companion, who still rode ahead, the beast beneath T'riss creaking and still leaking dust, dirt and insects. *Is she the truth of the Vitr? Is this the message we are meant to take from her? Ignorant of us and indifferent to our destruction? Is she to be the voice of nature: that speaks without meaning; that acts without reason?*

But then, if this were true, why the need for a messenger at all? The Sea of Vitr delivered its truth well enough, day after day, year upon year. What had changed? Faror's eyes narrowed on T'riss. *Only her. Up from the depths, cast upon this shore. Newborn and yet not. Alone, but Finarra spoke of others – demons.*

The hills drew nearer as the afternoon waned. They met no other riders; saw no signs of life beyond the stunted shrubs and the aimless pursuits of winged insects. The sky was cloudless, the heat oppressive.

The rough ground ahead slowly resolved itself in deepening shadows, the clawed tracks of desiccated, sundered hillsides, the gullies where

185

runoff had once thundered down but now only dust sifted, stirred by dry winds.

Faror's eyes felt raw with lack of sleep. The mystery posed by T'riss had folded up her mind like a tattered sheet of vellum. Hidden now, all the forbidden words of desire; and even her concern for the fate of the captain – as well as that of Spinnock Durav – was creased and obscured, tucked away and left in darkness.

Closer now, she made out a trail cutting into the ridgeline. It was clear that T'riss had seen it as well, for she guided her mount towards it.

'Be wary now,' Faror Hend said.

The woman glanced back. 'Shall I raise us an army?'

'What?'

T'riss gestured. 'Clay and rock, the dead roots beneath. Armed with slivers of stone. Below the deep clays there are bones, as well, and the husks of enormous insects all wonderfully hued.'

'Can you make anything from the land surrounding you?'

'If it had occurred to me,' she replied, reining in, 'I could have made guardians from the grasses, but in shape only that which I have seen. A horse, or one such as you and me.'

'Yet you fashioned a sword with which to defend yourself, before we met.'

'This is true. I cannot explain that, unless I have perhaps seen such a weapon before, only to have since forgotten. It seems my memory is flawed, is it not?'

'I believe so, yes.'

'If we are many, the outlaws will avoid us. So you said.'

'I did.' Faror hesitated, and then said, 'What power do you draw upon, T'riss, in the fashioning of such creatures? Does it come from the Vitr?'

'No. The Vitr does not create, it destroys.'

'Yet you came from it.'

'I was not welcome there.'

This was new. 'Are you certain of that?'

T'riss was still for a moment, and then she nodded. 'It assailed me. Age upon age, I fought. There was no thought but the struggle itself, and this struggle, I think, consumed all that I once was.'

'Yet something returns to you.'

'The questions you would not ask have given me much to think about – no, I do not read your mind. I can only guess them, Faror Hend, but I see well the battles they wage upon your countenance. Even exhaustion cannot dull your unease. I remember the pain of the Vitr: it remains, like a ghost that would swallow me whole.'

'Whence comes your power, then?'

'I do not know, but it delivers pain upon this world. I dislike this, but if necessity demands, I will use it.'

'Then I would rather you did not, T'riss. The world knows enough pain as it is.'

To that T'riss nodded.

'I suspect now,' Faror resumed, 'that you are Azathanai. That you sought to war against the Vitr, or, perhaps, that you set out seeking its source, its purpose. In the battle you waged, much of yourself was lost.'

'If this is true, Faror Hend, then my only purpose is my own – none other seeks to guide me, or indeed use me. Are you relieved? I am. Do you think that I will return to myself?'

'I don't know. It is a worthy hope.'

T'riss turned back and nudged her mount forward.

Faror Hend followed.

The trail was well used, and not long ago a score of shod horses had travelled it, coming round from the west along the range's edge, the most recent hoofprints heading in the same direction as the two riders.

'I think we shall find company at the spring,' said Faror Hend, moving up alongside T'riss. 'But not outlaws.'

'Friends?'

Faror's nod was cautious. 'A troop, I think. Perhaps a militia, out from Neret Sorr, or Yan Shake to the south.'

'Let us see.'

They rode on.

The path twisted between crags, climbing steeply in places before levelling out across the spine of the first line of hills. Ahead, a short distance away, the ruins of a gate marked the pass. Off to one side was a lone blockhouse collapsed on two sides, revealing a gut crowded with broken masonry, tiles and withered timbers from the roof. The scatter of shattered tiles crunched under the hoofs of Faror's plodding horse as they rode past. She saw her mount's nostrils flare, followed by a pricking of its ears. 'Not far now,' she said quietly.

Beyond the gate, they traversed the remnants of a cobbled road, the surface buckled in places; in others the cobbles buried under white dirt made silver in the dying light. Shortly later, they came within sight of the spring, a green-fringed pond half encircled by pale-trunked trees. Figures moved about and horses could be seen, tethered to a long rope strung between two ironwood boles.

T'riss reined in. 'I smell blood.'

The words chilled Faror. The men she could see were all dressed in light grey robes, hitched up round their legs to reveal supple sheaths of leather armour cladding their thighs, knees and shins. The bulk of their upper bodies hinted at more of the same beneath the thin wool.

Single-bladed axes hung from rope belts at their hips. The men were bareheaded, their hair shaggy, wild.

A dozen or so were busy digging graves, while others slowly converged upon that impromptu burial ground, dragging corpses splashed in blood.

T'riss pointed at one of the dead bodies. 'Outlaws?'

Faror Hend nodded. Two robed figures were approaching. The larger of the two by far was thick-limbed, the muscles of his shoulders slung down as if by their own weight. His nose, twisted and flattened, dominated his weathered face, but the blue eyes were bright as they fixed on T'riss's mount. Lying across this man's broad back was a two-handed axe, single-bladed and spiked, over which he rested his hands.

His companion was almost effete in comparison, his skin pale and his features watery in the manner of the oft-ill. The short axe tucked behind his belt bore a shattered haft, and the man's forearms were almost black with blood up to the elbows.

'Death rides their breath,' T'riss said in a cool voice. 'Are these your kin?'

'Monks of the Yannis Monastery,' Faror replied. 'We are within the demesne of Mother Dark. This is Kurald Galain.'

'They took no prisoners.'

Close to thirty slain outlaws – men, women and children – now lay beside the gravediggers. Off to one side of the pond, a makeshift village pushed through the trees, shacks like open sores, doorways gaping, possessions abandoned. Woodsmoke drifted.

The smaller of the two monks spoke to Faror, 'Warden, your arrival is well timed. Had you come here yesterday, you'd be the sport of little boys by now. I am Lieutenant Caplo Dreem, commanding this troop of Yan Shake. And this drooling fool at my side is Warlock Resh.'

Resh addressed T'riss, his voice melodious, like water on stone. 'Welcome, Azathanai. That is a fine horse you've made, but I wonder, can you hear its screams?'

T'riss turned to Faror Hend and her expression was grave. 'It seems that I shall be delayed somewhat in my journey to Kharkanas.'

'Not too long I should imagine,' the warlock said. 'Yan Shake is on the way to the Wise City, after all.'

Faror Hend straightened. 'Excuse me, but this woman is in my charge. I will deliver her to Kharkanas, and without delay.'

Caplo cleared his throat, as if embarrassed. 'Your pardon, but you must be Faror Hend. Calat has fifty Wardens out looking for you, not to mention Kagamandra Tulas, who happened to be visiting your commander's camp. Your presence is required by your commander, at once. To any who might come upon you, such was the message you were to receive.'

'This guest,' said Resh, with little in the way of welcome in his eyes as they held unwavering upon T'riss, 'is now under the protection of the Yan Shake.'

'I will convey my protest to Calat Hustain,' said Faror Hend, furious – but it was the best she could manage, so confounded were her thoughts. *Kagamandra Tulas? Has he come for me? How dare he! I am a Warden of the Outer Reaches, not some wayward child!*

T'riss spoke to her. 'My friend, it seems that we must part. For your company, I thank you.'

'This sits well with you?' Faror asked her, hands tight on the saddle horn to still their tremble.

'If I tire of their company, I will continue on to Kharkanas, to meet Mother Dark. With respect to my person, I am safe enough. This warlock thinks much of himself, but he poses no threat to me.'

Caplo coughed. 'Excuse me, but please, there is no threat in any of this. We are returning south, and without question Mother Sheccanto Derran will wish to meet this Azathanai, thus requiring a brief stay in Yan Shake. It is but a courtesy, I assure you.'

'You'd best keep it so,' Faror snapped.

T'riss was now studying the lieutenant. 'I see you are well acquainted with blood, sir.'

'I am, Azathanai. This band of cut-throats have well earned their fate, I assure you. Unpleasant tasks—'

'And the children?' T'riss asked. 'Were they too cut-throats?'

'Clay in twisted hands,' Caplo replied. 'They fought alongside their kin. The newborn were slain by their own, when we would have welcomed such waifs into our monastery.'

'Despair raises high walls,' Resh said, shrugging. 'Lieutenant, the Azathanai spoke in truth. She has immense sorcery within her, like a child waiting to be born. Best not twist her hands.'

'We shall display the utmost courtesy.'

'Then I shall ask of you a favour,' T'riss said to Caplo. 'Provide Faror Hend with an escort, and perhaps a fresher horse. I would no harm come to her now that she must return to her camp.'

'Unnecessary,' Faror said. 'But thank you, T'riss—'

'T'riss!' grunted the warlock, eyes widening. 'No gift from the Vitr, this woman!'

Faror Hend sighed, 'And in your denial you reveal what?' She faced Caplo again. 'Lieutenant, in the message you received from the Wardens, was there word of Captain Finarra Stone?'

'Yes. She will recover. But if there is cause for concern now, it must be for your betrothed, who rides with haste to the very shore of the Vitr itself.'

'That is his decision.' Even as she said it, she saw Caplo's brows lift.

'Be assured that he does not do so alone,' the lieutenant continued, once again looking embarrassed. 'A troop of Wardens accompany him, as does Sharenas Ankhadu.'

'Sharenas Ankhadu?'

'Your commander entertained guests – I am sure I mentioned that, did I not? No matter. We met Captain Hunn Raal upon the road, as he rode with three spare mounts for Kharkanas. Of his mission, alas, we know nothing.' But now his innocent gaze settled upon T'riss, and then he smiled.

*Abyss take all these games!* 'Was there word of Captain Finarra Stone's companion?'

'Safe and sound, I understand, though physically restrained from riding out in search of you.'

She thought she hid well her reaction to that, but then Resh said, 'A cousin, yes? This thickness of blood so inspires.' In his tone there was both amusement and faint derision.

Caplo cleared his throat. 'In any case, do rest with us this night, Warden. I see you are near to collapse—'

'I am well enough.'

'Spare pity for your horse, then, who so quivers beneath you.'

She studied him, but his innocent expression did not waver, not for an instant. 'I dislike sleeping in a place of close death.'

'As do we all, but our warlock here will see to the quelling of despairing spirits. None of us will succumb to fevers of the soul—'

'No matter how stained your hands,' T'riss cut in, dismounting and, ignoring them all, walking towards the water. 'It flows quiet,' she murmured, 'does it not?' Throwing off her makeshift garments, she strode naked into the water.

Faror Hend asked, 'Must you gape so, lieutenant?'

*          *          *

The shacks were torn down to provide firewood for the cookfires. Meals were prepared while monks went in twos and threes into the water, to bathe away the day's slaughter. None seemed too concerned if there was blood in the water they then drank. With a young monk attending to her horse, Faror Hend accepted the offer of a spare tent and made her own camp a short distance from the others. She had not yet decided if she liked Caplo Dreem. Warlock Resh, on the other hand, was a man used to his size. There were people, men and women both, who lived awkwardly in their selves, whether timorous of the space they took, or imagining themselves other than what they were and so prone to colliding with or breaking things. In the manner of walking was revealed a host of truths.

In the outlier camps of the Wardens, where so many misfits found a home, Faror often took note of their diffident first arrival, carrying with them the wounds of isolation, ridicule or social neglect; only to see that frailty gradually fall away as each, in time, found welcome. Confidence was a seed that could grow in any soil, no matter how impoverished. She had seen as much again and again.

No such weaknesses attended Warlock Resh of the Yan Shake. Instead, in presence alone he bullied. In demeanour he challenged. She had felt herself bridling the moment she set eyes upon him, and was determined to stand fast against him. Years ago she would have quailed, retreated with eyes downcast. Now, as a Warden of the Outer Reaches, she had met the mocking in his eyes with flat resolve. Men like him crowded the gutters of the world.

She built her own modest fire, to make tea, and was not displeased when T'riss, still dripping from her extended stay in the water, joined her.

'Faror Hend, are these men who sleep with men? Do they abjure women and so consort only with their brethren?'

Faror smiled. 'Some are like that. Others are not. The Shake monasteries are two sects. These are the Yan, Sons of the Mother. There also exist the Yedan, Daughters of the Father. Many sons are lifebound to daughters – a kind of marriage although not in the manner one usually views marriage. The lifebound can choose to lie with whomever they please. They can live apart and never attend to one another. But upon their deaths, they share a single grave.'

'What deity demands this of them?'

'None.' Faror Hend shrugged. 'I am not the one to ask. They are peculiar to my eyes, but of their martial prowess I have no doubt.'

'It seems that the ability to fight is important in this world, Faror Hend.'

'It has been and always will be, T'riss. We are savages in disguise, and let no pomp or indolence deceive you. At any moment we can bare our teeth.'

T'riss sat down opposite the Warden, her expression thoughtful. 'Is civilization nothing but an illusion, then?'

'Crowd control.'

'Excuse me?'

'That's all civilization is, T'riss. A means by which we manage the proliferation of our kind. It increases in complexity the more of us there are. Laws keep us muzzled and punishment delivers the necessary message when those laws are broken. Civilizations in decline are notable when certain of their members escape justice, and do so with impunity.'

'Are these a soldier's thoughts, Faror Hend?'

'My mother and father lived scholarly lives. An aberration among the

Duravs. Both were killed by a Jheleck raiding party, murdered in their home, which was then set aflame. The fate of my younger sisters was, alas, far worse.'

'And to answer such cruelty, you took up the sword.'

'I fled, if truth be known. What worth knowledge when the savage bares teeth? Thus, I fight to defend civilization, but know well the ephemeral nature of that which I defend. Against ignorance there is no front line. Against viciousness no border can hold. It breeds as readily behind your back as elsewhere.'

'What of life's pleasures? Its joys, its wonders?'

Faror Hend shrugged. 'Equally ephemeral, but in the instance, drink deep. Ah, the tea is ready.'

\* \* \*

The two-handed axe thumped to the ground and a moment later Warlock Resh joined it, grunting and taking a moment to crook his neck to each side. 'Killing gives me a headache,' he said in a low rumble.

'But dying hurts more,' Caplo replied. He twisted in his seat to regard the two women at the distant fire. 'I am prone to pettiness.'

'You are political.'

Caplo glanced back at Resh. 'I just said that.'

'Calat Hustain demands her immediate return? Utter rubbish.'

'Not entirely. I'm sure he does. In any case, I see some value in our being the ones to deliver the Azathanai to Kharkanas. Besides, Mother Sheccanto felt this one's arrival.'

'Felt the twist of her sorcery, you mean. As did I. The ground convulses beneath her. This delivery may earn revile.'

'That can prove useful, too.'

'And this is the talent of your mind, Caplo: to stand firm on all sides of a matter.'

'I accept the possibility, dear warlock, that we invite a viper into our nest. But then, we are hardly chicks waving stubby wings.'

'Speak for yourself. I keep checking to see that I'm not sitting in my own shit.'

'You've been doing that for years, Resh. This Azathanai – T'riss – is claimed as a spume-child of the Vitr, a most sordid birth for all her physical charms. What threat does she pose? What possible value the voicing of that threat? What portent her stated desire to travel to Kharkanas?'

'On these three legs you will totter, Caplo Dreem.'

'On three legs so do we all.'

'Sheccanto will lather you in grease and send you into the Citadel, if only to see from which crack you squirt back out. And this gives purpose to your life?'

'The Shake serve Kurald Galain. Note how Hunn Raal shied from our regard. He sought out Calat Hustain to the cause of Urusander, but not us. And, upon the other flank, when last did a nobleborn make formal – or even informal, Abyss fend – visit to our Mother or Father?'

'All anticipate our neutrality – why would you take offence from their expectation, Caplo, when it shall clearly prove accurate?'

'Offence lies in the assumption. The nest is sure, but how firm the perch upon the branch? How solid the roots of the tree?'

'I am of two minds,' Resh said, sighing as he leaned back on his hands. 'Eager to pluck unknown fruit. Yet chary of its taste. Does this define temptation?'

'No answer tempts my tongue. Thus, I leave you unassuaged.'

'Magic is awakening. I feel its heat. I tremble to its beating heart. I grow still as death upon hearing the slither of vipers. Twigs raise scant obstacle. Our lofty height proves no barrier. Someone is bleeding, somewhere.'

'Mother Dark?'

Resh snorted. 'Her power is too cold for fire, too black for warmth. Hers is a heart yet to drum awake. In her company, even the vipers are blind.'

'Then will she blind our guest, or will our guest come in fire and refutation?'

'Truth?'

'Truth.'

'I imagine to each other they will have very little to say.'

Overhead the swirl of stars was bright, modest in its fiery light, bold in its unlit absence. Caplo studied it for a time as his brethren settled down to sleep, and then said, 'Let us take a fresh grip upon the weapon and spare nothing in our charge upon a new slope, no matter its bristling facade. Note you the Warden's intrigue?'

Resh yawned. 'Her cousin is reputed fair indeed, although too winning for my tastes.'

'Not one to succumb to your insistence, then? I am sure Spinnock Durav will little spare the loss.'

'Her betrothed cleaves a forest of black grass in search for her.'

'Slays myriad wolves and less handsome denizens.'

'Seeks a suitable hole in which to drain ill Vitr Sea.'

Caplo sighed. 'And sets siege upon her blandish indifference.'

'All to no avail. Perhaps there is a thieving bird eyeing the stone mantel, where unknown words flow.'

'Words not yet written.'

'Some things need no chisel, no carver's hand.'

'True enough, O warlock. But I think this Azathanai has other purpose, not aligned to Faror Hend. Besides, dear T'riss has not a mason's talent, nor one's stolid comportment.'

Resh looked up, heavy brows lifting. 'You think not? Peruse yon knotted horse. Think not too hard on it, lest your pallor grow yet more sickly. If that is even possible.'

'Since I never heed your words, Resh, I will in fact give it further thought. But not now. All this killing has made me sleepy.'

'Bah, while my headache clatters a plain of spears.'

*    *    *

The horses' heads drooped. Sweat formed lather about their bits and made white streaks against their slick necks. They were through the forest of grass, out upon the lifeless verge with slumped knolls and rotted crags facing them. Sharenas Ankhadu had not thought such a ride possible, and these mounts were done. This thought irritated her. Kagamandra Tulas had succumbed to a kind of wilful disregard in his mad hunt for his betrothed. She glanced over at the others in the troop and saw well their drawn faces, their glazed eyes. They had gone in search of one of their own, yet no one life was worth the lives of these horses.

She never could understand the desperate elevation of a person's value over that of other, less privileged creatures, as if every sentient mind was a lofty citadel, a self-announced virtue the loss of which staggered the world.

True, some worlds were staggered. Death's kiss was always personal, and cold lips offered no solace. Unseeing eyes had a way of looking through and past those who dared meet them. Landscapes lost colour and breaths felt dry on the tongue. But all these feelings only stung in their mockery. They were echoes of sudden absence, the wail of the lost.

Animals knew the same grief. She had seen as much, time and again. Loss was universal. It was life's own language, after all.

No, she was not irritated. She was furious, and when Tulas took up the reins again, she snapped out a single word. 'No.'

He swung to face her.

'Unless you fancy a long walk home.'

After a moment, Kagamandra slumped.

'We have found the trail,' Sharenas went on. 'Leading back the way we came, although, granted, not the very same route we took. Lord Tulas, Calat Hustain dispatched these Wardens with more than one task in mind. Of course, we must discover the fate of Faror Hend. But also, we must confirm the tale of Captain Finarra Stone. We can return to this place upon our return journey, and so follow her track. But now, after a time of rest, we must set out for the shore – the trail here is plain. West.'

'I am of a mind to leave you to it, then,' Tulas replied.

The captain of the troop, a short, squat man of middle years named Bered, now cleared his throat, adding a dry cough before saying, 'It is best we remain together, Lord. These are hostile lands, and for all your courage you cannot claim familiarity with it. We accepted the pace, true, but with misgivings. Now we must walk our beasts and then rest. This air is foul and will only get worse.'

'She is my betrothed.'

'And she is our companion. A friend to each and every one of us here. But we have great faith in her abilities, Lord Tulas. Still, should she have fallen, then no haste on our part will avail what remains of her. We will trail her, but with the expectation that the trail shall find no grisly end. In the meantime, it is as Lady Ankhadu has said: we must make for the shore.'

'Besides,' Sharenas added, 'would you come this far only to deny yourself sight of the Vitr? Do you not wish to understand the purpose of Faror Hend's duty in this land? Should you not see for yourself her avowed enemy? I will do no less, if only to honour her memory.'

He flinched at that last statement, but voiced no protest.

Tulas had tasted death's kiss before. He could shoulder any new loss. She saw him find his resolve, like a man throwing on a cape of thorns, and saw too the hint of satisfaction, if not pleasure, in its bite. 'Truly spoken, Sharenas Ankhadu. I am pleased that you are here.' His lifeless gaze moved on to Bered and the other Wardens. 'You as well. I see the strain in each of you: that you might have lost a friend. It is clear that my betrothed has found a worthy world in which to live. In all that you have already done, you do her honour.'

Bered's reply was gruff. 'And we expect to jest without repent in her company, Lord, in a few days.'

Tulas drew his horse to one side. 'Will you take the lead now, captain, and read this faint trail?'

'Thank you, Lord.'

Sharenas and Tulas waited for the others to set out, and then fell in side by side into their wake.

'You must think me a fool,' he muttered.

'In matters of love—'

'Spare all of that, Sharenas. You read well my fragile verve. This betrothal is my reward, and Faror Hend's penance. Love does not rush between us. But I will give ease to her as best I can. My expectations are few and all chains I will cast away long before we join hands. She is welcome to take what lovers please her, and indeed to live out her days among the ranks of the Wardens. I begrudge her no decision.'

'Yet you would give your life in her defence.'

He shot her a look. 'Of course. She is my betrothed.'

'Dear me,' she replied, low, 'you really are a fool, Tulas.'

'What do you mean?'

'Rest your umbrage and I will speak honestly. No, I will wait for the heat to drain from your face. Listen well. This is not a question of dying for your betrothed. It is one of living instead. You should have refused the offer, knowing what you know – of yourself, of a young woman's dreams. This was, as you say, your reward, and as such was intended as a gift to match gratitude. In turn, House Durav was badly mauled in the wars, almost unto dissolution – and for those losses, another gift was offered. Accordingly, Faror Hend had no choice. She had to accept in the name of her family – she had to accept any husband of nobility offered her. And in turn, she is expected to produce heirs.' She studied him carefully, and then continued, 'It may be that you are gone. That all that remains of you is flesh and bone. But that will serve. Do you understand my meaning?'

'Why did you choose to accompany us? On this search?'

She grimaced. 'I admit to cruel curiosity. But there is so little left of you, Tulas, that the game palls in the deed. I was as much the fool here as you, I fear. So, let us smooth the sands between us and begin anew, if you will have that.'

His nod was understandably cautious.

She went on. 'If friends have left you, then I will be your companion. If companionship stings too much, then nod to my occasional smile, the meeting of my gaze. With me you can speak, on any matter, and I in turn avow myself a secure repository of your secrets.'

'And what of your secrets, Sharenas Ankhadu?'

'Alas, mostly venal, I admit. But if you enquire, you shall have them in abundance.'

To her astonishment, the weathered face creased in a smile. 'It is said that among the three, you are the cleverest.'

She snorted. 'Among the three that's hardly a triumph of wit.'

'Will you side with Urusander?'

'You waste little time, Tulas.'

Tulas made a strange sound, and then said, 'Time? In abundance it is no more than preparation. In short supply it is every necessary deed. We are hoarders of time's wealth, yet worshippers of its waste.'

'You have spent years now, preparing to die, Tulas. A waste? Most assuredly.'

'I'll bear the cut of your tongue and wipe away what blood may flow.'

She looked ahead through the grainy gloom. Another day was past and the time of failing light was upon them. 'Calat Hustain was a wall, against which Hunn Raal flung arguments. Stone after stone, shattering, raining down. His words were futile as dust. It was glorious.'

'Ilgast Rend was a bear among wolves, yet the wolves saw it not.'

'You knew his purpose?'

'I surmised. He is a conservative man, and only grows more hardened in his ways. Whatever he said to Calat was all the bulwark the commander needed and as you say: the walls did not so much as tremble.'

'My sister and cousin will back Urusander, if only to wound Draconus. Better a husband than a consort, if she is to rule us all.'

'Children cleave to the security of a formal union in the matter of parents,' said Tulas. 'It is in their nature to dislike their mother's lover, if that is all he is. There is a way among the Jheleck, when they have veered into their wolf form, that males are taken by a fever of violence and they set out to slay the pups of their rivals.'

Sharenas thought about that, and then smiled. 'We do the same and call it war.'

'No other reasons serve?'

She shrugged. 'Forms and rules serve to confound what is in essence both simple and banal. Now, you ask which way I will fall. I have thought about it, yet am still undecided. And you?'

'I shall side with peace.'

'Who among any of us would claim otherwise?'

'Many speak of peace, yet their hearts are torrid and vile. Their one love is violence, the slaying of enemies, and in the absence of true enemies, they will invent them. I wonder, how much of this hatred for Draconus comes from base envy?'

'I have wondered the same,' Sharenas admitted.

They rode on for a time then, silent. The caustic air, so near the as yet unseen Vitr, burned in the throat, made raw the eyes. They passed the carcasses of slain wolves, the beasts scaled rather than furred, and though only days old already the hide was crumbling, the jutting bones gnawed by the very air.

Deep into the night Bered called a halt. It was a wonder to Sharenas that the Wardens had managed to follow a trail this long. Now the captain dismounted and walked back to her and Tulas. 'Here, Finarra Stone emerged from among the rocks, coming from the shore. Her steps were laboured, her stride unsteady. We will rest here, as best we can in this foul atmosphere, and approach the Vitr with the dawn. Lady Sharenas, Lord Tulas, will you join us in a meal?'

*　　*　　*

The sun was like a wound in the sky, reflecting dully on the tranquil surface of the Vitr Sea. They were arrayed in a row upon the high bank, looking down through a scatter of pocked boulders. Just up from

197

the shore sprawled an enormous, headless carcass. Close to it was the mangled remains of Finarra Stone's horse.

'She spoke true, then,' Sharenas said. 'But how is it that a creature with its head cut away was able to live on, much less launch an attack?'

Bered, his face pale and drawn tight, dismounted and closed a gauntleted hand on the sword at his belt. 'Selad, Stenas, Quill, walk your horses with me. Lances out.'

Tulas grunted and then said, 'Captain, the beast is clearly dead. Its flesh rots. Its organs are spilled out and sun-cracked.'

Not replying, Bered set out down the makeshift trail between the boulders. The three named Wardens accompanied him, each picking his own path.

Tulas slipped down from his horse and followed the captain.

Pulling her gaze away, Sharenas stared out upon the Vitr. Its placid mien belied its evident malice. Rising on her stirrups, she scanned the length of shoreline, first to the west, and then to the east. She frowned. 'There is something there,' she said, and then pointed. 'A shadow, half in, half out of the water. No boulder could long survive that.'

One of the Wardens near her, second in rank behind Bered, guided his horse down to the left, out on to the strand. Sharenas glanced back at Bered and the others. They had reached the two carcasses, and Bered, sword sheathed, was pulling loose the saddle from the dead horse. He'd already retrieved Finarra's weapons and delivered them to one of his Wardens. Tulas stood a few paces back, watching.

Her chest felt tight, much like after a night with the pipe, and she could feel vehemence in the fumes flowing against her exposed skin. Eyes stinging, she set out after the veteran. Joining him on the strand she said, 'Nothing untoward with the captain. It seems the creature is finally dead. Let us ride to examine our find, and then we can be quit of this place.'

'The Vitr yields no detritus, Lady Sharenas.'

'It seems that now it does.'

The observation made him clearly unhappy. Sighing, he nodded. 'Quickly then, as you say.'

They kicked their mounts into a slow canter. The sharp sands beneath the horses' hoofs sounded strangely hollow.

Four hundred or so paces ahead, the object casting the shadow looked angular, tilted like a beached ship, but far more massive than any ship Sharenas had seen – although in truth she had only seen ships in illustrations, among Forulkan books and hide paintings, and scale was always dubious in such renderings, so eager were the artists to magnify personages aboard such craft.

From one of the two spars something like sailcloth hung down in torn shrouds. The other spar was broken halfway down its length, tilted with its tip buried in the sand.

But as they drew closer, both riders slowed their mounts.

Not a ship.

The Warden's voice was weak with disbelief. 'I thought them tales. Legends.'

'You imagine Mother Dark succumbed to invention? She walked to the End of Darkness, and stood on a spar surrounded in chaos. And when she called upon that chaos, shapes emerged from the wildness.'

'Is it dead, do you think? It must be dead.'

Illustrators had attempted to make sense of Mother Dark's vague descriptions. They had elected to draw inspiration from a winged lizard that had once dwelt in abundance in the Great Blackwood, before the trees in which they nested were all cut down. But such forest denizens were small, not much larger than a month-old hunting hound. They had been called *Eleint*.

The spars were the bones of wings, the sailcloth thin membrane. The sharp angles were jutting shoulder blades, splayed hips. At the same time, this was so unlike the beast that had attacked Finarra Stone as to belong to someone else's nightmare. It massed three times the size, for one.

*Dragon. Thing of myth, the yearning for flight made carnate. Yet ... see its head, the length of its neck so like a serpent's body. And those jaws could devour a horse entire. See its eyes, smeared black in blood like tears.*

The Warden reined in. 'Captain Bered must see this.'

'Ride back,' said Sharenas. 'I will examine it more closely.'

'I would advise against that, milady. Perhaps it is a quality of the Vitr that nothing dead stays dead.'

She shot him a look. 'An intriguing notion. Go on. I intend to be careful, as I happen to greatly value my life.'

He swung his horse round, kicked it into a canter, and then a gallop.

Facing the dragon again, she rode closer. At fifty paces her mount baulked, so she slipped down from the saddle and hobbled the horse.

The giant beast was lying on its side. Its flank bore wounds, as of ribs punching out through the thick, scaled hide, but she could see no thrust of white bone from any of them, and there were scores. The huge belly, facing her, had been sliced open. Entrails were spilled out in a massive heap, and these had been slashed and chopped at, savaged as if by a sword swung in frenzy.

Something else was lying near the belly wound, amidst disturbed sands. Sharenas approached.

Clothing. Armour, stained by acids. Discarded. A long, thin-bladed sword was lying close to the gear, black with gore. And there . . . foot-prints leading away.

Sharenas found that she was standing, motionless, unable to take another step closer. Her eyes tracked the prints up the strand to where they vanished between boulders crowding the verge.

'Faror Hend,' she murmured, 'who walks with you now?'

# EIGHT

'THERE IS NOTHING BOLD IN THE WEARING OF WEAPONS,' HAUT SAID, the vertical pupils of his eyes narrowed down to the thinnest of lines as he studied the array on the table's battered, gouged surface. 'Each one you see here is but a variation. What they share is of far greater import, Korya. They are all arguments in iron.' He turned upon her his lined, weathered face, and his tusks were the hue of old horn in the meagre light, the greenish cast of his skin reminding her of verdigris. 'You will eschew such obvious conceits. For you, iron is the language of failure.'

Korya gestured at the weapons on the table. 'Yet, these are yours, and by their wear, you have argued many times, master.'

'And won the last word each and every time, yes. But what has that availed me? More years heaped upon my back, more days beneath the senseless sun and the empty wind in my face. More nights under indifferent stars. More graves to visit, more memories to haunt me. In my dreams, Korya, I have lost the gift of colour. For so long now, in passing through my eyes the world is bleached of all life, and strikes upon my soul in dull shades of grey.'

'I must tire you, then, master.'

He grunted. 'Foolish child. You are my lone blaze. Now, heed me well, for I shall not repeat myself. We must quit this place.'

'Do you fear the return of the Jheleck?'

'Cease interrupting me. I have spoken now of the education awaiting you, but all that I have done has been in preparation. There are things you must now learn that are beyond my expertise. We journey south, to where powers are awakening.'

'I do not understand, master. What powers? Have not the Jaghut surrendered all claims upon such things?'

Haut took up a weighty belt bearing a sword in a heavy leather scabbard. He strapped it on, adjusted it briefly, and then removed it with a scowl. The weapon thumped heavily back on to the tabletop. 'Azathanai,' he said. 'Someone has been precipitous. But I must speak with my kin. Those who have remained, that is. The rest can go rot.'

'Why am I so important, master?'

'Who said you were?'

'Why then have you spent years preparing me, if I am to have little or no value?'

'Impertinence serves you well, Korya, but you ever risk the back of someone's hand across the face.'

'You have never struck me.'

'So, like some Jheleck mongrel, you play the odds, do you?' He lifted free a heavy halberd, stepped back and waved it about, until the blade bit into a wall, sending stone chips flying. He dropped the weapon with a clang, rubbed at his wrists.

'What will you discuss with your kin?'

'Discuss? We never discuss. We argue.'

'With iron?'

A quick, savage smile lit his features, only to vanish again a moment later. 'Delightful as the notion is, no.'

'Then why are you girded for war?'

'I fear too light a step,' he replied.

Korya fought the urge to leave the chamber, to head back up the tower. To stand beneath the morning stars and watch the sun slay them all. Haut had forbidden her any possessions beyond a change of clothes for this journey. Even so, she believed they would never return here.

Haut collected a double-bladed axe with an antler shaft and hefted it. 'Thel Akai. Where did I come by this? Handsome weapon . . . trophy or gift? My conscience makes no stir, so . . . not booty. How often, I wonder, must triumph drip blood? And is it by this that we find its taste so sweet?'

'Master, if it is not by iron I am to defend myself, then what?'

'Your wits, child. Now, can you not see that I am busy?'

'You told me to listen well, master. I remain, listening well.'

'I did? You are?'

'We are to travel south, among your kin. Yet the source of your curiosity will be found among the Azathanai. Thus, I assume we will meet with them as well. This promises to be a long journey, and yet we have but a small bag of food, a single waterskin each, two blankets and a pot.'

'I see your point. Find us a ladle.'

'Will you be passing me on to one of your kin, master? To further my education?'

'Who would have you? Get such absurd notions out of your head. We might as well be bound together in shackle and chain. You are the headache I cannot expunge from my skull, the old wound crowing the coming of rain, the limp that stumbles on flat ground.' He found a leather strap to take the weight of the Thel Akai axe. 'Now,' he said as he collected up his helm and faced her, 'are you ready?'

'The ladle?'

'Since you are so eager to be armed, why not? It hangs on a hook above the hearth.'

'I know that,' she snapped, turning round to retrieve it. 'I mislike mysteries, master.'

'Then I shall feed you nothing but, until you are bloated and near to bursting.'

'I despise riddles even more.'

'Then I shall make of you an enigma to all. Oh, just reach for it, will you? There. No, tuck it into your belt. Now you can walk with a swagger, bold as a wolf. Unless you'd rather carry the axe?'

'No. Weapons frighten me.'

'Then some wisdom at least I have taught you. Good.'

She did not want to leave. By far the greater host of her memories belonged in this tower, rather than in the place of her birth; but now it seemed she would make her pilgrimage, by a most circuitous route, back home. In her path, however, she would find other Jaghut, and then the Azathanai. Since the Jheleck visit, Haut had been animated by something, his mood mercurial, and it seemed that his infirmities were vanishing from his withered form, like skins in the heat. He bore himself like a warrior now, readying himself for an argument in iron.

She followed him to the door, frowning at it as if seeing it for the first time. All at once, she had no faith in what waited beyond it. A sweep of yellow grasses, the muted rise of worn hills ahead, a sky paling as if brushed with light – these would be as they always were. What then to fear?

As Haut reached out for the handle he paused and glanced back. 'You're learning.'

'I don't understand.'

The Jaghut flung open the door. Darkness swirled in like smoke around him, tendrils curling round his legs. He muttered something, but, turned away as he was from her, she could not make out the words.

Dread held Korya motionless. Her heart beat wildly, like a trapped bird.

This time, when Haut spoke, she heard him clearly. 'I begin to see now, what they did. It is clever, yet rife with risk. Very well, we shall walk it, and see where it leads.'

'Master – what has happened to the world?'

'Nothing . . . yet. Come along.'

Somehow she managed to step into his wake, the ladle banging at her thigh with each stride. Flickers of irritation sought to distract her, but she held her gaze upon the strange, smoky darkness. As it flowed up and around her, she was startled to realize that she could see through its ethereal substance. Haut marched ahead, his worn boots thumping and scuffing across gravel.

Crossing the threshold of the tower's entrance, she beheld a narrow path running along a ridge barely an arm's reach across. To either side there was nothing but empty space. She swallowed down a sudden vertigo. When she spoke, the vastness devoured her voice. 'Master, how can this be?'

Under her feet, she felt the gravel shifting unsteadily and looked down. She saw, in gleam and sparkle, jewellery: a thick carpet of gems, rings, baubles; a veritable treasure underfoot. Haut paid it no heed, kicking through the clutter as if it were nothing more than woodchips and pebbles. Crouching, she collected up a handful. The rings were all cut through, twisted as if pulled from senseless fingers. She held a neck torc of solid gold, bent and gouged as if by knife cuts. Snapped necklaces slithered down between the fingers of her hand, cool as serpents. Glancing up, she saw that Haut had stopped and was looking back at her.

Korya shook her head in disbelief. 'Wealth to make a noble less than a beggar. Master, who would leave such a trail?'

Haut grunted. 'Wealth? Is it rarity that warrants value? If so, of greater value than these trinkets are trust, truth and integrity. Of greater value still, forgiveness. Of greatest value among them all, an outstretched hand. Wealth? We live in paucity. And this here is a most treacherous path – and we must walk it with unerring step, child.'

Korya dropped the treasure and straightened. 'I fear that I might stumble. I might fall, master.'

He shrugged, as if the notion gave him no qualm. 'This is loot. A slayer's hoard. The path wends upward and who can say what waits at its very end? A keep groaning beneath melted sheaths of gold? A throne of diamond where sits a rotted corpse? Will you believe this path to be so obvious? Who defends this realm? What army kneels in service to gold and silver? How warm is their bed of jewels at night?'

'I said I dislike riddles, master. What realm is this?'

'Ah, such a nuanced word. *Realm.* An invitation to balance, all stationary, mote tilted against mote, the illusion of solidity. A place to walk through, encompassing the span of one's vision and calling it *home*. Did you expect the world you knew? Did you imagine the future awaits you no different in substance from the past? Where are the grasslands, you ask. Where is the tumble of days and nights – but of those, what more can I teach you? What more can be learned of them than any child of sound wits can comprehend after but a handful of years?'

With these words drifting back to her, and then out to the sides to fall away leaving no echo, Haut resumed his march.

Korya followed. 'This is Azathanai.'

'Very good,' he answered without turning.

'What do they mean by it?'

'Ask the Jheleck. Bah, too late for that. The fools left, tails between their hairy legs. And to think, they wanted you. Another bauble. I wonder – what will your kin do with a score of Soletaken pups?'

'I don't know. Tame them, I suppose.'

Haut's laugh was sharp, cutting. 'To tame something, one must take advantage of its stupidity. They will never tame those beasts, because savage though they may be, they are not stupid.'

'Then, as hostages, they will learn the ways of the Tiste, and see them not as strangers, nor enemies.'

'You believe this? Perhaps it will be so.'

The path continued its climb, though not so steep as to make uncertain their purchase. But her legs were getting tired. 'Master, did you expect this?'

'In a manner of speaking, yes.'

'What do you mean?'

'Child, we have been invited.'

'By whom?'

'That remains to be discovered.'

*     *     *

She knew her life was yet modest, but already she had a sense that most promises would, eventually, prove empty. There was nowhere to go but forward, but no one could avow that what lay ahead was a better life. Potential felt like a burden, possibility like wolves on her trail. Her dreams of godly powers were the frayed remnants of childhood; they trailed like wisps behind her, tired as the streamers of last year's fete. She thought back to the dolls in the trunk's silent, dark confines, the eyes staring at nothing, the mouths smiling at no one, now well behind her – long gone from reach, or a moment's rush across the floor. There was stillness in that place, as still as the room surrounding it, as still as the keep itself. And just as the dolls dwelt in their trunk, so too had she and Haut dwelt in the keep, and it might well be true that this realm was but another version, and that it was all a matter of scale.

The gods and goddesses were in their rooms. She could almost see them, standing at the high windows looking out and dreaming of better places, better times, better lives. And like the dolls, their eyes were focused on vast distances and nothing closer to hand could make them waver, not for a moment.

Yet stranger memories haunted her now. Her room in the tower, the dead flies lying in the grit of the stone windowsill, crowded up against the discoloured glass, as if in the frenzy to escape they had bludgeoned themselves to death trying to reach an unattainable light. She should never have swept the spiders' webs from the frame, for the spiders would have fed well on the flies' futility.

Was the future no more than a succession of worlds one longed to live in? Each one for ever beyond reach, with such pure light and vistas that ran on without end? Was frenzy and anguish really that different?

They had been ascending for what seemed half a day, and still the path ahead wended its way ever upward. Fires burned in the muscles of her legs, making her imagine peat fires – some childhood memory, a place where the forest had died so long ago it had rotted into the ground, in layer upon layer, all soaked through with water the colour of rust. She remembered bundles of sodden skins pulled out from the pools, dangling stone weights from black ropes. She remembered stuffing wiry as hair, and the day was cold and the air was thick with midges, and knives flashed as the bundles were cut open and the hides rolled out.

The memory, arriving now so suddenly, halted Korya in her tracks. *Jheleck skins.*

Haut must have sensed her absence behind him, for he turned about, and then made his way back down to her.

'Master,' she said, 'tell me of the first encounters between the Jheleck and my people.'

The Jaghut's pained expression filled her with dismay.

When he said nothing she spoke, her tone dull but relentless: 'I found a memory, master. We understood nothing of Soletaken, did we? That the giant wolves we slew were in fact *people*. We killed them. We hunted them, because it is a lust in our souls, to hunt.' She wanted to spit that last word, but it came out as lifeless as the others. 'We cut their hides from their carcasses and we cured those skins in the bogs.'

He gestured for her to walk and set out once again. 'The origin of the Jheleck is a mystery, hostage. When they have sembled into their walking forms, standing upon two legs, they bear some resemblance to the Dog-Runners of the far south. Their features are perhaps more bestial, but then, that should hardly surprise you – the frigid world of the far north is a harsh home, after all.'

'Do the Dog-Runners treat with them?'

'There are Jheck in the south now. It may be that they do.'

'We hunted them. For pleasure.'

'It is the legacy of most intelligent beings to revel in slaughter for a time,' Haut replied. 'In this we play at being gods. In this, we lie to ourselves with delusions of omnipotence. There is but one measure to the wisdom of a people, and that is the staying hand. Fail in restraint and murder thrives in your eyes, and all your claims to civilization ring hollow.'

'Is there such a legacy among you Jaghut?'

'There was a time, Korya, when the Jaghut ceased their forward stride.'

A faint chill came to her at that, as if he but plucked at her earlier thoughts with fullest knowing.

'We faced a choice then,' Haut went on. 'To resume our onward journey, or to turn round, to discover the blessing that is walking back the way we came. In our standing in one place, we argued for centuries, until finally, in our mutual and well-deserved disgust, we each chose our own paths.'

'And so ended your civilization.'

'It was never much of one to begin with. But then, few are. So, you recall a grim memory, and would now chew it. Your next decision is crucial. Do you spit it out or do you swallow it down?'

'I would walk from civilization.'

'You cannot, for it resides within you.'

'And not within you?' she demanded.

'Do not be a fool, Korya,' he replied, his voice drifting back soft as a knife edge on a whetstone. 'You saw well my array of weapons. Most arguments in iron are arguments of civilization. Which paint shall we wear? By which name are we to be known? Before what gods must we bow? And who are you to answer such questions on my behalf? I take up this axe to defend my savagery – but know this: you will hear the echo of such sentiments in every age to come.'

She snorted. 'You imagine that I will live through *ages*, master?'

'Child, you will live for ever.'

'A child's belief!'

'An adult's nightmare,' he shot back.

'You would I never grew up? Or are you happy to contemplate my eternal nightmare?'

'The choice is yours, Korya. Spit it out or swallow it down.'

'I don't believe you. I will not live for ever. Nothing does, not even the gods.'

'And what do you know of gods?'

'Nothing.' *Everything. I stood with them, at the window.*

In the dark of the trunk, the eyes saw nothing, yet knew it not. She could have taken the dolls out before she left. Set them out in a row upon the windowsill, among the dead flies, and pressed their flat faces against the grimy glass. She could have told them to see all there was to be seen.

But, goddess that she had once been, she was never so cruel.

*We are not flies.*

One day she had come to the window only to find all the flies gone. The sun's warmth had brought them all back to life. That day had been the most frightening day of her young life.

*I should have fed them to the spiders. If I had not swept their homes away.*

*In this place* . . . 'I have begun remembering things,' she said.

He grunted, not turning, not slowing his stride. 'And are these memories yours?'

'I think so. Who else's?'

'That remains to be seen, hostage. But it has begun.'

*Mahybe. The vessel waiting to be filled. Trunk of dolls. Reach in, quickly now! Choose one, upon your life – choose one!*

Another memory assailed her, but it could not be real. She was outside the tower, hovering in the hot summer air. Before her, the window, and through its grey glass, she saw row upon row of faces. She floated, looking upon them, wondering at their sad expressions.

*Now at last, I think I know what the gods and goddesses were all looking at.*

Jewels crunched and rolled under her feet. She imagined herself old, bent and broken, with at her hand all the gold, silver and gems of the world, and in her heart there was yearning, and she knew that she would give it all up . . . for one child's dream.

\*     \*     \*

Children died. Feren held those words in her mind, swaddled and snug-tight in bitter embrace. Some fell from the womb with eyes closed, and the warmth of the blood upon their faces was cruel mockery. They were expunged in waves of pain, only to lie still in dripping hands. No woman deserved that. For others, there were but a handful of years which only later seemed crowded, cries of hunger, small hands grasping, luminous eyes that seemed wise in the ways of things not spoken. And then one day, those eyes stared out from half-closed lids, seeing nothing.

Mischance was scurrilous. Fate had a way of walking into empty rooms with smug familiarity. Children died. The laments of the mothers were hollow sounds to anyone's ears. People turned away and studied the ground, or some feature upon the horizon, as if it were changing before their eyes.

She remembered the look on Rint's face, her beloved brother, and how it crumpled with comprehension. She remembered the old women working quietly, businesslike, and not meeting her gaze. She remembered her fury at the sound of youths laughing nearby, and then hearing the bark of someone hushing them. It was not that death was rare. In dogged step it ever remained close, cold as a shadow. The blunt truth was, the world beat upon a soul until bones bent and hearts broke.

Since then, she had been crawling away, and it had been years and for all that she had aged since that time she felt but a day older, the bruise of grief still fresh beneath her skin, with the echo of insensitive laughter hard in her ears.

As they travelled across Bareth Solitude, each night she took to her bed the young man, bastard son of Draconus, and told herself that it was because the Lord had asked it of her. But it was getting more and more difficult to meet her brother's eye. Arathan was pouring his seed into her, twice, three times a night, and she did nothing to prevent what might come of that; just as she had done nothing the night that she slept with Grizzin Farl, but at least then she'd had the excuse of being rather drunk. Something wayward had taken hold of her, a rushing towards fate, eager to sink into dire consequences.

She had no fear of her own future, and to be mired in circumstances of one's own making offered its own delusion of control. But she was claiming that which belonged to others – the years ahead of them, the lives they would be made to lead. Mothers who lost could become obsessed with protectiveness and that might well find Feren, and for that her child would suffer through life. Arathan could sire a bastard and so show his father a mirrored reflection, and the eyes in their self-regard would be cold and unforgiving. Her brother, disarmed anew, might flee from an uncle's love, stung by the pain of a loss still too sharp to bear.

Arathan was the same age her son would now be, a young man spread-eagled beneath the world, as all young men were. He was not her son, but he could give her a son. Indeed, she was certain that he would. Her brother had seen something of this strange, macabre compact in her mind, this blending of fates, one empty, the other fast filling. She was convinced of that.

It was one thing to use for pleasure. It was another thing entire to just use. She taught Arathan the ways of lovemaking, whispering of grateful women in the future. But who were these women, who would give thanks to Feren for all that she'd given the man in their bed? Where would he find these women, this frail bastard son, soon to be abandoned among the Azathanai? Not a question with which she need concern herself, of course; and she reminded herself of this often, to little avail. He would be what she made him, and in turn he would make in her what he could never be: a son. And afterwards, in the dark and the heat, she would stroke his hair, and make his hands into fists – soft tips and absent nails – which she then closed her own hands around – and in fleeting ecstasy, sick with guilt, she imagined the boy's fists to be smaller than they were, as if by the strength of her grip she could crush them down to proper proportions.

There was a kind of recklessness in women. To open her legs was to invite it in, and with the invitation came surrender. Each night, the taste of that surrender stole into her like a drug. Her brother could see it, and was right to fear it. A woman who does not care is a dangerous woman.

Each day, as they rode across the barren land, she longed for the night to come, for the boy's helpless eagerness, for the shudders of his body against hers, for the waves that seemed to steal away his life – so much of it, rushing into her. She meant to use that life.

Children died. But a woman could make more children. Sons were born and sometimes they died, but there were many sons. And even dreams of the future held in hands, places of darkness.

*    *    *

Riding at his sister's side, trapped in the silence between them, Rint studied the lie of the land, wishing that monuments might rise before them, erupting from the hard ground, halting them in their tracks. All forward progress denied: nothing to do but turn round and return to Kurald Galain.

When she took with child, she would flee, like a thief down a street, into hidden alleys, secret courses that none could follow. A prize in her womb, she would draw knife and hiss at any who drew near. Even her brother.

He cursed Draconus, cursed this entire venture; he felt his body weaken with anguish at the sight of young Arathan, riding so proud at his father's side. He'd thought better of his sister. The world, crowding close round this meagre party, had grown sordid.

The day was drawing to a close, shadows stretched into their path from the lead riders, ephemeral and misshapen. To either side the plain rolled out, rippled like a dislodged rug, threadbare on the rises where the winter winds cut like knives for months on end. The deeper basins were bleached white, made lifeless by leaching salts.

They had passed some ruins just after noon. Foundation stones of pitted granite formed a rectangle on a level span just above a broad, shallow basin. The scale of the structure seemed oversized for Azathanai, and Rint saw little sign of their legendary stone-working skills in the roughly hewn granite. The walls had long since tumbled, forming a scree down the slope on the basin side and lying in heaps

210

upon the opposite side. There was no evidence that anyone had ever harvested the rubble. Apart from the lone building, Rint saw no other signs of habitation – no pen walls, no field enclosures, and the ground bore no evidence of ploughing. He wondered at it as they rode by.

Only ignorance emptied the past. Fools built the world from nothing – the whim of a god, some bold acclamation of existence in the Abyss. None of these visions of creation did more than serve the vanity of those holding them. As if all was made for them; for their eyes to witness, for their wonder to behold. Rint did not believe it. The past had no beginning. Something always existed before, no matter how far back one reached. It was the conceit of a mortal life, which began and so must end, to then imagine all of existence following suit, as if cowed into obedience. In myriad forms all that existed had always existed.

His sister had made herself the lover of a bastard son who was of an age to match that of the son she had lost. Things twisted in thinking about that. Things peeled back, exposing ugly secrets in lurid half-light. The past had a face and it was a face she would make alive once more. Arathan deserved better and there was no cause to wonder at his innocence, his naïveté in these matters: he was in his age of foolishness, as came upon all young men. Dreams raged like fires of the sun, but high as those flames might carry him, the fall promised an endless plunge into despair. Subtlety was lost – these were Arathan's years of stumbling, awkward his limbs and overborne his mind, and the depthless love he now felt for Feren would soon turn to wounded hatred.

Such were Rint's fears and he felt helpless before them. Twisting in his saddle he looked back the way they had come, seeking sign of Ville and Galak, but the plain stretched unbroken into the eastern gloom. Even under the best of circumstances they were still a day or two away.

Somewhere ahead of them were the first settlements of the Azathanai. He imagined imposing keeps, castles and palaces. Gardens where water flowed up from the ground in ceaseless servitude. And upon walls and around solid doors there would be scorch marks, from fires set by Jheleck raiders; and within the airy chambers, where the furniture was poor and worthless, there would be a faint hint of old smoke – not the smoke of woodfires, but that of cloth and bedding, acrid and bitter. These would not be welcoming places, and he knew he would long to be quit of them as soon as possible.

Why would the Azathanai feel any need, beyond simple hospitality, to entertain Lord Draconus? There was a mystery here. Grizzin Farl had looked upon Draconus as he would an old friend, and the familiarity between them in that night of revelry was no false performance. But as far as Rint knew, the Lord had dwelt within Kurald Galain all his life, and his years away from the House had been spent fighting in the wars.

The Protector of the Azathanai had never visited the realm of the Tiste, as far as Rint could recall. How then did they meet?

There were hidden currents here. Draconus was not simply taking his bastard son away, even for reasons of blunting the ambitions of his enemies in the court. Something else was in play.

The day's heat was slow to fade. They arrived upon another set of ruins similar to the last ones, although here there was evidence of at least three buildings, all massive and each one seemingly constructed without account of the others. Angles were discordant, lines clashing, and yet from what Rint could determine, the three buildings had all been raised at once. The remains of the walls were chest high at the corners, half that height along the walls. Stones seemed to have fallen randomly, inside and outside the structures, and there were no visible remnants of roofing in any of the buildings.

Sergeant Raskan turned back to Rint and Feren. 'We will camp here,' he said.

Rint rose in his stirrups, looked about. 'I see no well, no source of water, sergeant.'

'Only what we carry this night, I'm afraid.'

Displeased with this information, Rint dismounted. He slapped dust from his leather leggings. 'Had you told us this in the morning, sergeant, we could have filled a few more skins.'

'My error,' said Draconus from a few paces ahead. The Lord still sat astride his horse, a figure in black mail and weathered leather, the ruins stark behind him. 'My memory was that this settlement was occupied.'

Startled, Rint looked round again. 'Not for centuries, I would say, Lord. Not for centuries.'

Grimacing, Draconus dismounted. 'We shall have to make do.'

'And on the morrow, Lord?' Rint asked.

Raskan shot him a sharp look at the question, but Draconus was easy in his reply, 'By midday, we should reach Herelech River which, unlike most in these lands, flows year round.'

'Very good, Lord,' Rint said.

Feren was removing the saddle from her horse, as if unmindful of the challenges facing them this night. The horses needed most of the water they carried. There would be little left for cooking and none for washing away the day's sweat and grime. Yet his sister seemed eager to yield to all these inconveniences.

He realized he was scowling as he watched her, and so turned away.

Arathan had slipped down from his gelding, standing with a little less of the unsteadiness he had shown before. He was finding himself on this journey. *More than he imagined, no doubt. But be wary, Arathan, that by this journey's end you do not lose far more than what you gained.*

212

Raskan watched the Borderswords readying the camp. Lord Draconus had walked up to wander in the ruins, while Arathan brushed down his horses, beginning with the gelding – though the young man's eyes strayed over to Feren again and again.

Now that Arathan rode at his father's side these days – ever since the night of Grizzin Farl's visit – the sergeant had found himself more or less alone, riding between Draconus and his son to the fore, and the two Borderswords behind him, yet he felt himself a bridge to neither. Rint and Feren were at odds, but in the silent manner of siblings wishing to hide their mutual enmity from outsiders, lest family secrets spill forth. And of the conversations the Lord held with his bastard son, well, it seemed that there were few of those, and when they did occur, Raskan could not make out the words exchanged between them.

The ease that had been Grizzin Farl's gift was crumbling. Deep in the night, Feren rutted with Arathan amidst gasps and low cries that sounded oddly desperate; and she was not content with a single grapple. He had heard her wake the boy up more than once, and it was beginning to show in the dark smudges under Arathan's eyes.

Raskan wondered when Draconus would intercede. Surely the Lord could see that something untoward was being forged between Feren and his son. She was twice his age, if not older. And Raskan thought he saw a weakness in her that had heretofore been well hidden. The veneer of professionalism was fraying in the Bordersword.

Nor was her brother oblivious of all this.

Tensions mounted.

Draconus reappeared. 'Jheleck,' he said, gesturing at the ruins behind him.

'They struck here, Lord?'

'All that they could carry, including the roof beams and slate tiles.'

Raskan frowned. 'It must have been long ago, Lord. Was it Grizzin Farl who assured you that this place was still occupied? Clearly he did not come along this trail.'

Draconus studied him briefly, and then nodded. 'As you say, sergeant. No matter. We shall make do, I am sure.'

'Of course, Lord. Shall I attend to your horse?'

'No, thank you. Leave me with something to do while supper is being prepared.' Draconus seemed to hesitate, however, and seeing this Raskan edged closer.

'Lord?'

'A quiet word with you, sergeant.'

They walked off a way, round the faint mound on which stood the ruins. Raskan was startled to see an avenue carved into the slope on this side, marking the entrance to a barrow. But before he could enquire as to it, Draconus spoke.

'The boy needs warning off.'

At once Raskan understood the Lord's meaning, and so he nodded. 'I fear so, Lord. It is natural zeal—'

'Her zeal is anything but natural, sergeant.'

He had meant Arathan's, but Draconus had cut to a deeper truth. 'I think she is eager to beget a child from this union, Lord. But I do not think it is to hold a blade above House Dracons.'

'No, I agree – that would be pointless.'

Raskan wondered at that comment, but knew no proper means of querying it. 'She advances in years, perhaps—'

'She is forty years of age, give or take a year. She can bear more children for decades to come, if not longer.'

'It is the capacity for love for a child that withers among older women, Lord,' said Raskan. 'Few choose to give birth once past their first century. Tracks deepen to ruts. Independence is hoarded with avarice.'

'This is not the source of her impatience, sergeant.'

He was not inclined to disagree with that assessment. He had ventured his observations in invitation to Draconus, that the Lord might choose them to mitigate his unease. But this man standing before him was not one to embrace delusions simply because they offered comfort. After a moment, Raskan said, 'One might wonder, since we do not know, if she has never been a mother before. But to my eyes, Lord, hers is a body that has carried a child to term, and fed it at the breast.'

'No doubt of that, sergeant.'

'I would warn him, then, Lord. But he is only half the problem here.'

'Yes.'

'As her commander I can—'

'No, sergeant. You show courage in assuming that burden, but it is not yours to bear. It is mine, and I will speak with her. Tonight, with darkness upon us. Take Arathan off, but away from this place here.'

'Yes, Lord. Back along our trail, perhaps?'

'That will do.'

\*      \*      \*

Arathan could not take his eyes off her. She had become his vortex, around which he circled, tugged inward with a force against which he had no strength. Not that he struggled much. In her heated embrace he thought he could vanish, meld into her flesh, her bones. He thought that, one day, he might look out from her eyes, as if she had devoured him whole. He would not have resented the loss of his freedom, the abandonment of his future. Her drawn breath would be his; the taste in her mouth would be his taste, the supple movement of her limbs his own.

They would look for him, in the morning, and find no trace, and he would hide well behind her eyes and she in turn would give nothing away, content in a glutted, swollen way. He wondered if what he was feeling was the definition of love.

Unfurling his bedroll, Arathan collected up the weights and set them near his saddle. He had thoughts of Sagander, and how his tutor now fared. It would seem strange to be delivering gifts from a scholar who had been left behind, and all the knowledge the old man so desired would remain beyond his reach. Questions never asked, answers never offered – these remained somewhere ahead of Arathan, formless as a low cloud on the horizon. The weights, carefully stacked on the dusty ground, looked useless. Out here, nothing could be weighed, nothing could be measured out; out here, so far now beyond the borders of Kurald Galain, there was a kind of wildness, swirling through every-one.

He felt every current and at times seemed but moments from drowning, swept under into something animal, something base. Such a fate, when he considered it, amounted to little or no loss. All that he had known, all that he had come from, now seemed small, banal. The sky was vast overhead, the plain unending, and in moving beneath, in crossing it, they made bold their desires. This motion he felt, day after day, seemed to him far grander than any raised keep, any ruined house. He remembered playing in a heap of sand behind the workhouse, when he was much younger. It had been brought in for the potter who was visiting on her rounds. Something to do with grit in the clay, and moulds for firing and shaping. The sand had felt soft, sun-warmed on the surface but cool underneath, and he recalled lying sprawled across it, reaching out with one hand, watching his fingers sink deep, and then dragging handfuls close, as if to bury himself.

Travelling across this world felt much the same, as if by movement alone all could be taken hold of, taken in grasp, and thereby claimed as one's own.

Musing on this, as he watched Feren building the fire for the night's meal, Arathan thought he found an understanding of the nature of war; one that might impress even Sagander. When more than one hand reached out; when there was challenge over what was claimed: then would blood spill. There was nothing rational in it. The sand slipped through the fingers, sifted down and away from the hands that would hold it, and it remained long after the claimant had left. Nothing rational. Just desire, raw as a body's release in the night.

'Arathan.'

He looked up. 'Sergeant Raskan.'

'The light fast fades. Come with me.'

Arathan straightened. 'Where are we going?'

'Back up the trail.'

'Why?'

'Because it is my wish.'

Bemused, Arathan followed the man. Raskan walked as if in a hurry to leave the camp. He had removed his worn-out boots and now wore the moccasins Draconus had given him – but so precious were they in Raskan's eyes that he had taken to wearing them only at day's end. Arathan could not be certain that this was the reason, but he suspected that it was. A gift from his lord. There was value in that. It made Raskan seem younger than he was, but nowhere near so young as Arathan felt when in the sergeant's company.

The track bore signs of their horses' passage. Torn grasses, hoof-prints stamped deep, a ragged line that did not seem to belong on this open, rolling landscape.

'Did you drop something on the trail, sergeant? What are we looking for?'

Raskan halted, glanced back at the camp, but all that was visible was the red and orange glow from the fire. The smell of its smoke reached them, thin and devoid of any heat. 'Your father wanted you to learn the ways of the flesh. To lie with a woman. He judged the Bordersword useful in that, without having to worry about anything . . . political.'

Arathan looked down at the ground, unable to meet Raskan's dark eyes. He brought a finger to his mouth to chew on the nail, and tasted the past night's lovemaking. He quickly pulled it away.

'But the feelings that can build, between a man and a woman . . . well, these things can't be predicted.' The sergeant shifted about, muttered a moment under his breath, and then continued, 'You'll not marry her. You'll not spend the rest of your life with her. She's twice your age, with twice your needs.'

Arathan looked off into the darkness, wanting to run there, lose himself. Let Raskan utter his cruel words to empty shadows.

'Are you understanding me?'

'There should have been more women with us,' Arathan said. 'So you could've had one, too.'

'Like a hole in the ground? There's more to it than that. There's more to *them* than that. It's what I'm getting at. She ain't a whore so she don't think like a whore. What do you think coin pays, when it goes between a man and a woman? It pays for no hard feelings, that's what it pays for. Your father thought it would serve you. A few nights. Enough to make you familiar with the whole thing. He didn't want you to take on a woman, half lover, half mother.'

Arathan trembled, wanting to strike the man, wanting to draw his sword and cut him to pieces. 'You don't know what he wanted,' he said.

'I do. He sent me to you – he knows what we're talking about right now. And there's more than that – he's taken Feren off, too. He's telling it to her as plain as I am to you. It's gotten too much, too important—'

'What's wrong with that?'

'She's taking your seed—'

'I know.'

'And when she's got it, she'll toss you aside.'

'She won't.'

'She has to. To keep you from claiming that child years from now. To keep you from stealing it once it comes of age, or once you decide it's time.'

'I wouldn't do that. I'll live with her—'

'Your father can't allow that.'

'Why not? What does it matter to him? I'm a bastard son and he's throwing me away!'

'Stop shouting, Arathan. I tried making you see. I tried using words of reason, but you're not ready for that, not yet old enough for it. Fine. See if you understand this: if you two keep it up, your father will kill her.'

'Then I will kill him.'

'Right, you'll want to, and he doesn't want that between you. So that's why it's got to end here and now. You're not to be given to a Bordersword woman just because you want it, and that's not because she ain't good enough for you or anything. It's because she only wants one thing from you and once she gets it, she'll hurt you bad.'

'Why do you keep saying that? You don't know anything about her!'

'I know more than you, Arathan. She's had a child and lost it – that's what I know. It ain't just a guess, either; there's something about her. And now, how she's taken you in. It's not right, none of it.'

'Is my father killing her right now?' Arathan stepped past the sergeant.

Raskan grasped him by the arm and pulled him round. 'No, he isn't. It's not what he wants, and I guarantee you, Feren's not acting as hot-blooded as you are at this moment. She's listening; she's hearing what he's saying. Your nights with her are done with and that will be the proof to my words.'

Arathan pulled free and set off back to the camp.

After a moment, Raskan followed. 'It's all right,' he said to the boy striding ahead, 'I knew it wouldn't be easy.'

\*       \*       \*

217

The moment she saw the sergeant lead Arathan away, Feren knew what was coming. When Draconus gestured, she straightened. To her brother she said, 'Don't burn the stew – it's already sticking.'

He grunted his understanding – of everything.

The Lord led her past the ruins, round to the base of the mound on which the houses had been built.

Feren was not interested in getting an earful. 'I have done as you asked of me, Lord.'

'Shed your iron.'

'Excuse me?'

'Your dagger. Your sword, and the belt.'

She made no move. 'You would disarm me, Lord Draconus? I would know: to what end?'

An instant later and she was lying on the ground, her bones aching from the impact. She was not sure what had happened – had he struck her? She felt no imprint from a fist or hand. Stunned, too weak to move, she felt him fumbling at her waist, then heard the rasp as he stripped the belt from her. Metal clanged some distance away. The dagger followed.

She fumbled at his hands, trying to push them away, and sought to draw her legs up to protect herself.

He gave an irritated grunt, and then she felt him grasp her left ankle. She was twisted on to her stomach, and then he was dragging her through the grasses. She wanted to cry out – to summon her brother – but then more blood would flow. Crimes would tear through them all – too many to countenance.

If Draconus was intent on raping her, she would permit it. Vengeance could lie in wait a long time.

He dragged her down into a channel lined with boulders, and in the grainy gloom she saw the stacked stones of a squat, wide doorway pass to either side, and all at once the night sky vanished into deeper darkness.

She was still weak, still helpless in his grasp. Was this sorcery? Was this the power from his lover, Mother Dark? To reach so far, to be so easily abused by this man, this Consort – no, it did not make sense.

In the low confines of the barrow, as the floor sloped sharply downward, Feren smelled death. Old, withered, dried out.

He dragged her alongside a stone sarcophagus.

Sudden fear ripped through Feren. 'Lord,' she gasped. 'I yield. There is no need—'

'Be quiet,' he hissed. 'We take a terrible risk here.'

He released her leg, used one foot to turn her on to her back, pushing her roughly up alongside the cold stone. 'Be still.'

She saw him lean over her, reaching into the sarcophagus – there

218

was, it seemed, no lid – and then there was the sound of rustling, creaks and faint pops, followed by a sifting, as of sand.

Draconus pulled the corpse on to the edge of the coffin. Dust rained down on Feren, covering her face. She coughed, gagged.

He used both his legs to hold her in place, pushed up against the sarcophagus, and she saw him fumbling with the withered corpse – the creature was huge, the limb bones long and thick. Black hair tumbled down to brush Feren's face, smelling of mouldy skin.

A bony hand was suddenly pressed down on to her belly.

Convulsions of agony took Feren, strong enough to knock Draconus away – he staggered, still holding the corpse by one leather-wrapped wrist. The body tilted, and then slid down to land heavily on Feren's legs.

'Shit!' he bellowed. 'Move away, woman – quickly!'

From the corpse's mouth came a moaning sound.

Terrified, the waves of pain from her belly fast fading, Feren pushed away from the body.

Draconus bent down and levered the huge corpse back into the sarcophagus. It thumped in a cloud of dust and cracking bones.

'That will have to do,' he muttered. 'Blessings on you, and begging forgiveness, O Queen. Crawl out now, Feren, and be quick about it.'

She did as he commanded, and moments later clambered out through the chute and saw above her the swirl of stars, bright as a gift. Stumbling clear of the ramp, she fell to her knees, gasping, spitting out rank dust.

Draconus joined her, brushing down his leggings. He drew off his gloves and tossed them to one side. 'Collect your weapons, Bordersword.'

'Lord—'

'I saw you flinch. I felt you flinch.'

Wondering, she nodded.

'Death and life, in there, do not welcome each other's touch. You are with child, Feren. The seed grows within you. Now, leave my son alone.'

Fumbling to retrieve her gear, fighting a return of the unnatural lassitude, she looked up at Draconus. She felt sullied; he might as well have raped her. She could still feel the imprint of that dead hand upon her belly. Feren bared her teeth. 'Take him then.'

\*       \*       \*

Rint sat alone at the fire. The supper had burned. Not enough water in the stew, not enough attention from the man tending to it. He had no doubts as to what was happening out there in the darkness, and he prayed that words would be enough – but his sister was a hard woman, not easily bullied. Lord or no, Draconus might find himself facing a viper. With that thought came to him bone-deep fear.

*Should you hurt her, you will have war. With the Borderswords. With me. I will take you down, Consort, and to the Abyss with the consequences.*

He heard a shout from Arathan, but not well enough to make out the words. Easy to guess, however. The Lord's son was far gone, pulled back from manhood into being a child once more. The way she wanted it. But it would not do. Draconus had not been blind to the twisting of his desires. While from beyond the ruins there was no sound at all.

A few moments later Arathan emerged from the darkness, into the fire's light. Seeing Rint he halted. Anger and shame seemed to roll from him in waves and he was shivering. For the briefest of instants their gazes locked, and then the son of Draconus looked away.

Raskan appeared behind him, went to crouch down beside the cook-pot. He leaned over, sniffed and then scowled.

'My apologies, sergeant,' Rint said. 'Not enough water.'

'It will have to do,' Raskan said, reaching for a bowl.

'Where are they?' Arathan demanded.

Rint said nothing, and Raskan busied himself ladling scorched stew into his bowl.

'You won't win. None of you will. She's not afraid of my father, and neither am I.'

This was taking too long. Rint struggled to keep from rising, from drawing his sword and setting out to find them. If he did that, Raskan would intervene, assert his authority, and things would break down. Two lovers in the night could unleash a war, take down an entire realm. They could not see past each other; they never did.

'Arathan,' he snapped as the young man made to leave the fire.

'I have no reason to listen to you.'

'Maybe not. But I was wondering, did your tutor ever speak to you about sacrifice? Yielding your wants in the name of peace? Did he speak of such things as he sought to guide you from childhood into adulthood?' Rint nudged the fire with one foot, sending sparks fleeing skyward. 'A man understands sacrifice. What needs surrendering.'

'You say this because you have no woman.'

'Arathan, I have a wife. She dwells in Riven Keep. When I return I will have a daughter or a son. I was late to it, you see, because I serve with the Borderswords, and we have known war.'

These words seemed to have an effect. Arathan stood unmoving, as if drained of strength, emptied of will.

'Had I known,' Raskan said to Rint, looking up from his bowl, 'I would have sent you back and found another among the Borderswords. You should have been with her, Rint.'

'Had an uncle whose wife knifed him when she was in the heat of labour. Too many platitudes and assurances.'

'She killed him?'

'No, she took his caressing hand and pinned it to the ground.' He hesitated, and then added, 'The story goes, he pulled the knife from his hand and went back to stroking her hair. But not for long, as the midwives dragged him from the room. So, it ended well.'

Raskan snorted.

Footsteps announced the return of Feren. Draconus was nowhere in sight.

The sergeant straightened. 'Where is the Lord?'

'He makes propitiations,' Feren replied. 'Rint, you burned it, damn you.'

'I did.'

'Propitiations?' Raskan asked.

'The barrow,' she said distractedly, selecting a bowl.

Arathan stood, his eyes upon her, but she paid him no heed as she filled the bowl, and Rint knew that his sister was done with the boy.

*  *  *

'No,' said Feren in the dark, 'it's finished.'

Arathan moved away, feeling lost. Tears blurred his vision. His father ruled everyone, and to rule meant to *use*. Everywhere he turned he saw his father's heavy hand. Pushing away, dragging along, holding down – where it struck there were bruises, aching wounds. This was the meaning of power.

He wanted to flee. Come the morning he could be gone. But Rint would track him down. Besides, some things he could not escape.

He edged past his bedroll, came to the weights stacked in their perfect measures. One by one, he threw them out into the night.

*  *  *

A day's travel west of Abara Delack, Grizzin Farl sat by the small fire he had made to roast the hare he had killed earlier that day. True hunters used slingstones, or arrows. Perhaps even a spear such as he carried in abundance. But Grizzin Farl was no hunter. He had run the creature down. Dogged it into panting submission. Even then, as he held the trembling thing in his arms, he had spent an inordinate amount of time stroking its soft fur, to calm its fear, and he had winced when he snapped its neck.

Death was terrible power. The delivering of suffering never quite washed off. He had seen, among hunters and herders, an undeniable coldness of spirit that made of necessity a virtue. Grief did not touch them in the slaying of creatures, whether those creatures walked upon two legs or ran upon four; whether they possessed wings or slid smooth

221

through water. Need was its own answer. One needs to eat, be it flesh or plant, and death was the currency.

He did not like that truth and this night, as he gnawed on small bones, his title of Protector felt mocking and hollow.

Earlier in the day he had seen two riders off to the north: the Borderswords who had taken the tutor to Abara Delack, presumably, now hastening to catch up with their companions. If they had in turn spied the Azathanai, they'd chewed and spat out their curiosity. The minds of some were shuttered things, singular of focus and thus narrow in their interests. They thrived as impediments to wonder. One day, he imagined, every place in every land might be filled with such men and women, each one busy draining colour from the world. He had no intention of living to see it. Rue the realm where bold laughter was met with disapproving frowns and sullen agitation! Serious people never stopped waging their war on joy and pleasure, and they were both relentless and tireless. In the making of his life he stood against them, and saw in his steadfastness a most worthy virtue. Protector indeed!

The thought brought a low rumble of laughter to him.

Alas, the hare had no reason to join in the amusement.

Before dusk descended into night, he had seen a lone figure walking up from the east. While it was true that chance could not be measured, this meeting to come was by no means accidental, and so in his mind he measured it out most carefully. Well to the west, a Thel Akai queen had been stirred from her eternal slumber, and her mood was still foul, no matter the efforts at placation.

The old so disliked the young, and at the extremes of both, why, the dislike stretched into genuine distaste. Regard as foul the fresh-born; see as crêped the laggard ancients, with disgust the mutual regard and well earned, too.

And now here, from the east, heavy footsteps drawing ever closer, came an old friend who would kneel to a child. These details did not so much balance out as wink at one another.

'So much to muse on,' he now said, loud enough to be heard by the one who approached. 'Yet all the ale is gone. I was never one to ration my gifts, poor me.'

'In words alone, Grizzin Farl, you could fill casks.'

'Ah, but mine own fill never tastes as sweet. Join me, old friend. I would wring from you a thousand confessions this night, till I nod drunk on wisdom. If not yours, then mine.'

His guest was nearly of matching bulk and girth. A cloak of silver fur rode his broad shoulders, shimmering in the starlight. 'I have come from a place of tribulation and dire portent.'

'In leaving did you, by chance, raid a wine cupboard?'

'The Tiste do well by wine, it's true. So much, then, for gifts carried a great distance.' With that he drew out from a satchel a fired jug.

Grizzin Farl smiled. 'Caladan Brood, I would kiss you if I were blind and only a smidgen more desperate than I am.'

'Hold the sentiment until you are well and truly drunk, but think not of me.'

'Who, then?'

'Why, your wife, of course. This wine was meant for her.'

'Thief of her heart! I should have known not to trust you! Her sloven'd gratitude, which I easily envision here in my skull, has the rank stench of a distillery. Truly you know the secret path to her bed!'

'Not so secret, Grizzin, but I shall say no more and thus protect your innocence.'

'By title I was named Protector and in said cause I now stopper my ears and shut my eyes. Come then, pass me this bottle and let's know the sting of portent.'

'My freedom,' Brood said, 'has been wrested away from me.'

Grizzin swallowed down three quick mouthfuls, and then gasped. 'You fool – how much did you pay for this? Your firstborn? Never have I tasted better! Upon my wife's tongue the shock of quality – she'll know not what to make of it.'

'So confesses her husband of centuries. Besides, I wager none of the three jugs I carry will last this night, so quality evades her yet again. My sympathy is unbounded, especially as I sit here looking upon you.'

'Well said, since it is a night for sordid confession. Freedom is nothing more than life stripped of responsibility. Oh, we yearn for it with reckless lust, but the shudders are short-lived, and besides, in sotted state she's a poor game in bed, and this I well know, since it's the only way by which she relents to my bluff pawing.'

'I grieve for your memories, Grizzin Farl. But more, I grieve in the hearing of them.'

'Let us not weep just yet. Here, numb thy throat and so steal pain from every word we utter.'

Caladan drank, handed the jug back. 'The First Son of Darkness has bound me to an oath, as I did to him in the making of a marriage stone for his brother.'

'It will never last.'

'What, the marriage?'

'The oath.'

'Why do you say that?'

'Well, I thought the lie would relieve you. Otherwise, could I even claim to be your friend? I think not. This bottle is done. Find us another, will you?'

'You've run far for this hare, Grizzin.'

'It was that or plucking weeds from around the house. Under critical eye, baleful and jaded. But now curiosity has me and I would see this dark woman's dark garden, weeds or no.'

'Think you not Draconus will stand in your way?'

'Ah, but he is well behind me, and well ahead of you, even as we speak.'

'He travels among the Azathanai? This surprises me, given the tensions in Kharkanas.'

'He goes to hide a bastard son, I think.'

'And for other reasons.'

Grizzin Farl raised his thick brows. 'You surmise from hidden knowledge. Here, drink more.'

'The Tiste put much in gestures,' Caladan said, taking back the jug. 'They would make of every deed a symbol, until the world carries benighted weight. By this means many walls are raised, many doors barred, and in meaning the realm becomes a maze to all who dwell in it.'

'No maze frightens me. I have run with hares.'

'You would weed her garden, then? Has she no decision to make on the offer?'

'Hah! Look upon me, friend, in the manner that would a true-blooded woman! See this golden hair? These bright dancing eyes? The grave assurance in my comportment? I am a mystery, a lure of well-hidden depths. To touch me is to brush jewels and gems; to stand too close is to swoon in heady spice – into my very arms. These gifts I have, friend, are not made of breadth or height; neither of weight nor robust presence. I could be a squirrel of a man and still women would fall in like bugs on a cup rim!'

'A fine speech, Grizzin.'

Grizzin nodded. 'Much practised,' he said, 'but yet to convince. I would change my tack, were I not certain the course is true.'

'I think it is time for the third jug.'

'Yes. Despondency was beckoned and lo, herein it slides. So morose, so knowing. If my vision were clearer, if my thoughts sharper, if my wit truly honed, I might find cause to drink and forget.'

'I know little of this Anomander Rake.'

'Then I shall bestir him for you. All that is to be known, and so you will find out who stands at the other end of your chain, and if the links be few in number, or beyond count, this too I will discover.'

'There is a surety about him, that much was clear,' said Brood. 'Beyond the gift of the title given him; and his closeness to Mother Dark. He possesses something deliberate and yet of great depth. He is, I think, a violent man, yet is not at ease with the violence in him.'

'A flagellant, then. I see before me the demise of my enthusiasm.'

'He avowed he would not drag me into their civil war.'

'That war is certain?'

Caladan Brood shrugged. 'They are a generation that has tasted blood, and where horror fades, nostalgia seeps in. In war all is simple, and there is appeal in this. Who among us is comforted by confusion, uncertainty?'

Grizzin Farl mulled on this for a time, and then shook his head. 'Is it as the Jaghut assert, then? In society we find the seeds of its own destruction?'

'Perhaps, but they miss the point. It is the absence of society that leads to destruction. When concord is lost, when arguments cease and in opposition neither side sees the other as kin, as brother and sister, then all manner of atrocity is possible.'

'You strew sharp stones upon my path of thought, old friend. Does Mother Dark will this dissolution?'

'I should think not, but in darkness she dwells.'

'The wine is gone. Only sour fumes remain. Drunkenness pretends to resolution. I would sigh and revel in lazy pondering. Do you return home, Caladan? Ah, I thought not. K'rul has begotten a child and the earth itself holds the memory of its birth-cry. Will you drink of K'rul's blood?'

Brood grunted, eyes on the failing fire. 'There is no need for that. As you say, the child is born, and will in turn beget many others before too long.'

'Did you not judge him precipitous?'

'That judgement is no longer relevant, Grizzin. It is done.'

'It was a thought of mine,' Grizzin Farl said, 'that Draconus journeyed in fevered rage.'

Brood looked up, eyes sharp. 'And?'

'Bloodied my feet for a time on that path. But in our night of meeting, which I revisit from all angles, I now conclude that my fears are unfounded. He is indifferent to K'rul. What drives him now is far more desperate.'

Brood nodded. 'Love will do that.'

'It may seem to you, by your comment and all its sharp edges, that I am fleeing from my beloved wife and our wastrel of a son. This gives great offence and I am of a mind to draw weapons and have at you.'

'Then you are even drunker than I had thought.'

'I am, and am also most hateful of truths that rear up ugly of countenance.'

'Most truths have that face, friend. But I was speaking of Draconus.'

Grizzin sighed. 'Guilt shouts loud at the most inopportune moment. Drunk and a fool – already the wine knocks about inside my skull, and I curse how you plied me with that Tiste poison.'

'Better you than your wife.'

'All my friends say that. I will be hungry come the dawn – have you spare food?'

'You brought none with you, Grizzin Farl?' Caladan Brood sighed.

'I have a pot,' Grizzin countered.

'Followed you out of the house, did it?'

'Eager to replace the head on my shoulders, yes. Long ago she swore to carry no blade, no cudgel, no iron-tipped spear. Yet made of her hands the deadliest of weapons, second only to her temper, but on occasion even they will deign to reach for something that will serve the instant. I have learned her ways, you see, and so was appropriately wary in my retreat.'

'And the argument this time?'

Grizzin sank his head into his hands. 'I went too far. I threw the boy out.'

'I am sure he gave cause.'

'He has fallen under the influence of my first progeny, Errastas.'

'There was always something of the follower in Sechul Lath,' said Brood. 'Errastas is ambitious and would be the master of the litter.'

'Setch is weak, is what he is. To have them both come from my loins shrinks my sack with shame.'

'Amend that defect before you stand naked before Mother Dark.'

'In so many ways I will give thanks to the darkness surrounding her. Now, my words remain bold as weapons, but my thoughts shy from reason. I am drunk and unmanned and the only retreat awaiting me is senseless slumber. Good night to you, old friend. When next we meet, it shall be Thel Akai ale and the gifting shall be from my hand to yours.'

'Already you dream of vengeance.'

'I do, and with pleasure.'

\*     \*     \*

'That nearly killed us,' gasped Sechul Lath, his right arm hanging useless and broken in at least two places. He leaned forward as far as he could and spat out blood and mucus, which was better than swallowing it, as he had been doing since the stubborn woman's death. The taste in his mouth belonged to violence and savage fear, and now it sat heavy in his stomach. 'And I am still of two minds.'

Errastas, kneeling nearby, finished binding the deep wound on his thigh and then looked away, back down the glittering trail. 'I was right,' he said. 'They're coming. Her Tiste blood flows true.'

'How will this work, Errastas? I am still uncertain . . .' Sechul Lath looked down at the corpse. 'Abyss below, but she was hard to kill!'

'They are at that,' Errastas agreed. 'But this blood – see it flow down

226

the path? See how it swallows gems, diamonds and gold, all of our stolen loot? There is power in this.'

'But not Azathanai power.'

Errastas snorted, and then wiped blood from his nose. 'We are not the only elemental forces in creation, Setch. I sense, however, that the power we spilled out here comes as much from outrage as anything else. No matter. It is puissant.'

'I feel,' said Sechul Lath, looking round, 'that this place is not for us.'

'Mother Dark dares to claim it,' Errastas said, sneering. 'Darkness – as if she could claim the domain as entirely her own! What arrogance! Look below, Setch – what do you see?'

'I see Chaos, Errastas. An endless storm.'

'We make this place a trap. Let its Tiste name stand. Spar of Andii it shall remain – it hardly confers a right to ownership. By our deeds we undermine its purity. K'rul is not the only one who understands the efficacy of blood.'

'So you keep saying, but I wonder if we truly know what we're doing.'

'Perhaps you don't, though Abyss take me I've tried explaining it to you often enough. *I* know, Setch, and so you'll just have to trust me. K'rul would simply give power away, freely, to any who might want it. By this, he undermines its value. He dislodges the proper order of things. We will best him, Setch. *I* will best him.' He pushed himself up against a boulder. 'We haven't long. They're coming, that Jaghut and his Tiste hostage. Listen to me. Mother Dark understands the exclusivity of power, though she reaches too far, revealing outrageous greed. We must draw her into this fray. We must awaken her to the threat these new Warrens pose – to us all. It's important that she resist him, and so occupy all of K'rul's attention. So distracted, he will not see us, and most certainly not comprehend our intentions, until it is too late.' He looked up at Sechul Lath. 'There, I have explained it yet again. Yet I see disappointment in your eyes – what now?'

'It felt blunt. Crass, even, the way you said it. It lacked subtlety.'

'I yield the meaningless secrets, Setch, to better hold hidden the important ones. Think of prod and pull, if you like. Explore the concepts in your mind, and muse on the pleasures of misdirection.'

Sechul Lath studied Errastas, lying there propped up against a boulder, beaten half to death. 'Are you truly as clever as you think you are?'

Errastas laughed. 'Oh, Setch, it hardly matters. The suspicion is enough, making fecund the soil of imagination. Let others fill the gaps in my cleverness, and make of me in their eyes a genius.'

'I doubt the veracity of your words.'

'Well you should. Now, help me up. We must leave here.'

'Exploiting the very freedom K'rul offers us.'

'I delight in the irony.'

Sechul Lath turned and looked down at the corpse of the Jaghut, lying so near the edge of the spar. It was a fell thing, to murder someone. Errastas was right: outrage swirled in the air, thick as smoke. It felt heady enough to make his head spin.

'I never knew,' said Errastas as Sechul, with only one working arm, awkwardly helped him to stand, 'that killing could be so much fun.'

Sechul shuddered. 'Errastas, look at what we have done. Invited her here under false pretences, and then set upon her like wild beasts. We have awakened the wrath of the Jaghut. Nothing good will come of that.'

'Night comes to the Jaghut, Setch. Their fury is as nothing now.'

'Too easy your dismissal, Errastas. We have just murdered his wife.'

'And Hood will weep – what of it? Now, let us go, before they draw close enough to hear us. Besides, it is not Hood who approaches, is it?'

'No,' Sechul Lath muttered, 'only his brother.'

＊　　＊　　＊

Haut paused on the trail, squinting upward.

Behind him, Korya sagged down in exhaustion. Circling the top of a tower did not make for much exercise. Three strides from edge to edge; such was her realm, the span of faith for her godly aspirations. It seemed paltry, small, and she had begun to suspect that the world ever delivered lessons in humility, even to gods and goddesses.

'It is not far now,' said Haut. 'I should have selected the sword; this axe grows heavy. Bold my pride; feeble my aged muscles.' He glanced back at her. 'Have you given more thought to this scattered treasure?'

'Was I to have given it more thought?'

'I await your wisdom.'

She shook her head. 'Of wisdom I have little, master. But I see it as a deliberate mockery of worth.'

'Yes, but why?'

'Maybe we are being told that only what awaits us at the end of this trail holds true worth.'

'Possibly. The Azathanai are curious creatures. They are not acquisitive. In fact, there is one among them who bears the title of Protector, yet protects nothing. The Jheleck came to their villages and stole all they could carry, and he but smiled.'

'Perhaps he protects what cannot be seen.'

'And what might that be?'

She considered, taking her time as it gave her further respite. 'There are many virtues that cannot be measured in a material manner.'

'Indeed? Name one.'

'Love.'

'Torcs and rings of gold, brooches and diadems; expensive gifts, a solid home and a roof that does not leak. A child.'

'From all those love can be stripped away, yet still they remain.'

'Excellent. Go on.'

'Trust.'

'Guard my wealth and I will pay you in return.'

'That is a transaction.'

'One that purchases trust.'

'Such material exchanges as you describe are meant to symbolize the virtues I mentioned. They are not the virtues in and of themselves.'

'But is this not the meaning of all wealth, hostage?'

'I think not. After all, greed is not a virtue.'

'Greed is the language of power, the hoarding of symbols.'

She shook her head. 'Virtues cannot be claimed; they are but shown.'

'Shown. How are they shown?'

Korya scowled. 'By the gifts you describe.'

Haut nodded. 'Listen well. You are right to not conflate the symbol with the meaning; but you are wrong in thinking that to do so is un-common.'

'Then I would say, the Protector defends the distinction, and so to make his point, he must stand aside when thieves take away the material symbols of the virtues whose sanctity and purity he defends.'

Haut grunted. 'A fine theory. I will consider—'

His abrupt stop made her look up. Haut was staring down at his feet. After a long moment he drew free his axe and then faced upslope once more.

'Master?'

'By what measure then, Azathanai wealth?'

'Master? What is—' Faint motion caught her eye, something glittering, and she looked down on the path. A thin, crooked stream was wending its way down through the twisted rings and cut gems. In the strange, colourless light it looked black as ink.

Haut set out, climbing once more with the axe readied in his hands.

Pushing herself upright and taking care to avoid the rivulet, Korya followed.

Another half-dozen strides upward and it became impossible to step around the draining liquid. *Is this blood I see?* She thought of gods and goddesses, the notions of sacrifice – so long ago abandoned by the Tiste – and this place at once seemed colder, crueller.

No more questions to ask Haut; this was not the time. She remained silent, but her mouth was dry and her heart beat fast in her chest.

The ascent ended just ahead in a broken tumble of stones that seemed to flatten, as if by weight alone they could force the trail level, but something was lying upon the verge – a corpse, sprawled and half naked, the limbs stretched as if the body had been dragged to the edge of the descent. From this contorted perch, blood ran down in thick ropes, drowning the last few scattered gems.

A Jaghut woman.

She could see the point of a long knife jutting from her chest, and her back was arched in a manner to suggest the handle protruding from between her shoulder blades.

'Karish.'

The word, coming from Haut who now stood before the body, was half prayer, half plea. A moment later he wavered, as if about to fall – and she drew up close, thinking to take his weight though, of course, she could never manage that. Haut staggered ahead, stumbled past the body, lifting the axe.

*'Karish!'*

Korya reached the corpse. She stared down at it – the first dead person she had ever seen. A proud-looking woman, her features even, perhaps beautiful by Jaghut standards, she seemed to be frowning at the formless sky. The tusks were white as goat's milk. The mouth was slightly open, crusted with froth and blood. The eyes bore a strange look, as if in seeing everything they found nothing worthy of regard. Above all, it was their stillness that shook Korya. *This is death. Death is stillness. And stillness does not belong among the living.*

A pinnacle beyond the tumbled boulders marked the end of the ascent – a span of level rock five, perhaps six strides across. A godly realm, but upon it stood only Haut. He was studying the ground, as if seeking to read the past.

*Not long past. She died only moments ago. The blood only now begins to slow.*

Now at last she found the need to speak. 'Where could they have gone? We passed no one.' When Haut made no answer, she walked to the edge and looked down. A seething storm swirled far below, argent yet sickly. Waves of nausea struck her and she backed away a step, almost toppling.

Haut's hand met her back, solid as stone. 'Unwise, hostage. To look upon Chaos is to yield to its invitation. For that, I am most sorely tempted. It is said,' he went on, the axe-head crunching on the bedrock as he let the weapon down, 'that Mother Dark did not hesitate. She leapt into that wild realm. And returned, but not the same woman she had been before. Now, she would turn her back upon Chaos, a champion of all that it is not.'

She wondered at his words, their rambling nature; their looseness in this moment.

'I wager it unwise,' Haut went on, 'to make of oneself a symbol, and if she be coveted, why is it a surprise to any?'

'Master. Who was she? The Jaghut woman? Who could have done this?'

'My brother's wife,' Haut replied. 'Karish. The greatest scholar among the Jaghut. She was lured here and then murdered.'

'By the Azathanai?'

'By one or more among them, yes.'

'Will there now be war, master? Between the Jaghut and the Azathanai?'

He turned at that, studied her for a moment, only to look away again. 'A war?' He voiced that word as if he had never heard it before, and only now comprehended its meaning.

'Master. When we began this journey, you said that we were invited. Was it to see this? If so, why?'

'She named it the Spar of Andii – your Mother Dark. And made of it a fist of Darkness. Hostage, what awaits us now is the challenge of making sense of these symbols. For this, your cleverness surpasses mine. It was ever my belief that you needed us. Now it seems that it is we who need you.' His face twisted and seemed to crumple before her. 'Korya Delath, will you help us?'

# NINE

HARAL, THE LEADER OF THE CARAVAN GUARDS WHO WOULD NOT BE called 'sir', had drawn up his horse to await them. Just beyond, the trail forked, with a cobbled track beginning there. To the left it climbed a hundred or more strides to the fortified walls of the Tulla Hold, an edifice carved into the cliffside. A dozen or more windows made rough holes in the rock facing above the heaped boulders that formed the defences. Along the uneven wall rose squat towers, four in all, each one twice as broad at the base as at the summit, with mounted arbalests commanding the platforms. To Orfantal's eyes Tulla Hold rose before him like a fortress of myth, and he imagined high-ceilinged hallways shrouded in shadows, through which grieving lords and haunted ladies walked, and the rooms that had once held children now had their doorways sealed and the cradles – rank with mould and thick with dust – rocked only to faint draughts in the deep of night.

He saw rusting weapons on hooks lining the walls, and tapestries sagging beneath their pins. The images were faded with age, but all bore the scenes of war, the death of heroes and murderers in flight. In every room such tapestries brooded like faint echoes of battle, filling the walls with corpses of sewn thread, studded with arrows or bearing lurid wounds.

Gripp riding at his side, Orfantal reined in opposite Haral.

The captain seemed to be eyeing Orfantal's nag with some regret. 'We will camp here,' he said after a moment. 'The Lady is not in residence, so we need not pay our respects, which is just as well, since that horse would never manage the climb.'

Orfantal set a hand against his horse's neck as if he could protect the beast from Haral's cruel words. Feeling the heat of the animal under his palm, he found it impossible to imagine life surrendering in this beast. He saw it as a loyal servant and knew that its heart would not falter in its strong beat. There was glory in final journeys and he was certain that his mount would carry him all the way to Kharkanas.

Gripp was squinting up at the distant citadel. 'Gate's opening, Haral. Tithe, do you think?'

Scowling, Haral said nothing. Dismounting, he led his horse to the stone-lined well off to one side of the fork. Beyond it stretched levelled ground studded with iron tent pegs, and a half-dozen fire-pits lined with rocks.

Orfantal looked ahead, to where the cobbled track led deeper into the hills. If there were bandits, they would be hiding among those bleached crags crowding the road. Perhaps even now steady eyes were fixed upon them. Come the morrow there might be an ambush. Peace suddenly shattered: shouts and weapons clanging, figures toppling from saddles and bodies thumping heavily in the dust. His heart beat fast in excitement – the world was so huge! They might kidnap him, demanding a ransom, and he might find himself trussed up and left in some hovel, but he would twist free of the bonds and dig his way out, slipping into the maze of rock and crevasse, there to live wild as a beast.

Years would pass, and then word would come from these hills of a new bandit chief, clever and rich, a wayfarer who stole young women and made them all his most loyal warriors; and theirs was a loyalty beyond challenge, for each woman loved their chief as would a wife a husband.

He would conquer Tulla Hold, sweep it clean of ghosts and broken hearts. He would burn all the tapestries. There would be many children, an army of them. All would be well, with tables groaning beneath roasted meats, until at last all the noble houses marched to lay siege to the fortress. They would come in their thousands and when the walls were surmounted, he would fight to the last on the battlements, defending his children – but someone had yielded the gate, with gold in hand, and the enemy was suddenly in the courtyard. Assailed on all sides, he would be driven down to his knees by a spear flung from behind, and twisting round to see his slayer, his betrayer, he would defy the gods and rise once more—

'Off your horse now for pity's sake,' said Gripp.

Orfantal started and then quickly slid down from his mount. Together with the old man who was his protector, they led their charges towards the well.

'That's a wagon comin' down,' Gripp said. 'And there's a highborn with them. Young. As young as you, Orfantal. You ain't curious?'

Orfantal shrugged.

'When the Lady is in residence, she sends down fine food and ale to whoever camps here. It's a measure of her honour, y'see? Haral was hoping and then he was disappointed, but now he's hopeful again. We could all do with fresh food. And the ale.'

Orfantal glanced over at Haral, who was now busy stripping his mount while the others prepared the camp. 'Maybe she's out hunting bandits.'

'Who?'

'The Lady of the Hold.'

The old man rubbed at the back of his neck, a habit of his that left a dirty line that no amount of washing seemed able to remove. 'No bandits this close to Tulla, Orfantal. A day into the hills, about half-way between here and Hust Forge, that's when things get risky for us. But we're not too worried. Word is, them Deniers are now making more money mining tin and lead and selling it to Hust – more than they ever could waylaying people like us. Mind you, mining's hard work and not something I'd want to do. It's all about weighing the risks, y'see?'

Orfantal shook his head.

Gripp sighed. 'Saddles off and some grooming while we feed 'em. Your nag's got a bad eye and it's weeping more with all this dust. Getting old's no fun at all and that's the truth.'

For the past two nights there had not been sufficient fuel for cook-fires, barring a single one upon which tea had been made, and so they'd eaten bread, cheese and smoked meat dry as leather. But this night three fires were built, using the last of the dung chips, and pots un-packed from under the wagons. By the time the tents were raised and bedrolls unfurled inside them, the visitors from Tulla Hold had arrived in the camp.

Orfantal finished brushing down his horse and then led it over to the rope corral. He watched for a time as the other mounts greeted the nag, wondering if they but felt sorry for it, and then he made his way over to the cookfires, where the strangers had drawn up.

He saw servants unloading charcoal and dung chips, which were then carried over to Haral's wagons, and bundles of food now crowded the cookfires. A highborn girl was standing beside Haral, dressed in a thick midnight blue cloak of some waxed material, and as Orfantal approached he saw that her dark eyes were upon him.

Haral cleared his throat. 'Orfantal, kin of Nerys Drukorlat, this is Sukul of the Ankhadu, sister of Captain Sharenas Ankhadu, spear-wielder of Urusander's Legion at the Battle of Misharn Plain.'

Orfantal eyed the round-faced girl. 'Are you a hostage like me?'

'A guest,' Haral explained before she could reply, as if embarrassed by Orfantal's question and fearful that she would take offence. 'Lesser Families exchange hostages only with their equals. Lady Hish Tulla is of the Greater Families and powerful in the court.'

The expression on Sukul's face had not changed.

Orfantal was unable to judge her age. Perhaps she was a year older than him, or a year younger. They were of similar height. Something in her eyes made him nervous. 'Thank you,' he now said to her, 'Sukul Ankhadu, for this gift of food and company.'

The girl's brows lifted. 'I doubt you learned such manners from your grandmother,' she said, derision in her tone. 'She showed no honour to Urusander's Legion.'

Haral looked uncomfortable, but at a loss, so he said nothing.

Orfantal shrugged. 'I did not know that my grandmother has dishonoured your family. I am sorry that she did, as you have shown yourself to be generous in Lady Tulla's absence from the Hold. For myself, I still thank you.'

There was a long moment of silence, and then Sukul tilted her head. 'Orfantal, you have much to learn. But for this night, I will take advantage of your innocence. Together, we shall leave the bitterness of our elders in their restless hands. Your kind words have touched me. Should the need arise in your life for an ally, you may call upon Sukul Ankhadu.'

'When I am a great warrior,' Orfantal replied, 'I shall welcome you to my side.'

She laughed at his reply and then gestured towards the nearest cook-fire. 'Join me then, Orfantal, and we shall eat like soldiers upon the march, and woe to the enemy awaiting us.'

Her laughter had made him uncertain, but the invitation was like a spark to dry tinder, as if she had unerringly set fire to his imagined future, and would readily take her place in it. He looked upon her most carefully now, imagining her visage – older, stronger – wrought in bold thread. A face to one side of the hero's face; a companion of years, loyal and sure, and as they strode past Haral and Gripp Orfantal felt that face, smiling and flushed, sink into his soul.

They would indeed be great friends, he decided. And somewhere still ahead, hazy and vague but dark with promise, awaited their betrayer.

*       *       *

They left the two of them to their own fire, and at first this had perturbed Orfantal. He was used to Gripp's company and thought of the old man as a wise uncle, or a castellan. But this was a matter of blood and purity, and although the Ankhadu line was lesser, still it measured far above that of Haral, Gripp and the others.

There was nothing in what Orfantal had seen while in the company of these guards and traders to make clear this distinction in class. Roughness of manner did not suffice, as it was, in Orfantal's mind, the way of the road for all travellers; and even Haral's brutal treatment of Narad befitted the man's insubordination.

But when Sukul seated herself – on a saddle-like stool brought out from the Hold's wagon – opposite him, and servants arrived bearing pewter plates on which steaming food was heaped, along with tankards of watered wine – in place of the ale being offered the others of the caravan – Orfantal was startled to realize that he had grown so accustomed to his companions on this journey that he had begun to see himself as no different from them, an orphan in their company, well liked by all and, indeed, one of them.

The sudden deference was unwanted, a reminder of all the rules of behaviour that made no sense; and watching how Sukul responded to it with such natural ease, all of his grandmother's impatient lessons returned home, unwelcome as a switch to his back.

'Orfantal,' said Sukul as she picked at her meal, 'tell me about yourself. But first, to save you time, this is what I know. Kin to Nerys Drukorlat, widow of the wars – she has a daughter, does she not? Once a hostage to House Purake. But of her family beyond her own estate, I have heard little. Indeed, it was my belief that the bloodline was almost extinct, like an ancient, once proud tree, with but a single branch left bearing leaves. You must have come far, then, from some half-forgotten brood at the very edge of Kurald Galain.'

Orfantal had been well versed in the tale he was to tell. But Sukul would be his companion, and as such there would be truth between them. 'Nerys Drukorlat is my grandmother in truth,' he said to her. 'My mother is Sandalath Drukorlat, who now dwells in Dracons as a hostage. My father died in the wars, at a great battle where he saved the lives of many famous highborn.'

The girl paused in her eating and regarded him steadily. 'Surely,' she said after a moment, her voice low, 'Nerys had for you a different story to tell.'

'Yes. But it made no sense. I don't know why I am supposed to pretend that I had a different mother and father. My mother is very kind to me and tells me many stories about my father. Theirs was a love only death could silence.'

'With whom will you be hostage, Orfantal?'

'To the Citadel itself, and the line of the sons and daughters of Mother Dark.'

She set her plate down, most of her supper untouched, and then reached for her wine. 'And all arrangements have been made for this? I am surprised – would Mother Dark now claim for her closest followers – her sons and daughters – the unity and honour of a Greater House?

What will the highborn make of that, I wonder? Bloodlines shall be crossed, and all for a cult of worship.'

Her words confused him. It was clear now that she was much older than him. 'I think, yes, it is all arranged.'

Her eyes flicked back to him, as intent as ever. She drank down half her tankard and held it out to be refilled. 'Orfantal, are we in truth now friends?'

He nodded.

'Then listen well to my advice. In a few days you will arrive in Kharkanas, and be delivered into the keeping of those who dwell in the Citadel. There will be teachers, and you will feel plucked one way and then another, and even those into whose care you have been given, well, they will be busy with their own tasks and interests. It may be, Orfantal, that you will find life lonely.'

He stared at her. Would they not all gather to welcome him, as they had his mother? What of Anomander Rake? And Andarist and Silchas Ruin?

'Seek out Lady Hish Tulla – she is there now. Before you leave tomorrow morning, I will send a servant down with a message that I will write to her, which you must carry upon your person, and then give into her hand.'

'Very well. But you are not a hostage. You are a guest – why are you a guest in Tulla Hold?'

Sukul made a sour face. 'My sister has a reputation in court, and our mother saw me upon the same wayward path. She endeavoured to prevent that. There was an old friendship, forged on the field of battle . . . well, my mother made a request and Lady Hish accepted. I am in her charge, being educated above my station, and under the protection of Hish Tulla – who herself has known the wayward life, only to have stepped back from its sordid path.' She drank more wine and then smiled. 'Oh dear, how I have confused you. Heed only this, then: blood is not the only loyalty in the world. Two spirits, matched of vision, can reach across any divide. Remember that, Orfantal, for on this night such a friendship has begun, between us.'

'This,' said Orfantal, 'has been a wonderful night.'

'Hish Tulla seeks to forge the same friendship, the same loyalty, between the highborn and the officers of Urusander's Legion. By this means she seeks peace in Kurald Galain. But I tell you this: many officers, like my own sister, have no interest in peace.'

Orfantal nodded. 'They have fought in wars,' he said.

'They sting to slights, both real and imagined.'

'Will you visit me in Kharkanas, Sukul Ankhadu?'

She drained her wine. 'If I am to stand at the side of a great warrior, why, I am sure we shall meet again, Orfantal. Now, finish your wine – you sip like a bird, when you should be filling your belly.'

'I wish,' said Orfantal, 'that I had a sister. And that she was you.'

'Better we be friends than siblings, Orfantal, as perhaps you shall one day discover. Upon friends you can rely, but the same cannot always be said for siblings. Oh, and one more thing.'

'Yes?'

'That tale your grandmother would have you tell? Make it a truth in your mind – forget all you have told me this night. No one else must hear the truth as I have. Promise me this, Orfantal.'

'I promise.'

'The older you get,' she said, in a tone that made her seem eye to eye with his grandmother, 'the more you discover the truth about the past. You can empty it. You can fill it anew. You can create whatever truth you choose. We live long, Orfantal – much longer than the Jheleck, or the Dog-Runners. Live long enough and you will find yourself in the company of other liars, other inventors, and all that they make of their youth shines so bright as to blind the eye. Listen to their tales, and know them for the liars they are – no different from you. No different from any of us.'

Orfantal's head was swimming, but in challenge to her words he heard a faint voice of protest, rising from deep inside. He disliked liars. To lie was to break loyalty. To lie, as the ghost of every dead hero knew, was to betray.

The night was sinking into confusion, and he felt very alone.

\*     \*     \*

'I am a great believer in invention,' said Rise Herat to the small girl beside him. Glancing down at her he added, 'But do be careful. It's a long fall from here and I would not survive the displeasure of the entire Hust clan should harm befall you.'

Seeming intent on ignoring his warning, Legyl Behust pulled herself up and on to the merlon. Feet dangling behind her, she leaned out, her face flushed with excitement, her eyes wide with wonder.

Rise took hold of the nearest ankle and held tight. 'I indulge you too much,' he said. 'But look well upon all that you see. The city holds its back to the river behind us, and indeed to the Citadel itself. We need not concern ourselves with those settlements upon the south shore, where you will find the factories, infernal with the stinks of industry. Hides into leather, the butchering of pigs, cattle and whatnot. The crushing of bones into meal for the fields. The throwing of clay and the deliveries each day from the charcoal burners. All the necessities of maintaining a large population.'

'I don't want to look there!'

'Of course you don't. Better these finer structures, this sad attempt at order—'

'But where are the spirits of the forest? Where is the forest? You talked about forests!'

He pointed. 'There, that dark line to the north. Once, it was much closer.'

'It ran away?'

'Think of Kharkanas as a beast crawled up from the river. Perhaps to sun itself, or perhaps only to glower at the world. Think of the long-tailed, beaked turtles – the ones the river folk bring to the markets. Gnarled and jagged shells, a savage bite and thick muscles upon the long neck. Claws at the ends of strong limbs. Skin tough as armour. An ugly beast, Legyl, foul of temper and voracious. Hear its hiss as you draw close!'

She was squirming about on the narrow stone projection. 'Where's its eyes? I don't see its eyes!'

'But dear, we are its eyes. Here atop the Old Tower. We are the city's eyes just as we are the world's eyes, and that is a great responsibility, for it is only through us that the world is able to see itself, and from sight is born mystery – the releasing of imagination – and in this moment of recognition, why, everything changes.'

She sagged back. 'But I don't want to be its eyes, Master Rise.'

'Why not?'

'Because I don't know what I'm seeing.'

He helped her regain her feet. 'That's fine, because none of us do. Brush the grit from your clothes. You venture into a difficult area, this idea of "knowing".'

'I wasn't going to ever fall,' she said, slapping at the stains on her tunic.

'Of course not. I had your foot.'

'Ever.'

'And you can be sure you may rely upon me, Legyl,' said Rise Herat. 'So, as you say, there are some things that can well be known. But tell me – did not the city seem alive to you?'

'I could see everyone. In the streets. They were tiny!'

Taking her hand, he led her back to the trap door and the steep steps leading down to the level below. 'Fleas from the mud, mites and ticks burrowing into the hide.'

'It was buildings and stuff. Not a river turtle at all.'

'I have shown you the city and to look upon the city is to look upon your own body, Legyl. And this Citadel . . . why, the eyes are set in the head and the head upon the body. This morning, you became the Citadel's eyes. Is your body not flesh and bone? Is it not a place of heat and labour, the beat of your heart, the breath you draw? Such is wise Kharkanas.'

At the bottom of the steps she pulled free her hand. 'Cedorpul's a better teacher than you. He makes sense. You don't.'

He shrugged. 'I forget the narrow perch of the child's mind. In pragmatism there is comfort, yes?'

'I'm going to play in my room now.'

'Go on,' he said, gesturing her along.

The temple's lone hostage scampered off, down the inner stairs to the next floor below. Rise Herat hesitated, and then turned about and made his way back up to the tower's platform. His morning ritual, this private contemplation of Kharkanas, might still be salvaged. Cedorpul had ambushed him in the corridor outside his chambers, thrusting this young student into his care. Hasty words regarding lessons and then the young priest was gone.

More rumours, more agitation to rush up and down the hallways of the Citadel. The sanctuary of the Old Tower was Rise Herat's place of strength amidst all this nonsense. Instead, he found himself left in charge of a girl he saw as almost feral and possibly simple-minded, so vast the temple's neglect. Ever passed on to the next, scores of teachers and no lessons ever returned to, Legyl's was an education of fragments, delivered in haste and out from airs of distraction. When he had looked down at her, however, he had seen sure intelligence in the large eyes staring back up at him.

As the court historian, he decided that history would be the lesson he delivered. Such ambitions proved short-lived, as her breathless scatter of comments and observations left him confused. She listened to his words as one might listen to a songbird in the garden, a pleasant drone in the background. Whatever she took in seemed randomly selected; but perhaps it was that way with all children. He rarely had any contact with them, and generally preferred it that way.

Rise looked out over Kharkanas. Thin smoke drifted above the cityscape, not yet lifting to the height of the tower. It softened all that lay beneath it, and he wondered at the loss he always felt when venturing into a vista, the way the vastness narrowed down to the immediate; the sudden insistence of details near to hand. There had been a time, a generation or so back, when the city's artists had taken to the countryside, to paint landscapes, and to Rise Herat's mind these paintings achieved what reality could not. A promise of depth and distance, yet one in which the promise remained sacred, for neither depth nor distance could be explored. To draw closer was to see only the brush strokes and dried paint upon the board; and with them the surrendering of the illusion.

Details cluttered the mortal mind, blinded it to the broader sweeps of history. He'd thought to reach this observation in his lesson with Legyl. It might have been, he now considered, that she was still rather too young for such concepts. But then, it was equally likely that age had little to do with comprehension. He need only descend the tower and plunge into the frantic world of the court to witness the same obsessions with detail and immediacy that sent Legyl Behust scurrying this way and that. If anything, he was, in making the comparison, being unkind to the child.

No matter. Thoughts unspoken left no scars upon others. The fate of the inner landscape of the one doing the thinking was, of course, entirely different. This was the procession, he knew, of the failing mind, and in that failure was found a place where many unspoken thoughts came to rest; and it was a place of prejudice, hatred and ignorance.

That said, he knew that he was a poor teacher. He wove his histories as if they were inventions, disconnected and not relevant. Worse, he preferred the sweeping wash of colour to obsessive detail, ineffable feeling over intense analysis, possibility over probability; he was, by any measure, a dreadful historian.

He could see a shadow upon the city below, not thrown down by the smoke; nor did it come from a cloud as the sky was clear. This was Mother Dark's indrawn breath, stealing the light from the world. What, he wondered, did she do with it? Was it as the priestesses said? Did she devour it, feed upon it? When light goes, where does it go?

The landscape painters of old became obsessed with light, and reputedly that obsession drove many of them mad. But surely it was much worse if all light was stolen away. His thoughts turned to Kadaspala, the finest of all portrait artists – was it any wonder that he lived beneath a cloud of fear and flung his rage at the world? The priestesses promised gifts with the coming of darkness, and that none would be blind within it. Such gifts came from sorcery and so they were never free. Rise wondered at the cost awaiting them all.

He heard scrabbling from the stairs and turned to see Cedorpul climbing into view. The young priest was out of breath, his round face and round body seeming to bob loosely, as if filled with air. Behind him, as he stepped on to the platform, another figure loomed into view.

Cedorpul looked round. 'She's not here? Where is she?'

'In her room. Playing.'

'Abdication of responsibilities!'

Rise Herat tilted his head to one side. 'My very thoughts when you left her with me, Cedorpul.'

The priest waved a hand and then spent a moment straightening his stained tunic. 'These matters are beneath argument. Her whereabouts are known: that is all that is relevant here.'

The other priest edged past Cedorpul and stood looking out over the city.

'Endest Silann,' Rise said to him, 'tell me what you see?'

'It is less what I see than what I feel, historian.'

'And what do you feel?'

'Up here, it is as if the world's weight falls from my shoulders. While in the corridors beneath us . . .' He shrugged.

'You are young,' said Rise. 'There is much for you to bear, but the gift of youth means you scarcely feel its weight. It distresses me to think that you are growing old before your time.'

Cedorpul said, 'You've not yet heard. A rider has come in from one of the monasteries. Warlock Resh leads a party of Shake. They are escorting a guest, who will meet Mother Dark herself.'

'Indeed? It is already known that she will grant an audience? This guest must be of considerable importance.'

'From the Vitr.'

Rise turned to Cedorpul, studied the flushed face and bright blue eyes, wondering again at the lack of eyebrows or any other facial hair – did the man simply shave it all off, as he did from his pate? It seemed an odd affectation. 'Nothing comes from the Vitr,' he said.

'We make bold claims at our peril,' Endest muttered from where he leaned over the wall.

Rise considered for a moment, and then said, 'It is said the Azathanai have fashioned stone vessels capable of holding Vitr. Perhaps entire ships can be constructed of the same material.'

'No ships,' said Cedorpul. 'Beyond that, we know little. A woman, but not Tiste.'

'Azathanai?'

'It would seem so,' Endest confirmed.

'They should approach the edge of the forest soon, I would judge,' Cedorpul announced, moving to position himself beside his fellow priest. 'We thought to witness their arrival from here.'

So much for a period of restful contemplation. 'I trust all is being made ready below.'

'Nothing grand,' Cedorpul said. 'This is not a formal visit, after all.'

'No polishing of buckles?' Rise asked. 'No buffing of silver?'

Endest snorted.

Puffing out his fleshy cheeks, Cedorpul slowly shook his head. 'Ill-chosen my company this day. I am assailed by irreverence. An historian who derides historical occasions. An acolyte who mocks decorum.'

'Decorum?' Endest twisted round on one elbow to regard Cedorpul. 'How readily you forget, that before dawn this morning I dragged you out from under three priestess candidates. Smelling like a sack of stale wine, and as for the stains upon your robes, well, I remain most decorous in not looking too closely!' To Rise Herat he added, 'Cedorpul finds the candidates when they're still waiting in the chaperon's antechamber, and informs them that their prowess in bed must be tested—'

'I avail myself of their natural eagerness,' Cedorpul explained.

'He's found an unused room and now has the key for it. Swears the candidates to secrecy—'

'Dear me,' said Rise. 'Cedorpul, you risk a future of scorn and righteous vengeance. I hope I live to witness it in all its glory.'

'Endest, you have failed me in every measure of friendship of which I can conceive. Into the ears of the court historian, no less! It will be the two of you who curse me to the fate the historian so ominously describes!'

'Hardly,' countered Endest. 'I envision a night of confessions – no, whom do I deceive? Dozens of nights and confessions by the hundred. Yours is a fate I do not envy—'

'You seemed thankful enough for my cast-offs last night, honourable acolyte. And every other night at that. Who was it who said that hypocrisy has no place in a temple of worship?'

'No one,' replied Rise Herat, 'as far as I know.'

'Indeed?' Cedorpul asked. 'Truth?'

Rise nodded.

'Oh my,' Cedorpul said, and then he sighed. 'These matters are beneath argument. Let us ignore, for the time being, the unfortunate circumstances driving the three of us into each other's company, and enjoy the view.'

'And what of young Legyl Behust?' Rise asked him.

'Surely there is a sound argument to be made regarding the educational value of play. Besides, that chamber beneath us is the traditional sanctuary of the Citadel's succession of hostages. May she bar the door in all assurance of privacy. Until the noon bell at the very least.'

It occurred to Rise Herat, somewhat ungraciously, that he would have preferred the company of Legyl Behust.

Cedorpul pointed. 'I see them!'

*     *     *

Sister Emral Lanear examined herself in the full-length silvered mirror. The faintly blurred woman staring back at her promised great beauty, and Emral longed for them to exchange places. With such a prayer answered, none could pierce the veil, and she need not guard herself at every moment, lest someone glimpse the tortured truths roiling behind her eyes; and in expression she would give nothing away.

The world held up its illusions. No one could see for ever, beyond horizons, through the thickest of forests and the solid mountains of rock, or into the depths of dark rivers, and so there were promises out there as well, inviting the longing reach, offering up vistas of grandeur. The illusions were borne by all who witnessed them in the name of sanity, perhaps, or hope. And so too could others see her: a

High Priestess taking her station in the altar room, with the other High Priestess at her side, both standing as representatives of Mother Dark, whose own veil of darkness none could pierce – they could indeed see this and so find whatever illusions of comfort they desired.

There was no cause to resent their expectations. Yet, for all that, she wished the image before her to step out from the mirror, leaving a space into which Emral could then plunge. Illusions held up the world, and she was so tired of holding up her own.

Behind her the lesser priestesses fretted, and the sound alone was sufficient to irritate her. They had fled their beds and the men lying in them as soon as the news reached them. In her mind she imagined them transformed, bright silks shed and in their place dark, oily feathers. Mouths twisting into beaks. Breathless, excited words dissolving into senseless cawing. And the musty heat of their bodies now filled the chamber, and the long-toed feet clacked and kicked through the white shit of their agitation, and in a moment Emral Lanear would turn from the mirror and look upon them, and smile at the death of illusions.

'A woman!' someone hissed.

'Azathanai! It is said they can take any form they wish.'

'Nonsense. They are bound by the same laws as the rest of us – you might well dream of escaping that ugly countenance of yours, Vygilla, but not even an Azathanai's power could help you.'

High-pitched laughter.

Emral stared at the blurred reflection, wondering what it was thinking, wondering what it was seeing. There must be a secret dialogue, she told herself, between thinking and seeing, where every conclusion was hidden away. But to look upon oneself in this mirror-world was to witness every truth; and find nowhere to hide. *Mirrors, I fear, are an invitation to suicide.*

'Sister Emral.'

At the familiar voice she felt something quail inside her. But the blurry reflection showed no sign of that, and Emral felt a flash of unreasoning jealousy. Yet she held that placid gaze and did not turn at the call. 'Sister Syntara, is it time?'

High Priestess Syntara's arrival in the chamber had, Emral realized, announced itself a few moments earlier, in the sudden hush among the priestesses. Such was the force of the young woman's power, a thing of polished gold and dripping blood. Emral could see her now, almost formless in the mirror, neither beautiful nor imposing. She suppressed an urge to reach up and wipe through the shape, smearing it from existence.

There was no need for two High Priestesses. The temple was ancient, once consecrated to a spirit of the river. The god's very name had been obliterated from all records. Pictorial representations had been effaced

244

from the walls, but she knew the Dorssan Ryl had been named after the spirit that once dwelt in its depths. In that ancient dawn, when the first stones of Kharkanas were set down, a single priest led the processions, the rituals of worship, and conducted the necessary sacrifices.

The Yan and Yedan cults were survivors of that time, but Emral saw them as little more than hollow effigies, where ascetics invented rules of self-abnegation in the mistaken belief that suffering and faith were one and the same.

Instead of answering Emral's soft query, Syntara spent a few moments sending all the others from the chamber. Now she turned to Emral once more. 'Will you gaze upon yourself until All Darkness comes?'

'I was examining the tarnish,' Emral replied.

'Set the candidates to polishing it, then.' Syntara's tone betrayed the first hint of annoyance. 'We have matters to discuss.'

'Yes,' Emral said, finally turning to Syntara, 'that does seem to be our principal task these days. The discussion of . . . matters.'

'Changes are coming, Sister. We must be positioned to take advantage of them.'

Emral studied the younger woman, the fullness of her features, the unnecessary paint round her elongated, seductive eyes, the perfect moulding of her lips; and she thought of the cruel portrait Kadaspala had painted of Syntara – although it seemed that only Emral saw it as cruel, and indeed the portrait's subject had uttered more than once her admiration of the rendition. But then Emral could not be certain that Syntara's admiration was not for the woman depicted, rather than the genius of Kadaspala. 'We must be positioned to *survive*, Sister Syntara. Seeking advantages is somewhat premature.'

'That you are old is not my fault, Sister Emral. Mother Dark kept you elevated out of pity, I suspect, but that too is her decision to make. We are creating a religion here, but instead of glorying in the possibilities, you resist at every turn.'

'From resistance comes truth,' Emral replied.

'What truth?'

'Are we now discussing matters, Sister Syntara?'

'An Azathanai has come from the Vitr. She even now approaches, as much as raised aloft by the Shake.'

Emral lifted her brows. 'To challenge Mother Dark? I should think not.'

'Did you know that Hunn Raal is in Kharkanas?'

'I have observed his petition for an audience, yes.'

'You should not have denied him,' Syntara replied. 'Fortunately, he sought me out and we have spoken. The Azathanai was found by a troop of Wardens of the Outer Reach, and it was a Warden who was escorting the woman here – before the monks intervened. The

Azathanai was brought directly into audience with Sheccanto, and was a guest of the monastery for two nights. Do you begin to understand?'

'I did not deny Hunn Raal. Rather, I saw no need for haste. He has brought you this tale? And what, do you imagine, might be his reasons for so eagerly filling your ear, Sister Syntara? Allow me to guess. He wishes to enliven the notion of this Azathanai woman posing a threat, and so receive from Mother Dark the command to once more muster unto arms Urusander's Legion.'

Syntara was scowling. 'She came from the Vitr.'

'She is Azathanai. Perhaps she did indeed come from the Vitr, but she is not *of* it. Since when have the Azathanai posed a threat to us? If Hunn Raal gets his way, how will the highborn react to the resurrection of Urusander's Legion at full strength? Particularly at this time when all of Kharkanas is talking about a holy marriage?'

'Holy marriage? I assure you, Sister Emral, the talk on the streets is all about Draconus, and what he might do should such a union be announced.'

'Only because they've thought further along this path than, it seems, you have, Sister. Draconus indeed – will it be his head on the plate offered to the highborn in appeasement? And how long will the pleasure of that last when a score or so of Urusander's lowborn cohort commanders tramp mud into the Citadel's Grand Hall? The banishing of Draconus from her bed is poor balance to the diluting of highborn power. The return of Urusander's Legion will be a drawn blade, held high over our heads. And you would dance for them?'

At these last words, Syntara's face darkened. The rumours of her childhood spent as an alley dancer – mouth round the cocks of drunken old men – never quite went away. Emral and her agents had done nothing to dispel them, of course. But then, Syntara's own talespinners never rested in assailing Emral's own reputation. *Accordingly, there are always matters to discuss.*

'It would appear,' said Syntara after a moment, 'that you've become well acquainted with alley rumours of late, Sister Emral.'

'Enough to know that the hatred of Draconus stems from jealousy—'

'And his growing power!'

Emral stared at Syntara. 'Are you now as deluded as the rest? *He has no power.* He is her lover, that and nothing more. A Consort.'

'Who has doubled the number of his Houseblades over the past three months.'

Emral shrugged, turning back to the mirror. 'In his place I would do no less. Hated by the Legion and the lowborn, feared by the highborn. To steal the threat from this, she would do no better than to marry him instead of Urusander.'

'It is well then,' snapped Syntara, 'that Mother Dark does not seek our counsel.'

'Upon that we agree,' replied Emral.

'But even that will change, Sister Emral. What then? Are we to stand before her snarling and spitting at each other?'

'With luck, you will have aged by then, and so found for yourself some wisdom.'

'Is that how you interpret the lines upon your face? Since you stare endlessly into that mirror, you must know those flaws well by now.'

'But Sister Syntara,' said Emral to the vague form standing behind her own reflection, 'it is not me that I am looking at.'

*     *     *

Caplo Dreem and Warlock Resh rode at the forefront of the train. Behind them, unflanked and trailed by a half-dozen Shake, rode T'riss, astride her horse of bound and twisted grass. The black of the grass blades had faded in death; the simulacrum was now grey and brown, and in drying the entire creature had tightened in form, until the grasses bore the appearance of muscle and raw bone, like an animal stripped of its hide. The holes of its eyes were now spanned by the webs of funnel spiders. Caplo repressed an urge for yet one more glance back to the Azathanai and her ghastly mount.

His hands were sweaty inside their leather gloves. Up ahead, the forest's edge was visible in a swath of dulled sunlight, as if the shadow of clouds resided in his own eyes, and he found himself fighting a shiver.

Beside him Warlock Resh was uncharacteristically silent.

As promised they had delivered T'riss to the Yan Monastery, riding into a courtyard filled with brothers called in from the fields and assembled to make formal greeting to the Azathanai. Many among the crowd had recoiled upon seeing the horse of grass – or perhaps it was its rider's growing power, which Resh said roiled about her in invisible yet palpable currents – or the blankness of her expression, the flatness of her eyes.

Little had been said on the journey back to the monastery. None knew what they were bringing into the community; none knew what threat this Azathanai posed to Mother Sheccanto. Born of the Vitr was a fearful notion. Caplo regretted the enmity of the Warden, Faror Hend – he would have liked to question her more about T'riss: the first moments of their meeting; the details of their journey through Glimmer Fate.

Politics was worn like a second skin, smooth as silk when stroked but bristling when rubbed the wrong way. Caplo was as quick to make enemies as friends, and he had chosen wrongly with Faror Hend. Now that she was upon the other side, he would have to give thought to diminishing her reputation. But he would need his talent for subtlety, since she was betrothed to a hero of the realm. It was all very unfortunate, but a spy was the repository of many unpleasant necessities. The profession was not all daring and romance, and at times even the mask of seduction could turn ugly.

His thoughts returned to that fateful meeting between Mother Sheccanto and T'riss. There had been no delay in ushering himself, Resh and the Azathanai into the chamber of the Mother, known as the Rekillid – the old tongue word for womb. The candles of gold wax lining the walls had all been lit, bathing the round room in soft yellow light that seemed to lift towards the domed, gilt ceiling. The vast woven rug, rich with earth tones, was thick enough to swallow the sounds of their march across it to where waited Mother Sheccanto, seated in the high-backed chair of her office.

With Warlock Resh upon the Azathanai's right and Caplo Dreem upon her left, they walked without speaking until halting five paces from the dais.

Caplo saluted. 'Mother, the bandits have been eradicated. In sorrow I must report that no children were saved.'

Sheccanto waved one wrinkled hand in dismissal, her watery eyes fixed upon T'riss, who seemed to be studying the rug underfoot. 'Warlock Resh,' Mother then said, making a command of the name.

Bowing, Resh said, 'Mother, the report of the Warden is that this woman emerged from the Vitr. Her escort named her T'riss.'

'A Warden versed in the old tongue, then.'

'Faror Hend, of the Durav, Mother.'

'She had wise and knowledgeable parents,' Sheccanto said, nodding. She'd drawn her hands into her lap and there they fidgeted, gripping one another as if to still an unseen tremble, but her gaze had yet to shift away from T'riss. After a moment, she lifted her chin and raised her voice, 'Will you be a guest among us, T'riss?'

The Azathanai looked up and then away again, now studying the walls. 'This light is pretty,' she said. 'I saw a fountain in the courtyard, but it seemed shallow. There is a dryness here that ill fits a mother's home.'

Breath hissed from Resh's nostrils in a rush, but a twitch from Sheccanto stilled the warlock, and then she said, 'If you will not be a guest among us, Born of the Vitr, then we shall not delay you longer. It is your desire to speak with Mother Dark? We shall provide you a suitable escort.'

'Your faith is empty,' said T'riss. 'But I expect you already know that. There was a spirit once, a god of sorts. From the river near here. It reached through the earth, pulsed in the well you bored in the courtyard. But now even the fountain is lifeless. In chaining and harnessing the power of the water, you bound the spirit and stole from it its life. The free shall live but prisoners shall die.'

'It would seem,' said Sheccanto – and now her trembling was beyond disguising – 'that you lack the usual Azathanai tact.'

'Tact?' Still her eyes cast about in the chamber, more wandering than restless. 'Mother, I am sure you mean amused condescension. Azathanai are amused by many things, and our superiority is not in question. Tell me, do we visit often? I imagine not, since the power that now grows from this realm called Kurald Galain is cause for consternation.' She had slipped her feet from the odd grass moccasins she had been wearing, and now dug the toes of one foot into the deep plush of the wool rug. 'Someone will come, soon, I expect.'

'Is that someone not you, then?' Sheccanto asked.

'You are dying.'

'Of course I am dying!'

'No god sustains you.'

'No god sustains any of us!'

'This is wool. It is the hair of animals. You keep these animals for their hair, although some you slay – the newborn and the very old. There is a smell to the meat when it is old, but the meat of the young is most succulent. Mother, the bandit mothers opened the throats of their children – they would give you nothing. Many of your monks are old. Your cult is dying.'

Sheccanto sagged back in her chair. 'Get her out of here.'

'I accept your offer,' T'riss said then. 'I will be your guest, for this night and the next. Then we shall depart for Kharkanas. It is my belief now that Mother Dark has made a grave error in judgement.' She turned back to the entrance. 'Now, I will bathe in the fountain.'

'Warlock Resh,' said Sheccanto, 'escort our guest to the fountain. Lieutenant, remain a moment.'

T'riss left her odd moccasins on the rug where she had kicked them off, and followed Resh from the chamber. As soon as the heavy curtains settled once more, Sheccanto rose from her chair. 'They murdered their own children? Next time, employ stealth. Attack at night. Kill the mothers first. Your failure here is a grievous wound.'

'We lost a generation to the wars,' said Caplo, 'and this cannot be replaced in a single day, nor from a single camp of wayfarers. Mother, they fought with the ferocity of wolves. We shall travel further afield next time, and employ the tactics you describe.'

Sheccanto was standing on the dais, tall and gaunt, a figure of wrinkled skin and prominent bones beneath her robes. Below the wattle of her neck, he could see the lines of her ribs, and the hollows beneath her jutting clavicles looked impossibly deep. *Of course I am dying!* This confession had shocked him. There was more to the Mother's frailty than her two thousand years of life. It was said that there were great healers among the Azathanai. Caplo wondered if some desperate hope had been blunted in this meeting with T'riss.

'I am not dead yet,' Sheccanto said, and Caplo saw how her eyes were fixed on him, sharp as knife points.

'Mother, it is my thought that T'riss is a damaged Azathanai. The Vitr has stolen much of her mind.'

'All the more cause for concern, lieutenant. Mad she may be, but her power remains, and it is unmitigated by the restraint of reason. She seeks an audience with Mother Dark? You shall be the Azathanai's escort. Keep your skills close to hand.'

'Mother, for all my skills, I do not think it possible to assassinate an Azathanai.'

'Perhaps not, and you may well die in the attempt. So be it.'

'Is Mother Dark so dear to us?' Caplo asked. 'Besides, it would astonish me to discover that one who would assume the title of Mother of Night is incapable of defending herself.'

'By darkness alone, she defends,' Sheccanto replied. 'By darkness alone, she preserves herself. And in that darkness she trusts but one man and that man does not belong to us. Indeed, I am told that he has left Kurald Galain. Westward, into the lands of the Azathanai. Old suspicions are awakened within me.'

Caplo studied her, the face now in profile, hawkish and sharp. 'Suspicions you have not shared with your chosen assassin, Mother.'

'Nor shall I, as no proof is possible. I will risk you, lieutenant, even unto losing you, for the sake of defending Mother Dark. It is not that we need her. We don't. What we do need from her, however, is her gratitude – and her certainty of our allegiance.'

'Paid in my blood.'

'Paid in your blood.'

'Not even the Azathanai can pierce the darkness enveloping Mother Dark.'

Ancient eyes fixed on his. 'You cannot be certain of that. Does not her gift steal among her closest children? It is said Anomander has no need for light in his private chambers – servants report candles filmed with dust, their wicks not even blackened. Yet books are left lying opened on the map table, along with scrolls bearing his own handwriting. We have no path into this sorcery of hers, but this is not to say it is an obstacle to others.'

'I am made uneasy, Mother, by this assignment. There are too many unknowns. Would it not be more prudent that I kill her here, in the monastery? Before she can pose any greater threat to our realm?'

'Her presence here is known, lieutenant. The Wardens have given her into our care.'

250

Caplo nodded. 'To persuade them to do so, we also made guarantee of the Azathanai's safety. But these matters are all contingent. There is sufficient precedent for the unpredictability of our guest to make believable a tale of her initiating violence. Perhaps upon you, or among the monks. Yes, we may weather a period of indignation and accusation, but in the absence of details our word would stand, and prevail. As you taught me many years ago, an assassin seeks to control as much as possible the moment of assassination. I fear that very loss of control when in the Chamber of Night, in audience with Mother Dark and who knows how many other advisers in attendance.'

'Those others, lieutenant,' Sheccanto said, 'will have uppermost in their minds the protection of Mother Dark, not the Azathanai.'

Caplo cocked his head. 'It has been many years since you last left the monastery, Mother. I have seen Anomander fight, and even in a chamber the size of Mother Dark's, it is my judgement that he would reach me before I could kill the Azathanai. If not him, then Silchas Ruin.' At her steady glare he shrugged. 'Perhaps it is a gift of Mother Dark's sorcery that has earned them such skills. Or perhaps their talent is entirely natural. Either way, I wager my chances at success as very low; in which case, if I understand you, my life is to be sacrificed as a symbol of Shake loyalty.'

'We were speaking of this T'riss posing a threat to Mother Dark. I ask that you hold yourself in readiness for such a possibility.'

'Of course I shall.'

'And I trust you will understand, should the moment come, that your sacrifice is entirely necessary. After all, we will be the ones delivering the Azathanai into an audience with Mother Dark.'

Caplo lifted his brows. 'Absolution of consequences? And if no one survives the battle but T'riss?'

'Then few would argue, lieutenant, that we are all lost. Now then, you will have other responsibilities when in Kharkanas. Hold still your thoughts while I explain.'

A short time later, Caplo emerged into the courtyard and made his way towards the fountain. Warlock Resh was standing at a respectable distance from T'riss, who wandered naked through the knee-deep water, droplets glistening on her burnished skin. There were signs of sunburn upon her shoulders, the patches of peeling skin reminding Caplo of shedding snakes. Apart from the warlock and the Azathanai, no one else was within sight anywhere in the courtyard.

*Children either flee the baring of flesh, or gawk. But it is unseemly to gawk. For me, I but admire.*

He came up to stand beside Resh. 'It is said that we are ever students, no matter our age.'

Resh grunted. 'Lessons oft repeated, never quite learned. I see before me a new treatise on life.'

'The critics will savage you.'

'They shall be as midges upon my hide. Frenzied in scale, but the scale is small.'

'Then I shall look with delight upon your pocked and wealed self.'

'It is your secret admiration of savages, Caplo, which your words now betray.'

'All betrayal will begin, or end, with words.'

'Savage ones?'

'I imagine so, Resh.'

T'riss had made her way to the far side of the fountain and now sat upon the broad ledge, face upturned to the sun and eyes closed.

'If Mother Dark had rejected the element of Night and taken the element of Silence instead,' mused Resh, 'there would be peace everlasting.'

'You suggest then,' Caplo asked, 'that all instances of violence involve some manner of betrayal?'

'I do, and it shall be first and pre-eminent in my list of lessons never learned.'

'The hawk betrays the hare? The swift betrays the fly?'

'In a manner of speaking, most certainly, my sickly friend.'

'Then we are all doomed to betray, since it seems implicit in the very act of survival.'

Resh faced him. 'Have you not witnessed for yourself the anguish of philosophers? The glee of their guilt, the eager admonition of their selves and all kin? We have all betrayed the promise of everlasting peace, and was there not an age, long ago, when death was unknown? When sustenance itself was without cost or sacrifice?'

That notion was an old joke between them. 'Warlock Resh,' Caplo now replied, 'all the philosophers I have seen are either drunk or insensate.'

''Tis the sorrows of loss, friend, and the wallows of recognition.'

''Tis weakness of will, I wager the more likely.'

'A will crumbled helpless to the assault of revelation. When we are driven to our knees, the world shrinks.'

His eyes on T'riss, Caplo sighed and said, 'Ah, Resh, but not all revelation arrives as an assault.'

'You give me reason to drink.'

'Then your reason is weak.'

'And lo, I am the only philosopher brave enough to admit it.'

'Only because you're sober, and I always question the courage of sobriety.'

They both fell silent as T'riss rose once again and made her way over.

Eyes flicking briefly to Caplo she said, 'Your Mother advised against my murder, then? It is well. You would not like my blood on your hands, lieutenant.'

Caplo said nothing for a long moment, and then he cocked his head. 'Guest, you surmise extreme conduct on our part. It is unseemly.'

She nodded. 'It is.'

'I am pleased that we agree—'

'Murder always is,' she continued. 'I tasted the distrust in my friend, Faror Hend, upon your intervention. There were many levels to her displeasure.'

'We mean you no harm,' said Caplo, 'but if we must, we will defend our own.'

'I see much room for debate, lieutenant, as to what constitutes "your own". Of course, you rely upon that ambiguity.'

'Does that comment refer to me personally, or people in general?'

Beside Caplo, Resh seemed to flinch.

'I do not know sufficient "people" to comment on them,' T'riss replied, sitting down before them and running a hand through the warm water. 'I believe you are a killer, and that you are both *given* reasons for the necessity, and assemble in private more of your own, bolstering such justifications as needed.'

Warlock Resh seemed to gag. Coughing, he said, 'Guest, I beg you, constrain your power.'

'You think this power is mine, warlock?' Smiling, she rose. 'I am weary. I see a monk in the doorway – will he suffice to guide me to my quarters?'

'A moment, please,' Caplo interposed, alarmed after a glance at his companion, who was gasping, half bent over. 'If not your power, then whose?'

'Your river god was dead. It is dead no longer.'

He stared in disbelief.

She met his eyes and this time held them. 'Now you must contend with what you purport to worship, and give answer to the many things you have done in its name. Is it any wonder your friend quails?'

She set off across the compound.

Caplo stepped close to his friend. 'Resh? Will you recover? Does she speak truth? What is it you feel?'

He looked up with savage eyes. 'Rage.'

Thereafter, in the midst of panic and chaos tearing through the settlement, the Azathanai guest remained in her rooms, taking her meals in private. Upon the third morning she appeared in the compound. Summoning her grass horse, she mounted up and waited for the others.

Mother Sheccanto was confined to her bed. She had lost all control over her body and could not move, not even to lift a hand. Her lungs were filling with fluid, her breaths came in shallow rasps and her eyes, Caplo recalled, darted like trapped birds.

*The hawk betrays the hare. The swift betrays the fly. God was bent to our will; and God now rages.*

Riders had already gone out to Yedan Monastery, by Resh's command, and word had come back the night before their departure for Kharkanas. Father Skelenal was on his way. Sisters had collapsed. The thirteen eldest among them had died. And in the Great Well of the Ancient God, the water boiled. The steam made a column that could be seen from the forest edge south of the convent.

When Warlock Resh announced that he would remain, awaiting the arrival of Skelenal, T'riss had turned to him and said, 'You will not be needed here. Your Mother will recover most of her faculties. She will speak in private with her lifebound mate. You will accompany me, Warlock Resh.'

'Why?' he had demanded, and it had shocked Caplo to realize that his companion had not even questioned the Azathanai's right to command him.

'Who dwells in the forest north of Kharkanas?' she asked him.

Resh shrugged. 'Cast-offs, half-wild folk. Poachers, criminals—'

'Deniers,' Caplo said.

T'riss said, 'Your Mother and Father need to prepare.'

'For what?' Caplo asked.

'For what I must show Warlock Resh, lieutenant. It shall begin in the forest, but also upon the river itself, and in the streets of Kharkanas – until such time as Mother Dark awakens to the challenge.'

'What will you say to her?' Resh demanded in a harsh voice.

'To Mother Dark?' T'riss gathered up the makeshift reins. 'I expect there will be no need for words, warlock. With my presence, she will understand.'

'Do you threaten her?' Caplo asked.

'If I do, lieutenant, there will be nothing you can do about it. Not you, not her guardians. But no, I myself pose no threat to Mother Dark, and upon this you have my word, to weigh or discard as befits your nature. What I bring is change. Will she welcome it or resist it? Only she can answer that.'

In silence they had ridden out from the monastery, on to the south road that would take them on a route well to the east of Yedan Monastery, before entering the much diminished easternmost arm of Youth Forest.

The last words T'riss spoke, just outside the monastery gates, were, 'I understand now the mystery of water. In peace it flows clear. When I stand before Mother Dark, turmoil will come to the water between us. But the promise remains – one day it shall run clear once again. Hold to this faith, all of you, even as chaos descends upon the world.' She faced Resh and Caplo. 'The river god tells me Dorssan Ryl's water is dark, but it was not always so.'

*It was not always so. The oldest of our scriptures say the same.*

*This Azathanai has resurrected our god. This Azathanai has spoken with our god. But what does she promise the Tiste?*

*Chaos.*

When they rode into the forest, however, Caplo had seen nothing unusual, nothing to give credence to the Azathanai's portentous words. He had turned to the warlock riding beside him, a question on his lips, but Resh forestalled him with an upraised hand.

'Not yet. It grows. Things stir. Dreams plague a thousand shadowed minds. Something is indeed awakening. We shall see its face upon our return.'

Caplo owned nothing of the sensitivity possessed by Warlock Resh and many of the others in the faith. Sheccanto once told him that even as a child he had knelt before pragmatism; and in so doing had surrendered his capacity for imagination. There existed a dichotomy between the two, and as forces of personality they often locked in combat. For some, however, there was an accord. Dreams defined the goal, pragmatism the path to it. Those who possessed that balance were said to be talented, but it did not make their lives any easier. The blunt of mind, who lived lives in which obstacles rose up before them with every step, were quick to raise similar obstacles before their 'talented' associates, and were often adamant in their belief that it was for the best, and justified their views with such words as 'realistic', 'practical' and, of course, 'pragmatic'.

Caplo held much sympathy for those who would, by advice and by ridicule, rein in the unfettered dreamers of the world. He saw imagination as dangerous, at times deadly in its unpredictability. Among the many victims he had murdered, it had been the creative ones who caused him the most trouble. He could not track them upon the paths of their thinking.

That said, so many other things had been surrendered in the loss of his own imagination. It was difficult to feel anything for the lives of others. He had no interest, beyond the professional, in searching out empathy, and saw no reason to shift his own perspective on matters of opinion, since his opinions were soundly rooted in pragmatism and therefore proved ultimately unassailable.

For all of this, as they rode into the thinned fringe of the ancient forest, with the tight creaking of the Azathanai's mount an incessant rhythm behind them, Caplo felt a chill that had nothing to do with the sudden falling off of sunlight. He glanced across at Resh to see the man's craggy face sheathed in sweat.

'Does she awaken her power again?' he asked in a low tone.

Resh simply shook his head, a singular gesture of negation so uncharacteristic of the warlock that Caplo was startled and, indeed, somewhat frightened.

He looked about, eyes narrowed upon the shadows between the trees lining the road. He saw rubbish heaped in the ditches, and there, thirty or so paces deeper into the wood to his right, a squalid hovel wreathed in woodsmoke, with what might be a figure sitting hunched behind a smouldering fire – or perhaps it was nothing more than a boulder, or a stump. The air was cool on the cobbled road, redolent with decay, acidic enough to bite the back of his throat with each breath he took. There was little sound, barring that of a barking dog somewhere in the distance, and the nearer clump of horse hoofs upon the muddy stones.

The other times Caplo had ridden through, on his way to and from Kharkanas, he had barely noticed this stretch of woodland. There seemed to be as many stumps as growing trees, but now he realized that this was only true of the area immediately flanking the road. Things grew wilder deeper into the forest, where the gloom was a shroud no gaze could pierce, and to travel through would require a torch or lantern. It was astonishing to think people lived in this forest, hidden away, confined to an ever shrinking world.

'They are free,' said Resh in a strained voice.

Caplo started. 'My friend, of whom do you speak?'

'Free in ways lost to the rest of us. You see their limits, their seeming poverty. You see them as fallen, forgotten, ignorant.'

'Resh, I do not see them at all.'

'What they are is free,' insisted Resh, his gloved hands making fists on the saddle horn where they gripped the reins. 'No tithes, no tributes to pay. Perhaps even coin itself is unknown to them, and every measure of wealth lies within reach of able hands, and within sight of loving eyes. Caplo, when the last forest is gone, so too will end the last free people of the world.'

Caplo considered this, and then shrugged. 'We'll not notice the loss.'

'Yes, and this is why: they are the keepers of our conscience.'

'It is no wonder then that I never see them.'

'Yes,' said Resh, his tone removing all the humour from Caplo's words.

Irritated, made uneasy by this wood, Caplo scowled. 'It avails us nothing to elevate the impoverished.'

'I do not speak of those who have fled our way of living,' replied Resh, 'although one might argue that by choice or by accident they walk towards truth, while we plunge ever forward into a world of self-delusion. No matter. Those I am speaking of are those who were never tamed. They live still in this forest – perhaps only a hundred or so left.

One cannot imagine their numbers any greater than that. We take their home, tree by tree, shadow by shadow. To know too much is to lose the wonder of mystery. In answering every question we forget the value of not knowing.'

'There is no value in not knowing. Roll that thick hide of yours, Resh, and shake free of this nonsense. The value of not knowing? What value?'

'You have no answer and so you conclude that none exists. And there in your reaction, O pallid wretch, lies the lesson.'

'Riddles now? You know how much I dislike riddles. Out with it, then. Tell me what I lack. What is gained by not knowing?'

'Humility, you fool.'

Behind them T'riss spoke up, her voice carrying with unnatural clarity. 'In ritual you abased yourselves. I saw it in the courtyard, many times. But the gesture was rote – even in your newfound fear, the meaning of that abasement was lost.'

'Please,' growled Resh, 'explain yourself, Azathanai.'

'I will. You carve an altar from stone. You paint the image of waves upon the wall and so fashion a symbol of that which you would worship. You give it a thousand names, and imagine a thousand faces. Or a single name, a single face. Then you kneel, or bow, or lie flat upon the ground, making yourselves abject in servitude, and you may call the gesture *humble* before your god, and see in your posture righteous humility.'

'This is all accurate enough,' said Resh.

'Just so,' she agreed. 'And by this means you lose the meaning of the ritual, until the ritual is itself the meaning. These are not gestures of subservience. Not expressions of the surrendering of your will to a greater power. This is not the relationship your god seeks, yet it is the one upon which you insist. The river god is not the source of your worship; or rather, it shouldn't be. The river god meets your eye and yearns for your comprehension – not of itself as a greater power, but comprehension of the meaning of its existence.'

'And that meaning is?' Resh demanded.

'Recall the gesture of abasement, warlock. You make it in recognition of your own humility. A god's powers are immeasurable and before them you are nothing. Therefore you would worship your god and surrender your life into its hands. But it doesn't want your life, and knows not what to do with your longing, helpless soul. In ritual and symbol you have lost yourselves. Could the god make you understand, it would make you understand this simple truth: the only thing worthy of worship is humility itself.'

Caplo snorted and then made to speak, to heap derision upon her assertion – but he did not even need Resh's gesture of admonishment to bite his tongue. It was true that he had no imagination, but even he could see the pattern of predictable behaviour, in this confusing of ritual and meaning, symbol and truth.

'Then,' said Resh in a rasp, 'what does our god want of us?'

'Dear child,' said T'riss, 'he wants you to be free.'

* * *

Caplo was not one to welcome revelation. He felt knocked askew, and what galled him the most was that he understood, with absolute clarity, the Azathanai's argument. Earlier, she had announced to them that they had killed their ancient river god. In binding water to mundane uses, in taking away its freedom, they had slain the very entity they sought to worship. It was only logical, then, that what the god wished for was freedom, and in that freedom, a life reborn.

He did not know how she had resurrected that river god, but there was no dissembling when she then said that change was coming to them all.

They rode on in febrile silence following her words, and when Caplo glanced across at Warlock Resh, he saw that his friend was silently weeping, and the glitter of the tears, so raw on his cheeks, was like a bitter gift in the gloom.

*In tears, water runs free.* One of the oldest poems in the scriptures, penned by an unknown hand. Generations had argued over the meaning, embracing both the prosaic and the profane; but in a handful of words from T'riss, that meaning was suddenly clear, and Caplo could almost hear the regret, echoing in the tormented scratching of quill upon parchment, from that unknown, heartbroken poet.

A truth buried in mysterious words. This was how imagination could be both gift and curse. For himself, he would rather have remained ignorant, but it was too late for that.

After a ride through the night, wrapped in silence and anguish, they reached the edge of the forest, and the city of Kharkanas rose before them, knuckled against the banks of the Dorssan Ryl, like a massive fist of black stone.

* * *

The old temple at the heart of the Citadel always made High Priestess Emral Lanear think of a closed eye within a deep socket. The bones spread out from this shuttered centre, in angular additions, the black stone heaped in a half-dozen architectural styles to fashion something like a crushed skull, flattened by its own weight, its innumerable burdens. There was nothing of beauty in the Citadel and for all the life that rushed through it, in corridors and chambers, on saddled steps and in musty cellars, it conjured in her mind an image of bugs trapped in that skull, desperate for a way out.

The stones were insensate, and so the eye remained shut. One could look upon a lifeless face for as long as one liked; if it was truly lifeless, it would never change. No flickering of the lids; no drawing of breath, nothing at all to shock the observer with the undoing of truth, or the unmaking of time.

She was walking beside Sister Syntara, in formal cadence, as they approached the Grand Hall that had once been the temple's nave. Behind them trailed a dozen priestesses, their fluttering excitement stripped away as, with each step, the way ahead grew darker, defying the candles, devouring the light from the flanking torches on the walls.

None could draw close to the presence of Mother Dark without slowing their steps, and even though preternatural vision was now common among the priestesses and those closest to their chosen goddess, there remained an ineffable pressure in the air, and a chill that reached deep into the bones. Hands could not help but tremble. Breaths grew shallow, the air biting the lungs.

Fifteen solemn strides from the entrance, Emral felt something strike her forehead, and then trickle down to her brow. An instant later she gasped as the wet streak froze against her face. Another drop landed upon her hand where it held the Scabbard, and she looked down to see the bead of water form instantly into ice, numbing the skin beneath.

There was no rain in the city beyond. These corridors were so dry they stole the vigour of health from the youngest priestesses – this was true of the entire Citadel.

Hisses of surprise and then consternation rustled behind her.

Sister Syntara stopped abruptly, proffering the Sceptre to Emral. 'Sheathe it, Sister. Something is happening.'

There could be no argument to that. Emral accepted the iron and blackwood rod, slipped it into its protective shell.

Droplets of freezing water now rained upon them all. Looking up, Emral saw the gleam of frost covering the rounded arch of the ceiling. Shock stole away her voice. Blistering cold water stung her upturned face.

All at once comprehension arrived, a flood in her mind, and with it came wonder. For all that, the taste was bitter. 'The eye has opened,' she said.

Syntara's glare was almost accusing. 'What eye? This is the Azathanai's work! She assails Mother Dark's domain. This is nothing but unveiled power, mocking the sanctity of the temple!'

'The sanctity of the temple, Sister? Indeed, but not in mockery.' She glanced back at the train of huddling, frightened priestesses. 'The procession is at an end. Return to your cloisters. The High Priestesses must seek private audience with Mother Dark. Go!'

They flapped and fluttered away like panicked crows.

'The procession was not for you to command,' snapped Syntara.

'Paint your lines in spit and fury, Sister, if that is as far as you can see. I am not—'

Heavy boots sounded from down the corridor and she turned to see Anomander approaching, behind him his two brothers. Frozen water droplets bounced from their armour like diamond beads.

'Emral,' said Anomander. 'The Azathanai is now through the gate of the city. The river is in flood and water streams down the streets. I would have your thoughts on this.'

'The Shake, Lord Anomander.'

A low curse came from Silchas Ruin. 'They invite a war of faiths? Are they mad?'

Syntara was looking back and forth between Emral and the brothers, her expression confused.

Anomander glanced to the barred doors just beyond them, and then he shook his head. 'That seems unlikely, High Priestess. Their cult looks inward. Not once have they revealed any ambition to reclaim the old temple.'

He well understood the matter, she saw. The quickness of his thinking surpassed even hers. 'Perhaps you are right, Lord. Then, they must be as disconcerted as are we. Sufficient to consider them as potential allies?'

'Not reliably, I should think,' he replied. 'The impasse is theirs – I imagine there is chaos in the monasteries. One thing the worship of a dead god assures, and that is unmitigated freedom for the priesthood.'

'But now . . .'

He nodded. 'Their plans are awry. They face challenge from a most unexpected quarter.'

'If they are nimble of thought,' Emral ventured, 'they will see the potential strength here, bolstering whatever position they take in matters of the realm.'

'Profane matters, yes.' He hesitated, still ignoring Syntara, and then said, 'I am informed that Mother Sheccanto lies gravely ill – in consequence, I should imagine. And that Skelenal hastens to her side. They are old but hardly foolish.'

Silchas said, 'Then we must look to Warlock Resh and Witch Ruvera to determine what is to come from the Shake.'

Another sharp mind, Emral noted. She could forgive Andarist's distraction, although she well knew that among the brothers, the depth of his introspection was a close match to Anomander's almost mythical talent in that area, although demonstrably slower in its steps. She said to Silchas, 'I am informed that the Azathanai's escort is Warlock Resh and Lieutenant Caplo Dreem.'

'Caplo,' said Silchas.

'Yes,' mused Anomander. 'Let us think on that.'

'Sheccanto is afraid,' concluded Emral. 'There can be no other reason for Caplo Dreem.' She regarded Anomander. 'His eyes will be upon the Azathanai, surely.'

'Agreed. But this is Sheccanto's panic, not ours, and I do not see the value of a messenger slain at the foot of Mother Dark.'

'Lord Anomander,' Emral asked, 'can you prevent it?'

'We have the advantage of expectation,' Anomander replied, with a glance at Silchas, who nodded and then shrugged.

'You all hesitate,' Emral observed.

Frozen rain still fell. Pellets like hail deepened on the floor.

Anomander sighed. 'With blade in hand, Caplo Dreem is faster than anyone I have ever seen. I could well stand beside him and still fail.'

'Then stand between him and the Azathanai,' hissed Syntara. 'They approach and here we blather on like old hens, wasting time! Mother Dark must be warned—'

'She knows and needs no more from us,' said Anomander. 'Sister Syntara, we hens have much to decide here, yet you persist in pecking the ground.'

'I am her chosen High Priestess!'

'Your elevation was intended to ease the burden of administration from Sister Emral,' Anomander replied. 'Little did Mother Dark realize your venal ambition, and if you think high tits and a damp nest are the surest paths to power, might I refer you to Gallan's poem, "Trophies of Youth"? By the poem's end, even the words fade.' He faced Emral. 'High Priestess, I will address the matter of Caplo Dreem before we enter the Grand Hall.'

'I am relieved,' she replied, struggling to hide her astonishment at Anomander's words to Syntara. An elevation to ease administration? She had not known this. *And now . . . is there regret?*

Silchas spoke. 'What, then, of this matter of an awakened river god?'

Relief was flooding through Emral. These brothers, the first chosen among Mother Dark's children, made fragile every fear and then shattered each one with sanguine confidence. Each time she looked upon them – Anomander, Silchas and especially Andarist – she saw their father, and the love within her, so shackled, so raw and bleeding beneath her obsessive flagellations, surged anew with defiant strength. Pleasure in anguish, hope in long-broken promises – she could almost feel years fall from her when in the presence of these three sons.

To Silchas's pointed question, Emral said, 'That depends, I now believe, upon Warlock Resh.'

'We shall await them here,' said Anomander.

'Too many of us here suggests weakness,' Andarist observed. 'I will withdraw. Silchas?'

Silchas turned to Anomander and smiled. 'The two of us together twice drowns the threat and what needs drowning twice? I am with Andarist. It's said Captain Kellaras has returned but is waylaid in a tavern by Dathenar and Prazek. Andarist, I suggest we join them. Anomander, shall we enquire from your good captain Hust Henarald's answer?'

'Why not?' Anomander answered. 'I am passing curious.'

Both his brothers snorted at that, and then they set off.

Emral knew nothing of the meaning of these last comments. Hust Henarald stood outside all political machinations. She wondered what Anomander might want of the man. *Foolish woman! What else could it be? My . . . if an iron cry sounds in the Citadel, the echoes will travel far.*

But there had been not a moment of hesitation in either Andarist or Silchas. Their trust in their brother's competence was breathtaking under the circumstances.

*Sons of the father.*

*But of their mother's flaws, I pray . . . none.*

'Are we to simply stand here, then?' Syntara demanded.

'You are not needed,' Anomander said to her. 'Seek shelter in Mother Dark's presence.'

'You invite me to private audience with our goddess?' Syntara smirked. 'I will accept, most assuredly.' She waved a pallid hand, dismissing them all. 'Surrender all decorum out here in the corridor, by all means. I shall remain above such awkwardness, since it seems that I alone understand the position of High Priestess.'

'Would that be on your knees, Syntara?'

Despite the paint on her face, and despite the gloom of the hallway, Syntara visibly paled. Fury burgeoned in her eyes and she spun from them, marching towards the doors. A moment later and she was through. As the echo of the door's closing drummed down the corridor, Emral shook her head. 'She'll not forget that insult, Lord Anomander, and for all her vanity, do not think her harmless.'

'I was unwise,' admitted Anomander. 'However, it is not me at risk of her ire, it is you. For that I apologize, High Priestess.'

'No need, Lord. I have cut deeper than that many times.'

'Yet in private, surely.'

She shrugged. 'With all the spies in this court, I doubt "privacy" even exists.'

'This is the danger of darkness,' said Anomander. 'The world made unseen invites intrigue.'

'It is no easy thing,' she said, 'to carve faith from secular ambition, Lord. The birth of any religion is bound to be tumultuous.'

'It would be more relaxed,' said Anomander, as the sounds of people entering the far end of the corridor reached them, 'if Draconus were here.'

And just as quickly, a single comment from him could uproot the world from beneath her feet. She made no reply, no longer trusting her own voice.

*Hold up no mirror, lest you like not what you see.*

\*       \*       \*

As the river crested its banks, pouring murky water into the streets and alleys of Kharkanas, and as shock and alarm rippled ahead of the tide throughout the city, Caplo Dreem and Warlock Resh escorted T'riss on to the main avenue that led out from the wood. Crowds were pushing up from the streets, funnelled by the rising water behind them, and gathering like flotsam along the high ridge that fringed the floodplain, halfway between the city's edge and the line of trees marking the forest.

Floods were seasonal events in Kharkanas, occurring in the spring. Here, in the depths of a dry summer, and arriving without warning, the upsurge was accompanied by a sense of superstitious fear.

Where the main avenue sloped downwards, crossing the bank of the ridge, refuse-littered water lapped the cobbles directly ahead. Caplo reined in and a moment later Resh followed suit. T'riss drew up immediately behind them. Beyond her, the Shake halted their mounts, silent and pale-faced, ignoring the queries from refugees nearby.

'Azathanai,' said Caplo. 'Will your mount suffer in form, should we ride through this water?'

'I will walk,' she replied. 'The river resists its imprisonment. In this it speaks a truth of nature.'

The warlock's voice was harsh as he asked, 'What will the river god demand of this city? Of Mother Dark herself? The banks are walled in stone. The bridges are built. The jetties and piers stand firm against the currents. Must it all be destroyed in the name of water's freedom?'

T'riss slipped down from the simulacrum. 'Mother Dark is awakened to its presence. She asserts her domain.'

'Is this to be a battle?' Caplo asked her.

The woman studied him briefly, and then glanced up at the sky, as if invisible words were carved across its vault, which she now read out loud. 'In stirring from sleep, the river god opens eyes upon a much changed world. Even the pillow upon which he rested his head is claimed by another – there is a temple within the Citadel, yes? It once belonged to the river god, but ownership has passed to another.' She looked down, frowned at the city before them – and of the hundreds of Tiste now climbing the ridge to either side of the avenue, she was oblivious. 'Even now the flood subsides. Mother Dark's power is impressive.'

She strode between the two men and moments later walked into the water.

Resh's sigh was rough. 'I'll keep my feet dry, if you please.'

Nodding, Caplo nudged his horse forward.

The procession resumed, this time led by the Azathanai, who cut a path through the swirling flood as if the river's rising was a gift to her. Above the Citadel, Caplo saw clouds lifting, roiling away. *Steam. Mother Dark banishes. We see here the truth of her growing power.*

They continued on, at a pace somewhat quicker than the subsidence, although by the high waterline on the building walls it was clear that the flood was fast draining. The sound of rushing water was everywhere, as if in the aftermath of a heavy shower.

T'riss spoke without turning. 'She must heed this lesson. To bind is to weaken. To hold is to make vulnerable, so that just as temples are focal points for worship and sacred gestures, so too are they weak points in a god's armour. They are where the skin is thinnest, where fingers can touch, one mortal the other immortal. The meeting of lips, the sharing of breaths. Believe with all your heart, but know that your kiss can kill.'

Resh said, 'Mother Dark is yet to sanctify the temple in her name, Azathanai. This is a matter of some contention. She may not need your warnings.'

They were approaching an intersection, opening out in a rectangular expanse. From windows on higher floors in the buildings to either side, people looked down, tracking their progress. Upon the far end reared the Citadel's City Gate. There was no one visible in the concourse.

T'riss halted, turned to Caplo. 'I have heard mention of highborn and lowborn, yet the Tiste acknowledge no royalty. How is this so?'

'There was a queen once,' Caplo replied. 'The last of the royal line. She died on the field of battle. Her husband was not among the nobility, yet greatly revered for his martial prowess. When he fell, mortally wounded, she led a charge of her Royal Wardens in an effort to retrieve his body from the field. It failed. Thereafter, her body was not found, although that of her husband was.'

T'riss was studying him. 'This queen was blood-kin to Mother Dark?'

'Half-sisters,' Resh said.

'She could not have claimed the throne?'

'No,' Caplo replied. 'An exception would have been made, however. There was precedent. But she was deemed . . . unsuitable.'

'Esoteric interests,' said Resh in a growl. 'No talent for politics. Idealistic, romantic – well suited, perhaps, to her elevation into godhood.'

'Then,' said T'riss, 'your throne remains unoccupied. I expect that this would indeed suit the highborn.'

'The throne is transformed,' said Resh. 'Its place of honour now is in the temple. Upon it sits Mother Dark, and by title it is no longer the Royal Throne, but the Throne of Night.'

'She will be seated upon it, then?' T'riss asked. 'When we have audience with her?'

Caplo shrugged. 'Who can say? In darkness she dwells.'

The Azathanai was now looking from Caplo to Resh and back again. 'The dead queen was the last of the royal line. By this you mean the direct line.'

'Yes,' said Resh, scowling.

'There remain distant relations.'

Caplo nodded.

'Lieutenant, I see little of the disingenuous in your comportment with me. You will give honest answer to my next question.'

'If answer I possess,' said Caplo.

'The Queen had other kin. They now hold the titles of Mother and Father, and their names are Sheccanto and Skelenal.'

'Yes.'

'Yet they are lifebound.'

'Without consummation, Azathanai,' replied Caplo. 'To be lifebound is not a marriage. It is something . . . other.'

'By rights they could claim the throne.'

Caplo shrugged. 'It could so be argued.'

After a moment she turned back, resumed her trek across the concourse.

The water was gone, leaving little more than a few puddles and patches of wet stone fast dwindling in the sunlight. As Caplo made to nudge his mount forward, Resh reached out a hand and stayed him.

They watched her walking onward for a dozen heartbeats.

'Warlock,' murmured Caplo, 'say nothing in the certainty of being unheard.'

'I won't,' Resh answered. 'But these matters – of lineage and blood – I see no advantage in her knowing them.'

'To firm her footing, I should think.'

'Nothing more?'

Caplo shrugged. 'The age of kings and queens is past, warlock. The lesson was lost on no one. By love aggrieved she cast the realm into chaos. This shall not happen again.'

'We should have left the Azathanai to the damned Wardens,' Resh said.

This time, Caplo could not but agree. 'She nears the gate,' he observed.

They rode to catch up, avoiding the puddles.

\* \* \*

Atop the Old Tower, Cedorpul, Endest Silann and Rise Herat watched the tiny figure of the woman walk towards the Citadel's City Gate. As the Shake escort, momentarily halted, now rode to catch up to her, Cedorpul grunted and said, 'That is Warlock Resh and Caplo Dreem. A curious pairing for this formality.'

Rise Herat glanced across at the young priest. 'Of course the warlock should be in attendance,' he replied. 'The river has breached its banks and washed the city—'

'As if to cleanse her path,' murmured Endest Silann.

'Faith can survive a little water,' said Cedorpul.

The historian heard the diffidence in that assertion. 'Do you sense this ancient awakening, priest?'

The round-faced man shrugged. 'In witnessing something both unexpected and . . . vast, there is a sense of awe, but that is perfectly reasonable. Such reactions are beneath argument, I would say. Is this synonymous with reverential awe? I think not.'

'Although we possess no documents,' observed Rise Herat, 'it is fair to assume that the seasonal rise and fall of the river was integral to the worship of the river god. Is it not clear that we have witnessed a miracle?'

'Yet the water retreats,' Cedorpul countered. 'The power here belongs to Mother Dark.'

'"Upon the field of battle, I saw peacocks."'

'The meaning of that, historian?'

'Only that the ground is contested now, priest. It may well be that Warlock Resh will make claim to the temple itself.'

'He dare not!'

Below, the Azathanai woman, of average height, thin, dressed in strange, colourless garb, now reached the gate. She made no pause and a moment later disappeared from sight. Her path would take her across a squat bridge to an inner gate, and from there into the Citadel itself. Behind her the two riders dismounted and followed, leaving their horses with the other monks – who, it seemed, would not be entering the Citadel grounds. Rise watched as the mounted warriors wheeled around and, leading the two riderless horses, set off back across the concourse at a fast trot.

'These matters are beyond us,' said Endest Silann. 'I am unbalanced and feel unwell.'

'Betrayed by your nervous constitution,' Cedorpul said. 'Mother Dark cannot be assailed at the very heart of her power.'

'Mother Dark is not the one at threat here,' said Rise, thinking of Caplo Dreem.

'What do you mean by that?' Endest Silann asked.

The historian shrugged. 'An idle thought. Pay it no mind. Instead,

266

consider this: it is only when opposed that some things find definition. Few would argue, I think, that Darkness is a difficult thing to worship. What is it we seek in elevating Mother Dark? What manner of unity can we find circling a place of negation?'

'Contentious questions,' Cedorpul said, his tone too light for the assertion.

Sensing the strain in the priest, Rise Herat spoke again, 'Religious practice rises from precedent, after all.'

'You would argue the matter of religious practice?'

'If it helps this moment, Cedorpul, then my answer is yes. My point is, you are all starving for guidance. For all of Mother Dark's power, there is no prescription. What form must ritual observance take? How is proper propitiation to be achieved and is it even desired by the one whom you would worship? In what manner do you announce obeisance? These are the issues occupying your priesthood, and the source of debate.'

'The resurrection of the river god offers us no worthy answers, historian. The faith died, did it not?'

'There was a rejection, yes; that much is clear. One need only look upon the determined defacing of the walls in the temple to grasp something of the rage surrounding that crisis. Yet, one could argue that it was the perceived death of their god that so triggered the frenzy of destruction.'

'What if it was guilt?' Endest asked.

'That suggestion,' snapped Cedorpul, his colour high, 'displeases me on countless levels, acolyte.'

'Not all thoughts are uttered to please,' Rise said. 'This does not diminish their value. Guilt is a powerful emotion . . . yes, I can see it gouging faces from walls, words from panels. If the god died, there is cause to ask why. Yet faith alone clearly proved insufficient sustenance, so we need not discuss its veracity, given the persistent presence of the Yan and Yedan Monasteries. And,' he added, 'the resurrection of this selfsame god.'

Cedorpul turned to Endest Silann. 'Acolyte, we have dallied up here long enough. The others will be gathering – they will be looking for me. Before us now is a challenge and face it we must. Historian, fare you well. Oh, will you look in on the child?'

Rise Herat smiled. 'I shall rattle the lock and demand entrance, and she shall cry me begone.'

Cedorpul's nod was brisk. 'That will do.'

*　　*　　*

High Priestess Emral Lanear stood beside Lord Anomander, awaiting the appearance of the Azathanai and her escort. Syntara had entered the inner chamber and now presumably communed with Mother Dark, although in truth Emral knew that such communion was notoriously frustrating. Perhaps an idealistic, romantic woman well and truly belonged at the heart of something as ephemeral as faith and worship. Perhaps indeed no virtue of pragmatism was possible in matters of the soul, and might even prove anathema to the very notion of the sacred.

Did not all prophets speak in riddles? Did not diviners slip like eels through an array of futures? Scriptures fraught with hard pronouncements might well be desired, but these were the ones most readily ignored, she suspected – although in truth she knew little of the religions of other peoples. One did not need to be a scholar to observe, however, that faiths were born of stone, water, earth, sun and wind, and should these forces prove harsh and inimical, so too the faith. Hard lives begat hard laws, not just in the necessities of living, but also in those of believing. She well understood that particular dialogue.

A river in seasonal flood, a forest to hold back the harshest winds, the plenitude of fish, crops and game: these did not describe a harsh world, a scrabble to live. The Tiste had traditionally recoiled from fast rules, as if such rules offended their nature. It was only war that changed this, and now, when Emral took a moment away from her mirror – when she looked upon the many now commanding positions of influence in the Citadel – she saw sharp edges in place of soft lines, and in a host of eyes there was stone instead of water.

Many were the natural forces to assail a people and give them shape; in her mind, she must now count among them war itself, no different from sun and wind.

'They are coming,' said Anomander. 'Will you give greeting first?'

'I see myself as more of a final escort into the presence of Mother Dark, Lord.'

'Very well,' he replied.

Motion at the far end of the corridor, and then a sudden bloom of light.

Ice cracked where it sheathed the stone walls, slid down in sheets. The glow surrounded the Azathanai, its golden hue deepening at its edges, reminding Emral of burning leaves. The power she unveiled as she drew closer made the walls groan and shift. Dust drifted down.

Emral found that she was trembling. *It is a wonder that the Azathanai are not worshipped as gods.*

Behind the approaching woman came Warlock Resh and Lieutenant Caplo Dreem. Neither man bore an air of confidence; instead, they looked beleaguered, exhausted by uncertainty.

With the light came warmth, cutting through the chilled air, devouring it. The Azathanai woman, slight of frame, attractive in a delicate way, her fair hair drifting in the swirling draughts, halted three strides from them. Her gaze fixing upon Anomander, she said, 'Night will claim your skin. Before your eyes, darkness will be revealed. But I will make visible the defiance within you, as a gift.'

Anomander frowned. 'Azathanai, I ask for no gifts. I offer no defiance.'

The woman's gaze drifted from him and settled upon Emral. 'Your sorrow, High Priestess, is lonely, and you are driven to share your truths. I advise against it. Give voice to your secrets and you will be rejected by those for whom you care the most.'

Heat flooded through Emral and she fought to control her tone. 'Azathanai, your words of greeting are presumptuous.'

Thin brows arched. 'I cannot be but what I am, High Priestess. I come to stir the waters, and for a time we shall all be blind. Will you now turn me away?'

Emral shook her head. 'She wishes to see you, Azathanai.'

'A desire I share. I have been called T'riss and this name I now take as my own. I do not know who I was before I was T'riss. I dwelt for a time in the Vitr. I am of the Azathanai, but I do not know what this means.'

'If you are here,' said Anomander, 'seeking answers to questions, you may be disappointed.'

'The Tiste view the Vitr as an enemy,' said T'riss. 'It is no such thing. It exists for itself. It is a sea of possibilities, of potential. It holds life in the manner that blood holds life.'

'Did it create you?' Anomander asked.

'No.'

'Yet it grows. It devours land – this indeed poses a threat to Kurald Galain.'

The woman shrugged. 'The sea does not dream of you.'

Emral's attention slid from the Azathanai's unperturbed equanimity, past her to Warlock Resh. The man's face was pale, drawn. 'Warlock Resh, you have brought us this guest. She has awakened your ancient god. What would Mother Sheccanto have you say to the followers of Mother Dark?'

'Nothing,' he replied, as if choking out the word. 'For the moment.'

'I will see her now,' said T'riss.

Emral stepped to one side. The Azathanai moved past her.

As Warlock Resh and Caplo fell in behind T'riss, Anomander's hands snapped out, grasped Caplo by the man's tunic, and threw him up against the wall. He held the monk pinned there, feet dangling.

Resh stumbled back in alarm, and then quickly shook his head and Emral saw the gleam of a knife blade half hidden in Caplo's left hand – which vanished as quickly as it had appeared.

Ahead, T'riss did not so much as turn round, instead pushing open the heavy door and striding into the chamber. The door, left open, reflected flashes of yellow light, and Emral could feel the Azathanai's power pushing through the darkness.

Anomander was speaking to Caplo. 'No blood to be spilled within, do you understand me?'

'Un-unnecessary, Lord,' Caplo said in a gasp.

Releasing the man to sag against the wall, Anomander faced Warlock Resh. 'Inform Sheccanto that we have no interest in sharing her panic. And should she ever again send her prized assassin into audience with Mother Dark, I will see his head spiked to the Citadel's wall, with hers to follow.'

'I will convey your message, Lord,' Resh replied, but his tone was distracted.

From the doorway, the light suddenly vanished. A moment later, High Priestess Syntara staggered into view. Her skin was the hue of alabaster, her dark eyes like pools of ink. When Emral moved to assist her, Syntara threw up a staying hand, and her face twisted into a mask of spite and venom. 'Do not touch me, you wretched hag! I chose my gift! I chose it!'

Pushing past the others, she rushed down the corridor.

Groaning, Warlock Resh set his back to the wall as would a man with too much drink in him. Eyes squeezing shut, he said, 'She's gone.'

Emral did not need him to elaborate. Bitter cold air was rushing into the corridor from the sanctum. The audience was at an end, and T'riss had vanished. The aftermath of the power unveiled in the last few moments made the air fiercely bitter, almost caustic.

Anomander faced the warlock. 'She was banished?'

Resh's eyes started open. 'Does she give you nothing? This precious new goddess of yours?'

'She may well give,' Anomander replied. 'But I do not ask.'

'Not banished. Time twisted in the sanctum – in there, they might well have spoken for days. There is no way of knowing. She brought the blood – I felt it – she brought *vitr* into that chamber. Lord, I did not know – it must have been within her.'

Anomander half turned to the yawning doorway. 'A weapon?'

'No, Lord. A gift.'

'Shake,' Anomander commanded. 'Await us here. High Priestess Emral, accompany me.' He strode into the sanctum.

Emral followed.

As the door was shut behind them, Emral noticed at once that something had changed. The darkness remained, yet somehow lacked its oppressive weight, and before her eyes it seemed almost pellucid. In growing astonishment, she realized that she could make out details of the chamber.

Before them, motionless on the Throne of Night, sat Mother Dark, black-clothed in loose silks, black-haired, and now black-skinned. The transformation left Emral stunned, her thoughts plucked loose from all that she saw, as if she beheld a dubious world with the eyes of a drunk, and could make no sense of it.

As if nothing could rattle him, Anomander faced the throne, and something in his demeanour hinted at the defiance T'riss had seen within him. 'Are you harmed, Mother?'

Her voice was soft, pitched low as if in weariness. 'I am not.'

'You sent her away?'

'Beloved Emral,' said Mother Dark, 'you now stand alone as my High Priestess. Syntara has chosen, and from this a schism now threatens us all. In matters of faith, waters will part. This cannot be undone.'

But Anomander was not easily set aside. 'Mother, the Azathanai resurrected an ancient god—'

'There is peace between us. You see too many enemies, First Son. We are not threatened from without; only from within.'

'Then we shall deal with it,' he replied. 'But I must understand what has happened here. I will defend what I believe in, Mother.'

'But what is worthy of your belief, Anomander? This is ever the question, isn't it?'

'What has T'riss done here? The darkness itself is changed.'

Again, Mother Dark made no answer to him, instead addressing Emral. 'Inform your sisters and brothers, High Priestess. This temple is sanctified.'

*This was the Azathanai's gift? Sanctified by vitr?* 'Mother Dark, what has driven Syntara from us? Her faith was unassailable—'

'Easily assailed,' countered Mother Dark. 'By ambition and vanity. The Azathanai can see deep into a mortal soul, yet she understands nothing of tact, nor the value of withholding truths.'

'And her gift?' Emral asked. 'She is made bloodless, white as bone.'

'She is beyond my reach now, beloved Emral. That is all.'

'But . . . where will she go?'

'That remains to be seen. I have thoughts . . . but not now. You both stand in the presence of Night. You are no longer blinded by darkness, and all who come to me will receive this blessing. Even now,' she observed, 'I see Night comes to your skin.'

When Emral looked to Anomander, however, she gasped upon seeing not the ebon hue of his skin, but the silver sheen of his hair.

Mother Dark sighed. 'You ever trouble me, First Son. One day I shall tell you of your mother.'

'I have no interest in her,' said Anomander. 'Love cannot survive the absence of memories, and for that woman we have none.'

'And has that not made you curious?'

The question seemed to startle him and he made no reply.

271

Emral wanted to weep, but her eyes remained dry, as if lined with sand. She struggled not to step back, to wheel and leave them to their bitter exchange. But she would not flee as had Syntara. Of vanity she had little, but ambition was another matter, twisted though its path might be.

Mother Dark's eyes were upon her, she now saw, but the goddess said nothing.

Anomander finally spoke, 'Mother, will you speak with the Shake?'

'Not yet. But I warn you this, First Son, do not oppose the gathering of believers. The Deniers were never without faith – they but denied a faith in me. So be it. I do not compel. The Shake will insist upon their neutrality in matters of the state.'

'*Then name your enemy!*' Anomander's shout echoed in the chamber, and behind it was exasperation and fury.

'I have none,' she replied in a calm voice. 'Anomander. Win this peace for me; that is all I ask.'

Breath hissed from him in frustration. 'I am a warrior and I know only blood, Mother. I cannot win what I must first destroy.'

'Then, above all, First Son, do not draw a sword.'

'How is it Syntara poses a threat?' he demanded. 'What manner of schism could she create? Her cadre is small – priestesses and a half-dozen spies among the servants. The Shake will not have her.'

'It is the gift she now carries,' Mother Dark replied, 'that will draw adherents.'

'Then let us arrest her, throw her and her lot into a cell.'

'The gift cannot be chained, First Son. I see how you both struggle to understand, but the schism is necessary. The wound must be made, so that it can be healed.'

'And what of Draconus?'

At Anomander's question Mother Dark grew very still, and the air in the sanctum suddenly crackled with cold. 'Leave me now, First Son.'

'Without him,' Anomander persisted, 'you set before me an impossible task.'

'Go.'

The way before him was indeed impossible and Emral could see that bleak knowledge in Anomander's dark eyes. He wheeled and marched from the chamber.

Emral's head spun. The air bit at her throat and lungs.

Mother Dark spoke. 'Beloved Emral . . . I once asked Kadaspala a question. I saw in his eyes that he knew this question, as if, long ago, it had been seared into his very soul. But for all that, he could give me no answer.'

'Mother Dark, what was the question?'

'One to be asked of an artist, a creator of portraits, whose talent is found not in the hands but in the eyes. I asked him: how does one paint love?'

*He knew the question. He asked it of himself.*

*But he had no answer.*

'Do you know,' Mother Dark went on, 'when you can see in darkness, nothing is hidden.'

If she wept now, the tears would freeze upon her cheeks, and burn leaving scars. For all to see.

'Nothing,' Mother Dark then added, 'but darkness itself.'

\*       \*       \*

Half drunk, Hunn Raal stared at the white-skinned woman who had come stumbling into his room. He saw the fear and fury warring in her eyes, but it was the alabaster bleaching of her visage that held him enthralled. Not even Silchas Ruin possessed such purity. He struggled to speak. 'H-High Priestess, what has become of you? You are glamoured – what new gift of sorcery has Mother Dark discovered?'

'I am cast out, you fool! Banished from Night! This was not her doing – the Azathanai said she could see into my soul. She said terrible things—' Syntara turned away, and he could see how she trembled. 'She reached out to me. There was light. *Blinding light.*'

He forced himself from his chair. The room tilted slightly and then righted itself. He drew a deep, steadying breath, and then moved close to her. 'High Priestess, I will tell you what I see when I now look upon you—'

'Don't.'

'I see a woman reborn. Syntara, you among all women do not belong in darkness.'

She looked up at him. 'The light is within me. I feel it!'

He nodded. 'And I see it shining through, High Priestess. There is nothing to fear – the truth of that is plain to my eyes.'

'Reborn,' she whispered. And then her eyes flashed. 'I demand sanctuary.'

'And you have come to me. I understand, High Priestess.'

'Where else could I go? I cannot stay here. I need the protection of the Legion . . .'

He straightened, saying nothing. He needed to think this through.

'Hunn Raal—'

'A moment, please. This is a complication—'

'Is that what I am? A complication? Hardly the grovelling stance you took yesterday, babbling how everything is in place!'

'Yesterday you were the High Priestess of Mother Dark,' he snapped. 'But now she'll not have you, Syntara. I must think of my master, and the future I seek for him. I must think of the Legion.'

She stood, faced him. 'Save that nonsense for the fools who will believe it. I see your ambition, Hunn Raal. I know your bloodlines. You long to walk these halls again, in your rightful place. Your master is simply the means, not the end.'

'We are not all as base as you, Syntara. Now, cease your raging. Give me time to see a way through this, to the advantage of all of us. Tell me truthfully now, why do you believe you need sanctuary?'

Her eyes widened. 'Look at me! See what she has done!'

'The Azathanai did this, not Mother Dark. You fled the chamber – why?'

'You were not there,' she hissed. 'You did not hear the horrible things the woman said of me.'

'Then,' he concluded, 'you fled in shame. Mother Dark did not cast you out.'

'Nor did she defend me! Her own High Priestess!'

He grunted. 'Fortunate for her then that she had two High Priestesses.'

Her slap against the side of his face sent him back a step, not from the weight of the blow, but in the shocked sobriety it delivered. One side of his face stinging, he studied the woman before him, and then sighed. '"Anger is the death of beauty." Who was it said that? Never mind. This has been a fraught day – the city streets flooding to announce the coming of the Azathanai, and I am told there was ice in the passage leading to the Chamber of Night. And now you . . . what do these things portend, High Priestess?'

But her gaze had slid past him, to the jug of wine on the table. She strode over, poured full a goblet and drank it down in three quick swallows. 'Are you too drunk to fuck me, Hunn Raal?'

*Said the woman who just slapped me.* 'Probably.'

'Men are so pathetic.'

'I have other things on my mind.'

She refilled her goblet and then faced him. 'Will Urusander take me?'

'As what?'

Instead of the anger he expected from his careless retort, she laughed. 'Now *that* would ruin your plans, wouldn't it, Hunn Raal? Don't you think I have had my fill of old soldiers? They are nothing but dumb need and you have no idea how tiring that is. No, Mother Dark is welcome to him.'

His nod was sharp. 'So we're clear on that. Good.'

'A god now stirs the mud of Dorssan Ryl,' she said, eyes narrowing, watching for his reaction over the rim of the goblet as she drank. 'It was dead but is dead no longer. What ancient laws have been broken this day?'

'Was this too a gift of the Azathanai woman? Then let us be plain.

274

These were not gifts. A city flooded? Ice in the Citadel? They amount to an assault upon Kurald Galain.'

She shrugged. 'Semantics.'

'Hardly. You are speaking to an old soldier, remember? Dumb we may be but us soldiers know the answer to such things.'

'Will you declare war upon the Azathanai?' She snorted, somewhat drunkenly. 'Not even Urusander is that foolish. Besides, the woman vanished – as if she opened a door in the very air itself, and then simply stepped through. The power of that made Mother Dark recoil.'

'Then we are indeed threatened, High Priestess.'

She waved a dismissive hand, turning to refill the goblet. 'We can do nothing about it. The Deniers will crawl out of the woods now, eager to lay sacrifice upon the banks of the river. Eager to walk the shore.'

'And Mother Dark permits this?'

'She is weak, Hunn Raal – why do you think she hides in darkness? Why do you think she draws close the three most feared warriors among the highborn and proclaims them her children? And why' – she faced him – 'did she take Lord Draconus to her bed? Sons may be all very well, but a man such as Draconus is another matter entirely. You understand nothing, Hunn Raal. You and your ridiculous plans.'

He saw the challenge in her eyes, glittering behind the alcohol, and felt something stir in him. *She is like me. She is the same as me, exactly the same.* 'You will take this to Urusander, High Priestess,' he said. 'You will tell him of the threat now facing Kurald Galain. You will explain to him her weakness, her vulnerability. But more than this, you will show him what must be done. The purity of your skin is now a symbol – the light within you is a power. Above all, High Priestess, tell him this: in darkness there is ignorance. In light there is justice.' He moved closer to her. 'Remember those words. This is what you must do.'

She leaned against the table behind her, a smirk playing on her full lips. 'I am to be a beacon, then? Still a High Priestess, but now in the name of light?'

'It is within you.'

She glanced away, still smiling. '*Liossan.* And who, then, are our enemies?'

'All who seek to hurt Mother Dark – we will fight in her name and who could challenge this?'

'And Draconus?'

'He but uses her. Another way of hurting.' He leaned over to grasp the jug of wine, and in the movement their faces came close, almost touching for a moment before he drew back. But he had smelled the sweet wine on her breath. 'The old religion is a direct threat. The Deniers. The brothers and sisters of the Monasteries.'

'There are more of them than you might imagine, Hunn Raal.'

'All to the better,' he said.

'Sheccanto and Skelenal could even make claim to the throne.'

'I wish they would. That would settle the sides quickly enough.'

She reached out and stroked his cheek, where she had slapped only a short time before. 'We will plunge Kurald Galain into civil war, Hunn Raal. You and I, and all that we now do.'

But he shook his head. 'We prevent one, High Priestess. Even better, once we have purged the realm, the end to all conflict is then offered to Mother Dark. By taking the hand of Lord Urusander. She will see that she needs such a man at her side. Strength to answer her weakness, resolve to stand firm against her whims. Light and Dark, in balance.'

'I want Emral dead.'

'You cannot have that. She is but your reflection. An imperfect one to be sure, but even then you fare the better between you. No, Syntara, you will be as equals, yet need share nothing but your titles.'

'Then I shall proclaim Urusander as Father Light,' said Syntara, her hand still upon his cheek. 'And the light within me shall be my gift to him.'

'If you can give it.'

'I can, Hunn Raal.'

He was still holding the jug. 'Now then, High Priestess, do we fuck or do we drink?'

'Which do you prefer?'

A dangerous question that he shrugged off. 'Either is fine with me.'

To his surprise she stepped away, and her stride was suddenly steady. 'There is not time for either, Hunn Raal,' she said, her words sharp. 'I must gather my followers and we will need an escort from the city. Best we do this without fanfare – I shall cloak myself and remain unseen. My return to Kharkanas shall be in triumph.'

'Of course,' he said, setting the jug back down on the table, feeling a fool for having been so easily played. 'I think I underestimated you, High Priestess.'

'Many do,' she replied. 'And you – you must send word to your people, wherever they happen to be hiding in the countryside.' Seeing the alarm on his face her smile grew cruel. 'Yes, I know that you are ready to pounce. But they must wait – your enemy is no longer the highborn. Nor the sons and daughters of Mother Dark. Not even Draconus – not yet, in any case. Why so troubled, captain?'

'I fear that it may already be too late.'

'Then sober up, you fool, and make sure that it isn't!'

\* \* \*

The troop of riders came upon the train, meeting at a sharp bend in the road. There had been little sound to betray them, despite the high cliff walls to either side. Orfantal saw, just past the strangers, the road opening out, sunken flats flanking the raised track: the signs of an old, extinct lake.

Haral was quick to draw up, and he twisted in the saddle and with a shout commanded the wagons to one side, to let the riders past.

Orfantal looked upon those unknown faces. He counted eleven men and women, all well armed and bearing none of the ragtag equipment he would have expected among bandits. Nor did the strangers accost them, but Orfantal felt their sharp eyes gauging the caravan and its handful of guards. Beside him Gripp was silent, head lowered as if in deference.

A few, Orfantal saw as they plodded past, wore the colours of Urusander's Legion, charcoal grey half-capes piped in gold, the high leather knee-guards that so faithfully copied Urusander's own armour. He knew this from his grandfather's kit, which he had examined countless times. Others seemed to be carrying the same gear, but rolled up and tied to the backs of their saddles.

'Hunting bandits?' Orfantal asked Gripp after the last rider had trotted past. 'There were Legion—'

'Quiet, boy!' rasped Gripp, and Orfantal saw how pale the old man was, his mouth pinched, the lips dry. He was staring ahead to Haral, awaiting the command to resume. 'Send us on, damn you!' he said in a hiss.

Orfantal twisted on his saddle to look back at the strangers.

'Turn round!' Gripp snapped. 'Now, let's go. Ride on, boy, ride on. Eyes forward!'

'What's wrong?'

Ahead, Haral had swung his mount round, watching the wagons rock back on to the centre of the road.

Orfantal could see Gripp's watery eyes fixed on Haral's, as if seeking a sign.

It came when Haral frowned, and then straightened in his saddle. A moment later he half rose on the stirrups, confusion writ plain on his features.

'That's it, then,' growled Gripp. He pulled his mount close alongside Orfantal's. 'Listen to me. They're coming back.'

'What? Why?'

'Because they shouldn't be here, that's why. At least three of them were from a disbanded unit.'

'But—'

'Ride ahead, Orfantal – and once you're on the straight, kick that hag of yours into a gallop and don't look back. No more questions!' he added as horse hoofs sounded behind them, fast approaching. 'Go, son, *ride.*' And he slapped the hag's rump, jolting the beast forward into a startled canter. The motion almost unseated Orfantal and he gripped hard the reins, which only slowed the beast.

'Kick her on!' Gripp shouted, and there was the sound of swords being drawn.

Punching the flanks with his heels, Orfantal pushed his mount back into a canter, and then a heavy gallop. Disorientated, he rocked in the saddle. He heard harsh shouts behind him. Someone screamed like a dying pig.

Mouth dry, heart hammering, he leaned forward. 'Oh, run! Run, you, oh run . . .'

The horse thundered beneath him, but it seemed so slow, the beast labouring. The scene jolted up and down, side to side, and he thought of Gripp, and Haral and the others. He thought of that scream, and wondered from whose throat it had erupted. He thought of dying, cut down from behind. He could hear a horse running behind him, catching up impossibly quickly. A whimper escaped him and he felt hot urine in his crotch, seeping down the inside of his thighs.

He didn't turn as the horse caught up, instead ducking down.

A moment later and the beast rushed past. Haral's own horse, riderless, its flanks black with spilled blood and lumps of gore.

Orfantal looked back – but he was beyond the bend and not even the wagons were in view. He saw two riders emerge, reining in to watch him flee. A moment later they set off in pursuit.

The nag was labouring, breaths gusting harsh and loud. Haral's horse was already twenty paces ahead. Desperate, Orfantal looked round. The sunken flats to either side formed a basin, but one edge was closer than the other – to his right – and he saw the fringe of an old stony shoreline, and then the ragged broken hillsides rearing up beyond. There were paths up there, places to hide.

Orfantal slowed his horse, and then pulled it down from the road. He glanced back to see the two riders drawing closer, their swords out.

The nag stumbled on the rocky slope, righted itself with a snort. Orfantal kicked it forward. The clay underhoof cracked and gave way, miring the horse in the thick mud hiding beneath the crust. The animal dragged itself clear, pushed on at Orfantal's frantic urging. Lunging, pitching, the nag fought onward.

They were halfway across when the horse sank down to its belly, lurching helplessly, head tossing, eyes rolling. Crying now, the tears half blinding him, Orfantal dragged himself free of the saddle. He looked back to see the two riders reined in at the roadside, watching his progress. In a flash he realized that neither dared venture on to the clay.

He worked his way clear of the sucking mud, rolled on to his side.

The nag had given up its struggle and looked across at him with dumb misery in its weeping eyes. He could see that it had sunk down now halfway up its shoulders at the front, and deeper still at the back. Its whole body trembled and flies swarmed its mud-spattered hide.

He crawled away, still weeping, his face smeared. He had killed his horse, his noble servant. He had betrayed the beast, as only a master could.

*But I'm not the betrayer – it's not supposed to be me. It was never supposed to be me!*

His weight was as nothing on the hard-packed clay crust. He made his way across it towards the pebble-studded old bank. Reaching it he straightened and looked back.

The riders were leaving, heading back up the road – and from beyond the bend two columns of thick, black smoke lifted into the sky, and Orfantal knew that his companions were all dead. Haral, Gripp, all of them. A disbanded unit, fallen into banditry and murder – but no, even that did not make sense. Those skins on the wagons were valuable. Bandits would not set them alight.

His gaze fell back to the nag.

The back end of the animal was now beneath the mud, and he could see how it struggled to breathe.

Orfantal ventured back out on to the clay, retracing his route.

When he reached the nag only its head and neck were visible. The crying left him weak, but he managed to throw his arms around that neck, holding on tight. The hide was hot and slick, almost on fire with life, and he felt the nag's cheek settle against the side of his head, and he wept so hard he felt as if he was emptying his own soul. His wails echoed back from the cliffs behind him.

The mud touched the underside of his left arm; he felt his elbow plunging into soft coolness. The neck muscles strained and the nag lifted its head, nostrils opened wide, air gusting out in a long stream. But it had no strength with which to draw a breath inside – the weight of the clay against its ribs was too vast. As the exhalation dwindled, he felt the nag shudder, and then begin to sag, the muscles relaxing and the head settling on the clay. The horse's eyelids dipped down half over the lifeless eyes, and stayed there.

Orfantal dragged his arms from the mud. With the nag's death, the anguish left him, and in its place was a vast hollow, a numbness that made him feel small.

Truth cared nothing for stories. The real world was indifferent to what people wanted to be, to how they wanted everything to turn out. Betrayers came from everywhere, including inside his own body, his own mind. He could trust no one, not even himself.

He faced the broken rocks and started crawling.

# TEN

R ISP WATCHED CAPTAIN ESTHALA THROW ON HER CLOAK AND TUG her gauntlets from her swordbelt. There was the taste of iron in the air, a pungent aura of panic spreading through the hidden camp. The day was fast drawing to a close, shadows engulfing the spaces between the crags. Esthala's husband, Silann, had dismounted to help down one of his wounded soldiers. Risp turned and studied the battered troop, seeing faces flushed and faces pale and taut with pain, seeing the blood splashed on most of the soldiers and the tenderness with which they pulled bodies down, and the way the horses stamped and tossed heads in the aftermath of battle. A moment later Esthala walked past her to accost her husband.

'Have you lost your mind?' she hissed, but not quietly enough to be missed by the nearby soldiers. 'This was not supposed to happen.'

He shot her a glare. 'A caravan. We recognized one of the guards, and for damned certain he recognized us!'

'What of it? A dozen old soldiers on the trail – that means nothing!'

'A disbanded unit once more under arms, you mean. And to that old man it meant something. I think even the one commanding those guards had marked us as being in the wrong place at the wrong time. But listen, Esthala, it's been taken care of. No survivors barring a child who was quick to run off – and who'd listen to a child? The caravan was struck by bandits and that is all.' His rush of words ended and he stood staring at his wife, his face smeared in dirty sweat.

'A child escaped you? Go back and hunt him down!'

'He'll never survive the hills. No food, no water. The night will

280

probably kill him – he looked no more than six years old. He rode out across a mudflat and lost his horse to it.'

'Then he should be easy enough to find,' said Esthala, crossing her arms.

Silann was scowling. 'I'm not in the habit of killing children.'

'I will lead a troop if you deem it necessary,' said Risp, drawing them both around. Fed up with this unprofessional display, where whatever marital problems they possessed continually overwhelmed all propriety, she continued in a reasonable tone, 'Silann's unit is all chewed up. They're tired and they have friends to bury.'

'And what think you Hunn Raal will say to this?' Esthala demanded. 'We're not yet ready for open bloodshed. You said so yourself.'

Risp shrugged. 'My cousin understands the risks. You have plenty of country to cross, and thinking you can do it unseen is unrealistic. I agree with Silann that we need not worry about some hysterical, shocked child, but if you wish it, captain, I will find that child and we can put this matter to rest. Silann,' she added, one brow lifting, 'it seems your soldiers are out of shape. A few caravan guards mauled you badly.'

'Veterans among those guards, Risp. And the old man was Gripp.'

'Gripp Galas?'

'The same. He killed the first two who came at him.'

'How did he fall?'

'A spear to the back.'

'Who fired the wagons?' Esthala demanded.

Silann turned away. 'That was a mistake.'

Risp said nothing. The venom between husband and wife was growing ever more vicious. There was a son who had left the family, Risp recalled, taking the priestly orders and so disappointing his ambitious parents. No doubt they each blamed the other, but it was likely not the least of their mutual irritations. Glancing away, she could see the pillars of black smoke in the distance to the south, rising above the rough rocks. 'Is Hish Tulla in residence at her keep? Does anyone know?'

'No,' replied Esthala in a tone that could dull knife blades. 'She is still in Kharkanas.'

'So it's not likely they'll investigate. As I recall, that old castellan of hers has no imagination and isn't one to abandon the keep on account of a little smoke. If he sends anyone, it'll be tomorrow and you'll be long gone from these hills. I'll catch you up on the north road.'

'Take six of your own,' Esthala told her. 'If you come upon anyone from Tulla Keep, offer to ride with them if any searching takes place, and do not take no for an answer. I doubt they will look beyond the scene of the fight itself. The burnt loot is a problem – that's a hoard of

281

wealth gone up in smoke, after all.' She fixed her husband with another iron glare. 'See to your soldiers, husband.'

Risp gestured to her sergeant who stood a few paces away. 'Ready the horses. Choose five with tracking skills and good eyes.'

'Yes sir,' the man replied.

She watched the old veteran walk back to her unit's camp. Hunn Raal had awarded her the rank of lieutenant and she was well pleased with it. Not her fault the best of the war was over by the time she reached an age suitable to soldiering. It was satisfying giving orders and seeing them followed without question, and this was just the beginning. Soon, they would all stand in the Grand Hall of the Citadel, eyes level with those of the highborn. She and her sisters were destined for the personal staff under Osserc, once he took command of the Legion. And it was clear that, even though Esthala technically outranked her, the real power here was with Risp, as she had just shown. She counted it among her own virtues that she could distil pleasure from the most extreme fiascos and disasters, and this mess was surely both.

*Gripp Galas. That was unfortunate. Once footman to Anomander himself and proven in the wars. Anomander should never have let the fool retire.*

Frowning, she watched two soldiers of Silann's troop stagger off with a body between them. They had to hold it carefully balanced as the man had been disembowelled by a single sword cut. Gripp was said to have a temper in a fight. She wagered that was his work. That man had died in pain. She walked over to Esthala.

'Captain, I am wondering about something.'

Distracted and perhaps, now that she'd cooled down, also embarrassed, Esthala shrugged. 'Go on.'

'I am wondering what in the name of the Abyss was Gripp Galas doing with that traders' caravan.'

Esthala faced her husband again. 'Silann! Tell me, did you examine Gripp's body? His gear?'

The man looked over and shook his head. 'The spear point in the back took him off his horse. His corpse rolled into a damned crevasse, fell right out of sight.'

Esthala stepped towards him. 'Didn't you go down after him? To make certain that he was dead?'

'He left a blood trail thick with gore – and that crevasse was bottomless.'

'Gore?' Risp asked. 'Whose gore? He was stabbed in the back. Silann,' she continued, struggling to control her panic, 'bring us the soldier who stabbed Gripp. I want to see the spear point. I want to hear how the blow felt – was Gripp wearing armour? Was Gripp wearing leather, as befits a caravan guard, or chain, as befits a covert agent?'

The blood had left Silann's face. 'That man died to the leader of the caravan guards – who was clearly another veteran.'

'The gutted one or the one with no throat left? That one? Have you his weapon?'

A few moments later one of Silann's soldiers collected up and delivered the dead man's spear; as Risp reached for the weapon, Esthala stepped close and took it instead. Ignoring Risp's scowl, the captain studied the iron point. 'Might have struck chain – I see the bite of snapped links. The tip's bloody, so it went through . . . about three fingers' worth. If it severed the spine then Gripp's dead or paralysed. Anywhere else and he's wounded but not fatally so.'

'He fell down a damned crevasse!' Silann shouted.

'Fell or rolled down it?' Esthala demanded. 'Did you see it happen?'

Swearing under her breath, Risp made her way back to her troop. 'Muster out six more, sergeant! This hunt has turned serious.'

*　　*　　*

The sun was low in the western sky when Sukul Ankhadu summoned Rancept to the top floor of the High Tower. Upon the castellan's wheezing arrival, she gestured to the large window. 'I trust you have been made aware of smoke to the east.'

Rancept, it was said, was the offspring of a drunken woman and a sadly sober boar. Such observations were rarely made to his face, of course, because Rancept had his father's temper, and enough brawn to make a bear cower. The castellan's face looked familiar with tavern floors, his nose broken and mashed by countless brawls in his youth, unfortunately pushed back to give it the appearance of a pig's snout. His teeth were uneven and stained and ragged from years of mouth-breathing. He was rumoured to be a thousand years old and as bone-weary as a man twice his age.

At her query he squinted at the window.

'You'll have to step closer to see it from here,' said Sukul.

He made no move. 'Mistress wants us stayin' put, milady. Says there's trouble on the way.'

'Closer than we think, yes? That smoke smells to me of burning hides.'

'Does it now, milady?'

'You will have to take my word on that, castellan.'

He grunted, still squinting at the window. 'Suppose I will at that.'

'There was a highborn riding with those wagons. A boy of five or six years of age. On his way to the Wise City. To the Citadel, in fact. A child of the Korlas family.'

Rancept pawed at the silver stubble on his jaw. 'Korlas? Good soldier. Always sad. Heard he killed himself.'

'Officially died in his sleep or something like that.'

'Festered wound I think it was, milady.'

'You're trying my patience, castellan.'

His squint narrowed until his eyes were thin slits. 'I do that, yes.'

'I want us to ride out – tonight – and catch up to that caravan. If there are bandits that close to us, we need to know.'

'Not bandits, milady.'

'I know that, you oaf! So who attacked them and are we under threat?'

He grunted a second time. 'Safe enough up here.'

'I insist we ride out! I want fifteen Houseblades, and a fist of tracking dogs!'

'You'll get one Houseblade, milady, and Ribs.'

'Ribs? That dog is constantly surprised by the smell of its own butt! And one Houseblade isn't enough – you are supposed to accord me proper protection.'

'And I will, milady,' and he now turned to her, showing his teeth. 'That one will be me.'

'Castellan, forgive me, but walking up the stairs to get here nearly burst your heart.'

'Hardly, milady. My heart's just fine and so is the rest of me, barring this nose you keep trying to not look at.'

'Abyss below. Then it shall be you and me, castellan.'

'And Ribs, milady.'

'Find yourself a horse—'

'On foot,' he said. 'It's quieter.'

'But look at me – I'm all dressed to ride!'

'Me and Ribs will be waitin' downstairs, milady.'

*    *    *

Orfantal crouched in a hollow surrounded by shattered boulders. The sky overhead was black, overcast, and the darkness on all sides had stolen away all the familiar features he had looked upon a short while earlier. In his imagination the world was now transformed, seething with motion. He heard strange sounds, stared helplessly into the blackness where he thought he saw something staring back at him.

He missed his blanket, and the fire of the caravan guards, which was kept alive through each night and which he'd find when awakening with a start, forgetting where he was and frightened – but that smudge of coals and the occasional flicker of flame seen through the tent's thin fabric always righted him again. But now there was nothing, no tent, no Gripp snoring and muttering under his breath. He was alone and he felt nothing like a hero.

Shivers raced through him. He remembered his daydreams of a bandit attack, and just as in that story he had fled into the night, into the hills. But the truth of it, here in this hollow, was nothing like that epic adventure. His feet were numb; his hands hung heavy and insensate at the ends of his wrists, and he felt the beckoning of sleep, as if the cold were drifting away.

He had not crawled far from the basin where his horse had died. The hills had seemed too vast, too threatening to venture deep into. If he lost sight of the basin, he'd lose sight of the road, and then he'd be lost. The truth was, his courage had failed him and he felt ashamed. The smell of his own urine mocked him. He could taste his own betrayal, bitter and sickening, and again and again the shudder of the horse echoed through him – the feel of life leaving it as he hugged its neck. It did not deserve that kind of end, driven forward in fear, pushed into exhaustion, guided by a foolish boy. What would he tell Wreneck? He would rather the bandits had cut him down instead.

He gave up on his fear of the night and closed his eyes. He'd stopped shivering and that was good.

A footfall on gravel dragged him awake. His heart pounded hard and seemed to swell inside his chest. He struggled to breathe.

From over his head, atop the boulder he leaned his back against, a voice drifted down. 'There you are.'

With a soft cry, Orfantal tried to lunge forward, but his legs gave way beneath him.

'Easy! It's me, old Gripp.'

The man edged down into the hollow, alongside Orfantal. A hand settled on his shoulder. 'You're chilled as the Abyss. I made up a camp nearby, scavenged some bedding. Can you stand?'

Tears were streaming down from Orfantal's eyes, but apart from that first cry no sound would come from him. Shame was flooding back into him. He tried to get up but failed again.

'You wouldn't have lasted the night. Good thing I found you. That thing with the horse, that was a smart move – no way they was going to follow you out there.' As he was speaking he gathered up Orfantal in his arms. 'Lie still. It'll be all right. I got to move slow, got a hurt back and a wrenched knee.' And now Orfantal could feel the man limping as he carried him; a rhythmic sagging to the left as Gripp tried to put weight on that leg. The old man's skin was slick with sweat, a detail that Orfantal could not understand. 'Just a little further. Can't have no fire, though.'

Orfantal found that his eyes were adjusting and he could now make out the looming shapes of rocks and sheer cliffsides as Gripp worked up along a narrow trail. He then angled left, off the path, wending slowly between boulders, his breaths growing harsh.

There was an odd echo to those gasps and Gripp settled down to one knee. 'We're here.'

They were in a rock shelter, a shallow cave. Beneath Orfantal, as he was set down, was dry, powdery sand, and he settled into it. Gripp moved away and came back with a rough woollen blanket. It was not the one Orfantal's grandmother had given him and it wasn't Gripp's own, which he remembered for its smell of the sage leaves which Gripp kept in a long cloth bag and folded into the bedroll when rolling it up every morning. This blanket stank of sweat and something else, pungent and musty. Once Gripp had wrapped Orfantal in its rough weave he began rubbing hard at the boy's limbs, beginning with his feet and working his way up to his thighs; and then repeating the same rapid motions along Orfantal's arms.

The effort brought warmth along with prickling irritation, and after a moment Orfantal pushed the hands away and curled up in the blanket.

'Shivering again. That's good, Orfantal. I was damned lucky to find you in time. I know you want to sleep but sleep's not good right now. Wait a bit, wait till you feel good and warm.'

'Where are the others? Did you fight them off?'

'No, we didn't fight them off. Though Haral gave a good account of himself. Migil and Thennis tried running off but got cut down from behind – fools. When you see it's hopeless that's when you stand. Breaking just sees you dead quicker and there's nothing more shameful than a death-wound to the back.' He paused and then grunted. 'Unless you're surrounded, of course. Then getting stabbed in the back is usually the way and there's no shame in that.'

'Heroes always get stabbed in the back,' said Orfantal.

'Not just heroes, Orfantal.' Gripp had eased himself down into a sitting position, tenderly settling against the stone wall. 'You know how to sew?'

The question confused him. After a moment he said, 'I have seen the maids doing it.'

'Good. Come light you've got some sewing to do.'

'Are we going to make me some more clothes?'

'No. Now listen, this is important. I need to sleep, too, and it might be that I don't wake up.'

'What do you mean?'

'I mean I don't know how bad off I am. I think the flow's eased but there's no telling what that means. We'll see. But if I don't wake up, you've got to follow the road, east – the way we were going – but listen, stay off it, stay under cover. Just move alongside of the road, you understand? And if you hear riders, hide. Keep going until you're out of the hills and then go to the nearest farm you see. Don't try to explain anything or even tell them your bloodline – they won't believe you. Just see if you can get a way into Kharkanas, even if it takes a week before a wagon of produce heads in. Once there, head straight for the Citadel.'

'I understand. I will.' And he felt for and found the tiny tin tube containing the missive Sukul had written for Hish Tulla, tucked into his belt pouch.

'They made a mistake,' Gripp continued, but now it seemed he was mostly talking to himself. 'More than one, in fact. Me. You. I saw Silann, Esthala's worthless husband. The fool never could command a unit in battle. But if he's there then Esthala's not far away, and she's sharp enough. They'll go back to the kill site, intent on tracking you from there and finishing things. But first they'll look for my body and not find it and that will bother them more than you getting away.' His head lifted and Orfantal sensed Gripp was looking at him once more. 'We're going to be quarry, you and me, as long as we're in these hills.'

'Hunted,' said Orfantal.

'Take your story to Lord Anomander, boy, no matter what.'

'I will. Mother told me all about him.'

'If they find our trail, I may have to lead them away from you. On my own, I mean.'

'All right.'

He grunted. 'You're figuring it out. That's fast, Orfantal. Good.'

'Gripp, did you kill any of them?'

'Two for sure and that pained me.'

'Why?'

'Wounded is better. I wounded two more and that was good. Haral tried for the same. Remember him, Orfantal. He saw you riding away. He knew he had to buy you time, and the more wounded the enemy had to deal with the better your chances. He took cuts to deliver cuts. Haral was a good man.'

Orfantal nodded. *A good man. A hero.* 'Did you see him die, Gripp?'

'No. I lost consciousness for a time – the crack I rolled into was deeper than I'd thought it would be. By the time I made my way back out the killers were gone.'

'They set fire to the skins.'

'Idiots, like I said. But I found Haral. They took it out on his body, if you catch my meaning.'

'That's a cowardly thing to do!'

'No, just undisciplined. But I got their faces burned into my brain. I got them in here, Orfantal, and if I live, they'll all regret what they did. Now, it's time to sleep.'

Orfantal settled down, warm inside the blanket. But notions of sleep seemed far away now. Gripp's story rocked and bounced through his thoughts. Warriors battling to the death, the air filled with desperation. And in the midst of it all, he saw this old man now sleeping beside him, and it seemed impossible to think of him as a warrior. He closed his eyes, and sudden as a flash, sleep took him.

*     *     *

Ribs was an old herding dog, at least twelve years old, with a grey muzzle, oversized ears that flicked and cocked with every quick turn of the narrow, fox-like head. The long fur was a dishevelled blend of grey and black, snarled with burrs and filthy. The beast's eyes were vaguely crossed.

Sukul stared down at it while Castellan Rancept checked the muting straps of his weapons one more time. Torchlight flickered across the courtyard. The gate guards stood waiting at a small postern door to the left of the gate tower. The air was cold and sharp.

Rancept lumbered up to her and nodded. 'Ready?'

'This thing's all bones.'

'Tapeworm, milady.'

'Aren't there treatments for that?'

'A few. But skinny dogs live longer.' With that he turned and made his way towards the gate, Ribs trotting along happily at his side.

Rancept had confiscated the sword she'd selected, along with the spear, leaving her a dagger. None of this was going as planned. The castellan was stubborn and too quick to take charge of things, when she'd wanted to be the one in command. Of course, it was something of a victory that they were going at all. He could have forbidden her outright. She followed him to the postern door and watched as the heavy bars were pulled. As soon as the door was drawn open, Ribs slipped out.

'Where's he going?' Sukul demanded.

'Scouting the trail ahead, milady.'

She grunted. 'He'll probably take us to the nearest squirrel hole.'

'Ribs knows what we're about.'

'How?'

They were outside now and the door was pushed shut behind them. She heard the thump of the bars falling back into place.

At her question, Rancept shrugged. 'I wander on occasion.'

'The hills?'

'If we need to talk to the Deniers. It's important to Lady Hish that there's no misunderstandings.'

'Deniers? Bandits, you mean.'

'It's a hard scrape living in these hills, milady. There's road taxes, if you like.'

'Extortion.'

'And Lady Hish's tithe on travellers? Extortion's a big word. It's only extortion when someone else is doing it.'

They were making their way down the rough-hewn steps. The heavy clouds that had come in with dusk were now breaking up, stars showing through here and there. The temperature was fast dropping.

'Tulla Hold was granted this land by royal charter,' said Sukul. 'A tithe is legal and necessary. Robbing people at the roadside isn't. But now you're hinting that Lady Hish had an arrangement with those thieves.'

Ribs was waiting at the middle landing, another half-dozen steps down. When Rancept and Sukul reached the dog, the animal suddenly left the descent, instead cutting across the boulders of the scree to the left of the stairs.

'As I said,' Sukul noted. 'Some rock rat's got Ribs hungry for more worms.'

But Rancept had halted. 'We're not taking the road, milady. There's a track running above it on this side. It's well hidden and don't start up for a ways. Follow me.'

'What kind of arrangement?' Sukul asked as they clambered over the boulders.

'Before they started working the mines,' Rancept said, once more wheezing, 'they made cheese from the goats they kept. And fine, soft leather, too. But more important, they kept an eye on the traffic. There's a track some travellers take that avoids Tulla Hold.'

'Cheating the tithe? That's pathetic.'

'Sometimes it's that. Sometimes it's just people who don't want to be seen.'

'What kind of people?'

Beyond the boulders, Ribs vanished between two sheer outcrops.

'We're at the trail now,' Rancept said. 'Time for the talking to end. Night carries voices, and the hills can channel sounds a long way. If you need my attention, just tap my shoulder. Otherwise, we move quietly now.'

'This is ridiculous – I can still see the keep's light from here.'

'If we're going to argue, milady, we can turn round right now. But I'll tell you this. Look at Ribs.'

The animal had reappeared and was seated just ahead. 'What about him?' Sukul asked.

'Strangers in the hills, milady. That's what Ribs is telling us.'

To her eyes the animal looked no different from any other time she'd seen it. There was no way to tell where it was looking with those crossed eyes. But as Rancept moved forward, the dog wheeled and raced up the trail again. Tugging tight her slightly oversized gloves, she followed.

For all his size, the castellan moved quietly, not once glancing back to see if she kept pace. This latter detail irritated her and she wanted to hiss at him, since she was getting tired and the trail seemed to go on for ever. Her boots pinched her feet; her nose was running and she'd begun using the back of one hand to wipe at it, and that was staining the fine leather of the glove. Even more annoying, there was nothing bold in this venture. She'd wanted a dozen well-armoured and grim-faced riders at her back, each one ready to give up his or her life at her word. She'd wanted the thunder of horse hoofs and the clatter of iron and wooden scabbards.

Beneath all of this was the conviction that an innocent little boy was lying dead somewhere ahead of them, killed for no good reason but the silence his death would ensure. She'd taken enough hints from Hish Tulla that there was trouble in the realm. The whole thing seemed ridiculous. Peace had been won, but she knew that the hunger for fighting was not yet done with. It was never done with, and there were people in the world who wanted nothing else, since lawlessness was their nature.

Sukul did not have to look far to see such people; she counted her sisters among them. They delighted in all manner of lusts, and the wilder their environs the more base their desires. If she was honest with herself, there was something of that in her as well. But the reality – including this cold, night-shrouded ordeal – was proving more crass than what the imagination offered in all those idle moments when boredom was a shout inside the skull.

She'd made promises to that boy, to that lost bastard of the Korlas line. They seemed both empty and wasted, and the rush of secrecy she'd felt, looking upon his wide, innocent eyes, was now a source of guilt. She'd played at being grown-up, but it had been a childish game none the less. What if they'd tortured Orfantal? Was Hish Tulla now in danger?

Half the night was gone, and still they padded along. All Sukul wanted to do now was stop, rest, even sleep.

The swirl of stars had spun half round when she collided with Rancept's back – she'd not been looking ahead, eyes instead on those now-dusty boots that were torturing her feet. Grunting at the collision, she stumbled back, but a hand snapped out to right her, and then that hand drew her close.

She smelled the lanolin of the thick sheepskin jacket he was wearing, and somehow the familiarity of it steadied her.

He leaned down. 'Riders ahead,' he said in a whisper.

Sukul looked past him, but Ribs was nowhere in sight.

'No questions,' he continued as she started to speak, and his other hand pressed against her mouth, but just briefly – before panic could take her. 'We wait for Ribs.'

Bandits had carved out numerous hidden trails through these hills, and Risp led her dozen soldiers along one of them that would bring them out on to the road close to where they'd seen the smoke. The old Denier camps they'd come across were abandoned, at least a season old, but she knew the cause of that: the Hust Forge's demand for ore had grown prodigious of late, for reasons not one of Hunn Raal's spies could glean. In any case, banditry had been given up and now those miners were growing wealthy with Hust coin.

Thoughts of the Hust Legion – perhaps soon to be bolstered by new recruits – left her disquieted. Every cry for peace was echoed by the beating of iron into blades. No one was fooled unless they willed it upon themselves. Civil war was coming. Hunn Raal meant it to be short; necessarily bloody, true enough, but short.

Urusander escorted to Kharkanas by his triumphant Legion, every enemy of the realm dispensed with and feeding the weeds; an end to the divisiveness and all these private armies; a grand marriage to bind the military and the faith: this was the proper path awaiting them. The Hust Forge would fall under the command of Urusander's Legion, and that cursed Hust Legion would be gone, disbanded, their dreadful weapons melted down into slag. Houseblades would be reduced to a modest family and estate guard, with prohibitions against re-arming. The Borderswords and the Wardens of the Outer Reach would be folded into the Legion, under Osserc's command. In this way, peace would be won.

The best solutions were the simple ones. Besides, she had liked the look of the Wardens of the Outer Reach, and had thoughts of commanding them at some point. Her first order would be the burning down of Glimmer Fate, followed by the killing of the naked wolves and whatever other terrible beasts dwelt in those black grasses. They could then face the Vitr directly, and meet its challenge from a position of strength. If an invasion from that sea was forthcoming, she would stand ready for it upon its very shore.

Urusander placed much value in merit; he cared not if the blood was low or highborn among his officers. That was why the nobles hated him so. Calat Hustain was highborn and this alone granted him the privilege and power of command – and Risp had well seen the result of that: the Wardens were little more than a rabble, devoid of discipline and far too respectful of eccentricity among the ranks. She would change all of that.

Assuming any survived the purge.

They emerged from a narrow, choked avenue between crags, moving on to a level clearing partly encircled by low stone huts. An old fire-pit marked the centre, ringed in flat slabs of shale. Off to one side, near the far end, was a heap of animal bones and rubbish. Risp reined in beside the fire-pit. She never liked places of abandonment. They seemed redolent with failure. People were generally disinclined to move; only necessity forced them from a place, whether it was pressure from stronger neighbours or the loss of clean water or sufficient game. For these herders who were, no doubt, occasional bandits, it had been the call of wealth. Everyone took the coin road sooner or later, with haunted, hungry eyes. She eyed the pile of bones and fought a shiver.

Her sergeant pulled up alongside her. 'Not far now, I should think,' he said in a soft growl.

She glanced across at him. He was one of Hunn Raal's men. He had lost most of his toes on both feet to frostbite in the wars against the Jheleck, and now wore boots inserted with wooden plugs. He walked badly but rode well. 'When we arrive,' she said, 'we should wait for dawn.'

He nodded, tugging at the strap of his helm. 'These hills don't seem as empty as they should, lieutenant. It's just a feeling, but I've learned to trust what my gut's telling me.'

'All right.'

'I'd advise two scouts ahead and two trailing, sir.'

'Do it,' Risp said, and watched as he communicated his orders with a half-dozen terse gestures. Two women rode ahead to where the trail resumed beyond the clearing.

The sergeant nodded to Risp.

They set out once more. The sky was paling with false dawn and the air was bitterly cold. Breaths plumed. Wending between crags again, the path began a stuttered descent and she guessed that they were nearing the road. The hoofs of the two horses ahead clopped and scrabbled on loose stones; the riders' silhouettes were hunched over, one to each side, eyes on the trail although surely it was too dark to see much. In any case, they were all making noise, loud enough to Risp's ears to announce their presence to anyone within a thousand paces in these hills.

The track levelled and a short time later they reached the road, riding up on to it. Here the stench of foul smoke was acrid in the air. 'East, I think,' said the sergeant.

They reached the site of the battle where the road made a sharp bend. The two wagons had burned down, although embers still gleamed amidst the charred wreckage and ash. The beasts that had drawn them were nowhere to be seen. The bodies of the slain formed a kind of row on the road, two of them blackened by their proximity to the fired wagons, their clothes burned off to reveal swollen limbs and split torsos, the hair roasted away and the skin of their pates curled back to expose smoke-blackened skulls.

Dismounting beside the two scorched corpses, Risp could feel the heat from the embers just beyond them, and the pleasure she gained from that warm breath felt perverse. Silann was a liability, and the proof of that was all around them. Gripp might well have been one of Anomander's spies, but to Risp's mind the news of a troop of disbanded Legion soldiers on the road heading west was not a back-breaker – both Gripp and his lord would have little more than questions, with few answers forthcoming. Besides, if Anomander was not yet prowling with hackles raised, then he was both blind and a fool, and that man was neither.

The spilling of blood here was the real disaster to her mind. Especially if old Gripp had escaped the carnage.

'Here, sir,' said the sergeant, and she saw him standing a dozen or so paces away, where the road's ditch dropped down against the outcropping that marked the bend.

Risp joined him. The man gestured to a crack at the base of the outcrop. 'He went down there, and I'd wager he rolled.'

'Rather than fell? Why?'

'There's a rise before the edge, rubble and dirt sifting down from the cliff. You don't slip uphill, sir. He'd have needed to work to get over that.'

She went to stand on the edge, leaning over to peer down. 'But he couldn't have guessed how deep, though.'

'True enough,' the man agreed. 'It's a good chance he broke his neck, if that goes down any distance. Or his legs, depending on how he landed.'

'They couldn't see all the way down,' Risp muttered. 'But they didn't drop a rope and make sure either.'

'Panic, sir,' said the sergeant. 'It can take anyone, like a hand to the throat. They had wounded and fallen comrades. They needed to get off the road, out of sight.'

Risp snorted. 'You're too forgiving, sergeant.'

'Just seeing how it was, sir. We ain't none of us immune to making mistakes.'

'I wouldn't have made this one,' she replied.

'No sir, we wouldn't have.'

*Not with you at my side, you mean. I'll earn your respect yet, old man.* 'I don't want to wait and wonder, sergeant. Lanterns, rope, let's get on with this.'

'Yes sir. You want it should be me climbing down?'

'No. I'll do it.'

'Lieutenant—'

'I'll do it, I said. Tie the rope's end to the lantern handle – we'll see if we can lower it straight down. Did he hit ledges on the way down? Anything to break his fall? The light will show us.'

'Yes sir.'

'And get a burial detail for these poor guards. It's the least we can do.'

*     *     *

When Ribs finally reappeared, the dog's burr-snagged tail was wagging. Rancept's grunt was soft. 'Caught the echoes,' he then said in a low voice.

'What?' Sukul demanded.

'Riders, coming down from the north. Heading for the road. And they ain't bandits.'

'And you know all this from a wagging tail?'

'That and the drooping left ear.'

There was no way to tell if he was serious and in any case she was already fed up with him and this whole venture. 'How many riders?'

He seemed to be studying her in the gloom, and he made no reply.

After a moment she sighed. 'Can we get going again? I'm cold.'

Ribs disappeared once again as soon as they rose. A short time later they came to a clearing. She saw the dog at the mouth of a trail to their right, just beyond a jumble of goat and sheep bones. Low stone houses offered up black doorways in an uneven ring around the expanse, like open, sagging mouths; she half expected to hear sorrowful moans drifting out from them.

'This is how bandits live?' she asked.

Rancept glanced back at her. 'They used it, yes. But those huts have been standing there for five thousand years at least.'

She looked at them with renewed interest. 'How do you know that?'

'They're old, milady. You'll just have to take my word for it. About a dozen horses crossed this clearing. Went down where Ribs is. We're about two thousand paces from the road here. They'll come out just down from the ambush, but it's a loose descent and there's a chance they'll hear us. There's a bend on the road, just east of here. We can use another trail to take us opposite it.'

Rancept swung left and made his way towards one of the stone houses. Ribs leapt up and scampered to the castellan's side, but halted at the threshold of the doorway.

Sukul saw the animal sink down, tail dipping.

'Back of the hut,' said Rancept when she joined him. 'There's a slab on the floor, with stone bosses set in a frame.'

'A tunnel?'

'A passageway,' said Rancept. 'But it cuts through rock we can't climb over. Took a bit of work but it's now clear enough for us to use.'

'Why did you do that?'

Instead of answering, he ducked and disappeared inside the hut. Ribs edged in after him.

294

When she followed, she found herself stepping down a sharp slope to a sunken floor of flat stones set in earth. The ceiling was high enough for her to stand without hunching, but she was short for her age. Rancept was bent over like a drunk looking for his feet. He made his way to the far end and began working loose the stone trap. She edged up alongside him. 'Do all the huts have these?'

'No,' he replied in a grunt, levering up the door.

Roots had made a tangled web across the tunnel and would have proved impassable but for Rancept's past efforts at hacking a way through. Sukul frowned. 'But there are no trees,' she said.

He lowered himself into the hole, and then paused to look up at her. 'The roots belong to a tree, but not the way you'd think.'

'What does that mean?'

'You'll see.' With those muffled words, he sank down and out of sight.

Sukul glanced at Ribs. The animal was shivering. 'You don't like this place, do you?'

The crazed eyes gleamed, catching the reflection from some unknown source of light. Noticing that, Sukul's frown deepened and she looked round. She should have been blind, lost in pitch black; instead, she could make out every detail in this hut: the way the angled flat slabs were perfectly fitted to make the sloped walls, with no signs of mortar; the pit in the centre, artfully ringed in stone, that would have once held a cookfire. But there was no obvious source of light. Shivering, she worked her way down the hole in Rancept's wake.

The cut ends of thick roots snagged her clothing and dug into her flesh. Tendrils dragged through her hair, earth sifting down. The air was close and surprisingly warm, smelling of mud. She had no idea how Rancept had managed to push his bulk through this tunnel, but he was little more than a vague smudge ahead and was still working his way forward.

Whatever faint, ethereal light had been emanating in the hut behind her, it did not reach far into this passage and soon she was groping her way, fingers brushing roots, and instead of lined stones to either side she found damp clay. There was nothing holding in place the walls or ceiling and she felt a thrill of fear rush through her. From ahead came a faint breath of cooler air.

She could hear Ribs behind her, scrabbling and snuffling.

A moment later her outstretched fingers found nothing and she froze in place. 'Rancept?'

'Let yourself adjust,' he said from somewhere ahead.

'Adjust to what? There's no light!'

'So stop looking with your eyes.'

'What else should I look with? My thumbs?'

The dog edged past her, dirty fur against her high boot and then the roll of ribs beneath the slack skin. The beast was aptly named. Hands still held out, grasping empty air, she sensed that they were in a cavern. Reaching up, she found no ceiling.

'This is Dog-Runner magic,' said Rancept.

'That's impossible. There were never any Dog-Runners this far east.'

'This wasn't always Tiste land, milady.'

That made no sense either. 'We were always here. No one argues with that, castellan. You've not had much schooling. That's not your fault, by the way. It's just how it turned out for you and your family.'

'Dog-Runner magic is all about fire, and earth. Dog-Runner magic fears the sky. Fire and earth, and tree and root. They're gone from here because the forests are gone.'

'Folk tales.'

But he went on. 'There's Dog-Runner blood in the Deniers, who hold on in what's left of the forests of the realm. Pushing them out was easy – just cut down the forests. Didn't need any war. Didn't need to round them up or anything. They just melted away. You call all that folk tales, milady. As you like, but this here is a Dog-Runner temple, and if you open your senses, it'll show itself to you.'

Ribs was back around her legs, trembling. 'Why is your dog so scared, Rancept?'

'Memories of the Ay,' he said in a mutter.

She had no idea what he meant. 'Just take my hand and lead me across. We have things to do, and lounging in some buried temple isn't one of them.'

'Sorry, milady.' A moment later he took hold of her right hand, with fingers gnarled and rough as roots. 'Just step, the ground's level.'

When he guided her forward, however, it was clear that he was taking a circuitous route. 'What are we going around, Rancept?'

'It don't matter, milady.'

'Tell me.'

'Easier to look than describe. Very well, uneducated as I am, I'll try. There's a Dog-Runner witch squatting on the altar.'

'What! Someone else is in here?'

'She won't bother you. Might be she's dead but I don't think so. She's sleeping, I think.'

Sukul pulled up. 'All right, you win. Tell me how to see.'

'Close your eyes—'

At that nonsensical beginning she snorted, in spite of her fear.

'Close your eyes,' he said again, this time more forcefully. 'Picture a cavern in your mind. Earthen walls, a sagging dome for a ceiling. Roots everywhere, even underfoot if you care to feel them. Pushed into the walls all around you are wolf skulls, but bigger wolf skulls than any you've ever seen. Big as horse skulls. Those are the Ay, who run with the Dog-Runners and give them that name. There's hundreds of them here. The roots grip them like the hands of the earth itself.'

Ribs's trembling had now taken her as well. Her mouth was dry and she felt currents tracking across her skin, caressing her face. 'The air is moving,' she whispered.

'Yes. It never stops moving down here. I don't know why, but I think it's the magic's doing, milady. This energy is restless. She was a powerful witch, I think.'

'Tell me more,' Sukul said. 'About the witch.'

'The altar she's sitting on is hard-packed earth. Clay, mostly, along with pretty stones—'

'Stones?'

'Pushed in. Offerings. Garnet, onyx, skystone, various raw metals. Gold and the like. And animal claws and fangs, bits of carved ivory. A few feathers. Chipped stone tools. This is how the Dog-Runners give offering to a beloved one.'

'I see it,' she said suddenly, her breath quickening.

'She's cross-legged on the altar,' Rancept went on. 'Or she was at first. Her bones are transformed, into wood, into roots, and what's left of her hide looks like bark. She grows out of the altar like a tree, milady, and all these roots – all the way up the passage and all around us here – they all grow out from her.'

She gasped. 'And you cut through them!'

'I wounded her, yes, in my ignorance. I wounded her deeply, milady.'

Sukul heard the anguish in his soft admission. 'I'm sorry, Rancept. Has she eyes left? Does she look upon you now?'

'They're grown over, so I don't know. I've troubled her dreams, though. I did that and I know it and if I could mend her, I would.'

'If she still lives, Rancept, they'll heal. The roots will grow back.'

'No sign of that yet, milady.'

'I have never seen a Dog-Runner. Describe her, please.'

He seemed grateful for the command. 'Her face is polished wood, a deep brown that seems to hold gold in its depths. The wood has grown over the bones of her face. Once, that face would have been fair-skinned, the features heavy but open to all pleasures and joys – this is how the Dog-Runners are. They laugh with ease and weep with even greater ease. Every word is a confession and they do not understand dissembling. To speak with a Dog-Runner, milady, is to be humbled and to feel blessed. Many among the Tiste found resentment in that.'

Though she doubted he could see, she nodded to that observation, well understanding how it would be so. 'We surrender nothing.'

'There is wisdom in you, milady, beyond your years.'

But she felt anything but wise at this moment. 'You believe the witch sleeps.'

'I believe she is the one, yes.'

'The one?'

His hand tightened slightly around hers. 'The Dog-Runners of the southwest speak of the Dreamer, the greatest witch of their kind – who remained behind when her people left. She stayed, to keep emptiness from the world.'

Sukul thought of Mother Dark, and that terrible hint of the Abyss that swirled around her presence in the sacred chamber where was found the Throne of Night. 'She resists Mother Dark?'

She felt the motion of his shrug. 'That might be so. That is beyond me.'

'Rancept, are you a Denier?'

'I do not stand against Mother Dark, milady.'

But that was not an answer; still, she knew that it was all he would give her, and she decided to respect that. Her question had been improper by any standards, made worse for coming from a child. 'Forgive me,' she said in a small voice.

'Do you see all that I have described?'

'Yes. I see it clear. I see the cavern, and all its roots coming from the walls – back to her, where she sits with a face of wood and eyes grown over and for ever closed. We stand inside the cavern, like errant thoughts inside a skull.'

The hand snapped tight, almost crushing the bones of her fingers and she winced.

'My apologies, milady. But those last words were not your own.'

She thought about that and then nodded once more. 'She dreams us. We are in her dreams and she is trying to make sense of us. Strangers inside her skull. In here, Rancept, our words could be her thoughts. In here, we are in danger of disappearing, of losing ourselves.'

'Yes, milady. I believe you are right, and I have felt this before. We must leave.'

She pulled her hand free. She no longer needed his guiding clasp; she could see the tunnel continuing on at the far end; could see its upward slope. Yet, still her eyes remained closed. 'Tell me,' she said, 'does this witch have a name?'

'In the language of the Dog-Runners, she is named Burn. She dreams so that we may live. All of us: Tiste, Dog-Runner, Jaghut, Thel Akai, even the Forulkan. She dreams, to give us our freedom.'

She had been making her way forward while Rancept was speaking, and she felt him move alongside her, but at his last words she drew up. 'Tell me, did you offer her anything?'

His mouth-breathing stuttered slightly. 'I would have to be a Denier to do that, milady.'

Sukul thought back, to the time before he had taken her hand. Was there movement from him? Was he standing near the witch? She did not know. Reaching for her leather purse, she loosened the draw-strings.

'Careful now,' said Rancept, and she realized that he was watching her, somehow – no, not 'somehow'. *He sees because he believes. In this temple Rancept worships. Yet, he chose to lead me here. There would have been other ways through, other paths. But he brought me here.*

She drew out a memory stone, found upon the banks of the Dorssan Ryl. *For the brother I lost to the wars.*

'Milady. Sukul Ankhadu, I beg you. This gesture must not be a careless one. Will you bind Mother Dark to the Sleeping Goddess of the Dog-Runners?'

Her breath caught. 'I am not a highborn, castellan. I am not a priestess.'

'Does your faith lie with Mother Dark? No, do not answer me. If it does, however, then surely you shall bind these two women. More than this, you shall bind the Deniers and the Tiste. There is no more holy place than this temple, but it is lost to the Deniers. I alone know of it – do you understand me?'

'And you are a man with secrets, yet bold or foolish enough to reveal this to me. Why?'

'Truth?'

'Truth, Rancept. Give me that at least.'

'Tiste schooling is rubbish,' he said.

She almost yelped her laughter, and it echoed loudly in the chamber. At the sound Ribs bolted past her and up the tunnel.

Beside her, the castellan's astonishment was palpable to her senses.

'Forgive me again, Rancept . . .' and then her words faded away.

The air had changed in the chamber and she felt her skin prickling. 'What is it?' she asked in a frightened whisper. 'What have I done?'

'Put the stone away,' said Rancept. 'She is a Dog-Runner still, it seems.'

'I don't understand – what is this I'm feeling?'

'Her blessing, child. What greater or more precious gift could you give her, but laughter? Breath of the Sleeping Goddess, you have healed her, Sukul Ankhadu.'

She started as the huge man knelt in front of her, and somehow – though still her eyes remained shut – she saw the glitter of tears on his cheeks. 'The roots no longer bleed,' he said gruffly. 'I thank you, milady, with all my heart.'

'For this learning,' she heard herself say, 'I make payment with pleasure.'

She felt his wry smile and smiled in return.

He rose and together they headed into the passage ahead.

When he took her hand again she welcomed it, though both knew she no longer needed any guidance from him. No, this was more like friendship, and the notion startled Sukul, so that she almost laughed again. Instead, she sent her delight back down the tunnel, back into that wondrous chamber, where flesh and wood were one, and eyes grown shut could see all there was to see.

As they clambered back towards the surface – where dawn's pale light made a plate of silver-blue above and ahead of them – Sukul said, 'Rancept, the Deniers who remain must be told of this temple. They deserve that much.'

'There is no need,' he replied. 'I shared her dreams below – yes, it is plain now and I will not dissemble. I am a Denier – though I deeply dislike that name. No matter. In sharing those dreams, I saw a truth, newborn and wondrous.'

'What did you see?'

They rose into the light of dawn and he looked back at her with a half-smile transforming his twisted features – an expression she had never before seen on him and one that she thought would stop the hearts of the castellan's guard should they ever witness it – and he said, 'Burn dreams of a river, milady. She dreams of a river.'

＊　　　＊　　　＊

Gloved hands gripping the rope, Risp made her way down the crevasse. Unfamiliar twinges assailed her shoulders and back. Climbing was not a common activity among the Tiste – a better excuse than her general unfitness, she decided. Below her the lantern anchored the rope, resting on broken rock. The air was dusty and chilled by eternal shadow, and she felt a kind of belligerence in this place, as if the stone walls resented her intrusion.

Just nerves, she told herself. And anxiety. The light had revealed no obvious body on the floor below, but it was clear that the crack extended to either side for unknown distances. Risp was certain that no cold corpse awaited her; the clenching of her gut was proof of her conviction. Men like Gripp Galas possessed that infuriating luck that seemed to ride the shoulders of old soldiers. He'd never fall in battle. When death took him he would probably be lying on a woman in some rank bordello.

She worked her way over a sloping bulge in the stone wall that showed signs of scraping, a few spots of blood now dried and black as ink, and two body-lengths below that she reached the bottom, boots scrabbling for purchase on the loose stones. More blood, spattered amidst dislodged rubble.

Looking back up the crevasse, Risp wondered how Gripp had ever managed to climb back out. She then turned and crouched, untying the lantern and taking the handle in hand. The smell of scorched leather came from her glove and she could feel the handle's heat. Ignoring the faint discomfort she straightened and set out to explore.

No body, but she'd already guessed as much. The fissure narrowed quickly at one end. In the other direction – eastward, she judged – the crevasse continued on, down a sloping, choked floor littered with dry branches, and the remnants of bird nests built from twigs, mud and snarls of goat hair.

She made her way forward. A dozen paces along, the walls leaned inward, tightening the passage so that she had to angle sideways to go further. Feeling the stone pressing in on her front and back triggered a momentary panic, but she fought it down and pushed ahead. The crevasse widened again and here the fallen rocks formed a slope leading upward. She made out a bloody handprint on a stone halfway up it.

Risp followed the obvious trail. The crevasse broadened out still more, and now huge broken boulders filled the space. Dust was scraped clear here and there, on obvious hand- and footholds. Dawn's light revealed the surface only a dozen paces onward. Moments later she scrambled into the clear. The road was thirty paces to her left, the span in between a wash of sand on which Gripp's bootprints were visible. One leg had been dragging.

Dousing the lantern, she walked to the road, scrambled up the bank and swung left. Just beyond the bend waited her troop, the soldiers dismounted and still busy building cairns over a row of bodies on the far side of the road. Her sergeant, she saw, was still at the crevasse, squatting and peering down. At a word from a nearby soldier he twisted round to see her approaching on the road.

'Alive,' she said upon re-joining them. 'But bleeding and with a bad leg. Looks like he came back here after Silann left. Where he went after that is the question, isn't it?'

'He went after the boy,' the sergeant replied.

'Why would he do that?'

'Maybe he wasn't just guarding goat and sheep skins, sir.'

'You think the boy was important?'

The veteran shrugged. 'Laskan was going through what the fire didn't burn. There was a soldier's trunk. Korlas crest, solid blackwood, which was why it mostly shrugged off the fire. But the lock melted. Boy's clothing inside, and what looked like lead soldiers all melted down into slag.' He paused, eyes on her. 'Korlas, sir. That would make the boy of that bloodline. There was a Korlas Houseblade who served as a captain in Urusander's Legion.'

'Can this get any worse?'

'If Gripp collects up the boy and they get out of these hills, yes, sir, it can get much worse.'

'A highborn child on his way to Kharkanas . . .'

'Yes sir, a hostage. To the Citadel. Captain, that boy was under Lord Anomander's protection, the moment he left the estate. *That's* why Gripp Galas was with that caravan of skin-sellers.'

Risp felt sick inside, a strange quavering that rose into her throat. If she gave sound to the feeling it would emerge as a moan. Her sergeant was staring at her, expressionless, and she felt the attention of the other soldiers in her troop – even the burial detail had drawn close. She was tempted to voice regrets that she'd ever volunteered to clean up this disaster. It was Silann's mess, after all. If that fool were at her side right now, she would kill him. She thought it unlikely that his wife would even object. *She'd probably hand me the knife.* 'There were a few high-born serving in Urusander's Legion,' she said.

The sergeant nodded. 'Greater Houses without enough wealth to assemble a decent cadre of Houseblades. If there were a chance, they'd end up with the Houseblades of other Houses. But Korlas was a proud man, as I recall.'

'You knew him?'

'Captain, I served under him. Same for Laskan, Helrot and Bishim. He was a good man. Died a hero.'

All at once a new fear took hold of Risp: the loyalty of this man standing before her. 'You said that Gripp and this hostage cannot be allowed to get out of these hills alive, sergeant.'

'No sir. I said things would get even worse if they did.'

'I see. Then what do you suggest?' *So much for exercising the power of command. My first test and I fail.*

'We need to find them, sir. And make it right.'

'How do we do that?'

'We let Silann hang, sir.'

'He just up and decided to become an outlaw? You can't be serious, sergeant. He still holds a rank in the Legion, and so do half his soldiers.'

'We don't have to know why he did what he did, sir. It's a mystery to all of us, maybe even his wife.'

'So, instead of hunting down and killing Gripp and the boy, ensuring that all of this goes away, you're advising we act in baffled horror and disgust. That we find the old man and this hostage and help them, maybe even escort them to Kharkanas.' She looked around, scanned the faces of her soldiers. She barely knew them, but Hunn Raal was certain of their loyalty. Nevertheless, under these circumstances, even that loyalty was being stretched – she could see as much in their expressions. Hostages were sacred, and this particular hostage was under Lord Anomander's protection, which added genuine fear to their discomfort. 'Esthala needs to know of this change in plans.'

'Yes sir.'

'Send Laskan and Bishim back to her. And then what, Silann's own wife arrests him?'

The sergeant shook his head, but said nothing.

Risp closed her eyes briefly and then looked away, up the road. 'No, she won't do that. Silann is too weak to keep his mouth shut. She'll have to kill him, and his soldiers.' She met the sergeant's eyes again. 'She'll understand the necessity, won't she? There is no other way out of this. Is there?'

Still he remained silent, watching her.

'Send them.'

'Yes sir.' The sergeant gestured and the two men mounted their horses and a moment later set off.

'Send Helrot to Tulla Hold,' she went on. 'To report the slaughter and make known our search for survivors. And to ask for assistance.'

'Yes sir.'

She would have to get rid of this sergeant. She didn't want him in her troop. He gave too little away; she could not tell what he was thinking and this unnerved her. His silence had felt like a judgement, and for all she knew she had failed in the balance.

'Collect up that trunk. We'll take it with us. Then we ride east. We eat in the saddle.'

'Yes sir.'

*       *       *

Rancept slid back down to where she huddled. 'Three riders dispatched,' he said. 'Two back the way they came and one up the road – likely on her way to Tulla. The rest are heading east.'

Exhausted, chilled and miserable, Sukul sighed. 'What does all that mean?'

'Not party to the killing, I'd wager, milady. They're all Legion, and that raises another question.'

'What are they doing out here?' Sukul said, nodding. 'Since no Legion troop ever rode within sight of Tulla Hold.'

'Not wanting to be seen.'

'But one is now riding to Tulla, you said.'

The castellan grunted, squinting at Ribs, who was curled up asleep against Sukul's feet – and the animal's heat now warmed her aching toes, and she looked upon the creature with a fondness she had not imagined possible.

'Should we go down to them?' she asked.

'Too late.'

'I told you we should have taken horses and just ridden the road.'

'In hindsight,' Rancept allowed, 'maybe so. But what doesn't change is that none of this feels right.'

She wasn't about to argue that point. The wheezing old castellan's feelings couldn't be dismissed this time. 'So who killed those traders?'

He shook his head, and then straightened. 'Let's go down. Maybe Ribs will tell us.'

'Castellan, he's just a damned dog, not a seer.'

'Milady, he's my dog.'

Her eyes narrowed on him. 'Are you some kind of priest of Burn, Rancept?'

'No priests among the Deniers, milady.'

'What about the Dog-Runners?'

'Witches and warlocks,' he replied. 'Bonecasters, they're called.'

'They throw bones?'

'No. Well, maybe, but I think the name goes more to what we saw in that temple, milady. Bone to wood, bone to stone. As if to ask, if we can be one why not the other? As if it's only a matter of how we talk to time.' He paused and then added, 'It's said they gave the Jheleck the gift of Soletaken, which is yet another way of seeing the casting of bones.'

Ribs lifted his head without any signal from Rancept, and she felt the unwelcome chill in her feet once more. Sighing again, she rose. 'Tell me they buried the bodies at least.'

'They did, milady. Cold stone on cold flesh and sorrow in the silence.'

She shot him a look. 'I think you surprise people, Rancept.'

'Yes, milady, I do that.'

They made their way down a side track, rounding the butte they'd mostly ascended in order for Rancept to look down on the road. 'I trust Lady Hish knows you well enough to value you.'

'Why do you ask?'

'If she doesn't, then I'll do my best to steal you away, castellan. You . . . and Ribs, too.'

'That's a kind thing to say, milady. But I will serve Lady Hish Tulla until my dying day.'

Something in those words told Sukul of a love beyond that of a castellan for his mistress, and the very notion threatened to break her heart.

Ribs snaked down the stony slope ahead of them. 'He's just a dog, isn't he?'

'Just a dog, milady.'

'Not Soletaken.'

Rancept snorted. 'If he once was, he's long forgotten his other body, leaving him what he is now, and that's just a dog.'

Once down on the road, they approached the site of the killing in silence, Ribs staying close on Rancept's left. Before reaching the scene both the dog and the castellan halted. Eyes on the ground, Rancept said, 'The killers rode past the caravan and then went back to them.

More proof that they weren't bandits. They were back up to a fast trot, two lines in close formation, before they turned round. Someone gave a command.'

'Disciplined, then.'

'To start with,' he replied, as he and Ribs set out once more. 'But I saw what was left of one of the guards. There was anger in that butchery.'

'Your eyes are that good?'

'Was easy to see. The ones doing the burying carried him over in pieces.'

She pushed down her imagination, squeezing shut figurative eyes upon the image. The smell from up ahead was foul, not just from the still smouldering ash heaps where the wagons had burned, but also the stench of bile and urine. A horse's carcass was lying on the road's flank, this side of the row of cairns. The beast had been stabbed in the gut, the slash vicious enough to spill out stomach and intestines, now stretched out and partly wrapped about the animal's hind legs as it had tried to kick free of its own ruin. Sukul found herself staring at the pathetic creature, seeing its terrible death and feeling pain as the scene seared into her mind. 'I will never be one for war,' she whispered.

Rancept, picking among wreckage, heard her and glanced over. 'It's an unpleasant business that's for sure, especially when the sack is opened.'

She pulled her gaze away. 'What sack?'

'You. Me. The sacks of our skin, holding everything inside.'

'Surely we are more than that!' Her words were harsher than intended. 'Even this horse was more than that.'

He straightened, wiping his hands. 'Milady, though you ain't asked for it, here's some advice. Most of the time – the best of times, in fact – it's good to think that. We're more than just a sack of blood and organs and bones and whatever. So much more, and the same for every animal, too, like that noble horse and even old Ribs here. But then comes a time – like this one – when you can't let yourself think that. When what you're looking at now is just a broken open sack, with stuff spilled out. Whatever was "more" inside of us is gone – it's gone from that carcass and it's gone from those bodies under those stones. It's not down to what we're worth—'

'No,' she snapped, 'it's down to what we've lost!'

He seemed to flinch and then he nodded, turning away once more.

Sukul felt bad, but she wouldn't take back her words. She understood his meaning, but she didn't like it. Seeing people and animals as just sacks of skin made ruining those sacks that much easier. If no one looked at the loss, they were left with no sense of the worth. In such a world not even life itself had any value. She looked over at Rancept once more. He was standing in the centre of the road, opposite the cairns, but his gaze was on the track ahead, beyond the road's bend. Ribs sat at his heel. There was something hopeless in the scene and she felt herself close to tears.

'Is there a smaller grave?' she asked, refusing to look too carefully at those cairns, not wanting her eyes to witness yet one more unpleasant truth.

He shook his head. 'The boy got away, at least to begin with. Our friends are just ahead, by the way. Trying to skirt the mudflat, and you need to be on foot to do that – no place for horses. I'm thinking the boy was being pursued and took his horse out on to it.'

'And?' She made her way towards him.

'There's a lake under that flat,' he said. 'A lake of mud and it's deep. His horse wouldn't have made it. Could be the boy went down with it.'

'Have they seen us yet?'

'No.'

'Step away, then.'

He frowned at her and then moved behind the butte once more. 'What are you thinking, milady?'

'When that rider comes to Tulla Hold not even the castellan will be there. Does anyone know where we are?'

'Sergeant Broot's commanding in my absence. He'll stare and blink and eventually that messenger will decide he's got rocks for brains.'

'And then?'

'And then the rider will leave, going back to wherever she needs to be. Done her duty and left the tale at the feet of Broot.'

'I think we need to make sure, if we can, whether Orfantal is still alive.'

'The boy was meant to be a hostage, milady?'

'Yes, in the Citadel itself.'

'And he was sent along with nothing more than a handful of caravan guards as escort?'

'Yes.' She hesitated, and then added, 'There might have been reasons for that.'

Rancept looked away again, his mouth hanging open as it always did, and the man's ugliness now struck her as something tender, almost gentle. *In that temple, in the vision in my mind, I could have made him beautiful.* She wished she had. She wished, with sudden ferocity, that she had made him anew.

'Castellan, can't they heal you? Your nose, I mean.'

He glanced at her. 'Best way is to break it all over again.'

'Why not try that?'

'Ever had your nose broken, milady?'

'No.'

He shrugged, looking away once more. 'Tried that. Six times.'

She realized that his attention was fixed on the cairns, and that it had not been a casual regard. As she made to speak he strode over to the makeshift cemetery, edging down into the ditch. Ribs followed him, tail dipped and ears drooping. Sukul joined them. 'What is it, Rancept? What have you found?'

'Found? Nothing, milady.' Yet he studied the cairns. 'When they camped below the Hold and you decided to go down and visit them, you commanded me to have the cook prepare four days' worth of decent meals, for seven people.'

She looked at the cairns. 'If there's only one body under each one . . .'

'Someone else got away,' he said, nodding.

'Then where did he go?'

'Milady, this is something old Ribs here can answer. But we're not equipped for more nights out here. So this is what I suggest.'

'Go on.'

'I send him on, milady.'

'To do what?'

'Whatever needs doing.'

'You told me – he's just a dog!'

Rancept shrugged. 'That's my suggestion, milady.'

Sukul threw up her hands. 'Oh, very well, whatever you say. He's *your* dog, after all.'

'We can take the road back to the Hold,' Rancept continued, 'but it might be that we'll meet that rider.'

'No, I don't want that. Find us another trail back.'

'As you wish.'

'Rancept,' Sukul asked, as a sudden thought struck her, 'there aren't any more secret temples hereabouts, are there?'

'Nothing we'd call such, milady.'

\*　　\*　　\*

Corporal Renth had ridden out from Kharkanas in the depths of night. He had been dispatched to deliver Hunn Raal's command that the unit commanders were to ensure that no violence was initiated, and that all contact was to be avoided. All plans were on hold, and Renth was relieved to hear it. He had never been easy with how things were going; even the thought of letting highborn blood to achieve their aims left him sick with dread and guilt.

It didn't help that his captain was at his worst when drunk, shaking loose the reins on his bloodlust and saying terrible things about the highborn and anyone else who wasn't Legion. Such guttural vehemence had a way of infecting those close to him. More than once, Renth had contemplated seeking out a soldier among Lord Anomander's House-blades, and betraying the whole cause.

But Urusander deserved better. Renth knew that the ugliness belonged to Hunn Raal, and if there were no irony in a man of fallen highborn blood now spouting vicious hatred against his own kind, then irony was a dead weed in the field of souls, and who would be foolish enough to claim that?

In his drunkenness, Hunn Raal revealed deeper currents; there was an ambition there that saw Lord Urusander as nothing more than a means to an end. The captain might well espouse the redress of justice when it came to the Legion and all who served or had once served in it, but something else lurked behind that pious fervour, and whatever that was, Corporal Renth did not trust it.

Changes had come to Kharkanas. The priestesses and priests had crowded the corridors and hallways deep into the night, but it seemed they had nothing but questions to exchange, a worthless currency when no answers could be found. He'd had trouble making his way out of the citadel without being noticed.

Out on the streets of Kharkanas, the residual mud of the river's flooding earlier that day had smeared the stones and painted the walls of the torchlit buildings he rode past, as if making a sullied pronouncement bold as blasphemy. His unease had only deepened in his passage through the city to the bridge that would take him west of the river. Faith was ever on the edge of crisis, but it seemed that this fated arrival of the Azathanai, and the dark, disturbing miracles that followed, had pushed everything over the edge.

Hunn Raal had argued that now, more than ever, was the time for Lord Urusander's ascension. Once he stood at Mother Dark's side, the unruly elements would be hammered into submission and whatever schism now threatened the faith could be addressed. It had seemed a contrary position, since he was in the process of dispatching riders out to all the units with orders to desist. Drunks had a way of spitting in two directions at once. The truth was, there was chaos in Kurald Galain and the sudden unleashing of bloodshed might shatter the entire realm, and Mother Dark with it. For all that, what had seemed relatively straightforward in Renth's eyes was now murky and confused, and a belligerent, red-eyed commander was hardly an inspiring send-off. Loyalty to Urusander alone kept Renth's hands on the reins, and his butt in the saddle.

But a long ride through the night gave him too much time to think. Renth had no compunction about slaughtering the Deniers because he did not see them as Tiste at all. They had surrendered that name in their squalid worship of old gods. The Tiste needed to unify their faith, with Mother Dark upon the Throne of Night. Refusing allegiance to Mother Dark had long ago stripped the Deniers of her protection, and so they deserved whatever befell them. He doubted that any hoary, mud-spattered river god of old could protect those lost fools. Lord Urusander understood necessity, and he would do what was needed to unify the Tiste and to cleanse the realm.

It was, in fact, simple. They would hunt down the Deniers and kill them. They would scour the last depths of the forests and root them out, and then feed their corpses to the river.

But the highborn were another matter. When the time came, however, Renth would do as commanded. He was a soldier after all, and soldiers needed to set aside their conscience on occasion, when necessity demanded hard choices. Besides, after the deed was done even remorse could be chewed dry and spat out.

The nearest of Raal's allies were attempting to move unseen through the Tulla Hills, just beyond the Old Forest. These units were his destination. Hunn Raal had scant faith in Captain Silann, but at least Esthala and Risp were there. Once Renth had delivered his message he would swing back, crossing the Dorssan Ryl once more, and then head northward to find the other units.

Mid-morning found him riding at a slow canter along the road that wound through the hills. His eyes were grainy from lack of sleep, but he would push on regardless. He had met no one since leaving the Old Forest.

He caught the sudden attention from his horse – the ears flicking forward – and looked up to see a small figure on the track ahead. A boy, filthy with mud, standing as if waiting for him.

Perhaps some brat from the Deniers said to be living in these hills. Scowling, Renth gestured the boy from his path as he drew closer.

But the boy remained where he was, in the centre of the road.

'What is this?' Renth demanded, reining in. 'Do you wish to be run down? Get away!'

'I am named Orfantal,' said the boy, 'of the House Korlas, and I claim the right of protection.'

'Highborn?' Renth snorted. 'That I doubt.'

'I was being escorted to the Citadel,' the boy said. 'But we were way-laid. Everyone else died.'

'A highborn would be better protected than—' He caught a flicker from the boy's eyes and then something punched through the chain shirt he was wearing, stabbing under his right arm. Sudden cold slid between his ribs, from which fire erupted. A hand took hold of his weapon belt and dragged him down from the saddle. Flailing, trying to push away from that blade buried in him, Renth fell to the ground.

He couldn't speak. Strength left him in a rush. He stared up into the face of an old man, a face twisted with venom, though the eyes, fixed on his own, were empty as pits into the Abyss itself.

309

'For Haral,' he heard the man say, twisting the blade before tugging it back out.

The effort jolted Renth's body, but the motion seemed to have nothing to do with him. *Haral? I know no one named Haral.* He wanted to tell the man that. He wanted to explain the mistake that had been made, but nothing came from his mouth except blood. Hot, tasting of the iron that had taken his life. Bewildered and hurt, he closed his eyes for the last time.

*       *       *

Orfantal stared in horror, and when he saw Gripp spit into the dead man's face, coldness filled his insides, and he knew it for the flood of fear. The old man had said they needed a horse. Because they were being hunted and people wanted to kill them both.

They'd seen the rider coming up the road, and Gripp had sent him out after telling him to say the things he had said.

Orfantal thought they were going to steal the horse at sword point, since they had no coin. But they would one day pay the man back, even give him a new horse, or two. They would make it right.

Now he watched the old man rise from the body, using the dead rider's cloak to clean the blood from his dagger. The horse had moved off a short distance and now stood trembling in the ditch. Murmuring under his breath, Gripp approached the animal and moments later held the reins. He faced Orfantal. 'Now we ride to Kharkanas.'

He scowled at whatever he saw in Orfantal's face. 'He was Legion and it was Legion that attacked us. They're the enemy now, hostage. We're in a civil war – do you understand me?'

He nodded, though he didn't – he didn't understand anything any more.

'I ain't hiding the body,' Gripp said. 'I want them to find it. I want them to know. More than that, I want them to know it was Gripp Galas who did this, and it's Gripp Galas who'll come for them.' He had drawn his knife with these words and now he handed Orfantal the horse's reins and limped back to the corpse.

He hacked off the head. Blood poured on to the dusty road. Gripp then carved his initials on the forehead. Once this was done he lifted the head by the hair and flung it on to the centre of the road.

After using the cloak again to clean the knife he re-joined Orfantal. 'Now, let me get up in the saddle before you – this knee is killing me.'

*All the heroes are dead.*

*I am lost.*

*We are all lost.*

The hand that reached down to pull Orfantal up was red, and the morning air filled with the smell of iron.

310

# PART THREE

*The proofs of your ambition*

# ELEVEN

ON ALL SIDES ARATHAN SAW DESOLATION. BENEATH A COLOURLESS SKY, houses huddled in their own ruin, and to look upon them was to draw inside all the details of failure, until they clogged his thoughts like greasy dust. Between the scattered buildings, low, smoke-blackened walls of stone rose from scorched grasses like smeared teeth. He weathered their skeletal grimaces as he hunched in the saddle, Besra plodding beneath him. The walls were without any order, and none of the haphazard enclosures they made held livestock.

This was nothing like any village he had seen. Trapped between walls as if snared in a giant web, the houses were far apart, defying the notion of streets. They refused to face one another and there was something shameful in this unwilling regard, as if community offered no gifts and necessity was cause for resentment. Most doorways were without doors and the blackness they framed seemed strangely solid; even in surrender something remained that was impenetrable, mystifying. They did not invite inside with the lure of curiosity; he felt pushed away, and whatever remained in the hidden rooms, behind shuttered windows and beneath sagging ceilings, was a secret tale written in wreckage.

This was the civilization of the Azathanai, desultory and forlorn. In its impoverishment it besieged the soul, and the most horrifying thing of all, to Arathan's eyes, was that some of these houses were still occupied. He saw solid doors, latched shut, and the smudged ember-glows of candles leaking through shutters. He saw figures standing in shadows, beneath porches made of huge granite stones so perfectly cut that no mortar was needed, and he felt the unyielding pressure of strangers' eyes upon him and his companions as they rode slowly through the settlement.

His imagination recoiled from the poison of this place, from all the rejections – the casting away of pointless possessions, the indifference to weed-snarled yards and the broken barrows of burnt wood that had once been buildings. This was not his world and to breathe of it, to look upon it and take inside each and every detail, whispered of madness.

The day's lifeless light was failing. Lord Draconus led them through tumbled gaps in the walls, cutting through the centre of the settlement. The horses walked as if exhausted by grief, and upon the dusty neck of Besra, the flies barely crawled.

When his father reined in opposite an oversized house of stone and timber, Arathan felt his spirits flinch. It stood a short distance away, somehow more alone than all the others, and upon its granite facade the grey stone had been carved in endless, meaningless patterns of what seemed to be circles or rings. The sawn ends of the wood rafters, forming a row above the squat, wide door frame and marching on to the very ends of the front wall to either side, all bore similar shapes, like the imprints left behind by raindrops on mud. Three low walls reached for the building but all seemed to have shattered or crumbled with the effort. The air around the house felt dead and cold.

'You might think,' said Draconus, half turning to regard his bastard son, 'that your thoughts are your own.'

Arathan blinked.

Behind him, Sergeant Raskan whispered something like a prayer, and then cleared his throat. 'My lord, is this sorcery, then, to so plague our minds?'

'The world around you speaks your language,' Draconus replied. 'It can do no else. All you see bears the paint of your words.' He paused, and then grunted, 'I wager none of you noted the flowers amidst the weeds, or the dance of the swifts above the old spring. Or how the sky, for but a moment, was like the purest porcelain.'

Unwilling to turn, to look upon Feren who rode at Rint's side, Arathan stared at his father, fighting with the meaning of his words. 'We are invited,' he said.

'Indeed, Arathan. You begin to comprehend the curse of the Azathanai.'

'The Jheleck do not raid here any more.'

Draconus shrugged. 'See you anything of value?'

A figure now stood in the doorway of the strange, carved house. Not tall but thin, and, from what Arathan could make out, barely clothed – and that clothing was little more than rags of the skins of small animals. All at once, to Arathan, the scene seemed perfect – perfectly rendered, and nothing was accidental. *Nothing ever is.*

Rint spoke and his voice sounded clumsy and rough amidst a sudden, fragile elegance. 'Do we make camp here, Lord Draconus? You mentioned a spring and we have great need of water.'

Draconus nodded. 'The horses will find it for you, but we shall camp just beyond the village, on the hill at the crossroads up ahead.' He dismounted.

Arathan did the same, trying not to shiver and struggling not to gasp: for all the perfection closing tight around him, it seemed the air surrounding the carved house could not feed his lungs.

Studying him, Draconus said, 'Draw nearer to me, Arathan, if you wish to remain.'

Rint and Feren had moved away. Raskan was hastening to gather up the reins of the other horses, his movements strangely panicked to Arathan's eyes.

Stepping closer to his father, Arathan found that he could once more fill his chest with sweet, blessed air. He returned his attention to the figure in the doorway. 'Who is he and how can he live in . . . in this?'

'Azathanai, of course,' Draconus replied, and then sighed. 'I know, the name is meaningless. No, it is more than that: it is misleading.'

When it seemed that he would not explain, Arathan asked, 'Are they gods?'

'If they are,' his father said after a moment's thought, 'they are gods in waiting.'

'Waiting for what?'

'Worshippers. But this confuses things, I would wager. Belief creates, Arathan. So you have been taught. The god cannot exist until it is worshipped, until it is given shape, personality. It is made in the crucible of faith. So claim our finest Tiste philosophers. But it is not that simple, I think. The god may indeed exist before the first worshipper ever arrives, but it does not call itself a god. It simply lives, of and for itself. Far to the south, Arathan, there are wild horses, and from birth until death they remain free. They have never tasted an iron bit, or felt the command of reins or knees or heels, and in that freedom, not once in their lives do they surrender their fear of us.'

Arathan thought about that, but found no words for those thoughts.

His father continued, 'What falls under our hand, Arathan, we bend to our will. The horses we ride worship us, as if we were gods. But you and I, we can taste the bitterness of that, because if we are gods then we are unreliable gods. Imperfect gods. Cruel gods. Yet the horse is helpless in the face of all that and can only yearn for our blessing. Should its master beat it, still it yearns, seeking what all living things seek: the grace of being. Still, its god ever turns away. You may pity that horse,' Draconus continued after a moment, 'but not its desire.'

*The grace of being.* 'Then what god would break us?' Arathan asked.

Draconus grunted a second time, but it seemed to be a pleased grunt. He nodded to the figure in the doorway. 'Not this one, Arathan.'

But Arathan's thoughts had marched on, relentless upon a fraught path. *Do gods break those they would have as worshippers? Do they set upon their children terrible ordeals, so that those children must kneel in surrender, opening their souls to helplessness? Is this what Mother Dark will do to her children? To us?*

'Most Azathanai,' Draconus continued, 'have no desire to be worshipped, to be made into gods. The confession of the helpless is written in spilled blood. The surrender that is sacrifice. It can taste . . . bitter.'

He and his father were now alone, facing the house and its dweller. Dusk fell around them like dark rain, devouring everything else, until the rest of the village took on the texture of worn, fading tapestries.

The figure then stepped out from the doorway, and a light came with him. It was not a warm light, not a light to drive back the gloom, and it hovered over the man's left shoulder, a pallid disc or ball, larger than a man's head, and if the man reached up, it would have remained beyond his touch, just past his fingertips.

That globe followed the man as he approached.

'Cold and airless is his aspect,' muttered Draconus. 'Stay close to me, Arathan. A step away from my power and the blood will freeze and then boil in your flesh. Your eyes will burst. You will die in great pain. I trust such details impress upon you the importance of remaining close?'

Arathan nodded.

'He has not yet decided on a name,' Draconus added. 'Which is a rather irritating affectation.'

The man was surprisingly young, perhaps only a handful of years older than Arathan himself. Here and there, in almost random fashion, ring-like tattoos adorned his skin, like the scars from some pox. His narrow, nondescript face bore no marks, however, and the eyes were dark and calm. When he spoke, his voice made Arathan think – incongruously – of pond water beneath a thin sheet of ice. 'Draconus, it has been how many years since we last met? On the eve of the Thel Akai's disavowal—'

'We'll not speak of time,' Draconus said, and the words rang like a command.

The man's brows lifted slightly, and then he shrugged. 'But one way, surely, this refusal? After all, the future is the only field still to be sowed, and if we are to stay our hands here, what point this meeting? Shall we throw our seeds, Draconus, or make blunt fists?'

'I did not think it would be you delivering the gift,' Draconus replied.

'Oh, that gift. You surmise correctly. Not me.' And with that he smiled.

Arathan's father answered with a scowl.

The stranger's laugh was low. 'Indeed. Impatience besets you, to no avail. You must trek farther still. The next village at the very least.'

'The next, or do you but mock me?'

'The next, I think. There has been much talk of your . . . request. And the answering thereof.'

'Already I have been away from the court for too long,' Draconus said in a frustrated growl.

'Such gestures fill the imagination of the bearer,' the man said, 'but the same cannot be certain of the recipient. I fear a great disappointment awaiting you, Draconus. Perhaps even a hurt, a deep wound—'

'I am not interested in your prophecies, Old Man.'

Arathan frowned at that strange name, so contrary to this figure facing them.

'Not a prophecy, Draconus. I would not risk that in your presence. Rather, I fear the value you have imbued in this gift of yours – it is, perhaps, dangerous in its extremity.'

'Who awaits me in the next village?'

'I cannot even guess,' Old Man replied. 'But a few will gather. Curious. This usage of Night, Draconus, was without precedent, and the fury of the believers is something to behold.'

'I care not. Let them worship stone if it pleases them. Unless,' he added, 'they would challenge me?'

'Not you, nor the hand with which you wielded your desire. Instead, Draconus, they weep and seek redress.'

'As I expected.'

Old Man was silent for a long moment, and then he said, 'Draconus, be careful – no, we must all be careful now. In the healing they seek, they reach deeply into the Vitr. We do not know what will come of this.'

'The Vitr? Then they are fools.'

'The enemy is not foolishness, Draconus, but desperation.'

'Who so reaches?'

'I have heard Ardata's name mentioned. And the Sister of Dreams.'

Draconus looked away, his expression unreadable. 'One thing at a time,' he muttered.

'Much to make right, Draconus,' Old Man said, smiling once more. 'In the meantime, my child approaches.'

'So you ever say.'

'So I shall say until I need say it no more.'

'I never understood why you were content with mere reflection, Old Man.'

The smile broadened. 'I know.'

He turned round then and walked back to his house, the globe following and taking with it the bitter cold, the empty promise of dead air.

Halfway back, Old Man paused and looked back. 'Oh, Draconus, I almost forgot. There is news.'

'What news?'

'The High King has built a ship.'

Arathan felt a sudden pressure, coming from his father, an invisible force that pushed him away, one step, and then another. He gagged, began to crumple—

And then a hand pulled him close. 'Sorry,' Draconus said. 'Careless of me.'

Half bent over, Arathan nodded, accepting the apology. Old Man had vanished within his strange house, taking the light with him.

'I'm never good,' said Draconus, 'with displeasing news.'

*　　*　　*

The noses of the horses found the spring readily enough, and Rint leaned forward over the saddle horn to study the stone-lined pond. As Draconus had predicted, there were swifts wheeling and darting above the still waters, and now bats as well. Beside him, Feren grunted and said, 'What do you make of that?'

A statue commanded the centre of the pool. A huge figure, sunk to its thighs, roughly hacked from serpentine as if in defiance of that stone's potential, for it was well known that serpentine wore well the finest polish – not that Rint had ever seen a solid block anything near the size of this monstrosity, more familiar with small game pieces and the like. None the less, this seemed a most artless effort. The torso and every limb were twisted, the stone seeming to shout its pain. The scum of dried algae stained its thighs, evidence of the spring's slow failing perhaps. The face, tilted skyward atop a thick, angular neck, offered the heavens a grimace, and this face alone bore signs of a skilled hand. Rint stared up at it, mesmerized.

Raskan moved past the two Borderswords, leading the horses to the pond's roughly tiled edge.

Sighing, Feren slipped down from the saddle, dropping the reins of her mount so that it could join the other beasts in drinking from the pool.

'I think it's meant to be a Thel Akai,' Rint finally said.

'Of course it's a Thel Akai,' Feren snapped. 'All that pain.' She held in one hand three waterskins and now moved to crouch down at the edge, and began filling them.

Feeling foolish, Rint pulled his gaze away from the giant's tormented face and dismounted. He collected more waterskins from where they hung flaccid from his saddle.

318

'What I meant was,' Feren resumed, 'why raise a statue in the middle of a watering hole? It's not even on a pedestal or anything.'

'Unless it sank in the mud.'

'And what monuments do *you* build on mud, brother?'

The water was cool and clear. Beyond the ledge, the pool seemed to drop away to unknown depths, but that was due to the failing light, Rint suspected. 'I don't trust magic,' he said. 'And this village reeks of it.'

Raskan grunted at that. 'I feel the same as you, Rint. It makes the skin crawl. If this is what waits this side of Bareth Solitude, well, it's little wonder we rarely visit these lands. Or the people who choose to live like this.'

Feren straightened and turned round. 'Someone comes,' she said.

Rint thought about spitting into the water and decided against it. He imagined Raskan was regretting his words, since it was likely that they had been heard by the Azathanai who now approached. Still crouching, he twisted to regard the newcomer. A woman of middle years, overweight but not grossly so; still, it seemed she sagged from every appendage, and the roll of fat overwhelming her belt had pushed away the front of her hide shirt and so hung exposed, the skin white as snow and creased with stretch marks. She had, Rint decided, once been much fatter.

The woman halted a few paces away, scowling. 'You do not know me,' she said in the Tiste language, but with a thick, muted accent.

Feren cleared her throat. 'Forgive us, Azathanai. We do not.'

'The Dog-Runners know me. I am found among them, on winter nights. They see me in the fires they light. I am worshipped and I see the worship in their eyes, the reflected flames of their eyes.'

'Then,' said Rint, 'you have travelled a long way to come here.'

The scowl faded and the woman shrugged. 'I would choose a shape of beauty. Instead, they feed me until I can barely move.' With these words she reached to her belly, pushed her hand inside, and Rint realized, in horror, that what he had taken to be stretch marks were in fact scars – now wounds, one of them splitting open as she pushed her hand deeper. When she withdrew it, slimed with blood and ichor, she held in her hand a small clay figurine, bulbous in form. She tossed it at the feet of Feren, who involuntarily stepped back.

Rint stared as the wound closed, and the blood ran from the skin watery as rain, until once more the belly was alabaster white.

Feren was looking down at the clay figurine and after a moment she bent down and picked it up.

Glancing over at what his sister held, Rint saw that it was female, with a nub of a head – barely shaped – above huge breasts and a round belly. The legs were pressed together below an exaggerated vulva.

'They feed the fire,' the woman said. 'And I grow fat.'

Raskan was mute and pale; he stood like a man who wanted to flee. The woman walked over to him. 'Do I frighten you? Do you not want to feel my weight upon you? The wetness of my gift?'

Rint saw that Raskan was trembling.

'I could make you kneel to me,' continued the woman. 'Such is my power. You think you understand beauty. You dream of women thin as children, and see nothing perverse in that. But when one such as I comes to stand before you, I sense your hunger for worship, even as that hunger shames you. Lie upon the ground, Tiste, and let me teach you all about power—'

'Enough!'

The command rang in the air. Rint was spun round by it. Draconus had appeared, Arathan a step behind him.

The Azathanai woman edged back, her scowl returning, and with it a spasm of venom that just as quickly vanished. 'I was but amusing myself, Draconus. No harm.'

'Begone, Olar Ethil. Skulk your way back to the Dog-Runners. These people are under my protection.'

She snorted. 'They need it. *Tiste.*'

That word dripped with contempt, and dropping the figurine Feren reached for her sword, but Rint stepped close and stayed her hand.

Raskan staggered away, his hands covering his face. He almost collided with Draconus who moved aside just in time, and then fled onward. Now Rint could see the Lord's fury.

The woman named Olar Ethil studied Draconus, unperturbed. 'I could take them all,' she said. 'Even the woman. And you would not be able to stop me.'

'When last we crossed paths, Olar Ethil, that might have been true. I invite you to quest deeper.'

'Oh, no need, Draconus. Night rides your breath. I see where you have gone and what you have done and you are a fool. All for love, was it? Or am I being too . . . romantic. More like *ambition*, which, since we are not fools, you could not appease among us.' She made a faint gesture with her blood-stained hand.

The clay figurine exploded with a sharp *crack.*

Feren cursed, reaching a hand up to her cheek and drawing it back smeared in blood. 'You fat hag!'

Olar Ethil laughed. 'Touched by the goddess! You carry a child, woman, yes? A girl . . . and oh, the hue of her blood is *most* unusual!'

Draconus stepped closer and Olar Ethil faced him again. 'You wanted a grandson?' she asked. 'How disappointing for you. Come no closer, Draconus! You have my attention now. Gaze into the flames at night for too long, and I will steal your soul – you all have felt it.

Your words die and the fire fills your mind. Draconus, I will look out from the flames. I will watch you, and listen, and discover your secrets. Although, granted, I already know most of them. Shall I utter your truths, O Suzerain of Night?'

Draconus halted his advance. 'If you come to the flames of our campfires, Olar Ethil, even once, we shall do battle. Until but one of us remains alive.'

The woman's eyes widened with shock. 'Well now,' she murmured, 'all that armour . . . for naught. Death, Draconus? Be careful – the word alone is an unholy summons these days.'

'What do you mean?'

'I mean an Azathanai has taken a life. Spilled the blood of a very powerful . . . innocent. Around this deed, chaos now dances like carrion flies – why do you think I returned?'

'An Azathanai has committed murder?' The belligerence was gone from Draconus now, and when he stepped closer to Olar Ethil, Rint understood – as well as she evidently did – that no threat was intended.

Her expression was now grave. 'Not a Tiste, Draconus, which absolves you of vengeance. Nor a Dog-Runner, or so I have since discovered, which absolves me of the same. Nor a Thel Akai – although that would have been interesting. Neither Jheck nor Jheleck. *Jaghut*, beloved. Karish, mate to Hood, is dead. Slain.'

The sudden anguish in the Lord's face was terrible to behold. Rint edged back, pulling Feren with him. He saw the boy watching from a dozen or so paces away, but not watching his father; nor was he watching Olar Ethil. Instead, Arathan's eyes were fixed on Feren.

*Abyss take us all. He's made a child with her. A girl.*

Feren had half turned, only to be snared by Arathan's eyes.

Rint heard her whisper, 'I'm sorry.'

In a harsh voice Draconus spoke. 'Olar Ethil, come to my fires.'

The woman nodded, strangely formal. 'I would never have done so,' she said, 'if not invited, Suzerain. Forgive me. I have been too long among the Dog-Runners, who prove so easy to bait that I cannot help myself.' She cocked her head. 'It seems that I am a cruel goddess.'

'Be more mindful, then,' Draconus replied, but there was no bite in his words; rather, a kind of tenderness. 'They are vulnerable to deep hurts, Olar Ethil.'

She sighed regretfully. 'I know. I grow careless in my power. They feed me with such desperation, such yearning! The Bonecasters voice prayers in my name, like biting ants beneath the furs. It drives me mad.'

Draconus settled a hand upon her shoulder, but said nothing.

She sank against him, resting her head against his chest.

Rint was dumbfounded. *Draconus . . . who are you?*

'And,' Olar Ethil continued, her voice muffled, 'they make me fat.'

321

With an amused snort Draconus stepped away. 'Do not blame them for your appetites, woman.'

'What will you do?' she asked him.

'Where is Hood?'

'I have heard that his grief has driven him mad. Lest he proclaim war upon the Azathanai, he was subdued by kin and is now chained in a cell in the Tower of Hate.'

'The Jaghut have gathered? To what end?'

'None can say, Draconus. The last time they gathered they argued themselves into the abandonment of their realm.'

Draconus seemed distracted for a moment, and then he shook his head. 'I will speak to the Lord of Hate. Tell me, do we know the slayer among the Azathanai?'

'Not yet, Suzerain. Some are missing, or in hiding.'

Draconus grunted. 'Nothing new in that.'

'No.'

As they were speaking, Feren had been pulling at Rint's grip on her arm. Finally her efforts drew his attention. But she was not interested in leaving his side. Instead, as he released her, she sagged to the ground, leaning hard against his legs. He felt the shudder of her silent weeping.

Rint felt sick inside. He wished they had never agreed to accompany the Consort. He wished that Ville and Galak would finally catch up with them, so they could all leave – break this contract and to the Abyss with the consequences. He wanted no more of this.

Draconus said, 'Rint, help your sister tend to her wound, and then make camp upon the hill.'

'Yes, Lord.'

'Arathan.'

'Sir?'

'Find Raskan. Help him.'

'Help?' The boy's eyes were wide with sudden fear.

Draconus frowned. 'I meet your eyes. You are the son of Draconus. Go to him.'

\*       \*       \*

Arathan found Sergeant Raskan crumpled against a wall, his face ravaged by grief. As he drew nearer, the man looked up, wiped roughly at his eyes and made to stand, only to sag once more on the wall. He looked away as if shamed.

'Rint and Feren are going to where we will make camp,' said Arathan. 'They have all the horses.'

'Go away, boy.'

'I cannot.'

'I said go away!'

Arathan was silent for a long moment, and then he said, 'I wish that I could, sergeant. This should be a time for you to be alone. I do not know what she did, but I can see that it was cruel.'

'Keep your distance,' Raskan said in a low rasp, 'lest I harm you.'

'Sergeant, my father has met my eyes. I am his son. I am not here to ask you. I am here to command you. I will lead you to the camp. It is my father's wish.'

Raskan looked up, eyes hooded in the gloom, his cheeks streaked and his beard glittering. 'Your father,' he hissed, making the words a curse. 'This was Ivis's task, not mine! Maybe he could have weathered it, but I cannot!'

'What did she take from you?'

His laugh was harsh and bitter, but he straightened from the wall. 'I am not the fool he thinks I am. She knows him from long ago. I begin to *see.*'

'What do you mean? What do you see? Sergeant Raskan, tell me – what do you see?'

'Azathanai blood is what I see. It needs chaining and that's what he's done. Chained it down. By his will alone you are held back, made normal to our eyes. You fool – not once did she look at you!'

Arathan stared at the man, trying to comprehend. And then he backed away a step. 'Why should she? Raskan! Why should she look at me at all?'

But the man levered himself from the wall and staggered in the direction of the hill beyond the village. After a moment, Arathan stumbled after him. He heard the sergeant muttering under his breath.

'How can it be a secret when even I did not know it? No, I have dreamed no sordid dreams, longed for nothing immoral. There is no cause for disgust. I could kneel above the water – I could look down on my face. And see nothing evil. She lied. I deserve no shame!'

The man was speaking nonsense. Arathan wondered if his mind had been broken by the witch's magic. His own thoughts felt unhinged. *My father knew her long ago. I don't know what that means – it means nothing. It seems all of the Azathanai know my father. Grizzin Farl. Old Man. And now this witch. Each one we meet knows him. They call him the Suzerain of Night. They fear him.*

*I am his son. Bastard no longer.*

*Why did he wait? Why did he bring me out here to say that?*

They clambered over the last of the settlement's walls. Ahead the track resumed, climbing to a crossroads flanked on one side by a humped, rounded hill on which stood half a dozen trees, forming a half-ring. In the cup they formed stood Rint and Feren. Neither Draconus nor Olar Ethil could be seen – he wondered where they had gone. Were they still at the pool?

The horses were tied to the trees and stood with heads lowered beneath gnarled boughs that seemed tangled with black lichen.

Raskan ascended the hillside as if it were the face of a hated enemy, tearing at the grasses, pulling aside rocks and leaving them to tumble and roll so that Arathan had to jump from their path. The manic fury of the man was frightening.

Halfway up Raskan halted and wheeled to glare down at him. 'Some truths should never be revealed! Look at me!'

'There is nothing to see, sergeant,' Arathan replied. 'Nothing but anger.'

The man stared as if in shock.

'You are the gate sergeant of House Dracons, Raskan. You wear my father's old moccasins and you have ridden at his side. He sent you to me, remember? And you said what needed to be said.'

Each statement seemed to strike the man like a blow, and he sat down on the slope.

'Stand up!' Arathan snapped. 'You taught me how to ride Hellar. You fed Sagander blood-broth and saved his life.'

Raskan drew a deep, shuddering breath, squeezed shut his eyes for a moment, and then regained his feet. 'As you say.'

'They're getting a meal ready. We should join them.'

But Raskan hesitated, and then he said, 'I am sorry, Arathan. I misspoke.'

'You made no sense.'

'That is true enough. No sense, none at all. Forgive me.'

Arathan shrugged.

Raskan resumed the climb, but slowly this time, without vehemence. After watching for a moment, Arathan tried to follow, but his legs would not move. She was up there, and she carried his child. A girl had been made, by him and her. In the heat and wet, in the hunger and need, a child had been made. The thought terrified him.

He managed a step, and then another, although it seemed, all at once, that this was the hardest climb of his life. Feelings swarmed him in chaotic confusion, until they all blended into a solid roar; he felt that sound then rush away, leaving only a numbed silence, too weary for hope, too exhausted for expectation. All that remained was the taste of the terror he had experienced earlier, dull now, metallic.

They had made a child, but Feren needed nothing more from Arathan. She already had all she had wanted from him. In giving her one thing, he had thought it only right to give her everything, all of him. The foolish were ever too generous – he had heard Sagander say that often enough when stuffing scrolls and manuscripts into a chest that he then locked. His private writings, the culmination of his life as a scholar. Kept, for none to see. Arathan understood that now. *What is given away for free comes back wounded. Value is not always shared and some hands are rougher than others.*

*Father, this is what Old Man said to you, in warning.*

*I don't think you were listening.*

*     *     *

Feren touched the wound on her cheek. Rint had pulled from it a shard of clay, sewing the gash shut with gut thread. The bitch had laughed and that laugh still echoed in her skull, sharp as claws. Her mind felt full of blood, as if the wound from the clay fragment still bled, but only inward now, in unceasing flow.

Rint crouched nearby, building the cookfire, but she could see that his hands were shaking.

The witch had only confirmed what the corpse in the barrow had told them: she was seeded. A child was spreading roots through her belly. But now it felt alien, monstrous, and this sensation made her spirit recoil. The midwives were clear on this: *love must line the womb.* Love, forming a protective sheath. Without love, the child's soul withers, and she so wanted to love this creation.

The seed had been given in innocence. The hunger for it had belonged to her alone, hoarded like a treasure, a chest she wanted filled to the brim. And it had seemed that, night after night, she had cast in the boy's precious gifts by the handful, only to find that chest still gaping come the dawn. An illusion, she realized now. She was swollen with wealth and this sense of pallid impoverishment was her failing, not his.

She recalled looking upon pregnant women in the Bordersword villages, not too long ago, and seeing in them the sated satisfaction that she had, on occasion, derisively called *smug.* She had been a fool, quick to forget when she had known the same, when she had sauntered bold as a glutton – but such memories delivered spasms of pain and grief: it was no wonder she rejected all of what she too had known, leaving nothing but contempt and spite.

But now all she could feel was the girl curling like a fist inside her. *Around blood* most *unusual!* The boy had been more than just a boy. He was the son of Draconus, and the witch knew something – a secret, a buried truth. The unknown mother was not unknown to her, or so Rint now believed.

The wound in Feren's face stung as if licked by flames. It throbbed, shouted with pain in the centre of her cheek. It had torn her beauty away – what beauty she possessed and she'd never gauged it a thing to admire or envy – and she felt marked now, as if with a thief's brand. *She stole the seed of a lord's son – see her! There is no hiding the truth of that!*

She wanted to love the child growing within her: that first gift of

325

protection offered up by all mothers, and if the shock of birth was as much the surrendering of that protection as it was labour's own pain, she was a veteran to both and nothing awaiting her was unfamiliar. She had no cause to fear: every desire had been appeased; every prayer answered in the white stream's perfect blessing.

A girl, damned in conception, and when Feren imagined looking upon its newborn face, she saw her own, cheek gashed and bleeding, with eyes that knew only hate.

The torment of her thoughts shredded and spun away when Raskan clambered into view and she saw what had been done to him. He looked aged far beyond his years, his motions palsied and febrile as those of an ancient with brittle bones as he tottered to the fire and slowly sat down. He looked more than shocked; he looked ill, and Feren wondered if the witch's brutal sorcery had stolen more than peace from his soul.

Rint was stirring a broth on the fire. He did not look up when he spoke and his words were gruff. 'Every witch has cold hands. The touch wears off, sergeant.'

'She is Azathanai,' the sergeant replied, making the statement a rejection of all that Rint had offered him.

'A witch all the same,' Rint responded doggedly. 'Even the Jheleck know of this Olar Ethil, who looks out from flames and yearns to meet your eyes. They call her power *Telas*. We have all felt it, when the night slumps just before dawn, and we look upon the hearth, expecting to see nothing but embers, and are shocked at the sight of fresh flames.' He nudged another stick into the fire. 'And then . . . other times . . . who hasn't fallen silent when sitting round a hearth, eyes trapped by the deadly spirit in the flames? You feel the cold on your back and the heat on your face, and it seems that you cannot move. A trance grips you. Your eyes are locked, and in your mind, moving like half-seen shadows, ancient dreams stir awake.'

Feren stared across at her brother, half in wonder and half in fear. Rint's face was twisted into a grimace. He stirred the broth as if testing the depth of mud before his next step.

Beside Feren, Raskan's breathing was harsh and rapid. 'She has touched you, Rint.'

'She has, though I knew it not at the time. Or perhaps I did, but kept the truth from myself. We are ever made uneasy by what we do not know, and there is no virtue in recognizing that, since it speaks only of our own ignorance.'

'Better ignorance than this!'

With that hoarse admission from Raskan, Arathan arrived. He halted a few paces from the fire, and Feren saw how he would not look at her. This was a relief, since the single glance she had just cast his way burned like a knife blade in her chest. She felt her eyes drawn to the flickering flames and quickly looked away, off into the night.

*Better ignorance than this! Voice that cry as if the words were holy, for they are surely that. Words to haunt our entire lives, I should think.*

Rint rose. 'Feren, if you would, the bowls are here.'

She did not object, as it gave her something to do. She set about ladling the broth into the bowls, while Rint moved off to his pack. When he returned he carried a flask which he offered to Raskan. 'Sergeant, I'm of no mind to test your command this night. Nor shall Feren.'

The man frowned. 'Meaning?'

'Get drunk, sergeant. Get good and drunk.'

A faint smile cracked the man's features. 'I am reminded of an old saying and now wonder at its source . . .'

Rint jerked a nod. 'Yes. "Drown the witch," sergeant, with my blessing.'

'And mine,' Feren said.

When Raskan reached for the flask he suddenly hesitated and looked up at Arathan. 'Lord Arathan?'

'Mine, too,' Arathan said.

Feren settled back on her haunches, closing her eyes.

*'Lord Arathan.' It is done, then. He met his son's eyes and knew them as his own.*

'Of course he'd know them,' she muttered under her breath. *They just needed a few hundred wounds first.*

*　　*　　*

'You did not expect me,' said Olar Ethil. When he did not answer she looked across at him, and then sighed. 'Draconus, it pains me to see you like this.'

'What I shall deliver to Kharkanas—'

'Will heal nothing!' she snapped. 'You always see too much in things. You make symbols of every gesture and expect others to understand them, and when they do not, you are lost. And, Draconus, you do not fare well when you are lost. She has unmanned you, that doe-eyed, simpering fool.'

'You speak ill of the woman I love, Olar Ethil. Do not think I will yield another step.'

'It is not you I doubt, Draconus. You gave her Darkness. You gave her something so precious she knows not what to do with it.'

'There is wisdom in her indecision,' Draconus replied.

She studied him. The night felt starved of faith, as if he had taken it all inside, and now harboured it with undeserved loyalty. 'Draconus. She now rules, and ascends into godhood. She sits on that throne, face to face with necessities – and I fear they have little to do with you, or what you desire. To rule is to kneel before expediency. You should fear her wisdom.'

If her words found tender places, he had the will and the strength to not flinch, but there was pain in his eyes. She knew it well, from long ago. 'There are Jaghut among the Dog-Runners.'

He looked at her. 'What?'

'Those who rejected the Lord of Hate. They amuse themselves ordering and reordering what does not belong to them. They make fists and call them gods. Spirits of water, air and earth flee before them. Burn dreams of war. Vengeance.'

'Must it all crumble, Olar Ethil? All that we have made here?'

She waved a dismissive hand. 'I will answer with fire. They are my children, after all.'

'Making you no different from those Jaghut, or will you now claim Burn as your child, too?'

Scowling, Olar Ethil set her hands upon her distended belly. 'They don't feed *her*.'

They were silent for a few heartbeats, and then he said, 'Feren did not deserve that.'

'I said I was a cruel goddess and I meant it, Draconus. What care I about who does or who doesn't deserve anything? Besides, she was already well used. You will have a grandchild to play with and let us be plain: I don't mean tossing on one knee. How are they, by the way? Our wretched spawn?'

'If they had a fourth sister she would be called Venom,' Draconus replied. 'As it is, alas, they have no need for a fourth sister.'

'Three memories of pain. That is all I have of them. Will you visit his mother, then?'

'No.'

'You and I, Draconus, we are cruel in love. I wager Mother Dark is yet to discover that.'

'We shall not make love tonight, Olar Ethil.'

She laughed harshly against the sting of those words. 'A relief, Draconus. Three pains are enough for me.'

'Old Man says . . . the next village.'

'And then?'

He sighed. 'I shall send the others back and ride on to the Tower of Hate.'

'Your son?'

'He shall ride with me. I believe his tutor left him with gifts for the Lord of Hate.'

'They will be ill received, I predict. Does the boy return to Kharkanas with you?'

'He cannot, and the means with which I shall hasten that journey are for me and Calaras and none other.'

'Then he knows nothing.'

'Nothing.'

'Draconus, must all your seeds be errant? Left to grow wild, for ever untamed? Our daughters will be the death of you – you keep them too close, smothered by your neglect. It is no wonder they are venomous.'

'Perhaps,' he admitted. 'I have no answer to my children. All of myself that I see in them is but cause for concern, and I am left wondering why parents give to their children so freely their flaws, yet not their virtues.'

She shrugged. 'We are all misers with what we believe we have earned, Draconus.'

He reached to her and rested his hand upon her shoulder, and that touch sent a tremble through her. 'You wear your weight well, Olar Ethil.'

'If you mean my fat then I call you a liar.'

'I did not mean your fat.'

After a moment she shook her head. 'I think not. We are no wiser, Draconus. We fall into the same traps, over and over again. For all that I am fed by my Dog-Runners, I do not understand them; and for all that I nurtured Burn, at my own breast, still I underestimated her. I fear it is that fated disregard that will see the end of me some day.'

'Will you not see your own death?'

'I choose not to. Best it come in an instant, unexpected and so not feared. To live in dread of dying is to not live at all. Pray that I am running on my last day, fleet as a hare, my heart filled with fire.'

'So I shall pray, Olar Ethil. For you.'

'What of your death, Draconus? You were always one for planning, no matter how many times those plans failed you.'

'I will,' he replied, 'die many deaths.'

'You have seen them?'

'No. I have no need for that.'

She looked out upon the water of the spring. Night made it black. Caladan Brood's sculpture of the Thel Akai still lifted a tormented face to the sky, and would do so for ever. It was aptly named *Surrender*, and he had forced that sentiment upon the stone itself, refusing all subtlety. She feared Caladan Brood for his honesty and despised him for his talent.

'I see his mother in his face,' she said after a time. 'In his eyes.'

'Yes.'

'That must be hard for you.'

'Yes.'

She pushed her hand into her belly, feeling the skin split, and then the sudden heat of blood and the steady beat of her heart – almost within reach. Instead, her hands closed about the baked clay form of a figurine. She pulled it out. She crouched to wash it clean and then straightened and offered it to Draconus. 'For your son.'

'Olar Ethil, he is not yours to protect.'

'Even so.'

After a moment he nodded and took it from her.

Draconus then squeezed her shoulder and began walking away.

She brushed fingers across her belly but the wound had closed once more. 'I forgot to ask, what name did you give him?'

Draconus paused and glanced back at her. When he told her, she made a startled sound, and then began laughing.

*    *    *

Arathan slept fitfully, haunted by dreams of the corpses of children floating on a pool of black water. He saw ropes coming from their bellies, as if each one had been tied to something, but those ropes were severed, the ends hacked and shredded. Staring upon this scene, he felt a sudden certainty – in the way of dreams – that the spring, far beneath the surface, spilled out not water but these drowned babies, and the flow was endless.

When he walked out upon them he felt their soft bodies give under his weight, and with each step he grew somehow heavier, until, with a sound like breaking ice, he plunged through—

Only to awaken, slick with sweat, his chest aching from a breath held overlong against imaginary pressures.

He sat up to see that it was still night. His father was standing near the horses under the strange trees, and it seemed that he stared eastward – into the village or perhaps beyond it. For all Arathan knew, Draconus might be looking upon Kharkanas itself, and the Citadel, and a woman hidden in darkness seated on a throne.

Throne of Night. He settled back into his blanket and stared up at the stars overhead. Their twisted pattern made him think of fevers, when nothing was right with the world and the wrongness was terrifying – tormenting a small boy who was already filled with confused visions of icy cold water and shards of ice and who cried out for a mother who never came and never answered.

He had been that boy once. But even questions had a way of going away, eventually, when no answers were possible. He thought of the gift he would bring to the Lord of Hate, and knew it to be paltry, useless enough to be an insult. But he had nothing else to give.

Raskan believed that Olar Ethil was Arathan's mother, but he knew that she was not. He had no reason for his certainty; still he did not question it. If anything, the witch reminded him of Malice, when she was younger and fatter – in the days when the girl first walked and was in the habit of wandering everywhere, smiling and singing since she did not yet know the meaning of the name she had been given. Something in their faces, young and old, seemed to be the same.

Bootsteps sounded and he tilted his head to find his father standing over him. After a moment Draconus sank into a crouch. He was holding in his hands a clay figurine, a thing that seemed to cry out sex, in an excess of sensuality that struck Arathan as grotesque. One of the witch's gifts.

'For you,' Draconus said.

Arathan wanted to refuse it. Instead he sat up and took it from his father's hands.

'It will be light soon,' Draconus went on. 'Today I send back Rint, Feren and Raskan.'

'Back?'

'You and I shall ride on, Arathan.'

'We leave them behind?'

'They are no longer needed.'

*And somewhere ahead, you will leave me behind, too. No longer needed.* 'Father,' he said, hands clutching the figurine, 'don't hurt her.'

'Hurt who?'

'Feren,' he whispered. *And the child she carries. My child.*

He could see his father's frown, and how it slowly twisted into a scowl. It was, he realized, never too dark to see such things. 'Don't be foolish, Arathan.'

'Just leave them alone, please.'

'I would do no other,' Draconus said in a growl. He quickly straightened. 'Go back to sleep if you can,' he said. 'We have far to ride today.'

Arathan settled back on to the hard ground once more. He held the figurine like a baby against his chest. He had stood up to his father. He had made a demand even if it had sounded like a plea. A true son knew to draw lines in the sand and claim what he would for himself, for his own life and all that he deemed important in it. This was what growing up meant. Places to claim, things owned and things defended. It was a time of jostling, because the space was never big enough for the both of them, for both father and son. There was pushing and there was pulling, and comfort went away if it had ever existed; but maybe someday it would come back. If the father permitted it. If the son wanted it. If neither feared the other.

Arathan wondered if he would ever stop fearing his father, and then he wondered, as he studied the swirl of stars fading in the paling sky overhead, if there would come a time when his father began fearing him.

He thought he heard the witch whisper in his mind.

*For the fire, boy. When your love is too much. Too much to bear. For the fire.*

The smooth curves of the figurine felt warm in his hands, as if promising heat.

When he closed his eyes the nightmare returned, and this time he saw a woman at the bottom of the pool, reaching into her belly and dragging free babies, one after another. She bit through the ropes and sent the babies away with a push. They thrashed until they drowned.

Along the edge of the pool now, women had gathered, reaching down to collect the limp, lifeless forms. He watched them stuff those bodies inside their bellies. And then they walked away.

But one woman remained, and the water before her was clear – no corpses in sight. She stared down into it, and he heard her singing in a soft voice. He could not understand the words, only the heartbreak in them. When she turned away and walked, he knew it was to the sea. She was going away and she was never returning to this place, and so she did not see the last boy rise up, still thrashing, fighting shards of ice, reaching for a hand that was not there.

And upon a stone, overlooking all this, sat his father. Cutting ropes. Into, Arathan surmised, manageable lengths.

\*       \*       \*

Raskan woke late in the morning, the sun's light lancing into his brain like jagged spears. Cursing his own fragility, he slowly sat up.

The two Borderswords were sprawled out in the shade of the trees. Behind them stood the horses, still tethered, but some, he realized, were missing. He wondered why, but a terrible thirst rose from within and he looked round, with sudden desperation, for a waterskin. Someone had left one within reach and he dragged it close.

As he drank, perhaps too greedily, Rint sat up and looked across at him. 'There's still some breakfast,' the Bordersword said.

Raskan lowered the waterskin. 'Where have they gone?' he asked.

Rint shrugged.

*I have shamed my lord.* 'Where have they gone?' he demanded, pushing himself to his feet. The pain in his head redoubled and he gasped, feeling his guts churn. 'What was I drinking last night?'

'Mead,' Rint replied. 'Three flasks.'

Feren had climbed to her feet, brushing grasses and dried leaves from her clothes. 'We're to go back, sergeant. They went on without us. It was the Lord's command.'

After a long moment, Raskan realized that he was staring – stupidly – at the woman. He could see the beginning of a swell on her, but that was impossible. Perhaps, he told himself, she'd always carried some extra weight. He tried to recall, but then gave up on the effort.

'Something changed,' Rint said to him. 'We do not know what it was. He discharged us and orders you to return to House Dracons. That is all we know, sergeant. For most of the journey back, it seems reasonable that we should travel together, and so we waited.'

Raskan looked away, but then he nodded. *I failed him. Somehow – no, do not lie to yourself, Raskan. It was that witch's curse. It was how you broke, fled like a coward. Draconus will throw you away, just as he did Sagander.* He thought then of Arathan, now riding at his father's side, and shot another glance at Feren.

But she was carrying her saddle to her horse.

*The boy commanded me. I remember that much at least. He showed his father's iron, and yet, in his words to me, he was generous. Arathan, fare you well. I do not think I will see you again.*

'Clouds to the south,' Rint said. 'I smell the approach of rain.' He turned to Raskan. 'Get some food in your stomach, sergeant. If we are lucky we can ride free of the rain, and, if Mother Dark wills it, we shall meet Ville and Galak.'

Feren snorted. 'Dear brother,' she said, 'she may well be a goddess now, but Mother Dark sets no eyes upon us, not here. We are not in Kurald Galain and even if we were, do you truly believe she is omniscient?'

'Wherever there is night,' he said, glowering.

'If you say so,' she replied as she led her horse out from under the trees. 'I'll wait for you at the spring.'

Raskan winced, and saw that Rint was now staring at his sister with an expression of dread.

'If I see that witch,' Feren said to her brother, one hand reaching up to the stitched gash on her cheek, 'I'll be sure to say hello.' Swinging into the saddle, she loosened the sword in the scabbard belted at her side, and then set out, back towards the village.

Rint hurried over to his own saddle. 'Wake up, sergeant – I'm not leaving her alone down there with that witch.'

'Go, then,' said Raskan. 'Do not wait for me. I will find you on the other side of the village.'

'As you will,' he replied. 'But she's right in one thing – you'll need to water your horse first.'

'I know.'

＊　　＊　　＊

Feren didn't know if it was possible to kill an Azathanai, but she meant to try. She hoped the witch was wandering, as she had been the night before, since Feren had no desire to begin kicking down doors in this wretched village. She'd had enough of feeling used. The Azathanai did not understand propriety – even Grizzin Farl had pushed into her world of secrets, and if he laughed to soften the insult, an insult it remained.

She had suffered the touch of a dead Thel Akai, and now bore the scar of a witch's curse. She had earned the right to fight back.

She knew what she was doing; she knew the value of anger, and how it could scour away other feelings. In her rage she did not have to think about the child growing within her; she did not have to think about Arathan and what she – and Draconus – had done to him. She did not have to think about the hurts she had delivered to her own brother. This was the lure of violence, and violence did not begin at the moment of physical assault; it began earlier, in all the thoughts that led up to it, in that storm of vehemence and venom. Rage beckoned violence, like those call-and-answer songs among the Deniers.

She rode through the village, through cool morning air, using the crumbled gaps in the walls as they had done the day before, and guided her mount down to the spring with its ugly statue and depthless waters. But she did not find the witch. Instead, she found Ville and Galak, watering their horses.

At the sound of her horse's thumping hoofs as she approached, both men turned. And the smiles they gave her shattered the fury within her, and she rode out from it as if from under a cloud.

\* \* \*

In the night just past, as Rint lay in his sleeping furs and listened to Arathan's soft moans from the other side of the fire – and Feren's soft weeping much closer to hand – he had thought about killing Lord Draconus. A knife to the throat would have done it, except that it seemed the man never slept. Again and again through the night Rint had opened his eyes and looked across to where the huge figure was standing, seeing only that he remained, motionless, a silhouette strangely impenetrable.

Shivering under his furs, Rint began to believe in the power of Night, in the inescapable breath of Mother Dark. Wherever the sun set, she would then rise, as if bound now to the raw truths of the universe. She had ceased being a Tiste. Even the title of goddess now seemed paltry and insufficient to evoke what she had become.

He did not understand how a mortal could make that journey, could become something *other*. But clearly she had done so. And Lord Draconus stood at her side and, Rint now suspected, shared something of the power his lover possessed.

The Azathanai met Draconus eye to eye, as equals, and even, on occasion, in deference. The Suzerain of Night: he had heard that title used for Draconus before, but it was not a popular one among the Tiste, who objected to its presumption, its arrogant impropriety. Well, as far as Rint was now concerned, they were all fools to denigrate Draconus's claim to that title. Whatever it meant, it was a thing of power, brutally real and profoundly dangerous.

There was no question now in Rint's mind that Draconus posed a threat. The highborn were right to fear the Consort and his influence in the court. They were right to want him ousted, and if not ousted, then brought down, discarded and driven away in disgrace.

Months past, Urusander's agents had come among the Bordersword villages. They had argued their case – the need for a husband for Mother Dark, rather than a consort, and the obvious choice for that husband: Vatha Urusander, commander of the Legion. Those agents had gained little ground among the Borderswords. Their cause rode currents of conflict, and the Borderswords had lost their thirst for war. Those fierce fools had left in frustration.

Rint knew that his opinion counted for something among the loose council of his people, and he vowed that the next time such an agent visited, he would lend his support. Draconus needed to go. Even better, someone should kill the man and so end this deadly rise to power.

He had seen enough, here on this journey, to choose now to stand with Urusander. Hunn Raal and his comrades were not so blinded by personal ambition as Rint and his kin had believed. *No, the next time will be different.*

When Draconus announced that the contract had ended, concluded to the Lord's satisfaction, Rint had struggled to hide his relief. Now he could take Feren away from all this: from the Lord's cruel needs and the son's pathetic ones. They would accompany Raskan as far as Abara Delack, because the man deserved that much – it was hardly Raskan's fault that he served a beast.

They could now leave the lands of the Azathanai.

He rode hard to catch up to his sister, only to find his fears unfounded and, better still, that she was in good company.

*       *       *

'I am not always cruel.'

Raskan spun round at the words. The saddle slipped from his hands and he staggered back. 'No,' he moaned. 'Go away.'

Instead Olar Ethil drew closer. 'Yours is an unhealthy fire,' she said. 'Let me douse it. Let me heal you.'

'Please,' he begged.

But this denial she received as an invitation. She reached out, as Raskan sank to his knees, and took his head in her hands. 'Poisons of desire are the deadliest of all. I can cure you and so end your torment.' She paused and then added, 'It will give me pleasure to do so. Pleasure such as you cannot conceive. You are a man and so cannot know what it is to be sated – not in those few panting breaths following release that is all you can ever know – but the swollen bliss of a woman, ah, well, Gate Sergeant Raskan, this is what I seek and it is what I can offer you.'

The hands, pressed against the sides of his head, felt cool and soft, plump and yielding as they seemed to meld into his skin, and then the bones of his face, the fingers reaching through his temples. The heat of his thoughts vanished at their touch.

'Open your eyes,' she said.

He did so and found only her bared belly. It filled his vision.

'Whence you came, Raskan.'

He stared at the scars and would have turned his head but she held him fast. He reached up to pull away her hands but found only her wrists – the rest had flowed into him, merging with the bones. In horror, he felt his fingertips track a seamless path from the skin of her wrists to his own face.

She drew him closer to her belly. 'Worship is a strange thing,' she said. 'It seeks . . . satiation. Revelation is nothing without it. As you are fulfilled, I am filled. As you revel in surrendering, I delight in your gift. You need no other gods than this one. I am your only goddess now, Raskan, and I invite you inside.'

He wanted to cry out but no sound came from his throat.

She pressed his face against her belly, and he felt a scar open, splitting ever wider. Blood smeared his cheeks, leaked past his lips. Choking, he sought to draw a breath. Instead, fluids filled his lungs.

He felt her push his head into her belly, and then the edges of the gash tightened round his neck. His body was thrashing, but her power over him was absolute, even as the wound began to close, cutting through his neck.

His struggles stilled. He hung limp in her grip, blood streaming down his chest.

A moment later, in a sob more felt than heard, his body fell away. Yet he remained, blind, swallowed in flesh. And in his last moments of consciousness, he touched satiation and knew it for what it was. The blessing of a goddess, and, with it, joy that filled his being.

*    *    *

Olar Ethil wiped her bloodied hands on her distended belly, and then stepped over the headless corpse crumpled at her feet.

She went to the nearest tree and clambered up into its branches. The strange black lichen enwreathing those branches now gathered round her, growing in answer to a muttering of power from her full, blood-tinted lips. Thoroughly hidden now, she waited for the return of the dead man's companions. She wanted to see the pregnant woman again, and that sweet wound on her cheek.

Not always cruel, it was true. *Just most of the time.*

*　　*　　*

'It was boredom that had us riding half through the night,' Ville was saying as they rode back to find Sergeant Raskan. 'That and finding water. Without that spring we would've been in trouble.'

'The sooner we're gone from these lands the better,' Galak said, glancing at the stone houses they rode past. 'I don't mind us riding all this way only to turn round and go back again. I don't mind it at all.'

'The tutor?' Rint asked.

'Quiet the whole way,' Galak replied. 'Seemed happy enough to see the monks.'

Something in the man's tone made Rint look over at his friend.

But it was Ville who grunted and said, 'Galak decided he didn't trust the old man. Saw no reason for it myself.'

'Something in his eyes,' Galak said, shrugging. 'Something not right.'

They reached the base of the hill.

'I see his horse,' Feren said. 'Did he go back to sleep?'

Rint shook his head. The witch had wounded the poor man and a night of mead did not heal. It just offered the peace of oblivion. Nothing lasted, of course. The spirit struggled back to the surface, gasping the pain of living.

The four of them cantered up the hillside, crested its summit.

He saw Raskan, lying curled up – but something was wrong. The air stank of spilled blood. Reining in, Rint made to dismount, and then fell still.

The Borderswords were silent – their horses halted and the beasts jerking their heads, nostrils flaring.

Feren slipped down and walked over to where the headless body was lying. Rint saw her studying Raskan, and then the ground around the corpse. All at once she lifted her head towards one of the trees. Her sword scraped free.

Rint's mouth was suddenly dry as dust. Eyes narrowing, he sought to see what Feren was staring at, but the snarl of lichen cloaking all the branches revealed nothing. Dismounting, one hand on his knife, he drew closer to his sister.

'Feren?'

'She's there,' Feren whispered.

'What? I see nothing—'

'*She's there!*'

Rint looked down at the body. The severed end of Raskan's neck looked pinched, and the cut was ragged. He did not think it came from an edged weapon. But then, what? A wave of cold swept through him and he shivered. He turned as Galak and Ville came up behind them. Both men had drawn their weapons, and they looked to all sides, their faces desperate, seeking an enemy though there was none to be found.

'I just left him,' Rint said. 'There was no one about – he was alone up here. I swear it.'

'She's there!' Feren cried, pointing with her sword. 'I see her!'

'There is nothing there,' Ville said in a growl. 'No woman, at least. Feren—'

'Azathanai! Witch, come down and meet my sword! You so liked my blood – give me some of yours!' Feren marched up to the tree and swung her sword at the tree's gnarled bole. The edge rebounded with a metallic shout and the blade was a flash of dull silver flying out from Feren's hand. The weapon spun past Rint and then landed, burying its point in the earth – where Raskan's head would have been had it remained. Feren staggered back as if she had been the one struck, and Rint moved to take her in his arms.

She thrashed in his grip, glaring up at the tree. 'Murderer! Olar Ethil, hear me! I curse you! In the name of an innocent man, I curse you! By the blood you took from me, I curse you!'

Rint dragged her back. He shot a glare at Ville and Galak. 'Wrap up the body and throw it on the horse! We need to leave!'

The woman in his arms fought savagely, her nails raking deep gashes across his forearms. All at once he remembered a child, thrashing in blind fury, and how he had to hold her until her rage was spent in exhaustion. She'd clawed him. She'd bitten him. She'd been terrible in righteousness. A cry broke from his throat, filled with anguish at all that was lost, and for all that never changed.

His cry stilled her sudden as a breath, and then she was twisting round in his arms and embracing him, and now it was her strength that he felt, and his weakness that he gave in return.

'But where's the head?' Ville shouted, half panicked.

'It's gone!' Feren snapped.

Brother and sister held each other tight, and all at once Rint knew that they were doomed, that their lives were now wrapped round this moment, this wretched hill and these haunted trees – the headless body of an innocent man. Awaiting them he saw only blood and murder, cascading down like rain. He saw fires and could taste the bite of smoke in his throat.

He heard Ville and Galak carrying the body to the horse, and then Ville cursed when he saw that the mount had yet to be saddled. 'Set him down! Set him down, Galak!'

Feren pulled herself free. Rint stood, arms hanging as if life had been torn from his embrace, and now only empty death remained, watching dully as his sister stumbled over to her sword. She tugged it free and sheathed it, every motion febrile, moving like a woman who knew eyes were fixed upon her – but in chilling hunger, not admiration. His chest ached to see her this way again.

When she had found her husband – his body and his useless, pathetic escape from the hardships of grief – when that man had simply left her alone and with staring eyes and open mouth shouted out his cowardice in a voice that never came and would never come again – she had moved as she did now, busying herself with tasks, with necessities.

He felt tears filling the beard on his cheeks.

Something sailed down from the tree's black canopy and thumped on the ground almost at Rint's feet. He looked down to see a clay figurine, slick with fresh blood. And from the impenetrable tangle overhead he heard a soft laugh.

Rint straightened. Ville and Galak had saddled the mount and were heaving the corpse over it. They took up leather strings to tie Raskan's hands to his feet, one man to either side of the animal as they passed the string ends under the horse's belly. They tied the strings to the laces from the moccasins – Lord Draconus's own – and cinched tight the knots.

Rint stared at the heels, at how the thick hide was unevenly worn. *Just like his boots.*

'Feren,' he said, 'lead them down the hill.'

'Rint?'

'Take them, sister. I won't be long.'

But she drew close, her eyes wide with fear. 'What are you going to do?'

'Something meaningless.'

Whatever she saw in his face seemed to answer her needs and after a moment she turned away, hurrying back to her horse.

Rint went to his own horse and rummaged in the saddle bags. As his friends mounted up and rode away, Ville leading Raskan's horse with its lifeless burden, Rint drew out a flask of oil. They would have dry whetstones for the rest of this journey and would have to be mindful of rust and dulled edges, but there was nothing to be done about it.

He walked up to the tree, collecting wood, grasses and dried leaves along the way.

'I know,' he said as he built up the tinder round the base of the tree. 'I know I but send you back into the flames. And in fire there is doubtless no pain for one such as you.' He splashed oil against the bole of the tree, emptied the flask. 'Unless . . . the desire behind the fire has power. I think it does. I think that is why a raider's firing a house is a crime, an affront. Burning to death – malicious hands touching the flame to life – I think this has meaning. I think it stains the fire itself.'

He drew out his tinder box and found the embers he had this very morning collected from the cookfire. 'I do this wanting to hurt you, Olar Ethil. And I want that to matter.'

He set the embers down beneath a thick twisted bundle of grasses, watched as the smoke rose, and then, as flames licked to life, Rint stepped back.

The fire spread, and then found the oil. Like serpents the flames climbed the trunk of the tree. The lowest branches, with their nests of black lichen, burst alight.

Rint backed away from the heat. He watched as the flames surged from branch to branch, climbing ever higher. He watched as branches from the trees to either side caught, and the sound was a building roar.

When he heard her begin screaming, he walked back to his horse, climbed into the saddle, and rode away.

Her shrieks followed him down the hill.

*     *     *

Feren stared up at the burning trees. She could hear the witch's frantic screams and they made her smile.

When Rint re-joined them they turned as one and made their way back through the village.

This time Azathanai were emerging from their homes, to stare up at the wall of flames commanding the hilltop, and the grey smoke rising from them. Then they turned to watch the Borderswords riding past, and said nothing.

Feren held her smile, and offered it to every face turned her way.

*     *     *

Father and son rode side by side through the morning, saying little. Shortly after noon Draconus reined in suddenly and twisted in the saddle. He peered eastward, in the direction they had come. Arathan did the same, but could see nothing untoward.

'Father?'

Draconus seemed to hunch slightly. 'Raskan is dead.'

Arathan said nothing. He did not want to believe his father's words, but he did not doubt the truth of them.

'She saw it as mercy,' Draconus continued after a moment. 'Does that make a difference?'

*The witch killed him?* He thought of the clay figurine in his saddle bag. He had not wanted to take it from his father's hands. He wished now that he had refused him. *When your love is too much to bear. For the fire, boy, for the fire.*

'They found the body,' Draconus said. 'It is their rage that I now feel. I was careless. Unmindful, my thoughts elsewhere. But I made plain my

340

protection. Olar Ethil mocks me. Too often we strike at one another. From the ashes of our past, Arathan, you will find sparks that refuse to die. Be careful what memories you stir.' He drew a deep breath then, and let it out in something like a shudder. 'I admire them,' he said.

'Who?' Arathan asked.

'The Borderswords. I admire them deeply. They have struck back at her, not in my name, but because it was right to do so. Olar Ethil will be scarred by this. Terribly scarred. Arathan,' he added, taking up the reins once more, 'she who bears your child is a remarkable woman. You are right to love her.'

Arathan shook his head. 'I do not love her, Father. I no longer believe in love.'

Draconus looked across at him.

'But,' Arathan allowed, 'she will be a good mother.'

They resumed riding. He wanted to think about Raskan but could not. He was leaving a world behind, and the faces that he saw in that world remained alive in his mind. It seemed to be enough. The day ahead stretched before Arathan, as if it would never end.

# TWELVE

'**D**O YOU KNOW WHO I AM?'
The young woman stood on the roadside, looking up at him. She was old enough to have had her first night of blood, and there was a looseness about her that invited lust. At his question she nodded and said, 'You are Lord Urusander's son.'

By any measure, her respect was less than satisfying, verging on insult. Osserc felt his face reddening, a trait of his that he despised. 'I am riding to my father,' he said. 'I deliver words of great import. From this day,' he continued, 'you will see changes come to the world. And you will remember this chance meeting on this morning. Tell me your name.'

'Renarr.'

'My father awaits me with impatience,' Osserc said, 'but for you I will make him wait.'

'Not too long, I should think,' she replied.

'What do you mean by that?'

'Only, milord, that I am sure the world is eager to change.'

He stood in the stirrups and scanned their surroundings. He had just crossed the ford of the nameless stream that half encircled Neret Sorr, although from here the settlement remained hidden behind the low hills directly ahead. Scrub flanked the stream's basin, growing over the stumps of cut trees. The bushes seemed filled with birds, chattering in a thousand voices.

By the wet upon her leggings Osserc surmised that she too had been down at the stream, although she carried no skins or buckets. But he

342

saw that she held something in one closed fist, and could guess at what it was. That alone made him feel ugly inside. 'Are you from the village, then? I've not seen you.'

'I don't spend my evenings in the taverns, milord.'

'Of course you don't. But it seems that you know that I do.'

'It's known.'

'Women fight to sit in my lap.'

'I am happy for you, milord.'

'What you are is insolent.'

Her expression faltered slightly and she looked down. 'I am sorry that you think so, milord. Forgive me.'

'It's not your forgiveness that I want.'

And he saw then how his words frightened her, and that was the last thing he desired. 'What do you hide in your hand?'

'I – I do not hide it, milord. But it is personal.'

'A stone from the stream.'

Eyes still downcast, she nodded.

'A boy in the village?'

'He is past being a boy, milord.'

'Of course he is, to have earned your affection.' Osserc drew up his spare horse. 'You can ride? I will escort you back to the village. The day is hot and the road dusty, and I see that you wear no shoes.'

'That is a warhorse, milord—'

'Oh, Kyril is gentle enough, and most protective.'

She eyed the roan beast. 'I did not know you gelded warhorses.'

'Kyril would fight with my father's horse, and that could not be permitted, as it endangered both of us – me and my father, that is – and distracted the other mounts. Besides,' he added, 'I grew tired of fighting him.' After a moment, she still had made no move, and Osserc dismounted. 'I was, of course, intending for you to ride Neth, since, as you say, it's safer.'

She nodded. 'You will be most impressive, milord, riding Kyril into the village. All will see that the son of Lord Urusander has returned, pursuing important matters of state. They will see the dust upon you and wonder what lands you have travelled.'

Osserc smiled and offered her the reins.

'Thank you, milord,' she said, pausing to sweep back her golden hair and deftly knot it behind her head; then she accepted Neth's reins and drew close to the horse.

She waited for Osserc to swing into Kyril's robust saddle before lithely leaping astride Neth's back.

'Ride at my side,' Osserc said, guiding his mount alongside her.

'I must not, milord. My beloved—'

Osserc felt his smile tightening and there was pleasure when he hardened his tone. 'But I insist, Renarr. You will humour me in this small gesture, I am sure.'

'Milord, if he sees—'

'And if he does? Will he imagine that we dallied by the stream?'

'You may wish him to think so – him and others, milord. And so make sport of him. And me.'

Osserc decided he disliked this young woman, but this made her only more attractive. 'Am I to be challenged on my father's own lands? By some farm boy? Will he think so little of you to imagine you unable to resist my charms?'

'Milord, you are Lord Urusander's son.'

'And I am far from starved of the pleasures of women, as he must well know!'

'Also known to him, milord, is your insatiability, and your prowess.'

Osserc grunted, feeling his smile return, but now that smile was relaxed. 'It seems I have a reputation, then.'

'One of admiration, milord. And perhaps, for young men, some envy.'

'We shall ride side by side, Renarr, and should your beloved appear I will speak to put him at ease. After all, we have done nothing untoward, have we?'

'You have been most gracious, milord.'

'And you need never fear otherwise. As proof of that, I insist that you call me Osserc. I am my father's son and we are humble before what modest privileges our family possesses. Indeed,' he continued as they trotted up the road, 'we take most seriously our responsibilities, which seems to be too rare a virtue among the highborn. But then, we are not highborn, are we? We are soldiers. That and nothing more.'

To this she said nothing, but he found her silence pleasing, since it told him that she was listening to his every word.

'I will tell your beloved that he should be proud to have won your love, Renarr. The Abyss knows, I am too wayward and my future too uncertain, and besides, I have no freedom in such matters. For me, marriage will be political, and then there will be hostages and commissions and postings in border garrisons and the like. I see my future as one of service to the realm, and have made my peace with that.'

When he glanced across at her he saw that she was studying him intently. She quickly looked away. 'Milord, there are some in the village – sour old women, mostly – who do not approve of your nightly visits with – to the taverns, I mean.'

'Indeed?'

'But by your words I see that you must find what pleasures you can, and I will speak against their harsh judgement, on your behalf. A life of sacrifice awaits you, milord.'

He laughed. 'Then once again I am forgiven in your eyes?'

'Please excuse my presumption, milord. A village is like a tree filled with birds all talking at once. All manner of things are said.'

'I don't doubt it.'

They approached the slope of the last hill before the settlement. Off to the right, forty or so paces from the road and at the end of a rutted track, was an old stone house that had been abandoned generations past, its roof long since collapsed. Osserc slowed his mount and eyed the climb of the road. 'You may not believe this,' he said, 'but I value your forgiveness, Renarr. In my mind, these are my last days of freedom, and with the news I bring, that claim feels starker than ever before. But I tell you,' and he looked across at her, 'I do yearn for a tender touch that I have not paid for.'

She met his eyes, and then turned her mount on to the rutted track. The glance she cast back at him was veiled. 'I think your father and the world can wait a while longer, milord?'

He nodded, not trusting himself to speak.

'*When you want a woman to give freely of herself, Osserc, let her know that the privilege is yours, not hers. Be tender in your touch, and afterwards, make no boasts to anyone. There are many kinds of love. Some are small and brief, like a flower, while others last much longer. Value each one, for too few are the gifts of this world. Are you listening, boy?*'

'*I am, Hunn Raal. I always listen to what you have to say . . . until you're too drunk to say anything worth listening to.*'

'*But boy, I ain't never that drunk.*'

Halfway to the abandoned house, he saw her let the polished stone slip from her hand. It vanished in the yellowed grasses.

*   *   *

They hobbled the horses behind the house, out of sight from the road, and Osserc took Renarr's hand and led her in through the gaping doorway. The grasses were thick on the floor, lumpy with wooden remnants from the rotted, fallen roof. He spent a short time clearing a space and then laid out his cloak.

She stood watching him as he stripped off his armour and then set aside his sword belt. He was not ashamed of his body, for it was lean and he bore the muscles of a fighter. When he had pulled off his sweat-stained linen shirt he looked over to see that she had slipped out from her tunic. She wore no undergarments, telling him that she had bathed in the stream; perhaps to wash away a night of lovemaking with her beloved, and perhaps she still felt his clumsy, rough hands upon her body, his desperate kisses.

He would sweep away such memories, and in so doing would cause her beloved to begin to pall in her eyes, and she would find herself longing for a more seasoned touch – for in the ways of lovemaking the whores had taught him all he needed to know.

She was not thin, yet wore her weight as if she belonged in it, and no life of idyll or tug of years pulled down upon her. The curves were round and he had a vision of her in the future, swollen with child yet pretty much the same as she was now.

Osserc wondered, as he drew her to him, if she made use of the herbs the whores employed to ensure that a man's seed took no root. As far as he knew, he'd yet to sire a bastard, though it was known that some whores went away and did not return, suggesting that the herbs were not foolproof. He had no aversion on that count, though his father would be less than pleased. Still, Urusander knew of his son's trips down to the taverns – no doubt Hunn Raal kept his lord informed, perhaps in detail.

She was tentative at first, until her desire awoke to his measured caress, and much as he wanted to throw her down on the cloak and rut like a boar, he held himself back.

'There's an art to torturing women in bed, Osserc. You want to tease . . . like a lake's waves rolling on to the shore, with each wave reaching farther, only to slide back and away. You offer the flood, you see? And keep offering it, but not giving it, not until she begs to be drowned – and you'll know it by how she holds you, her clutching hands, her gasps. Only then do you take her.'

When at last he slid into her, she cried out.

He felt something give inside her and wondered what it was, and only when they were at last done, and he rolled away and saw the blood, did he comprehend. She knew nothing of herbs, and her beloved was a man kept at a distance, and what he longed for Osserc had just stolen. The poor fool was finished.

Lying on his back, staring up at scudding summer clouds, he wondered how he should feel about all of that. 'Renarr,' he finally said. 'If had known . . .'

'I am glad, milord, that it was you.'

He heard her hesitation halfway through her confession, and knew that she had almost voiced his name; but in the wake of what they had done a new fragility had arrived, and Osserc knew enough to say as little as possible. He did not want this peasant girl walking up to the keep, belly distended, and shouting out his name.

His father would take her in – if only to spite his son. Things would get complicated. Besides, he had told her as much, hadn't he? His future, the service and the sacrifices awaiting him? She understood well enough.

'I will not ride with you into the village,' she said.

He nodded, knowing she was up on one elbow and studying his face.

'I need to go back to the stream.'

'I know.'

'Alone.'

'If you think it best,' he replied, reaching down to find her hand. He squeezed it and then held it up to his lips. 'I will remember this day,' he said. 'When I ride the borderlands and grow old under the sun and stars.'

Her laugh was soft and, he realized after a moment, disbelieving. He looked across and met her eyes. She was smiling, and there was something both tender and sad in it. 'I think not, milord, although it is kind of you to say so. I was . . . clumsy. Unknowing. I fear you must be disappointed, although you hide it well.'

He sat up, still holding her hand. 'Renarr, I do not lie to make you feel better – I will not do that. When I say I will remember this day, I mean it, and above all, it is you that I will remember. Here, upon this cloak. To doubt me is to hurt me.'

Mute, she nodded, and he saw the glisten of tears in her eyes.

Suddenly she looked much younger. He studied her face. 'Renarr, when was your night of blood?'

'Almost two months past, milord.'

*Abyss take me! No wonder her beloved only yearned!* He climbed to his feet, reached for his shirt. 'Your lips are puffy, Renarr. Use the cold water of the stream to ease them. I fear my beard has scratched your chin.'

'I will pick berries and make more scratches.'

'Upon your face? Not too many, I hope.'

'A few, and on my knees, as if I had stumbled and fallen.'

He pulled on his leggings and reached for his armour. 'By your wit, Renarr, I had judged you older.'

'By my wit, milord, I am.'

'Name your father and mother.'

She blinked. 'My mother is dead. My father is Gurren.'

'The old smith? But he was married to Captain – Abyss below, *she* was your mother? Why did I not know you?'

'I have been away.'

'Where?'

'Yan Monastery, milord. In any case, I doubt you saw my mother much, and she died on the campaign against the Jheleck.'

'I know she did,' Osserc replied, buckling on his sword. 'Renarr, I thought you just a girl – a woman, I mean – from the village.'

'But I am.'

He stared at her. 'Your mother saved my father's life on the day of the assassins. She and Hunn Raal—'

'I know, milord, and I am thankful for that.'

'Thankful? She died.'

'She did her duty,' Renarr replied.

He looked away, ran both hands through his hair. 'I need to think,' he said.

'There is nothing,' she said. 'I too will remember this day. That is all we need, is it not?'

'And if you take my seed?'

'I will make no claims upon you, milord.' She paused and then added, 'Most of the stories I've heard about you, milord, come from my father—'

'Who hates us, and we do not blame him for that, Renarr – he should know that. He lost the woman he loved. My father still weeps to remember that day.'

'It is all right, milord. It was my father's unreasonable opinions of you that made me first curious, enough to see for myself. And, as I suspected, he is wrong about you.'

He thought to say more, but nothing came to him. She drew close and kissed him and then turned away. 'I will wait here until you are well gone, milord.'

Feeling helpless, Osserc left the ruined house. He collected up both horses and led them on to the rutted track.

He caught sight of the polished pebble in the grasses, hesitated, and then continued on.

Three paces later he turned round and went back. He picked it up and slipped it into the pouch at his belt.

Once back on the road, he mounted the warhorse, and – Neth trailing – they took the hillside at a canter.

*     *     *

Ahead on the track, just past the village, a flag was being raised at the Tithe Gate at the bottom of the hill, announcing Osserc's return. Seeing the banner climb skyward and then stream out in the wind pleased Osserc as he rode past the trader carts and the figures edged to one side of the road, standing with heads bowed. The flag's field was sky blue studded with gold stars, and so marked one of Vatha blood. A second pole alongside the familial one remained bare, as it had done ever since Urusander ordered his Legion to stand down.

Houseblades – veterans of the Legion one and all – were pushing people from the gateway as Osserc approached. He rode through without slowing, nodding at the salutes from the old soldiers. The way ahead was steep and Kyril was blowing hard by the time they reached the keep's High Gate.

He rode into the courtyard, hoping to see his father upon the steps – he would have been informed of his son's return – but only retainers

348

stood there. There had been a temptation, briefly entertained, to rein in at the Tithe Gate and order the Legion flag hoisted; but he had feared a refusal from the Houseblades. He imagined closed expressions looking up at him, and the sergeant telling him that only the Legion commander could order such a thing. Osserc's authority was fragile enough, a thin shell left untouched out of respect for Urusander. So he had dismissed the idea. But now he wished he had insisted; that second flag would surely have brought his father out to meet him.

It seemed that he ever chose to do the wrong thing, and that each time boldness offered itself up he turned away from it; and to ride past the veterans with stern regard and silent resolve now struck him as diffident, if not pathetic. Self-possession, when nothing more than a pose, bared a prickly hide over a host of failures and all confidence could sink away leaving no trace: to hide weakness behind bluster was to hide nothing at all. He carried himself as if all eyes were upon him, and they gauged with critical judgement that hovered on the edge of mockery; Osserc imagined words muttered behind his back, laughs stifled when faces were turned away. He had earned nothing in his young life, and the airs he held to, he grasped with desperation.

Reining in at the steps, scowling as the grooms rushed in, he dismounted. He saw Castellan Haradegar – a man only a year or two older than Osserc – standing near the doors. Quickly ascending the steps, Osserc met the man's eyes. 'Where is my father?'

'In his study, milord.'

Osserc had not yet eaten this day, but he knew his father forbade any food or drink anywhere near his precious scrolls. He hesitated. If he ate at once, then the import of his words would lose all vigour, but already a headache was building behind his eyes – he did not do well when hungry. Perhaps a quick bite first and then—

'He awaits you, milord,' Haradegar said.

'Yes. Inform the kitchens I will eat following my meeting with my father.'

'Of course, milord.'

Osserc strode inside. The lower floor was crowded with workers – masons and carpenters and their flit-eyed apprentices – and the air was filled with dust, the stone paving underfoot coated in sawdust and the crumbled plaster that was all that remained of the old friezes that had once adorned every wall. He was forced to step round men and women, their tools and the blocks of marble and beams of rare wood, and these obstacles only darkened his mood. When he reached the study, he thumped heavily on the door and entered without awaiting invitation.

His father was standing over his map table, but this scene lost its martial pretensions in the details, since he leaned over an array of fired clay tablets, and the clothing he wore was ink-stained and spotted with dried droplets of amber wax. Urusander was unshaven and his long hair, streaked with grey, hung down in greasy strands.

Osserc strode forward until he stood opposite his father, the broad table between them.

'You are in need of a bath,' Urusander said without looking up.

'I bring word from Hunn Raal, and Commander Calat Hustain.'

Urusander glanced up. 'Calat Hustain? You were in the Outer Reach? Why did Hunn Raal take you there?'

'We were visiting, Father. In the company of Kagamandra Tulas and Ilgast Rend, as well as Sharenas Ankhadu.'

Urusander was studying him. 'Then where is Raal? I think I need a word with him.'

'He rides in haste to Kharkanas, Father. There is dire news, which sent him to the Citadel, to audience with Mother Dark, and this same news sent me here, to you.'

Urusander's expression was severe and it seemed to age him. 'Out with it, then.'

'A new threat, Father. Invasion – from the Sea of Vitr.'

'Nothing comes from the Vitr.'

'Until now,' Osserc replied. 'Father, this was of such importance that Sharenas and Kagamandra both rode out across Glimmer Fate to the very shore of the Vitr to see for themselves. Hunn Raal carried the news to the Citadel. Kurald Galain is under threat. Again.'

Urusander looked down but said nothing.

Osserc stepped closer to the table, until he felt its worn edge against his legs. 'Mother Dark will have no choice,' he said. 'She will need the Legion once more. Sevegg, Risp and Serap have all ridden out, to carry word to the garrisons and to the decommissioned. Father, the flag must be raised—'

Urusander was studying the clay tablets, but at that he shook his head and said, 'I have no interest in doing so.'

'Then I will stand in your stead—'

'I – you are not ready.'

'In your eyes I will never be ready!'

Instead of replying to that accusation, instead of easing Osserc's deepest fear, Urusander stepped away from the table and walked to the window behind him.

Osserc glared at his father's back. He wanted to sweep the tablets from the tabletop, send them on to the floor to shatter into dust. For the briefest of instants, he wanted to drive a knife into his father, deep between the shoulder blades, straight down into the heart. But he did none of these things; he but stood, trembling against all that his father's silence told him. *Yes, son. You will never be ready.* 'What must I do to convince you?' he asked, hating the weakness in his tone.

Urusander folded his hands behind his back but did not turn from whatever he was looking at through the murky window panes. 'Give me one thought not made in haste, Osserc. Just one.' He glanced over a shoulder, momentarily, and there was grief in his eyes. 'And I will cling to it as if it were the Spar of Andii itself.'

Uncomprehending, Osserc shook his head. 'Will you keep your only son beneath the respect of everyone? Your own soldiers? Why? Why do that to me?'

'And if I make you commander of the Legion, you will have all the respect you so need?'

'Yes!'

Urusander had turned back to the window. He now reached up and rubbed a smudge on the frail glass. 'By title and the burden of responsibility, you will find all you yearn for? You will find this "respect" you've heard so much about, from old veterans and drunk fools; from the poets and what you think you see upon the wood panels so finely brushed into likenesses – from historians and other whores of glory?'

Osserc feared for his father's mind. He struggled to return Urusander to this world, where matters of import needed to be discussed. 'Father, listen to me. Mother Dark will summon you.'

'I imagine that she will.' But when he faced Osserc once more Urusander's eyes were grave and wounded. 'And in you, where there was weakness, there will be strength. And where there was strength, there will now be inflexible certainty. Doubts will drown, humility throat-cut and left face down in the mud, and on all sides they will salute you and hang upon your every word – which they must do, since you will hold their lives in your hands, Osserc. Not just your soldiers, but all of Kurald Galain. Every child, *every child* – do you comprehend any of this?'

'You think me afraid? I am not, Father.'

'I know, but I wish you were. Afraid. Terrified.'

'You would have me frozen as a hare beneath a hawk's shadow?'

'I would have you afraid, Osserc. I would see you afraid – here, before me in this moment. I would see you realize that fear, and yet take its vast weight upon your shoulders, and stand strong. Resolute. I would see command humble you.'

'Then, Father, I ask you. How will you ever see any of that if you do not give me command?'

'Still you do not understand, do you?'

'Because you offer, only to take away!'

'Is it only commanders who know fear? What of the crippled widower who can no longer support his family? Or the widow with too many children to feed? What of the lone wanderer who spends a night without shelter when the wolves are hunting? What of the broken man who must rise to face every morning when all love is dead and all hope is lost? Tell me, who does *not* live with fear?'

'Father, you give me nothing with these words. What fears have I faced, when you have kept me locked up here instead of riding with you and your soldiers?'

Urusander sighed. 'You will find a soldier's fear in your time, Osserc. I never doubted your courage with blade in hand and self-preservation the wager.'

Even a compliment from his father could sting in its utterance. Before he could muster a reply, however, his father continued. 'Osserc, why did you ever imagine that I would give you the Legion?'

The question struck like a blow against his chest. Osserc felt his knees weaken and he almost reeled. 'But – Hunn Raal said—'

Urusander's brows lifted. 'Hunn Raal? He's like a lame dog I can't keep from under my feet. He's an Issgin – of course he does nothing but sniff my heels for any scrap he can find. The Issgin yearn for a return to the court, and he's the closest of their brood to that and no doubt he imagines himself almost within reach of it. He rode to bring word to Mother Dark? He seeks an actual audience with her?' Urusander shook his head. 'The man is a drunk with a drunk's bloated self-image – Abyss knows, drunks think themselves clever, and measure the prowess of their wit by the genius of their rationalizations. Of course, the first fool they deceive is themselves. There will be no audience with Mother Dark. Not for Captain Hunn Raal.'

'But I am your son! Who else should inherit the Legion?'

'Inherit? Is Kurald Galain's only standing army a thing to be inherited? Like a keep, or a precious bauble? Is it a mine? A forge? A fine horse? A throne? Have you understood nothing? One cannot inherit the Legion – one must earn the right to the privilege of commanding it.'

'Then why didn't you prepare me for that? I could earn *nothing* here in this keep while the rest of you were out fighting! You have doomed me, damn you!'

Urusander leaned back at his son's tirade. Then he said, 'Because, son, for you I wanted something better.'

\*     \*     \*

Osserc did not even recognize the room he found. It was small, crammed full of rolled-up tapestries from the rooms above. The bare stone floor was littered with moth carcasses and the air was rank with the smell of mould. Locking the door he threw himself down on a musty heap piled up along one wall. Shudders took him as he wept. He hated his weakness: even rage unmanned him. He thought back to Renarr, and saw anew the look in her eyes – which had not been tenderness. It had been pity that he saw. Even now, he suspected, she was spinning the tale to her giggling friends.

He wrapped his arms about his folded-up legs and rested his forehead on his knees, still fighting the tears, but now they marked his shame, his helplessness. His father held to glory as a miser clutched the world's last coin. There was nothing here for Osserc; nothing for a son chained to childhood.

*He would seal me in wax. Place me upon the highest shelf in some dusty room. To lie there, like some preserved memory. My father remembers innocent days and yearns for a return to his own childhood. But as that cannot be, he would make me what he once was, and keep me there: Vatha Urusander before the wars.*

*I am his nostalgia. I am his selfishness made manifest.*

*I will leave here. Tonight. Tomorrow. Soon. I will leave and not return. Not return until I am ready, until I have made myself anew. Indeed, Father, I am to inherit nothing from you, nothing at all. Especially not your weakness.*

*I will set out. Seeking truths. Seeking my place, and when I return I shall blaze with triumph, with power. I shall be a man such as . . . as Anomander himself. You think me not clever, Father? But I am. You think me unwise? You are to blame for what wisdom I lack, but no matter. I shall find my own wisdom.*

*I shall leave Kurald Galain.*

*And ride alone into the world.*

To such bold claims, he saw in his mind his father's face, and that look of disappointment as the old man said, *'Alone, son? Weren't you listening? Your fears will run with you, like a pack of wolves howling to bring you down. The only true solitude, to any man, to any woman, to any thinking being, is death.'*

'I know that,' he whispered in reply, lifting his head and wiping at his cheeks. 'I know that. Let the wolves close in – I will kill them all, one by one, I will kill them all.'

His head pounded; he was hungry, but all he could manage was to lie down upon the rolls of cloth and close his eyes. Pain had its own teeth, sharp and eager, and they sank deep into him. Bite by bite, they could tear him away – they were welcome to all that was lying here – until nothing was left.

The shell was gone, shattered by an old man who had tried to convince him that a cell was a palace, and imprisonment a gift. Even Hunn Raal had lied to him. Hunn Raal, an object of contempt to the man whose very life he had saved. Was it any wonder the fool drank to excess?

*But he's been very busy, Father. Speaking in your name. That part was easy, since all he had to fill was silence. You do not even know it, but he has your future all mapped out. You've surrendered all choice, dear Father.*

*I am glad you didn't raise the flag. The Legion is no longer yours, although you do not yet know that, either. It will march in your name, however. That it will do.*

*Changes are coming, coming to us all.*

*     *     *

Over the next two days Osserc avoided his father, taking his meals in his chambers. He gathered together all that he would need, selecting two swords, including a hundred-year-old Iralltan blade – that forge, rival to the Hust, had been destroyed by the Forulkan, the family slaughtered and the keep fired. The mines had been later taken over in yet another example of Henarald's acquisitive greed. The weapon had been a gift from Hunn Raal, and it was finely made, bearing an elegance of line that no Hust weapon could match. Osserc had never used it when sparring, although his practice weapon was a perfect match in balance, reach and weight. His other sword was from a secondary family forge, under the ownership of the Hust but tasked with making weapons for Urusander's Legion. It was plain but serviceable, and held its edge well, although twice the bars of the hilt had been replaced after cracking round the grip.

Many veterans claimed that the Hust had deliberately supplied inferior weapons to Urusander's Legion, but this was the subject of guarded mutterings in the barracks, since Lord Urusander, upon hearing that opinion, had revealed a rare loss of temper, publicly dressing down the officer who had voiced the suspicion.

Osserc believed the soldiers, although apart from the bars, his Legion sword bore no flaws in workmanship. The iron was free of tin pits and the blade was impressively true.

In addition to these weapons, he selected a hunting knife, a dagger and three lances. The armour he chose was not the full dress set: silver filigree invited a thief's eye and besides, it was too heavy to suit his fighting style. Instead, he selected a thick but supple leather hauberk, studded over the thighs to pull its weight down. Stained black, it was reinforced beneath the leather on the shoulders and the back of the neck with iron strips bound to the quilting of the inner layer. The heavily studded sleeves ended at his elbows where they were joined by thick straps to his vambraces, which were of matching black leather but banded in bared iron. Over all of this he wore a grey cloak, since the leather of his armour did not fare well under the harsh sun.

The helm he chose was a light skullcap of blued iron with a chain camail.

At two bells past midnight on the third night, he carried his gear down to the stables, making use of side passages to avoid the main rooms where the occasional guard wandered. He had done as Hunn Raal had asked of him. He had delivered the news of the Vitr. His responsibilities were at an end, and whatever might now happen in Kurald Galain, he would play no part in it. In fact, he had ceased to care.

He reached the stables undiscovered, and once there he set about saddling his two horses. They had been reshoed since his return and he took a moment to examine the work. Satisfied, he loaded his camp gear on to Neth's broad back, including two of the lances and the Legion sword. From this moment forward, he would wear the Iralltan blade.

He led both mounts outside and swung on to his warhorse. Both animals were restless as he rode across the courtyard. At the gate two guards emerged.

'Late to be riding, milord,' one said.

In the gloom Osserc could not recognize the man, although his voice was vaguely familiar. 'Just open the gate,' he said.

The men complied and moments later Osserc rode through and out on to the track. For a change, the route down into the town was unobstructed. Once among the low buildings he eased Kyril into a slow trot. At one point he thought he heard running feet off to his left, crossing an alley, but when he turned he saw little more than a dark shape, quickly vanishing from sight.

He thought nothing of it until, upon reaching the last buildings on the north edge of the settlement, he found a figure standing in the lane before him. Curious, Osserc reined in.

'You have business with me?' he asked.

There was some light bleeding out from a house on one side, enough for Osserc to see that it was a man who was blocking his path. Young, heavy-set, breathing hard from his run. It seemed his hands were stained and they hung half curled at his sides.

'She told me everything,' the man said. 'It took a while, but she told me everything.' He stepped forward. 'Y'think I couldn't see? Couldn't tell that she'd changed? Y'think I'm blind? I been waitin' for you, sir. Keepin' an eye on the road. I knew if you lit out, it'd be in the dark.'

Osserc dismounted. He approached the man, and saw now, clearly, the welts and cuts on the man's knuckles, the kind made by someone's teeth.

'You shouldn't of done that, sir. She was sweet. She was pure.'

As Osserc continued advancing, the man's eyes widened slightly, his nostrils flaring. When he began tugging free his knife Osserc leapt forward. He blocked the draw and closed one hand tightly on the wrist, forcing it down. His other hand found the man's throat. He squeezed hard and continued squeezing, even as the man reached up and fought to pull free.

355

'You beat her?' Osserc asked. 'That sweet, pure woman?'

The eyes before him were bulging, the face darkening. Osserc drew out the man's knife and flung it away. The man's legs gave out before him and his weight yanked at Osserc's grip, so he brought up his other hand to join the first one. He saw the man's tongue protrude, strangely black and thick.

His struggles weakened, and then ceased entirely.

Osserc studied the lifeless eyes. He was not sure if he had intended to kill the fool. But it was done now. He released his grip and watched as the body crumpled on to the dirt track.

*I killed someone. Not in battle – no, it was in battle. Well, close enough. He went for his knife. He came to me, thinking to stab me. To murder me. And he beat Renarr – I saw the proof of that. He beat her like a coward. Might be he killed her – would I have heard? I stayed in my room, stayed away from the taverns. I know nothing of what's happened in town.*

*He beat her to death, but justice was mine, mine to deliver.*

He found himself back on his horse, riding clear of Neret Sorr, winding tracks, low stone walls and farmhouses before him. He was trembling and his left hand ached.

He had been counted strong, even by the soldiers he'd sparred with. And he had, with one hand, just crushed a man's throat. A grip that had seemed filled with rage, with almost mindless fury – if only it had blinded him; if only he'd not been able to see the man's face, his eyes, his open mouth and the jutting tongue. Somehow, even that ghastly mask had simply made him squeeze harder.

Osserc could not understand what had happened, how any of this had happened. He had meant to ride away unseen by anyone, setting forth on a new life. Instead, in his wake they would find a dead man, strangled, a parting gift of horror from the Lord's son.

Thoughts of his father struck him then, like blows to the body that left him sickened. He urged Kyril into a fast canter, fighting to stifle a moan.

The night, so vast around him, seemed to mock him with its indifference. The world held no regard for his feelings, his fears; the mad cavort of all the things filling his head. It cared nothing for the ache in his left hand and how it felt as if it still grasped that throat – the throat with its hard muscles that slowly surrendered to the ever-tightening pressure of his grip, and the way the windpipe finally crumpled into something soft and ringed that moved too easily, too loosely. All these sensations roiled in his fingers, in the flattened throb of his palm, and though he dared not look down, he knew he would see murder's own stain – a stain invisible to everyone else but unmistakable to his own eyes.

356

Hunched over, he rode on. And there came then a bleak thought, repeating in his mind amidst the thumping drums of horse hoofs.

*The darkness is not enough.*

       \*      \*      \*

Beneath bright morning light, Serap rode into Neret Sorr from the south track. Once on the high street, she swung her horse left and made for the keep road. But the way ahead was blocked by a flat-bed wagon, the ox rigged to it, and a small crowd. Three of the town's constabulary were there, and Serap saw two young men approach from a lane opposite, carrying a body between them on a canvas tarp. They clutched the corners but kept losing their grip. Though other men walked with them none made a move to help.

Reining in, Serap looked to the nearest constable and saw that the man was studying her. After a moment he stepped forward.

'Lieutenant Serap.'

She studied him. 'Ex-Legion, yes? Ninth Company.'

'Sergeant Yeld, sir. I was on Sharenas's staff.'

'What has happened here?'

'Murder last night, sir. A local got strangled.'

'If you've a mind to hunt down the killer,' she said, 'I have some experience at that. Has he run or he is holed up somewhere?'

All at once the sergeant looked uncomfortable. 'Not sure, sir. No witnesses.'

'Is there a seer in town?'

'Old Stillhap up at the keep, sir. We haven't sent for him yet.'

Serap dismounted. Her back was sore. She'd ridden hard from Kharkanas, bearing the latest news along with Hunn Raal's usual exhortations to ensure that she spoke directly with Lord Urusander. Although the news she had been instructed to give him made her uneasy, since much of it was close to a lie, she was now committed. Still, a minor delay here in town might give her time to compose her thoughts, quell her misgivings, before seeing Urusander. 'I will examine the body,' she said, walking over to where the two men had finally reached the wagon with their burden.

The sergeant joined her. 'Mason's apprentice, though his master tells us he ain't been showing for work up at the keep the past two days, and no one recalls seeing him in that time either. He was up to something, I suppose.'

The body was on the bed now and Serap climbed aboard the wagon. She drew the canvas to one side, revealing the corpse.

Yeld grunted. 'Ugly way to die, sir.'

'Not a rope or garrotte.'

'No sir. Was hands that done that.'

'Not hands, sergeant. One hand.'

Mutters sounded from the crowd now gathered round.

Serap straightened. 'Takes a strong man to do that. I see a knife sheath at his belt but no knife.'

'Found a dozen paces away, sir,' said Yeld.

'Blood on it?'

'No. But look at his hands – seems he fought back.'

'Anyone with a bruised face in this mob?' Serap asked with a half-smile as she scanned the townsfolk. 'No,' she added. 'That would be too easy.'

Someone spoke from the crowd. 'Anyone seen Renarr?'

'Who's Renarr?' Serap asked.

'The woman he was courting,' Yeld replied. 'From what I gather.'

'Millick was courtin' and plannin' t'marry,' someone else said.

'Where does this Renarr live?'

Yeld pointed to a solid stone house at the western end of the high street, close to the Tithe Gate.

'Send anyone over there yet?'

'Sir, she's Gurren's daughter. Gurren was married to Captain Shellas.'

'And?'

'And Gurren's got no love for Legion. Or ex-Legion. I doubt we could get in the door.'

'But she needs to be told, sergeant. Out of decency, she needs to know.'

'I expect she knows, sir. It's been on everyone's tongue all morning, this whole mess.'

Serap returned to her horse. She gestured Yeld close and kept her voice low as she said, 'Was this Gurren's work? Did the boy – Millick – rape his daughter, you think? Knock her up?'

Yeld clawed at his beard, squinting at the ground. 'Gurren's got a temper. And he used to be a smith – still has a hand in, so long as it ain't Vatha or Legion work. But sir, no one wants to lose a smith. This town's only got the one who ain't working day and night for Lord Urusander. I admit, living here now, I'm pretty reluctant to stir up a wasp nest—'

'A mason's apprentice was murdered in the street, sergeant.'

'And no one's looking at Old Smith Gurren. That's the problem.'

'What do you mean?'

'Meaning I heard from one of last night's High Gate guards that Osserc rode out two bells past midnight, trailing a spare mount and kitted for a journey. He ain't come back, and it gets worse.'

'How?'

'Clean horse tracks on the lane up to and then around the body. Freshly shoed, just like Osserc's mounts were. Osserc's probably the

358

strongest man I know, lieutenant. Take all that and add to rumours from a few days ago, about Renarr coming back late from the stream – same track as Osserc rode in on earlier that morning . . . so you see, right now there's rumours and just rumours and still plenty of mysteries. It's a wasp nest no matter which side we kick at it.'

Serap cursed under her breath. 'That gate guard been talking?'

'Just to me.'

'And those horse tracks?'

'I took note, since I was put in mind of Urusander's boy riding out. But I don't think anyone else noticed. Get plenty of riding back and forth, and I obscured the path that went round the body. Scuffed it up, I mean.'

'I know what you meant,' she replied, irritated with the detail. 'Has Lord Urusander been informed of any of this?'

'Not yet, sir. I was on my way when you arrived.'

'You could clear Gurren by making him put his left hand round the dead man's neck – see if the imprint fits.'

'Yes, sir, I could, though the body's starting to swell up some.'

'But if you did and Gurren was cleared of suspicion, you'd be left with one choice—'

'Yes, sir, and it's a rumour already out here. Going after Gurren would make it worse, if you see what I mean. Worse for Lord Urusander. Worse for the Legion.'

'You've thought this through, Yeld.'

The sergeant shrugged. 'We can't make it go away, sir, but we can let it rust.'

Serap swung into the saddle. 'I will report all this to Lord Urusander.'

'All of it?'

'All that he needs to hear. There's been a murder. No witnesses and no suspects. The rest is just base speculation. The loss of a mason's apprentice will be a hardship on the family, and no doubt the mason, too, and we both know that the commander will do what's necessary to ease their loss.'

The sergeant nodded up at her. 'Very good, lieutenant. Oh, and welcome.'

She eyed him jadedly at that, but he seemed sincere. She edged her horse past the wagon and then through the crowd. The mood around her wasn't yet ugly, which was something. She did not envy Yeld and his squad.

Riding on, she drew opposite Gurren's stone house and reined in. She eyed the shuttered windows, and then the faint wisps of smoke rising from the chimney. Dismounting, Serap left her horse standing on the track and made her way to the front door. She thumped on the blackwood.

359

There was no response.

Serap waited for a time and then made her way round to the back yard. Pushing through the gate, she saw Gurren hunched over the forge, stirring the coals.

She approached, but from one side, to give him the opportunity to see her. He offered up a single glance then returned to his work.

'Old Smith,' she said. 'We've not met, but I know of you and, of course, of your wife. You have my deepest sympathies.'

He made no reply.

'Gurren, where is your daughter?'

'In the house.'

'She does not come to the door.'

'Ain't surprised.'

'Why?'

He faced her. He was not as old as his local title suggested, but he was bowed; the muscles from a lifetime with hammer and tongs were still visible but the skin around them was slack, as if he had been ill for a long time. The watery grey eyes were like broken glass. He spat yellow mucus on to the ground and said, 'Night before last she barely made it back to the door, beaten half t'death. Witch Hale comes over and works on her, and comes out and tells me. Broken jaw, broken cheekbone; won't see good outa her left eye ever again.'

'Someone killed the man who did that, Gurren.'

'I know. Hale got the girl to talk.'

'What did she say?'

Gurren's face was impossibly flat, impossibly empty of all expression. 'From what Hale could make out, Urusander's lad plucked her, but tenderly. But Millick saw enough to guess and took the rest out on her. And now Millick's dead, choked in North Lane last night, and Osserc's gone.'

'That's right,' Serap said, seeing no need to dissemble. 'Some rumours are going around that you might have been the one doing the killing.'

Gurren nodded. 'I set those out, lieutenant.'

'To muddy the trail.'

He eyed her, and then said, 'I been holding a long hate for your lord, and your Legion that saw my wife killed, taken from me and Renarr.'

She nodded. 'Poets have written of Urusander's grief over your wife's death.'

'Poets can go fuck themselves.'

'Well . . .'

'I'm dying,' Gurren said. 'Witch Hale says it's too late. Had my doubts about Millick all along, but she was set on him, you see, and with me leaving and all . . .'

'I'm sorry how it turned out—'

'I'd be a lot sorrier,' he snapped, 'leavin' her to a lifetime of beatings and maybe worse. So it's like this. I owe Osserc and if I could, why, I'd kneel before him, take that murdering hand of his, and kiss it.'

Serap stared, struck silent.

Gurren turned back to the forge. 'Tell your lord this, lieutenant. Between us, now, the water is clear.'

'I will tell him,' she whispered.

'But I want my daughter taken care of.'

She nodded. 'I will swear to that.'

He shot her a hard look. 'Legion vow?'

'Legion vow, Gurren.'

The man suddenly smiled, and years vanished from him, despite the sickness behind his eyes. 'I'll be seeing my wife soon. There's nothing like waiting, when the waiting's about to end. Go on with you, then. I got me some chains to melt down for the nailmonger, and this fire ain't nearly hot enough yet.'

*　　*　　*

'Commander, it is good to see you again.'

Vatha Urusander seemed to study her for a moment before gesturing her to sit. They were in the room Hunn Raal called the Vault. Shelves lined all the walls, reaching to the ceiling. Scrolls, bound books, manuscripts and clay tablets bowed every shelf. A single work table dominated the room. Two chairs were pushed up against it, while the lower, padded chairs they now occupied stood like sentinels to either side of the low doorway.

The positioning was awkward in that Serap could not face Urusander unless she perched sideways on the seat. As expected, the commander seemed indifferent to this detail. There was an air of distraction about him that Serap had seen each time she had visited over the past two years, and she gauged it as the look of a man slowly losing himself. It pained her.

'How are Sevegg and Risp?' Urusander asked.

Startled, Serap shrugged. 'They fare well, sir. Busy.'

'Busy with what?'

'Sir, I have news from Kharkanas.'

He glanced away, as if to study the archives lining the shelves opposite. 'Hunn Raal has sent you.'

'Yes sir.'

'And no doubt Risp and Sevegg are running horses into the ground to deliver word to the garrisons.'

'Sir, there is need, once again, for the Legion. There is need for you.'

'There will be no invasion from the Sea of Vitr. The very idea is ridiculous.' He met her eyes and his gaze was sharp and hard. 'Hunn

361

Raal would have the realm stirred in panic. He sows fear with the sole aim of resurrecting the Legion – not to meet this imagined threat, but to coerce the highborn, Draconus and ultimately Mother Dark. He still bears the wound of our dismissal.'

'I will not lie, sir, he does bear that wound. We all do.'

'Old soldiers cannot fit in a peaceful world,' Urusander said. 'They feel like ghosts and they hunger for the zeal of life, but the only life they know is one of violence. War is a drug to them, one they cannot do without. And for many others, to see an old soldier is to know of sacrifices they never made, and to feel an obligation they come to resent, and so they would rather not see that old soldier. They would rather forget. For yet others, Serap, an old soldier reminds them of their own losses, and the grief stings anew. It is right that we go away, but more than that, it is right that we embrace silence and solitude. We have devoured horror and now we are as ghosts, because we stand next to death and we cannot leave its side.'

Serap stared at her commander. His words, delivered leaden as pronouncements, felt cold inside her now, an unwelcome gift filled with unwelcome truths. 'Sir, an Azathanai emerged from the Sea of Vitr, a woman. She was found by a Warden and escorted through Glimmer Fate. That Warden named her T'riss. Monks of Yan Monastery intercepted them and commandeered the protection of the Azathanai. They brought her to their Hold. This proved a grave error. Sir, the woman resurrected the long-dead river god worshipped by the Yan and the Yedan. She then marched, in the fearful company of monks, to Kharkanas. Upon entering the city she raised the river in flood. Water dripped from stone to the very door of Mother Dark's Chamber of Night.'

'A moment,' cut in Urusander. 'You describe an assault upon Mother Dark.'

'I do, sir. There were casualties.'

'Who?'

'The High Priestess Syntara—'

'She is dead?'

'No. In the Chamber of Night T'riss assailed the High Priestess and left her . . . sullied, in Mother Dark's eyes. She was forced to flee and now seeks sanctuary with the Legion—'

'Hold!' Urusander rose suddenly. 'What you say makes no sense. Mother Dark is not cruel. She would not cast out her own High Priestess! What you describe is madness!'

'Perhaps I misspoke,' Serap said. 'We cannot know for certain what occurred in the Chamber of Night, in the moment of confrontation between the Azathanai and Mother Dark. Even Lord Anomander was late in arriving. But Syntara fled the chamber. She sought out Hunn

Raal – sir, the High Priestess is changed, manifestly changed. It may be that what she now possesses – and what Mother Dark's servants proclaim – is indeed a curse. But perhaps it is the very opposite. It may in truth be a gift. Sir, she is coming here, to you—'

'And you imagine I will grant her sanctuary – from Mother Dark? Have you all lost your minds?'

'Sir, she comes to you, not as the commander of the Legion, but as a scholar, as one who has delved the histories. She comes begging for your knowledge. What is this that she now holds within herself? Is it a curse as her rivals say, or is it a gift?'

'Where is the Azathanai now?'

'Banished by Mother Dark.'

'Has Draconus returned from the west?'

Serap blinked. 'No, he has not yet returned, not even to Dracons Hold, where awaits the army he has raised.'

'Army? Don't be absurd – the Consort seeks consolidation, lest any highborn take advantage of perceived weakness. He knows how precarious his position is, and how resented he is as well. Do you think I am unable to see through Hunn Raal's incessant reports? No, Serap, and I sense Hunn Raal's subtle twisting of all that you tell me here.'

The coldness inside her worsened and she had to struggle not to drop her eyes from his unwavering regard. 'Sir, there is no twisting to the truth that the Deniers are awakened to their old faith. That the ancient river god has summoned its worshippers, and indeed has made both the Yan and the Yedan kneel to its suzerainty. The cult of Mother Dark is under threat. Kharkanas, upon the banks of Dorssan Ryl, is in danger of inundation. The old temple in the very heart of the Citadel has been usurped. If all this is not alarming enough, sir, we have reports – sketchy ones, to be true – of demons upon the shore of the Sea of Vitr. Captains Sharenas and Kagamandra Tulas are even now returning from the Sea of Vitr, and they ride not for the forts of the Wardens – they ride here, sir, to you.'

Urusander had been standing, his hands upon the back of the chair he had been sitting in earlier, through all that Serap recounted. When she finished she saw the knuckles of his hands bloom white, and then, in a blur, the chair was sent across the small room. It collided with the heavy table and broke apart as if struck by a siege stone. The sound of the impact, the shattering and splintering of wood, hung in the air.

Serap felt driven back into her seat by the ferocity of Urusander's fury. Struck silent, she made no move, not wanting to draw his attention in any way.

He was staring at the wreckage he had made. Without looking at her, he spoke in a low tone, 'What else?'

She fought to speak evenly. 'Sir, there are rumours. Deniers among

363

the Hust Legion. Deniers among the Wardens of the Outer Reach. Deniers among the Borderswords. Even among the highborn. All who refuse the cult of Mother Dark. We face a religious war, sir, and we are compromised on all sides. We cannot even be sure if all this was not long in planning, from the rise of the Azathanai to the rebirth of the river god. What is undeniable is this: Mother Dark is weakened, and neither Draconus nor Anomander and his brothers nor even all the remaining – loyal – highborn and their Houseblades will be enough – not against a peasant uprising in the countryside, an uprising bolstered by the Hust, the Wardens and the Borderswords.'

'I do not want this,' Urusander whispered.

'There is a way through this, sir.'

'I am done with it, all of it.' He glared at her. '*I do not want this!*'

Serap rose. 'Commander, we both know well Captain Hunn Raal's ambitions, and so we must always view his zeal with caution. But he is no fool and his loyalty to you is absolute. We are not as unprepared as you might fear.'

'I know why he sent you,' Urusander said, turning away. 'Not Risp, with her bloodlust. Not Sevegg, who can't think past her crotch.'

'Kurald Galain needs you, sir. Kurald Galain needs the Legion. However, I am neither blind nor deaf. Name a successor to the command and—'

Urusander snorted, but it was a bitter sound, and then he said, 'There is no one.'

'Sir, it is as you have said many times: you have done your duty. You have found a new life, with new interests, and they are yours by right—'

'Abyss knows they are that!'

'Sir—'

'I know Hunn Raal thinks me unmanned. He fears I have lost the necessary edge, that I am dulled by inactivity.'

'He does not discuss his fears with me, sir. If he did, I would tell him, in no uncertain terms, that he is wrong.'

'Save the flattery, Serap. He might well be right. I have hidden myself away here. I sought to make a new . . . a new . . . setting. For my – for me and my son. The Legion is behind me, where I left it, and there I wanted it to stay.'

'Sir, about your son—'

'He is gone. We argued . . .' Urusander shook his head. 'He is gone.'

'It may be, sir, that you have underestimated him.'

'I have made mistakes.'

'I have a tale to tell you, then, about Osserc. About your son.'

He waved a dismissive hand. 'Not now. You tell me there is a way through this.' He faced her. 'The highborn are not my enemy. I will not be the deliverer of civil war to Kurald Galain.'

'We can win over the loyal highborn, sir.'

Urusander's sneer was ugly. 'By turning on Draconus.'

'He is no friend of yours.'

'He is the man Mother Dark loves.'

'I doubt that, else she would marry him.'

'If she did the highborn would surely rise and where would that put us? The Legion will defend Mother Dark. If this means defending Draconus too, then so be it. Thus: civil war.'

'This must be the reason, then,' said Serap, 'why she does not marry him.'

'Probably,' Urusander growled. He bent down and picked up the back of the shattered chair. Fragments of the arms hung from it. 'Wedding gift,' he muttered, 'these.'

'They will accept a husband for Mother Dark, sir, but not from among their own. Someone from the outside, who curries no favours, who owes not one among them and would remain immune to their advances.'

'Ridiculous.'

'Mother Dark is not blind to expedience, sir. And if I may be so bold, neither are you. We stand in service to Mother Dark. We did so once, and now we shall do so again.'

He let the chair-back fragment fall to the floor, and then eyed her. 'You say we are not unprepared.'

'No sir, we are not.'

'I must speak with Mother Dark, before I do anything else.'

'Sir, forgive me, but there may not be time. That said, sir, I am at your disposal.'

'I was going to send you after my son.'

'I think it best we let him alone. For a time.'

'What do you mean?'

'The tale I spoke of earlier, sir. Will you hear it now?'

He strode to the doorway. 'Walk with me, Serap. The air is too close in here and I need the feel of light upon my face.'

'Of course, sir.'

'Speak to me, then, of my son.'

\*       \*       \*

The sound of many horses reached Gurren as he was shovelling coal, and upon hearing the mounts drawing up on the street in front of his house, he dropped the shovel, dusted his blackened hands, and made his way towards the side passage.

He was halfway along when he saw the soldiers, at least a dozen, and among them two Legion healers. Coming to the corner he saw that Witch Hale had emerged from the house and stood blocking the front door. Gurren pushed between a pair of soldiers. One of the healers moved close to Hale and the two began talking.

An officer spoke to Gurren. 'Old Smith, forgive us this intrusion—'

'I might,' he said, 'or I might not.'

'Lord Urusander sent us, sir—'

'Don't "sir" me.'

'My apologies. I did not mean to imply rank, only respect.' Gurren's eyes narrowed. The officer went on. 'Your daughter has suffered injuries.'

'Witch Hale's seen to them.'

'Lord Urusander holds the utmost regard for Witch Hale,' the officer replied. 'But our Legion healers are trained in the mending of bones and the purging of infection. Cutter Aras, who speaks with the witch, apprenticed under Ilgast Rend. They have discovered sorceries—'

'As you say,' Gurren interrupted, and then he moved past the officer, walking over to where stood Hale and Aras. Ignoring the Legion cutter, Gurren edged close to Hale. 'You can tell 'em to all go away, witch.'

The woman shook her head. 'You stubborn whorespawn, Gurren. You ain't been listening. This is *Denul* he's talking about here. If Ilgast Rend had made it to your wife before her last blessed breath, she'd still be alive. The cutter says he can mend the broken bones and even save her eye. The cutter can give her back her future, Gurren, so wipe that miserable scowl off your face and let 'em inside.'

Gurren stepped back. Numb, he nodded at Aras. The man quickly slipped past, followed by the second Legion healer.

Witch Hale said, 'And listen to me. Your rotted lungs – might be Aras can—'

'No. I'm going to my wife.'

'And you'll just up and leave Renarr all alone?'

'She's known it was coming. My girl's got protection now. Legion protection. I'm going to my wife.'

'Town needs a smith—'

'I'm going to my wife.'

Snarling something Gurren couldn't make out, Witch Hale went back into the house.

Gurren found he was wiping his hands over and over again, but all he managed was to smear them evenly with sweaty coal dust. With his mind he felt inside his body for the places of sickness. They sat like empty absences in his chest, things that felt nothing even as they sickened everything around them. He saw them as lumps of coal, and the blood he coughed up showed the black from those lumps. Those numb gifts were carrying him to Shellas. He loved them dearly.

Renarr would grieve. That had been the worst part in all of this. Grieving and alone, their little girl. He looked over at all the soldiers, wondering why they had all come down just to deliver a pair of healers. He saw how they had ranged out, watchful – but not watching Gurren or the house; instead, they faced outwards, and something about them made him shiver.

They would take care of their little girl, and might be Shellas would be happy with that, with them being Legion and all. She could rest easy and look kindly on him, and might be she'd step forward after watching him crawling towards her for so long, long enough to confirm that his love for her had never died – she'd step forward and lift him up, and reach into his chest, and pull out those black lumps of grief. He'd watch her throw them away, so that he could breathe again, without coughing, without feeling the horrible tightness.

*Heal me, my love, as only you can.*

Another two riders were coming down from the keep. Gurren squinted. The Lord himself, and at his side that woman from the morning. They cantered through the Tithe Gate, pausing there for the Lord to issue some orders, and then rode on to draw up within the rough semicircle made by the soldiers.

Urusander's grey-blue eyes were fixed on Gurren, and the old man saw in them raw pain which was what he always saw in them, which was why he could never meet them for long. And he remembered how sick that weakness had made him feel. Urusander could not have loved Shellas the way Gurren did. Urusander had no right to weep for her death; he had no right to take from Gurren his own pain.

The Lord dismounted and walked straight to him. 'Gurren—'

But Gurren pointed at Serap. 'She made a Legion vow.'

'I know,' Urusander replied.

'I bless your son,' Gurren said, feeling his face set stubbornly – and all at once he could meet Urusander's eyes, and feel nothing. 'I bless him, sir, and nothing you ever say will change that.'

If there was anguish in the commander's eyes before, it was as nothing to what Gurren saw in them now. But still he felt nothing, and was astonished when it was Urusander who broke the gaze.

'She will be taken care of,' the Lord said then.

'I know. It was promised.'

'Will you come to the keep, Gurren?'

'What? What for?'

'I want you both under my roof. I want your daughter to find you there, with her, when she mends.'

'I got work to do here.'

'I will release one of the smiths to stand in your stead.'

'For how long?'

'For as long as needed.'

'Until I die? Has to be until I die, sir, and afterwards, too. Town needs a smith, more than you do.'

'If you would keep an eye on the work going on at the keep, Gurren, then we have a deal.'

'I can do that. Until I get too sick. And don't say nothing about your healers working on me.'

'I wouldn't do that,' was Urusander's soft reply.

Gurren jerked a nod.

'We will send a wagon down for you and your daughter.'

'Want some of my tools, too. The best ones.'

'Of course. As many trips as needed.'

'When I'm gone then, sir, what of my girl? Back to this empty house?'

'If you would permit it, Gurren, I would formally adopt her.'

'You would, would you?' Gurren glanced away, studied the small crowd of townsfolk who'd been drawn to the commotion. 'She's not a girl any more, though. She's a woman and that's how she needs to be treated. You don't call her "daughter" or nothing either. She's our daughter – me and Shellas made her.'

'I know,' replied Urusander.

Gurren nodded.

'Gurren,' said Urusander, louder, more formal, 'how is the water between us?'

Gurren met the man's eyes and was surprised to see the anguish gone, the eyes now filling with warmth. He nodded again. 'The water is clear, Lord.'

\*　　　\*　　　\*

Serap held back. She saw Lord Urusander transformed; she saw the commander she had always known. All indecisiveness had vanished. There were things to be done and, at last, orders to be issued. Her only regret was Osserc's absence. She imagined that he had fled after murdering Millick; fled thinking he was now an outlaw and almost certainly disowned by his father for the crime. The boy did not understand his father at all. But then, that baffled regard was mutual.

How could it be otherwise, with so much mud in the water between them? Mud and swirling currents, the endless, helpless stirring of silts so that nothing could ever come to rest.

But on this day, she had seen a dying old man and a heartbroken, guilt-ridden commander stand face to face, and make peace with each other.

They walked now, as would old friends, up to the house, and then disappeared inside.

*Mother Dark, you have found a worthy husband here. A most worthy husband.*

When she swung round to return to her horse, she looked up and saw, whipping hard in the breeze, the Legion's banner, high above the gatehouse.

It was done.

Urusander's Legion had returned to Kurald Galain.

Against the bright blue, cloudless sky, the banner was like a golden blade, torn from the sun itself. She squinted at it. Painters called that colour *liossan*.

*  *  *

In the wake of terrible fever, in a strange, warm stillness that filled her being, Renarr opened her eyes. She saw her father, and with him strangers. The twisted, damaged vision that had claimed her left eye was gone now, and everything seemed impossibly clear. Even the pain of her swollen face was fast fading.

Her father leaned closer. 'Little girl,' he said, his eyes wet. 'Do you see who's here? It's Lord Urusander himself.'

Her gaze slipped past her father, to the man standing near, and in the Lord's face she saw the son. Renarr looked away.

'Changes, little girl,' said Gurren, in a tone she'd never before heard from him. 'In your whole world, Renarr. Changes, blessed changes.'

There was no denying that. Millick was dead. The man she loved was dead, murdered by the Lord's son. And now here stood the Lord, and her father babbling about how they were going to live in the Great House, and how she would be taken care of from now on, and the Lord was smiling and nodding, and all she could think about was Millick, to whom she had told everything because he saw that she wasn't the same any more – Millick, weeping and drunk and feebly trying to put her face back together, on his knees beside her telling her how his cousins had got the story of her confession out of him after a cask of ale, and how they laughed at him and called her a whore to his face, until he was driven to madness. Blind rage, he kept saying, trying to explain himself, how his fists just lashed out unseeing when she came upon him beating Eldin and Orult behind the house, how he punched not knowing whom he punched.

And how Witch Hale got her story all wrong, because Millick had gone in hiding from his cousins and their friends, and Renarr got fevered and had to crawl home in the middle of the night, and Renarr's jaw was too swollen and she couldn't get the right words past her broken mouth.

*Changes.* It was a day of changes all right.

# THIRTEEN

K ADASPALA WAS NOT A BELIEVER IN GODS, BUT HE KNEW THAT BELIEF could create them. And once made, they bred in kind. He had seen places where discord thrived, where violence spun roots through soil and flesh both, and the only propitiation left to those who dwelt there was the spilling of yet more blood. These were venal gods, the vicious spawn of a stew of wretched emotions and desires. There was no master and no slave: god and mortal fed on each other, like lovers sharing a vile fetish.

He knew that there was power in emotion, and that it could spill out to soak the ground, to stain stone and twist wood; that it could poison children and so renew the malign cycle, generation upon generation. Such people made of their home a god's lap, and they curled tight within its comforting, familiar confines.

Kadaspala wanted none of it, and yet he was never as immune as he would have liked: even the pronouncement that he stood outside such things was itself an illusion. He was not a believer in gods, but he had his own. They came to him in the simplest of all forms, eschewing even shape and, at times, substance itself. They came to him in a flood, with every moment – indeed, even in his sleep and the dream worlds that haunted it. They howled. They whispered. They caressed. Sometimes, they lied.

His gods were colours, but he knew them not. They bore heady emotions and before them, in moments of weakness or vulnerability, he would reel, or cry out, seeking to turn away. But their calls would bring him back, helpless, a soul on its knees. At times he could taste them, or feel their heat upon his skin. At times he could smell them, redolent

370

with promise and quick to steal from his memories, and so claim those memories for their own. So abject had his worship become that he now saw himself in colours – the landscape of his mind, the surge and ebb of emotions, the meaningless cascades behind the lids of his eyes when shut against the outside world; he knew the blues, purples, greens and reds of his blood; he knew the flushed pink of his bones, with their carmine cores; he knew the sunset hues of his muscles, the silvered lakes and fungal mottling of his organs. He saw flowers in human skin and could smell their perfumes, or, at times, the musty readiness of desire – that yearn to touch and to feel.

The gods of colour came in lovemaking. They came in the violence of war and the butchering of animals, in the cutting down of wheat. They came in the moment of birth and in the wonder of childhood – was it not said that newborn babies saw naught but colours? They came in the muted tones of grief, in the convulsions of pain and injury and disease. They came in the fires of rage, the gelid grip of fear – and all that they touched they then stained, for all time.

There was but one place and one time when the gods of colour withdrew, vanished from the ken of mortals, and that place, that time, was death.

Kadaspala worshipped colour. It was the gift of light; and in its tones, heavy and light, faint and rich, was painted all of life.

When he thought of an insensate world, made of insensate things, he saw a world of death, a realm of incalculable loss, and that was a place to fear. Without eyes to see and without a mind to make order out of chaos, and so bring comprehension, such a world was where the gods went to die. Nothing witnessed, and so nothing renewed. Nothing seen, and so nothing found. Nothing outside, and so nothing inside.

It was midday. He rode through a forest, where on all sides the sun's light fought its way down to the ground, touching faint here, bold there. Its gifts were brush-strokes of colour. He had a habit of subtly painting with the fingers of his right hand, making small caresses in the air – he needed no brush; he needed only his eyes and his mind and the imagination conjured in the space between them. He made shapes with deft twitches of those fingers, and then filled them with sweet colour – and each one was a prayer, an offering to his gods, proof of his love, his loyalty. If others saw the motions at the end of his right hand, they no doubt thought them twitches, some locked-in pattern of confused nerves. But the truth was, those fingers painted reality, and for all Kadaspala knew, they gave proof to all that he saw and all that existed to be seen.

He understood why death and stillness were bound together. In stillness the inside was silent. The living conversation was at an end.

Fingers did not move, the world was not painted into life, and the eyes, staring unseen, had lost sight of the gods of colour. When looking upon the face of a dead person, when looking into those flat eyes, he could see the truth of his convictions.

It was midday. The sun fought its way down and the gods fluttered, dipped and filled patches of brilliance amidst gloom and shadow, and Kadaspala sat on his mule, noting in a distracted fashion the thin wisps of smoke curling round his mount's knobby ankles, but most of his attention was upon the face, and the eyes, of the corpse laid out on the ground before him.

There had been three huts on this narrow trail. Now they were heaps of ash, muddy grey and dull white and smeared black. One of the huts had belonged to a daughter, old enough to fashion a home of her own, but if she had shared it with a husband his body was nowhere to be seen, while she was lying half out of what had probably been the doorway. The fire had eaten her lower body and swollen the rest, cooking it until the skin split and here the gods sat still, as if in shock, in slivers of lurid red and patches of peeled black. Her long hair had been thrown forward, over the top of her head. Parts of it had burned, curling into fragile white nests. The rest was motionless midnight, with hints of reflected blue, like rainbows on oil. She was, mercifully, lying face down. One rupture upon her back was different, larger, and where the others had burst outward this one pushed inward. A sword had done that.

The body directly before him, however, was that of a child. The blue of the eyes was now covered in a milky film, giving it its only depth, since all that was behind that veil was flat, like iron shields or silver coins, sealed and deprived of all promise. They were, he told himself yet again, eyes that no longer worked, and the loss of that was beyond comprehension.

He would paint this child's face. He would paint it a thousand times. Ten thousand. He would offer the paintings as gifts to every man and every woman of the realm. And each time any one man or woman stirred awake the hearth gods of anger and hate, feeding the gaping mouth of violence and uttering pathetic lies about making things better, or right, or pure, or safe, he would give them yet another copy of this child's face. He would spend a lifetime upon this one image, repeated in plaster on walls, on boards of sanded wood, in the threads of tapestry; glazed upon the sides of pots and carved on stones and from stone. He would make it one argument to defy every other god, every other venal emotion or dark, savage desire.

Kadaspala stared down at the child's face. There was dirt on one cheek but otherwise the skin was clean and pure. Apart from the eyes, the only discordant detail was the angle between the head and the body, which denoted a snapped neck. And bruising upon one ankle, where the killer had gripped it when whipping the boy in the air – hard enough to separate the bones of the spine.

The gods of colour brushed lightly upon that face, in tender sorrow, in timorous disbelief. They brushed light as a mother's tears.

The fingers of his right hand, folded over the saddle horn, made small motions, painting the boy's face, filling the lines and planes with muted colour and shade, working round the judgement-less eyes, saving those for last. His fingers made the hair a dark smudge, because it was unimportant apart from the bits of twig, bark and leaf in it. His fingers worked, while his mind howled until the howling fell away and he heard his own calm voice.

'Denier Child . . . *so I call it. Yes, the likeness is undeniable – you knew him? Of course you did. You all know him. He's what falls to the wayside in your triumphant march. Yes, I kneel now in the gutter, because the view is one of details – nothing else, just details. Do you like it?*

*'Do you like this?*

*'The gods of colour offer this without judgement. In return, it is for you to judge. This is the dialogue of our lives.*

*'Of course I speak only of craftsmanship. Would I challenge your choices, your beliefs, the way you live and the things you desire and the cost of those things? Are the lines sure? Are the colours true? What of those veils on the eyes – have you seen their likeness before? Judge only my skill, my feeble efforts in imbuing a dead thing with life using dead things – dead paints, dead brushes, dead surface, with naught but my fingers and my eyes living, together striving to capture truth.*

*'I choose to paint death, yes, and you ask why – in horror and revulsion, you ask why? I choose to paint death, my friend, because life is too hard to bear. But it's just a face, dead paints on dead surface, and it tells nothing of how the neck snapped, or the wrongness of that angle with the body. It is, in truth, a failure.*

*'And each time I paint this boy, I fail.*

*'I fail when you turn away. I fail when you walk past. I fail when you shout at me about the beautiful things of the world, and why didn't I paint those? I fail when you cease to care, and when you cease to care, we all fail. I fail, then, in order to welcome you to what we share.*

*'This face? This failure? It is recognition.'*

There were other corpses. A man and a woman, their backs cut and stabbed as they sought to hold their bodies protectively over those children they could reach, not that it had helped, since those children had been dragged out and killed. A dog was stretched out, cut in half just above the hips, the hind limbs lying one way, the fore limbs and head the opposite way. Its eyes, too, were flat.

When travelling through the forest, Kadaspala was in the habit of leaving the main track, of finding these lesser paths that took him through small camps such as this one. He had shared meals with the quiet forest people, the Deniers, although they denied nothing of value that he could see. They lived in familiarity and in love, and wry percipience and wise humility, and they made art that took Kadaspala's breath away.

The figurines, the masks, the beadwork – all lost in the burnt huts now.

Someone had carved a wavy line on the chest of the dead boy. It seemed that worship of the river god was a death sentence now.

He would not bury these dead. He would leave them lying where they were. Offered to the earth and the small scavengers that would take them away, bit by bit, until the fading of flesh and memory were one.

He painted with his fingers, setting in his mind where all the bodies were lying in relation to one another; and the huts and the dead dog, and how the sun's light struggled through the smoke to make every detail scream.

Then, kicking his mule forward, he watched as the beast daintily stepped over the boy's body, and for the briefest of moments hid every detail in shadow.

In the world of night promised by Mother Dark, so much would remain for ever unseen. He began to wonder if that would be a mercy. He began to wonder if this was the secret of her promised blessing to all her believers, her children. *Darkness now and for evermore. So we can get on with things.*

A score or more horses had taken the trail he was now on. The killers were moving westward. He might well meet them if they had camped to rest from their night of slaughter. They might well murder him, or just feed him.

Kadaspala did not care. He had ten thousand faces in his head, and they were all the same. The memory of Enesdia seemed far away now. If he was spared, he would ride for her, desperate with need. For the beauty he dared not paint, for the love he dared not confess. She was where the gods of colour gathered all the glory in their possession. She was where he would find the rebirth of his faith.

Every artist was haunted by lies. Every artist fought to find truths. Every artist failed. Some turned back, embracing those comforting lies. Others took their own lives in despair. Still others drank themselves into the barrow, or poisoned everyone who drew near enough to touch, to wound. Some simply gave up, and wasted away in obscurity. A few discovered their own mediocrity, and this was the cruellest discovery of all. None found their way to the truths.

If he lived a handful of breaths from this moment, or if he lived a hundred thousand years, he would fight – for something, a truth, that he could not even name. It was, perhaps, the god behind the gods of colour. The god that offered both creation and recognition, that set forth the laws of substance and comprehension, of outside and inside and the difference between the two.

He wanted to meet that god. He wanted a word or two with that god. He wanted, above all, to look into its eyes, and see in them the truth of madness.

*With brush and desire, I will make a god.*

*Watch me.*

But in this moment, as he rode through swords of light and shrouds of shadow, upon the trail of blind savagery, Kadaspala was himself like a man without eyes. The painted face was everywhere. His fingers could not stop painting it, in the air, like mystical conjurations, like evocations of unseen powers, like a warlock's curse and a witch's warding against evil. Fingers that could close wounds at a stroke, that could unravel the bound knots of time and make anew a world still thriving with possibilities – that could do all these things, yet tracked on in their small scribings, trapped by a face of death.

Because the god behind the gods was mad.

*I shall paint the face of darkness. I shall ride the dead down the throat of that damned god. I, Kadaspala, now avow this: world, I am at war with you. Outside – you, outside, hear me! The inside shall be unleashed. Unleashed.*

*I shall paint the face of darkness. And give it a dead child's eyes.*

*Because in darkness, we see nothing.*

*In darkness, behold, there is peace.*

\*      \*      \*

Narad's fingers brushed the unfamiliar lines of his own face, the places that had twisted or sagged. Haral's fists had done more than bruise and cut. They had broken nerves. He had looked upon his face reflected in a forest pool, and barely recognized it. The swelling was gone, bones mending as best they could, and most of the vision had returned to his left eye, but now he bore another man's visage, thickened and pulled down, stretched and dented.

He had known Haral's history. He had known that the bastard had lost his family in the wars, and that there was a cauldron of rage bubbling and popping somewhere inside the man. But for all that, Narad had been unable to stop himself, and finally – the day with that highborn runt – all of his verbal jabs and prods had pushed the caravan captain too far. It wasn't hard to remember the look in Haral's face, in the instant before he struck, the raw pleasure in the man's eyes – as though a door had been thrown open and all the fists of his anger could now come flying out.

There was plenty of anger among the Tiste, swirling and on occasion rising up to drown sorrow, to overwhelm what was needed to just get along. Or maybe it was a force that existed in everyone, like a treasure hoard of every humiliation suffered in a lifetime of broken dreams and disappointments, a treasure hoard, a chest, with a flimsy lock.

Narad was an ugly man now, and he would think like an ugly man, but one still strong enough to keep sorrow's head down, beneath the surface, and find satisfaction each and every time he drowned it. He wasn't interested in a soft world any more, a world where tenderness and warmth were possible, rising like bright flowers from beds of skeletal lichen and sun-burnt moss. He needed to keep reminding himself of all of that.

He sat listening to the conversations in the camp around him, the words coming from those gathered round the fire, or outside the tents. Jests and complaints about the damp ground, the fire's wayward but vengeful smoke. And he could hear, in rasping susurration, iron blades sliding on whetstones, as nicks were worked out and blunt edges honed sharp once again. Narad was among soldiers, true soldiers, and their work was hard and unpleasant, and he now counted himself one of them.

The troop awaited the return of their captain, Scara Bandaris, who along with a half-dozen soldiers had gone on to Kharkanas, to deliver the Jheleck hostages. Left behind by the caravan, still rib-cracked, still face-swollen, still half-blind, Narad had stumbled upon this troop and they had taken him in, cared for him, given him weapons and a horse, and now he rode with them.

The war against the Deniers had begun, here in this ancient forest. Narad had not known such a war was even threatening; he had never been impressed by the forest people. They were ignorant, most likely inbred, and meek as lambs. They weren't much of an enemy, and it didn't seem to be much of a war. The few huts they had come upon yesterday had been what Narad would have expected. One middle-aged man with a bad knee, a woman who called him husband, and the children they'd begotten. The girl who'd been hiding in the hut might have been pretty before the fire, but she was barely human after it, crawling out like she did. The killing had been straightforward. It had been professional. There had been no rapes, no torture. Every death delivered had been delivered quickly. Narad told himself that even necessity could be balanced with mercy.

The problem was: he was having trouble finding the necessity.

Corporal Bursa told him that he and his troop had cleaned out most of the Deniers in this section of forest – a day's walk in any direction.

He said it had been easy as there didn't seem to be too many warriors among them, just the old and mothers and the young. Bursa reminded Narad of Haral, and already he had felt his instinctive response to a man bad at hiding hurts, but this time he kept quiet. He had learned his lesson and he wanted to stay with these men and women, these soldiers of the Legion. He wanted to be one of them.

He had drawn his sword in the Deniers' camp, but none of the enemy had come within reach, and almost before he knew it the whole thing was over, and the others were firing the huts.

Where the girl had hidden was something of a mystery, but the smoke and flames had driven her out, eventually. Narad had been close by – well, the closest of any of them – and when she'd crawled out Bursa had ordered him to put the creature out of its misery.

He still remembered edging closer, fighting the gusts of heat. She was making no sound. Not once had she even screamed, although her agony must have been terrible. It was right to kill her, to end her torment. He told himself that again and again, as he worked ever closer – until he hunched over her, staring down at her scorched back. Pushing the sword into it had not been as hard as he thought it would be. The thing below him could as easily have been a sow's carcass, roasted on a spit. Except for all the black hair.

There was no reason, then, that his killing her should be haunting him. But he was having trouble laughing and joking with the others. He was, in fact, having trouble meeting their eyes. Bursa had tried telling him that these forest folk weren't even Tiste, but that was untrue. They were – the lame man they'd cut down could have been from Narad's own family, or a cousin in a nearby village. He felt confused and the confusion wouldn't go away. If he could get drunk it'd go away, for a time, but that wasn't allowed in this troop. They drank beer because it was safer than the local water, but it was weak and there wasn't that much of it and besides, these soldiers weren't like that. Captain Scara Bandaris wouldn't allow it; by all accounts, he was hard and ferociously disciplined, and he expected the same of his soldiers.

Yet these men and women worshipped the captain.

Narad was jealous of them all. He'd not even met the captain yet, and he wondered what he would see in this Scara Bandaris to make sense of this killing of Deniers, and this whole damned war. Narad had grown up on a farm lying just outside a small hamlet. He knew the reasons everyone gave when hunting vermin – the rats brought disease, the hares ate the crops and riddled the ground, and so all that slaughter was necessary. He knew that he should think of these Deniers in the same way, as an infestation and a threat to their way of life. Even rats minded their own business, but that didn't save them; that didn't stop them from being a problem; that didn't keep the beaters and their dogs away.

He sat on a log outside the tent he had been given. Every now and then he would look down at his hands, and then quickly away again.

It wasn't murder. It was mercy.

But he was an ugly man now and the world was just as ugly, and this face wasn't his and if this face wasn't his then neither were these hands, and yesterday was someone else's crime. He wondered if that girl had been beautiful. He believed that she had. But beauty had no place in this new world. This world that Haral had delivered him into. This was Haral's fault and one day he would kill that bastard.

He looked up, his eyes catching movement from the trail. A man had appeared, astride a mule.

Others took note, and Narad saw Bursa approach. The corporal caught Narad's eye and a hand waved him an invitation. Narad straightened, feeling the weight of his sword at his hip, a weight he had always liked but never quite felt comfortable with, but it was there now and it wasn't going away. He made his way over to Bursa's side.

The stranger had not even paused upon finding the camp, and by his dress Narad could see that he was highborn, although his mount and the stained boxes strapped to it suggested otherwise.

Bursa, with Narad now on his left, positioned himself directly in the stranger's path, forcing him to rein in.

It came to Narad suddenly that the trail this man had come from led straight back to the Deniers' camp. His eyes narrowed on the stranger's bland, utterly fearless expression.

'You wander obscure paths, sir,' said Bursa, hands on his hips.

'You have no idea,' the stranger replied. 'Cleaned your blades yet? I see that you have and so must acknowledge your discipline. You wear the livery of Urusander's Legion, but I suspect he knows not what you do in his name.'

The challenge of this left Bursa momentarily speechless, and then he laughed. 'Sir, you are mistaken—'

'Corporal, I have just ridden from Vatha Keep. I have been Lord Urusander's guest for much of this past month. The only "mistake" here is your assumption of my ignorance. So I ask you, since when does Urusander's Legion make war upon innocent men, women and children?'

'You have, I fear, been somewhat out of touch,' Bursa growled in reply, and Narad could see the anger bubbling up, a fizzling froth that this stranger seemed blind to, or indifferent.

Narad put his hand on the grip of his sword.

The stranger's eyes flicked to him then away again, back to Bursa. 'Out of touch? What you are touching I want nothing to do with, corporal. I am returning to my father's estate. It is regrettable that you are in my way, but as I have no wish to share your company I will continue on.'

'In a moment,' Bursa said. 'I am under orders to make note of travellers in this area—'

'Whose orders? Not Lord Urusander's. So I ask again, who gives orders to Urusander's Legion in his name?'

Bursa's face was reddening. In a tight voice he said, 'My orders came by messenger from Captain Hunn Raal not three days past.'

'Hunn Raal? You're not of his company.'

'No, we are soldiers under the command of Captain Scara Bandaris.'

'And where is he?'

'In Kharkanas. Sir, you ride in ignorance. An uprising is under way.'

'I see that,' the stranger replied.

Bursa's lips thinned into a straight, bloodless line. Then he said, 'Your name, please, if you wish to pass.'

'I am Kadaspala, son of Lord Jaen of House Enes. I have been painting your commander's portrait. Shall I tell you how much I see in a man's face when studying it day after day after day? I see everything. No dissembling evades my eye. No malice, no matter how well hidden, can hide from me. I don't doubt you are following Hunn Raal's orders. The next time you see that smirking drunk, give him this message from me. It will not do to imagine that Lord Urusander is now little more than a mere figurehead, to be pushed this way and that. Manipulate Vatha Urusander and he will make you regret it. Now, we have the measure of each other. Let me pass. It's getting late, and I ride in the company of ghosts. You'll not wish us to linger.'

After a long moment, Bursa stepped to one side. Narad did the same, feeling his heart pounding in his chest.

As the artist edged past them, he turned to Narad and said, 'I can see the man you once were.'

Narad stiffened, biting back his shame.

Kadaspala continued, 'But all I can see is this. What was inside is now outside. I feel sorry for you, soldier. No one deserves to be that vulnerable.'

He then rode on, through the camp and the crowd of other soldiers – all of them silent and hooded, as if cowed by this unarmed boy of an artist. A few moments later, he disappeared into the far end of the clearing, where the trail picked up once more.

'Shit,' Bursa said.

Narad wanted to ask a question, but seeing the expression on Bursa's face silenced him. The corporal had paled, looking to where the artist had gone, and in his eyes there was confusion and something like sick dread. 'Captain told us to sit tight,' he muttered. 'But Hunn Raal's whore said—' He stopped then and glared across at Narad. 'That'll do, soldier. Back to your tent.'

'Yes sir,' Narad replied.

Moving quickly, eyes on the log lying in front of his tent, Narad reached up to brush the lines of his broken face, and for the first time, he felt fear at what his fingers found.

*　　*　　*

Drought had dried the field and the hoofs of horses had driven like mattocks into the soil, tearing up the grasses until nothing was left alive. Master-at-arms Ivis walked from it covered in gritty dust. His leathers were stained, his jerkin sodden under his arms and against his back. Behind him the brown clouds of dust were slow to settle over the clearing and the troop he'd been training had all retired to the trees, desperate for shade and a rest. There wasn't much talk left in them: Ivis had driven that out. Some were crouched down, heads hanging. Others were sprawled on the grassy verge, forearms covering their eyes. Armour and half-emptied waterskins were scattered about like the aftermath of a battle, or a drunken night of revelry.

'Take what's left of that water and cool down your horses. Those animals need it more than any of you.'

At his words, the men and women stirred into motion. Ivis studied them a moment longer and then turned to where the warhorses stood beneath the trees. The only movement that came from them was the swishing of their tails against the swarming flies, and the occasional ripple of their sleek hides. The beasts looked strong, stripped down of all fat. As the Houseblades moved in among them, Ivis felt a spasm of sadness and looked away.

He didn't know if animals dreamed. He didn't know if they knew hope in their hearts, if they longed for things – like freedom. He didn't know what looked out through their large, soft eyes. Most of all, he didn't know what teaching them to kill did to them, to their spirits. Habits and deeds could stain a soul – he'd seen enough of that among his own kind. He'd seen broken children become broken men and broken women.

No doubt scholars and philosophers, puttering in their cosy rooms in Kharkanas, had devised elaborate definitions of all those intangible things that hovered like clouds of stirred-up dust above hard and battered ground – things nobody could really grasp or hold on to. Ideas about the soul, the hidden essence that knew itself, but knew itself incompletely, and so was doomed to ever question, to ever yearn. No doubt they had arguments and defences, built up into impressive structures that were more monuments to their own brilliance than stolid fortifications.

He remembered something his grandfather used to say. '*The man patrolling his prejudices never sleeps.*' As a boy, Ivis had not quite understood what Ivelis had meant by that. But he thought he understood now. No matter. The philosophers dug deep moats around their definitions of things like the soul; moats that no animal could breach, since animals spoke the wrong language and so could never argue their way across. Still, when Ivis looked into a horse's eyes, or a dog's, or a felled deer's in the last moments when the beast shudders and blinks with eyes filled with pain and terror, he saw the refutation of every philosopher's argument.

Life did more than flicker. It burned with fire. He knew it to be a fire for the simple reason that eventually it burned itself out. It ate up all the fuel it possessed, and dimmed and waned, and then was gone.

But were life and soul one and the same? Why the division at all?

Anyone could draw circles in the dust, but in the greater scheme of things, it made for a pathetic moat.

His Houseblades had pushed away their weariness and were attending to their mounts. Saddles were pulled off, brushes drawn. Hands stroked down the length of muscles, felt along tendons and brushed bones under stretched hide. The animals stood motionless: Ivis never knew if they but tolerated the attention, or were comforted by it. He'd seen mischief in animals, but none of them could smile. And always, their eyes were but wells of mystery.

Corporal Yalad moved up alongside him. 'Sir, they wheeled with precision, didn't they? Never seen anything so perfect.'

Ivis grunted. 'You want compliments, corporal? Maybe even a kiss? Go find that maid you keep rocking up the wall back of the stables. I'm the wrong man to make you feel good, and if I wanted a conversation I'd find someone with more than half a brain.'

Yalad backed a step. 'Apologies, sir.'

The captain knew that his foul mood was the subject of plenty of barracks talk. If no one knew the cause of it, all the better as far as Ivis was concerned. It just made them work harder trying to please him, or at least avoid a dressing down. If they knew, they'd think him mad.

There was something in the air, in this summer heat, that felt . . . wrong. As if malice had a smell, a stink, and even the hot winds blew through it and left it untouched, and the sun could not beat it down and all the ripening crops could not burn it away.

Days like this were making his skin crawl. He'd seen lone riders skirting the estate grounds, cutting fast and hard across Dracons land. He'd caught the faint smell of bad smoke, the kind of smoke that came from burnt clothes, burnt possessions, burnt hair and flesh – but never enough to be entirely certain, to even so much as sense a direction or possible source.

He had taken to watching sunsets, wandering out into the trees or drifting along the forest's edge, and in the failing of light he found moments of frightening stillness, as if even in a held breath some breath was lost, the faintest exhalation, smelling of something wrong.

If all life possessed a soul, then perhaps it too was a burning fire, and just as life burned out when it had used itself up, so too did a soul. But maybe it took longer to wink out. Maybe it took for ever. But just as life could sicken, so too could a soul – sometimes one could tell, if there were eyes to look into, if there was an easy focus to that wrongness. When he walked through the dusk, along the forest's dark line, he thought he could feel the land's soul – a soul made up of countless smaller souls – and what he felt was something sickening.

Ivis turned to Corporal Yalad. 'Round everyone up and head back. Walk the horses on to the track, then everyone dog-trot up to the gate. Shake out those muscles. Everyone cleans up before mess.'

'Yes sir.'

'I'll be in later.'

'Of course, sir.'

The forest, preserved by an edict from Lord Draconus, ran like a curled finger between hills, following the line of an ancient valley's riverbed. Its tip, where it was thinnest, was at this field's edge, where it stretched to almost touch Dracons Hold. If he walked northward, up the track of that finger, the forest thickened, and if one persisted in the simile, spread out to form the hand where the valley opened on to a floodplain. This was the forest's ancient heart.

It had been years since Ivis last ventured there. Few people did, as Draconus had forbidden the harvesting of its wood or the hunting of whatever animals dwelt within it. Ivis had been instructed to patrol its edges on a regular basis, but at random intervals. Poaching was always a risk, but the punishment was death and that punishment could be carried out by the patrols, and this discouraged the petty hunters and wood cutters. But the real deterrent was the Lord's own generosity. No one starved on his lands, and no one had to brave the winter without fuel. It was, to the captain's mind, extraordinary what was possible when those people who could do something, did. He knew that not everyone appreciated it enough. Some poachers just liked poaching; they liked working outside the laws; they liked secrecy and deceit and that sense of making fools of their betters.

Ivis suspected that there weren't many of those people left on the lands of Lord Draconus, or they were biding their time. The last hanging of a poacher had been three seasons past.

He walked through the forest. The few game trails he came across had been made by small animals. The larger game had been hunted into extinction long ago – long before the arrival of Draconus. There was a kind of deer, no higher than the captain's knee, but they were nocturnal and so rarely seen. He'd heard the eerie cries of fox and had noted owl scat, but even these signs could not disguise the impoverishment of this remnant forest. His senses felt the absence all around him, like the pressure of silent, unrelieved guilt. He'd once enjoyed wandering these woods, but no longer.

The day's light was fading. As if searching for something he knew he wouldn't find, Ivis pushed on, deeper into the forest, where it spread out and occasional ancient trees still remained, their black bark sweating in the shadows. He saw slashes of red here and there, from trees that had toppled and split. The flesh of the blackwood was too much like muscle, like meat, to the captain's eyes. It had always unnerved him.

He wondered at his own impulse, at this seemingly thoughtless push to continue onward. Was he fleeing what he knew was coming? There was nowhere he could run to. Besides, he had duties. His lord relied upon him, to train these Houseblades, to prepare them for the sudden loss of control that was civil war. Lord Draconus did not make use of spies. Dracons Hold was isolated. Unknown events swirled around them.

He found himself upon a trail, this one clear to a man's height. The boles of the trees lining it looked misshapen. Ivis stopped. He studied one, peering through the gathering gloom. The trunk made a shape, as if hands had moulded the wood itself. It bulged outward. He made out a vaguely feminine form, but bloated. He saw something similar in the next tree, and upon others, all lining this trail. A chill crept through him.

He had not known that there were Deniers living in this forest; but then, never before had he walked into its ancient heart. He knew that he had nothing to fear from them, and that they would probably hide from him. It was likely that he had already been seen. But that sense of sickness would not leave him.

Mouth dry, he continued on.

The avenue of trees opened out on to a glade studded with wooden stakes, driven into the ground in a tight pattern, impenetrable and threatening. They stood high as his hips. In the centre of this spiral was a body, impaled through its back, through its arms and its legs. The tips thrusting up through the broken flesh glistened in the faint starlight.

It was a woman, stripped naked. She was lying horizontally above a score of shafts; her head level as if it too had been pierced by a stake. He did not know why she had not simply slid down.

There was no obvious path to her. A stables cat might wend its way through but no grown man could. Ivis edged closer – he could see no one else about. With one boot he kicked at the nearest stake. His foot rebounded from it, proof that it had been driven deep.

'I am not for you,' the woman said.

Cursing in disbelief, Ivis stepped back. He drew out his sword.

'Iron and wood,' she said. 'But iron never has anything good to say to wood, does it? It delivers the shout of wounding, and then it promises fire. Before iron, wood can only surrender, and so it does, each time, every time.'

'What sorcery is this?' Ivis demanded. 'You cannot remain alive.'

'How big do you imagine the world, Tiste? Tell me, how vast is darkness? How far does light reach? How much will shadow swallow? Is it all that your imagination promised? Is it less than you hoped for, more than you feared? Where will you stand? When will you stand? List for me your enemies, Tiste, in the name of friendship.'

'You are no friend of mine,' he growled. He had seen her breath in her words, pluming up into the night, and he could just make out the spike buried in the base of her skull. If that stake was the same height as all the others, then its tip pressed against the bone of her forehead, driven straight through her brain. She could not be alive.

'It is, I think,' she said, 'the other way round. But then, I did not invite you. You are the intruder here, Tiste. You are the unwelcome guest. But I am here and that cannot be denied, and so I am bound to answer your questions.'

He shook his head.

'The others are done with me,' she said.

'What are you?'

'I am you when you sleep. When your thoughts drift and time is lost. I am there in each blink of your eyes – so swift, so brief. In that blink is the faith that all will remain as it was before, and the fear that it won't. I lie with you when you're drunk, when you are senseless, and your flesh meets mine and I rut with you all unknown, and take from you one more sliver of your life, for ever gone. And so you awaken less than what you were, each time, every time. I am—'

'Stop!'

She fell silent.

He saw runnels of blood flow down the shafts beneath her, saw the gleaming pool those runnels flowed into. But none of this could be real. 'Tell me your name.'

'The Tiste have no name for me.'

'Are you a goddess of the forest?'

'The forest knows no goddess. The trees are too busy singing. Even as they die, they sing. They have no time for gods in the face of all this death.'

'Who did this to you?'

'Did what?'

He slashed with his sword, hacked through a broad sweep of the stakes. Splinters flew. He kicked at the stubs, pushed them aside, and stepped into the maze.

'What are you doing?' she asked.

He did not reply. Some things could not be countenanced. No decent man or woman could withstand the brutality of this apparition. Ivis no longer believed his own eyes. He did not think this night was his own. He did not think he was still in the world he knew. Something had happened; something had stolen his soul, or guided it astray. He was lost.

His blade scythed through stakes. He drew closer to her.

'Iron and wood,' she said.

Limbs aching, sweat sheathing his face, he reached her side. He looked down at her face and met the woman's eyes.

She was not Tiste. He did not know what she was. Her eyes were slits, tilted upward at the outer corners. Her skin was white with blood loss. The tip of the stake piercing her skull had pushed through her forehead just above the eyes, breaking the skin. She smiled.

Ivis stood, chest heaving from his frenzied attack on the forest of stakes. He bled from splinters driven into his hands and forearms. This woman should be dead, but she wasn't. He knew that he could not move her.

'I don't know what to do,' he whispered.

'There is nothing you can do,' she said. 'The forest is dying. The world comes to an end. All that you know will break apart. Fragments will spin away. There is no need to weep.'

'Can you not – can you not stop it?'

'No. Neither can you. Every world must die. The only question is: will it be you who wields the knife that slays it? I see an iron blade in your hand. I smell the smoke of woodfires upon your clothes. You are of the people of the forge, and you have beaten your world to death. I have no interest in saving you, even if I could.'

Suddenly he wanted to strike her. He wanted her to feel pain – his pain. And all at once he realized, with a shock, that he was not the first one to feel as he did. The anger collapsed inside him. 'You tell me nothing I do not already know,' he said, face twisting at the bitterness he heard in his own words.

'This is my gift,' she said, and smiled again.

'And in receiving that gift, all we can do is hurt you.'

'It is not me whom you hurt, Captain Ivis.'

'Then you feel no pain?'

'Only yours.'

He turned away then. A long walk awaited him, back to the keep; a walk from one world to another. It would take the rest of the night. He wanted to believe the best of people, even the Deniers. But what they had done appalled him. He could make no sense of the sorcery they had awakened, or what ghastly rites they had conducted in this secret place. He did not know how they had found her; if they had conjured her up out of the earth, or from the blood of sacrifices.

He reached the edge of the clearing, made his way up the avenue of deformed trees, feeling as if he was being spat out, flung back into a colourless, lifeless world. The forest was suddenly dull around him, and he thought, if he dared halt, if he dared pause and draw a breath, he would hear the trees singing. Singing as they died.

*  *  *

Malice sat with her sisters in the bolt-hole they had found under the kitchen. Directly overhead was the bakery, and the stone foundation of the huge oven formed the back wall of the tiny room. Where they crouched now, milled flour sifted down from the floorboards each time someone thumped past overhead, and in the low light from the small lantern set on a ledge, it seemed the air was filled with snow.

'If only she wasn't a hostage,' Envy said. 'I'd cut her face.'

'Drop coals on it when she's sleeping,' Spite said.

'Make her ugly,' Malice added, enjoying the game even though they played it all the time, hiding in the secret rooms of the house, drawing close together like witches, or crows, while people walked above them all unknowing and stupid besides.

'Poison would be perfect,' Spite began but Envy shook her head and said, 'Not poison. Malice is right. Make her ugly. Make her have to live with it for the rest of her life.'

Weeks past, they had hidden in the corner tower opposite the one Arathan used to hide in, and had watched the arrival of the new hostage. Envy had been furious when Malice had commented on how pretty the woman was, and this had begun things: the plans to ruin that beauty. So far, of course, nothing had been done – just words – since it was as Envy had said. Sandalath Drukorlat was a hostage and that meant she couldn't be touched.

But it was still fun planning, and if accidents happened, well, they just happened, didn't they?

'She's too old to be a hostage,' Spite said. 'She's ancient. We were supposed to get a proper hostage, not her.'

'A boy would have been best,' said Envy. 'Like Arathan, only younger. Someone we could hunt down and corner. Someone too weak to stop us doing anything we wanted to him.'

'What would we do?' Malice asked. She was the youngest and so she could ask the stupid questions without her sisters beating her up too badly, and sometimes they didn't beat her up at all, or put things in her that hurt, and that was when she knew that her question had been a good one.

Spite snorted. 'What do we do to you?' she asked, and Malice could see the gleam of her smile and it was never good when Spite smiled. 'We'd fill him up, that's what, and keep doing it until he begged us.'

'Begging never works,' Malice said.

Envy laughed. 'You idiot. Beg us for more. We could make him our slave. I want slaves.'

'Slaves were done away with,' Spite pointed out.

'I'll bring them back, when I grow up. I'll make slaves of everyone and they'll all have to serve me. I'll rule an empire. I'd kill every pretty woman in it, or maybe just scar them for ever.'

'It feels like we'll never get older,' Malice said, sighing.

She caught a silent look between her sisters, and then Envy shrugged and said, 'Scrabal birds. Malice, you ever heard of scrabal birds?'

Malice shook her head.

'They make small nests, but lay too many eggs,' Envy explained. 'All the chicks then hatch and at first it's all right, but then they start growing.'

'And the nest gets even smaller,' said Spite, reaching out and walking her fingertips down Malice's arm.

Envy was watching, her eyes bright. 'So the biggest ones gang up on the little ones. They kill them and eat them, until the nest isn't crowded any more.'

Spite's walking fingers made their way back up the arm, edged closer to Malice's neck.

'I don't like scrab birds,' said Malice, shivering at the touch.

'Scrabal,' corrected Spite, still smiling.

'Let's talk about the hostage again,' Malice suggested. 'Making her ugly.'

'You were too young to understand Father,' said Spite, 'when he talked to us about how we were going to grow up. Eight years, just like the Tiste, and nobody knows any different. We grow up like the rest of them. But just for those first eight years. Or nine.'

'That's because we're not Tiste,' said Envy in a whisper.

Spite nodded, her hand sliding round Malice's throat. 'We're different.'

'But Mother was—'

'Mother?' Spite snorted. 'You know nothing about Mother. It's a secret. Only me and Envy know, since you're not old enough, not important enough.'

'Father says it's in our natures,' Envy added.

'What is?' Malice asked.

'Growing up . . . fast.'

'Scary fast,' Spite said, nodding.

'Arathan—'

'He's different—'

'No he isn't, Spite,' Envy said.

'Yes he is!'

'Well, half different, then. But you saw how he grew past us.'

'After the ice.'

'And that's the secret, Spite. You have to nearly die first. That's what I meant, before. That's what I meant.'

Malice did not understand what they were talking about. She disliked the way Spite was holding her throat, but she dared not move. In case Spite decided to not let go. 'We hate Sandalath Drukorlat,' she said. 'Who says hostages have to be special? Get her drunk and then cut her face, and use coals to pock her cheeks and forehead, and burn away her hair. Put a coal on one of her eyes. Burn it out!'

'Do you want to grow up?' Spite asked her.

Malice nodded.

'Grow up fast?' Envy pressed, leaning forward to stroke Malice's hair. 'Faster than us? Do you want to grow right past us, little one? If you did that, you could boss us around. You could make us lie with dogs and like it.'

Malice thought about the dog, the one that Ivis had to kill. She thought about what they did to Arathan when he was little, so little he couldn't fight the dog off, not with the three of them holding him still. She wondered if he remembered all of that.

'Don't you want to make us lie with dogs?' Spite asked her.

'Jheleck,' answered Malice. 'Grown ones. And I'd make you like it, too, and beg for more.'

'Of course you would,' Envy murmured. 'Unless we decide to grow right past you again, and make you littler than us all over again. Then we'd give you to the Jheleck.'

'I wouldn't let you!'

'But there's two of us,' pointed out Spite, 'and only one of you, Malice. Besides, we already make you like lots of things.'

But Malice only said that she did. The truth was, she hated everything they did to her. She wanted to kill them both. She wouldn't be content with making them lie with dogs or Jheleck or old drooling men. When she grew up, she would murder her sisters. She would cut them into pieces. 'Make me grow up fast,' she said.

Spite's smile broadened, and her hand tightened about Malice's throat.

When she couldn't breathe, she began struggling, trying to scratch Spite's face, but Envy lunged close and grasped her wrists, pushing her arms down. Malice kicked, but Spite moved round and sat on her. And the hand kept squeezing, and it was terrifyingly strong.

Spite laughed, her eyes shining. 'I dreamed this last night,' she whispered. 'I dreamed a murder far away. It was wonderful.'

Malice felt her eyes bulging, her face growing impossibly hot. Blackness closed in around her, swallowing everything.

*     *     *

Envy heard something break in Malice's neck and tore Spite's hands away. Their little sister's head lolled back, as if to show them the deep imprint on her throat – the ribbons made by the fingers, the white knobs made by knuckles and the crescent cuts from nails digging in.

Neither said a word as they stared down at Malice.

Then Spite grunted. 'It didn't work,' she said. 'Not like with Arathan. It didn't work at all, Envy.'

'I'm not blind,' Envy snapped. 'You must have done it wrong.'

'I did what you told me to!'

'No – the choking was your idea, Spite! From your dream!'

'Now,' whispered Spite, 'now I've done it twice. I've killed twice, both times the same way. I choked them to death.'

'That's what you get for going too far in your dreams,' Envy said. 'I told you to stay closer to home. You look through too many eyes.'

'I didn't just look,' Spite said. 'I made him like it.'

'That's your power then. Father said we had powers. He said we had *aspects*, that's what he said.'

'I know what he said. I was there.'

'You make them like it. I make them want it.' Envy looked down at Malice's body. 'I wonder what her aspect was.'

'We'll never know,' said Spite. 'And neither will she.'

'You killed her, Spite.'

'It was an accident. An experiment. It's Father's fault, for what he said.'

'You killed Malice.'

'An accident.'

'Spite?'

'What?'

'What did it feel like?'

*     *     *

There was a niche under the foundations of the oven, where someone had pulled away a number of stones at the base as if to hide something, but nothing was there. It was just about big enough to fit Malice's body, and once they pushed, sitting down and using their feet, and once a bone or two had snapped, they managed to get all of her inside.

389

The stones that had been pulled away were the ones they always used to sit on. Now Spite and Envy pushed them back to at least block the niche.

'Hilith is going to be a problem,' Spite said. 'She'll want to know where Malice has gone.'

'We'll have to do what we said we'd do, then.'

'Now?'

'We don't have any choice. It's not just Hilith, is it? It's Atran and Hidast and Ivis.'

Spite gasped. 'What about the hostage?'

'I don't know. That's a problem. We can't stay here, anyway. Not for too long. Besides, look what Father's done with Arathan. He took him away. For all we know, he's killed him, cut open his throat and drunk all his blood. He'll come back for us and do the same. Especially now.'

'We should go to the temple, Envy. We should talk to him.'

'No. He could reach through – you know he can!'

'That's not him,' Spite said. 'That's only what he's left behind. It wears his armour. It paces back and forth – we heard it!'

'You can't talk with that thing.'

'How do you know? We've never tried.'

Envy's eyes were wide. 'Spite, if we let that thing out, we might never get it back inside. Let me think. Wait. Can you give it dreams?'

'What?'

'If I make it want something, can you make it like it?'

Spite hugged herself, as if suddenly chilled despite the oven's dry heat. 'Envy. This is Father's power we're talking about. *Father's.*'

'But he's not here.'

'He'll know anyway.'

'So what? You said we're going to have to run no matter what.'

Spite sat back. She shot her sister a glare. 'You said it would work, Envy. If she got close enough to death, the power would reach inside her and wake everything up.'

'It's awake in me.'

'Me too. So, you had it the wrong way around.'

'Maybe. You don't look any more grown up.'

Spite shrugged. 'I don't need to. Maybe when I do, I'll grow. Everything feels in reach. Do you know, I could take down all of Kurald Galain, if I wanted to.'

'We might have to,' said Envy, 'to cover our trail.'

'Daddy will know.'

'Remember Ivis killing that rut-mad hunting dog? How he came up behind it and sliced through the tendons of its back legs, with one slash of his sword?'

'Sure I remember. That dog howled and howled, until I thought the sky would crack.'

Envy nodded. 'Father doesn't scare me. We just need to give people a reason to be Ivis.'

'Daddy's the dog?' Spite snorted. 'Hardly. He's got Mother Dark. No need to rut everything in sight, with her around.'

'You don't get my meaning, sister. You're not subtle enough. You never were.'

'Maybe you think that, but you don't know anything about me.'

'I know that you're a murderer.'

'Now, try saying it like you think it's awful, Envy.'

'You didn't get my meaning, but what you said has given me an idea. But I need to work on it some more. First, though, there's the people in the house to deal with.'

'Tonight?'

Envy nodded. 'It has to be, I think.'

Spite smiled knowingly. 'You just want to know what it feels like.'

To that, Envy only shrugged.

A moment later and they were on their way, rushing down the hidden passages between the walls.

Accidents happened, and when accidents happened, the most important thing to do was cover them up, and fast – but not so fast as to make mistakes and so give it all away. Hiding the truth was Envy's special talent – among many special talents, she reminded herself. Spite was good at the practical matters, the things that needed doing. But she needed guiding. She needed direction.

The night ahead was going to be glorious.

\*       \*       \*

In the house of Draconus, there was war. Even in those rare moments when she was alone, when she no longer struggled on the battlements, Sandalath felt the title of hostage close about her, like clothes long outgrown, and their constriction was suffocating.

House-mistress Hilith stalked the corridors day and night. As far as Sandalath could tell, Hilith slept when demons slept, which was never. The hag cast a huge, devouring shadow upon this house, and even that shadow had claws. At night, Sandalath dreamed of death-struggles with the woman, all blood, spit and handfuls of hair. She dreamed of pushing knife blades deep into Hilith's scrawny chest, hearing ribs pop, and seeing that horrid face stretched in a silent scream, the black tongue writhing like a salted leech. She woke from these dreams with a warm glow filling her being.

It was all ridiculous. Once Lord Draconus returned, Hilith's empire would collapse in a heap of rubble and dust. In the meantime, Sandalath did her best to avoid the old woman, although certain daily rituals made contact inevitable. The worst of these were meals. Sandalath would sit at the end of the table opposite the unoccupied chair where Lord Draconus would have sat, had he been present. As hostage, she was head of the house, but only because the Lord's three daughters were not yet of age. Sandalath rarely saw them. They lived like ghosts, or feral kittens. She had no idea what they did all day. For all that, however, she felt sorry for them, for the names Lord Draconus had given them.

It was the Lord's practice to assemble most of his heads of staff for these repasts. When the household was intact, Ivis and Hilith would be joined by Gate Sergeant Raskan, Master of Horses Venth Direll, Armourer Setyl, Surgeon Atran and Keeper of Records Hidast. Among these notables only the surgeon was of any interest to Sandalath, although she'd yet to meet Raskan as he was riding with the Lord and his bastard son. Venth stank of the stables and often entered with horseshit under his boots and still wearing his stained leather apron. His hands were filthy and he rarely spoke, busy as he was shovelling food into his mouth. The few times he did say something, it was to complain to Captain Ivis about exhausted horses, listing the animals that went lame in accusing tones. Sandalath had heard from her maids that Venth slept in the stables. Setyl, the armourer, never spoke at all, for part of his tongue had been cut away by a sword thrust back in the wars. The scarring on his lower face was terrible to look at and he struggled to keep food in his mouth, and never met anyone's eyes. The keeper of records, Hidast, was a small man with a sloping forehead and an oversized lower jaw, giving him a pronounced underbite. His obsession was with the household accounts, and the Lord's vigorous expansion of Houseblades was a burden that he took personally, as if all of the Lord's wealth in fact belonged to Hidast rather than Draconus. He looked on Captain Ivis with open hatred, but this was a siege he was losing. Most mealtimes Hidast complained of stomach pains, but every offer from the surgeon to treat his ailment was met with a rude shake of the head.

Atran was a clever woman, inclined to ignore Hilith while flirting with Ivis – to his obvious discomfort – and inviting Sandalath to join in the conspiracy of torturing the hapless master-at-arms. This had offered the only entertainment during these meals. In the captain's absence, however, Atran seemed to sink into depression, taking to drinking to excess, in morose silence, and by the meal's end she had trouble standing, much less walking.

Sandalath had mapped out these people and their places in the household. It was all too complicated and fraught and rather ridiculous. The boredom that assailed her was relentless. She did not know how things would change once Lord Draconus returned, but she knew that they would, and she longed for that day.

It was almost time for the evening meal. She sat alone in her room, waiting for her two maids to arrive. They were late and that was unusual but not unduly so. No doubt Hilith had found for them something that needed attention, and the timing was deliberate. Inconveniencing the hostage had become one of Hilith's special pursuits.

The house was quiet. Rising, she went to the window that overlooked the courtyard. Captain Ivis had not yet returned. Supper promised to be dreadful, with the surgeon getting drunk and Hidast and Venth taking turns to slander the master-at-arms in his absence, subtly encouraged by Hilith, of course. Sandalath could almost see the gleam of approval and satisfaction in the hag's eyes, as the knives clinked and scraped and the prongs jabbed into tender meat.

She hoped Ivis came back in time. His presence alone was like a fist thumping the table, silencing everyone but Atran. Sandalath was jealous of the surgeon's ease in teasing the captain, making her lust almost playful in its obviousness, and she could well see the discomfort it caused in Ivis, which hinted that his eye was perhaps fixed elsewhere.

Sandalath considered herself pretty; she had seen soldiers follow her with their eyes when she walked the courtyard, and she remembered how gentle his hands had been outside the carriage, when the heat of the journey had proved too much. He'd told her that he had a daughter, but she knew now that this was untrue. He was only being solicitous. She imagined that she'd needed that at the time, and it was this generosity in him that she found so compelling.

But where were her maids? The bell was close to sounding. The first courses were even now being prepared in the kitchen and Sandalath was hungry. She would wait a short while longer and then, if neither Rilt nor Thool showed, why, she would go down to the meal dressed as she was, and do her best to ignore Hilith's quiet triumph.

She continued looking down on the empty courtyard.

*Oh, Ivis, where are you?*

\*     \*     \*

Hilith stepped out from her quarters and marched up the corridor. She saw dust where there should be no dust. Rilt was due for a whipping, on the backs of the thighs where it hurt the most and where the welts and bruises couldn't be seen under the maid's tunic. And Thool wasn't fooling Hilith at all – the maid was meeting two or three Houseblades a night, behind the barracks, earning extra coin because she had ambitions of getting away from all this. But Hilith had found where Thool hid her earnings, and when there was enough to make it worthwhile she would steal that cache and say nothing. A little extra come the winter would suit her fine, and if that meant Thool spreading her legs ten times a night with tears in her eyes, well, a whore was what a whore did.

Turning on to the corridor that led to the stairs she saw Spite on the floor ahead of her, crying over a blood-smeared knee. *Clumsy whorespawn, too bad it wasn't her skull. Nasty creature, nasty nasty.* 'Oh dear,' she crooned, smiling, 'that's a *nasty* scrape, isn't it?'

Spite looked up, eyes filling with tears all over again.

This was new. Hilith had never before seen any of these wretched daughters of the Lord ever cry. They'd been left to run wild, too privileged for a caning although Hilith longed to do just that – beat the things into being proper and meek. Children should be like frightened rabbits, since only that taught them the ways of the world, and showed them how to live in it.

'It hurts,' whined Spite. 'Mistress Hilith, it might be broken! Can you look?'

'I'm about to eat – do you think I want filthy blood on my hands? Go find the surgeon, or a healer in the barracks – they'll love having you in there.'

'But mistress—' Spite rose suddenly, blocking Hilith's path.

Hilith snorted. 'So much for broken—' There was a sound behind her and she began turning. Something punched her back, pulled free and punched again. Pain filled Hilith's chest. Feeling unaccountably weak, she reached out one hand to grip Spite's shoulder, but the girl, laughing, twisted away.

Hilith fell to the floor. She didn't understand. She could barely lift her arms and her face was against the polished wood, and there was grit and dust between the boards. Rilt needed a whipping. They all did.

*   *   *

Envy looked at the small knife in her hand, saw how the blood from the miserable old witch sat on the polished iron blade in beads, like water on oil. Then she glanced down at Hilith who was lying on her stomach, head to one side and the eye that Envy could see staring sightlessly.

'Stop gawking,' Spite hissed.

'We need a bigger knife,' said Envy. 'This won't do for the men.'

'It did fine for Hidast!'

'He wasn't much of a man, but Venth is. So is Setyl. Ivis—'

'Ivis is away,' said Spite. 'I sent him into a dream. I can do that now. It's easy.'

They had been busy. Slaughter in the laundry room. Murder in the maids' cells. Dead cook, dead scullions – the knife in her hand they had stolen months past and Envy had thought to find something better in the kitchen, but the ones in there were too big to wield. She wished

394

she were stronger, but so far everything had worked, and as long as she could strike from behind, with Spite distracting the victim, being a murderer was easy.

'The men will be trouble,' she said again.

'Stab them in the throat,' Spite said. She dipped a finger into a pool of blood creeping out from Hilith's body and smeared her knee again. 'Atran's next. Let's go, before the supper bell sounds.'

*     *     *

She'd heard from Corporal Yalad that Ivis had wandered into the forest, and for Atran the night ahead had fallen through a hole, and somewhere down there was oblivion, luring her, tempting her to find it. She decided that she wouldn't wait for that first goblet of wine at the start of the meal, and so went into the surgery where she poured out a healthy measure of raw alcohol into a clay cup. She added a little water and then a small spoonful of powdered neth berries. She drank down half of the concoction and then stood, tilting back until she was against a wall, waiting for the burning shock to pass. Moments later she felt the first effect of the berries.

A dab of the black powder on an unconscious man's tongue could stand him upright in a heartbeat, but she had been using it for so long that her body simply expanded, smoothly, warmth filling her limbs. Drinking invited sleep but the powder kept her awake, wildly invigorated. Without the alcohol in her blood right now she knew that she would be trembling, nerves twitching, vision fluttering. She'd seen a man punch through a solid door when spiked on neth powder.

The oblivion awaiting her was a delicious kind, especially when she could walk straight into it. The fall from the neth berries was swift and savage, and she would not move for at least a day from wherever she happened to collapse, but neither would she dream. And that was the bargain and she was content with it.

Ivis was gone for the night. Whatever haunted him she could not touch, and though she made her love plain to see, he was simply uninterested in her, and it was that disinterest that so wounded Atran, straight down through her body like a spear pinning her soul to the ground. She knew he took women to his bed – if his tastes had been for other men, then she would have understood and it would not be so bad. But it was *her* that he had no feelings for.

She was not ugly. A little too thin, perhaps, and getting thinner as the neth berries devoured her reserves, but her face was even, not too lined, not too wan or sunken. She had green eyes that men professed to admire, and the sharpness which had once made the same men uneasy was long gone, drowned away and for ever done with. Sharpness wasn't a gift when bluntness was what was desired.

Spite limped into the surgery. 'Atran? I hurt my knee! Come quick – I can't walk any farther!'

The surgeon blinked. 'Rubbish,' she pronounced without moving.

The girl frowned. 'What?'

'That's arterial blood and it's smeared, not spurting. Did the cook slaughter another pig? You're a sick little wretch, you know that?'

Spite stared at her, and then slowly straightened. 'Just fooling,' she said.

'Get out of my sight.'

The girl scowled. 'Father won't like it when I tell him how you talk to me.'

'Your father doesn't like *you*, so why would he give a fuck how I talk to you?'

'We're going to kill you,' said Spite. Envy stepped out from behind her and Atran saw the bloody knife in her hand.

'What have you fools done? Who did you hurt? Where's Malice?'

Envy rushed her, knife upraised.

Atran's hand was a flash, catching the girl's wrist and snapping it clean. She then picked up the child by the throat and threw her across the room. Envy struck the cutting table, her back arching, folding around the table's edge – a table that was bolted to the floor.

Shrieking, Spite flung herself forward.

A slap sent her sprawling. Atran turned to see Envy picking herself up from the floor, and that was impossible – the girl's back should have broken, snapped like a twig. Instead, something dark and vile was bleeding out from the girl, from her limbs, her hands, from her dark eyes. The tendrils of this dread sorcery reached out, curling like talons. The broken wrist was visibly mending, flesh writhing under the red skin.

Spite scrabbled to her feet, and in her Atran saw similar power. 'You're nothing!' the girl hissed. 'A useless drunk bitch!'

Sorcery lashed out from both of them, the tendrils whipping, scything into Atran. At their touch flesh burst, blood sprayed hot as melted wax. Atran held up her hands, shielding her eyes, and then lunged at Envy. The neth powder was roaring in her body, fuelling a rage that swept away the agony. Her groping hands found Envy's face, took hold like a raptor's claws and lifted the girl from her feet. When she threw Envy this time, it was with all her strength. The girl hammered into a wall, the back of her head crunching wetly. The sorcery enveloping her winked out.

Spite's attack continued, lancing into her back, rending flesh down to the bone. Gasping, Atran wheeled, staggered forward.

The girl suddenly bolted for the doorway, but Atran's boot caught her in the midriff. Spite skidded and struck the door frame. Her face bulged as she fought for air. Atran advanced, caught a flailing arm, and spun the girl around, into the wall behind her. Bones shattered at the impact, and Spite fell to the floor in a disordered heap.

The pain of her wounds tore at Atran's mind. Moaning, trembling uncontrollably, she reached up and fumbled along a shelf bearing battle medicines. She found a vial of rellit oil, pushed the stopper from the bottle and quickly drank down its contents. The pain vanished like a candle's flame under a bucket of water. Her clothes were shredded and soaked in burnt blood – but that heat had cauterized the wounds even as they had been delivered. She had no idea what was left of her back, but she knew that it was bad. Still, that would have to wait.

From both girls, there was motion. Bones were knitting before Atran's eyes.

She had little time. On a peg affixed to one end of the cutting table were her surgeon's tools. Stumbling over to the leather satchel, she plucked it free and unfolded it on the table. Taking a tendon knife in one hand, she went over to Envy. Picked her up by one limp arm and dragged her over to the table. She lifted the girl's body and flopped it down on to the tabletop then pinned the girl's left hand against the wood and drove the knife into the palm with all her strength.

Envy's body jolted and the eyes fluttered. Atran selected another knife and nailed Envy's other hand to the table. Then she collected up Spite and flung her down at the table's opposite end. Two more knives pinned her hands to the table like her sister's.

A part of Atran, lodged cowering in one corner of her mind, watched and knew that she had snapped inside. Madness had spilled out to fill the room and still it boiled. Those wide eyes staring out from that dark corner looked on in horror and disbelief, even as she stalked over to collect a cloak, pulling it over lacerated shoulders.

The girls wouldn't stay put for long. Whatever sorcery filled them was too powerful, too eager for freedom. She needed to save as many people as possible. Get them out of the house – and then burn the house down to the ground.

Her strides jerky, wobbly, she made for the doorway.

Malice stepped into it, holding above her head a block of masonry. She threw it as if it were a brick. The massive stone slammed into Atran's chest, shattering ribs. She fell, hit the floor on her back as if thrown down, her head snapping and crunching hard. Light blinded her. She could not breathe and she felt heat filling her lungs and she knew that she was already dead, her lungs drowning in blood. The light faded suddenly and she looked up to see Malice, her throat swollen black and blue and green, dried blood at the corners of her mouth. She had collected the huge stone and was lifting it again.

The eyes that met Atran's in the moment before the stone descended on her face were empty of life – a look the surgeon had seen a thousand times before. *Impossib—*

* * *

Atran's skull squashed flat, with gore spurting out to the sides. Malice stared down at what she had done. On the cutting table, her sisters were thrashing, trying to pull their hands from the knives pinning them to the surface.

Malice turned to them. 'I'm mad at you,' she said. 'You took the lantern with you. You took away the light and left me all alone!'

'Never again,' hissed Envy. 'We promise, never again!'

'Now be a good girl and help us!' Spite begged.

* * *

Venth stumped into the dining room. Only Setyl had arrived before him and the armourer sat glumly at the table, which had not yet been set. The master of horses frowned. 'The bell's sounded, by the Abyss. I do not even smell cooking – where are the staff? Where is everyone?'

Setyl blinked up at him, and then shrugged.

'Did you not think to look?' Without waiting for a reply – which wouldn't ever come in Setyl's case, anyway – Venth made his way to the service door that led to the kitchen. Something wasn't right. He'd been looking forward to this meal, once he'd learned that Ivis would not be attending. He was furious with the captain. The horses were being pushed too hard – the wretched animals weren't smart enough to resist a tyrant, and Ivis was surely that.

*You'd think a damned war was coming—*

He pushed open the door. There were bodies lying on the tiled floor, and pools of blood. He stared for a moment longer, trying to make sense of what he was seeing, and then he spun round and rushed back to the dining room.

'Setyl!'

The scarred man looked up.

'Get the Houseblades. Get Corporal Yalad. Someone's murdered the staff. And look – *look at us* – where's everyone else? Abyss take me – where is the hostage? Go! The Houseblades! And make sure they're armed.'

As Setyl rushed out, Venth crossed the chamber and plunged into a side passage, the one leading to the hostage's quarters. His shock was giving way to dread. Nothing was more sacrosanct than the safety of a hostage of the House. If he found her dead, the Lord would never survive the consequences. Even Mother Dark would be unable to protect him. *Things go slack when Ivis isn't around. The damned fool, wandering off into the wood all night! And now . . .*

398

He told himself that he knew nothing, since the alternative made him recoil inside. Someone, an assassin, must have found a way into the house. This was an attack upon Dracons – the Lord was away and horror was being visited upon his home. *Cowards.*

Passing the maids' cells he paused, and then knocked upon the door of the nearest one. There was no reply. *Somewhere else or dead.* Venth continued on. He found that he had drawn his knife.

Shouts sounded from the front entrance. The Houseblades were inside. As he drew closer to the hostage's door, he wondered if it wasn't already too late. *They've killed her.*

Still five paces from the door, he saw the latch suddenly turn and the door was thrown open. The hostage stood in the threshold. 'Venth? What has happened? I saw running, in the courtyard—'

'Mistress, please go back inside your room,' Venth said.

She noted the knife in his hand and stepped back and he saw fear in her eyes.

Venth shook his head. 'Assassins, mistress. There has been slaughter in this house. Go back. I will guard this passage until a Houseblade arrives.'

'Slaughter? Who? My maids?'

'I don't know about them, mistress, but I fear the worst. Only Setyl and me arrived in the dining hall – no one else. Not Atran, or Hidast or Hilith.' He turned at the sound of someone running up the corridor. Heart suddenly pounding hard, he readied himself. He would give his life here, defending her. And he'd hurt the bastard—

But it was Corporal Yalad. The young officer was pale and he had drawn his sword. He pulled up when he saw Venth, and then Sandalath. 'Good,' he said with a shaky nod. 'Both of you, with me—'

'Corporal,' said Venth, 'would it not be better if the hostage remained in her—'

'No, I want every survivor with me, in the dining room. I know – I could post guards, but to be honest, until we know the nature of our attacker, I'll not split up my squads.'

'Corporal, you have six hundred Houseblades at your disposal—'

'The squads I know and trust, horse master. The rest are locking down the grounds.'

'I don't understand,' said Sandalath.

'Mistress,' replied Yalad, 'if we're in time, then the assassins are still with us. But no matter what, to get into the house . . . it is quite possible that there are co-conspirators. Indeed, given the number of new recruits we've been taking on, the assassins could well come from among the Houseblades. I am even now determining if anyone cannot be accounted for. For now, however, I want all the survivors in one place, where I can keep them safe. So please, both of you follow me.'

Venth gestured Sandalath between himself and Yalad, and in this formation they quickly made their way towards the dining hall.

'Why is this happening?' Sandalath asked.

When Yalad did not reply, Venth cleared his throat and said, 'The Lord has enemies in the court, mistress.'

'But he's not even here!'

'No, mistress, he isn't.'

'If he had been,' growled Yalad ahead of them, 'we'd be looking down at the corpses of however many assassins got in here tonight. And dead or not, Draconus would get answers from them.'

Venth grunted. 'He's no warlock, corporal. I don't know where those rumours came from, but I ain't never seen anything to suggest he is – and I wager neither have you.'

'He is the Consort,' Yalad countered. 'Or would you deny Mother Dark's ascension, horse master?'

'I would not,' Venth replied.

'I may not have seen anything,' Yalad said, 'but Captain Ivis has.'

'I wish the captain was here,' said Sandalath.

'You're not alone in that,' Yalad said in a growl, and Venth could not tell if the young man had taken offence. There were times when this hostage displayed all the tact of a child.

The corporal looked in each of the maid cells, but his glance was brief and he was quick to close the doors behind him before moving on. 'I don't get this,' Venth heard him mutter. And then he halted.

Venth almost collided with the young man. 'What is it, corporal?'

'His daughters – have you seen them? Anywhere?'

'No, but then, I rarely do,' Venth replied. *And I'm grateful for that.*

'Stay here,' Yalad said, and then he edged past them, returning to the last of the cell doors. He went inside, and when he reappeared there was blood on his hands. He moved to pass them but Venth blocked him, and the thing he did not want to contemplate was now burning like a wildfire in his mind.

He met Yalad's eyes. 'Well?'

'Not now, Venth.' The corporal roughly pushed past. 'Let's go.'

'But what about those little girls?' Sandalath demanded. 'If they're out there with an assassin on the loose, we need to find them!'

'Yes, mistress,' Yalad said without turning. 'We need to find them.'

*         *         *

It was just past dawn when Ivis stepped on to the track wending its way up to the grounds. He was exhausted, and in his mind, haunting him, was the face of the goddess who had been impaled on the stakes in the clearing. He remembered her smile and the absence of pain in her eyes – as if wounds meant nothing. Yet each time he saw that face, taking

400

form in his mind's eye as if reassembled from pieces, he thought about cruelty, and all the other faces he had seen in his life then crowded his skull as if clamouring for attention.

He feared the attention of gods. They had the faces of children, but these were not kind children, and all that was revealed in them, why, he could see it mirrored among the many men and women he had known. The same venality. The same unashamed indifference.

Cruelty was the bridge between mortals and the gods, and both sides had a hand in building it, stone upon stone, face upon face.

*We are – each and every one of us – artists. And this is our creation.*

When he came within sight of the keep wall, he saw Houseblades swarming the grounds, and a moment later a half-dozen of them were rushing towards him. Looking like children, when something has gone wrong. The sun's light was hard and strangely harsh, as if every colour was paint, and every hue and every shade held in it, somewhere, a hint of iron. Ivis paused, and then made his way across the moat bridge to meet his Houseblades.

# FOURTEEN

WHEN HE WAS YOUNG AND STILL LIVING WITH HIS FAMILY ON THE Durav estate, Cryl remembered one summer when a tree-fall blocked a stream in the wood of the grounds. Water backed up to form a pool, and then a pond. He recalled seeing the mound of an ant nest in the path of that rising water. Day after day he returned to it, watching one side of the nest slowly crumbling to the seep of water. Atop the mound the ants continued their usual frenetic activity, as if blind to what was coming. On the last day of his visit, he discovered only a sodden heap of mud and twigs where the nest had been, and in the black muck he saw eggs and drowned ants.

He thought of that nest now, inexplicably, as he stood staring at the smear of smoke above the forest to the east, watching it spread across the sky. The procession had drawn to a halt while Lord Jaen rode out with a dozen Houseblades to investigate, a venture from which they were yet to return. Cryl remained with the carriage, ostensibly in command of the remaining eight Houseblades, although there were no orders to give.

Upon this journey, to the place of the wedding, Enesdia was required to remain cloistered, hidden from sight by the closed shutters on the carriage windows, and communicating only via a tube with her maid, Ephalla, who sat beside the driver on the bench. Somewhere, on the north road out from Kharkanas, Lord Andarist would be similarly bound to solitude, assuming they had departed the city yet. There were symbolic meanings to this ancient tradition, but Cryl wasn't much interested in them. As the poet Gallan once said, traditions hid the obvious and habits steadied the world.

When next he rested eyes upon Enesdia, she would be facing her future husband, on the threshold of the edifice Andarist had built to proclaim his love for her. And Cryl would smile, from where he stood at her father's side – a hostage made brother and a brother filled with brotherly love.

*But I am not her brother.*

There was virtually no traffic upon the road, and the line of trees off to their left, gap-holed by the beginnings of trails, seemed empty of life: wood like bone, leaves like flakes of ash. The river on the right showed them a mud-clotted bank where plants had torn away in unseasonal currents and high water. As they had travelled down from Enes House, they had almost kept pace with Dorssan Ryl's southward flow, but now the familiar water seemed to have rushed past and in its place was something darker, stranger. He knew that such notions were nonsense. The currents were unending, and whatever sources of the river existed high in the mountains of the north, they too never ceased.

After one more long searching study of the trail mouth in which the troop had vanished some time earlier, Cryl turned and strode down from the road to draw closer to the river. The black water held hidden every promise, and even to reach down into it was to find nothing to grasp. He thought of its chill touch, and the numbness waiting in its depths. *River god. Your water does not run clear, and so you remain blind to the shore and the lands beyond. But I wonder . . . do you hunger? For all that you cannot have? All that you cannot defeat? The traditions of current, the habits of flooding, and the mysteries you guard: these are the things the Deniers would worship. And I see no crime in that.*

This wedding would be his last responsibility to the Enes family. His days of being a hostage were coming to an end. He felt like a crow lost in a flock of songbirds, beleaguered by gentle songs and shamed by his own croaking call. The Duravs had given themselves to the sword, had made their lives traditions of violence and habits of killing, and though Cryl had yet to end someone else's life, he knew that should the necessity arise he would not hesitate.

He thought back to Captain Scara Bandaris and his troop, and the miserable, snarling pack of Jheleck children they had been escorting. He had felt comfortable in their presence. Understanding the mind of a soldier was a simple task; even meeting the feral eyes of those savage pups had proved an exercise in recognition, despite the shiver that ran up the back of his neck.

The Enes family now felt alien to him, and his ties to it were stretching, pulling apart, fraying like rotted tendons. He was ready to draw a blade and slash through the last of them. *I am done with flighty young women and sad old men. I am done with foul-tempered artists who see too much. Done with giggling maids who flash bared flesh my way at every opportunity, as if I am but a slave to temptation. I leave Osserc to such legendary prowess – if Scara's tales are of any worth on that account.*

*Spinnock, where are you now? I would ride at your side, and feel at home.*

He might even join Scara's troop. The Greater House of Durav was dying. It might already be dead, slipping into the shadow of their cousins, the Hend, who were surely on the rise. Cryl had been isolating himself and besides, he had no loyal retainer to bring rumours to him – rumours and opinions none would dare utter to Cryl himself. But he suspected that his station was low, his prospects few. In any case, even the thought of prowling the Citadel, like a cur hunting noble blood, disgusted him.

The river slid past before his eyes. If he surrendered, here and now, and offered up a prayer to the river god, his plea would be modest. *Swallow up the turmoil in my skull. Pull it all away and send it down to the dark mud, the furred snags and slimy boulders. Take this all away, I beg you.*

*A single slash of the sword and love dies.*

He heard horses behind him. Riding at a heavy canter. Turning away from the river, his prayer unspoken and no surrender yielded to the bank – his knees free of stains – he made his way back on to the road.

Jaen's visage was dark, and Cryl immediately saw a pall over the Houseblades behind the Lord. Faces were closed in beneath the rims of helms. Swords rattled loose in their scabbards as the troop reined in. His eyes fixing once more upon Jaen, Cryl was shocked to see a man transformed. *The songbird opens wings of black, and in his wake wheel a dozen crows.*

*I am such a fool. He is a man from the wars – how could I have forgotten this?*

Lord Jaen dismounted. Ephalla had bent to set an ear to the tube mouth and was now attempting to snare Jaen's attention, but the Lord ignored her as he made his way over to Cryl. A gesture invited the young Durav to return once again to the river's bank.

Upon the muddy fringe, Jaen halted alongside him and stood silent for a time, eyes on the current's taut twisting, the bulges rising to the surface. Then he drew off his gauntlets. 'This was a fell intrusion, Cryl Durav.'

'There has been violence,' said Cryl.

'A Denier – well, I was about to say "village", but I dare say a half-dozen huts scarcely warrant such a name.' He fell silent again.

'Lord, the wedding waits. If there are raiders—'

'This is *my* land, hostage.'

'Deniers—'

'Cryl,' Jaen's voice was harsh, grating like a notched blade on rough stone, 'they could worship a toadstool for all I care. All who dwell on my land are under my protection. This was an attack on House Enes. Raiders? Bandits? I think not.'

'Sir, I do not understand – who else might have reason to slay Deniers?'

Jaen shot him a gauging look. 'This is what happens when you hide down a hole dug by your own hands. Surely you've kneaded the life out of that broken heart by now? Bury it in that hole, Cryl Durav. The world shakes awake and you sleep on at your peril.'

Cryl was shocked into silence. Never before had Jaen been so abrupt, so cruel. He looked out over the water, his face burning, though with shame or anger he knew not. The Lord's next words snapped his attention round.

'The wedding.' Jaen's face twisted. 'A gathering of the highborn. All in one place, all away from their lands. Abyss take me, we're blind fools.'

'Sir, you hint of an enemy in our midst. Is it Draconus?'

Jaen blinked. 'Draconus?' He shook his head. 'Cryl, I advance you to the rank of lieutenant in my Houseblades – no, you will have to swallow down your impatience to leave us for a time longer. Take my twelve and ride back to the estate. Muster the entire company under full arms and prepare for an attack.'

'Sir?'

'The civil war is upon us – must I strike you about the head to stir your brain to life? You make me doubt your training, not to mention my bold elevation of your rank. Is this all too much for you, Cryl Durav? Be truthful.'

'No sir. But I am not convinced. Urusander's Legion would not slaughter innocents – not even lowly Deniers.'

'There were fears that the Deniers were . . . enlivened. The river god lives again – that much is certain. Do you truly imagine the Legion cannot justify this war? They do so in the name of the cult of Mother Dark. They raise high banners of faith.'

'But House Enes has nothing to do with—'

'I harbour the heretics on my land, Cryl. And I am hardly alone in that – most of the Houses and all the Holds tolerate the Deniers, if only out of pity. But every face has changed. The old masks are discarded.'

'Sir, we entertained Captain Scara Bandaris and his officers in your very dining hall – and now you would condemn them as murderers. This is beyond countenance.'

'Bandaris? He's a man with his own mind, and not one to heel to Hunn Raal. I cannot say for Scara Bandaris, but then, what other troop of armed soldiers has passed down this road of late?'

'Sir, that enemy could have come from anywhere, even from deeper in the forest. I will accept that there may now be renegade units of the Legion. But Lord Urusander is an honourable man.'

'He is, if we accept woeful ignorance on his part, Cryl. But if he is not, if he shutters his own eyes to what his lapdog is up to in his name, I will know the truth of him the moment I stand before him and can look him in the eye. For now, renegade units or not, there is malice at loose in the realm.'

Cryl shook his head. 'Yet you pronounce a conspiracy. Lord, if you are right and the timing of all of this is deliberate, then would not the true target be the wedding itself?'

'They dare not,' Jaen said. 'Not yet – not while they still kill in Mother Dark's name. The marriage of Andarist? Not even Hunn Raal would risk the personal ire of Anomander and Silchas.'

*Not yet?* Shaken, Cryl drew a deep breath. 'I will lead your twelve back to the keep, sir, and prepare for siege.'

'Tell me it is not preferable to watching her take his hands in wedlock.'

Cryl frowned and then straightened. 'Sir, it is not.'

Jaen's nod was sharp. 'Just so. I knew your courage, Cryl Durav. Go, then.'

'Very well, Lord. I would a word with your daughter—'

'No. Leave her. We must move on.'

Cryl bit back a protest, and then felt something crumble inside. Jaen was right. Anything he might say would frighten her, or worse, he might be tempted to invite that fear into his own fate, into whatever awaited him back at the keep. He could not be that selfish, much as it might please him to leave a lingering prick of blood upon her conscience. *As a child might do, all unknowing, all uncaring. Or worse, in pleasure of giving hurt.*

Saying nothing more, they climbed the bank and returned to the others.

Cryl went to his horse and swung into the saddle. He looked across to the twelve Houseblades who had ridden with Lord Jaen. Their regard was gauging, almost cold. As if all friendship was now gone, and in its place was a new officer, abilities unknown, talents untested. The sudden pressure of their pending judgement was almost physical, descending heavily across his shoulders. Yet he met their eyes levelly, accepting their expectations. 'Two to point and keep all weapons loose,' he said. 'Right flank eyes on the forest line.'

The troop sergeant, Agalas, a sour-faced woman with flat eyes, simply half turned in her saddle and two Houseblades swung their mounts round and set off up the road.

Cryl glanced over at Lord Jaen, but the man had drawn off his eight remaining Houseblades. Whatever he said was a source of obvious agitation among those men and women, some of whom responded with a look back at their comrades. Cryl understood. *We may be headed into battle, but you have a young woman to protect, and a lord to serve. Duty is not always worn with ease.*

He nodded to the sergeant and together they rode out from the train. As he passed the carriage he thought he heard echoing shouts from Enesdia, muted by wood and curtain, and he saw Ephalla flinch and then cast Cryl a panicked look. In response Cryl shook his head, and then he was past.

*     *     *

Galdan sat in the alley with his back to the tavern wall, his kingdom arrayed before him, his subjects the rats busy scuffling through the rubbish. All kings, he decided, should have but one arm, and thus but one grasping hand. The nightmares were gone, finally, but still the air felt thick as blood. He lifted into view his sole hand and studied its minute trembles. Perhaps he was seeing nothing but the shuddering of his own eyes. Chaos could make the world bright, but blindingly so, painfully so. He felt emptied out, his skin a shell protecting hollows and red-hued darkness. If he could roll back his eyes and look inward, he would see the cavern of his skull, and rats among the rubbish, and a throne on which sat the dried-up husk of his life so far.

Soldiers were in the village, wearing livery Galdan knew all too well. They had drunk all the wine and there was no more to be found, not anywhere. When Galdan had crept into the tavern to beg his share, they'd laughed and then he'd been beaten – but not with any vigour. Lying in the dirt, he had sweated out everything inside him. It had begun with foul, wretched oil, beading flushed flesh, and then bile, followed by blood and then rancid meat, rotting organs, fragments of bone and clumps of brain. Everything had come out until there was nothing left to come out. He could hear a moaning wind inside, tracking the tubular length of his arm, swirling in the flaccid sacks of his legs, sliding up through his neck and into his head.

Moaning, he decided, was the song of absence.

Legion soldiers occupied the village and everyone was afraid. Soldiers had no reason for being in Abara Delack and there were too many of them. So many that they had drunk all the wine.

Muttering filled his head; it sounded far in the depths of his skull, but it was trying to come closer, with urgency. He wanted to turn away; he wanted to run from that voice, but from where he sat he could see all the borders of his kingdom, and in his realm there was nowhere to hide.

She had been sent into the north and east. He knew that much. Sent to the Consort, or so went the rumour though none knew for certain, but the demesne of Lord Draconus was indeed in that direction.

The soldiers – what did they want?

He could hear the voice now, louder although still incoherent; and yet, for all its unintelligibility, its timbre of fear was undeniable. It was trying to warn him, crying out frustrated and helpless, and he needed to do something.

He watched his legs draw up under him, watched as they pushed at the ground, shifted for balance. The alley rocked when he stood and then leaned hard against the tavern wall. His subjects froze for a moment, tilting questing noses in his direction, and then went back to their feasting.

'The king,' Galdan gasped, 'is always free with his bounty.'

*One arm, only the one. Where is the other one? She took it – no, she didn't. But she can give it back. She can do that.*

*There is danger. Someone is screaming, here in my head. There is danger. She's in danger.*

*The Legion is awake. The Legion is on the rise.*

*Lord Draconus. She's in danger.*

He would leave his kingdom for a time. The realm would thrive without him. Wealth in unending repast. It was time to set out in search of more wine.

Galdan staggered out from the alley, into the street. He paused, reeling as the bright sunlight assailed him. Few people in sight; and those he saw moved quickly, fearfully, with all the furtiveness of hunted vermin. Soldiers filled the tavern and the fine inn down the street. They occupied houses that had been abandoned in the wake of the war. The community pasture was crowded with horses and the air stank of their shit. Smoke rose from unchecked fires at the town's rubbish heap in the old Denier temple – the one that had been torn down years ago when the monastery went up – out at the western edge where there had once been a grove of old trees. Wood from that grove now held up the ceiling of the fine inn.

He heard laughter from the front steps of the tavern as he stumbled across the street.

The old lady's bribe had failed. There was no more wine. The deal was finished with. Galdan was finished with it. This is what came when things emptied out.

He wanted nothing to do with horses. *But we knew that.* He would have to walk. He needed to find her. He needed to save her. *Behold, the one-armed king. We go to find our queen. The one hand that reached for wealth now reaches for love.*

Galdan knew that the rats would bless him, if they could.

Wreneck wandered up on the high hill overlooking Abara Delack. His ma had told him about the soldiers and this reminded him of the last time he had seen an armed man, the one who'd come for Orfantal's mother. But that man had been a Houseblade, in the service of a lord. Soldiers were different. They served something else, something vast and maybe even faceless. But his ma had said that these ones who now stayed in the village were here to start trouble.

Lady Nerys Drukorlat was virtually alone in that big house. She had taken to hatred for even the sight of Wreneck, and the night before last she had beaten on his back with a cane. He wasn't sure what he'd done to deserve it, but she'd said terrible things about him, things that weren't even true. Although maybe they were and he just didn't know it yet.

With the last horse gone, Wreneck had no work. He had already collected up the last of the dried dung from the pastures, to stock up on fuel, but there wasn't nearly enough to last the winter. Once the soldiers were gone, she'd said, his laziness would end and he would have to go down and collect in the community fields, but he would have to do that at night, so no one saw. *'House Drukorlas shall not be poor in their eyes. Do you understand me, you brainless oaf? Spare me, dear Abyss! Look at those dull eyes – Orfantal had more wits in one finger than you have. You'll collect in the fields at night.'* He had nodded to show that he understood, thankful for the promise that he'd still be one of the household staff, even if she never let him into the house.

But the soldiers hadn't left yet, leaving him nothing to do, and that frightened him. She might see how lazy he was and forget what she'd said. He needed to get to those fields, somehow. Though it was probably already too late. The dung wouldn't even be cured by the time the rains and snows came, and they had nowhere dry to store it except for one blockhouse and that was full of drying brush and sheaves of bark.

He hadn't eaten yet today. He scanned the high grasses, switch in hand. He'd taken to hunting jump-mice, and if he caught a few he would make a small fire from twigs and grasses, roast the fur off them and finally put something in his aching belly.

Distant motion caught his eye and he looked up to see a half-dozen soldiers coming out from the village, up on the keep road. They were riding at a slow canter, unevenly. As he watched, he saw one loosen the sword in the scabbard at her side. The effort almost toppled her from the saddle and the others laughed upon seeing that, the sound drifting up to where Wreneck stood.

The Lady didn't like visitors. There was nothing to feed them.

If he ran, he might reach the house in time, to at least warn her. Switch still in one hand, he set off at a lumbering run. He had been clumsy all his life, not like Orfantal, who was like a jackrabbit under the shadow of an owl or a hawk. His knees sometimes knocked together when he ran and that was painful, and the work shoes he had been given were too big, driving his toes hard forward with each stride, and at any moment one of them might fly off.

His breath ached in his chest and he could feel how hot the effort was making him, but on he ran, stumbling once when a foot struck a sunken stone in the grasses. Slowly, he realized that he would not make it in time. The horses were on the climb already.

She might well hide. Pretend to not be there, sending Jinia out to say that her mistress was away, or maybe unwell, and they would leave. She would tell them to visit on another day, maybe in a week or so. So, he was running for nothing. Jinia was smart and besides, he loved her, though she teased him all the time for being slow and stupid, when she was neither and older besides.

At nights, under his blanket, he made himself wet thinking about Jinia, like pee but not pee, wishing she didn't tease him and wishing that he was let in the house so that he could see more of her and she wouldn't always complain that he stank of horse shit. If he could be let in the house she might one day fall in love with him and when he was older, as old as she was, they could get married and have children and he would name one Orfantal. If it was a boy, of course.

He reached the pasture fence and slipped through it. He could see the dust from the horses at the front of the house, though he was coming up on the building from its back. They had arrived, and dismounted, and there was more laughter and then a shout, but the shout didn't sound right.

Then he heard Jinia scream.

Wreneck ran again and came round the corner of the house. The scene before him made no sense. The door of the house was open. A little way from the steps, three of the soldiers stood around Jinia and one gripped her by her upper arm, holding her up so that only the tips of her leather-clad feet touched the ground. Another one, a woman, had her hand up the maid's tunic. The third soldier, a man, was unbuckling his weapon belt and tugging down his trousers.

The other soldiers must have been inside the house, since there were sounds coming from there, along with crashing. The lady's harsh voice brayed but it was answered by a barking laugh.

Wreneck rushed towards Jinia, raising the switch in his hand.

Someone collided with him from one side, throwing him off his feet. Winded, Wreneck lay on his back. Above him he saw another soldier – the woman who had loosened the sword. She was grinning. 'Look here! Another damned Denier – you can tell by the shit on his face.'

Aching to draw breath, Wreneck rolled on to his side. He saw Jinia looking at him, but her eyes were dull. The woman with her hand up the maid's tunic was making pushing motions, but her other hand was gripping her fellow soldier's stallion, making the same motions. The third soldier, the one holding Jinia, was using his free hand to lift and twist Jinia's breasts. Wreneck stared into his love's eyes and saw nothing, nothing living.

Air rushed back into his lungs. He pushed on to his hands and knees, trying to get up.

'Mother Dark isn't good enough for you?' the woman asked, advancing on him. She kicked him, up into his gut, hard enough to lift him from the ground. Once more the air was driven from his lungs. He curled up in the grit and dust.

Lady Drukorlat was shrieking now, and Wreneck saw one of the soldiers reappear in the doorway, dragging the old woman out by the back of the neck. He propelled her through the air over the steps and she fell hard on the cobbles. Something broke, a bone, and the Lady screamed in pain.

'Too old to fuck, this one,' pronounced the soldier as he came down the steps behind Nerys. 'And the house is fucking near empty, though Pryll's still looking. No other staff that we could see either. It's pathetic.'

The woman standing over Wreneck had not moved. Her hands were fists and those fists rested on her hips and it seemed she was watching what was being done to Jinia. She was breathing fast and her face was red. She smelled of wine.

Jinia's eyes had closed and her head lolled, and if not for the soldier holding her upright she would have fallen over. Wreneck was sure that she was dead. When the woman pulled her hand out from under the tunic, it was red with blood. The man she had been gripping had spilled out the pee that wasn't pee, and he backed away, pulling free as she laughed at him.

The woman spoke above Wreneck, her voice loud and commanding. 'Sort this up, all of you. If the captain sees or hears of this, we'll all hang.'

The man from the steps said, 'Only one way to sort this, sergeant.'

'So get on with it,' she replied. 'Maybe nobody comes up here like they was saying, but these servants got families somewhere, I bet. Thing is, we need to clean it all up, leave no sign of anything.'

There was blood on the ground, and Lady Nerys had rolled on to one side but her leg or hip was broken and she moaned and moaned.

'Fine, only how do we do that?'

The sergeant sighed. 'You really have no brain, do you, Telra? Bodies into the house and burn the fucker down to the ground. We saw the smoke, didn't get here in time to save anyone. Tragic mess. Farab, did you kill the girl?'

411

The woman with the blood-smeared hand and forearm shrugged. 'Probably. In any case, she won't be coming round any time soon.'

'Into the house, then.' The sergeant looked down at Wreneck. He tried meeting her stare but she wouldn't let him. She drew her sword, pointed it at him. Wreneck tried to curl tight. She pushed the blade into him anyway.

It sliced through his left shoulder, cutting the muscle down to score along the bone, and from there the sharp but rounded tip slid into his chest. It bumped along his ribs, then down into his lower belly, driving up against his hip. When she yanked the weapon free, the pain exploded in Wreneck.

*     *     *

He woke up coughing. Each cough was agony. There was blood everywhere. His left arm was senseless, pinned to the floor under him by his own weight. When he pulled back, more blood spurted, then slowed to a dribble through black smears of dried blood. Smoke filled the room. He was in the house. Looking around, eyes burning, he saw flames everywhere. Jinia was lying beside him, motionless, terribly pale. He reached for her. Her skin was cool, but there was life in it.

He was clumsy, but he wasn't weak. Long ago he used to lift Orfantal with one arm, to make the boy squirm and squeal. Jinia was heavier, though, and there was a new weakness in him that he didn't quite understand, but he managed to angle her limp form over his uninjured shoulder. When he stood, gasping under her added weight, he was blinded by the smoke. But he thought he had seen a way through, down the main corridor. He staggered in that direction.

The heat tore at him from both sides but he wouldn't let himself flinch, since she might fall if he did. So he bore the burns, the lashing tongues that flared in his hair and made him scream.

To the right, at the far end: smoke but no flames. He went that way.

A door hanging open. He stumbled through into a room – Sandalath's room – he could tell by the window's shutters. There were no furnishings left, not even wall hangings. The bed had been broken up for firewood. There was nothing to burn. Wreneck made his way to the window.

He was putting it all together. They'd left them on the upper floor. Set fire to everything they could on the ground level. He hadn't seen the Lady's body, but he knew it was in here somewhere. He knew also that he had no hope of finding it. He couldn't be a hero this day. All he could do was save himself and Jinia, the maid he loved.

He set her down beneath the window, and lifted the latches and pushed the shutters back. He looked out and down. Orfantal had once jumped from this floor, from a storeroom above the kitchen, landing

412

catlike on the kitchen wastes. He had stained his clothes and Wreneck had been whipped for letting him do it.

Now, with the floor under him burning the soles of his feet – right through the thin leather of the worn work shoes – he leaned out and looked down. Curing dung was stacked there, because this was the window that wasn't opened any more, and the wall was sunward and that kept everything dry. He turned and, one-armed, picked Jinia up, pushing her limp form over the sill, feet first. He lost his grip on her and she fell before he was ready. He looked down to see that she had landed in the dung. He couldn't tell if the fall had broken anything – not with all the blood covering her legs.

Wreneck clambered out and leapt. He went a bit too far and landed on the edge of the heap, and the impact was hard enough to throw him forward, and the stabbed side of his hip gave way under him. He landed on his good shoulder, and that hurt as much as the burns and cuts.

Standing, he limped back to Jinia and pulled her clear of the dung. He saw her eyelids flutter and then grow still again, but she was breathing and that was good – that meant that everything was all right.

Lifting her again was harder this time, since now both shoulders were full of pain, but he managed it. Staggering, he made his way towards the ruins of the burnt-down stables. Heat gusted at his back for most of the way across the cobbles. He slipped in through a gap in the stone foundation wall and here the air was cooler and free of smoke. Laying Jinia down, he sat beside her, leaning his back against the wall.

He stared at her pretty face. She had a wandering eye when she got tired but with her eyes closed he couldn't see it. Even when he did, he thought it was cute, and this made her even prettier. The trouble now was thinking of what to do next. The people in the village would see the smoke and know that the keep was burning down. But they wouldn't do anything about it. There wasn't enough of them. The only people that might care was his ma, and Jinia's lame uncle.

So, he would wait for them.

And when he got better he would make a spear, the way Orfantal showed him from what he'd learned from somewhere. Finding a shaft of stout wood, heating and trueing it and heating it some more to harden the wood, especially at the point. Once he had his spear, he would go out and hunt down the sergeant who had stabbed him, and then the three who had hurt Jinia, and then the ones in the house who had killed Lady Nerys. He would find them because he had three names. Telra, Farab and Pryll.

He stared down at his scraped knees; and the welts of red from the burns and all the body hair that was now white and fell to dust when he brushed his skin, and all the splashed blood where flies now danced.

413

He could see his pain, inside his head, and it was all red, but he decided to stay away from it.

*She called me a Denier, but I never denied nothing. I was never even asked anything, so I couldn't deny anything, could I? I seen that monastery once, the one on the other side of the river, and it looked like a fortress, or a place where they send criminals. It scared me.*

He'd wanted to be a hero. Saving everyone. Saving Lady Nerys just like Orfantal would have done. Nothing ever went right in his life.

*She should never have stabbed me. That hurt worse than any caning. One day I'll stab her and see how she likes it.*

When he heard his ma's thin voice wafting up, calling his name in helpless anguish, Wreneck shouted wordlessly to bring her to him, and when at last he saw her and she saw him and hurried towards him, he began bawling and could not stop.

∗ ∗ ∗

Tutor Sagander leaned hard on the crutch. The padding did nothing to ease the ache in his shoulder, but his one remaining leg hurt even more. He had no idea there could be so much pain in one poor body, and every twinge and spasm rode bitter waves. He imagined everything inside, beneath his skin, to be black as pitch, fouled by the pain and the hatred that seemed locked in a savage embrace, like lovers wanting to devour each other. But this was not torment enough. He could still feel the leg that was no longer there, could feel its outrage, its incessant demands. It haunted him, rushing through sensations of brutal cold and searing heat, maddening itch and deep ache.

He stood now, resting, in the narrow corridor, trying to hear the words being spoken at the front gate. From the window of his small cell he had seen Legion soldiers. Things were happening in the outer world, the marching of unheard footfalls; and the isolation he had willed upon himself, in the name of healing, now constricted him, tight enough to unleash a howl in his mind.

That cry battered him. There were Legion soldiers in Abara Delack. A dozen or more had ridden out to the monastery; he'd seen monks mustering under arms, and now it seemed that there was a confrontation at the gate.

And here he was, almost too weak to make his way outside.

The boy had a lot to answer for. Better he had drowned under the ice years ago. And as for the three daughters, well, he'd witnessed enough to know that their father should have slit their throats at birth. House Dracons was cursed, by its own blood, by all its secret histories the Lord guarded so well. But the tutor felt close to some truths. He had not wasted all his time here in the monastery.

He'd rested enough. The pain wasn't going anywhere. Lurching into motion, Sagander made his way down the corridor. Cell doors were open on both sides, evidence of haste. Within he saw modest possessions, nothing of worth, little of interest.

The cult was reborn. He knew that much. The well in the compound had overflowed. The fountain in the garden ran red for days. That had been unnerving. Kharkanas was probably in an uproar. The Citadel itself had been built around an ancient temple to the river god. Sagander felt a certain satisfaction when thinking about all of that. When one viewed such matters from a distance, it was clear to see that Mother Dark and her cult were but upstarts, and all the blustering and displays of power hid paucity at the heart. His growing sense of contempt for Mother Dark was new, but he found pleasure in its cultivation.

Gasping, he reached the corridor's end where it opened out to a high-ceilinged intersection. Off to his left ran the colonnaded transept leading to the assembly hall and beyond that the Vigil Chamber and then the front doors. A year ago and he would have traversed this distance in a few score heartbeats. Now it seemed impossible.

He saw no one about, none upon whom he could call for help – although of late they had been less inclined to give it. Their hearts were hardening to him, as he knew they would. Sympathy surrendered to pity and pity gave way to contempt and disgust. He would have to leave here soon. They might well decide to stop feeding him, or bathing him, or carrying him about. People were the same everywhere, no matter what lofty vows they proclaimed. Help was given only in the hope of its being reciprocated. Expectations of reward lurked behind every act of altruism. But he had nothing to offer them, nothing but more need, more weakness, more misery.

They saw his body and thought his mind crippled. And they were fools to think that way.

He intended to use that in bringing down House Dracons, and then his rival scholars in their rich homes and crowded lecture halls, and then, if he could, Mother Dark herself.

*Yes, everything has changed. There is a virtue to imperfection, a place of hidden strength and will. The broken find cunning in the confession. The wounded unveil their wounds and sup well on the pity. See this hitching gait. Follow me down into death.*

He reached the front doors and paused. Red blushes filled his head in pulsing waves. He was layered in sweat and its smell was wretched. His remaining leg quivered under him. *None to carry me. They will pay for that.* He struggled with the latch. Nothing was easy any more. They should have given him a servant.

*I've fallen through the ice.*

The thought made him scowl. He finally managed to open the door.

415

Beyond, in radiating heat, the packed white dust of the compound was blinding, making Sagander flinch. He waited for his eyes to adjust, but it seemed that he could not slow his breathing, which remained fast and tight.

Thirty paces opposite him was the main gate. A small grilled window was at head-height and the mistress stood at it, with armed monks flanking her. More of the brothers lined the wooden walkways near the top of the defensive wall. On the crenellated roofs of the corner towers, the arbalests were loose on their swivels, bolts loaded and the heavy weapons held at the ready by watchful crews. The raw belligerence of the scene shocked him.

He made his way out, angling slightly sideways to take the steps. He saw a brother standing nearby. The young man was rethreading a strap on his left vambrace. Sagander lurched over to him. 'Are we at war, brother?'

The man glanced up. 'Tutor. You have made quite a journey to come out here. I commend you, sir.'

Sagander fought back a sneer. 'Next you'll be expecting me to join you hoeing the rows.' The answering smile was simply irritating. 'You did not answer my question, brother.'

'Our faith is being tested,' he replied, shrugging.

'With whom does the mistress treat?'

'An officer of the Legion company, I would imagine.'

'Urusander's Legion – yes, I know that. But which company? Who commands? Is this one of the disbanded companies or a garrison gone astray?'

The man shrugged a second time. 'If you will excuse me, sir, we're to make a showing along the wall.' He set off at a jog.

Sagander reached up and wiped sweat from his brow. The sun and heat were making him feel ill.

The window's door thudded shut at the gate and he looked over to see the mistress wheel about and march back towards the abbey. *She comes straight to me. I could have stayed in the doorway, in the shade.* Watching her approach, he saw fury in her dark visage and almost quailed before it.

Before he could speak, she said, 'Get under cover, tutor. This could get messy.' And then she was past him, up the steps and inside.

Sagander glared after her, feeling a fool. He'd thought she was coming to speak to him, but the truth was, he'd simply been in her path. *Another slight. One of many. These things add up.* Ignoring her command, he set out across the compound, towards the gate.

Horses thundered briefly on the other side, but the sound quickly drew away. The delegation was retreating back to Abara Delack. He cursed under his breath and then reconsidered. *No. Better this way.*

Only one monk remained at the gate itself and he regarded Sagander curiously. 'Nothing to see any more, sir,' he said.

'I'm leaving.'

'Sir?'

'You have all been most gracious to me. Do convey my appreciation to the mistress and to all of your brothers. But I have no desire to be trapped in a siege. This is not my battle and I am needed in Kharkanas.'

'I see that you have none of your possessions, sir—'

'Send them on when you next have the opportunity. Is it safe beyond this gate – there is no risk in lifting the bar for me?'

'None, sir. They have left for the moment. Tutor, I feel I should perhaps speak with the mistress first.'

'I just did, brother – did you not see? She has given me leave. Now, you must understand, the walk into the town will be arduous enough for me. I would venture it now, while I still have the strength, for I tire greatly once dusk arrives.'

'Then fare you well, sir. I regret we cannot take you down in a wagon.'

'I fully understand, brother. Do you not all insist I take as much exercise as possible?'

'But you refused more often than not, sir. I wonder if you are ready.'

'I eschew exercise for its own sake, brother. Necessity is all I need to become fit.'

The monk lifted the latch and pushed open one of the gate doors.

His smile fixing against all the aches and the misery, Sagander made his way past the man, hobbling through with as much haste as possible. He feared at any moment a shout from the compound, and then hands dragging him back. Instead, he heard the door shut behind him, followed by the heavy settling of the bar.

*As easy as that. Mistress, your children are fools.*

If servants of Mother Dark were eager to spill Denier blood, they were welcome to it. They could spill all they wanted here, until the blood ran in rivers down this treacherous cobbled road. But the river god was old, appallingly old. It had power and it would understand rage, and vengeance. *I have read enough to know. The old cults are blood cults. They thrive on it. They feed on savagery and violence. The god's river will hold ten thousand bloated corpses on its bosom, and still yearn for more.*

*Mother Dark, strike your first blows. Kill the brothers and sisters. Slay the mistress here, it's all she deserves. But this war's last blow will not be yours.*

*River god, I will deliver the blood you need. This I promise.*

He would find the commander of this company. Crippled though Sagander's body might be, his mind was not.

417

There were hidden ways into the monastery, and he knew them all.

A blood bargain, in the name of vengeance. The river god understood. The river god blessed him in this betrayal.

Every step was torture. The commander would feed him, offer him wine. Find him a comfortable chair and a bed and a woman or two – why not? He would earn such rewards. *A religious war, when what we had feared was something different, something more confused. Instead, we get this. Simple, the lines sharply drawn and mutual slaughter the only way through.*

He imagined himself, at the end, emerging from the smoke and ashes, on a road like this one, with naught but charred bones left in his wake. His rivals dead, their opinions meaningless, their judgements a wasted breath. Draconus: Consort to a corpse. Arathan, gutted, with his entrails wrapped round the shaft of a spear. Raskan – so gentle in pouring hot blood down Sagander's throat – well, he would drown in the same. And as for the Borderswords . . . Ville and Galak had been kindly enough, though misers with their commiseration. In return, he would spare them little when their time came.

The triumphs ahead, at the end of this cobbled road, shone with a sceptre's light, raised high as a torch in the darkness. *Flames closed the mouth of my leg – that horrid stump – seared it for ever shut, trapping the howls inside me. I will let them out another way.*

*By sceptre's light, this I vow.*

Mounted soldiers were gathering below, emerging from the village. It seemed he would not have to walk all the way after all.

* * *

They saw a rider ahead of them on the road. The horse was walking and the figure was slumped as if half asleep in the saddle. Their two scouts had reined in halfway between the parties and now faced Cryl and his troop of Houseblades.

Beside Cryl, Sergeant Agalas grunted and then said, 'No uniform.'

'We'll question him.'

The scouts fell in as they continued on.

The man looked up as they cantered closer, as if startled awake. His face was badly bruised and its bones poorly knitted from what must have been a savage beating. One eye was shot with red. Dirt stained his clothes, as did blackened spots of dried blood. He halted his horse.

Agalas gestured and the troop drew up and formed a line behind her and Cryl. The two of them then rode forward to rein in before the stranger.

'You've seen some trouble,' said Cryl.

The man shrugged. 'I lived.'

Agalas spoke. 'Have you seen soldiers of the Legion on this road?'

'Urusander's Legion or the Hust Legion?'

Cryl blinked. 'Hust? No, Urusander's, sir.'

The man shook his head. 'Seen no one and been riding all day.'

'Riding where?' Agalas asked.

'Kharkanas. Thought I might hire on. Did some caravan guarding once, might do it again. The country's unruly these days.'

Agalas seemed annoyed with this response. 'Where did you come down from?'

'Riven Keep. Thought to try the Borderswords, but they wasn't looking to take anyone on, now that peace has come.'

'That's a long journey,' Cryl observed.

The man nodded. 'Sorry I can't help you. Of course,' he added, 'if there was soldiers about, there'd be less trouble on the roads.'

Cryl turned to the sergeant. 'Let's go. We'll see what we see.' To the stranger he said, 'There's an armed procession ahead of you. You'd be safe enough near to them if you rode a little quicker, sir.'

'Thank you,' the man replied. 'That's a decent offer.'

Agalas waved the Houseblades forward and they all rode past the stranger.

'That wasn't much help,' Cryl said as they continued on up the road.

'Sorry, sir,' said Agalas, 'but I'm not buying it.'

'What do you mean?'

'I mean, sir, he wasn't quite right. Not sure.'

'I could see him as a caravan guard.'

She nodded. 'But his horse was a damned good animal, well groomed and well fed, and the tack was clean.'

Cryl considered. 'Any man long on the road would do well to take care of his mount and tack.'

'As to that, sir, he wasn't carrying much gear. I don't know, is all I'm saying.'

'Wonder who gave him that beating. He was armed, after all.'

She shot him a look and then reined in hard. The Houseblades veered past her, drawing up in confusion. Cryl halted his own horse and swung round to face the sergeant. 'What is it?'

'His sword, sir. It was Legion issue.'

Cryl frowned. 'Hardly surprising – those weapons must have flooded the market stalls after the disbanding.'

'You'd think so, sir, but they didn't. Maybe you heard different, but I'm saying they didn't. Soldiers kept their gear.'

'No, I believe you. I only assumed.' He looked back down the road but the stranger was already out of sight. 'So he's ex-Legion. Might be riding to join up with a renegade troop—'

'Sir, we went with the Lord this morning. We saw the Deniers, that village, it was a place of slaughter. The killers just cut 'em all down. Children too. It was butchery.'

'So what was he, then?' Cryl asked. 'A scout? If so, he was coming from the wrong direction and heading the wrong way.'

'I don't know, sir. I don't know what to think, but it feels all wrong here. All of it.'

He studied her weathered face, the flat eyes. If she was in an excited state, he'd not know it from looking at her. 'Sergeant, a word alone, please.'

They rode on ahead and then reined in again.

'Sir?'

'I don't know what to do,' Cryl confessed. 'Lord Jaen commanded us to return to Enes House. He fears for his household. If that lone rider's a scout, then the renegades must be somewhere ahead and that would mean that they'd already hit the estate – assuming they were planning on doing so. But I see no dust above the way ahead, and we're not close enough to see smoke if they attacked the Lord's house.'

She said nothing, watching him, her gloved hands folded on the saddle horn.

'But they wouldn't attack a wedding procession,' Cryl said.

'We need to keep an eye on the road, sir. Study the tracks ahead. Lone rider or lots of riders? Headed which way? Problem is, sir, there's trails through the forest, some of 'em running parallel with this road.'

'Is this your suggestion, sergeant?'

'We can reach Enes House before dusk, sir.'

'They wouldn't attack a wedding procession,' Cryl said again. 'Deniers – well, you've seen the proof of that.' Still he hesitated. Lord Jaen had promoted him, given him this command, and the orders were explicit. Return to Enes House. Muster the full garrison of House-blades. Prepare for an attack. 'Abyss below, one lone stranger on the road and suddenly nothing is clear!'

'I told you he was wrong, sir. And he is. All wrong.'

'That beating was days old—'

'More like a week, sir, or even two. That wasn't swelling, just dead nerves.'

Cryl fidgeted, hating himself, hating his indecision. Lord Jaen had but eight Houseblades in that train. 'I don't know what to do,' he said again.

She frowned. 'Sir, you got your orders. Lord Jaen rides to a gathering of highborn.'

'And no one would dare attack a wedding procession.'

'Unless they've lost their minds. Sir, it's all down to that rider.'

'Should we ride back and question him?'

'If you give me leave, sir, me and two of my Houseblades will do just that. If I have to, I'll ask my questions with the point of my knife. Why's he riding south? That's the key to it all. It don't make sense.'

'Take two with the strongest mounts, sergeant, and waste no time,' Cryl commanded. 'We will continue on and you ride to catch us up – or you send one rider and take yourself and the other to Lord Jaen, if – well, if it's necessary. No, wait, take four, not two.'

'Yes sir. We shouldn't be long.'

'If he's an innocent, I feel for him,' Cryl said.

'If he's an innocent,' Agalas replied, 'his run of bad luck ain't ending soon.'

They rode back. Cryl watched the sergeant select four Houseblades and set off at a gallop. He eyed the eight who remained. She'd left him Corporal Rees, a round-faced veteran with a caustic sense of humour, but there was little amusement in the man's visage today. 'Corporal Rees, I'll have you ride at my side.'

'Send scouts ahead, sir?'

'Yes. But we will now ride without rest.'

'Understood, sir,' Rees replied. 'Don't worry about the sergeant, sir – she'll get the bastard to talk.'

'I hope so.'

'Agalas's been on the other end of torture, sir.'

'She has?'

Rees nodded severely. 'I got drunk one night and cornered her. Told her my whole life story, sir. But she survived. Most of her sanity intact, too.'

Cryl shot the corporal a look. 'It's already a day of blood, corporal. I really don't think you'll win much laughter with comments like that one.'

'Wasn't thinking about laughter, sir.'

Cryl let it pass.

They cantered on, horse hoofs thundering under them.

*　　*　　*

Ever since the huts and their dead, and the soldiers he'd found camped further along the trail, everything had gone wrong for Kadaspala. His mule had plunged a hoof down a burrow hole and snapped its foreleg in half. The artist had toppled from the animal's back, landing awkwardly on his paint box, and then received a solid kick from the braying, thrashing beast, leaving his left thigh so bruised he could barely walk.

He had considered making his way back to the soldiers, but by then they had been a half-day behind him – assuming they'd not moved on. His agitation deepened when he realized that he had lost track of the date – that he was, perhaps, at risk of arriving too late to accompany the procession from Enes House. Once his father and sister arrived at the site of Andarist's new estate, there would be two days of preparations before the ceremony. Even half lame and loaded down with equipment as he was, he expected to reach them before the ceremony. It was, he decided, the best he could hope for.

Cutting the mule's throat had proved messy and brutal, leaving him sprayed in blood and sickened by the deed.

When he looked down at his stained hands and clothes, he felt as if he had caught a curse from the Deniers' camp, and blood was now following him everywhere, a trail of culpability steeped in death and dying. The child's dead face returned to him, no longer ghostly, no longer sketched in the air by the fingers of one hand, but hard with accusation now. That child had made him a consort with the ending of lives, Tiste and beast, the wild into the tamed and the tamed into the decrepit, and all was sullied, all was ruined.

He limped on through the afternoon, the straps rubbing his shoulders raw, the insects biting through his sweat – but with all that he carried he could not brush or wave them away, forcing him to suffer their frenzy.

Art failed reality. Each and every time, it failed in the essence of experience. A work could but achieve the merest hints of what was real and immediate: the tactile discomforts, the pangs of disequilibrium, the smells of endeavour and the shaky unease of a rattled mind. It pawed bluntly at immediate truths and fumbled blindly through all the lies one told oneself in every passing instant, every eternal moment.

He saw now that there was no beginning to anything, and no end, either. Moments fell forward in seamless progression and then fell behind in gathering haze. Colours washed away the moment the observing eyes lost appreciation; or they grew stark and hard when the senselessness of things struck home. He saw now, at the ends of his scraped and stung arms, one hand that etched out creation, and the other that erased it: and by these twin measures he existed, and his entire purpose in living was to insist that he was here, and that this was now, and once those hands fell still, eternally still, all that he proclaimed of himself would vanish.

In his irretrievable absence, they could walk the halls between his paintings; they could walk as things of flesh and heat, blood and bone, thought and unthought, while to either side ran windows on to flattened worlds and reduced lives that were in total all Kadaspala had ever achieved, and with sharpened nail they could poke through those false worlds, and behind them find naught but mortar and stone.

*I have always been a liar. I cannot help what I am – and that is the first lie, the one I uttered to myself long ago. Others accepted it, by virtue of my talent, and in accepting it, they let me live the lie. Sweet of them, and such a relief – that I fooled them – and if my contempt now dogs their shadows, wherever I walk in their wake, well, it is no surprise.*

*Give me the lie and I will take it.*

*And then give it back to you. In vibrant otherworldly colours – that godly language uttered by ungodly tongues – and yearn for the adoration in your eyes. It's what I feed on, after all. Give me what I need, to keep the lies alive. To keep me alive.*

He kept his honest thoughts to himself, for himself. He risked nothing that way, because if artists were liars first and foremost, in close second were they cowards.

One day he would paint beauty. He would capture its essence, and once it was captured, at the pinnacle of his talent, he could lie back, close his eyes, and drift into death. He would be done, and done with the world. It would have nothing left to give him.

But for now, he would paint in blood.

The trail opened ahead, in tangled scrub and severed stumps, and beyond that was the raised river road.

*I leave the wild behind me, with all its perils of raw truth and senseless death. I step into civilization, its shaped stones and lifeless wood, its sun-baked clay and its crowded streets filled with furtive moments we boldly name people.* If he had a free hand, his fingers would awaken to paint the scene, in all its desultory glory, and so make things anew, in all the old ways.

*If the colours are gods, then another god waits in the death of all colour; in black lines and swaths of drowned light. My hand and my eye are creators of entire worlds, creators of new gods. Behold, artist as creator and world upon world to unfurl, inscribe, delineate, destroy.*

He clambered slowly up on to the road, wincing, and swung left – south – and set off.

To a wedding, where beauty was offered up to the sole promise of being sullied, made mundane by mundane necessities and the drudgery of day upon day, night upon night, the host of insipid demands that pulled flesh down, dulled the eyes, made puffy and irresolute the regard – no, he would never paint beauty. It was already too late.

But the scene haunted his mind. The flower petals upon the path, tears of colour already wilting and trodden upon, the bright eyes of the two now bound as one and the lascivious envy of the onlookers. Enesdia's was a transient beauty, its perfect day almost done, almost in the past. Handfuls of crushed petals thrown into the river, riding the currents down and away. Tree branches hanging low over the water as if weighted with sorrow. The colours watery and muted, as if seen through cold tears. A sky empty of life. *The Wedding of Andarist and Enesdia.*

If he could – if he dared – he would steal her away. Lock her in a tower like some mad lover in a wretched poem fraught with twisted notions of possession. His hands alone knew the truth of her, and brother or not he would show her every one of those truths, in pleasures she had never imagined – oh, he knew the crimes of such thoughts, but thoughts lived well in realms of the forbidden – he'd seen as much in the eyes of every victim he painted. He could play out his defiance of taboos here in his mind, as he walked this road, and imagine the brush of his fingers as they painted skin and flesh, as they painted gasp and ecstasy, lurid convulsion and spent sigh. Before his talent everything would surrender. *Everything.*

There had been riders on the road. He saw scores of hoof prints in the dust and dirt, leading in both directions. But the air felt dead, empty, drained of urgency. Here and there, in faint streaks beneath the signs of riders, he saw the tracks of a carriage.

He was indeed behind the procession then, but despite all the traffic suggested by the hoofprints, Kadaspala walked alone and no one else was in sight.

*The Wedding of Andarist and Enesdia.* Painted with rage. *The Wedding of Andarist and Enesdia.* Erased by fury. He had the power of both, here in his hands. Such thoughts lived well in this forbidden realm.

*Behold, artist as god.*

Bruised and scraped and stung, he limped down the road beneath his burden of paints and brushes.

The smell of smoke rode the wind, the smell of dying colours.

*       *       *

Once the Houseblades were out of sight, Narad nudged his mount into a fast trot. Sweat trickled down beneath his shirt, but he felt chilled. He had seen the suspicion in that woman's hard eyes. Corporal Bursa had sent him on to the road, while the troop travelled along a parallel track in the forest. They needed to know how many were ahead, and Narad now had good news for them. A full dozen Houseblades and an officer were riding back to Enes House.

His nerves were ruined. This wasn't what he wanted. He had heard that other companies were on the move, and even now death was being delivered across Kurald Galain. This had gone beyond the Deniers, the wretched poor in their foul huts. Things were spiralling out of control. Urusander's Legion had saved the realm. They were heroes. But they had been treated badly; they had grievances.

He thought about Haral, that old Legion veteran. He thought about the emptiness in that bastard's eyes when he was breaking Narad's face – and the others watching, like that ogre, Gripp, as if fists were proper arguments, as if brutality belonged in the company of men and women, and children. That nobleborn brat, with Gripp on his shoulder like a sour crow – who said that that boy was better than anyone else? What made him worth more than Narad, or any of those dead Deniers?

The world was full of lies. *And people keep telling us we need them, all in the name of peace. But the peace we got was poison. It's all kept in place to feed the few – the ones in charge, the ones getting rich off our backs, our sweat. And they sell us the virtue of obeying, and keeping our heads down, and not taking what we want – what they got and we don't got. They say they worked for it but they didn't. We did, even when we did nothing – by staying in the shadows, in the alleys, in small filthy rooms, by shovelling the shit they dump on us when they walk past noses in the air.*

*None of it's right. So maybe things do have to go down. Maybe it all needs tearing apart, every one of those lies. And maybe brutality is what'll make us all equal.*

Still, he dreamed of killing Haral. And Gripp and that boy.

*Every face is ugly. Even the perfect ones.*

Horses behind him. He twisted round to see that woman and four others. Coming for him. Terror spasmed in Narad's chest, throbbed into the cracked bones of his skull like fists punching from the inside out. He drove his heels into his mount's flanks and leaned forward in the saddle as the beast surged forward, knowing that he was now riding for his life.

*She's another Haral. Abyss spare me – I saw it in her. I saw in her what he had. Those eyes. I can't take any more beatings. I can't.*

He felt his bowels loosening, and each jolt in the saddle warmed his crotch.

None of this was fair. He was just trying to get by, to get through. Instead, he felt as if he were sliding down, and down, and no matter how he grasped or dug in his nails, he kept sliding. The scene before him was jarred and rocked with every clash of hoofs on the old cobbles. As if the world were breaking apart.

But his horse was fresher. He was outdistancing his pursuers – he could hear it. Once he was out of sight again he would cut into the forest, plunge into it and take any trail he found. He would lose them in the wild. He shot a look over one shoulder.

In time to see a score from Bursa's troop surge up the bank and hammer like a fist into the five Houseblades. Animals went down with shrill screams. Bodies fell, bounced and flopped on the road.

One Houseblade sought to wheel round, to flee back up the road, but it was Bursa himself who hacked down between the man's shoulder and neck, sword blade cutting through bone. The blow flung the victim forward, so that he pitched from the saddle and tore the weapon from the corporal's grip.

Narad had let his mount slow, and now he reined in and pulled the beast round. The five Houseblades were all down, along with two of their horses. Soldiers had dismounted to make certain none still lived. He watched them push their swords into bodies, Tiste and animal, and it seemed there was no difference between the two – the actions were precisely the same, methodical and final.

He trotted towards them. He had fouled himself and this shamed him, but the relief upon seeing his comrades overwhelmed him and he looked through watery eyes.

Bursa had dropped down from his horse to recover his sword, and now he walked towards Narad. 'You left a heady wake, Narad.'

The others laughed, but to Narad's astonishment those laughs were not cruel.

'There's the river, soldier,' Bursa added, pointing. 'Get yourself cleaned up.'

'Yes sir. It was the thought of another beating—'

'We know. In your place I'd be the same. We all would. And you can be sure they would have tortured you to get their answers.'

Narad nodded. He dismounted and almost sat down on the road. His legs wobbled under him, but he forced himself to walk down the slope to the river's bank. Behind him, soldiers were dragging the corpses from the road, back into the forest. Others were tying ropes to the dead horses. For all their efforts, only a blind fool would not see that something terrible had happened here. Blood and gore littered the span, staining black the white dust on the cobbles.

The water was deep, the bank dropping off sharply. He pulled off his boots and leggings and, naked from the waist down, held on to a branch and settled into the bitter cold water. The currents would cleanse him – they would have to as he was not about to let go or risk trying to hold on with one hand. He did not know how to swim.

Bursa edged down the bank. 'We had someone keeping an eye on you.'

'I didn't know that,' Narad replied in grunts, still gripping the branch and feeling his feet and legs growing numb.

'Standard doctrine,' Bursa replied. 'No one is left on their own, even if it looks like they are. You're a soldier of the Legion now, Narad. Initiated on a stream of shit and piss.' He laughed again.

Shaking his head, Narad clambered free of the river. He looked down at his pale, thin legs. They seemed clean enough. He went to the soiled clothing.

'Throw the trousers away,' Bursa said. 'I've got a spare pair that you can have, with a rope belt which I think you'll need.'

'Thank you, sir. I'll pay you back.'

'Don't insult me, Narad. This kind of debt means nothing in the

Legion. Who knows, maybe one day you'll make the same offer to someone else, and so it goes.'

'Yes sir. Thanks.'

'Come back up with me. We have a wedding to attend.'

Narad followed Bursa back on to the road. Seeing his nakedness, the men laughed and the women crowed.

'That water was cold,' Narad explained.

*    *    *

The afternoon light was fading. Hobbling on blistered feet, the swelling on his thigh now reaching to the knee, Kadaspala made his way down the slope of the road's bank. He was spent, too weary to go on. He could see a battered lean-to among the young trees at the forest's edge. It would have to do for this night.

Arriving, he paused to study the old camp. The ancient necessity for shelter was simple in its beginnings, he reflected, before it strived for such elaborations as to achieve absurdity. But there was nothing elaborate or absurd about this humble construction. It would need work to keep the rain from him, but he knew that there would be no rain, not this night. Beyond that, this shelter's only surviving function was to comfort the mind.

With a small fire flickering before it, smoke wafting in along with the heat, to keep the insects at bay, he would sleep like a king, albeit a hungry, battered one. When he arrived at Andarist's house, he would appear like a pauper, a destitute wastrel. Would anyone even recognize him? He imagined a familiar Houseblade grasping him by the scruff of the neck and marching him behind an outbuilding, for a lesson in propriety.

He saw his father's disgust, his sister's shock. Hostage Cryl would laugh and drape an arm across his shoulders. All this on the morrow, then. A return to civilization for the wandering artist, the mad painter of portraits, the fool and his brushes.

But even this scene, conceived so tenderly in his mind, was but an illusion. Tiste were killing Tiste. *Today's righteous cause is religion. The gods are paying attention, after all. Wanting you to die in their name. Why? To prove your loyalty, of course. And what of their loyalty, you might wonder? Has your god blessed you and your life? Answered your every prayer? Given proof of its omnipotence?*

*Where is this god's loyalty to you? Not loyal enough to spare your life which you give in its name. Not loyal enough to steer you past tragedy and grief, loss and misery. Not loyal enough to save your loved ones. Or the children who had to die as proof of that selfsame loyalty.*

*No, today the sack is filled with religion. Tomorrow it will be something else. The joy lies in beating it.*

'Poor Enesdia,' he muttered as he sat down beneath the flimsy shelter. 'The wrong wedding. At the wrong time.' *Bruised petals on the black currents.*

He had asked, once, to paint a portrait of Lord Anomander. This in itself was almost unprecedented. Kadaspala was asked: he did not ask. But, that one time, he had, because he had seen something in that young highborn. Something different. He knew that he would find no answer to this mystery without day upon day devoted to piercing the mien of Anomander of House Purake, to slicing it away sliver by sliver with each stroke of his brush, down to the bone and then through that bone. No one, not even a highborn, should possess what Anomander possessed – that almost ancient assurance, and eyes that saw across a thousand years in an instant.

In other flesh, he would see it as madness. As tyranny, or an historian's jaded, cynical regard, or both, since surely every historian was a tyrant at heart, so fiercely armed were they with the weapons of fact and truth; and if tyranny did not thrive in delusion and self-delusion, then it thrived nowhere at all. He would know the first honest historian he saw – the one broken and weeping and well beyond words or even a meeting of gazes. Instead, those he knew were mostly smug with their presumed knowledge, and on board or canvas their visages were as flat as anyone else's.

But he saw no cynicism in Lord Anomander. He barely saw privilege, and the notions of strength and weakness blended in confusion, until Kadaspala wondered if he had not, all through his life, somehow inverted the meanings of each. A man who could offer weakness in strength was a man at peace with power.

Still, Kadaspala was haunted, when thinking of Anomander, by fears and unnamed, faceless dangers. If the lord had not refused him his request, he would now know the truth, from the surface through to the very roots, and all mysteries would be gone, revealed and exposed on board or canvas, and nothing would be quite as dark as it was.

*Do not haunt me, Anomander. Not on this night, the night before your brother takes her hand and steals her from me. Not on this night, I beg you, when I curse the growing darkness and the mother who died in order to birth perfect beauty. Died and broke her husband, died and broke her son. Not on this night, when everything ends and nothing new begins.*

*Andarist, to be the hand that creates. Silchas, the hand that but waits to destroy. Anomander, who owns them both yet stands as would one defenceless and yet impenetrable. You three! War comes and it comes now. How will you answer?*

*Anomander, where is your weakness, and how can it be in truth your strength? Show this to me, and I in turn promise to not haunt*

*you as you now haunt me. Fail in what comes, however, and I vow to
never leave your soul in peace.*

If there was one thing he could not deny, it was that, sullied and
ruined as she would be, Enesdia would at least be safe. With Andarist
and his gentle ways. Safe, but not preserved. The thought sickened him.

He drew his cloak around him and settled into the shelter. Too tired
for a fire, too weary for false comforts, he closed his eyes and tried to
sleep.

∗     ∗     ∗

There was a hill overlooking Enes House. A watchtower had once
commanded it, but some ancient conflict lost in the family's history
had seen it burned, and then fully dismantled until only the foundation
stones remained. The ground surrounding the ring of stones and the
rubbish-filled pit was mostly denuded, covered in a gravel of fire-cracked
rocks and broken crockery. A single track led down the southeastern
side of the hill to the road.

From the summit, Cryl studied the estate. The light was fast fading.
The river bent away from the road, circling this hill, and it ran like a
black serpent behind the house and its grounds. All looked peaceful.

Beside him, Corporal Rees was studying the ground. A moment
later he dismounted and crouched. 'Lieutenant, it's as you said on the
road – they rode up here, a dozen or so in all. To do just what we're
doing.'

Cryl continued studying the estate. He saw the pole bearing no
banner. He could see the front courtyard of the house and the carriage
stable, its doors open. Smoke rose from the chimneys of the mess hall.
A few figures moved about, and the two guards at the gates were out
on the sward, watching them.

'Scouting,' Rees said. 'The Lord was right to fear for his home.'

'I don't think so,' Cryl replied.

'Sir?'

'They came up here, studied the estate. They saw it was under-
manned. They saw that the Lord was not present, and the carriage was
gone.'

'A perfect time to attack.'

'Yet they didn't, did they? Why not?'

'Loss of nerve?'

Cryl shook his head. Dread was a cold fist tightening in his chest.
'The estate wasn't their target, corporal. They didn't attack, because
the procession had already left.'

'Sir, they would not do that. It is one thing to launch a purge against
the Deniers, but what you suggest – against highborn, against a Greater
House – they could never justify that in Mother Dark's name.'

429

'Those highborn who harbour Deniers on their lands,' said Cryl. 'The Lord spoke of this.'

'But sir, we are speaking of the bride of Lord Andarist.'

Cryl looked down at the corporal, bemused.

Rees had pulled off his helm, running a hand through his sparse hair. 'Sorry, sir. It's just . . . I have friends in the Legion. Dear friends. Men and women I fought alongside. What you're saying – none of them I know would ever agree to that. You're describing a crime. Raw murder. Lord Urusander would be the first to hunt down the killers and hang them all.'

'Renegades,' said Cryl. 'Bandits, even, or perhaps the blame will be laid upon the Deniers. If proper signs are left behind. Abyss knows, they could even implicate Draconus. Deceit is their weapon, and every act of murder and chaos will simply impress upon everyone the need for more order – the need for the Legion's return.'

'They would not do that,' Rees whispered.

'They need to strike quickly,' Cryl went on, 'before those coming up from Kharkanas reach the wedding camp. Don't you understand, Rees? Strike the brothers to anger – no, to blind rage – and by whose hand will this civil war be unleashed?' He gathered up his reins. 'Mount up. We ride to the estate, and there I will hand you over to the castellan.'

'And you, sir?'

'A fresh horse. No, two. I will ride through the night – Sergeant Agalas should have caught up with us. Something has happened to them. If the attackers wait for dawn, I should reach Lord Jaen in time—'

'Sir, don't you think they'd have watchers on the road?'

'If I take the other side of the river, there is a ford—'

'I know the one, sir, but the river is high – no one dares it and for good reason.'

'Which is why they'll post no watchers upon it.'

'Sir, you should not go alone.'

'Corporal, it may be that Lord Jaen is right and indeed that I am completely wrong. You need to ready yourselves. Explain it all to Castellan Delaran.'

'Yes sir.'

They swung their weary horses round and set off down the hill.

*     *     *

The night sky was clear and the swirl of stars bright overhead when Narad dismounted with the others in Bursa's troop. Awaiting them in a glade was another troop of Legion soldiers, although none wore uniforms. From this unlit camp an officer strode out to meet them.

She was tall, well shaped, yet she moved in a loose way, dissolute,

430

and Narad wondered if she was drunk. But when she spoke, her words were sharp and precise.

'Corporal Bursa, what news do you bring me?'

'Small troubles only, sir. Taken care of on the road. But we can be certain that no reinforcements from the north will reach them in time. Has Captain Scara Bandaris responded to the rider I sent?'

'I intercepted your messenger, I'm afraid.'

'Sir?'

'Too great a risk, corporal. I deemed it more prudent that no Legion soldier ride to Kharkanas. I understand that you wish for confirmation of your orders. That you feel troubled by events, but you may take the word of Infayen Menand that all we do here is necessary. These first acts, each one but a small letting of blood, are intended to prevent more bloodshed later.'

'Yes sir.'

'Now, divest yourselves of all Legion attire. There is spare clothing awaiting you.'

Narad had stood close enough, among his comrades, to hear this exchange. He assumed that the officer was this Infayen Menand, although he could not be sure. When Bursa turned back to them, however, Narad could see, even in the darkness, his troubled mien.

'You heard the lieutenant, then,' he said to them. 'Head over to that heap of clothing and be quick about it. Once changed, you can try to get some sleep. We'll be back on the move, on foot, well before dawn. Supper's cold tonight. Go on, all of you.'

Narad joined the others in making his way to the spare clothing. When he began picking through it, he felt sticky blood stains on some items.

'Denier shit,' the woman beside him muttered. 'In case any of us get cut down.'

'We get left behind?' Narad asked.

'That's the way of it, Waft.'

Narad didn't much like the nickname they'd given him, but he knew enough to not complain, which would only make it worse. *Just another lie.*

The woman shot him a look. 'You say something?'

'No.'

'Glad for that,' she snapped under her breath, shaking out a tunic and holding it up. 'Spent four years going hungry after getting discharged. Four nobleborn boys once caught me worse for wear on a country road. Said I stank and damned near drowned me giving me a bath in the river. They laughed and pawed me and left me lying naked in the mud. I risked my life to see them safe and that was what they did to me? It wasn't right, and now they're going to pay.'

Narad stared at her. Others had paused to listen, but he suspected that they'd all heard the tale before. They probably had their own. Lists of wrongs could bind tighter than blood. *And I got my face ruined by a Legion veteran, so go to the Abyss all of you.* He stood studying a shirt he'd pulled out, and then dropped it. 'Just realized I don't need anything from here, since I ain't wearing any uniform.'

She snorted a laugh. 'Lucky you. Go get some sleep, Waft. Killing comes with the dawn.'

*       *       *

They were camped in the clearing in front of the new Great House of Andarist, which stood silent, unoccupied but ready. In the darkness, with the Houseblades ranged out to form a protective circle, Enesdia was at last permitted to climb out from the carriage. She was swathed in a thick robe and hooded and the weight of this covering pulled at her.

It was late and her father stood alone by the fire, his eyes upon the huge edifice of the Great House. She moved up alongside him, feeling strangely hollow, almost frightened by what would come in the days ahead.

'A fine home awaits you,' Lord Jaen said, reaching out to take her hand.

She felt the warmth of that grip and found strength in it, but also a painful longing. She would leave his side, and everything would change between them. All at once, Enesdia yearned for her life left behind. She wanted to wear the rough clothes of her childhood, and run laughing with Cryl in heated pursuit, the stains of the soft fruit she'd thrown at him all down the front of his new tunic. She wanted to feel the heat of the sun in its younger days, when it never blinked behind a single cloud, and the air smelled of freedom in ways she'd never fully grasped back then, and now would never know again.

'I am sorry I sent him away,' her father said then.

He had told her of his fears for his home, but she thought them unwarranted. They were highborn, and to strike at them would be seen – by Andarist, and by Anomander and Silchas – as an act of war. The Legion would not dare that, for they would risk losing all favour in the realm, beginning with that of Mother Dark herself. In truth, she believed her father was being dishonest with her, even if it was with her best interests in mind.

'It is probably better this way,' she said, using the words to push down the hurt she was feeling, this wretched sense of abandonment – when she had needed Cryl the most. 'He was not happy. Hasn't been for weeks, maybe even months.'

'Well,' he said, 'it's understandable.'

432

'No it isn't,' she retorted.

'Beloved daughter—'

'Why can't he be happy for me? If it was the other way around, I'd be happy for him!'

'Would you? Truly?'

'Of course I would. Love is such a precious gift, how could I not?'

Her father said nothing.

After a time, she frowned, reconsidering his silence. 'It's just selfish,' she concluded. 'He's as good as my brother, and no brother would be unhappy for me.'

'True, no brother would. But then, Cryl is not your brother, Enesdia.'

'I know that. But that's not the point.'

'I'm afraid that it is.'

'I'm not dense, Father. I know what you're implying, but it isn't true. Cryl can't love me that way – he knows me too well.'

Jaen coughed – but no, not a cough. Laughter.

His reaction should have angered her, but it did not. 'You think I don't comprehend my own vanity? The shallowness of my thoughts?'

'Daughter, if you comprehend such things, then your thoughts are anything but shallow.'

She waved the objection away. 'Who is the least of the brothers of the Purake?' she asked. 'Who among them lacks ambition? Who is the first to smile for no reason?'

'He smiles because he is in love, daughter.'

'Before me, I mean. When I first saw him, he was smiling.'

'His love is for life itself, Enesdia. This is his gift to the world, and I would never consider it of less value than those offered up by his brothers.'

'Oh, that wasn't what I meant. Not really. Never mind. It's too late and I'm tired and overwrought. But I will never forgive Cryl for not being here.'

'Unfair. I was the one who sent him back.'

'I doubt he argued overmuch.'

'On the contrary, he did.'

'But he went anyway.'

'Yes, because he would not disobey me. But I think I understand now. All of this. You are punishing him, and you wanted him to see it. So, in your mind, Enesdia, Cryl must have hurt you somehow. But the only way I can think he could have done that leads me to a place where I should not be – not now, only days from your wedding.'

Despite her robes, Enesdia felt herself grow cold. 'Don't say that,' she whispered.

'Do you love Andarist?'

'Of course I do! How could I not?'

433

'Enesdia.' He faced her, took hold of her shoulders. 'To say that I do not value the gift that Andarist possesses, by his very nature, could not be more wrong. I value it above most other qualities among a man or a woman. Because it is so rare.'

'Did Mother have it? That gift?'

He blinked down at her, and then shook his head. 'No. But I am glad for that, for otherwise her loss would be impossible for me to bear. Enesdia, speak truth to me here and now. If you do not love him enough, your marriage to him will destroy his gift. It may take decades, or centuries, but you will destroy him. Because you do not love him enough.'

'Father—'

'When one loves all things of the world, when one has that gift of joy, it is not the armour against grief that you might think it to be. Such a person stands balanced on the edge of sadness – there is no other way for it, because to love as he does is to see clearly. *Clearly.* Andarist smiles in the understanding that sadness stalks him, step by step, moment by moment. If you wound him – a thousand small wounds of disregard or indifference – until he stumbles and weakens, sorrow will find him and cut through to his heart.'

'I do love him,' she said. 'More than enough, more than any one man needs. This I swear.'

'We will return home upon the dawn, daughter, and weather all that comes.'

'If we do that, Father, then I wound him when he is at his most vulnerable. If we do that, I destroy his gift, and his life.'

He studied her, and she saw in his eyes that he knew the truth of her words. That it was already too late.

'Cryl did the honourable thing, Enesdia.'

'I know,' she replied. 'But I wish he hadn't!' These last words came in a welter of tears and she fell against him.

Her father drew her into a tight embrace. 'I should have acted,' he said, his voice gruff, almost broken. 'I should have said something—'

But she shook her head. 'No, I'm the fool. I have always been the fool – I showed him that often enough.'

She wept then, as there was nothing more for either of them to say.

There was no sense in the world, she decided, much later when she lay sleepless under furs in the carriage. No sense at all. It had surrendered to the facile creatures like her, gliding through life in a glowing penumbra of petty self-obsession, where every unclear comment was a slight, and every slight personal, and spite and malice bred like vermin, in whispers and hidden glances. *That is my world, where everything close to me is bigger than it really is. But the truth is, I know no other way to live.*

She would never let Andarist doubt her, never give cause to hurt. Only in imagination would she free herself to betray, and dream of a son of the Durav in her arms, and the face of a young man who knew her too well.

*　　*　　*

Narad dreamed of women. Beautiful women who turned away from him in revulsion, in disgust. They were crowding close on all sides, and each recoil jostled him. He struggled to hide his face, but it seemed as if his hands were not his own, and that they were helpless in their efforts to find what he sought to hide.

He had not been born with much. He could not recall once basking in the admiring regard of a woman. There was no point in counting all the whores, since they were paid to look pleased; besides, they never held his gaze for very long. Desire was a thing no eye could fake, and its absence was plain enough to unman the boldest man.

Blinking awake, he stared up through the motionless branches and leaves that seemed to fracture the night sky. He would never be desired – even the small hope he had cherished in the wasted years before the beating was now dead.

Not even the gods offered fairness, not without a bargain to be made first. There were tears in his eyes, blurring the scene overhead. *Bargain? I have nothing to give up.* If gods looked down on him now, their regard was flat, unfeeling. Even pity demanded a soul dropping to its knees, and he would not give that up for so poor a reward. *I get pity enough here among the mortals.*

*The beautiful women look away, look past. Their eyes glide over and that has always been the way of it, long before my face was broken. All they want is a mirrored reflection, another perfect face to match the admiration that is the only wealth they understand.*

*Behind this broken face waits an honest man, a man capable of love. He wants only what so many others have. Something beautiful to hold on to.*

*I ask for it, but the gods do not answer. No light or warmth finds their flat eyes. They blink cold. They look away, find something else, something more interesting, more original.*

There were no ugly gods. Their first expression of power was in the reshaping of their selves, into forms lovely to behold. Had he the power, he would do the same. He would take this clay in his own hands and mould it into perfection.

But no such gifts awaited him.

He heard low voices, and then a figure moved close to him, one hand reaching out to nudge him. 'Up, Waft, it's time. Cold breakfast and then weapons and armour on.'

435

It was the woman who had spoken so bitterly the night before. He turned his head, studied her dark form. Wishing she was both beautiful and blind, even her fingers senseless and dumb. Wishing he could lie to her and convince her and then slide into her and afterwards feel at peace.

'You awake?'

'Yes,' he replied.

'Good.' She moved on to the next sleeping form, and he knew that she had been oblivious of his thoughts.

Just as well. He'd had enough of their laughter.

A short time later, over a hundred armed figures were moving through the forest. Narad was among them, a few steps behind Corporal Bursa. He had drawn his sword but the hand that held it was cold. He was shivering under his clothes yet his skin was slick with sweat, and in his mind there was turmoil.

He saw his life unfurled behind him: all the times when he cut people with words, mocking all their pretensions. When he had viewed with disdain every gesture of kindness or supposed sincerity. It seemed to him now that he had been fighting a war all his life. Nothing was real enough to believe in; nothing was good enough to fight for, barring the patch of useless ground he stood upon, and the flimsy borders of his contempt.

And now he found himself in the company of murderers, just one more shadowy form threading between silent boles. Somewhere ahead slept innocent people. Assuming innocence even existed, and of that he had a lifetime of doubt gnawing the edges of his faith. No matter. Their dawn was about to be shattered in a sudden descent into violence and brutality.

He did not want this, and yet something in him hungered for what was to come, the ugliest part of himself – the outside pulled in and made still more venal, still more disgusting. Among all the soldiers in this midst, he alone bore the physical truth of what was hidden inside each and every one of them.

They had their lists, their grievances, just as he had his own.

Moving through the wood, as it drew the darkness down and around them all. There were different kinds of purity, different kinds of pain, but in the gloom every distinction was lost, made the same. He was no uglier than anyone here, they no more beautiful or handsome than he. *We're all the same.*

*Every cause is just when it is your own, when feelings count for something. But sometimes, among some people, feelings count for nothing at all.*

This was the soldier's gift, he supposed.

He staggered then, down to one knee, and his breakfast came back up his throat, sprayed out on to the black earth. The convulsions continued, until there was nothing left inside. Head hanging, threads of mucus and bile dangling from his twisted lips, he sensed people moving past him. Heard a few low laughs.

A gloved hand rapped him on the shoulder and the woman who'd woken him leaned down and said, 'Rancid meat, Waft. Been fighting to keep it down all the way. Get up, stay with me, we're almost there.'

He pushed himself upright, wondering at her invitation. Had Bursa put her up to this? Did they think him a coward, someone they needed to keep an eye on? Shamed, he wiped his mouth with a sleeve, spat out the bitter taste, and set off, the woman falling in beside him.

'We're going to make this a horror, Waft.'

He nodded, a gesture she could not even see.

'As bad as can be. You can't let it get to you. You got to shut it all down, understand? Do but don't think, that's the soldier's creed. If you think of anything at all, think of the peace to come, a year or two from now. Think of a new way of things in Kurald Galain, the nobles knocked down and weak, real people – like you and me – living well and living respected.'

*Living respected. Empty Abyss, woman, you think that'll take the place of self-respect? It won't. You're fooling yourself. We all are.*

'You with me, Waft?'

'Yes,' he said.

There was a lightening of the way ahead, the trees thinning, stumps rising from beaten down grasses. A bulky shape – a carriage – and a row of horses tied to a rope stretching between two upright banners. The glimmer of an ebbing fire.

And figures at the clearing's edge, motionless, seeming to stare directly at Narad.

Sudden shouts, the hiss of iron on scabbard rims—

'*Let's go!*' barked the woman.

And then they were running into the clearing, upon the open grounds of the Great House of Andarist.

\*     \*     \*

Lord Jaen had stood the night, fully dressed, as if in vigil. He had walked the round, checking on his Houseblades, sharing a few quiet words. Andarist and his retinue were at least a day away, with the guests to follow the day after. The night was measured by his circling strides, a slow spiral that, eventually, brought him once more to his position beside the waning fire.

His heart ached for his daughter, for the blindness of youth. And every thought of hostage Cryl was a twisted pressure deep inside him:

437

fear for the young man who might have to defend Enes House from an attack; pain for the wounds his daughter had delivered upon him.

Regret was an empty curse. He had let age take hold of him, as if ennui was an old man's final gift to himself – the blessed embrace of indifference in the guise of wisdom. Weariness awaited every unmindful soul, no matter its age, no matter its station. He knew that centuries of life awaited him, but that was a truth he could not face without blinking, without shying away. The true curse, the one curse that could fill a soul to bursting, was weariness. Not of the flesh, although that played its part; but of the spirit. He had come to recognize in himself a kind of hapless impatience: the affliction of a man waiting and wanting to die.

Loss and broken hearts could be borne by the young, the strong of will, the robust in spirit. He possessed none of those traits, and so he stood, soon to give away his only daughter, soon to pass into her hands all the promises of youth and none of the unspoken regrets, as befitted a father fading from the light. *I am left behind and I am content with that. As content as any old fool can be content. Perhaps I'll take to drink. Some sordid poison of forgetfulness to plunge days and nights into oblivion.*

*No longer needed . . . why should such things feel so cruel?*

He stared at the spent fire, the cooling coals that held to their old shapes of stick and branch. Every dying hearth was home to fragile ghosts, and all that glowed on was but the memory of living. That and nothing—

A sense of motion drew him round. A Houseblade shouted – he saw his guards draw weapons, saw them contract to form a tight line. And from the forest edge, dark shapes boiling out – a gleam of bared iron—

Appalled, disbelieving, Lord Jaen tugged his sword free. He lunged towards the carriage and drove the pommel of his weapon against the door. 'Out! Now! *Out!*'

The maid, Ephalla, crawled from under the carriage, groggy with sleep. Jaen grasped her arm and lifted her to her feet. He shook her. 'Listen to me – take my daughter – flee to the house. Do you understand? To the house!' He flung her hard against the side of the carriage and then wheeled.

His Houseblades were retreating, closing in around the carriage on the side facing the forest.

Behind him he heard the door swing open; heard his daughter's frightened cry as Ephalla dragged her from the carriage.

'We withdraw!' Jaen shouted to his Houseblades. 'Back to the house. Fall back!'

His guards formed a curved line, backing quickly. Jaen glanced over a shoulder and saw the two women running for the house.

The attackers were rushing closer. There were too many of them.

'Slow them down!' he commanded.

The first line of the enemy reached his Houseblades. Weapons clashed, blades slashed down. Two of his guards fell, overwhelmed. The others fought on, desperately hacking at the swords slashing and thrusting towards them. Another fell, his skull crushed.

The ones who remained continued to retreat. Lord Jaen backed up with them, helplessly trapped between his Houseblades and the two women striving to reach the house. Another moment's hesitation and then, with a curse, Jaen spun round and ran after his daughter and the maid. He would hold the door if he could, knowing that the gesture meant nothing.

Andarist had not built a fortress. A grand home and nothing more. Jaen doubted the bar would even hold.

The women reached the door. Ephalla tugged it open and pushed Enesdia through.

*Before her husband – not side by side – ill omen, a marriage doomed—*

The thought tore through him on a spasm of absurd guilt.

He heard scores of footfalls thudding on the ground behind him, fast closing. *My Houseblades are dead. Another dozen would have made no difference. Oh, Cryl—*

He reached the gaping doorway, saw the terrified faces of his daughter and the maid in the hallway inside. He met Ephalla's eyes and nodded.

She slammed the door shut, even as Enesdia shrieked.

Jaen wheeled on the threshold, readying his sword.

\*　　\*　　\*

He had lost one of the horses to the river, watched it swept downstream with its head raised and neck straining. Grainy-eyed, feeling leaden, Cryl clung to the remaining beast as it finally reached the far bank and stumbled up the slope. Without a pause he kicked the creature's flanks and it struggled against its own exhaustion, building into a plodding canter up and on to the road. Still he kicked and somehow the horse found the will to stretch out into a gallop.

He would be coming up to the house from the south. Before him the road was empty, with dawn only now edging the sky.

In the distance he heard shouts and then the clash of blades.

Above a line of trees, he saw the freshly tiled roof of Andarist's house. Cutting down from the road, he drove his horse hard across an open sward, and then through brush and into the shadow of the trees. Before him, as he rode towards the back of the house, he saw figures spilling to the sides at the run. He understood that Jaen had retreated into the house – his only choice, for there were scores of attackers.

439

Cryl's eyes fixed on a shuttered window on the main floor, to the left of the back door. He pushed his mount to even greater speed, riding straight for it.

Someone shouted – they had seen him, but that did not matter. He was almost there.

He kicked his boots free of the stirrups. He clambered up until he was perched on the saddle. At the last moment, as the horse veered of its own accord to avoid colliding with the back of the house, Cryl launched himself across the intervening distance, angling his shoulder down and protecting his face with his arms.

He struck the shutters and wood exploded around him.

Splinters lanced into him as he landed on the floor and skidded across slate tiles. Picking himself up, he drew his sword and rushed towards the front of the house. He could hear hammering against the front door and the sound of splitting wood. The rooms blurred past unseen as he ran.

Enesdia screamed as the front door was battered down.

Cryl plunged into the hallway – saw Enesdia. Ephalla had drawn a dagger and was standing before her mistress. A sword lashed out, the flat of the blade striking the maid's forearm, breaking bones. Another blade punched into her chest, lifting her from the floor—

Cryl rushed past Enesdia. He did not even register the faces of the figures before him. His sword flickered out, opened the throat of the man who had murdered Ephalla, tore free to bury half its length in the gut of a second attacker.

'Run to the back!' he shouted. 'Get on the horse! Go!'

'Cryl!'

More attackers were pushing into the hallway.

From somewhere off to his right, in another room, a window was being broken through. 'Go!' he screamed, flinging himself at the three attackers.

He was a Durav. The blood was on fire in his veins. He split the face of one man, sliced through the kneecap of another. A blade stabbed deep into his right thigh. He staggered back, pulling himself free of the weapon. Strength poured out of that leg. Cursing, he stumbled. More were coming in, eager to reach him. He blocked a thrust, felt his blade slice up the length of someone's arm. And then something slammed into the side of his head and the world flashed white. As he fell forward, twin punches met his chest, pushed him back upright. He looked down to see two swords impaling him.

Another blade slashed, cut through half his neck.

He saw himself falling, in the hallway, almost within reach of the entrance threshold and the hacked body of Lord Jaen lying beyond, where boots and legs crowded past and drew close. Someone stepped on his hand, breaking fingers, but he only heard the sound – the feeling was a sense of wrongness, but there was no pain.

There was only a growing emptiness, black as the river. He waited for it to take him. He did not have to wait long.

\* \* \*

They had caught the nobleborn woman in one of the back rooms, trying to climb out through a window, and dragged her into the main hall. And then the raping began.

When Narad was pushed forward – his sword unblooded and hanging from his hand – the woman who had run with him laughed and said, 'This one to finish her! She's a beauty, Waft, and she's all yours!'

To the crass urgings of a dozen onlookers he was shoved to where she was lying on the hearthstone. Her clothes had been torn away. There was blood on the stone under her. Her lips were split from hard kisses and bites, and the once unmarred flesh of her body now bore deep bruises left by hands and fingers. He stared down into her glazed eyes.

She met them unblinking, and did not turn away.

The woman behind Narad was tugging down his trousers, taking him in hand to wake him up. Laughing, nuzzling the side of his neck, she pulled him down until he was on top of the nobleborn.

He felt himself slide into a place of blood and torn flesh.

Having delivered him, the woman stepped back, still laughing.

The nobleborn woman's body was warm under his, and for all the bruises it was wondrously soft. He reached to hold her tight – to the howls of the others – and he whispered in her ear, asking for forgiveness.

Much later, they told him that she had breathed out her last breath while under him, and Narad had then realized that on that morning, upon the hearthstone, beauty had died in his arms.

\* \* \*

Kadaspala woke with a start. He sat up. In his mind there remained the echoes of screaming – a terrible dream he could not even remember. He rubbed at his face, looked down in the pale morning light to see that his bruised thigh had swollen to twice the size of the other. Groaning, he sank back down.

But the faint echoes of the screams did not fade away. They did not fade at all.

*No. Oh, no no no no—*

Paint and brush boxes left lying on the ground, Kadaspala somehow found himself on his feet, limping through blinding waves of agony, scrabbling up into the road. Trying to run, leg dragging, lurching under him, his breaths raw in his throat.

The sun climbed up through the trees. He hobbled on, wondering what madness had taken him. He could not have heard anything real. The distance was too far – he had been running on this road for ever. Leagues, tens of leagues – but no, the air was still cold from the night just past. Mist clung to the river's surface like smoke.

He could barely walk, much less run.

When he came within sight of Andarist's house, he halted. He could see the carriage, but the horses were gone. There was no movement – not a single Houseblade or servant. He limped forward.

Bodies on the ground. His father's Houseblades and others. He saw faces he had known all his life, each one flat as the thinnest paint, the eyes half-lidded and blank. And everywhere, in lurid hues, gaping wounds. When he brought his hands to his face, he felt only numbness, as if even sensation was in retreat.

Fingers now stabbing the air, he staggered on.

The front door of the house was broken, torn from its hinges.

A sound was coming from Kadaspala, an inhuman sound, a sound of something sliding into a pit, an abyss, a fall into depths unending. The cry surrounded him, greeted the empty morning and its senseless light, and the blood on the earth made shadows beneath motionless bodies. He saw the open carriage door and more bodies beyond – more Houseblades, more strangers in filthy rags, eyes staring as dead eyes always did.

A shape on the steps of the house, a thing in a fine woollen cloak as blue as midnight. Grey hair clotted with black gore. The fingers on the end of Kadaspala's hand danced in frenetic motion, jerking slashes of the invisible brush, and all the while the cry continued, like a soul in retreat, a soul plummeting for ever.

He stepped over his father's body, and then over Cryl Durav's. And saw Ephalla's still, stained form.

He came to stand before the hearthstone.

This was not her. This . . . thing. *Not her. Never her. I don't know who this is. It's not—*

The face was all wrong. The bloodless cheeks, the swollen lips cracked and torn. He had never seen this woman before. She was staring at the ceiling. He felt himself pulled over her, stepping forward, shifting to intercept that empty gaze. He heard his own howl of protest. Still he leaned closer, watching the play of his own shadow sliding up over her face. He met her eyes.

The fingers of his hands curled into claws. The keening sound filled the chamber, ran wild, was trapped in corners, jolting free and careening against the ceiling. Its pitch was building, climbing ever higher. A sound tasting of blood, a sound smelling of horror. He staggered back and fell to his knees.

442

*Enesdia.*

*Don't look at me like that. Don't—*

His fingers reached up, as he stared at the forlorn figure sprawled on the hearthstone, and the invisible brushes stabbed.

Deep into his eyes.

Pain was a shock, rocking his head back, but the artist would not let go – the brushes dipped deeper, soaked in red paint. The cry was now shrieking in a chorus of voices, bursting from his mouth again and again. He felt his fingers grasp hold of his eyes, felt them clench tight, crushing everything.

And then he tore them away.

And darkness offered its perfect blessing, and he shuddered as if in ecstasy.

The babbling in his skull fell away, until a lone, quavering voice remained. *It is the one question that haunts every artist, the one question we can never answer.*

*How does one paint love?*

The brushes had done their work. The gods of the colours were all dead. Kadaspala sat slumped, with his eyes in his hands.

# FIFTEEN

'FIRST SON, TAKE THE SWORD IN YOUR HANDS.'
Kellaras stood near the door, his eyes on the magnificent weapon that Hust Henarald had unwrapped. It seemed to divide the table it rested on, as if moments from splitting the world in half. Lord Anomander, his face hooded as if in shadow, made no move to reach for the sword.

Kellaras could see his commander – the man he had always known – through the midnight pitch of his skin, and the long hair that had been black and was now silver, the hue of polished iron, yet capable of trapping every colour in its strands. The glow of the lanternlight was gold deepening to red, rippling like water as Anomander slowly leaned forward. The shadows within it were blue, on the very edge of inky black, and the way the hair fell reminded Kellaras of rain, or tears. He still struggled to comprehend this transformation.

Henarald spoke again, his features all sharp angles, a glitter in his eyes that might have been fear. 'First Son, are you displeased? The blade is silent, its tongue severed at the root. If it howls for you, only you can hear it.'

'I hear it,' Anomander whispered.

Henarald nodded. 'The weapon waits only for the blessing of Mother Dark.'

'You will see nothing,' said Silchas Ruin from where he leaned against the wall opposite Kellaras.

Henarald shook his head. 'Then I shall hear that blessing, sir. Or taste it. Or touch it, like a rose melting on to the blade, and I will feel warmth in the turning away of light. My head shall fill with the scent of the holy.'

'You shall emerge,' Silchas said, 'with the skin of midnight.'

The Hust Lord flinched.

Anomander straightened, and still he did not reach for the weapon. Instead, he faced Andarist. 'Well, brother, what think you of this sword?'

Andarist was seated at one end of the table, like a man chained down against his will. His need to be gone from the city, to be on the road that would lead him to the woman he loved, was like sweat on his body, an emanation of impatience that seemed to crackle about him. His eyes flicked to the sword, and then up to his brother's face. 'I am a believer in names, Anomander. Power unfolds on the tongue. A word sinks claws into the mind and there would hold fast. Yet the Hust Lord tells us this blade is without a voice. Still, brother, you say that you hear its howl. I would know: by what name does this sword call itself?'

Anomander shook his head. 'None. I hear only the promise of purity.'

'In its will,' said Henarald, 'it demands the purest hand. To draw a weapon is to announce an end to uncertainty. It brooks no doubt in its wielder. It is, sirs, a sword for the First Son of Darkness. If he should deny it, in seeing weakness or flaw, or in sensing malign intent in its clear song, then I shall shatter it, and cast the shards across the world. No other shall claim this blade. Understand this of this sword: in the hands of a king, he is made tyrant. In the hands of a tyrant, he is made abomination. In the hands of the broken, he breaks all that he touches.'

The words hung in the small chamber, like echoes that wouldn't die.

Hust Henarald stood tall before Anomander: an apparition of soot and weals, scars and mottled skin, and Kellaras was reminded of his first meeting with the Lord, when it seemed that iron hid beneath Henarald's flesh and blood; that he was held in place by twisted bars still glowing from the forge. For all of that, Kellaras saw fear in the old smith's eyes.

Silchas Ruin spoke into the heavy silence, 'Lord Hust, what have you done?'

'There is a secret place,' Henarald said, 'known to me. Known to certain Azathanai. There is a forge that is the first forge. Its heat is the first heat. Its fire is the first fire, born in the time before the Dog-Runners, in the time of the Eresal who have long since vanished into the grasslands of the south, where the jungles crawl down to unknown seas. There is no death in these flames. Often they have dimmed, but never have they died. It was in this forge that this weapon was made. One day, I knew – I know – I will be a child again.' He turned to fix Kellaras with a hard stare. 'Did I not say so, good sir?'

Kellaras nodded. 'You did, Lord, but I admit, I did not understand then. I do not understand now.'

Henarald looked away, and to the captain's eyes he seemed to deflate, as if struck to pain by Kellaras's admission – his ignorance, his stupidity. One gnarled hand waved as if in dismissal. 'The child knows simple things,' he said in a near whisper. 'Simple emotions, each one solid, each one raw. Each one honest in its bold certainty, no matter how cruel.'

*It is the madness of iron. This weapon has been forged by a madman.*

'Purity,' Henarald continued, uttering the word in the tones of a lament. 'We are not ready for it. Perhaps we never will be. Lord Anomander, be sure in your reply to this – is Mother Dark pure in this darkness she has spun about herself? Is the darkness pure? Do doubts die where they are sown? For ever starved of light, with no soil to take their roots? Tell me, will her blessing be as that of a child?'

Slowly, Anomander shook his head. 'Lord Hust, I cannot answer these questions. You must ask them of her.'

'Are you not the First Son?'

Anomander's shrug bespoke frustration. 'What do children know of their parents?'

Andarist started at that, enough to make his chair creak. And then he rose. 'Brothers, I must make ready. We are late as it is. I would come to her upon her second day in waiting, with the sun high and every shadow in retreat. Anomander, either take the sword or deny it. Be as simple as a child, even as Lord Hust said, and decide upon the cut.'

'Every child wants, first and foremost,' replied Anomander, and now at last Kellaras could see his master's doubt. 'But not all wants should find answer.'

'I give you the blade,' Henarald said. 'The commission was accepted, as Kellaras is my witness. I bring it to you now. We are all honed well on promises, First Son, are we not?'

'Then I would not dull your virtue, Lord Hust,' said Anomander, and he reached down and closed his hand about the weapon's leather-wrapped grip.

Silchas pushed away from the wall and clapped Andarist on one shoulder. 'See? We are done as promised, O impatient groom, and so you can be off. But I must catch you up. Captain Scara Bandaris has petitioned my presence in the matter of a score of mongrels in the keeper's yard.'

Anomander withdrew his hand from the sword. 'Lord Hust, I will lead you now into the presence of Mother Dark, and by Darkness she will bless this weapon.'

'I will find you at the gate,' Andarist said to him.

His brother nodded. 'Prazek and Dathenar await you below. I would have Kellaras with me.'

'And I, Galar Baras,' said Henarald, 'who attends us without.'

Andarist followed Silchas out of the chamber.

These were fraught days and nights, ever since the mysterious meeting between the Azathanai woman and Mother Dark. The silts left by the flooding river still stained the foundations of the city's buildings, truly the soiled hand of an ancient god. A dozen citizens had drowned, trapped in cellars or swept from their feet by withdrawing currents and then battered by stone and wood. The fisherfolk who plied Dorssan Ryl had all departed – not a boat remained in Kharkanas, and it was said that the forest now seethed with Deniers on the march – to where, none knew.

Within the Citadel there was confusion and discord. The High Priestess Syntara, skin bleached of all life and seeming health, was said to have fled, seeking sanctuary in some unknown place.

Kellaras understood little of it. He felt as if the world had been jostled, throwing them all about, and balance underfoot remained uncertain, as if even nature's laws were now unreliable. The priesthood was in chaos. Faith was becoming a battlefield and rumours delivered tales of blood spilled in the forests, Deniers murdered in their huts. And in this time, as far as Kellaras could tell, his lord had done nothing. *Planning his brother's wedding, as would a father, if the father still lived. Awaiting his new sword, which he seems disinclined to hold, much less use.*

*Prazek and Dathenar get drunk every night, taking whores and priestesses to their beds, and if their eyes are haunted – when caught in a moment of reverie – then in that private silence is where dwells the frightful cause, and nowhere else.*

Kellaras now walked with his lord, with Henarald and Galar Baras behind them, and the corridors seemed damp and musty, the tapestries smelling of mould, the stone slick underfoot. Kellaras imagined a swamp rising to take Kharkanas, a siege of water against soil and every wall undermined beneath placid surfaces.

The rumours swirling round Urusander's Legion were, to the captain's mind, the most disturbing ones of them all. Entire companies had departed their garrisons, and the standards of disbanded companies had been seen above troops in the outlands. Hunn Raal had left Kharkanas in the night and his whereabouts were unknown.

*When faiths take knife in hand, surely every god must turn away.*

He had never given much thought to the Deniers. They were people of the forest and the river, of broken denuded hills. Their skin was the colour of whatever ground they squatted upon, their eyes the murky hue of streams and bogs. They were furtive and uneducated, bound to superstitions and arcane, secret rituals. He could not imagine them capable of the conspiracy of infiltration now being levelled against them.

They approached the Chamber of Night, where the air in the corridor was unseemly cold, smelling of clay.

'She is indeed assailed,' said Henarald behind them.

Anomander raised a hand and halted. He faced the Lord of Hust. 'This is indifference, sir.'

'No reverence given to stone and avenue, then? Even should they lead to her presence?'

'None by her,' the First Son replied, studying Henarald and the wrapped weapon cradled in the old man's arms.

'What of her temples?'

'The priests and priestesses know them well, sir, and by their nightly moans and thrashing would sanctify by zeal alone. You will have to query them directly as to their measures of success.'

'First Son, then it seems we are in tumult.'

'Lord, where is to be found the Hust Legion?'

Henarald blinked, as if caught off guard by Anomander's question. 'Afield to the south, First Son.'

'When last did you have word of them?'

'The commander departed from Hust Forge some days back.' He turned to Galar Baras. 'Were you not present at her leaving, Galar?'

The young man looked suddenly uncomfortable, but he nodded. 'I was, Lord. Toras Redone rides to the legion, but not in haste. At that time, there was nothing untoward upon the horizon.'

Anomander's gaze settled on Galar Baras for a moment, and then he swung round and resumed walking.

Kellaras moved to catch up, hearing, behind them, Henarald address Galar Baras. 'When we are done here, lieutenant, you will ride in haste to the Hust Legion.'

'Yes sir. And what news shall I bring them?'

'News? Has life in the city dulled you so, sir? Heed well my words if you choose to heed not the First Son's. Civil war is upon us, lieutenant. Mother Dark calls upon the Hust Legion. Tell this to Commander Toras Redone: the scales are awry and Urusander steps blind, but each step remains one on the march. The weight of the Hust should give him pause, and perchance a moment of reflection and reconsideration.'

'None of this is Urusander,' pronounced Anomander without turning.

Henarald snorted. 'Forgive me, First Son, but only the man who knows well his warhorse gives it freedom of rein.'

'If Hunn Raal is a warhorse, Lord Hust,' said Anomander, 'then pray Urusander's boots are firm on the stirrups, for indeed does he ride blind.'

They reached the doors and once more Anomander paused. 'Lord Hust, it is as my brother Silchas said. Such is her power that you shall not leave the chamber the man who entered it.'

Henarald's shrug did little to convey calm. 'My hide is too long whetted on iron and age, sir, to have me regret new stains.'

'I spoke nothing of stains, sir.'

The old man lifted his head sharply, as if affronted. 'Shall I fear faith upon her threshold, First Son?'

'This place above any other place, Lord Hust.'

'Would I had never accepted,' Henarald said in a frustrated rasp, his eyes glaring as they fell to the sword in his arms. 'See how I hold this as if it were a child? Even unthinking, I betray a father's terror, and you dare question my faith? I am unmanned too late to challenge this birth, and so must take every next step like a soul condemned. Galar Baras, will you bear the weight of an old man on this threshold?'

'No sir, but I will bear the strength of my lord's will and not easily yield.'

Henarald sighed. 'As the future carries the past, so the son carries the father. Will it take a sword such as this one to sever that burden, I wonder?'

Anomander seemed shaken by these words, but he said nothing and turned, reaching for the latch.

✳   ✳   ✳

When Silchas Ruin, coming upon the captain from behind, set a hand upon Scara Bandaris's back, the man flinched and stepped quickly to one side. Seeing who stood behind him, he relaxed and smiled. 'Ah, friend, forgive me. These pups have been snarling and squabbling all morning, and my nerves are fraught. Even worse, I must teach myself anew the cadence of the court, for I have been among soldiers for too long and have the bluntness of their manner upon me, like the dust of travel. Thus, you find me out of sorts.'

Silchas looked down into the courtyard. 'I see well the cause of your skittishness, Scara, and now fear that fleas ride you and so regret I ever came close.'

Scara laughed. 'Not as yet, Silchas, not as yet. But you see why I long to be quit of these rank charges. To make matters worse, none here in the Citadel will take the leashes.'

'And so you importune my attendance on the matter. I understand your desperation.'

'By any gauge, Silchas, my desperation cannot be measured in full. Tell me, did we ever expect the Jheleck to accede to our demand with these hostages?'

'Some smug negotiator thought it a sharp retort, no doubt,' Silchas mused, eyeing the score of filthy, snarling youths in the yard. 'I would wager he rides an overburdened wagon into the hills even as we speak.'

Scara grunted, and then said, 'Such betrayal warrants tracking hounds, I say, and let him beg on his knees the presumption of his suggestions, as if I will show mercy.'

'The scribes will see the end to us sooner or later, Scara, with numbers in column and fates aligned in ordered lists, and on that day it shall be you and I on the run, with howls on our heels and nowhere civil in which to hide our sorry selves.'

Scara nodded agreement. 'And under dark skies we shall fall, side by side.'

'In companionship alone, I welcome such an end.'

'And I, friend. But name yourself my salvation here, if you can, and I'll know eternal gratitude.'

'Careful, Scara. Eternity has teeth.' He crossed his arms and leaned against one of the pillars forming the colonnade surrounding the keeper's yard. 'But I have for you a delicious solution, in which I hear echoes of old pranks and cruel jests from our days on the march and our nights before battle.' He smiled when he saw his friend's eyes alight in understanding, and then he nodded and continued, 'It is said his familial estate is vast in expanse, feral upon the edges as befits its remote position, and given his pending marriage to a woman too beautiful and too young, why, I imagine dear Kagamandra Tulas will thrill to the challenge of taming these infernal whelps.'

Scara Bandaris smiled, and then he said, 'Lacking his own, why, no better gift could we give him to celebrate his marriage! I happily yield to your genius, Silchas. Why, we'll envigour the old man yet!'

'Well, let us hope his new bride serves that purpose.'

'And here I pondered long on what gift to give our old friend on his wedding day,' said Scara, 'and had thought of a settee to suit naps and the like, of which no doubt he'll need many in the course of his amorous first week or so.'

Silchas laughed. 'Generous in counting weeks, not days, friend.'

'As his friend, could I be less generous?'

'No less indeed. Now I regret the dismissal of the settee.'

'It would fail in surviving a score of pups gnawing upon the legs, and so I could not give him a gift so easily destroyed. I would dread causing him guilt and grief. Why, then he might begin assiduously avoiding me, and that I would not enjoy, much.'

Silchas nodded. 'We do miss his bright disposition, Scara.'

'Speaking of brightness,' Scara said, eyeing the man before him, 'I see your skin still resisting the caress of Mother Dark.'

'I have no answer for that, friend. I knelt alongside my brothers and so pledged my service.'

'And you are without doubt?'

Shrugging, Silchas glanced away.

There was a moment of silence, and then Scara said, 'I am told Kagamandra now rides for Kharkanas.'

'So I have heard. In the company of Sharenas.'

'A wager that he has not once availed himself of her charms, Silchas?'

'If you need coin you need only ask for it, sir. You dissemble and so risk our friendship.'

'Then I withdraw the gamble at once.'

'Tell me,' said Silchas with a nod to the Jheleck hostages, 'have you seen them veer yet?'

'I have, to smart the eyes with foul vapours. These will be formidable beasts in their maturity, and do not imagine them not clever—'

'I would not, as I can see how they regard us even now.'

'Think you Kagamandra can tame them?'

Silchas nodded. 'But amusing as it is for us to contemplate Tulas's expression upon the receipt, I admit to having given your dilemma much thought, and I believe that Kagamandra alone could heel these hounds, and indeed, that he alone would take great pride in doing so.'

'May he return to us enlivened then and so double the miracle.'

'A gift in kind would indeed bless this gesture,' Silchas said, nodding. He straightened from the pillar. 'Now, I must re-join my brothers. And you, Scara?'

'As it is, now that we have a solution here, I can leave my soldiers to oversee the pups until Kagamandra's arrival. Once I have penned a worthy note to him, I shall ride north to those of my company I left in the forest. From there, we shall return to our garrison.'

Silchas studied his friend for a moment. 'You have heard of the other companies stirring about?'

The query elicited a scowl. 'I even argued with Hunn Raal, before he departed here. Silchas, I tell you this: I want none of this. I see how this persecution of the Deniers is but an excuse to recall Urusander's Legion. The cause is unworthy.'

'The Deniers are not the cause being sought, Scara.'

'I well know that, friend. And I will not lie in saying to you that there are rightful grievances at work here. But such matters cannot be addressed by the sword, and I believe that Lord Urusander agrees with me.'

'Be most cautious, then,' Silchas said, his hand once more upon Scara's back. 'I fear Urusander is like a blind man led upon an unknown path, and the one who leads has ill ambition in his heart.'

'They'll not follow Hunn Raal,' Scara said.

'Not knowingly, no.'

The captain shot him a quizzical look then, and a moment later his eyes narrowed. 'I had best write that letter. Mayhap we shall meet on the north road beyond the gates.'

'That would delight me, friend.'

Two of the pups fell into a scrap just then, teeth flashing and fur flying.

*     *     *

Lady Hish Tulla sat in the study of her Kharkanas residence, contemplating the missive in her hands. She thought back to the last time she had met the three brothers, and the unease surrounding her imposition upon their grief at their father's tomb. There had been rain that day and she had sheltered beneath a tree until the clouds had passed. She recalled Anomander's face, a hardened visage when compared to the one she had known when sharing his bed. Youth was pliable and skin smooth and angles soft as befitted a memory of happier times, but on that day, with the rain still upon his unguarded features, he had seemed older than her.

She was not one for self-regard. Her own reflection always struck her to strange superstition and she was wont to avoid instances when she might catch herself in a mirror or blurred upon contemplative waters: a ghostly shadow of someone just like her, the image seemed, living a life in parallel wherein secrets played out unseen, and all the scenes of her imagination found fruition. Her fear was to discover in herself an unworthy envy for that other life. Most disturbing of all, to her mind, was to meet the gaze of that mysterious woman, and see in those ageing, haunted eyes, her private host of losses.

The missive trembled in her hands. Men such as Anomander deserved to be unchanging, or so she had always believed, and she would hold to that belief as if it could protect the past they had shared. His rumoured transformation within the influence of Mother Dark's mystical power frightened her. Was there not darkness enough within the body? But it was only the memory that did not change, of the time before the wars, and if these days were spent assailing it, she knew enough to blame none other than herself.

How would she see him this time? What might she say in answering this personal invitation from an old lover, to attend his arm upon the wedding of his brother? His face had hardened, defying even the soft promise of the rain; and now he would appear before her like a man inverted, with no loss of edges, and no yielding of the distance between them.

She feared pity in his gesture and was shamed by her own weakness before it.

Servants were busy downstairs, cleaning the last of the silts and refuse from the flood. The missive she held was days old, and she had not yet

452

responded to it, and this in itself was impolite, and no rising water could excuse her silence. Perhaps, however, he had already forgotten his offer. There had been tumultuous events in the Citadel. As First Son it was likely that he felt besieged by circumstance, sufficient to distract him from even his brother's wedding. It was not impossible, in fact, to imagine him late upon attendance and seeking naught but forgiveness in Andarist's eyes. A woman upon Anomander's arm at such a moment promised embarrassment and little else.

The appointed time was drawing near. She had things to do here in the house. The cellar stores had all been ruined and the sunken room was now a quagmire of bloated, rotting foodstuffs and the small furred bodies of mice that had drowned or died mired in the mud. Furthermore, on the day of the flood her handmaid's elderly grandmother had died, perhaps of panic, before the rush of the dark waters into her bedchamber, and so there was grief in the damp air of the rooms below, and a distraught maid deserving of consolation.

Instead of attending to all this, however, she sat in her study, dressed not in the habit of the mistress of the house, nor in the regalia of feminine elegance proper to attending a wedding. Instead, she was girded for war. Her armour was clean, the leather supple and burnished lustrous with oil. All bronze rivets were in place and each shone like a polished gem; every buckle and clasp was in working order. The weapon at her side was a fine Iralltan blade, four centuries old and venerated for its honest service. It wore a scabbard of lacquered blackwood banded at the girdle in silver, with a point guard, also of silver, polished on the inside by constant brushing against her calf.

A cloak awaited her on the back of a nearby chair, midnight blue with a high cream-hued collar. The gauntlets on the desk before her were new, black leather banded with iron strips that shifted to scales at the wrists. The cuffs remained stiff but servants had worked the fingers and hands until both were supple.

In the courtyard below, a groom holding the reins of her warhorse awaited her arrival.

There could be insult in this, and she saw once again the hard face of Anomander, and behind it Andarist's fury. Sighing, she set the invitation down on the desk and then straightened, walking to her cloak. She shrugged it over her shoulders and fixed the clasp at her throat, and then collected the gauntlets and strode into the adjoining room.

The old man standing before her was favouring a leg, but he had refused her offers of a chair. The boy behind him was fast asleep on a divan, still in his rags and wearing filth like a second skin. She contemplated the child for a moment longer, before settling her gaze on Gripp Galas.

'On occasion,' she said, 'I wondered what had happened to you. Anomander gives loyalty as it is given him, and yours was above reproach. You did well to ensure your master and I had privacy in our times together, even unto distracting his father when needed.'

Gripp's eyes had softened as if in recollection, but the surrender was momentary. 'Milady, my master found other uses for me, in the wars and thereafter.'

'Your master risked your life, Gripp, when what you truly deserved was gentle retirement in a fine country house.'

The old man scowled. 'You're describing a tomb, milady.'

The boy had not stirred throughout this exchange. She studied him again. 'You say he bears a note on his person?'

'He does, milady.'

'Know you its contents?'

'He is most protective of it.'

'I am sure he is, but he sleeps like the dead.'

Gripp seemed to sag before her. 'We lost the horse in the river. We nearly drowned, the both of us. Milady, he knows it not, but the note he carries in its tin tube is now illegible. The ink has washed and blotted and nothing can be made from it. But the seal impressed upon the parchment has survived, and surely it is from your own estate.'

'Sukul, I wager,' mused Hish Tulla. 'He is of the Korlas bloodline?'

'So we are to understand, milady.'

'And is intended for the Citadel?'

'For the keeping of the Children of Night, milady.'

'The children,' said Hish, 'have all grown up.'

Gripp said nothing to that.

Now and then, as their gazes caught one another, Hish had sensed something odd in Gripp's regard, appearing in modest flashes, or subtle glints. She wondered at it.

'Milady, the boy insisted that we find you first.'

'So I understand.'

'When I would have gone straight to my master.'

'Yet you acquiesced.'

'He is highborn, milady, and it was my service to protect him on the journey. He is brave, this one, and not given to complaint no matter the hardship. But he weeps for dying horses.'

She shot him another searching look, and then smiled. 'As did a child of Nimander, once, long ago. Your horse, I recall. A broken foreleg, yes?'

'A jump that child should never have attempted, yes, milady.'

'At the cost of your mount's life.'

Gripp glanced away, and then shrugged. 'He is named Orfantal.'

'An unwelcome name,' she replied. Then, catching once more that

454

odd expression on Gripp's lined face, she frowned. 'Have you something to say to me?'

'Milady?'

'I was never so wrathful as to make you shy. Speak your mind.'

His eyes fell from hers. 'Forgive me, milady, but it's good to see you again.'

A tightness took her throat and she almost reached out to him, to show that his affection was not unwelcome and that, indeed, it was reciprocated, but something held her back and instead she said, 'That leg is likely to collapse under you. I insist we summon a healer.'

'It's on the mend, milady.'

'You're a stubborn old man.'

'Our time is short if we are to meet them.'

'You see me standing ready, do you not? Very well, let us bring your unpleasant news to your master, and weather as best we can Andarist's outrage at our martial intrusion. The boy will be fine here in the meantime.'

Gripp nodded. 'It was ill luck, I wager, and not an attempt at assassination. The boy has little value after all, to anyone.'

'Except in death on the road,' she replied. 'The unwanted child as proof of unwanted discord in the realm. I would we had for him another name. Come, we will ride for the Citadel gate.'

\* \* \*

Galar Baras was blind, but he sensed Henarald still standing at his side. The darkness within the Chamber of Night was bitter cold and yet strangely thick, almost suffocating. As he stared unseeing, he heard the Lord of Hust draw a sharp breath.

A moment later a woman's soft voice sounded, almost close enough for Galar to feel its breath upon his face. 'Beloved First Son, what value my blessing in this?'

Anomander replied, but Galar could not sense from where the words came, or where he stood. 'Mother, if we are but your children, then our needs remain simple.'

'But not so easily met,' she returned.

'Is clarity not a virtue?'

'You will now speak of virtue, First Son? The floor beneath your pacing holds firm underfoot, and you would trust in that.'

'Until I trip, Mother.'

'And you think this blade will ease your doubts? Or is it my blessing that will serve you thus?'

'As a blade sliding into a scabbard, Mother, I would have both.'

Mother Dark was silent for a moment, and then she said, 'Lord of Hust, have you thoughts on virtue?'

'I know of virtues,' Henarald answered, 'but I fear my thoughts are little better than hounds nipping their heels, receiving only a hoof's kick in reward.'

'But dogged they remain . . . those thoughts?'

Henarald's grunt may have been an appreciative laugh, but Galar could not be certain. 'Mother Dark, might I suggest now, and here, that the finest virtues are those that flower unseen.'

'My First Son, alas, paces not through a garden, but on hard stone.'

'His boots strike expectantly, Mother Dark.'

'Just so,' she replied.

There was a frustrated hiss from Anomander. 'If you have found new strengths, Mother, then I beg to know of them. If not in form then in flavour. In this realm of yours, so like a void desperate to be occupied, we all await the fulfilment of our faith.'

'I cannot but retreat before your desires, First Son. The more I come to understand this gift of Darkness, the more I comprehend its refusal as necessary. The risk, I now believe, is to be found in the chaining of what must not be chained and the fixing in place of that which must be free to wander. After all, in the measure of every civilization, wandering must one day end; and when it ends, so too ends an unchanging future.'

'If nothing changes, Mother, then hope must die.'

'Lord of Hust, would you call peace a virtue?'

Galar felt the old man shift uneasily beside him, and suspected that the sword cradled in Henarald's arms was growing heavy. 'My peace is ever an exhausted peace, Mother Dark.'

'An old man's answer,' she murmured, without derision or scorn.

'I am that,' Henarald replied.

'Shall we consider exhaustion a virtue, then?'

'Ah, forgive me, Mother Dark, this old man's retort. Exhaustion is no virtue. Exhaustion is failure.'

'Even if it wins peace?'

'That is a question for the young,' Henarald said, his tone sounding abrasive.

'One day, Hust Henarald, you will be a child again.'

'Then ask me again, Mother Dark, when that time comes, and I will give you the simple answers you seek, as seen from a simple world, a life lived simply as only a child can live, where a question can drift away before fades the echoes of its utterance. Ask the child and he may well bless you in the name of unknowing peace.'

'First Son,' said Mother Dark, 'there is war in Kurald Galain.'

'Give me leave to take up the sword, Mother.'

'In my name? No.'

'Why not?'

'Because, dear son, I am the prize. What is it you seek to protect? My sanctity? I yield its blunting borders. My virtue? That horse has flown and even the dogs have ceased their howl. My holiness? I knew a life of flesh and blood and not so long ago as to forget. In any case, I admit to not understanding the very notion of holiness. Where is the sacred to be found except in each and every one of us, and who can find it in anyone else when they cannot find it in themselves? The conceit is to look outward, to quest elsewhere and to dream of better worlds beyond this one. For ever at the edge of your reach, brushing the tips of your fingers, and how you all stretch and how you all yearn! I am the prize, First Son. Reach for me.'

'You will not bless this sword, then?'

'Dear Anomander, the weapon was blessed in its making. It waits for you, in the trembling arms of the Lord of Hust, for whom this exhaustion is neither peace nor virtue. A most restless child, that blade.'

'Mother,' said Anomander, 'where has Draconus gone?'

'He would bring me a gift,' she replied.

'It seems that is all he does.'

'Do I hear resentment, First Son? Be careful. Draconus is not your father and therefore cannot suit being your target in such matters. Though there is no shared blood between you, nevertheless he is mine and wholly mine. As are you.'

'You go too far,' said Anomander then, in a rasp. 'By title I call you so, as you ask of me, but mother to me you are not.'

'Then wash the darkness from your skin, Anomander Purake.'

Her cold tone shivered through Galar Baras. Beside him, he heard Henarald gasping like a man in pain. Galar moved closer to him, felt contact, and reached to take the sword from his lord's failing arms. As the full weight of the weapon settled in Galar's hands, he grunted – it felt as if he was holding up an anvil.

Henarald sank to his knees beside Galar, shuddering uncontrollably.

Anomander spoke. 'Devoid of sanctity, lost to virtue, and oblivious of all that's holy, what manner of prize are you?'

'If you would seek me, look inward.'

'Perhaps that satisfies the priests, Mother, and you to see their feathers twitch above the vellum as if to mock the flight of your fancies. But I am a warrior and you name me your protector. Give me something to defend. Tell me not my enemies, for I already know them well. Advise no strategies, for that is my garden and it is well tended. Touch lips to no banner I raise, for all honour is found in the warrior at my side and my pledge to him or her. Give me a cause to fight for, Mother, to die for if need be. Shall we war over faith? Or fight in the name of justice or against injustice? A sword striking down the demons of inequity? A campaign to save the helpless, or just their souls? Do I fight for food

457

on the table? A dry roof and a warm bed? The unfettered promise of a child's eyes? Name yourself the prize if you must, but *give me a cause.*'

There was silence in the chamber.

Galar started at an oath from Anomander – close to his side – and he felt the sword taken hold of and then pulled from his hands, snatched away light as a reed.

Boots sounded behind him and suddenly the door was swung open and pale light spilled on to the stone floor around his feet. He looked across to see Kellaras, his skin the breath of midnight, stumbling into his master's wake as Anomander strode from the chamber.

Galar crouched to help lift Henarald to his feet.

The old man seemed barely conscious, his eyes closed, his head lolling, and the spit hanging from his mouth had frozen solid. 'What?' the Lord of Hust whispered. 'What has happened?'

*I know not.* 'It is done, Lord.'

'Done?'

'The sword is blessed, Lord.'

'Are you certain?'

Galar helped Henarald across the threshold, and then reached back to pull shut the door. He looked around and saw that Anomander and Kellaras were already well down the corridor. 'All is well,' he told the Lord of Hust.

'The child . . . the child . . .'

'He has it, Lord. In his hands. He has the sword.'

'Take me home, Galar.'

'I shall, Lord.'

The old man he helped down the corridor was not the old man who had walked into the Chamber of Night, and in this comprehension Galar did not for an instant consider the ebon cast to Henarald's skin.

\*       \*       \*

A soul made weary of life longed for sordid ends. Rise Herat climbed for the tower, his refuge from which any escape was downward, and the height of which reduced entire lives to smudges crawling on faraway streets, like insects examining the crevices between pavestones. He had earlier this day walked those streets, wandering through stained Kharkanas and its uneasy multitudes. He had looked upon faces by the hundred, watching people hide in plain view, or cleave close to companions and loved ones while offering suspicious regard to every stranger who dared look their way. He had witnessed smug wealth, worn like precious cloaks of invulnerability, and saw in those visages the wilful guarding of things that could not be guarded. He had seen the poverty that every concourse exhibited, figures like bent and tattered standards of ill-luck and failure, although to all others that measure of ill-luck was in itself failure. He had seen flashes of envy and malice in veiled glances; he had heard laughter loud enough to draw the attention of others, and knew it for the diffident bravado it was – that child-like need for attention like a weed's root wanting water – but no confidence grew straight and bold from such things, and the eyes ever gave it all away, in pointless bluster and ready challenge.

And those rare gestures of recognition and kindness, they appeared like remnants left behind from a better age. The modern guise was indifference and self-absorption, with every face offering a mask of imperturbability and cynical pessimism.

Rise was an historian who wrote nothing down, because history was not in ages past, not in ages either gilded or tarnished. It was not a thing of retrospection or cogent reflection. It was not lines scratched on parchment, or truths stained deep in vellum. It was not a dead thing to reach back towards, collecting what baubles caught one's eye, and then sweeping the rest from the table. History was not a game of relevance versus irrelevance, or a stern reordering of convictions made and remade. Nor was it an argument, nor an explanation, and never a justification. Rise wrote nothing, because for him history was the present, and every detail carried its own story, reaching roots into antiquity. It was nothing more than an unblinking recognition of life's incessant hunger for every moment, like a burst of the present that sent shockwaves into the past and into the future.

Accordingly, he saw nothing that he had not seen before and would not see again, until such time as death took him away, to shutter at last his weary witnessing of the rancorous, motley mess.

He opened the trap door and climbed up on to the tower's heat-baked, shadowless roof. Even solitude was an illusion. Conversations in clamour, lives crowding now in the ghostly haunts of memory, his mind's voice babbled without surcease and could torment him even in sleep. It was easy for him to imagine the Citadel below as but an extension of that chaos, with the priests hunting faith like rat-hunters in the grain, with liars tending their seeds under lurid candlelight in all the small rooms that so cramped their ambitions, and the foragers who plucked rumours from the draughts as if whipping nets through the air.

If history was naught but that which was lived in the present, then it was history's very unruliness that doomed the players to this headlong plunge into confusion. None of the future's promises ever quite drew within reach; none resolved into something solid or real; and none made bridges to be crossed.

He looked down at the river, winding its way through Kharkanas, and saw it as a metaphor of the present – hardly an original notion, of course – except that to his eyes it was crowded beyond measure, with the swimming and the drowning, the corpses and those barely holding on, all spun about and swirling on unpredictable currents. Those bridges that reached into the future, where dwelt equity, hope and cherished lives so warmly swathed in harmony, arced high overhead, beyond all mortal reach, and he could hear the wailing as the flow carried the masses past every one of those bridges, into and out of those cool shadows that were themselves as insubstantial as promises.

Such shadows could not be walked. Such shadows offered no grip for the hand, no hold for the foot. They were, in truth, nothing more than ongoing arguments between light and dark.

He could fling himself from this tower. He could shock innocent strangers upon the courtyard below, or the street, or even the bridge leading into the Citadel. Or he could vanish into the depths of Dorssan Ryl. A life's end sent ripples through those that remained. They could be vast, or modest, but in the scheme of this living history, most were barely noticed.

*We are all interludes in history, a drawn breath to make pause in the rush, and when we are gone, those breaths join the chorus of the wind.*

*But who listens to the wind?*

Historians, he decided, were as deaf as anyone else.

A soul made weary longed for sordid ends. But a soul at its end longed for all that was past, and so remained trapped in a present filled with regrets. *Of all the falls promised me by this vantage, I will take the river. Each and every time, I will take the river.*

*And perhaps, one day, I will walk in shadows.*

He looked out upon the haze of smoke above the forest beyond the city, the foul columns lifting skyward, leaning like the gnarled boles of wind-tilted trees. That wind made cold every tear tracking down from his eyes, and then gave him a thousand breaths to dry each one.

He thought back to the conversation he had just fled, down in a candlelit chamber far below. As witness he was but an afterthought, in the manner of all historians. Cursed to observe and cursed again to reflect on the meaning of all that was observed. Such a stance invited a sense of superiority, and the drudging internal pontification of the coolly uninvolved. But he knew that for the sour delusion of a frightened fool: to think that he could not be made to bleed, or weep, or even lose his life as the current grew wild with rage.

There were a thousand solutions, and each and every one was within grasp, but the will had turned away, and no exhortation or threat would turn it back.

'We have lost a third of our brothers and sisters,' Cedorpul had announced upon entering the chamber, and the candles had dipped their flames with his arrival – surely not the portent of his words. Behind him was Endest Silann, looking too young for any of this.

High Priestess Emral Lanear stood like a woman assailed. Her face was wan, her eyes sunken and darkly ringed. The strength of her title and eminent position had been swept away along with her faith, and every priest and priestess lost to Syntara clearly struck her as a personal betrayal.

'Her cause,' Cedorpul said then, his small eyes grave in his round face, 'is not the Deniers' cause. We can be certain of that, High Priestess.'

Rise Herat still struggled with the physical transformation among Mother Dark's children in the Citadel, this birth of the *Andii* that even now spread like a stain among her chosen. Night no longer blinded, or hid anything from sight. *And yet still we grope.* He had always believed himself the master of his own body, barring those vagaries of disease or injury that could afflict one at any moment. He had not felt Mother Dark's touch, but that she had claimed him could not be denied. There had been no choice in the matter. *But I now know that to be wrong. People have fled her blessing.*

When Emral Lanear said nothing in response to Cedorpul's words, the priest cleared his throat and resumed. 'High Priestess, is this now a war of *three* faiths? We know nothing of Syntara's intentions. She seems to position herself solely in opposition, but that in itself offers modest cause.'

'And probably short-lived,' Endest Silann added.

Emral's eyes flicked to the acolyte as if without recognition, and then away again.

The glance Cedorpul then turned on Rise Herat was beseeching. 'Historian, have you thoughts on any of this?'

*Thoughts? What value those?* 'Syntara sought refuge in Urusander's Legion. But I wonder at the measure of their welcome. Does it not confuse their cause?'

Cedorpul snorted. 'Is it not confused enough? Beating down the wretched poor to challenge the eminence of the highborn could not be more wrong-footed.' He faced Emral again. 'High Priestess, it is said they strike down Deniers in Mother Dark's name. She must disavow this, surely?'

At that Emral seemed to wince. Shakily she drew out a chair from the table dominating the chamber, and then sat, as if made exhausted by her own silence. After a long moment she spoke. 'The faith of holding on to faith . . . I wonder' – and she looked up and met the historian's eyes – 'if that is not all we have. All we ever have.'

'Do we invent our gods?' Rise asked her. 'Without question we have invented this one. But as we can all see, in each other and in such mirrors as we may possess, our faith is so marked and gives proof to her power.'

'But is it hers?' Emral asked.

Cedorpul moved forward, and went down on one knee beside her.

He took hold of her left hand and clasped it. 'High Priestess, doubt is our weakness as it is their weapon. We must find resolve.'

'I have none,' she replied.

'Then we must fashion it with our own hands! We are the Children of Night now. An unknown river divides the Tiste and we fall to one side or the other. We are cleaved in two, High Priestess, and must make meaning from that.'

She studied him with reddened eyes. 'Make meaning? I see no meaning beyond division itself, this ragged tear between ink and unstained parchment. Regard the historian here and you will see the truth of that, and the desolation it promises. How would you want me to answer our losses? With fire and brutal zeal? Look well upon Mother Dark and see the path she has chosen.'

'It is unknown to us,' snapped Cedorpul.

'The river god yielded the holy places,' she replied. 'The birth waters have withdrawn. There is no war of wills between them. Syntara was not driven away; she but fled. Mother Dark seeks peace and would challenge none in its name.'

Cedorpul released her hand and straightened. He backed away a step, and then another, until his retreat was brought to a halt, against the tapestry covering the wall. He struggled to speak for a moment, and then said, 'Without challenge, there can only be surrender. Are we so easily defeated, High Priestess?'

When Emral made no answer, Rise said, '"Beware an easy victory."'

Emral looked up at him sharply. 'Gallan. Where is he, historian?'

Rise shrugged. 'He has made himself a ghost and walks unseen. In times such as these, no poet is heeded, and indeed is likely to be among the first to hang from a spike, in clacking consort with crows.'

'Words win us nothing,' Cedorpul said. 'And now Anomander leaves the city, and with him his brothers. The Hust Legion is leagues to the south. The Wardens crouch in Glimmer Fate. The nobleborn do not stir, as if disaster and discord are beneath them all. Upon which threshold do they stand, and which step taken by the enemy is a step too far?' He no longer held pleading eyes on Emral Lanear as he spoke, and Rise understood that the priest had dismissed her, seeing in the High Priestess an impotency that he was not yet ready to accept. Instead, he glared at the historian during the course of his tirade. 'Is this our curse?' he demanded. 'That we live in a time of indifference? Do you think the wolves will hold back, when all they see before them is weakness?'

'The wolves are true to their nature,' Rise said in reply, 'and indifference plagues every age and every time, priest. Our doom is to be driven to act when it is already too late, and to then give zeal to our amends. And we beat our brows and decry that indifference, which we never own, or loudly proclaim our ignorance, which is ever a lie.

And old women drag brooms through the streets and graves are dug in even rows, and we are made solemn before the revealed fragility of our ways.'

Cedorpul's eyes tightened. 'Now even you advise surrender? Historian, you mock the value of past lessons, making you worthless in all eyes.'

'Past lessons deserve mockery, priest, precisely because they are never learned. If you deem that stance worthless, then you miss the point.'

Anger darkened Cedorpul's round face. 'We blather on and on – even as poor dwellers in the countryside fall beneath blade and spear! At last I understand what we are – we who hide in this chamber. You know of us, historian, you must! We are the useless ones. It is our task to fritter and moan, to cover our eyes with trembling hands, and bewail the loss of everything we once valued, and when at last there is no one else left, they will crush us like snails under their marching heels!'

Rise said, 'If the wolves are indeed loose among us, priest, then we surrendered some time ago. Yet you berate my mockery of lessons unheeded. Vigilance is an exhausting necessity, if one would protect what one values. We lose by yielding in increments, here and there, a slip, a nudge. The enemy never tires in this assault and measures true those increments. They win in a thousand small victories, and know long before we do when they stand over our corpses.'

'Then climb to your tower,' Cedorpul said in a snarl, 'and leap from its edge. Better not to witness the dregs of our useless demise.'

'The last act of an historian, priest, is to live through history. It is the bravest act of them all, because it faces, unblinking, the recognition that all history is personal, and that every external truth of the world is but a reflection of our internal truths – the truths that shape our behaviours, our decisions, our fears, our purposes and our appetites. These internal truths raise monuments and flood sewers. They lift high grand works as readily as they fill graves. If you blame one appetite you blame all of our appetites. We all swim the same river.'

'In which,' muttered Emral, 'even the wolves will drown.'

'"Destruction spares no crown and I say this unto the lords behind every door, from hovel to palace."'

'Gallan again!' spat Cedorpul. He swung to Endest Silann. 'Let us go. Like keepsakes, they will rest upon shelves even as the flames enter the room.'

But the young acolyte hesitated. 'Master,' he said to Cedorpul, 'did we not come here to speak of Draconus?'

'I see no point,' the priest replied. 'He is but one more keepsake. Mother Dark's own.'

Emral Lanear stood as one who would at last face her accuser. 'Do you now go to join Sister Syntara, Cedorpul?'

'I go in search of peace. I see in you the tragedy of standing still.'

He left the chamber. Endest bowed to the High Priestess but made no move to depart.

Sighing, Emral waved a hand. 'Go on, keep him safe.'

When he slipped out, looking more broken than ever, she turned to Rise. 'You said nothing of value, historian.'

'Daughter of Night, the other has made me hoarse.'

Emral studied the tapestry Cedorpul had been leaning against. 'She is young,' she said. 'Rigour of health and polish of beauty are seen as righteous virtue, and by this Syntara triumphs. Over me, surely. And over Mother Dark, whose darkness hides every virtue and every vice and so makes of them both a singular aspect . . . and one that yields nothing.'

'That may be her intention,' observed Rise.

She glanced at him and then back to the tapestry. 'You claim to have written nothing, historian.'

'In my younger days, High Priestess, I wrote plenty. There are fires that burn bright and so make youthful eyes shine like torches. Any wood pile, no matter how big, will one day be gone, leaving only memories of warmth.'

She shook her head. 'I see no end to the fuel, sir.'

'For lack of a spark, it does rot.'

'I do not understand this image here, Rise.'

He drew up alongside her and studied the tapestry. 'Creation allegory, one of the early ones. The first Tiste heroes, who slew a dragon goddess and drank of her blood and thus became as gods. So fierce was their rule and so cold their power, the Azathanai rose as one to cast them down. It is said that all discord reveals a touch of draconean blood, and that it is the loss of our purity that wields the hand of our ills in all the ages since that time.' He shrugged, eyeing the faded scene. 'A dragon with many heads, according to this unknown weaver.'

'Always the Azathanai, like a shadow to our conscience. Your tale is obscure, historian.'

'A dozen or more creation myths warred for eminence once, until but one survived. Alas, the victor was not this one. We seek reasons for what we are and how we imagine ourselves; and every reason strives to become justification, and every justification a righteous cause. By this a people build an identity and cleave to it. But it is all invention, High Priestess, to make clay into flesh, sticks into bone, and flames into thought. No alternative sits well with us.'

'What alternative would you have?'

He shrugged. 'That we are meaningless. Our lives, our selves, our pasts and most of all, our existence in the present. This moment, the next, and the next: each one we find in wonder and near disbelief.'

'Is this your conclusion, Rise Herat? That we are meaningless?'

'I try not to think in terms of meaning, Daughter of Night. I but measure life in degrees of helplessness, and in the observation of this, we find, in totality, the purpose of history.'

She sent him away when she began to weep. He did not object. There was no pleasure in witnessing the very helplessness of which he had spoken, and so a single gesture had set him to flight.

Now he stood, upon the tower, and from the gate below there came the creaking of massive doors, and out on to the bridge rode two Sons of Darkness and their entourage. Pure was Anomander's black skin, and pure silver his long mane, and as the day's light died, Rise thought he could hear, on the wind, that sundering of light – there, in the rumble of horse hoofs – and before it, on the street, barely discerned figures scattered from its path.

*    *    *

The dog, a bedraggled mess of mud and burrs, was entangled in a chaotic web of roots, branches and detritus, just beneath the eastern bank of the river. It was limp with exhaustion, struggling to keep its head above the water, as the currents tugged at its limbs.

Unmindful of the bitter cold water and pushing through the current – the stony bottom beneath the undercut bank shifting with every step – Grizzin Farl worked his way closer.

The dog swung its head towards him and he saw its large ears dip as if in shame. Reaching its side, the Azathanai lifted clear his travel sack and flung it over the bank, and then reached down and gently extricated the hapless creature.

'Most bravery, dear little one,' he said as he pulled the dog from the water and rested it across the back of his thickly muscled neck, 'is marked by a strength less than imagined, and a hope farther from reach than one expects.' He took hold of the roots above and tested to see if they would hold their weight. 'One day, friend, I will be asked to reveal the heroes of the world, and do you know where I shall take my questioner?' The roots held and he pulled himself up, out of the dragging current. The dog, still clinging atop his shoulders, licked the side of Grizzin's face and he nodded. 'You are quite correct. A cemetery. And in there, before every marker of stone, we shall stand, looking down upon a hero. What think you of that?'

He clambered on to the bank and then sank down on to his hands and knees – since the crossing had proved more onerous than he had thought it would – and the dog slid and scrambled down from his shoulders. It came round in front of him and then shook the water from its fur.

'Aai, foul creature! Did you not see how I struggled to keep my hair dry? This mane need only glance at water and forest to twist into hopeless snarls and tangles. Beastly rain!'

Faintly crossed eyes regarded him, head cocking as if the dog were considering Grizzin's bluster, and finding it far from threatening.

The Azathanai frowned. 'You are a most starved specimen, friend. I'd wager you share every meal and the servings unfairly apportioned. Have we rested enough? I see yon road venturing south and it beckons. It ventures north, too, you say? We shall see none of that with our backs, however, will we? No, with eyes and intention let us narrow the world before us.'

Collecting his sack, he climbed grunting to his feet, and when he set off the dog fell in beside him.

'Providence well understands me,' Grizzin said, 'and knows how better I fare for wise and wisely silent company. Lacking the pleasure of hearing my own voice is a torture I would not wish upon my worst enemy – had I enemies, and a worst one among them, whoever they may be. But think of the dread such an enemy would feel to hear me draw near! A true nemesis am I to him, or her – but no, we shall swing wide of her, lest we envisage a face for this imagined foe, and a pot wielded by a less than dainty yet no less vengeful hand. Him, then, this enemy cowering before us. Do you see a single bone of mercy in me, friend? One you would care to snatch away and bury? Of course not. My heart is cold. My eyes are ice. My every thought is unyielding as solid stone.'

The dog ran off ahead for a dozen or so paces. Grizzin sighed. 'I can make an enemy of mice, it seems. To speak is to wield a weapon, with which I bludgeon friend and foe, friend unto foe, I mean, and lacking victim, why, I but wave it fiercely in the air, bold enough to shy a god. Tell me dog, have you any wine?'

It seemed the beast would trot in advance of him down this road, in the manner of an animal that well knew a master. The smell of smoke was in the evening air, and Grizzin had seen the grey pillars above the forest for much of this day's travel. He disliked the meaning of such details, since they reminded him of all the places he had protected in the past. Strangers stepped carelessly in every garden he had ever tended, and that was a sad admission on all sides. 'For they value only what is theirs, and covet all that is mine, and should we meet we might invent economy, or theft, or both. Dog!'

The beast paused and looked back at him, ears cocked, eyes askew.

'By the confusion of your vision, friend, I name you Providence. Is that too long a name for a scrawny thing like you? No matter. Perversity pleases me, unless it is too perverse, upon which I am known to bark a laugh. You can join me in this, if you care to. But I call you not to call you names, friend, but to tell you that I am tired and hungry and in my sack is a fish, or two, and I see certain herbs that entice my eyes. In short, since I see you fret impatient, we shall make camp in some suitable glade or clearing in the forest upon the left. Thus: keep an eye out for a likely roost.'

When the animal resumed its trot, Grizzin smiled and continued walking.

A short time later the dog loped into the line of trees and vanished from sight.

The Azathanai shrugged, not expecting to see its return. He was thankful for the brief companionship, however, and thought the animal well named for that brevity.

The creature suddenly reappeared, tail wagging. It halted just outside the forest's ragged edge.

Grizzin stood on the road and squinted at the dog. 'Can it be you gleaned my desire? Your stance is most expectant, yet you draw no nearer. Very well, show me a place to sleep and show me, indeed, that Providence can do no less.'

He moved down from the road and approached. The animal spun round and bounded back into the forest.

A short distance in waited a glade, the grasses thick and soft, barring in the centre where the blackened stones encircled an old campfire.

Grizzin ventured into the clearing, up to the old hearth, where he set down his sack. 'You alter the course of this night's conversation, friend,' he said to the dog, now lying near the stones. 'I did anticipate the pleasure of not being understood, thus freeing me to heights of appalling honesty and blue confession. Instead, I now fear fleas will carry the tale, and so must be circumspect. And I fear more the matching of wits with you, and losing the game, O Providence. Now, rest here while I collect wood, herbs and the like. We shall feast tonight, and then pick clean our teeth with fish spines, and make fresh our breaths with the twigs of bitter juniper. What say you?'

But the dog was already asleep, legs twitching as it swam through dreams.

\*　　　\*　　　\*

Hish Tulla watched Gripp Galas gingerly lift himself on to the saddle of his horse. She met his eyes and he nodded. They rode out from the small courtyard, ducking as, Hish in the lead, they passed beneath the gate's heavy lintel stone. The street they trotted onto revealed similar gates lining its winding length, and stationed before a number of them were guards, their eyes shadowed by the visors of their helms.

The river might have receded, but currents of fear lingered. She wondered how many of these guards they rode past had once been soldiers in Urusander's Legion. Questions of loyalty haunted every street, even here where dwelt the highborn behind high walls. This matter of grievances irritated Hish, since they seemed so ephemeral. If by way of recognition of their service to the realm, these soldiers would now demand coin and land, then the matter of compensation could readily be addressed. Negotiations and honourable brokering could take the place of belligerence. But it was not that simple. From what she could determine, the soldiers yearned for something more, of which coin and land were but material manifestations.

Perhaps it was no more than a meeting of the eye, every station made level, as if birthright were irrelevant. A laudable notion, but one she knew to be unworkable. A realm of nothing but highborn would quickly crumble. Without servants, without workers of crafts – potters and weavers and carpenters and cooks – civilization could not function. But even here, this was not part of the new world as envisioned by the decommissioned soldiers. What they sought was only for them and what they sought was an elevation of their profession, to a level of social importance matching that of the highborn.

It was this that so disturbed her. Soldiers already possessed the means and the skills to impose violence or brandish its threat. To yield and heap wealth and land on them could only nurture the gardens of greed and ambition, and these were poison fruit that every highborn well understood.

Position and privilege imposed responsibilities. Unquestionably the defence of the realm was also a great responsibility. *But defence against whom? With all enemies beyond the borders vanquished, who remains to stand in their stead, but those within our borders? An army is a fist poised to strike, but that clenching of fingers and focus of desire cannot be held for ever. It is made to strike and strike it must.*

The poor Deniers of the forests and hills were now dying, but these were the lowest of the believers. How soon before the Legion struck the monasteries, and put to flame temples and abbeys? And who could not but see this in the most venal light? None were safe within the borders of Kurald Galain, from the very army created to defend them.

She thought of the highborn as the counterweight to Urusander's Legion. *But we present a sordid example, all things considered. Squabbling among ourselves, scrabbling for the highest elevation above our neighbours, and spitting venom upon the one who stands at Mother Dark's side, as if questions of justice and propriety did not curdle on our own tongues!* No, this was a wretched mess and in many respects the highborn had only themselves to blame. If a soldier risked her or his life, then it should be in defence of worthy things: family, promise, comfort and freedom from strife. But if a trench were cut across such virtues, where so many were left to scramble for the paltry leavings of those who most profited by that soldier's sacrifice, then it was no wonder that scarred hands should itch.

They rode through the highborn district, with its clean cobbles and ornate gates, its blackwood carriages and healthy horses, its scurrying servants burdened beneath wares they did not own, and of which they would not partake. And the wealthy strolled – fewer than usual – through the dusk, warded by bodyguards, and, as always, contentedly unmindful of the world beyond their ken. She had travelled through the lower quarters of the city; she had seen the destitution and disease breeding in the airs of neglect. But such boldness was rare among her kin.

It would be easy to blame the dwellers for the filth in which they lived, and to see that wreckage as a symptom of moral weakness and spiritual failure; as, indeed, proof of the inequity of blood and the making of privilege a birthright. In the manner of horses, breeding would tell, and if nags struggled before creaking wagons and bore whip marks upon their flanks, and warhorses knew only fields turned muddy with blood and gore, and the upper terraces of the city offered dry even cobbles under well-filed, iron-shod hoofs, then surely this marked a natural order of things?

She had begun to doubt. Too comforting by far these assumptions. Too self-serving the pronouncements. Too inhuman the judgements. The trenches were deepening, and the eyes that looked up and across that gulf were hardening. The privileged had a right to fear these days, just as the dispossessed had a right to their resentment.

But Urusander's Legion stood nowhere between that divide. They stood apart, wanting only for themselves, and they now gathered into ranks with weapons on hand, to take what the poor did not have and the rich had not earned.

She would be the first to scoff at the notion of hard work among her own kind. Tasks of organization were devoid of value without those being organized; without workers herded together with eyes downcast and the next day no different from this day and this life no different from the next one. She knew that she had been born to her wealth and land, and she knew how that inheritance had skewed her sense of the world, and of people – especially those in their hovels, who huddled in a fug of fear and crime and dissolution. She knew, and was helpless before it.

They approached the bridge and saw before them a large party of highborn, and Hish caught sight of Anomander – the silver hair, the mother's legacy of his skin.

Gripp Galas rode up beside her on the concourse and said, 'Milady, I am as unsuited to this company as the tale I bring to my master.'

'Nevertheless, sir.'

Still he hesitated.

Hish Tulla scowled. 'Gripp Galas, how long have you served your lord?'

'Since he was born, milady.'

'And how do you weigh the words you bring?'

'An unwelcome burden on this day, milady. They journey to celebration.'

'Think you your lord not aware of the violence in the countryside? He rides into smoke and ash this evening.'

'Milady, the Deniers are a feint. The Legion but clears the field in preparation. They intend to march Urusander into the Chamber of Night. They intend, milady, a second throne.'

She studied him, chilled by the raw language of his assertion.

After a moment, Gripp continued, 'I don't know my master's awareness of this situation. Nor do I know if my report will twist pleasure from his brother's day. We all know a paucity of joyous memories and I wouldn't assail this one.'

'Must it always be paucity, Gripp Galas?' Her question was asked softly and yet it seemed to strike him like a slap to the face.

He looked away, eyes tightening, and Hish Tulla sensed the gulf that stretched between her and him, a gulf he had acknowledged in acquiescing to the child Orfantal's insistence that he deliver the boy to her first. This was a man who had stood in the highborn shadow: a servant, a bodyguard, his life subservient and dependent upon the very privilege he was avowed to defend. By this measure, one of mutual necessity, all of civilization was defined. The bargain was brutal and implicitly unfair and it sickened her.

Gripp said, 'Milady, there's enough to worry about without thinking too much. Too much thinking ain't never but bred problems. A bird builds a nest, lays her eggs and feeds and defends her chicks, and there's no thinking to any of it.'

'Are we birds, Gripp?'

'No. The nest is never big or pretty enough, and the chicks disappoint at every turn. The trees don't give enough cover and the days are too short or too long. The food's short on supply or too stale and your mate looks uglier with every dawn.'

She stared at him in shock, and then burst out laughing.

Her reaction startled him and a moment later he shook his head. 'I do not expect my master to do my thinking for me, milady. We must each of us do that for ourselves, and that's the only bargain worth respecting.'

'Yet you will take his orders and do his bidding.'

He shrugged. 'Most people don't like to think too hard. It's easier that way. But I'm content enough with the bargain I've made.'

'Then he would know your thoughts, Gripp Galas.'

'I know, milady. I simply rue what he will lose in the telling.'

'Would he rather you said nothing? That you wait until after the marriage?'

'He would,' Gripp acknowledged, 'but will face what he must and voice no complaint, nor blame.'

'You are indeed content with your bargain.'

'I am.'

'You remind me of my castellan.'

'Rancept, milady? A wise man.'

'Wise?'

'Never thinks too hard, does Rancept.'

She sighed, eyeing the retinue once more. 'I wish to be back in my estate, arguing with my castellan over his cruelty to his favoured dog. I wish I could just hide away and discuss nothing more significant than a dog's wretched tapeworms.'

'We would mourn your absence, milady, and envy the castellan your regard.'

'Will you seduce me now, Gripp Galas?'

His brows lifted and his face coloured. 'Milady, forgive me! I am always honourable in my compliments.'

'I fear I mistrust men who make such claims.'

'And so wound yourself.'

She fell abruptly silent, studying the man's eyes, seeing for the first time the softness in them, the genuine affection and the pain he clearly felt for her. These notions only deepened her sorrow. 'It is my fate to lose the men for whom I care, Gripp Galas.'

His eyes widened slightly and then he looked down, fidgeting with the reins.

'In what comes,' she said then, 'take care of yourself.'

There was a shout from the party, and at once riders and carriages were crossing the bridge.

Gripp squinted at the group and then drew a deep breath. 'It is time, milady. I thank you for the clean clothes. I will of course recompense you.'

She thought back to the torn, bloodstained garments he had been wearing on the night of his appearance at her door, and felt tears in her eyes. 'I did not sell them to you, Gripp. Nor loan them.'

He glanced at her and managed an awkward nod, and then urged his mount towards the party.

Hish Tulla guided her warhorse into his wake. When he drew nearer, she would angle her mount to one side, seeking to join the procession at the rear. With luck, Anomander would not notice her arrival and so be spared embarrassment.

Instead, he caught sight of them both while still on the bridge, and as suddenly as the procession had begun moving it was stopped by a gesture from Anomander. She saw him turn to his brother Silchas. They spoke, but she and Galas – both now reined in – were too distant to make out the exchange of words. Then Anomander was riding towards them, with the attention of all the others now fixed upon the two interlopers.

Lord Anomander halted his horse and dropped down from the saddle. He strode to stand before Hish Tulla.

'Sister of Night,' he said, 'our Mother's blessing well suits you.'

'In the absence of fair hues my age is made a mystery, you mean.'

Her comment silenced him and he frowned.

*And so wound yourself.* She evaded his eyes, regretting that she had made him stumble.

Gripp Galas spoke, 'Forgive me, master—'

But Anomander raised a hand. Eyes still on Hish, he said, 'I see the gravity your tale wears, Gripp, and would not discount it. I beg you, another moment.'

'Of course, master.' He clucked and guided his horse away, towards the head of the train.

Hish stared after him, feeling abandoned.

'Will you dismount, Lady Hish?'

Startled, she did so and stood beside her horse's head, the reins in her hand.

'You gave no reply to my invitation, Lady. I admit to feeling shame at my presumption. It was long ago, after all, and the years have stretched a distance between us. But I still feel a child in your eyes.'

'You were never that,' she said. 'And the shame was mine. See me here, yielding to the pity of your gesture.'

He stared at her, as if shocked.

'I have been speaking with Gripp Galas,' she said. 'He is blunt in his ways, but I grew to appreciate his honesty.'

'Lady,' said Anomander, 'Gripp is the least blunt man I know.'

'Then I am played.'

'No, never that. If he is made to guard his feelings, Lady Hish, he is known to grow discomforted. There is a tale, I expect, in his riding to you before me. The last I knew of him, he was on the road down from House Korlas, safeguarding a young hostage. It is not like him to disregard such a charge.'

'Of course it isn't,' and she heard a faint snap to her retort. 'The child is in my keeping for now, and yes, there is a tale, but it belongs to Gripp.'

'Very well.'

'I am not one for unbridgeable divides, Lord Anomander.'

He considered that and seemed to relax. 'If you imagine him to view you as would a father, you have stepped wrongly.'

'I begin to comprehend that,' she replied, 'and now all footing is uncertain beneath me.'

'That said,' Anomander continued, 'I am confident in believing Gripp Galas to be generous of spirit, and so he would not burn to see you upon my arm at my brother's wedding.'

'Will he have a place to stand in witness to the ceremony?'

'Always.'

She nodded. 'Then, Lord, I am here to take your arm.'

He flashed a smile. 'And girded for war, no less. I did not think me so formidable.' Then, instead of waiting for her to draw near, he stepped forward, and his eyes met hers, and he said, 'Lady, your beauty leaves me breathless as ever, and once again I feel a wonder at the privilege of your regard, now and all those years past.' I fear Gripp might not be so pleased with my words here, but I speak only in admiration.'

All words left her, spun beyond reach.

'Pity, Lady Hish Tulla? I only pity those who know you not.' He offered his arm. 'Will you honour me by accepting my invitation?'

She nodded.

His wrist was solid as iron, as if it could bear not only the weight of an entire realm, but also her every regret.

*       *       *

When Anomander dismounted before Hish Tulla, Silchas Ruin twisted in his saddle and waved Kellaras closer. Leaving the company of Dathenar and Prazek, the captain rode up to the white-skinned warrior.

Silchas was smiling. 'For a beautiful woman, your lord will make even a groom wait.'

'There was an invitation, sir,' Kellaras replied.

'We did not think that she would accept, else I would have attempted the same and set myself as my brother's rival. We might have come to blows. Crossed swords, even. Scores of dead, estates in flames, the sky itself a storm of lightning and fire. All for a woman.'

'A thousand poets would bless the drama and the tragedy,' Kellaras observed.

'They'll sift the dust and ashes,' Silchas said, nodding, 'for all the treasures they can only imagine, and in vicarious ecstasy they'll invite wailing mourners into their audience, and make of every tear the most precious pearl. In this manner, captain, do poets adorn themselves in a world's grief.' He shrugged. 'But the feast of two brothers warring over a woman is one too many poets have attended already. 'Tis easy to grow obese on folly.'

Kellaras shook his head. 'Even poets must eat, sir.'

'And folly is a most pernicious wine, always within reach with sweet promises, with no thoughts of tomorrow's aching skull. Alas, it is not only poets who attend the feast of our condition.'

'True, sir, but they chew longer.'

Silchas laughed. And then, when Anomander stepped forward to take Hish Tulla's hand on his arm, the Lord's brother grunted and said, 'What think you of that old gristle waiting in the wings?'

'His presence disturbs me,' Kellaras admitted. 'Gripp Galas had other tasks and I fear his presence here marks failure.'

'Let us hope not,' Silchas said in a mutter.

Kellaras lifted his gaze, considered the northern sky. 'I also fear for the estates upon the edge of the forest, sir. Too many fires and no rain in many days. Bogs are known to swallow flames but not kill them. Should the wind veer . . .'

'The river god battles those flames, captain. It will only fail when dies the last Denier in the forest.'

Kellaras glanced across at Silchas. 'The Houseblades but await the command, sir.'

Silchas met his eyes. 'Will you risk your life defending non-believers, captain?'

'If so commanded, sir, yes.'

'And if Mother Dark deems the Deniers her enemy?'

'She does not.'

'No, she does not. But still I ask.'

Kellaras hesitated, and then said, 'Sir, to that I cannot speak for anyone else. But I will not follow any deity who demands murder.'

'Why?'

'Because we know murder to be wrong.'

'Is it as simple as that, captain? Are there not exceptions? Do we not draw circles in the sand and claim all outside them to be less than us, and by this distinction do we not absolve ourselves of the crime of murder?'

'Sophistry, sir.'

'Yet, as a warrior, captain, you have committed murder in the name of our people, and in the name of your lord.'

'I have, but in the taking of life I appease no god's command. The crime is mine and upon no other shoulders do I set it. If I did – if we all did – then no god could withstand the burden of those crimes. But more than that: we have not the right.'

'Urusander's Legion disagrees with you, captain.'

'With sword I stand ready to make argument, sir.'

Lord Anomander and Lady Hish Tulla were on their horses now, and Kellaras saw Gripp Galas join them. A moment later the procession lurched into motion once more. The captain wondered if Andarist, ensconced in the lead carriage, had chafed at the delay, or sought explanation from his servant. His eyes then fixed on the sword now strapped at his master's hip, encased in a lacquered blackwood scabbard. A weapon blessed by a goddess, forged to take life. *But she refuses to tell him which life. Who will die in her name?*

But the blade was un-named, and so it would remain until after Andarist's ceremony. There would be no omens attending this marriage scene. If perfection were possible, Anomander would seek it for his brother and Enesdia. Or die in the attempt.

Beside him, Silchas said, 'Andarist is the best among us.'

Kellaras understood the meaning of that 'us'. Silchas was referring to his brothers, as if his thoughts had followed parallel tracks to the captain's own.

'For him,' the white-skinned *Andii* continued, 'we will bring peace to the realm. By all that follows, captain, you may measure the fullness of a brother's love. Like you, Kellaras, Anomander will not murder in her name.'

*It is well then that the sword has no voice.*

As they rode out from Kharkanas and on to the north road, Captain Scara Bandaris arrived with his troop. Greetings were called out and jests followed. The sun was low in the western sky and the night promised to be warm.

*       *       *

Long before they came within sight of the estate the dog began to cower, casting glances back at Grizzin Farl, as if to question their chosen course down the road. By this sign, the Azathanai's steps slowed, and it was with deep trepidation that he continued on.

He had no words with which to ease the dog's growing distress, since he could find none for himself. The title of Protector was not an honorific, and not one he willingly chose for himself. The things he guarded against none could withstand, but he would be first to stand in their path, first to weather their storm, and first to bleed. He knew that few understood him, even among the Azathanai. And among the Jaghut, the Lord of Hate was the only one to turn away, avoiding his gaze.

The dog halted at a new track that led from the road, where brush had been cleared and stones left in piles to either side. When Grizzin Farl joined it, he reached down and settled a hand upon its sloped head. 'I am sorry,' he murmured, 'but this is my path. My every desire is a conceit, and where the road ends is where it begins again. Providence, forgive me.'

He set off down the track. The morning air smelled of blood and putrefying meat, but the rot held that sweetness that told him that

475

it was still relatively fresh. A day or two, no more. The dog stayed at his side as he came out upon the clearing. He studied the carriage with its open door, and then the bodies sprawled in the grasses. A fox stood over one, frozen in fear at the sight of the dog. An instant later it bolted, vanishing into the wood. The dog gave no sign of wanting to chase, instead pressing against the side of Grizzin's leg.

He walked past the corpses, pausing every now and then to study one. He scanned the tracks of beaten-down grasses, the places where blood had spilled. Flies buzzed the ground and crows took wing, croaking as they fled his and the dog's approach.

The estate's entranceway was splashed black with gore and a body was lying on the threshold. Grizzin Farl continued walking, until he stood in front of the open door, and the grim offering before it.

A highborn Tiste by the richness of his garb, a man with grey hair. Crows had plucked holes through one cheek, to get at the tongue. He had fallen to at least a half-dozen wounds, and those attackers whom he had killed were heaped to either side of the steps, five in all, dragged out of the way by their comrades but otherwise ignored.

Grizzin ascended the steps and walked past more corpses on his way into the main hall. Here he found the body of a woman, a maid, and there, upon the hearthstone, another young woman, lying on her back. The blood about her left no question as to what had befallen her. He drew closer, seeing that she was upon an Azathanai hearthstone, and seeing now what the blood had obscured: she wore the traditional dress of a bride in waiting.

Hearing a sound to his right, Grizzin turned. A figure was huddled on the floor, in the far corner of the room. Its legs were drawn up under the chin, but one side of its face was pressed against the stone wall, with a stained hand up beside it, the blackened fingers splayed against the stone. Shadows hid any further detail.

Grizzin walked closer. A young man, dressed neither in the fashion of the attackers nor like those who had defended this house. There was dried blood crusting his face, blackening the entire cheek and filling the socket of his eye with darkness. He wore no helm and his hair was long, hanging in greasy strands over his brow. With each step the Azathanai took, the man flinched and pushed deeper into the corner, seeking to grind his head between the stones of the wall until skin tore.

'I mean you no harm, friend,' said Grizzin Farl. 'We are alone in this place, and I would help you.'

The head swung round and Grizzin beheld what had been done to the man's eyes.

His gaze dropped to the man's hands, and then lifted again to that clawed, disfigured face. 'Oh,' he sighed, 'that was no answer.'

The cry that broke from the man was that of a wounded animal. Grizzin moved forward. Ignoring the fists that beat at him, he took the man in his arms and held him tight, until the screams died away and the body ceased its struggles and then, slowly, sagged in his embrace.

After a time, the dog came to lie down beside them.

*      *      *

They had travelled through the night. Breaking fast in the saddle, they continued on as the sun climbed into the sky. When it was high overhead, the procession reached the last stretch of the road before the track.

Anomander, Hish Tulla and Silchas were in the lead, riding abreast. Behind them rode Gripp and at his side was Captain Kellaras. There was no telling how many others had since joined the procession: highborn and their servants and guards, cooks and their pot-wagons, the tent-bearers and the musicians, the poets and artists, apprentices of all sorts; Gripp had seen Silchas's old war-time companion, Captain Scara Bandaris, moving to take up the rear with his troop. By tradition, none had spoken since the dawn, and the solemn air accompanied them as if to protect the day's light and warmth, lest a voice shatter the peace.

Gripp's thoughts were on the woman riding ahead of him, and when guilt drove those thoughts back he thought of the boy, Orfantal. There were fates within reach, and those beyond reach. A wise man knew the difference and Gripp wanted to be a wise man. He welcomed this silence, after the seemingly endless questions his lord had asked, seeking every detail from his recollections of the attack, the flight and the hunt and the escape that followed. Lord Anomander was never one to reveal his emotions, nor allow the extremity or depth of those feelings to tighten his throat or stilt the words he uttered. And so Gripp had no sense of his master's reaction to his tale. At the end he but thanked Gripp for saving the hostage, and this drew Gripp's thoughts back to the boy.

Orfantal should have been accompanying this procession, riding his nag of a horse and knowing nothing of death or murder, or fear, or nights of weeping in the cold. By luck more than anything else, his fate had been within Gripp's reach. But there was a score Gripp needed to settle, in that boy's name, and settle it he would.

They drew within sight of the track.

It was then that Gripp noticed the carrion birds wheeling above their destination. Cold dread filled him, sudden as a flood. Without awaiting command or offering explanation, he kicked his horse into a canter, and then a gallop, rushing past the startled trio at the column's head. An instant later his lord and his lord's brother were following.

Gripp yanked savagely to wheel his horse from the road on to the

477

track. Ahead, he saw the carriage – but no tents, no pavilion, no festive standards and no figures awaiting them.

But there were bodies lying on the sward, and a beaten retreat was marked out in dead Houseblades and matted grasses, straight to the house, and there, upon the steps—

Behind him someone cried out, but he did not recognize the voice.

The world was impossibly sharp around him, yet shaking as if jarred by repeated blows – but those sounded in his chest, and each beat was a fist against the cage of his ribs. The wound on his back bled anew. If a heart could have tears, then surely they were red.

He rode to the house and was down from his horse before it had stopped its frantic skid in the gore-flattened grasses. Limping past the body of Lord Jaen, through the doorway. The splash of blood on the walls, thick as mud on the tiled floor. Stumbling into the room, eyes struggling to fight the gloom, the brutal plunge from light into dark. One last fallen Houseblade – no, that was the Enes hostage, Cryl Durav, his chest broken open by sword-thrusts, one leg caked in blood, one hand mangled as it seemed to reach back towards the centre of the house. His face was twisted and almost unrecognizable, swollen and lined as an old man's. Gripp stepped past him.

'No further, I beg you,' said a deep voice from the shadows of the main chamber.

Gripp reached for his sword.

'I have kin to the fallen,' continued the stranger. 'Sadly injured. Asleep, or perhaps unconscious – I dare not test the gauge between the two.'

Behind Gripp, boots sounded at the entranceway.

'I am come late to this scene,' the voice said, 'but not as late as you, friend.'

Gripp realized that he had sunk down to his knees. His injured leg threatened to give way entirely and he set a hand down to steady himself. He heard his own breathing, too harsh, too dry, riding grief and fighting horror.

A dog trotted out from the shadows of one corner, where Gripp could now make out huddled forms. The half-starved creature halted before him, and then sat with ears laid back. Gripp frowned. He knew this dog.

'Ribs,' he heard himself say. 'I missed you at the Hold. You and Rancept both.'

A scrabbling sounded from the corner and a moment later a figure staggered into view, both hands held out and groping in the air. '*Who comes?*' the figure shrieked. The cry echoed in the chamber and Gripp flinched. No question could sound more plaintive; no need could sound so helpless, and yet none answered.

Behind Gripp stood Anomander – a presence sensed but not seen, but Gripp did not doubt. His lord spoke. 'Kadaspala—'

The blind man lunged towards Anomander, and only then did Gripp see the dagger in Kadaspala's hand.

He rose swiftly and grasped hold of Kadaspala's wrist, and twisted hard.

Another shriek rang through the room, and the knife clattered on the stones. Gripp forced Kadaspala to the floor and held him there as he would a raging child.

Straining against the hold, Kadaspala lifted his head, and blood-crusted sockets seemed to fix unerringly upon Anomander. The mouth opened and then closed, and then opened once more, like a wound. Red teeth offered up a ghastly smile. 'Anomander? I have been expecting you. We all have. We have a question, you see. Just one, and we all ask it – all of us here. Anomander, *where were you?*'

Someone began howling at the hearthstone, a braying, hoarse howl that erupted again and again.

Kadaspala struggled and tried to reach for his knife on the floor. Gripp dragged him back and threw him down on to the pavestones. He set the weight of one knee on the man's chest and then leaned close. 'Another move like that,' he said, 'and I'll cut you down. Understand me, sir?'

But Kadaspala's mouth was gaping, as if he could not breathe. Gripp drew his knee away. Still the man gaped, those horrid sockets bleeding anew. All at once, Gripp understood what he was seeing. *He cries. Without sound, without tears, he cries.*

Another figure stood in the gloom. Huge, brooding. Gripp looked up and his voice was a rasp, 'Who is that? In the shadows? Come forth!'

'It is only Grizzin Farl,' the stranger replied, stepping closer. Though tears glistened in his red beard, he somehow smiled. 'I am known as the Protector.'

Gripp stared up at the giant, unable to speak. Shattered by that smile, he tore his gaze away and looked across to his lord.

Anomander stood with his head turned, his eyes fixed upon the prostrate form of Andarist. He was motionless, as if carved from onyx. His brother's howls continued unabated.

Silchas appeared, halted a half-dozen paces back from the hearthstone. He stared down at Enesdia's body, lying motionless and ruined beside Andarist. Behind him came others. None spoke.

Beneath Gripp, Kadaspala continued his silent, horrifying weeping. The fingers of his right hand made small scribing patterns against the floor. Shudders rippled through the man, as if fevers burned in his skull.

When Anomander drew the sword from the scabbard at his side,

Andarist lifted his head, his howls cutting off abruptly, although the echo of the last lingered for what seemed an impossibly long time.

Anomander walked towards Andarist, his strides uneven – as if he was drunk – and halted near the hearthstone. Before he could speak, Andarist shook his head and said, 'I will name it.'

Anomander stiffened at his brother's cold pronouncement.

Silchas spoke. 'Andarist, the weapon is not yours—'

'The wound is mine and I will name it!'

Beneath Gripp, Kadaspala cackled softly, and held his head cocked, to better hear the words being spoken now by these three brothers.

Anomander said, 'And if I name my future, Andarist, will you doubt me? Will you challenge me?'

'Not now,' whispered Silchas to Andarist. 'Not on this day, I beg you.'

'Where were you?' Kadaspala asked again, in a broken voice. 'Blind in the darkness – I warned you all but you refused to heed me! I warned you! Now see what she has made!'

On his knees, Andarist moved up alongside Enesdia's body. With tenderness that was aching to witness, he gathered her up in his arms and held her head against his breast. He did all this without once breaking his gaze upon Anomander. 'I will name it,' he said.

'The sword is drawn, brother, as you can see. I am awakened to vengeance, and so shall this weapon be named. Vengeance.'

But Andarist shook his head, one hand stroking Enesdia's hair. 'Anger blinds you, Anomander. You take hold of vengeance and you believe it to be pure. Remember Henarald's words!'

'The road is true,' Anomander said.

'No,' said Andarist, and tears glistened in streams down his cheeks. 'Vengeance deceives. When you see its road to be narrow it is in truth wide. When you see it wide the path is less than a thread. Name your sword Vengeance, brother, and it will ever claim the wrong blood. In this blade's wake, I see the death of a thousand innocents.' He paused, looked round woodenly, as if not even seeing what met his eyes. 'Who is to blame for this? The slayers who came to this house? Those who commanded them? The lust of battle itself? Or was it a father's cruelty to his child a dozen years ago? A stolen meal, a dead mother? An old wound? An imagined one? Vengeance, Anomander, is the slayer of righteousness.'

'I need not reach to a childhood's tragedy, brother, to know who has made himself my enemy on this day.'

'Then you shall fail,' Andarist said. 'Vengeance is not pure. It rewards with a bitter aftertaste. It is a thirst that cannot be assuaged. Leave me to name your sword, Anomander. I beg you.'

'Brother—'

'Leave me to name it!'

'Then do so,' Anomander said.

'Grief.'

The word hung forlorn in the chamber, amidst breaths drawn and then surrendered, and it stung like smoke.

'Andarist—'

'Take this name from me, Anomander. Please, take it.'

'It has no strength. No will. Grief? Upon iron, it is rust. In fire, it is ash. In life, it is death. Brother, I will take nothing from that word.'

Andarist looked up with bleak eyes. 'You will take my grief, Anomander, or never again shall I look upon you, or call you brother, or know your blood as mine own.'

Anomander sheathed the sword. 'Then you shall but hear the tales of the justice I will mete out in your name, and the vengeance I will exact – which I here swear upon the still body of your beloved, and upon her father's cold flesh.'

Andarist lowered his head, as if his brother had just vanished before his eyes, and Gripp Galas knew that he would not look up – not until Anomander had departed this place.

Silchas stepped into the chamber, and as Anomander marched past him he reached out and spun his brother round. 'Do not do this!' he cried. 'Take his grief, Anomander! Upon your blade, take it!'

'And so dull every edge, Silchas? I think not.'

'Will you leave him to bear it alone?'

'I am dead in his eyes,' Anomander said in a cold tone, pulling free. 'Let him mourn us both.'

Beneath Gripp Galas, Kadaspala laughed softly. 'I have him now,' he said in a hiss. 'His portrait. I have him, at last, I have him. His portrait and his portrait and I have him, on the skin. On the skin. I have him. Wait and see.' And the mouth beneath those empty sockets twisted with joy, and with the fingers of his hand he began painting the air.

From the hearthstone Andarist wept, and then words spilled from him, loose and filled with despair. 'Will no one share my grief? Will no one mourn with me?'

Silchas said, 'I will bring him back.'

But Andarist shook his head. 'I am blind to him, Silchas. Choose now.'

'I will bring him back!'

'Then go,' whispered Andarist.

Silchas rushed from the chamber.

Kadaspala struggled free of Gripp, pushing with his feet. He rose, tottering, fingers cutting at the air. 'Listen to them!' he shrieked. 'Who sees here? Not them! Only me! Kadaspala, who has no eyes, is the only one who can see!'

'Kadaspala,' called Andarist. 'I hold your sister in my arms. Join me here.'

'You weep alone,' the man replied in a voice empty of all sympathy. 'She was never for you. You made for her this path, with your pathetic words of love and adoration, and she walked it – to her death! Look on me, O forgotten Son of Darkness, for I am your child, your malformed, twisted spawn. In these holes see your future, if you dare!'

'Enough,' growled Gripp, advancing on the fool. 'Your mind is broken and now all you do is lash out.'

Kadaspala spun to face him, grinning. 'I am not the one wielding vengeance, am I? Run to your master, you grovelling cur of a man. There's more blood to spill!'

Gripp struck him, his blow sending the artist sprawling. He moved forward again.

'Stop!'

He looked over to see Hish Tulla, and stepped back. 'My pardon, milady. I am dragged across a jagged edge. It cuts upon all sides.'

Kadaspala was lying on the floor, quietly laughing and muttering under his breath.

Hish Tulla walked up to Andarist. 'Do you see my tears?' she asked him, kneeling and resting a hand against the side of his face. 'You do not mourn alone, Andarist.'

And she took then the last brother into her arms.

# PART FOUR

---

*The forge of Darkness*

# SIXTEEN

'BELIEF,' SAID DRACONUS, 'NEVER FEELS STRANGE TO THE BELIEVER. Like an iron stake driven deep into the ground, it is an anchor to a host of convictions. No winds can tear it free so long as the ground remains firm.'

Riding beside his father, Arathan said nothing. The land ahead was flat, marked only by clusters of low cairns made from piled stones, as if signifying crossroads. But Arathan could see no crossroads; he could barely make out the path they travelled. The sky overhead was a dull blue, like burnished tin, through which vast but distant flocks of birds could be seen, scudding like clouds on high winds.

Draconus sighed. 'It is the failure of every father to impart wisdom to his child. No paint adheres to sweating stone. You are too eager, too impatient and too quick to dismiss the rewards of someone else's experience. I am hardly blind to the surge of youth, Arathan.'

'I have no beliefs,' said Arathan, shrugging. 'No anchor, no convictions. If winds take me, then I will drift.'

'I believe,' said Draconus, 'that you seek your mother.'

'How can I seek what I do not know?'

'You can and you will, with a need that overwhelms. And should you one day find that which you seek, you no doubt imagine an end to your need. I can warn you that disappointment lies ahead, that life's most precious gifts always come from unexpected sources, but you will not waver from your desire. Thus, from me you learn nothing.'

Arathan scowled, realizing that he could not hide anything from his father. Deceit was an easy path, but the moment it failed only a fool would stay upon it. 'You sent her away,' he said.

'Out of love.'

They rode past another heap of stones, and Arathan saw a scatter of finger bones along its nearer edge, bleached white by the sun. They made rows like teeth. 'That makes no sense. Did she not love you in return? Was it in the name of love that you chose to break her heart? No, sir, I see no wisdom from you.'

'Is this how you baited Tutor Sagander?'

'I never baited him—'

'Behind your innocent guise you make every word a weapon, Arathan. This may have worked with Sagander, since he refused to see you as anything but a small child. Among men, however, you will be known as dissembling and treacherous.'

'I do not dissemble, Father.'

'When you feign ignorance of the wounds your words deliver, you dissemble.'

'Do you always send away the ones you love? Must we always journey through the ruins of your past? Olar Ethil—'

'I was speaking of belief,' Draconus replied, with iron in his tone. 'It will make your path, Arathan, and I say that with certainty, because it is belief that guides each and every one of us. You may imagine it as a host and you may well feel the wayward tug of every conviction, and convince yourself that they each summon with purpose. But this is not a mindful journey, and the notion of progress is an illusion. Do not trust the goals awaiting you: they are chimeras, and their promise salves the very belief that invented them, and by this deception you ever end where you began, but in that end you find yourself not young, not filled with zeal as you once were, but old and exhausted.'

'What you describe is not a worthy ambition. If this is your wisdom's gift then it is a bitter one.'

'I am trying to warn you. Strife awaits us, Arathan. I fear it shall reach far beyond the borders of Kurald Galain. I did what I could for Mother Dark, but like you she was young when first I gave my gift to her. Every step she has taken since then she believes to be purposeful and forward. This is one anchor we all share.' He fell silent, as if made despondent by his own words.

'Is that how you view love, Father? As a gift you bestow upon others, only to then stand back to watch and see if they are worthy of it? And when they fail, as they must, you discard them and set out in search of the next victim?'

His face darkened. 'There is a fine line between fearless and foolish, Arathan, and you now stride it precariously. The gift of which I spoke was not love. It was power.'

'Power should never be a gift,' Arathan said.

'An interesting assertion, from one so powerless. But I will listen. Go on.'

'Gifts are rarely appreciated,' Arathan said, and in his mind he was remembering his first night with Feren. 'And the one who receives knows only confusion. At first. And then hunger . . . for more. And in that hunger, there is expectation, and so the gift ceases being a gift, and becomes payment, and to give itself becomes a privilege and to receive it a right. By this all sentiment sours.'

Draconus drew up. Arathan did the same a moment later and swung Besra around to face him. The wind seemed to slide between them.

His father's gaze was narrow, searching. 'Arathan, I think now that you heard Grizzin Farl's warning to me.'

'I don't recall, sir, if I did. I don't remember much of that evening.'

Draconus studied him a moment longer and then looked away. 'It seems,' he said, 'that every gift I give is carved from my own flesh, and by every wound and every scar upon my body, I map the passage of my loves. Did you know, son, that I rarely sleep? I but weather the night, amidst aches and sore repose.'

If this confession sought sympathy from Arathan, he judged himself a failure. 'I would evade that fate for myself, sir. The wisdom you have offered me is not the one you intended, so I cannot but view it as a most precious gift.'

The smile Draconus then swung to him was wry. 'You have re-awakened my pity for Sagander, and I do not refer to an amputated leg.'

'Sagander's iron stakes pinned him to the ground long ago, sir. Legs or not, he does not move and never will.'

'You are quick to judge. What you describe makes him no less dangerous.'

Arathan shrugged. 'Only if we walk too close. He is in my past now, sir. I do not expect to see him again.'

'I would think not,' Draconus agreed. 'But I wonder if I have not wronged him. You are far from easy company, Arathan. Now, a house awaits us.'

Following his father's gesture, Arathan looked ahead. Plain in sight, as if conjured from the ground less than a hundred paces distant, was a low structure. Its long roof sagged in the middle and a few gaps were visible as black holes amidst the lichen-covered slate tiles. Beneath the projecting eaves, the stone walls were roughly hewn and streaked with red stains. The yard around the house was devoid of grass and looked beaten down.

'Is it conjured?' Arathan asked.

'Suggested is the better word,' Draconus replied.

They set off towards it. The house appeared to be abandoned, but

Arathan was certain that it was not. He squinted at the black patches made by the windows to either side of the solid door – which seemed to have been hacked from a single slab of grey stone – but could make out no movement in the shadows within. 'Are we expected?'

'More than expected, Arathan. Necessary.'

'Necessary for this house to be?'

'Just so.'

'Then surely, Father, belief has more power than you credit it.'

'I never discredited the power of belief, Arathan. I but warned you that it can offer dubious charms, and rarely does it invite self-analysis, much less reproach.'

'Then sorcery must never be examined too closely? Lest it lose its power?'

'Lest it cease to exist, Arathan. What is it to be a god, if not to hold the unfettered willingness to believe?'

'Now you grant belief omnipotence. I can see how that would charm anyone, even a god.'

'With each day, son, I see you grow more formidable.'

The observation startled Arathan. He already regretted his brutal words to his father. *As if I can speak of love. The only game I knew to play was one of possession. It does ill to treat love as would a child a toy. Feren, I am sorry for all that I did, for all that I was, and was not.* 'I am anything but formidable, Father. I but flail with weapons too large to hold.'

Draconus grunted. 'As do we all.'

There was motion from one window as they drew closer, and a moment later a figure clambered out from it. A man: not much older than Arathan himself. He was dressed in bloodstained clothing, loose and made from silks. A half-cape of deep green wool covered his shoulders, its collar turned up. He was dark-haired, clean-shaven, not unhandsome, although his face bore a frown as he worked free of the window and found his feet.

At the edge of the barren yard, Draconus reined in and Arathan did the same. His father dismounted. 'Join me, Arathan,' he said, and there was a strange timbre to his voice, as if awakened to excitement or, perhaps, relief.

A flock of the unknown birds was drawing closer, swarming the sky behind the house. Their flight was strange and the sight of them made Arathan uneasy. He slipped down from Besra.

The stranger – another Azathanai, no doubt – had walked halfway across the yard and now stood, eyes upon Draconus, and in place of the frown there was a mocking smile that stole the grace from his visage. Arathan imagined his fist driving into that smile, obliterating it. Satisfaction warmed his thoughts.

The stranger's gaze snapped to Arathan's and that unctuous smile broadened. 'Would you rather not kiss it from me?' he asked.

Beside Arathan, his father said, 'Yield nothing to this one's baiting, son. The soil ever shifts beneath him.'

The stranger's brows lifted. 'Now, Draconus, no need to be cruel in your judgement. My artistry is what binds the two of us, after all.'

'For scarce a breath longer, Errastas. The gift is made, by you it seems, and I will have it.'

'Gladly,' Errastas replied, but he made no move; nor, Arathan noted, was the man carrying anything that might contain a gift. *Perhaps he gives as I will give.*

'You wear blood, Errastas,' Draconus observed. 'What grim passage is behind you?'

Errastas looked down at the stains on his silks. 'Oh, it's not mine, Suzerain. Well, most of it isn't, that is. The journey you set upon me proved fraught. I have never before bound power to an object where in its making I give nothing of myself. It proved most . . . enlightening.'

'Night is not unwelcome, Errastas, and chaos needs nothing of blood, nor can it be made to spill it.'

Arathan sensed a growing tension in the air. The flock of birds was rushing closer, and with it came a seething sound, not of wings but of voices, uncannily high-pitched. He still could not make out their breed. His body was tensing and his mouth had gone dry. He did not like Errastas.

To his father's words, Errastas had but shrugged. Then he cocked his head. 'Scarce a breath, Draconus? You cannot imagine the discoveries I have made. My journey was eventful, as Sechul Lath would attest, since he accompanied me, and you might imagine its reward is now awaiting your hand this day. For you, surely it is. But for me, why, I have just begun.' He held out an angular black disc, barely larger than the palm of his hand. 'Behold, Suzerain, the folding of Night.'

'I will have it.'

Smiling once more, Errastas strode closer. 'Have you even considered the precedent set in the making of this, Draconus? I doubt it. You're too old. All acuteness has dulled in your mind, and by love alone you are blind as these hunting bats.'

'They hunt you, Errastas? Then you had best flee here.' So saying, Draconus reached out and took up the object.

'This is consecrated ground, O Lord. They wheel, sensing me near, but they cannot find me. These things I am now able to do, and much more besides. Will you understand this at least? What we have done – you by your demand and me by the answering of it – will see the death of the old ways. The death of wandering itself.' He gestured with his now empty hand. 'Our kin who kneel before the Azath, and so make deities of insensate stone, will find new assurance in what they worship, because like it or not, we have made true their faith. Power will find those places now, Draconus, and though the worshippers will remain ignorant of its source, it is all by our hands.' He laughed. 'Is that not amusing?'

'This gift is singular, Errastas.'

The young man shrugged again. 'Indeed it is.'

'You have made none other?'

'Of course not.'

'Where is Sechul Lath?'

'Near, but he has no wish to speak with you.'

'If I find that you deceive me here, Errastas, I shall hunt you down, and with far greater efficacy than these helpless trackers.'

'No doubt. But I tell you the truth. I have made no rivals, neither of Night's aspect, nor of any other's.'

Draconus was silent, studying Errastas.

'I swear it!' the Azathanai laughed. 'Look at me! Do you think I would willingly repeat the ordeal I have suffered in the making of this *Teron*? How do you imagine I bound so much power to those crushed leaves? You above all others will comprehend the limits of wood, the atrocious absence of subtlety in stone, and the infuriating elusiveness of water and air. Did you truly think Night would readily yield to such binding? And by what coin could I make such purchase?' He stepped back and essayed a grand bow. 'See how I wear my wealth, O Lord?'

All at once Draconus staggered as if struck.

Before them Errastas, still in his bowing pose, was fading, like a ghostly apparition. Behind him the roof of the house suddenly slumped, collapsing inward in a dusty crash.

Bats thundered in, a chaotic maelstrom descending upon the site. Ducking, buffeted by wings, Arathan moved to the shelter of Besra's side – but the beast was tossing its head in fright, dragging him across the ground in its panic. The warhorse Hellar, however, stood fast, and though Besra could with ease drag Arathan, it was drawn up short when the lead between it and Hellar snapped taut. Sheltering between the two beasts, Arathan covered his head, crouching low.

A sudden concussion erupted.

Moments later the air was clear – entirely empty, as if the bats had simply vanished.

Shaken, Arathan looked up, and then across to where stood Draconus.

His father had the bearing of a wounded man. His broad shoulders were hunched, his head lowered. For all his girth and height, he suddenly seemed frail. Then Arathan heard Draconus whisper a single word, a name that he had heard before.

'*Karish.*'

All at once Arathan remembered the scene between his father and Olar Ethil: the sudden sheathing of verbal knives, the dismissal of threats. *'An Azathanai has committed murder.'* A woman among the Jaghut. *Her name was Karish and Father knew her, enough to be shocked by the news, enough to grieve and seek comfort from his old lover.*

'Your gift to Mother Dark,' said Arathan, 'is soaked in blood.'

When his father said nothing to that, he continued, 'Errastas needed it, he said. To achieve what you wanted. Now he wears his raiment plainly, and in that boldness he reveals his thirst for more . . . more blood, and the power that comes from it.'

'She will make this gift pure,' Draconus said, without turning. 'When Night unfolds once more, it will scour clean the binding – it will purge this poison.'

'And so hide the crime from her eyes. You will not tell her, will you, Father?'

'Nothing stays broken for ever.' These whispered words were like a promise. He turned to face Arathan. 'You think to hold this secret over me?'

Arathan shook his head. He felt suddenly exhausted and wanted only to turn away from all this. 'Kurald Galain,' he said, 'is not for me. Neither is Mother Dark, nor you, Father. None of it is for me. Offer her your flawed gift if you must. I care not. I wish I could spit out this secret we now share, and if Errastas were here to read my thoughts at this moment, he might have cause to fear.'

Draconus snorted. 'Most creatures of this world understand that fear can be a virtue. Errastas does not. If you seek him, he will wait for you and know your every thought. It is not a worthy path, Arathan. You are not ready to challenge Errastas.'

'Who hunts him, Father?'

'I don't know.'

Distrusting that reply, Arathan shifted his attention back to the ruined house, where the dust was slow to settle. 'Who once lived there?'

'Does it matter?'

'Errastas used it. I would know the workings of his mind.'

Draconus strode back to Calaras. 'Leave it, Arathan.'

'You told Olar Ethil that you would seek the Lord of Hate. Will you still do so, Father?'

'Yes.' Draconus pulled himself into the saddle.

'Will you lie to him as well?'

To that Draconus said nothing. Instead, he kicked his warhorse into motion.

Arathan chose Hellar instead of Besra and mounted up, and then set off after his father.

Draconus had grown so large in Arathan's eyes. Now he grew small again. His father broke the women he loved, and yet feared that Mother Dark would break him. He was but a Consort; resented by the highborn and feared in the Citadel. He had forged an army out of his Houseblades and so earned the suspicions of Urusander's Legion. He stood as a man beset on all sides.

*Yet he leaves her, seeking out not a gift of love, but one of power. He thinks love is a toy. He thinks it shines like a bauble, and he makes every gesture a demand seeking love in return. Therefore, each and every thing that he does must be a thing of many meanings.*

*But he does not understand that this is his private language, this game of bargaining and the amassing of debts no one else comprehends.*

*I begin to understand the many lives of my father, and in each guise new flaws are revealed. I once vowed to hurt him if I could. A foolish conceit. Draconus knows nothing but hurts.*

*Did you love Karish once? Tell me, Father, will the blood of one lover feed the next? Is this the precedent Errastas spoke of? Or did he speak as a god, flush with the lifeblood of a mortal?*

Arathan fixed his eyes on his father, who still rode ahead. In days past he would have spurred his mount until he was at his side, and they would converse like a father and son in search of each other, and every wound would be small and every truth would weave its way into the skein between them. He would think this both precious and natural, and value the moments all the more for their unfamiliarity.

Now he chose to remain alone, riding in a reluctant wake, on a path he no longer desired. His thoughts reached back to his memories of Feren – not the bitterness of their departure, but those times when he had shared her warmth. He wished he could surrender to her again. Night after night, if only to show his father a love that worked.

In the months to come, she would swell with the child they had made, and in her village she would fend off the questions and turn away from all the cruel comments stalking her. Her brother would come to blows defending her honour. And all of this would play out in Arathan's absence, and he would be judged accordingly. Such venom never lost its virulence.

If he had been older, he would have fought for her. If he'd had any other father – not Lord Draconus, Consort and Suzerain of Night – he would have found the courage to defy him. Instead, the father made himself anew in his son. *And I bow to it. Again and again, I bow to it.*

None of this armour he wore made him strong. It but revealed the weakness of flesh.

*Feren. One day I will come for you.* He would weather the scorn of her neighbours, and they would ride away. They would find a world for their child.

A world that did not feed on blood.

*     *     *

Korya and Haut walked. Low square stone towers studded the landscape, crouched against hillsides, rising from ridges and crowding hilltops. They filled the floodplain to either side of the old river, their bulky shapes shouldering free of the tree-line where the forest had grown back, or hunched low on sunken flats where marsh grasses flowed like waves in the breeze that swept down the length of the valley.

As they passed among them, skirting the high edge of the valley's north side, Korya saw that most were abandoned, and those few that showed signs of habitation were distant, and it seemed that Haut's route deeper into the now dead Jaghut city deftly avoided drawing too near any of them.

She saw no evidence of industry, or farming, or manufacture. There were no outbuildings to be seen, either for storing food or stabling animals. For sustenance, these Jaghut must have supped on air.

Her thighs and calves ached from all the walking. The silence from Haut was oppressive and there was a steady pain behind her eyes and blood had soaked through the pad of moss between her legs. She awaited a word from him, something to snap at and so feel better, but he strode ahead without pause, until she felt as if he'd bound an invisible leash round her neck and was simply pulling her along like a reluctant pet. She wanted him to tug on that leash, draw her too close and so come within reach of her claws.

Not that she had any. Nights of cooking over campfires had made scorched and smudged bludgeons of her hands. And for all her vehemence, her strength was gone, withered away by this seemingly endless trek. Her clothes and hair were filthy and stank of smoke.

Another square tower was just ahead, and this one Haut was making no effort to avoid and so she assumed that it too was abandoned. *Another monument to failure. How I long for Kurald Galain!*

When her master reached it, he halted and turned to Korya. 'Prepare camp,' he said. 'Tonight we will sleep within, since there will be rain.'

She glared up at the cloudless sky, and then at the Jaghut.

'Will the child doubt the adult in all things?' he asked.

'I trust,' she said as she dropped the pack from her shoulders, 'that was rhetorical.'

Haut pointed at a stunted tree outside the gaping entrance to the tower. 'That shrub is called ilbarea.'

'It's dead.'

'It does appear that way, yes. Collect a bag full of its leaves.'

'Why?'

'I see that you are in discomfort and ill-humour and so would remedy that. Not as much for your sake as for mine, since I have no desire to dodge barbs all night.'

'I have questions, not barbs.'

'And to grasp each one is to behold thorns. Collect the driest of the dead leaves and know that I do this for both of us.'

'You just said—'

'Bait to test your mood. The trap is sprung yet you still profess to a backbone and raised hackles. I will see you calmed and no longer so sickly-looking.'

'Well, we can't have your sensibilities so offended, can we?' She rummaged in her pack and found a small sack that had once held tubers – ghastly tasting things even when boiled to a mush: she had thrown the rest away after the first night.

'It is better,' said Haut, 'when you cook with enthusiasm.'

'I thought we were hunting murderers,' she said as she walked over to the shrub. 'Instead we just walk and walk and get nowhere.' She began plucking the dry, leathery leaves. 'This will make wretched tea.'

'I'm sure it would,' he replied behind her. 'Once you have filled the bag, we shall need a fire. There should be a wood pile behind the tower, in the yard. I have held on to a single bottle of wine and for that you will thank me, once you rediscover a thankful mood.'

'I suggest you hold your breath while awaiting its arrival,' she said, tugging at the leaves.

He grunted. 'I have failed you with too much shelter, I now see. You are resilient in civil settings, yet frail in the wilds.'

'You call this wild, master?'

'You would deem it civilization, hostage?'

'Civilization on its knees – if that roof proves dry to the non-existent rain. I am far from enamoured, master, exploring this legacy of surrender. But this is only the wildness of neglect, and that is ever sordid for the tale it tells.'

'True enough, there is nothing more sordid than civil failure, in particular its way of creeping up on one, in such minute increments as to pass unnoticed. If we are to deem civilization a form of progress, then how should it be measured?'

She sighed. Still more lessons. 'You would engage an ill-tempered woman in debate, master?'

'Hmm, true. Woman you are. Child no longer. Well, as I am bored, I will gird my armour and march into the perilous ferment of a woman's fury.'

She so wanted to dislike him, but again and again it proved impossible. 'The progress of civilization is measured in its gifts to labour and service. We are eased by the coalescing of intent, willingness and capability.'

'Then how does one measure the stalling of said progress? Or indeed, its decline?'

'Intent remains. Willingness fades and capability is called into question. Accord dissolves but blame is impossible to assign, leading to malaise, confusion and a vacuous resentment.' The bag was stuffed full. Eyeing the shrub she was startled to see that upon every branch she had stripped bare new shoots had appeared, just as brown as the leaves they replaced. 'What a ridiculous tree,' she said.

'Its disguise is death,' said Haut. He had removed his gauntlets and was shrugging out from his surcoat of mail. 'Give me the ilbarea, thus freeing your hands to collect wood.'

'That is kind of you, master. But I wonder, if I am to be a mahybe, a vessel to be filled, why fill it with mundane tasks and seething frustration?'

He sat on a stone near the old firepit and then glanced up at her. 'Have you ever held a stoppered bottle under water? No? Yes, why should you? No matter. Pull the stopper and what happens?'

'If the bottle held air, then the air bubbles out and is replaced with water. If it held liquid, then I imagine a certain slow admixture with the water. These are the experiments suited to a child in a tub. But, master, as you can see, I am not under water, nor am I as empty as you would think me.'

'These disciplines, hostage, are for your own good in that they bring ease and comfort to my being. I have been too long in civilization to understand the mundane cogitations of its basic requirements.'

'You are intent without capability and entirely lacking in will.'

'Just so, and I would not be a teacher of worth, if in neglect I led you into a life similarly devoid of useful knowledge.'

She eyed him for a long moment and then made her way to the back of the tower. Instead of an overgrown garden, she found a massive hole in the ground. It was four or five paces across and when she ventured to its edge and peered down, she saw only blackness. Collecting up a rock, she held it out and dropped it. The stone struck something after a few heartbeats, and then bounced and clattered until the sounds faded away.

The wood was stacked up against the wall, enough for a dozen nights at the campfire. That thought left her despondent. She collected an armful and returned to where Haut sat expectantly. He had set his last remaining wine bottle on the ground beside him. Eyes on the bottle, Korya contemplated smashing it over Haut's hairless pate. Instead, she crouched and set down the wood beside the firepit, and then went off in search of kindling.

A short time later, she had the fire lit and sat waiting for a decent bed of embers. The cookpot sat waiting, filled with water and a handful of dubious vegetables.

Haut rummaged in his pack and removed three goblets, which he set to polishing with a silk handkerchief she had never seen before. He lined up the goblets in a perfect row in front of the bottle.

A sound from the tower made her turn. A Jaghut was standing in the doorway. He was taller than Haut by more than a hand, broad across the shoulders and long-limbed. His tusks were stained almost black, except at the upthrust tips, where they faded to red-tinted amber. An old but savage scar seamed a ragged path diagonally across his face. He wore nothing but a colourless loincloth that failed to hide the lower half of his manhood. The vertical pupils of his eyes were thin as slits.

'I kill trespassers,' he said.

Haut nodded. 'We shall warn any who come near. Korya Delath, this is Varandas. I thought he was dead.'

'Hoped, I'm sure,' said Varandas, stepping forward. 'A wondrous fire,' he observed. 'I need only glance upon it to see the path to our demise. Well lit every stride we take, until sudden darkness falls. But then, to live is to stumble, and to stumble is to plunge headlong and ever forward. Is it any wonder death takes so many of us?'

'But not you,' Haut said. 'Not yet, in any case. Sit then, if you must intrude upon our peace, and pour out the wine.'

'She is too young to drink—'

'She has known wine from her mother's tit.'

'—too young to drink to, I was going to say. As for broaching the bottle, are you still so useless with your hands, Haut, that you need help with so simple a task?'

Korya snorted.

Varandas glanced at her, as if judging her anew. 'That's a woman's laugh.'

'She is Tiste,' explained Haut. 'She might be a thousand years old and you'd know it not.'

'Surely she isn't.'

'No, but that was not my point. Useless with my hands I might be, but I note the persistent inefficacy of your wits, Varandas, telling me that your affliction of stupidity is indeed eternal.'

'I do claim stupidity as an illness,' Varandas said with a nod, 'and have written a fine treatise arguing my point. Badly, of course.'

'I've not read it.'

'No one has. I am satisfied to think of writing as a desire worth having, whereas its practical exercise is a turgid ordeal I leave to lesser folk, since I have better things to do with the sentient fragments of my brain.'

'Thus the argument of a thousand useless geniuses, each one quick to venture an opinion, particularly a negative one, since by their own negativity they can justify doing nothing but complain.'

'Good company one and all,' said Varandas, taking up the bottle and inspecting its unmarked clay body. 'I pronounce this singular in quality.'

'So it is,' agreed Haut.

'Have you anything else?'

'No.'

'Oh well.' He plucked free the stopper and poured, filling each of the goblets to the brim.

'You would have us spill upon our hands?'

Varandas sat back. 'No, I would have us simply observe them and so appreciate the perfection of my measure.'

'I fear Korya was able to gauge that some time ago.'

'Oh?'

'Your diaper is too small, Varandas.'

'That is a matter of opinion, Haut. I will not apologize for the prodigiousness of my famous prowess. Now, let us embark on sticky hands and the smacking of lips and such. Tiste, do precede us.'

'As far as I know,' said Korya, reaching for the first goblet, 'my mother's tit was not full of wine. I refuse to be responsible for my master's opinions.'

Varandas regarded her. 'Her mood is foul, Haut. How do you put up with it?'

'Mostly I hide, but as you can see, this is presently difficult to achieve. I have a solution, of course.'

'Speak on, O spiteful one.'

Haut pulled out a clay pipe. 'Ilbarea leaves, from your own tree, Varandas.'

'Oh? I thought it was dead.'

*     *     *

'That,' said Varandas a short time later, 'is an expression I will never forget.'

Haut frowned, reached out and picked up the pipe from where it had fallen from Korya's senseless hand. He sniffed at the smoke still drifting up from the bowl, and his head snapped back. 'Oh dear, this would challenge the constitution of a Thel Akai. How long have those leaves ripened on the vine?'

'I can't say for certain, since I never picked them off. Decades, I would think. Or perhaps centuries – why do you ask me such challenging questions? You delight in making obvious the symptoms of my stupidity and this makes me cross and prone to belligerence.'

'Well, one hopes she will awaken on the morrow refreshed and full of vigour.'

'Or perhaps the following day, or the next one after that. That was a lungful to melt iron ore. See how she still exudes white tendrils with each breath? But I will say this, her ill-disposition no longer offends us and so I judge this a pleasing outcome.'

'The bottle is empty,' Haut observed, 'and I am no longer hungry, which is good since my cook lies supine.'

'Then we must walk to the back of the tower, Haut.'

'Very well, if you insist.'

'We have things to discuss.'

They rose and left the motionless form of Korya, although Haut paused to fling a blanket over her as he passed by.

Varandas led the way to the edge of the vast hole in the yard. Haut joined him. They stared down into the pitch black and said nothing for a time.

Then Haut grunted and said, 'I fear for Hood.'

'I fear the precedent,' Varandas replied. 'An Azathanai now truly stands apart, and would make a bold claim to godhood.'

'What is to be done?'

'This question is asked by everyone, Haut. Barring Hood himself, who speaks not a word and languishes still in chains.'

'In chains?'

'The Lord of Hate has the care of him.'

'In chains?'

'This was deemed a mercy. An act of compassion. We await Hood, I now believe – all of us who choose to care. We await his word.'

'And you?'

Varandas shrugged. 'It has been a long time since I took up the sword, and now I view the gesture as one of bluster. What do I recall of war? What do I know of fighting? I will listen to Hood, however, and give him the openness of my judgement until I can weigh his words.'

Haut nodded. 'That is honourable, Varandas. How many others will join you on that day, I wonder?'

'A handful, I would think. We keep small gardens and pluck weeds with uncommon vigour. After all, the Lord of Hate only spoke the truth, and by this made infernal argument none could oppose.'

They were silent then for a long time, until Varandas turned to Haut and asked, 'And you?'

'Mahybe Korya.'

Varandas's brows lifted. 'Indeed? A Tiste mahybe? Unprecedented and bold.'

'I am otherwise helpless,' said Haut.

Varandas gestured to the hole. 'What do you think of this?'

'I have been thinking of it, I admit,' confessed Haut. 'How did you come by it?'

'No idea,' Varandas answered.

They studied it some more.

*     *     *

'The worship of stone,' said Errastas, 'is a plea to longevity, but that's a secret stone never yields.'

Sechul Lath continued pulling rocks from the rubble, swearing as his fingers brushed the occasional stone that was still blistering hot. Steaming earth sifted down as the mound continued to settle. The air was rank with a smell he could not identify, but which he imagined to be outrage.

Nearby, Errastas crouched at a heap of broken slate tiles, rummaging through them and setting aside certain ones, arranging even stacks as if counting coins. 'They claim,' he went on, 'that the buildings simply grew from the ground. At first they were little more than piles of rock, but still they rose from the earth, and soon new ones found the shape of hovels. Here and there, a wall or line. Others made circles. And then, as if all these pathetic efforts somehow merged and found each other, houses were born. Well, not just houses as we now know. But towers to match those of the Jaghut. And others that bore the semblance of wood, as you might imagine a Tiste would make. While yet others took to earth itself, in Thel Akai fashion, or hides like the huts of the Dog-Runners.'

Sechul adjusted his grip on a particularly large boulder and pulled on it. It came away with a grinding lurch. He rolled it to one side and studied the hole where the stone had been. And then twisted round to look at his companion.

'But this is the struggle towards order,' Errastas continued, frowning at a shattered tile. 'The imperative of organization, which is both laudable and pathetic. We have all resisted dissolution, in our own ways, and thus make of our lives bold assertions to purpose and meaning.' He flung the tile away, and then picked up another one. 'This pose we insist upon, Setch, is substance constructed as argument. Our flesh, our blood, our bone, our selves. I for one am not impressed.'

Sechul returned to the mound of rubble. He tugged loose rocks and swept up handfuls of earth. He made the hole bigger.

'You can argue with nature and of course you will lose. You can argue with someone else and unless the wager is one of life or death, then the exercise is meaningless. Nature awaits us all, with emphatic solidity. All that is won is an illusion. All that is lost, you were doomed to lose anyway, eventually. They call the houses the Azath, and from this the Tiste name us, but we are not all worshippers of stone, are we, Setch?'

499

'It seems,' said Sechul, leaning back and wiping dirt from his battered hands, 'that you have won this particular argument, Errastas.'

Grunting as he rose, Errastas made his way over. 'I knew as much,' he said. 'Not even a Jaghut tower could withstand half a hill of earth and rock descending on it.'

Sechul Lath thought back to the power of his companion's conjuration. The sorcery was brutal, and the sound it had made – like a clap of thunder inside the skull – still reverberated through his bones. 'This could begin a war,' he said.

'I have purpose,' Errastas replied, dropping into a crouch to peer into the small cave dug into the mound. 'This may seem madness – murder often does. But this table I set will see multitudes gathering to the feast, dear brother of mine.'

'Half-brother,' corrected Sechul Lath, feeling the need to assert the distinction. 'Will they thank you?'

Errastas shrugged. 'They will gorge, friend, and grow fat and think not once upon the farmer, or the herder, or the one crushing the grapes. Nor will they muse on the maker of the utensils they wield, or the hand that hammered out their pewter plates. They will sit upon chairs that creak to their weight, and give no thought to the carpenter, or indeed the tree. They will listen to the rain upon the roof, and give no thanks to the mason. I do not seek notoriety, friend. I do not yearn for adulation. But I will remain the bringer of feasts.'

Sechul Lath rose, arching to work out the aches in his body, and then stepped back as Errastas crawled partway into the hole. His companion emerged dragging out the crushed corpse of the unknown Jaghut who had lived in the tower. The splintered ends of bones jutted from bruised and bloody flesh, making the broken body and its limbs look like shredded sacks. Some falling chunk of masonry had crushed the skull almost flat.

Errastas pulled the corpse into full view and then straightened, anchoring his hands on his hips. 'I felt his death,' he said, face flushed, 'like a hand on my cock.'

Turning, half in disgust, Sechul Lath scanned the sky. It looked wrong to his eyes, but in a way he could not fathom. 'I see no searchers,' he said.

'We have time,' Errastas agreed. 'K'rul gropes. He has not yet seen our faces. He does not yet know his quarry.'

'This is his gift you abuse,' Sechul observed. 'I will not welcome his ire when he discovers what we are about.'

'I will be ready for him. Don't worry. A man bled out is a man left weak and helpless.'

'I am already weary of running.'

Errastas laughed. 'Our flight is about to become frenzied and desperate, Setch. Draconus comprehended – there, at the very end, I am sure of it. And even now he travels to the Lord of Hate. Will he confess his role in that first murder? I wonder.'

'If he chooses silence,' said Sechul, 'then he will make the Lord of Hate his enemy.'

'Do you not relish the thought of those two locked in battle? Mountains would break asunder, and seas rise to inundate half the world.' Errastas took hold of two broken limbs and resumed dragging the corpse towards the heap of tiles.

'Just as likely,' said Sechul, 'they join in alliance, and seek out K'rul as well, and then all set themselves upon our trail!'

'I doubt that,' Errastas said. 'Why would you even think the Lord of Hate feels any affinity for his murdered kin? I see him sitting across from Draconus, weathering the Suzerain's furious tirade, only to then invite the fool to a cup of tea. Besides, Draconus must return to his precious woman, bearing his precious gift, and in exquisite ignorance will he give it to her.' With the body now beside the stacks of tiles he had singled out, Errastas knelt. He selected the tile from the top of the stack nearest him and, finding a large enough wound on the body, pushed it inside. 'There is no ritual beyond repetition and a chosen sequence, yet we deem ritual to be a vital component to sorcery. Well, this new sorcery, that is. Of course, ritual does not create magic – all we do with ritual is comfort ourselves.'

'It is the habit that comforts,' Sechul Lath said.

'And from habit is order found. Just so. I see a future full of fools—'

'No different from the past, then. Or the present.'

'Untrue, brother. The fools of the past were ignorant, and those of the present are wilfully obtuse. But the future promises a delightful rush into breathtaking idiocy. I charge you to become a prophet in our times, Setch. Be consistent in your predictions of folly and you will grow rich beyond avarice.'

'A fine prediction, Errastas.'

Errastas was busy covering tile fragments in gore, studding the torn corpse with the flat stones. 'Nature mocks all certainty but the one it embraces.'

'Can you keep hiding us, Errastas?'

'I doubt it. We must truly flee the lands of the Azathanai and the Jaghut.'

'Then do we travel to the Jheck? The Dog-Runners? Surely not the Thel Akai!'

'None of those, for the borders they share with the Azathanai. No, we must cross the sea, I think.'

Sechul Lath started, and then scowled. 'Whither fled Mael? He will not welcome us.'

501

'Indeed not,' Errastas agreed. 'I think . . . beyond his realm, even.'

'The High Kingdom? Those borders are closed to the Azathanai.'

'Then we must bargain our way into the demesne, friend. There must be good reason why the King is so beloved among his people. Let us make this our next adventure, and discover all the hidden truths of the High Kingdom and its perfect liege.'

Sechul Lath looked down at his friend. Blood painted red the man's hands, but upon the soaked tiles the same blood had etched arcane symbols. No two tiles were alike. The rank smell of outrage was thick in the air. 'Errastas, I was wondering, where did all that earth and rock come from?'

Errastas shrugged. 'No idea. Why?'

'I don't know. Nothing, I suppose.'

＊      ＊      ＊

Korya could hear rain rushing down stone in a steady torrent. She opened her eyes. It was dark. She was lying on a floor of cold pavestones that felt greasy to the touch. There was a heavy animal smell to the air, reminding her of the Jheleck. Bewildered, struggling to find her memory, she sat up.

Varandas was seated at a table, hunched over something he was working on. The tower's interior was a single chamber, with an old wooden ladder rising from the centre of the room, leading to the roof. Haut was nowhere to be seen.

She coughed, and then coughed again, and all at once she recalled sitting at the fire, setting an ember to the pipe bowl as Haut had instructed, and then drawing hot smoke into her mouth, and then down into her lungs. Beyond that moment, there was a void. She glared over at Varandas. 'Where is he?'

The Jaghut glanced over. 'Out. Why?'

'I will kill him.'

'There is a queue for that, mahybe. But he meant you little harm and the cause was just and indeed agreeable to all present—'

'Not to me!'

'Well, you excused yourself forthwith, as I recall. We had a passably benign evening. I even boiled up that pot of wrinkled things you imagined to be vegetables. While we did not partake of the broth, the exercise made work for my restless hands.'

She felt rested, virulently awake. 'I will allow,' she said, 'it was a good night's sleep.'

'And a day,' said Varandas. 'In oblivion, time is stolen, never to be returned. Imagine, some people actually welcome the losses. They measure them out as victories against what, boredom? The banal consideration of their own mental paucity? The wretched uselessness of their lives? The sheer pall of their dyspeptic thoughts? I am considering a thesis. On the Seduction of Oblivion. My arguments will be senseless, as befits the subject.'

'I did not think it possible,' Korya said.

'What?'

'I now believe Haut to be exceptional among you Jaghut.'

Varandas seemed to consider the observation for a moment, and then he grunted. 'I do not disagree, although I find the notion disagreeable. Tell me, has he explained why the Lord of Hate is so called?'

She picked herself up from the filthy stone floor. 'No. I need to pee.'

'There is a hole out back, but beware the crumbling edge.'

'I'm not a man, you fool.'

'Fret not. It is large enough to mean that you do not have to aim, dear.'

Moving near the table as she made for the doorway, she paused, eyes fixing on the objects arrayed in front of the Jaghut. 'What are you doing?' she asked.

'Playing with dolls. Why?'

'I recognize those,' she whispered.

'Of course you do. Your master bought a dozen for you the week you came into his care. I make them.'

She found it impossible to speak, but tears filled her eyes, and then she rushed outside.

Standing in the rain, Korya lifted her face to the sky. *Oh, goddess, they were not your children after all.*

From the doorway behind her, Varandas said, 'He deems you his last hope.'

She shook her head. In the valley below, lightning was flashing and she heard the mutter of thunder through the rain.

'The slayer of Karish,' continued the Jaghut, 'set you upon a trail. There was purpose in that. The killer wishes to stir us to life, or so Haut believes. But I wonder if that path was not made for you instead.'

'That makes no sense,' she retorted, angered by the thought. 'No one knows anything about me.'

'Untrue. You are the only Tiste to ever live among the Jaghut. Your arrival awakened debate and conjecture, not just among the Jaghut, but also among the Azathanai.'

She faced him. 'Why?'

'He has made a sorcery for you—'

'Who? Haut? He's done nothing of the sort. I am his maid, his cook, his slave.'

'Lessons in humility. But no, I was not speaking of Haut. I was speaking of Draconus.'

'The Consort? I have never even met him!'

'Ah. By "you" I meant the Tiste. Draconus has given the Tiste the sorcery of Darkness. He has walked the Forest of Night, and the very shores of Chaos itself. It is within you, mahybe, and your progress has been observed by many.'

'That makes no sense. There is no sorcery in me.'

'Unfortunately,' Varandas went on, 'some of those observers possessed inimical thoughts, and unpleasant ambitions. They saw the precedent of the Suzerain's manipulation of power. By the path you were set upon, there at the Spar, you were mocked. Draconus was too patient. Mother Dark is lost within his gift to her. The Tiste are blind to their own power.'

'I did not know that cooking and washing floors could awaken sorcery, Jaghut.'

'The greatest gift of education, Korya, is the years of shelter provided when learning. Do not think to reduce that learning to facts and the utterances of presumed sages. Much of what one learns in that time is in the sphere of concord, the ways of society, the proprieties of behaviour and thought. Haut would tell you that this is another hard-won achievement of civilization: the time and safe environment in which to learn how to live. When this is destroyed, undermined or discounted, then that civilization is in trouble.'

'You Jaghut are obsessed with this, aren't you? Yet you threw it all away!'

'We were convinced of the inherent madness of codified inequity. All cooperation involves some measure of surrender. And coercion. But the alternative, being anarchy, is itself no worthy virtue. It is but an excuse for selfish aggression, and all that seeks justification from taking that stance is, each and every time, cold-hearted. Anarchists live in fear and long for death, because they despair of seeing in others the very virtues they lack in themselves. In this manner, they take pleasure in sowing destruction, if only to match their inner landscape of ruin.' He moved out to stand beside her, huge and almost formless in the close gloom of the downpour. 'We rejected civilization, but so too we rejected anarchy for its petty belligerence and the weakness of thought it announced. By these decisions, we made ourselves lost and bereft of purpose.'

'I would think,' she said, 'that despair must stalk every Jaghut.'

'It should have,' Varandas said. 'It *would* have, if not for the Lord of Hate.'

'It seems that he was the cause of it all!'

'He was, and so in return he took upon himself our despair, and called it his penance. He bears our hate for him and our self-hate, too. He holds fast to our despair, and laughs in our faces, and so we hate him all the more.'

'I do not understand you Jaghut,' Korya said.

'Because you seek complexity where none exists.'

'Where has Haut gone?'

'He is upon the roof of my tower.'

'Why?'

'He watches the battle in the valley below.'

'Battle? What battle? Who is fighting?'

'We're not sure. It is difficult to see in this rain. But come tomorrow, he will take you to the Lord of Hate.'

'What for? Another lesson in humility?'

'Oh, an interesting thought. Do you think it is possible?'

Korya frowned.

Lightning flashed again, and this time the sound of thunder rumbled through the ground beneath her feet, and she heard things rattling in the tower behind her. She was soaked through, and she still needed to pee. 'Do you think he can see anything from up there?'

'Of course not. I am afraid I am to blame, as I bored him witless talking about my new series of dolls. They please me immensely, you see, and soon I will set them free to find their own way in the world.'

'I locked mine in a box,' she told him.

'To what end?'

Korya shrugged. 'Perhaps to keep guard over my childhood.'

Varandas grunted. 'That is a worthy post, I think. Well done. But not too long, I hope? We must all earn our freedom eventually, after all.'

She wondered if the Jaghut standing beside her, this maker of dolls, was perhaps mad. 'So,' she asked, 'when will you set your new creations free?'

'Well,' he replied, 'they need to wake up first.'

*I was right. He's mad. Completely mad.*

'Skin and flesh, blood and bone,' Varandas said, 'sticks and twine, leather and straw are all but traps for a wandering soul. The skill lies in the delicacy of the snare, but every doll is temporary. My art, mahybe, is one of soul-shifting. My latest dolls will seek out a rare, winged rock ape native to the old crags of a desert far to the south. I name this series *Nacht*.'

'And what did you name the series you gave to me?'

'*Bolead*. But I fear I made too many of them, especially given their flaws.' He paused, and then said, 'Creation involves risks, of course, but what is done is done, and by these words one can dismiss all manner of idiocy and atrocity. I utter the epigraph of tyrants without irony, are you not impressed?'

'Very.' She set out towards the side of the tower, out of the Jaghut's sight.

Almost directly below, a tower erupted in a blinding concussion, staggering her. As she stumbled against the stone wall she felt it

505

trembling against her. From the doorway Varandas called, 'Not too far, mahybe! The argument below grows fierce.'

Korya shivered, but the rain was suddenly warm. She decided that she had gone far enough and crouched down to empty her bladder.

Thunder shook the hillside again.

'Make haste,' Varandas said. 'The argument approaches.'

'Frightening me doesn't help!' she retorted.

The hillside was thumping, as if to giant footsteps.

She straightened and quickly made her way back to the doorway.

Haut had joined Varandas, and Korya saw that he was in his armour and helm again, and in his gauntleted hands he held his axe, all of him glistening as if oiled. A massive shape was clambering up the slope, straight for them.

'Ware!' Haut bellowed.

The figure halted, looked up.

Varandas raised his voice to be heard over the rain, 'I dwell here, Azathanai, and I have guests. But you do not count among them in your agitated state. Begone, unless you would see Captain Haut displeased unto violence.'

The huge figure remained motionless, and silent.

But no, not entirely silent: Korya thought she heard sniffling sounds drifting up the slope.

'You are driven from the valley,' Varandas continued, 'and you bear wounds and so would unleash your temper. There are plenty of towers about that are unoccupied, and they will suffer your fury with poetic indifference. Alter your path, Azathanai, and recall the lessons in the valley below.'

The creature sidled sideways along the hillside, seeming to use its hands as much as it did its feet to move across the ground. Every now and then one of those hands reared back and punched the earth, sending thunder through the hill. The tower swayed to each impact with an ominous grinding of stone.

Slowly, the rain obscured the Azathanai's form, and then stole it away, although the thumping punches continued, diminishing with distance.

Glancing across at Haut, Korya saw him leaning on the axe. Water ran like a curtain from the rim of his helm, parting round the upthrust tusks but otherwise obscuring his face. She advanced on him.

'Your name alone scared off a giant who's been knocking down towers with his fists,' she said.

Varandas grunted. 'She accuses you, Haut, of notoriety. What say you in defence?'

'Her,' he replied. '*Her* fists.'

'Very good,' nodded Varandas, who then turned to Korya. 'Thus, you

506

have your master's answer. I would continue to arbitrate this debate, but alas, I am getting wet. I go to light a fire in the hearth within—'

'You don't have a hearth within,' said Korya.

'Oh. Then I shall have to make space for one, of course. In the meantime, I suggest you thank your master for fending off the wrath of Kilmandaros. Why, I hear even her husband, Grizzin Farl, flees her temper. And now I see why.' He then went inside.

Korya glared at Haut. 'Who drove her from the valley?' she demanded.

'You should thank me indeed,' he replied, 'and be mindful of my courage these past few days. Twice now I have stood fast before the perilous ferment of a woman's fury.' He shouldered the axe. 'As to your query, I suppose we shall find out soon.'

Something small and bedraggled darted out from the tower, scampered like a hare down the slope and was quickly lost from sight.

'What was that?'

Haut sighed. 'Varandas has been playing with dolls again, hasn't he?'

*       *       *

With Arathan trailing his father, they rode among abandoned towers. The ground grew more uneven, the flatlands giving way to rounded hills. After a time, as the square edifices became more numerous, it occurred to Arathan that they were entering what passed for a city. There were no streets as such, nor was there any particular order to the layout of dwellings, but it was easy to imagine thousands of Jaghut moving to and fro between the towers.

The sky, a dull grey, was descending over them, and as they travelled onward the first drops of rain began falling. In moments, a deluge engulfed the scene. Arathan felt the water soaking through, defeating with ease the armour he wore, and a chill gripped him. He could barely make out his father ahead, the faded once-black cape like a patch of mist, Calaras like a standing stone that refused to draw nearer. The ground grew slick and treacherous and Hellar slowed her trot to a plodding walk.

Arathan fought a desire to slip still further back, to lose sight of his father. The strangeness of this city offered an invitation to explore, while the rain promised the mystery of all that remained unseen and, perhaps, unknowable. He felt moments from cutting a tether and drifting away.

Ahead, Draconus drew up before a tower and dismounted. Taking the reins in one hand, he led Calaras in through the gaping doorway.

Arathan arrived. He slipped down from Hellar, intending to follow his father into the tower, but instead he hesitated, feeling a presence nearby. His warhorse's ears flicked as she caught a sound off to the right – the splash of heavy feet thumping through the mud. Moments later, a huge form appeared: a woman, yet far more massive in girth and height than even Grizzin Farl. Her arms seemed over-long and the hands at the ends of them were huge and battered. Her long hair hung in thick braids, clotted with mud, as if she had fallen only moments earlier. She wore bedraggled furs black as pitch, also mud-stained. As she edged closer, seeming to squint at Arathan, he beheld a broad, flat face, the mouth wide and full-lipped, the eyes buried in puffy slits.

He saw no weapons on her. Nor was she wearing armour. She walked up and reached out, snaring thick fingers under the strap of his helm, and then dragged him close. He strained as she lifted him from the ground to peer into his face. Then, before he began choking, she lowered him down and released him. Saying nothing, she stepped past and made her way into the tower.

Arathan still felt her hard knuckles under his jaw. The muscles of his neck and back throbbed with pain. Fumbling, he unstrapped the helm and dragged it from his head, and then pulled off his leather cap. The rain pelting his head was like ice. He turned and looked out into the city, until Hellar nudged him.

Collecting up the reins, he led his mounts through the doorway.

Within was a single room, at least fifteen paces across. Calaras stood near the wall opposite, and his father had been emptying a bag of feed in front of him. Draconus had turned and straightened with the strange woman's arrival.

She was divesting herself of her furs near the centre of the room, dropping them to the stone floor around her feet. Beneath them she was naked. 'Of all your spawn, Suzerain,' she said in a thin voice, 'I sensed no madness in this one.' She looked up with an almost shy glance and added, 'I trust you killed all the others. A big stone to crush their skulls, and then you wrenched free their heads from their bodies. Dismembered and fed into the fires of the hottest forge. Until nothing but ashes remained.'

'Kilmandaros,' said Draconus. 'You are far from your home.'

She grunted. 'No one ever visits. For long.' Her attention swung to Arathan as he edged his horses past her. 'Is he awakened?' she asked.

'No,' Draconus replied. 'And yes.'

'Then you did not save him for me.'

'Kilmandaros, we met your husband upon the trail.'

'And my son, too, I expect. With that wretched friend of his, who did what you asked of him.'

To that Draconus said nothing, turning instead to his son. 'Arathan, ready us a small fire when you are done with your horses. There is fuel against the wall to your left.'

Discomforted, struggling to keep his eyes from the woman's nakedness, Arathan set down his helm and concentrated on unsaddling Hellar and Besra.

'We also met your sister in spirit, if not blood,' Draconus said.

Kilmandaros made a hissing sound. 'I leave her to grow fat on superstitions. One day the Forulkan will hunger for Dog-Runner land, and we will resume our war and, perchance, end it.'

'You would make weapons of your followers?'

'What other good are they, Suzerain? Besides, the Forulkan do not worship me. They have made illimitable law their god, even as they suffer its ceaseless corruption at their own hands. At some point,' she said, moving close to stand directly behind Arathan, 'they will deem manifest their right to all that the Dog-Runners own, and make of this law a zealotry to justify genocide.'

'Foolish,' Draconus pronounced. 'I am told that there are Jaghut among the Dog-Runners now, assuming thrones of godhood and tyranny. Did the Forulkan not suffer sufficient humiliation against the Tiste, that they would now make bold claims against both Dog-Runner and Jaghut?'

'That depends,' she said, 'on what I whisper in their ears.'

Feeling the breath of her words on the back of his neck, Arathan quickly went to the other horse and began removing the tack.

She came close again.

'Tyranny breeds,' Draconus said from across the room, 'when by every worthy measure it should starve.'

'Scarcity begets strife, Suzerain, is what you meant. It was hunger that sent my children against the Tiste—'

'Hunger for iron. The need was manufactured, the justification invented. But this is a stale argument between us. I have forgiven you, but only because you failed.'

'And so I weigh your magnanimity, Suzerain, and find it light on the scales. But as you say, this is behind us now.'

When her hand slipped round, over Arathan's left hip, and slid down to his crotch, Draconus said, 'Leave off, Kilmandaros.'

The hand withdrew and Kilmandaros moved away. 'The night is young,' she said, sighing. 'I know his desires and would satisfy them. This is between him and me, not you, Suzerain.'

'I have words that will drive you away,' Draconus said.

'You would do that to me? And to him?'

'Arathan will cease to concern you, I'm afraid. But that is a consequence of what I must tell you, not its purpose.'

'Then leave it until the morning.'

'I cannot.'

'You never did understand pleasure, Draconus. You make love fraught when it should be easy, and fill need with intensity when it should be gentle. Perhaps one day I shall proclaim myself the goddess of love – what do you think of that, O Suzerain? Would not this aspect welcome you, as love welcomes the night and as a caress welcomes the darkness?'

Finished with the horses for the moment, Arathan carried the cook-pack to the centre of the chamber. Here he lit a lantern and set out a pot, utensils and food. Sometime in the past four pavestones had been removed to make a firepit. Lifting the lantern, Arathan looked up, but the light could not reach high enough for him to see the ceiling. Still, he could feel an upward draught. He made his way over to the supply of fuel his father had indicated, and found a few dozen large, seasoned dung chips.

Through all of this, and even when he returned to the firepit, he felt her eyes tracking him.

'What think you, son of Draconus?' she asked him. 'Would I make you a good goddess of love?'

He concentrated on lighting the fire, and then said, 'You would offer a vastness of longing none could satisfy, milady, and so look down upon an unhappy world.'

Her breath caught.

'Come to that,' he said, watching smoke rise from the tinder, 'you may already be the goddess of love.'

'Suzerain, I will have your son this night.'

'I fear not. His is the longing that afflicts the young. You offer too much and he yearns to be lost.'

Arathan felt his face grow hot. His father could track every thought in his mind, with a depth of percipience that horrified him. *I am too easily known. My thoughts walk well-worn paths, my every desire poorly disguised. I am written plainly for all to see. My father. This Azathanai woman. Feren and Rint. Even Raskan found no mystery in my tale.*

*One day, I will make myself unknown to all.*

*Except Feren, and our child.*

'By your words,' said Kilmandaros, 'you reveal the weakness of the Consort. You are found in love, Draconus, yet fear its humiliation. Indeed, I am this fell goddess, if in looking into your eyes I see a man made naked by dread.'

'In the company of Errastas, your son has committed murder,' said Draconus.

Arathan closed his eyes. The flames of the small fire he crouched over reached through his lids with light and heat, but neither offered solace. He could hear her breathing, close by, and it was a desperate sound to his ears.

'By what right do you make this accusation?' she demanded.

'He and his half-brother are the slayers of Karish. They found power in her blood, and in her death. They now walk the lands stained with her blood, and as my son noted to me earlier, they bear it proudly. Perhaps your son less proudly, since he would not show himself to us. No matter. That which Errastas made for me was forged in blood.'

'Sechul,' Kilmandaros whispered.

'You are too wise to doubt my words,' said Draconus. 'If there is dread in my eyes, then it now matches your own.'

'Why do you not flee, Suzerain?' she asked. 'Hood will not turn from your complicity in the slaying of his wife!'

'I will face him,' said Draconus. 'He is chained in the Tower of Hate.'

'Then you had best hope those chains hold!'

Hearing her thump towards his father, Arathan opened his eyes and turned to watch her. He saw her hands close into fists and wondered if she might strike Draconus. Instead, she halted. 'Suzerain, will you ever be a child in this world? You rush to every breach and would fling your body into the gap. You offer up your own skin to mend the wounds of others. But there are things not even you can repair. Do you not understand that?'

'What will you do?' he asked her.

She looked away. 'I must find my son. I must turn him from this path.'

'You will fail then, Kilmandaros. He is as good as wedded to his half-brother, and even now Errastas weaves a web around K'rul, and the sorcery once given freely to all who would reach for it is now bound in blood.'

'He is poisoned, my son,' she said, hands uncurling as she turned away. 'The same for Errastas. By their father's uselessness, they are poisoned unto their very souls.'

'If you find them,' Draconus said, 'kill them. Kill them both, Kilmandaros.'

She put her hands to her face. A shudder rolled through her.

'You'd best leave us now,' said his father, his tone gentle. 'No walls of stone can withstand your grief, much less soft flesh. For what it is worth, Kilmandaros, I regret the necessity of my words. Even more, I regret my complicity in this crime.'

To that she shook her head, though her face remained hidden behind her hands. 'If not you,' she mumbled, 'then someone else. I know them, you see.'

'They will seek to twist you with their words,' Draconus said. 'Be wary of their sharp wits.'

'I know them,' she repeated. Then she straightened and shook herself. Facing Arathan she said, 'Son of Draconus, let not your longing blind you to what you own.' She gathered up her sodden furs and turned to the doorway, and was motionless for a moment, staring out into the hissing torrent of rain. Her hands became fists. 'Like the rain, I will weep my way across the valley,' she said. 'Grief and rage will guide my fists with thunder, with lightning, as befits the goddess of love. All must flee before my path.'

'Be careful,' said Draconus. 'Not every tower is empty.'

She looked back at him. 'Suzerain, forgive my harsh words. Your path ahead is no less treacherous.'

He shrugged. 'We are ever wounded by truths, Kilmandaros.'

She sighed. 'Easier to fend off lies. But none comfort me now.'

'Nor me,' Draconus replied.

She slung her furs about her, and then set out into the gloom beyond.

'I wish,' said Arathan into the heavy silence that followed the fading thud of her footsteps, 'that you had left me at home.'

'Grief is a powerful weapon, Arathan, but all too often it breaks the wielder.'

'Is it better, then, to armour oneself in regrets?' He glanced up to see his father's dark eyes studying him intently. 'Perhaps I am easily understood,' Arathan continued, 'and to you I can offer no advice. But your words of caution which you offered her, well, I think she gave them in return. You can't fix everything, Father. Is it enough to be seen to try? I don't know how you would answer that question. I wish I did.'

From somewhere in the distance sounded the rumble of thunder.

Arathan began preparing their evening meal.

Moments later a thought struck him, and it left him cold. He glanced over to see his father standing in the doorway, staring out into the rain. 'Father? Have Azathanai moved and lived among the Tiste?'

Draconus turned.

'And if so,' Arathan continued, 'are they somehow able to disguise themselves?'

'Azathanai,' said his father, 'dwell wherever they choose, in any guise they wish.'

'Is Mother Dark an Azathanai?'

'No. She is Tiste, Arathan.'

He returned to his cooking, adding more chips to the fire, but the chill would not leave him. If a goddess of love had cruel children, he wondered, by what names would they be known?

*        *        *

The morning broke clear. Still wearing his armour and shouldering his axe, Haut led Korya down into the valley, and the Abandoned City of the Jaghut. Varandas had departed in the night, whilst Korya slept and dreamed of dolls clawing the insides of the wooden trunk, as she wept and told them again and again that she would not bury them alive – but for all her cries she could find no means of opening the trunk, and her fingers bled at the nails, and when she lifted her head she discovered that she too was trapped inside a box. Panic had then startled her awake, to see her master sitting beside the makeshift hearth Varandas had made in the night.

'The wood is wet,' he had told her as she sat up, as if she had been responsible for the rain.

Trembling in the aftermath of the dream, she had set about preparing a cold breakfast. The chamber stank of the smoke that had filled the tower the night before, since there had been no aperture to draw it away except for the entrance, where the rain had formed a seemingly impenetrable wall. As they chewed the dried meat and hard bread, Korya had glared across at her master and said, 'I have no desire to visit anyone known as the Lord of Hate.'

'I share the sentiment, hostage, but visit him we must.'

'Why?'

Haut flung the crust of the bread he had been gnawing on into the hearth, but as there was no fire the crust simply fell among the wet sticks and soaked logs. The Jaghut frowned. 'With your vicious and incessant assault upon my natural equanimity, you force upon me the necessity of a tale, and I so dislike telling a tale. Now, hostage, why should that be so?'

'I thought I was the one asking questions.'

Haut waved a hand in dismissal. 'If that conceit comforts you, so be it. I am not altered in my resolve. Now tell me, why do I dislike tales?'

'Because they imply a unity that does not exist. Only rarely does a life have a theme, and even then such themes exist in confusion and uncertainty, and are only described by others once that life has come to an end. A tale is the binding of themes to a past, because no tale can be told as it is happening.'

'Just so,' Haut nodded. 'Yet what I would speak of this morning is but the beginning of a tale. It is without borders, and its players are far from dead, and the story is far from finished. To make matters even worse, word by word I weave truths and untruths. I posit a goal to events, when such goals were not understood at the time, nor even considered. I am expected to offer a resolution, to ease the conscience of the listener, or earn a moment or two of false comfort, with the belief that proper sense is to be made of living. Just as in a tale.'

Korya shrugged. 'By this you mean to tell me that you are a poor teller of tales. Fine, now please get on with it.'

'It may surprise you, but your impertinence pleases me. To an extent. The young seek quick appeasement and would flit like hummingbirds from one gaudy flower to the next, and so long as the pace remains torrid, why, they deem theirs a worthy life. Adventure and excitement, yes? But I have seen raindrops rush down a pane of glass with similar wit and zeal. And I accord their crooked adventure a value to match.'

She nodded. 'The young are eager for experience, yes, and seek it in mindless escapade. I grasp your point. Only a fool would bemoan an audience with someone called the Lord of Hate, if only to boldly survive the enticement of his regard.'

'I pity all the future victims in your path, hostage. Now then, the tale, which I will endeavour to make succinct. What are the Azathanai? Observe the brevity of my answer: none know. Whence did they come? Even they cannot make answer. What is their purpose? Must they have one? Do *we*, after all? Do you see how the seduction of the tale invites such simplistic notions? Purpose – bah! Never mind. These things you must know: the Azathanai are powerful, in ways not even the Jaghut understand. They are contrary and ill-inclined to society. They are subtle in their proclamations, so that often what they claim to be is in fact the antithesis of what they are. Or seem to be, or not.'

Korya rubbed at her face. 'A moment, master. Is this the tale?'

'It is, wretched girl. I seek to give you knowledge.'

'Useful knowledge?'

'That depends.'

'Oh.'

'Now. The Azathanai. Even that name is in error, as it implies a culture, a unity of form if not purpose. But the Azathanai do not wear flesh as we do, trapped as we are within what was given us and what we can make of it. No, they can choose any form they wish.'

'Master, you describe gods, or demons, or spirits.'

Haut nodded. 'All of your descriptions are apt.'

'Can they be killed?'

'I do not know. Some are known to have disappeared, but that is all that can be said of that.'

'Go on, master. I am intrigued in spite of myself.'

'Yes, the hint of power is always seductive. So. Among the Azathanai there was one who now names himself K'rul.'

'Now? By what name was he known before?'

'Keruli. The transformation lies at the heart of this tale. Among the Dog-Runners, the name of Keruli is understood to be living, of the present, as it were. But in passing, in turning about and striding into the past, Keruli must become K'rul.'

'Keruli died and so became K'rul? Then the Azathanai can die after all.'

'No. Rather, yes. This is difficult enough without your questions! I'd rather you threw some more wood on the fire.'

'What for?'

'Yes, I am aware that it is not burning. But fire marks the passage of time in that it demonstrably offers us the transition of one thing into another. It is like the music that accompanies a bard's voice. Without the damned flames between us it seems the tale must stall, like a word half uttered, a breath half drawn.'

'You were telling me about an Azathanai named K'rul.'

'Not even his fellow Azathanai understand what he did, or even why. Perhaps he but tests his own immortality. Or perhaps ennui drove him to it. Here we skirt the chasm of intentions. He gives no answer to entreaty.'

'What did he do?'

'He bled, and from the wounds he opened upon himself, in the blood itself, he gave birth to mysterious power. Sorcery. Magic in many currents and flavours. They are young still, vague in aspect, only barely sensed. Those who do sense them might choose to flee, or venture closer. In exploration, these currents find definition.'

'It is said,' Korya ventured, 'that the Jaghut possess their own sorcery. As do the Dog-Runners, and the Thel Akai, and even the Forulkan.'

'And the Tiste?' Haut asked.

She shrugged. 'So Varandas said, but I have never seen anything of that.'

'You were very young when you left Kurald Galain.'

'I know. I admit, master, that I am sceptical of Tiste magic.'

'And what of Mother Dark?'

'I don't know, master. Anything can be worshipped and made into a god, or goddess. It just takes collective fear – the desperate kind, the helpless kind, the kind that comes from having no answers to anything.'

'Then is the absence of belief the same as ignorance?'

'As much as the presence of belief can be ignorant.'

Haut grunted, and then nodded. 'The blood leaks from him, in thin trickles, in heavy drops, and so his power passes out into the world and in leaving him becomes a thing left behind, and so Keruli became known as K'rul.'

'The Dog-Runners expected him to die.'

'They did. Who does not die when bleeding without surcease?'

'But he lives on.'

'He does, and now at last, I suspect, the other Azathanai begin to comprehend consequences of K'rul's gift, and are alarmed.'

'Because K'rul offers anyone a share in the power they once held only for themselves.'

'Very good. What value being a god when each and every one of us can become one?'

She scowled. 'What value being a god when you bully all those with less power than you? Where is the satisfaction in that? If it exists at all, it must be momentary, and pathetic and venal. Might as well pull the legs off that spider on the wall behind you – it's hardly worthy of a strut, is it?'

'Hostage, are not all gods selfish gods? They make their believers cower, if believers they choose to have; and if not, then in the hoarding of their power they become remote and cruel beyond measure. What god offers gifts, and does so freely, without expectation, without an insistence upon forms and proscriptions?'

'That is K'rul's precedent?' Korya asked, and the very notion made her breathless and filled with wonder.

'Long ago,' Haut said, groaning as he climbed to his feet, 'there were Jaghut markets, back when we had need of such things. Imagine the consternation in such a market, should one hawker arrive bearing countless treasures, which he then gave away, asking for nothing in return. Why, civilization could not survive such a thing, could it?'

'Master, is K'rul the Lord of Hate?'

'No.'

'Is your tale at an end?'

'It is.'

'But you ended nowhere!'

'I did warn you, hostage. Now pack up, as we must be off. The day promises an air cleansed of all things behind us, and a bold vista to entice us forward.'

And now they walked, down the tiers of the valley's side, and in the distance there was a tower, rising above all others. It was white, luminescent as pearl, and it drew her gaze again and again.

* * *

Arathan followed Draconus out on to an expanse that in any other city would have been called a square. A high tower rose amidst a cluster of lesser kin directly opposite. Where the others were squat and angular and made of grey granite, the tower before them was faced in what looked like white marble, round-walled, smooth and graceful. The buildings gathered at its foot seemed as crass as hovels.

Draconus reined in before one such lesser tower, and dismounted. He turned to Arathan. 'Hobble your horses. We have arrived.'

Arathan tilted his head and let his eyes travel the height of the white edifice. 'I do not understand,' he said, 'why such a beautiful thing should be called the Tower of Hate.'

Pausing for a moment beside Calaras, Draconus frowned at his son. Then he gestured to the low doorway of the squat tower. 'In here,' he said. The aperture was narrow and low enough to force him to duck when he stepped within.

After hobbling Besra and Hellar, Arathan followed.

The chamber was dark and vaguely rank, its low ceiling bearing smoke-blackened rafters and beams stained with what looked like bird guano. A high-backed chair was positioned in a corner close to three vertical slits in the wall that passed for windows. The light spilling through ran like bars across a small, high desk, on which sat a stack of vellum as tall as the wine goblet that stood beside it. Roughly made feather quills were scattered about on what remained of the desk's flat top, with more littering the stone floor underneath the wooden legs. In the corner to the left of the chair, a trap door in the floor had been lifted back, and from somewhere below pale light drifted upward like dust.

Draconus drew off his leather gloves and tucked them behind his sword belt. He looked around, and then said, 'Wait here. I will go and find us some chairs.'

'Do we seek an audience, Father? Are we in the gatekeeper's tower?'

'No,' he replied, and made his way outside.

There was a scuffing sound from the trap and a moment later a figure climbed into view. Arathan had never before seen a Jaghut, as he knew this creature to be. Tall, gaunt, with skin the hue of olives, bearing creases and seams similar to those on lizard hide. The tusks curled as they swept up from the lower jaw to either side of a wide, slit mouth. Heavy brow ridges hid the eyes. The Jaghut was wearing a frayed robe of wool, unevenly dyed a watery purple. In one hand he held an ink bottle. His fingers were stained black.

Ignoring Arathan, the Jaghut walked to the desk and set the ink bottle down, and then, as if exhausted by the chore, he sat in the cushioned chair and leaned back to rest his head.

A flicker of dull gold marked his eyes as he studied the desktop. When he spoke, his voice was deep but rough. 'Some write in wine. But others write in blood. As for me, why, I prefer ink. Less painful that way. I invite no excesses but moderation, but some would view even moderation to be a vice. What think you?'

Arathan cleared his throat. 'We seek audience with the Lord of Hate.'

The Jaghut snorted. 'That fool? He bleeds ink like a drunk pissing in the alley. His very meat is sodden with the bile of his dubious wit. He chews arguments like broken glass, and he bathes all too infrequently. What business would you have with him? None of any worth, I imagine. They come seeking a sage, and what do they find? Look at that heap of writing there, on the desk. He writes a suicide note, and it is interminable. His audience blinks, too filled with self-importance to choke out a laugh. Death, he tells them, is the gift of silence. One day we will all roll into that crypt, where the painted walls hide in darkness and even the dust will not stir. Tell me, do you long for peace?'

'My father seeks out some chairs,' Arathan said. 'He will be back shortly.'

'You bear the trappings of a Tiste. No one doubts the power of the

Suzerain of Night, yet many doubt his will, but it is not his will that so endangers everyone. It is his temper. Tell them that, Tiste-child, before it is too late.'

Arathan shook his head. 'I will not return to my people,' he said. 'I mean to stay here.'

'Here?'

'In the Tower of Hate,' he answered.

'And where might that tower be?'

'The tall one, of white marble, where dwells the Lord of Hate.'

'Have you visited that tower yet, Tiste-child? No? A secret awaits you, then. A secret most delicious. But I see your impatience. If one must build an edifice of hate, what manner of stone should be selected in its construction?'

'Something pure?'

'Very good. And to build a tower for all to see, it should shine bright, yes?'

Arathan nodded.

'Thus. White marble, or, in the case of the tower you mentioned, opal. Of course, no Jaghut could build such a thing. We've not the talent to squeeze opal from rubble and dust. No, for such a miracle, one needs an Azathanai mason. One with an appropriate sense of humour. Why, you ask? Well, because humour is necessary, once the secret is made known. So tell me, how many floors should this tower have? Name for me the levels of Hate.'

'I cannot, sir,' said Arathan. 'Is hatred not a thing that blinds?'

'Hmm. What make you of a suicide note that never ends?'

'A joke,' he replied.

'Ah, and do you appreciate it?'

Arathan shrugged, wondering where his father had gone to. 'I appreciate the irony, I suppose.'

'Just that? Well, you're young still. Hate will blind, yes. There are no levels to it at all. You spoke of purity, and now we have discussed the matter of singularity. What of windows? What manner of door should be cut into this pure, singular thing?'

'Windows are not needed, because all that lies outside hate matters not to the one within.'

'And the door?'

Arathan studied the Jaghut for a moment, and then he sighed. 'The tower is solid stone, isn't it? But that's not right. There must be a way in.'

'But no way out.'

'Until you bring it down in . . . in conflagration. But if it is solid then none can live within it.'

'None do. Not what any sane person would calling living, anyway.'

518

Draconus appeared in the doorway. 'You've gone and burned all the furnishings in every home nearby,' he said, striding into the chamber.

'The winters are cold, Suzerain. We were just discussing Gothos's Folly, your son and I. See the trunk beside the doorway? In there you will find wine of passing quality. And Thel Akai ale, if you would invite insensibility.'

'I would speak with Hood,' said Draconus, walking over to the trunk. The lid creaked as he lifted it. He peered within for a moment and then withdrew a clay jug.

'Excellent choice, Suzerain,' said the Jaghut.

'It should be, as it was my gift to you, the last time we met.'

'Saved for your return. The Tiste have some worth in the world after all, given their talents in the making of wine.'

Draconus withdrew a pair of alabaster goblets and studied them. 'Caladan Brood has a subtle hand, does he not?'

'He does, when he so chooses. It is curious. Upon the heels of my proclamation, and in the midst of the dissolution that followed, I am showered with gifts. How can one fathom the minds of the Azathanai?'

'Does Hood remain below?' Draconus asked as he poured wine into the two goblets.

'I cannot get rid of him, it's true.'

His father offered Arathan one of the goblets. Startled, he accepted. Draconus then went to the desk, picked up the goblet there and sniffed at the wine. He flung the contents against the wall and refilled the goblet from the clay jug, then handed it across to the Jaghut.

'Your son wishes to remain in the keeping of the Lord of Hate.'

Draconus nodded. 'He would make of himself a gift to you.'

'As what, a keepsake? An ornament? What function could he possibly serve?'

'He is trained in letters well enough,' Draconus mused, sipping at the wine. 'How many volumes have you compiled thus far, Gothos?'

'An even dozen stacks to match the one on the desk. Written in an execrable hand, every word, every line.'

Draconus frowned across at their host. 'Not in Old Jaghut, I trust!'

'Of course not! That would be . . . ridiculous. A language for the compilers of lists, a language for tax collectors with close-set eyes and sloping foreheads, a language for the unimaginative and the petty-minded, a language for the unintelligent and the obstinate – and how often do those two traits go hand in hand? Old Jaghut? Why, I would have killed myself after the first three words!' He paused and then grunted. 'If only I had. I confess, Suzerain, I have indeed written in Old Jaghut.'

'Easily taught, that written script.'

'And you charge me to subject your only son to such an ordeal? To what end?'

'That he might transcribe your writings into a more suitable language.'

'Tiste?'

Draconus nodded.

'He will go blind. His hand will wither and fall off to lie on the floor like a dead bird. He will need more than chains to keep him here. Even the Lord of Hate has limits, Suzerain.'

'Until such time as he awakens unto himself. This seems as safe a place as any, Gothos, and I trust you to be an even-handed master.'

'I am to be the vault to your treasure? Dear me, Draconus, but I see hard weather ahead.'

'The thought was his, not mine,' Draconus said, and turned to Arathan. 'If you still mean to stay.'

'I will, Father.'

'Why?' barked Gothos. 'Speak, Tiste-child!'

'Because, sir, an unending suicide note cannot but be a proclamation on the worth of living.'

'Is it, now? I will argue against you, Tiste-child. Night upon night, page upon page, I will attack your belief, your faith, your certainty. I will assail you without pause for breath, and seek to crush you under the heel of my hard-won wisdom. What have you that dares to claim the strength to withstand me?'

'Lord,' said Arathan, 'I have youth.'

Gothos slowly leaned forward, his eyes glittering. 'You will lose it.'

'Eventually, yes.'

The Lord of Hate slowly leaned back. 'Draconus, your son does you proud.'

'He does,' his father whispered.

Gothos then held up a large, ornate key. 'You will need this, Suzerain.'

Nodding, Draconus set down his empty goblet and took up the key. Then he went below.

The Lord of Hate continued eyeing Arathan. 'Never doubt your father's courage.'

'I never have, sir.'

'How has he named you?'

'Arathan.'

Gothos grunted. 'And do you?'

'What?'

'Walk on water, for such is the Azathanai meaning of your name.'

'No sir. Even upon ice, I broke through, and came near to drowning.'

'Do you now fear it?'

'Fear what, sir?'

'Water? Ice?'

Arathan shook his head.

'Your father means to free Hood. What do you imagine he desires from such a perilous act?'

'I would think, sir, some form of redemption.'

'Then it was indeed by Errastas's hand, the slaying of Karish and now others. Alas, your father does not understand the Jaghut. He imagines that Hood will set out to hunt down the wayward Azathanai. He would see the legendary rage of my people unleashed upon this upstart with blood on his hands. But that shall not come to pass.'

'Then what will Hood do?'

'He grieves for the silence she now gives him, Arathan. I fear, in truth, that he will announce a war upon that silence. All to hear her speak again, one more time, one last time. He will, if he is able, shatter the peace of death itself.'

'How is that even possible?'

Gothos shook his head. 'Since I am the one who flees death tirelessly, I am not the one to ask.' The Lord of Hate waved one ink-stained hand. 'We wage war with our follies, Hood and me, and so are repelled in opposite directions. I chase the dawn and he would chase the dusk. I do not begrudge his resolve, and can only hope that my fellow Jaghut choose to ignore his summons.'

'Why wouldn't they? It is impossible. Madness.'

'Attractive qualities indeed. Impossible and mad, yes, but most worrying of all, it is *audacious*.'

'Then in truth, you fear they will answer him.'

Gothos shrugged. 'Even a few could cause trouble. Now, more wine, please. I believe the bottle bred another in the trunk, somewhere. Do go and look, will you?'

Instead, Arathan glanced at the trap.

Sighing, Gothos said, 'It bodes ill that you already tire of my company. Go on, then, and appease your curiosity.'

Arathan approached the trap and looked down. The steps were made of wood, warped and worn with age. They were steep. The light coming from below was pale. He made his way down.

After the twelfth step, he reached the earthen floor. It was uneven, with roots snaking across it like a tangled web. He could see no walls. The light was pervasive but without any obvious source. He saw his father standing at the edge of a pool fifteen paces ahead. In the centre of the pool was an island, only a few paces across, where sat a Jaghut. He seemed to have torn away his clothes, and raked claws through his own flesh. Heavy manacles bound his wrists, the chains plunging into the island's rocky surface. Arathan made his way to stand beside his father.

Draconus was speaking. '. . . I mean to purge the gift, and give it to

521

the Night. I know that this offers no absolution.' He paused, and then said, 'K'rul is not alone in seeking justice for the murder, Hood. I can think of no Azathanai who is not outraged by Errastas's crime.'

Hood was silent, eyes downcast.

'I would release you,' Draconus said.

A low laugh came from the imprisoned Jaghut. 'Ah, Draconus. You sought from Errastas a worthy symbol of your love for Mother Dark. To achieve that, he stole the love of another, and made from black-wood leaves the gift you sought. By this we are all made to bow before your need.' Hood lifted his head, his eyes catching the strange silver reflection from the pool. 'And now you stand before me, struggling to constrain your rage, a rage you feel on my behalf. But you see: I do not blame Errastas or his foolish companion, Sechul Lath. Nor do I look upon you with vehemence. Be a sword if you will, but do not expect me to wield it.'

'My fury remains, Hood, and I will curse Errastas for his deed, and for my own role in it. I will forge a sword and make of it a prison—'

'Then you are a fool, Draconus. I ask no redemption from you. I seek no compensation and am as unmoved by your sympathy as I am by your rage. Your gestures are your own.'

'Quenched in Vitr—'

'Cease this sordid description! What I will do, once I am freed, will unwind all of existence. Your fevered remonstrance is without relevance. Your gestures are reduced to petty exercises bolstering little more than your sense of self-importance, and in this I see you join the chorus of a million voices, but the song is sour and the refrain rings false. Give me the key, then, and begone.'

'Hood, you cannot defeat death itself.'

'You would know nothing of that, Draconus. I shall call for companions. My enemy shall be the injustice of mortality. I am certain that I will gather a few to my cause. The grieving, the lost, we shall be a solemn handful – but none will doubt our resolve.'

'And where then will you find the shores of that unknown sea, Hood? What bridge can you hope to cross without releasing your soul to the very oblivion you seek to destroy?'

'Heed well the lessons I will bring, Draconus, in my argument with death.'

'I fear that we will not meet again,' Arathan's father said.

'There are greater fears, Draconus. Make your regret modest and we'll never have cause to curse one another, and in that may we find peace between us.'

'You break my heart, Hood.'

'Voice no such confessions, lest Gothos hear you and be incited to mockery. I never refused his arguments, though he might well choose to believe otherwise. Nothing of what he dismantled with his words was worth keeping. We are never eased for long by the accoutrements of self-delusion. Not that you will heed that.'

Draconus tossed the key across to Hood.

The Jaghut caught it. 'Gothos chained me out of love,' he said, eyeing the key he held. 'And here you seek to free me in its name, but I am dead to such things now. One day, Draconus, I will call upon you, in Death's name, and I wonder: how will you answer?'

'When that moment arrives, Hood, we shall both learn what that answer will be.'

Hood nodded. He reached down and unlocked the first manacle.

Draconus turned to Arathan. 'We are done here.'

But Arathan said to Hood, 'Sir.'

The Jaghut paused, looked across. 'What would you tell me, son of Draconus?'

'Only of my faith,' he replied.

Hood laughed. 'Faith? Go on, then, I will hear it.'

'I believe, sir, that you will prove Gothos wrong.'

The Jaghut grunted. 'And is that a good thing?'

'His argument, sir. It is wrong. You all failed to answer him and so ended your civilization. But that argument never ends. It cannot end, and that is what you will prove.'

'An argument as endless as his confession? Hah! You are bold, son of Draconus. Do you also have faith that I will win my war?'

'No, sir. I think you will fail. But I will bless you for trying.'

There was silence, and then Arathan saw tears track crooked paths down the Jaghut's lined cheeks. Draconus set a hand upon his son's shoulder and drew him back. The hand was heavy, but the grip promised no pain. Reaching the steps they paused and his father said, 'Arathan, I regret not knowing you better.'

'Father, from all sides you have been warned away from the path you are taking. Why do you persist?'

'Because, son, I know no other.'

'This is what Hood said of his own path,' Arathan replied. 'And Gothos. And Kilmandaros and Olar Ethil. It's what all of you say, even when you don't say it.'

'Climb, Arathan. My time with you is almost done. I must return to Kharkanas. I have been gone too long as it is.'

Arathan ascended, his father following.

The Lord of Hate was still seated in his chair and seemed to be dozing, with an empty goblet in one hand.

Ignoring him, Draconus continued on. Outside, he collected up his horse's reins and swung into the saddle. Looking down at Arathan he said, 'Select an empty tower nearby to stable your mounts. There is a

Jaghut living near. He is named Cynnigig. He is strange but harmless, and has great love for horses. He will ensure that your mounts are well fed and watered, and indeed exercised, but of the latter, do not lose your ties to Hellar.'

'I won't.'

'Find somewhere near to sleep and make the best home you can. Do not unduly isolate yourself, and do not forget that a world exists beyond that of Gothos, and the Jaghut. When you feel ready, depart. You are a far greater gift than Tutor Sagander ever intended.'

'Father, be careful in Kharkanas. They think they know you, but they don't.'

Draconus studied him. 'And you do?'

'You are an Azathanai.'

His father collected up the reins and swung Calaras around. He rode out into the centre of the clearing, and as he did so the light faded around him, as if night itself had been summoned and now drew close to welcome its suzerain. In the moments before all light vanished, swallowing Draconus and his mount, Arathan saw a transformation come to Calaras. The stallion's black hide deepened, his form blurring at the edges, his eyes flaring as if suddenly lit with lurid flames.

Then they vanished within impenetrable darkness. A moment later the day's dying light swept in once more, revealing an empty clearing.

*No embrace. No words of love to seal this farewell. He's gone. My father is gone.*

He stood, alone, feeling lost. Feeling free.

Drawing out the clay figurine, he studied it. Olar Ethil's gift, passing to him through the hands of his father. For all that it comforted him with its roundness and its weight, he wished that he did not have it. But it was all that remained, the only thing left that marked this vast journey, from the moment Sagander had made him halt and look back upon the gate of House Dracons, to this last, solitary instant, in the empty wake of his father's departure.

*Another gift soaked in blood.* Hearing a sound, he looked up.

From across the clearing, two figures had appeared. A Jaghut in armour, and beside him a young Tiste woman, thin and sharp-featured. He watched them approach.

When they reached him the Jaghut spoke, 'Is he within?'

'He is, sir. Sleeping in his chair.'

The Jaghut snorted, and then strode inside. A moment later his voice echoed loud and harsh: 'If you're not yet dead, Gothos, wake up!'

The woman met Arathan's eyes, and then shrugged apologetically. A moment later she frowned. 'What are you doing here? Who are you?'

The challenge in her eyes made him recoil a step. 'I am a guest.'

'A guest of the Lord of Hate?'

He nodded, putting the clay figurine back into the pouch at his belt.

'Was that a doll?'

'In a manner of speaking. A gift.'

'It's ugly. I had prettier dolls, once.'

He said nothing, made uncomfortable by the directness of her gaze.

'Do you always do that?'

'What?'

'Chew your nails.'

Arathan dropped his hand and wiped his fingers on his thigh. 'No,' he said.

# SEVENTEEN

'DID HE EVER SPEAK OF FAMILY?'

Feren said nothing to Ville's question, and after a moment it was Rint who said, 'Not that I recall. He talked only of House Dracons. It was the home he had made and if there was something before then, they were ashes he would not stir among us.'

'Why should he?' Galak demanded. 'Sergeant or not, he was our commanding officer. I don't see how our ignorance excuses anything. We may well be discharged from the Lord's compass, but this does not absolve us from decency.'

'He is not a Bordersword,' Rint said in a growl. 'I have no desire to ride back to House Dracons just to deliver a headless corpse. I have a newborn child and would see it.'

Feren held her gaze fixed on the way ahead, the rolling grasses and the dark wavy line that marked hills to the northeast. They had already left the trail they had made when venturing west. If Ville and Galak won this argument, they would have to cut across, straight east, to reach Abara Delack.

Their horses were tired, and the wrapped body of Gate Sergeant Raskan made pungent every wayward gust of wind.

'We can build a cairn in the hills ahead,' said Rint. 'We can surrender his empty flesh to the realm of Mother Dark, and make all the necessary propitiations. There is nothing dishonourable in that. And if need be, we can send a message back to House Dracons, specifying the location of that cairn, should someone wish to come and collect the body.'

'How could such a message not be deemed an insult?' Ville said. 'I don't understand you, Rint. If we cannot hold to courtesy, what is left to us?'

'I am past courtesy,' Rint snapped. 'If you and Galak feel it is so important, then deliver him. But I am returning home.'

'Feren?' Galak asked.

'She took him,' Feren replied. 'The witch stole his soul. It matters not where you leave what's left, or even that you make propitiation. Mother Dark will never receive his soul. Raskan is gone from us.'

'The rituals serve the conscience of the living,' Ville insisted. 'Mine. Yours. His kin.'

She shrugged. 'I see no salve in empty gestures, Ville.'

Galak grunted in frustration, and then said, 'Would that we had never parted. You and me, Ville, we tell ourselves and each other that we ride in the company of two old friends. They well look the part.'

Everyone fell silent then, and the thumping of horse hoofs filled the cool afternoon air. Feren half closed her eyes, settling back into the rhythmic roll of her mount's slow canter. In a short while they would slow their pace back down to a walk, and the distant hills would seem no closer and the homeland beyond would remain lost in longing and fearful uncertainty – as if distance alone could call its very existence into question.

There were ways of resenting the world that she had never known before, never sensed, and she would never have believed anyone's claim to their veracity. She cursed the stretch of grassland. She cursed the pointless immensity of the sky overhead, its painless blue of daytime and its cruel indifference at night. The wind's ceaseless moaning filled her head like the distant wailing of a thousand children, and every harsh breath bit at her eyes.

With the coming of dusk she would sit huddled with the others, and the fire they made would mock with every tongue of flame. And she would hear the witch's laughter, and then her terrible screams which now came to Feren and sank in, stealing her satisfaction, her pleasure at what her brother had done. Instead, that sound of pain haunted her, leaving her feeling belittled and shamed.

The easy camaraderie among the Borderswords was gone. Her brother would sit with bruised eyes that caught the reflection of the fire, and she remembered the cry of anguish that had been torn from him when she had held on to his rigid body. She could not imagine what he had taken from her in that moment, to give him the strength to strike back at the witch. For the scar she now bore. For the murder of an innocent man. She had no courage to match his, and if he would now ride for home, she would ride with him and voice no objection.

She told herself that Rint was as he had once been: the brother who would always be there, protecting her from the world and its cruel turns. But the truth was that she doubted her own convictions, and for all of her gestures, her willingness to follow Rint, she felt herself falling behind him. She was a child again, and that was no place to be, with what she carried in her womb. Somewhere, in this vast landscape, the woman that she had been – strong, resolute – now wandered lost. Without that woman, Feren felt bereft and weak beyond measure, even as her brother seemed to be rushing towards an unknown but terrible fate.

She'd had no final parting words for Arathan, and this too shamed her. Few would not scorn the notion of an innocent father. After all, the guilt was in the conception, the act of wilful surrender. But she saw him as innocent. The knowledge and the wilfulness had belonged solely to her, and she suspected that she would have seduced him even without his father's command.

The sky was deepening its hue, remote in its unchanging laws, its crawling progression that looked down with blind eyes and gave no thought to wounded souls and their hopeless longing for peace. If self-pity was a depthless pool then she skirted its muddy, slippery bank on hands and knees, round and round. Awareness made no difference. Knowledge was useless. She held innocence in her womb and felt like a thief.

Ville spoke. 'A cairn it shall be, then. You two are not the only ones longing for home.'

She saw her brother nod, but he said nothing, and she felt the silence that followed Ville's words harden about them all. Submission without a word of thanks made plain the surrender, and that could only sting. Rifts were forming and widening and soon, she knew, they would not be able to cross them. She shook herself, straightening in the saddle. 'Thank you both,' she said. 'We are in a broken place, my brother and me. Even Rint's vengeance stretches too far behind us, while poor Raskan draws so close we might as well be carrying him on our backs.'

Ville's eyes were wide when she glanced at him.

Galak cleared his throat and spat to one side. 'That's a taste I am well rid of. My thanks, Feren.'

Abruptly, Rint shuddered, sobbed, and began weeping.

They all reined in. 'That's it for today,' Feren said, her voice harsh. She slipped down from the saddle and went over to help her brother dismount. He had curled in around his torment and it was a struggle to get him down from his horse. Both Ville and Galak arrived to help.

Rint sank to the ground. He kept shaking his head, even as sobs racked him. Feren gestured Ville and Galak away and then held her brother tight. 'We're a useless pair,' she muttered softly to Rint. 'Let's blame our parents and be done with it.'

A final sob broke, ended in a ragged laugh.

They stayed clenched together, and he stilled in her arms.

'I hate him,' he said with sudden vehemence.

Feren glanced over at Ville and Galak. They stood over their packs, staring, frozen by Rint's words.

'Who?' she asked. 'Who do you hate, Rint?'

'Draconus. For what he's done to us. For this cursed journey!'

'He is behind us now,' she said. 'We are going home, Rint.'

But he shook his head, pulling himself loose from her arms and rising to his feet. 'It's not enough, Feren. He will return. He will take his place at Mother Dark's side. This user of children, this abuser of love. Evil is at its boldest when it walks an unerring path.'

'He has enemies enough at court—'

'To the Abyss with the court! I now count myself his enemy, and I will speak against our neutrality to all the Borderswords. The Consort must be driven out, his power shattered. I would see him slain, cut down. I would see his name become a curse among all the Tiste!'

Her brother stood, trembling, his eyes wide but hard as iron as he glared at Feren, and then at Ville and Galak. 'That witch was his lover,' he continued, wiping at the tears streaking his cheeks. 'What does that tell you about Draconus? About the cast of his soul?' He marched over to where Raskan's body was bound across the back of the sergeant's horse. 'Let's ask Raskan, shall we? This poor man under the so-called protection of his lord.' He tore at the leather strings, but the knots resisted him, until he simply tugged the moccasins from the dead man's feet, and then dragged the corpse free. His foot caught and he fell back with the wrapped form in his arms. They landed heavily. Swearing, Rint pushed the body away and stood, ashen-faced. 'Ask Raskan what he thinks. About his lord, his master and all the women he has taken into his arms. Ask Raskan about Olar Ethil, the Azathanai witch who murdered him.'

Feren released her breath. Her heart was thumping fast. 'Rint, our neutrality—'

'Will be abused! Is already being abused! It is our standing to one side that yields ground to the ambitious. Neutrality? See how easily it acquires the colours of cowardice! I will argue an alliance with Urusander, for all the Borderswords. Sister, tell me that you are with me! You bear visible proof of what that man has done!'

'Don't.'

'Take his coin and surrender your body – that is how Draconus sees it! He respects nothing, Feren. Not your feelings, not the losses in your past, not the wounds you will carry for the rest of your life – none of that matters to him. He sought a grandchild—'

'No!' Her cry echoed, and each time her voice came back to her from the empty plain it sounded yet more plaintive, more pathetic. 'Rint, listen to me. I was the one who wanted the child.'

'Then why did he drive you away from his son once he determined that you were pregnant?'

'To save Arathan.'

'From what?'

'From me, you fool.'

Her reply silenced him and she saw his shock, and then his struggle to understand her. Weakness took her once again and she turned away. 'I was the one walking an unerring path, unmindful of the people I hurt, Rint.'

'Draconus invited you into his world, Feren. He did not care that you were vulnerable.'

'When he cut me from Arathan, he saved both of us. I know you can't see it that way. Or you won't. You want to hurt Draconus, just as you hurt Olar Ethil. It's just the same, and it's all down to your need to strike out, to make someone else feel the pain you're feeling. My wars are over with, Rint.'

'Mine are not!'

She nodded. 'I see that.'

'I expected you to stand with me, Feren.'

She turned on him. 'Why? Are you so certain that you're doing all this for me? I'm not. I don't want it! I just want my brother back!'

Rint seemed to crumple before her eyes, and once more he sank down to the ground, covering his face with his hands.

'Abyss take us,' Ville said. 'Stop this. Both of you. Rint, we will hear your arguments and we will vote on them. Feren, you are with child. No one would expect you to unsheathe your sword. Not now.'

She shook her head. Poor Ville didn't understand, but she could not blame him for that.

'We have far to go,' Galak added in a soft tone. 'And on the morrow, we shall reach the hills, and find a place for Raskan's body. A place of gentle regard to embrace his bones. When we return to our homelands I will ride on to House Dracons and inform Captain Ivis of the location. For now, my friends, let us make camp.'

Feren looked out on the plain to the south. There was a path there, distant now and fading, that trekked westward into strange lands. There were patches of ground with soft grasses that had known the pressure of a man and a woman drawn together by unquenchable needs. The same sky that was above her now looked down on those remnants, those faint and vanishing impressions, and the wind that slid across her face, plucking at the tears on her cheeks, whipped and swirled but flowed ever southward, and sometime in the night would brush those grasses.

Life could reach far, into the past where it grasped hold of things and dragged them howling into the present. And distance could breed resentment, when all the promises of the future remained for ever beyond reach. And the child shifting in her womb, as the day died, felt like a thing lost in the wilderness, and as its faint cries reached her from no known place she knelt, eyes closed, hands over her ears.

*    *    *

Rint dared not look again at his sister; not to see her as she was, on her knees and broken by the words they had flung between them. He left Ville and Galak to make ready the camp, and sat staring into the northeast, trapped in his own desolation.

It was a struggle to envisage the face of his wife. When he imagined her sitting wrapped in furs with a newborn child against her breast, he saw a stranger. Two strangers. His hands would not cease trembling. They felt hot, as if they still held the fires they had unleashed in that moment of fury, so fierce with brutal vengeance. He did not regret the pain he had delivered upon Olar Ethil; but when he thought of it, he saw himself first, a figure silhouetted by towering flames, and the screams filling the smoke and ashes rising into the air became the voice of the trees, the agony of blackening leaves and snapping branches. He stood then, like a god, face lit in the reflection of his undeniable triumph. A witness to the destruction, even when that destruction was his own. Such a man knew no love, not for a wife, not for a child. Such a man knew nothing but violence and so made of himself a stranger to everyone.

Insects spun through the dusk. Behind him he heard Ville muttering something to Galak, and the smoke from the cookfire drifted past him, like serpents escaping another realm, fleeing off into the gathering darkness. He looked across to where he had left Raskan's cloth-wrapped body. The hands were stretched out, bruised and swollen, and where the leather strings were tied round the wrists they now bit deep. Beyond them were the moccasins, lying on the grass. Draconus was free with his gifts indeed.

Urusander would find a way. He would crush the madness and force peace upon Kurald Galain. But blood would flow and the struggle would be arduous. If only the guilty died, then such deaths could be deemed just, and so make of each unfortunate murder an act of execution. Justice was at the heart of retribution, after all.

For too long had the highborn lounged, smug and complacent with the privileges that came with the wielding of power. But nothing of worth was given for free. Privilege was a bright weed growing on the spilled blood of the enslaved, and Rint saw nothing precious in such bitter flowers. When he looked ahead, he could think of nothing but smoke and flames, the only answers he had left.

It was Draconus's noble blood that had yoked them all, dragging them through misery and unfeeling abuse. Without his title, he was no different from any of them. And yet they had bowed before him. They had knelt in deference, and by each and every such act they but served to confirm the Lord's own sense of superiority. These were the rituals of inequity, and everyone knew their role.

He thought back to Tutor Sagander's nonsense – the appalling lessons the old man had thrust upon Arathan on the first days out. The self-righteous could argue unto their last breath, so certain were they of their stance, and yet with outrage would they view any accusation of being self-serving. But smugness filled the silence after every pronouncement they made, as if condescension were virtue's reward.

The Borderswords were men and women who had rejected the stilted rigidity of Kharkanas and sought out a rawer truth in the wild lands upon the very edge of civilization. They claimed to live under older laws, the kind that bound all forms of life, but Rint wondered now if the very sentiment had been forged on an anvil of lies. Innocence withered before knowing eyes just as it had once withered behind them. The first foot set upon virgin ground despoiled; the first touch stained; the first embrace broke the bones of the wild.

Outside House Dracons, it had been Ville – or was it Galak – who had bemoaned the slaughter of the beasts, and yet dreamed of taking the last creature by spear or arrow, if only to bring an end to its loneliness. That was a sentiment breathless in its stupidity and tragedy. It arrived as punctuation, and only idiotic silence could follow. And yet Rint knew the truth of it, and felt its heavy reverberation, like a curse to haunt his kind down the ages.

He would fight for justice. And, if need be, he would expose to the Borderswords the sordid delusion of their so-called neutrality. Life was a war against a thousand enemies, from the sustenance carved from nature to the insanity of a people's will to do wrong in the name of right. His hands trembled, he now knew, from the blood they had spilled, and their eagerness to spill yet more.

There was a truth that came with standing as would a god, with eyes fixed upon the destruction his malign will had wrought. To be a god was to know utter loneliness, and yet find comfort in isolation. When one stood alone with nothing but power in one's hands, violence was a seductive lure.

*And now, dear Ville, I long for a spear to the back, an arrow to the throat.*

*Give me war, then. I have walked from complex truth to simple lie, and I cannot go back.*

*It is no crime to end a life that sees what it has lost.*

The sun was a red smear to the west. Behind him, Galak announced

532

that supper was ready, and Rint climbed to his feet. He looked across to his sister, but she had not turned at the invitation. He thought of the child growing within her, and felt only sadness. *Another stranger. Blinking and then wailing to a new world. Only innocent before the first breath drawn. Only innocent until the birth of need and its desperate voice. A sound we all hear and will hear for the rest of our lives.*

*What god would not flee that?*

'We have company,' said Ville, and, straightening, he drew out his sword.

Five beasts were approaching from the west. Tall as horses, but heavier in the way of predators. Black-furred with heads slung low, bearing collars of iron blades. Insects swarmed in clouds around them.

'Sheathe your weapon,' Rint told Ville. 'Jheleck.'

'I know what they are,' snapped Ville.

'And we are at peace.'

'What we are, Rint, is four Borderswords alone on the plain.'

One of the huge wolves held the carcass of an antelope in its massive jaws. The antelope seemed small, like a hare in the mouth of a hunting dog. Rint shook his head. 'Put the weapon away, Ville. If they wanted to kill us, they would have rushed in. The war is over. They were vanquished, and like any beaten dog they will yield to our command.' But his mouth was dry, and the horses shifted uneasily as the Soletaken drew closer.

He felt something come to his eyes, stinging, and saw the five forms blur, as if melting into the dusk, only to reappear as fur-clad savages. They paused to remove their collars, the one bearing the carcass now throwing it over a shoulder. The cloud of flies lifted briefly, and then swept down once again.

During the wars, there had been few opportunities to look upon the Jheleck in their upright, sembled form. Even when a village was attacked, the fleeing non-combatants had quickly veered to aid their escape, and Rint recalled riding down many of them, pinning them to the earth with his lance and hearing their cries of pain amidst the snapping of their jaws. There had been much to admire and respect in the wolves they fought and killed. Individually, they were far more formidable than a Forulkan. Massed as armies, however, they had been next to useless. Jheleck were at their deadliest in small packs, such as the one that now drew to within a dozen paces of their camp.

Looking upon them now, however, Rint saw five savages, rank with filth and mostly naked under loose fur skins. The one bearing the antelope stepped closer and set the carcass down. Showing filthy teeth in a smile, he spoke in guttural Tiste. 'Meat for your fire, Bordersword.' Dark eyes shifted over to Ville. 'We saw the flash of your blade and it amused us. But where is your memory? Our war is done, is it not?' He waved a hand. 'You cross Jheleck land and we permit it. We come to you as hosts, with food. But if you would rather fight, why, we will happily accept the challenge. Indeed, we even agree to stand against you on two legs, as you see us, to more even the odds.'

Rint said, 'You offered us meat for our fire. Will you join us in the repast, Jhelarkan?'

The man laughed. 'Just so. Peace and hostages, like jaws around the throat. We'll not twitch, until it is time for the slave to turn on the master, and that time is not now.' He looked back to his companions and they came forward. Eyes fixing on Rint once more, the savage said, 'I am Rusk, blood kin to Sagral of the Derrog Clan.'

'I am Rint, and with me are Feren, Ville and Galak.'

Rusk nodded at his sister. 'We can use her tonight?'

'No.'

'Oh well,' Rusk said, shrugging. 'In truth, we did not expect you to share. Not the Tiste way. But if not her for the meat, then what gift will you offer us?'

'Something in return, Rusk, at some other time. If that is not acceptable, then take back your gift and with it the word itself, for gift it is not.'

Rusk laughed. 'Tell the Borderswords, then, of my generosity.'

'I will. Galak, take care of the carcass. Rusk, Galak is skilled with the skinning knife. You will have a decent hide at least.'

'And useful antlers and useful bones, yes. And full bellies. Good. Now, we sit.'

The other Jhelarkan lumbered up and sat in a rough half-circle facing the Borderswords. Except for Rusk, they were young, and seemed ignorant of the Tiste language. Their leader squatted, the grin never leaving his dirt-smeared face. With Feren forbidden him, he now ignored her, and Rint was glad.

'We do not agree with giving hostages, Borderswords,' Rusk now said, 'but we have done so. Fine pups one and all. If you harm them, we shall slaughter the Tiste and burn Kharkanas to the ground. We shall split your bones and bury your skulls. We shall piss on your temples and rut in your palaces.'

'No harm will come to the hostages,' Rint said, 'so long as you remain true to your words.'

'So you Tiste keep saying. Even the Jaghut nod and say it is so. But now we hear that Tiste kill Tiste. You are a pack with a weak leader, and too many among you eager to take his place. There is blood in the mouth and fur on the ground in Kurald Galain.'

Rint held his gaze on the Jheleck and said, 'We have been away for some time. Do you voice rumours or have you witnessed the things you describe?'

534

Rusk shrugged. 'War rides the winds and lifts the hackles. We see you wound yourselves, and we wait to strike.'

Ville grunted. 'So much for keeping your word!'

'We fear for the safety of our pups, Bordersword. Just as you would your own.'

'With you upon our borders,' Ville retorted, 'we had cause for fear.'

'But that is done now,' Rusk said, still grinning. 'We live with the new peace, Bordersword. The peace of empty villages and empty lands. Often, we look upon your hunting packs, as they travel with impunity across our homeland, seeking the last of the wild beasts. And when those beasts are gone, what shall the Jheleck eat? Grass?' He nodded. 'Peace, yes, plenty of that, written in bleached bones in old camps.'

Galak hacked at a hind joint.

'You have pups with you,' Rint said, nodding at the others.

'I teach them how to hunt, and so we all learn to go hungry, and come to understand all that we have lost. One day, they will be savage killers, and this night they take your scent and will keep it for all time.'

Feren said, 'If you are going hungry, why offer any to us?'

Rusk scowled. 'A host can do no less. But you Tiste do not comprehend honour. Only four days ago, the Borderswords gathered and rode out on to our land. They have word of a bhederin herd coming down from the north, and would make slaughter. They ride past our villages and laugh as they race our warriors to kill-sites. And when they have killed hundreds of the beasts, will they offer any to us? No. They will claim those carcasses as their own and take the meat, hides and bones away. We watch. We smile. And we vow to remember all that we see.'

'The Bordersword villages need meat for the winter,' Ville said.

'And long before the war, you took all you could from our lands, and so we made war—'

'And lost it!'

Rusk smiled again and nodded. 'We lost, and you may believe that you won. But when all the beasts are gone, will your victory fill your bellies? Will it taste any less bitter than our defeat? What you own you must nurture. But you Tiste do not understand that. All that you own you use, until it is used up, and then you cast your vision past your borders, and scheme to take again, this time from others.'

'I have hunted on your lands,' Ville said. 'I saw no nurture passing through your kill-sites.'

'Then you did not look carefully enough. We take the weak and leave the strong.'

'You took every beast,' Ville said.

Rusk laughed. 'We were defeated. We learned your ways of killing, but we found the winters long when we had naught but ghosts to hunt. You killed thousands of us. You made us few, and the irony of that is that it returned us to our old ways. And now we breed but rarely, and keep only the strongest pups. And when at last all the Tiste are dead, then we shall nurture the herds, until their numbers are vast once more, and we will make each new day the same as the day past, for all time, and know contentment.' He held up his hands. 'So we dream. But then your hunters pour over the border and the wise ones among us see the truth awaiting us. Yours is the language of death, and it will speak to us.'

Meat sizzled on skewers over the fire. The night had drawn close. Rint pushed away Rusk's words and stared into the flames. He thought he could see the witch's face, twisting with pain, the mouth opened to an endless shriek he could not hear but felt in his bones. He had wanted to spend this night alone, saying little and quick to take to his bedding. Instead, he found himself face to face with a filthy half-beast who smiled a smile devoid of humour, and whose dark eyes belonged to a wolf.

'Rusk,' said Galak, 'when did you see the Bordersword hunters?'

'Hunters, butchers, skinners, bone-splitters. Dogs, horses, mules and oxen pulling wagons. On another day their numbers would make them an army. They rode armed and wary, with scouts tracking our own hunters.' He waved a greasy hand. 'Days past now.'

'How many days? Five? Ten?'

Rusk sat forward, forearms on the knees of his crossed legs, and offered Galak that same, hard smile. 'We have kin, scouting your lands. They move at night and remain hidden. We have seen armies on this side of the river. One rode into Abara Delack. Another gathers in the hills of House Dracons—'

'That one is the Lord's own,' said Galak. 'You evade answering, Rusk.'

'I am indifferent to your need, Bordersword. I tell you what I choose to tell you. Your civil war has begun. We rejoice and sniff the wind for smoke, and look to the skies for the carrion birds. You killed us before, but now you kill each other and this pleases us.'

It was not long before the carcass was stripped down to the bones. Galak rolled up the antelope's hide and offered it to Rusk, along with the antlers and the long bones. Grunting, the Jhelarkan leader gestured to his hunters and as one they rose.

'Your company is bitter,' he announced. 'We return to the night. Remember our generosity, Borderswords, and tell the tale of this meeting to your hunters, so that they may at last understand courtesy.'

'It is a thought,' Rint allowed, 'that we might work best together. To hunt the great herds and to share in the bounty.'

'Rint, there are no great herds.'

The figures withdrew from the fire's light, and in moments were gone.

Ville spat into the flames. 'I think he lied,' he said in a growl. 'About those armies. He would stir us to alarm and fear.'

Galak said, 'We well know that there is an army at House Dracons, Ville, just as he described. He may have thrown more than a few truths into his words to us.'

'And Abara Delack? Why would any army, rebel or otherwise, occupy Abara Delack?'

'We don't know,' Rint said, wanting to end this debate. 'We've been away for too long. There is no point in speculating. Listen, our bellies are full for the first time in months. Let us sleep now, with the aim of riding hard on the morrow.'

'I hope,' said Ville, 'the hunt went well.'

\* \* \*

Lieutenant Risp studied the blockish silhouette that was Riven Keep. The solitary tower, which rose from a clutter of lower buildings huddled around it, showed a single, faint light, coming from a room on the top floor, just beneath the peaked roof. There was a low wall, she had been told, surrounding this ancient fort, marked by banked revetments. To assault Riven Keep an army would find itself descending steep ditches forming a treacherous maze beyond the walls, all under arrow fire from the revetments, and crowding into chokepoints where the ground underfoot would be uneven and even retreat would prove impossible. It was well, she concluded, that they were not facing an enemy aware of the threat drawing close.

The village below Riven Keep formed a half-circle round the hill, and these houses sprawled to the very edges of community pastureland. Risp could smell the smoke in the cool night air. Twisting in her saddle, she squinted at the waiting soldiers of her own troop. Weapons were drawn but held at rest across saddles and thighs. No one spoke and the only sound came from the occasional shift or snort from a horse. Beyond her unit waited others, all equally silent, gathered in mounted squares in the basins to either side of the road.

Upon the road itself, Captain Esthala led the centre unit, with her husband further along to the woman's right. The thought of that still left a bitter taste in Risp's mouth, but she told herself that Silann was not her problem, and if Esthala continued to refuse to do what was needed, well, she would answer to Hunn Raal. For once, Risp was relieved to find herself outranked. Better still, Esthala's ambitions were now doomed: she would never be promoted, or welcomed among the higher ranks in the Legion.

*Stupid woman. All for the sake of love. All for a fool better suited to hoeing vegetables than swinging a sword. Not only didn't you execute him; you didn't even demote him, or throw him out. Instead, we must all suffer his incompetence and pray to the Abyss that it doesn't kill us. When she took over command here . . .*

The sergeant cleared his throat and edged his mount up to her side. 'Sir, this doesn't sit well with some of us.'

*And I know which, too. Your days are numbered, sergeant. You and your old cronies.* 'We must divide our enemies,' she said, shrugging. 'Deceit is an essential component of military tactics. Furthermore, what creditable commander does not take advantage of surprise, or the miscalculations of the enemy?'

'The enemy, sir? I am sure that they are unaware that they are anyone's enemy. Is this the miscalculation to which you are referring?'

She heard the awkward formality in his words and was amused. 'One of them.'

'Most of the combatants are not here,' the sergeant said, nodding towards the village. 'Occupation will suffice to eliminate the Bordersowrds as a threat to the Legion, by virtue of holding their families under guard.'

'That is true, but at the expense of committing a defendable force to oversee those hostages, for an unknown period of time.'

'Few would resist overmuch,' the sergeant countered. 'They are neutral as it stands. Instead, we give them reason to reject that neutrality.'

'Indeed,' she agreed.

'Then I do not understand.'

'I know,' she said. 'And you don't need to, sergeant. Take your orders and leave it at that.'

'If we know what we're about, sir, then there's less chance of doing the wrong thing.'

'Sergeant, with what is about to come down to that village, there's nothing you could do that would earn our wrath.' She looked across at him. 'Barring disobeying orders.'

'We won't do that, sir,' the old man said in a growl.

'Of course you won't.' But even as Risp said that, she felt the hollowness to the assertion. It was hard to know where their orders were coming from. Was this still Hunn Raal's gambit, or had Urusander finally taken to the field? Where was Osserc? For all they knew here, the entire plan might be in ruins somewhere behind them, lying lifeless behind Hunn Raal's unseeing eyes in some muddy field, or upon the old spikes of the Citadel's riverwall, making what they were about to do a crime and an inexcusable atrocity. She knew her own unease with what was to come.

There would always be miscalculations in any campaign. The Tiste had faced near disaster against the Forulkan on more than one occasion, when miscommunication or the outright absence of communication had sent elements to the wrong place at the wrong time. There was nothing more difficult than linking up armies and manoeuvring such large forces into position. Ensuring that they acted effectively and in concert was a commander's greatest challenge. It was no accident that commanders were at their most comfortable when they could amass all the forces at their disposal. Of course, once battle commenced, everything changed. Upon the field, the company captains and their corps of officers were crucial.

She looked again at the distant keep, and that lone light upon the top floor. Had someone fallen asleep in a soft chair, with the candle burning down? Or was there a guard stationed in the tower, acting as a lookout? The latter did not seem likely, as light in the chamber would make it impossible to see anything outside. Perhaps some cleric or scholar was working through the night, muttering under his or her breath and cursing failing eyesight and aching bones. Risp could feel the chill in the wind coming down from the mountains to the north.

The Borderswords were welcome to this remote, cold place.

'Sir,' said the old sergeant.

'What now?'

'Once we are done here, will we be returning to besiege House Dracons?'

She recalled the day and the night during which they had camped at the very edge of the estate. The Lord's Houseblades had ridden out in strength, as if to challenge this unwelcome army camped on its door-step, but Esthala had been indifferent to the gesture, instead sending a rider to the Houseblade Commander, assuring him that her Legion units intended no violence upon the holdings of the Consort.

The Houseblade captain had been unappeased by these pronounce-ments, and had maintained his forces in readiness for all the time that the Legion remained on Dracons land, even going so far as to ride parallel to their column for a time, once it resumed its northward journey. Lord Draconus had assembled a formidable company, heavily armoured and impressively disciplined. Risp was in truth relieved that the Consort's Houseblades were not among Esthala's targets.

'Sir?'

'No, sergeant, we will not be returning to House Dracons. We have done what was needed. We have left a column trail back to his estate.'

There was a sound from the road and Risp glanced over to the vanguard and saw the standards of House Dracons being raised aloft.

The sergeant swore under his breath, and then said, 'With us out of uniform, I was assuming we'd be laying the blame on the Deniers. Now I see how this will be played.'

'We need deception,' Risp said. 'More to the point, we need our enemies divided and at each other's throat.'

'Then there are to be survivors.'

'It would be foolish to think no one will escape the slaughter, sergeant. And yes, we are relying upon that.' She met his eyes. 'We must do what is necessary.'

'Yes sir.'

'As every soldier understands.'

He nodded, reaching up to adjust the strap on his helm.

The command rippled out from unit to unit to begin the advance. Behind them, the sun was just beginning its rise, copper red from the smoke above the forest to the east. She readied her lance. *My first battle. My first engagement. Today I will spill blood for the first time.* Her mouth was dry and she could feel her heart thumping in her chest. She set her heels to her mount's flanks and they began to move.

*     *     *

Krissen let the scroll fall fluttering to the floor, joining a dozen others, and reached up to rub her eyes. She felt exhausted in her mind and weak in her flesh, but currents of excitement remained. There was no doubt in her mind now. Forty years ago she had travelled alone among the Jhelarkan, into the fastnesses high in the mountains and to the tundra beyond. Moving from clan to clan, she had made her way westward until arriving among the giant Thel Akai, the Keepers of Songs, and from there southward, into Jaghut lands. She had collected stories, legends and songs from the Jhelarkan and the Thel Akai, and had read through the dispirited but enlightened writings of the Jaghut before the originals had been destroyed following the Lord of Hate's murdering of Jaghut civilization.

In every tale, truths could be found, dull as river stones in a gem-laden mosaic. They needed only prising loose, out of the gaudy clutter and poetic trappings. Among the ancient songs, locked by the extraordinary memory of the Thel Akai, secrets waited.

Krissen understood the First Age now; not in its details, but in its broadest strokes. Everything began with the Azathanai, who walked worlds in the guise of mortals, but were in truth gods. They created. They destroyed. They set things into motion, driven by a curiosity which often waned, leaving to the fates all that followed. They displayed perverse impulses; they viewed one another with indifference or suspicion, yet upon meeting often displayed extraordinary empathy. They held to unwritten laws on sanctity, territorial interests and liberty, and they played with power as would a child a toy.

She could not be certain, but she suspected that one of them had created the Jaghut. That another had answered in kind with the Tiste. Forulkan, Thel Akai, perhaps even the Dog-Runners, were all fashioned by the will of an Azathanai. Created like game pieces in an eternal contest, mysterious in its conditions of victory, in which few strategies were observable. Their interest in this contest rarely accounted outcomes.

But even as they stood outside time, so too did time prove immune to their manipulations, and now, at last, they had begun suffering its depredations. Deeds accumulated, and each one carried weight. She was certain that the Jaghut had created the Jhelarkan, elaborating on the Azathanai gift of Soletaken, and among the Dog-Runners there were now Bonecasters, shamans powerful enough to challenge the Azathanai. Gods were rising from the created peoples – their own gods. Whatever control the Azathanai had once held over their creations was fast tearing free.

She had heard about the mysterious Azathanai who had come to Kharkanas, and even now, among sages and priests, an awareness was emerging that unknown powers were within the reach of mortals. The world was changing. The game had broken away from the players.

Krissen saw before them now the beginning of a new age, one in which all the created peoples could define their own rules.

Hearing something like low thunder from the window, she rose, arching to work the kinks out of her back, and then walked to the lone window where the dawn's light now paled the sky beyond. She looked down to see hundreds of riders converging on the village below.

For a long moment she simply stared, unable to comprehend what she was seeing. The riders broke up to pour into the streets, and down alleys and tracks. She saw figures appearing from their homes, saw some running from the path of the riders, and then came the flash of iron, or the thrust of lances, and bodies fell to the dirt.

*Like pieces on a board. Moves made and then countered. Pieces falling.* Faintly now, she could hear screams, and the first column of smoke lifted into the morning sky.

She had nothing of Gallan's artistry with words, and the more she saw, the more words failed her, each one arriving in her mind listless and pallid. She was a scholar, one whom ideas inspired more than execution, and to put her thoughts into words, upon parchment, had always been a struggle.

Even in her head, her sense of the Azathanai was almost formless, a thing of impressions and strange upwelling emotions. Her failure had always been in the marriage of imagination with the pragmatic. And now, as she watched the slaughter below, and saw the first riders climbing the cobbled track leading up to Riven Keep – an edifice undefended and virtually unoccupied – she felt incapable of binding these details to any personal impetus.

A new age was upon them. *How can you not see that? How can you*

*not understand? I have made discoveries. It was all there, in the stories
and the songs. Such discoveries!*

*The keep gate isn't even closed.*

*       *       *

Instincts had reared, beast-like, and now Risp felt herself knocked
about on her saddle, her lance dragging and stuttering heavily on the
cobbles, yanking her arm back. Impaled on the weapon was a boy of
about five years of age. He had darted out from behind a rag cart,
almost into her path, and she had struck without thought, and now his
limp body was skewered, his limbs flopping as his weight pulled at her.

A sob broke from her throat, a sound broken with horror. She bit
back on it. The lance head stabbed into the ground again and this time
she relaxed her grip, releasing the weapon. Directly ahead was a heavily
pregnant woman, pulling two children with her as she ran down the
alley.

Something cold and empty drove all thoughts from Risp, and she felt
her hand draw free her longsword, saw the blade flash in front of her.

As she closed on the three, she saw the woman throw both children
ahead of her, screaming *'Run!'* And then she spun round, leaping into
the path of Risp's horse.

The impact sent the woman flying back, to land stunned on the
cobbles.

Risp's horse staggered, coughing, forelegs folding under it. As it
collapsed, Risp kicked her boots free of the stirrups and rolled from
the saddle. She struck the ground on her right shoulder, felt the sword
clatter away from a senseless hand, and came up against the wall of a
building. Looking up, she saw her sergeant ride past, slashing down at
the nearest of the two children, who fell without a sound. The other
child, a girl of about four, wheeled to rush to her fallen sister, and came
within reach of the sergeant's sword. He cut down across the back of
her neck and she crumpled like a doll.

Picking herself up, Risp collected her sword, left-handed, and
awkwardly readied the weapon. Only now did she see the handle of
a knife, its blade embedded in the chest of her dying horse. Fury took
hold and she advanced on the pregnant woman. 'You killed my horse!'
she shouted.

The pregnant woman lifted her head and met Risp's eyes. Her face
twisted and she spat at Risp.

She hacked the woman down with repeated blows.

Beyond them, at the alley mouth, the sergeant had reined in and
spun his horse round. He seemed about to shout something, and then a
figure leapt down from the roof to the sergeant's left, colliding with the
veteran and dragging him from the saddle. Blood sprayed the moment

542

before they struck the cobbles, and the figure rose into a crouch, glaring across at Risp.

A young woman of sixteen or so. She dragged free a long-bladed knife from under the sergeant's ribcage, and then advanced on Risp.

Sensation was returning to the lieutenant's right hand and she quickly changed grips, but her shoulder was throbbing and weak. She backed away.

The girl bared her teeth. 'You armoured and all! Don't run, you filthy murderer!'

Another rider came up behind Risp, but had to slow his mount since Risp's dead horse blocked the alley. 'Back up, sir!' he snapped. 'Leave the pup to me!'

She saw that he was one of the sergeant's comrades, Bishim. His face looked almost black beneath his helm, contorted with rage. He slipped down from his horse and drew his shield to the ready as he advanced on the girl, pointing with his sword. 'For Darav, I'm going to make this hurt.'

The girl laughed. 'Come at me, then.'

Bishim charged behind his shield, slashing with his sword.

The girl somehow slipped past and then was clambering on to the man's kite shield. Her weight pulled it down and she stabbed her knife into the side of his neck. The point burst out the other side in a welter of blood. As Bishim fell to his knees, the girl sliced through the biceps of his weapon arm and laughed as the sword clanged on the stones. Then she stepped over the dying man and advanced on Risp.

The lieutenant threw her sword at the girl and then ran, grasping the reins of Bishim's horse as she went. With the beast between her and the girl in the narrow alley, she knew that she had a few moments in which to—

The girl used one wall to rebound from as she leapt to land astride the horse. Her knife slashed down and Risp felt her arm snap upward. Staggering, confused, she looked to see that its hand was gone, sliced clean off at the wrist, and blood was gushing out. Moaning, she fell back against the nearest wall. 'Don't,' she said.

The girl swung round the horse's neck to land in front of the beast, and then advanced on Risp. 'Don't? Don't what? I'm a Bordersword. You attacked us. What is it you don't want me to do?'

'I was following orders,' Risp pleaded, pushing with her boots as if she could somehow back through the wall behind her.

'Draconus just kicked the wrong nest,' said the girl.

Risp shook her head. 'It's not – we're not what you think! Spare me and I will go with you to your commander. I'll explain everything.'

'Commander? You understand nothing about us. Today, right now, right here in this alley, I'm in command.'

'Please!'

The girl stepped forward. She was pathetically scrawny, more boy than girl, and in her eyes there was nothing Risp recognized.

'I'll explain—'

The knife went into the side of her neck like a sliver of fire. Choking, she felt the blade turn, and then the girl sliced through her windpipe, and all at once Risp felt the back of her helmet slam into the stone wall as tendons were cut. Hot blood filled her lungs and she began to drown.

The girl stared down at her for a moment, and then moved off.

Risp tried turning her head, to follow her killer's flight, but instead felt her head sink back down. She looked down to see the stump at the end of her right wrist. The blood had stopped spilling out. Soldiers survived worse. She could learn to fight with her left hand. Wasn't easy, but she was young – *and when you're young, these things are possible. So many things are possible.*

*I doubt she was sixteen. If she was sixteen she'd have been off with the hunters. Fifteen.*

The need to breathe was a distant shout in her mind now, and she found it easy to ignore. Until black smoke rolled in, obscuring everything, and then it was time to go away.

*     *     *

'We think she fell down the stairs,' said the soldier.

Captain Silann studied the corpse of the woman lying at the foot of the tower steps. 'This is Krissen,' he said. 'A scholar of highest repute.'

The soldier shrugged, sheathing his sword. 'Life's full of accidents,' he said, moving off.

Silann felt sick inside. 'Highest repute,' he repeated in a whisper. 'What was she doing here?' After a long moment he settled to his knees beside the body. Her head was tilted at an impossible angle; her eyes were half open, her mouth parted with the tip of the tongue protruding. Her hands were filthy with coal dust or the powder that sometimes came from old ink.

The soldier he had been speaking to earlier now returned. 'None left alive in here, sir. Place was damned near abandoned as it was. It's time to fire the keep.'

'Of course.' But still Silann studied the woman's face.

'Do you want we should take the body, sir? For proper burial, I mean.'

'No, the pyre of this keep will suffice. Was there anything at the top of the tower?'

'No sir, nothing. We need to go – got another village to hit.'

'I know,' Silann snapped. He straightened and then followed the soldier back outside.

On the keep road, just outside the gate, his wife had arrived with her vanguard. Her thighs were red with splashed blood, and Silann well knew the look on her face. Tonight there would be fierce lovemaking, the kind that skirted the edge of pain. It was, she had once explained, the taste of savagery that lingered from a day of killing.

'Lieutenant Risp is dead,' Esthala announced.

'How unfortunate,' Silann replied. 'Do we have wounded?'

'Few. Lost seven in all. There was at least one Bordersword in the village, a woman, we think, but we've not found her.'

'Well, that's good, then,' he said. As her expression darkened he added, 'A witness, I mean. That's what we wanted, isn't it?'

'Depends on what she figured out, husband,' Esthala replied, in that weary tone that he was all too familiar with: as if she were speaking to a dim-witted child. 'Better some terrified midwife or pot-thrower.' She turned in her saddle to survey the village below. Houses were burning in a half-dozen places. 'We need to burn it all down. Every building. We'll leave out a few of our losses, but with their faces disfigured. Nobody they might recognize.' She looked across to Silann. 'I leave all that to you and your company. Join us at Hillfoot.'

Silann assumed that was the name for the next village, and so he nodded. 'We will do what's needed.'

'Of course you will,' Esthala replied, taking up the reins.

She had refused to see her husband executed and Silann knew that among the soldiers that had been seen as weakness. But he alone was aware of how close she had been to changing her mind, and that still left him rattled. Lieutenant Risp's death delighted him, since she had been the source of all this talk about executions and crimes; and it had been her troop that had brought back the carved-up head of one of Hunn Raal's messengers. Silann still cursed the name of Gripp Galas, although it was a curse riding a wave of fear.

He watched his wife gesture and then she was riding down the road with her troop.

Glancing back, he saw smoke coming from the keep's slit windows, and drifting out from the open front doorway. It was not as easy to burn such edifices as one might think, he knew, since they were mostly stone. He turned to the soldier at his side. 'I trust you are confident that it will burn down.'

The man nodded, and then shrugged: 'Nobody will want to live in it, sir.'

'Let's head down to the village, then, and be on with it.'

'Yes sir.'

'I want to look upon the lieutenant's body.'

'Sir?'

'To pay my respects.'

\*     \*     \*

Captain Hallyd Bahann, Tutor Sagander decided, was an unpleasant man. Handsome, with grey in his short-cropped hair, he had about him an arrogance that, for some odd reason, women liked. No doubt he could charm, but even then his commentary was sly and verged on cutting. It baffled Sagander that Captain Tathe Lorat shared the man's tent. She possessed a beauty that left the tutor breathless, and looking upon her – the laughter in her eyes and the ever ready smile on her full, painted lips – it seemed impossible that she would delight in killing and, even more appalling, that she would keep in her company a daughter sired by her first, now dead, husband, and that then she would do . . . this.

They sat in the command tent, the two captains and Sagander, and Hallyd Bahann's dark eyes glittered with something like barely contained mirth. At his side, Tathe Lorat was refilling her goblet with yet more wine, and the flush of her cheeks held its own glow in the faint lanternlight.

'I see,' she said in a slurred drawl, 'that you are struck speechless, tutor, which must, I am sure, be a rare occurrence. Do you wonder at my generosity? Good sir, even now, behind you on the tent wall, we can make out the flames from the monastery. True, the monks fought with uncommon vigour and we took disturbing losses despite your betrayal, but this nest of Deniers is now destroyed, and for that we are pleased to reward you.'

'It may be,' Hallyd said, half smiling, 'that the tutor prefers boys.'

Tathe's perfect brows lifted. 'Is this so, tutor? Then I am sure we can find—'

'No, captain, it is not,' Sagander replied, looking down. He sat on a camp stool, and with but one leg to anchor himself he felt poorly perched upon the leather saddle of the seat. The imbalance he felt in his body was like an infection, spreading out to skew the entire world. 'Did none of them surrender?'

Hallyd snorted. 'Why should the fate of the Deniers concern you now? You showed us the old tunnel to the second well. By your invitation, we visited slaughter upon the occupants of that monastery. However, I will assure you none the less. Not one knelt except to more closely observe the ground awaiting their final fall.'

'And the Mother?'

'Dead. Eventually.' And his smile broadened.

'Is it,' Tathe asked, 'that you do not find my daughter attractive?'

'C-captain,' Sagander stammered, 'she rivals even you.'

Tathe slowly blinked. 'I am well aware of that.'

There was something ominous in her tone and Sagander felt his gaze drop yet again.

'We tire of your indecision,' said Hallyd Bahann. 'Do not think she will be unfamiliar with her purpose. She is no virgin and is indeed now well into her womanhood. We do not approve of consort with children and among our soldiers we count it a heinous crime punishable by castration or, in the case of women, the branding of their breasts. Now then, will you accept our offer or not?'

'A most generous reward,' Sagander said in a mumble. 'I – I am pleased to accept.'

'Go then,' said Tathe Lorat. 'She awaits you in her tent.'

As always, it was a struggle to climb upright, using his crutch like a ladder, and then tottering as he found his balance. Breathing hard with the effort, he made his way out of the command tent.

The stench of smoke filled the air, drifting down into the streets and alleys of Abara Delack. Here and there walked squads of Legion soldiers, still loud and boisterous in the aftermath of the battle, although more than a few could be seen who were silent, for whom the end of the killing saw a second battle, this time with grief. Sagander looked upon them all as savages, filled with brutal appetites and the stupidity that marked bullies. Every civilization bred such creatures and he longed for a time when they could, one and all, be done away with. A civilization for ever within easy reach of a blade had little to boast about.

No, the only hope for humility was in the disarming of everyone, and with it the end of the threat of physical violence. He knew he could well hold his own in a society where words alone sufficed, where victories could be measured in conviction and reasoned debate. Yet here, on these streets in this cowed village, it was the thugs who swaggered drunk on ale and death, their faces alive with animal cunning and little else. With them, he could win nothing by argument, since in the failing of their wits they ever had recourse to the weapons at their sides. Was it not Gallan who had once said *'At the point of a sword you will find the punctuation of idiots'*?

He hobbled towards the tent where awaited Tathe Lorat's daughter. Shame had driven him to this, step by stuttering step. A hundred or more lives had been taken away this night, all by his own hand. In some ways, it would have been worse had he been whole, rather than the maimed, pain-filled wretch that he was now. Because then he would have no excuses, no justifications for the betrayals his wounded heart had unleashed. Still, he was committed to this path, and at its very end there would come what he desired most: vengeance against Lord Draconus and his pathetic whelp of a bastard son.

The Legion knew its enemies, after all.

Reaching the tent, he fumbled one-handed at the flap. A sound from within made him pause, and a moment later a long-fingered hand appeared to pull to one side the heavy canvas.

Ducking, Sagander hobbled inside. He found he could not look at her. 'Forgive me,' he whispered.

'What for?' the young woman asked. She stood close and yet still in shadow. The lone lantern cast little light from its shortened wick. He could smell rosewater on her breath.

'I am old. Since I lost my leg, ah, I beg you, do not mock me, but I am able to do . . . nothing.'

'Then why accept me as your reward?'

'Please, I would sit at least.'

She gestured to the cot. He kept his gaze averted from her as he made his way over to it. 'I am no fool,' he said. 'Your mother knows you as her rival and would see you used, damaged even. Broken and dissolute. You must find a way to win free of her.'

Her breathing was soft, and he thought he could feel the heat from her body – but that was unlikely. 'I am not at risk of dissolution, tutor Sagander, and against me my mother can only fail. Because she is old and I am young.'

'Yet she delights in casting you into the arms of men, some of whom might be cruel, even violent.'

'None dare, and this will not change. I am not my mother, tutor, and nothing that I give of myself I value overmuch. I can out-wait her.'

Trembling, he looked up and met her eyes. They were clear, but not languid. They held sympathy, but not empathy. This, he realized, was a woman who had learned how to protect herself. 'If you ever need my help, Sheltatha Lore,' he said, 'I am yours.'

She smiled. 'Be careful with such promises, tutor. Now, if you are incapable of making love, will passing a night in the arms of a woman please you?'

\* \* \*

*This one to finish her! She's a beauty, Waft, and she's all yours!* The soldier's voice laughed the words in Narad's head. He measured his paces by them as the company moved through the smoke-filled forest. He sat hunched beneath them when the Legion camped for the night, his back to the cookfires, his hands reaching up again and again to probe the bulges and indents of his face. They echoed in the darkness when all had bedded down on damp ground and insects whined close to draw blood from whatever was exposed. In his dreams he felt her again, in his arms, her skin impossibly soft and still warm – he knew the truth of that no matter what they told him – and how she had yielded to his awkwardness and so made of herself a welcome embrace.

She had been past all hurting by then. He told himself this again and again, as if by incantation he could silence that soldier's laughing voice, as if he could impose a balance between cruelty and mercy. But even this haunted him, since he could not be sure which was which. Was there pity and mercy in that soldier's gleeful invitation, and cruelty in Narad's answering it? Had he not sought to be tender, to show a gentle touch when taking her? Had he not thrown his body over hers to shield her from their laughter and their raw jests, their eager eyes?

What had they fed on that day, in that hall, when looking upon what they had done to that poor bride? Not once had he felt a part of it; not once did he imagine himself truly belonging to this company of killers. He asked himself how he had come to be among them, sword in hand, padding out from the night into a horror-filled dawn.

There had been a boy once, not ugly, not filled with venom or fear. A boy who had walked into town with his small paw nestled inside someone else's hand, and that boy had known warmth and impossible freedom – with all the sands ahead smooth and clean. Perhaps, suckling on the tales of war, he had filled his head with dreams of battle and heroism; but even then, his place in every scene had been unquestioned in its righteousness. Evil belonged to the imagined enemies, for whom viciousness was sweet nectar sipped with wrongful pleasure, and all vengeance awaited those enemies by the toy sword he held.

In the world of that not-ugly boy, he was the saviour of maidens.

Anguish filled Narad at the thought of the boy he had once been, and at the thought of the crooked path he now saw crossing blood-splashed sands behind him.

There was slaughter in the forest. There was the smoke of fire and burnt-out glades and blackened patches, and endless ash drifting in the air. He had lost all sense of direction and now followed his comrades blindly, and for all their bluster it still felt like flight. Sergeant Radas, who led his squad with her ever flat eyes and bitter expression, had told them that they were trekking north, and that their destination was a stretch of land on the other side of the river from House Dracons, where they would at last rendezvous with Captain Scara Bandaris.

Captain Infayen had led her company eastward the day after the attack, apparently seeking to link up with Urusander himself, who it was said intended to march on Kharkanas.

In truth, Narad could not care less. He was a soldier in an unwanted war, faceless to his commanders but necessary for their ambitions; and all the tumult filling his skull – these careening thoughts so riddled with horror – were as nothing to them. In this company, each man and each woman surrendered too much of themselves, melding into a faceless mass where life and death was measured in numbers.

It was one thing to learn to see the enemy as less than Tiste, as abominations in fact; but the truth was, Narad realized, every commander could not but view every soldier in that way, no matter the colour or cut of their uniforms. Without that severing of empathy, no sane person could send anyone into battle, could wager the lives of others. When he thought of what was surrendered in the coming of war, he thought of that not-ugly boy and the warm hand he held suddenly torn away. He thought of soft and yielding flesh beneath his weight slowly growing cold and lifeless.

Who could return from such things? Who could walk back across the sands, smoothing his own wake, and every other sign of atrocity, to then reach out and take the hand of a child, a son, a daughter?

He walked with his ugliness for all to see, and perhaps this relieved the others since they imagined that they could hide the ugliness they had inside. Instead, he was their banner, their standard, and if they haunted him, then surely he must haunt them as well – behind their laughter, behind their mockery. It was difficult to imagine otherwise.

They loped through another burnt-out cluster of huts, stepping round blackened corpses. None of these dead Deniers had ever held hands, or dreamed of heroic deeds. None had slept in a mother's arms, or felt the caress of a lover and shivered in the realization that fortune favoured them by each precious touch. None had whispered promises, to others or to themselves. None had ever broken them. None had ever wept over a child's future, or caught the morning song of a bird hidden in the trees, or felt cool water sliding smooth down their throat. None had prayed for a better world.

Narad spat the bitterness from his mouth.

Just ahead, Corporal Bursa glanced back. 'That dead kiss again, Waft?'

The others in the squad laughed.

Every crime committed was a betrayal of some sort. The first barrier breached was one of propriety, and this could not occur without the dismissal of respect and all those things that courtesy comprised. It took a hardening of the soul and a chilling of the eyes to do away with respect. The second barrier, he realized, was all the easier to overcome after the fall of the first. It was marked by the sanctity of the flesh, and when flesh meant nothing then harming it was no difficult task.

People could measure crimes by the levels of betrayal achieved. And from that, they could create laws and devise punishments. All of this, he understood, belonged to everyone. It was society's way of working, and it had a way of melding faces into one, for the good of all. It had nothing to do with what he needed the most – what every criminal needed – and that was the opportunity for redemption.

Where would he not go to find redemption? What would he not

sacrifice? And in the end, for all that he did to repair what could not be repaired, what greater torment could he feel?

*I am not like the others here. I am filled with regret when they are not. For them, no redemption should be offered. Take their lives in return for what they did.*

*But I yearn to make it all right again. I dream of doing something, something to unravel what happened, and what I did. I whispered to her. I begged her, and she answered with her last breath. Was there a word in it? I don't know. I will never know.*

*There was a man who loved her, who sought to marry her. But I was the last man in her arms. Ugly Narad, shuddering like an animal. I know you hunt me, sir, whoever you are. I know that you dream of finding me and taking my life.*

*But you'll not find me. I'll do that much for you, sir, because I tell you, taking my life will offer you no release, no peace.*

*Instead, and this I vow, I will find something right to fight for, and set my life into the path of every murderer, every rapist, until I am finally cut down.*

The echoes of laughter reached through his silent promises and he cringed. His was the face of war. His was the body that raped the innocent. And every desperate whisper to the fallen was a lie, and the way ahead was filled with smoke and fire, and he moved through it like a standard, a banner awaiting the rallying cry of killers.

There had been a boy once, not ugly . . .

\* \* \*

Rint watched as the last stone was placed atop the cairn. Ville stepped back, slapping the grit from his hands. The short grasses on the hill glistened with morning dew, like diamonds scattered on the ground. Here and there flowering lichen lifted short stalks holding up tiny, bright red crowns, each one cupping a pearl of water.

He thought again of that headless body and found it difficult to recall Raskan's face. The moccasins were folded and bound and lying nearby. They would accompany the messenger to House Dracons. Rint's gaze drifted over them, and then he spoke. 'Headless and bared of feet, we yield what remains of Raskan. We leave him alone now, upon this hill. But he has no eyes with which to see, no voice to utter his losses, and not even the voice of the wind will mourn for him.'

'Please, Rint,' said Galak. 'Surely there must be softer words for this moment.'

'He lies under stone,' Rint replied, 'and so knows the weight of that. What soft words would you like to hear, Galak? What comforts do you yearn for? Speak them, if you must.'

'He was a child of Mother Dark—'

'His soul abandoned to foreign fate,' Rint cut in.

'He served his lord—'

'To be made a plaything for his lord's old lover.'

'Abyss take us, Rint!'

Rint nodded. 'It surely will, Galak. Very well then, heed these soft words. Raskan, I give voice to your name one more time. Perhaps she left some of you in the embers of the morning fire. Perhaps you looked upon us through flames, or when the wind's breath fanned the coals, and you saw us bearing your body away. I doubt you think of honour. I doubt you are warmed by what respect we muster for the body you left behind. No, I see you now as made remote to all our needs, to all our mortal concerns. If you look upon us now, you feel only a distant sorrow. But know this, Raskan, we who still live will carry your regrets. We will wear the burden of your untimely death. We will harvest the unanswerable questions and grow lean on what little they offer us. And still you will not speak. Still you will grant us no comfort, and no cause for hope. Raskan, you are dead, and to the living, it seems, you have nothing to say. So be it.'

Ville was muttering under his breath through all of this, but Rint ignored him. Finished with his words he turned away from the cairn and walked over to his horse. Feren followed a step behind him and before he set foot in the stirrup her hand settled on his shoulder. Surprised, Rint glanced at her. 'What is it, sister?'

'Regret, brother, is gristle you can chew for ever. Spit it out.'

He glanced down at her belly and nodded. 'Spat out and awaiting a new mouthful, sister. But in you I have reason to pray. I look forward to seeing you a mother again.'

She withdrew her hand and stepped back. He saw her lips part as if she was about to speak; instead she turned away, striding to her horse and mounting up.

'None of us are unfamiliar with death,' Galak said in a bitter hiss as he swung on to his horse. 'We each face the silence as we must, Rint.'

'Will you face it with every word in winged flight, Galak?'

'Better that than harsh and cruel! It seems all you do is cut these days.'

Rint settled into the saddle and took up the reins. 'No, all I do is bleed.'

They set out, pushing deeper into the ancient hills. The old lines of rise and descent had been carved through in places by thousands of years of hoofs from migrating herds, and down these tracks floods had rushed in the wet seasons, exposing bedrock and an endless wash of bleached bones and the crumbling cores of broken horns.

Rint could see the old blinds, constructed from piled stones, arcing in fragmented lines along slopes overlooking the old migration tracks.

He could see signs of runs where beasts had been cut away from the main herd and driven off cliffs. Here and there, massive boulders rested atop hills, each one bearing painted scenes of beasts charging and dying, and stick figures wielding spears; and yet upon not one of these wrinkled tableaux was there a line denoting solid ground. Instead, these remembered hunts, these eternal images of slaughter, all floated in a dream world, uprooted and timeless.

Only a fool would not see death in such art. No matter how enlivened the beasts depicted, they were all long gone, slain, carved up and devoured, or left to rot. To look upon them, as he did when he and his companions rode past, was to see a dead hand's longing for life, but a life belonging to the past. Every scene was a broken promise, and upon these hills now had settled a pall of silence.

If the dead spoke to the living, they did so in an array of frozen images, and this doomed them to themes of loss and regret. He well understood Feren's warning. This was a gristle one could chew without end.

Lifting his gaze, his eyes narrowed. The eastern sky was grey, smudging the line of the horizon. He thought back to the Jhelarkan's words and felt something grow taut within him.

'Is that smoke?' Ville asked.

Rint nudged his mount to a faster pace, and the others joined him. There was nothing worth saying. The chattering of speculation would simply give voice to fear and so fill the gut with bile. Smoke hung above Riven Keep. It could be as simple as a grass fire, spreading out across the plain.

His home was in the village below the fortification. There he would find his wife and his child, and discover anew their place in his life. Nothing needed to be the same as it had once been. Their nights of indifference and hard silence would be behind them now. Rint finally understood the gift she was to him, and now that they had made a child he would look with clear eyes upon all that was precious and sacred.

No longer would he flee her company, escaping into the wilds. He would make the future different from the past. For every person, change was within reach. He had made his journey and it would be the last one he would make. His future was at his wife's side.

*I have sworn vengeance against Draconus. But I will join my sister and put away my sword. I, too, am done with this.*

By midday, they had ridden out from the hills on to flat land. The way ahead was wreathed in smoke. The smell did not belong to a grass fire. It was rank, oily.

The four Borderswords broke into a fast canter.

In his head, Rint uttered a list of vows to his wife and to his newborn child. The list began and ended with a vision of him standing with her, in a home emptied of his anger, the temper he could never quite control. And he saw the guardedness leaving her eyes, her hand leaving the grip of her knife which she had drawn countless times to defend herself against his rages. He saw a world of peace, floating as if painted on stone. The hand that could paint the past could paint the future. Rint meant to prove it.

'Riders on our left!'

At Ville's shout Rint turned, rose on his stirrups. Directly north was the long line of a dust cloud.

'Must be the hunting party,' Galak said. 'Abyss below! There was no one at Riven!'

*My wife. My child.*

The distant riders were converging on them, and Rint now saw that they were Borderswords. *No. No.* He pushed his mount into a gallop, fixed his eyes eastward, to that dark smudge that was Riven Keep. But the tower was mostly gone, only one wall rising to two-thirds its original height, black as charcoal against the grey sky.

*It was just one more damned argument. I rushed out, thinking only of escape lest I tear the knife from her grasp. And there was the call, a summons from Lord Draconus, who wanted an escort into the west. I found Feren. I badgered her into joining me. We needed to get away.*

*My wife's face is burned in my mind. It was fear that made it a stranger's face. It had always been fear that took away the face I knew.*

*I was running. Again.*

*Life was easier out there. Simpler. Feren was rotting, drinking too much. I had my sister to think of—*

All at once, there were more riders crowding them, the thunder of horse hoofs almost deafening. As if from a vast distance, Rint heard Ville shouting.

'Traj! What has happened?'

'Lahanis found us – she escaped the slaughter – the villagers, Ville – they're all dead!'

Someone howled, but even that sound was muffled, quickly swept away. The hammering of horse hoofs upon hard ground was a roar in Rint's skull. Lahanis. He knew that name. A young woman, fast with her long-bladed Hust knife, but too young still to ride with the adults. A Bordersword in waiting who lived up the street.

'Who attacked us, Traj? The Legion?'

'She saw standards, Ville! House Dracons! We ride to it now. We ride to war!'

Blackened, scorched and in ruins, the village surrounding Riven Hill was beneath a shroud of smoke. He looked for his house, but the scene was jarring up and down, wheeling as vertigo took hold of him. He pitched to one side but was quickly brought up by a firm hand. Wild-eyed he looked across to see his sister – her face was wet with tears and the tears were black with dirt.

*She's had her fill of those. But it's over now. At least she saw her baby, and held it in her arms. A living thing, nestled in her arms. That's why I led her away – no, the wrong face, the wrong woman. Where is my wife? Why can't I remember her face?*

Then they were riding through the remains of the village, riding past bloated bodies. Feren's fist, still holding him upright in the saddle – her knee stabbing into his thigh as she forced her horse to remain close – now tightened around a handful of cloak. If not for that grip, he would have fallen. He would have plunged down into the ashes, down among the dead.

*Where she waits for me. And the child. And my child. My family, of which I will never again speak.*

*We ride to war—*

# EIGHTEEN

CALAT HUSTAIN PACED THROUGH THE BARS OF LIGHT THAT SHOT through the slats of the window's shutters, and such was the frown on his angular features that Finarra Stone remained silent, reluctant to speak. From the main hall outside the room and from the compound through the window behind the commander, there was a seemingly endless clamour of shouting and the thump of footsteps, as if chaos had arrived like a fever among the Wardens.

'You will not be accompanying us,' Calat said suddenly.

'Sir?'

'I will take Spinnock with me, but I want you and Faror Hend to ride to Yannis Monastery.'

Finarra said nothing.

Her commander continued pacing for a few moments longer, and then he halted and turned to face her. 'Captain, if I were a man who was plagued by night terrors, the worst nightmare I could imagine befalling the Tiste is a descent into a war of clashing religions. Faith is a personal accord between a lone soul and that in which it chooses to believe. In any other guise it is nothing more than a thin coat of sacred paint slapped over politics and the secular lust for power. We each choose with whom to have our dialogue. Who dares frame it in fear, or shackle it in invented proscriptions? Is a faith to be so weak that its only definition of strength lies in raw numbers and avowals of fidelity; in words made into laws and pronouncements, all of which need to be backed by an executioner's sword?'

He shook his head. 'Such a faith reveals in its violence of flesh and spirit a fundamental weakness at its core. If strength must show itself in a closed fist then it is no strength at all.' He lifted a hand, made as if to punch the shutters of the window behind him, and then lowered it again. 'You will deliver from me a message to Sheccanto. The Wardens defy the call to pogrom. Furthermore, if the brothers and sisters of the old orders should find need for assistance, they need only request it and we shall answer.'

Finarra blinked. 'Sir, does that include military assistance?'

'It does.'

'Commander, we hear word now that the Legion has assembled against the Deniers and their ilk. Indeed, that Urusander himself has taken to the field.'

Calat Hustain resumed pacing. 'Once you have delivered my message, captain, you are to send Faror Hend south. She is to ride to the Hust Legion, but avoid Kharkanas.'

'And her message to Toras Redone, sir?'

'I will give that to her myself, captain. I cannot risk you knowing the details, since once you have completed your mission at the monastery, you will ride north to intercept Lord Urusander. You will demand an audience with him.'

'Sir, if they deem us their enemy then I may well be arrested.'

'This is possible, captain, if all military propriety is dispensed with, and I admit I am no longer as confident in the upholding of such rules as I once was.' He eyed her. 'I understand the risk to you, captain.'

'What do you wish me to ask Lord Urusander?'

His mouth twisted slightly at the honorific. 'Ask him: what in the name of the Abyss does he want?'

'Sir?'

'For all his flaws,' Calat said, 'Urusander is not a religious man. His obsessions are secular. Has he lost control of his Legion? I begin to wonder. Thus. I will know from him his intentions.'

'When do you wish us to leave, sir?'

'Immediately.'

'Sir, given the nature of my message to Mother Sheccanto, is it wise for you to relinquish your command here, even for a short time?'

'I will know the truth of the new threat posed by the Vitr,' he replied. 'I will see for myself what remains of this dragon.'

She heard the faint scepticism in his tone and glanced away. 'Sir, for what it is worth, I do not doubt a word of Sergeant Bered's report.'

'And the Azathanai?'

'A sword and a woman's armour were found beside the carcass, sir. Faror Hend has examined them and judges both well suited to the Azathanai.'

Calat Hustain sighed, and then shook his head. 'I will see for myself. In the meantime, Ilgast Rend will command here, with the able assistance of Captain Aras.'

This detail still left Finarra with a sour taste in her mouth. Ilgast Rend was not a Warden. Even more disturbing, he had ridden in with Hunn Raal, only to become ensconced at Calat's side for the past few weeks.

'Find Faror Hend, captain, and send her to me. Ready your mounts.'

'Yes sir.'

She stepped out into the main hall of the longhouse and into the midst of Wardens and servants rushing to and fro. The faint touch of panic among her comrades was disturbing, and she began to comprehend something of Calat Hustain's unease: his evident disequilibrium. Were there Deniers among the Wardens? Fanatic worshippers of Mother Dark who would shed no tear at the slaughter of non-believers? Even here, she realized, this war could tear friend from friend, brother from sister.

Finarra saw Spinnock and Faror Hend seated at the far end of the long table dominating the hall. They were drawn close together, presumably to better hear each other through the cacophony as the rest of the table was being used by Wardens laying out the trappings of their armour for one last inspection. Finarra could see how Faror Hend had positioned herself to ensure that there would be incidental contact between her and her cousin. A spasm of resentment rushed through the captain, which she struggled to shake off.

Perhaps Calat Hustain had seen what she herself had seen. He had been explicit in telling her that he was taking Spinnock Durav with his company on their expedition to the Vitr. And he was sending Faror onward, down to the Hust Legion. *But avoiding Kharkanas, where her betrothed is likely to be. A curious detail. I wonder what it means.*

She made her way over to them. Was that a flash of guilt in Faror's eyes when she looked up?

'Sir.'

'The commander wishes to speak with you, Faror.'

'Very well.' She rose, nodded cautiously to her cousin, and then made her way from the table.

Finarra pulled out the vacated chair and settled in it. 'Spinnock, it seems you are to return to the Vitr without us.'

'Sir?'

'Your cousin and I are being sent elsewhere. It may be some time before we see each other again.'

The young man's face displayed disappointment, but she saw no guile in that expression: no hint of darker regrets quickly hidden. Was he truly blind to his cousin's unnatural attentions? 'It would seem,' she said, 'that Calat Hustain no longer considers you a raw recruit,

Spinnock. You are well measured by your deeds in saving my life, and it would not surprise me to hear of your promotion in rank before too long.'

His only response to that was an enigmatic smile.

* * *

Calat Hustain said, 'It is my understanding that your betrothed rode with Sharenas Ankhadu to Kharkanas.'

Faror Hend nodded. 'So I have been told, sir.'

'In his zeal to discover your fate at the Vitr, Kagamandra Tulas revealed the virtues for which he is well known.' The commander eyed her. 'In failing to cross paths, Warden, you have missed an opportunity.'

She frowned. 'I would not think it the last, sir.'

'That does not help me now, however. Does it?'

It took a moment, but then she understood him. 'Sir, my betrothed was elevated and now counts himself a noble.'

'But he began as a captain in the Legion.'

'Yes sir. He did.'

'Then where, I wonder, does his loyalty lie?'

'Perhaps, sir, Lord Ilgast Rend could better offer an opinion on that matter.'

'You will ride with your captain to the Yannis Monastery, Warden, where she will deliver a message on my behalf. Immediately thereafter, you will part ways with her and ride to the Hust Legion encampment. While I have no doubt that Commander Toras Redone remains loyal to Mother Dark, it does not necessarily follow that she now sends her soldiers against Deniers. You will ascertain her stance and then return to me.'

'Yes sir.' It struck Faror, suddenly, that in Calat Hustain and his wife, Toras Redone, she saw a possible fate for her and Kagamandra Tulas. It seemed they knew little of each other and were content to keep it that way. That Calat did not know his wife's mind on the matter of her faith, and what it might lead her to do with her legion, struck her as pathetic, and, in this instance, potentially disastrous.

'One last thing,' Calat Hustain said, 'you are to bypass Kharkanas. Cross the river well downstream and avoid contact with Legion garrisons or troops.'

She thought back to her commander's earlier words. 'Sir, I could seek out my betrothed in the city, if only upon my return from the Hust Legion encampment.'

'You could, but you shall not. Kharkanas is about to become a web. With an indifferent mistress at its centre, I foresee a convergence of . . . males, each one eager for her embrace.'

'Sir, your analogy invites the notion that whoever wins will end up being devoured . . . by Mother Dark. This seems an odd victory.'

He grunted. 'Yes, it does, doesn't it?'

Neither spoke for a time, until Faror Hend began to wonder if she had been dismissed.

Then Calat spoke. 'You were displeased when the Yan Shake assumed responsibility for the Azathanai. I imagine they now regret their presumption.'

She thought back to Caplo Dreem with his airs of superiority, and Warlock Resh's bludgeoning presence. 'It would be pleasing to think so, sir. But then, by the Azathanai's will, their river god was resurrected.'

'Just so, and from this added injury to their ambitions, Warden, I wager your name has been cursed more than once.'

'Sir, you imply a taint of cynicism to the brothers and sisters of the cult.'

'You think me pessimistic by nature, Warden? Perhaps you are right. When Captain Finarra Stone is busy speaking with Mother Sheccanto, take the measure of the Shake. I will value your opinion on their determination.'

'Sir, I am already of the opinion that Urusander's Legion will regret antagonizing the Shake.'

'If they rely upon the neutrality of the Wardens, then indeed they will.'

Shock rippled through Faror Hend and then she nodded. 'We delivered T'riss to the Shake, sir, it is true. Rather, I did, and so I must bear some responsibility for all that has happened.'

'Hardly. The Azathanai set out seeking an audience with Mother Dark. She would have managed it sooner or later even if unaccompanied.'

'But would she have resurrected the river god if she had not encountered the Shake?'

He shrugged. 'That we will never know. We deceive ourselves if we imagine that we proceed through life with any semblance of control over what is to come, and we should be thankful for the humility. For if it had been otherwise, if indeed every event in history were guided by our hands, then we have long since relinquished any claim to virtue. Every triumph we might weigh would be little more than a redressing of scales to answer our own crimes in the past.' He gestured, as if dismissing not only his own words, but all of history and its host of sordid truths.

'Sir, when I depart the monastery, will Spinnock Durav remain with the captain?'

'Spinnock Durav will be riding with me to the Sea of Vitr, Warden.'

'Oh. I see.'

He studied her. 'Observe well the likely failure of my intercession, Faror Hend, and consider for yourself the crimes your loss of control shall force upon not just you, but many others.'

She felt herself grow cold and was unable to respond.

Calat Hustain looked away. 'Dismissed,' he said.

Faror Hend stepped out back into the main hall, her thoughts in turmoil. She saw her captain seated in her place at Spinnock's side. The thought of joining them sickened her. *This is Finarra's work. She's spun lies in Calat's ear. Spinnock needs no mothering from you, captain, and by age alone you are a poor meet to his challenge.*

Fury warred with shame in her. *And now I must ride with you, obedient at your side. I am no child to be so curbed, and one day I will show you all the truth of that.*

Glancing up, Finarra Stone caught Faror's eye. The captain rose and approached.

'Our mounts are being readied, Warden,' she said.

'Very good, sir. I will see to my kit.'

'There is a pallor to your cast,' Finarra said. 'Are you unwell?'

Faror shook her head. 'No sir.'

The captain ventured a faint smile. 'I dread to think that the substance of the message you are to deliver to the Hust Legion has so stolen the life from your face.'

'No sir, although I will admit that we seem caught upon a current—'

'And see naught but rocks ahead, yes. We have our orders, Warden, and by these we will be guided.'

Faror nodded. 'Sir, I must see to my kit.'

'Do not take too long. I will meet you near the gate.'

*    *    *

Finarra Stone watched her Warden set off, and felt some surprise to see the woman studiously avoiding her cousin. She saw Spinnock's gaze following Faror's departure from the main hall, and then the young man rose, as if to set out after her. The captain moved forward.

Perhaps Calat had warned Faror away from her cousin. The woman had emerged from her meeting with a ghostly visage and had stood visibly shaken. If there was truth to this supposition, then their imminent journey together would be strained.

'Spinnock.'

The young Warden turned. 'Sir. It seems that my cousin is upset.'

'Not upset,' she replied. 'Distracted. We are to leave at once and she must get herself ready.'

'Ah, of course.'

'Are you eager to return to the Vitr, Warden?'

He shrugged. 'It did not top my list of immediate ambitions, sir. I regret no longer being under your command.'

'We face difficult times, Warden. It may be some while before things return to normal and we can resume our routines. You will be in the care of Sergeant Bered while in the commander's train.'

'Yes, sir.'

'You need not worry overmuch. He is a veteran of Glimmer Fate and the shores of the Vitr.'

Spinnock nodded, and then sighed. 'I will miss you, captain.'

She felt something deep inside rise in answer to his words, and the sensation left her feeling momentarily weightless. She glanced away. 'Let us hope Bered is better proof to your charms, Warden, than I am.'

Spinnock stepped closer. 'Forgive me, sir. When I carried you back from the Vitr, ill as you were, well, I never tired of the embrace.'

'Yet another reason,' she muttered, 'to regret my fever. Spinnock, be careful now.'

But he shook his head. 'I know I am young. Perhaps too young in your esteem. But we—'

'Enough of that, Warden. This is not the time.'

'But it is all we have, Finarra.'

The figures moving past them seemed but blurs, like a host of wraiths bound to otherworldly tasks. She dared not meet Spinnock's eyes, even though she knew that only in them could she right herself and rid her senses of the wheeling vertigo that threatened to take her. 'It shall have to wait,' she said. 'Please, step back. There is proper decorum to consider.'

He did so, with a half-smile. 'I do not regret my impulse, sir. At least now you know my feelings.'

*And here I thought to seduce Faror, and find for Spinnock another woman's arms.* Confusion roiled in her and yet she felt almost drunk. 'Be safe, Warden, and we shall one day resume this conversation.'

'In private, I hope.'

'That,' she allowed, 'would be best.'

Out in the compound, she paused, drawing deep, steadying breaths. She recalled little of that ride through the night, as Spinnock bore her back to the fort. Had he spoken to her? Cajoled her to keep her from slipping away? She had been bound to him, knotted by leather straps. She remembered the heat coming from him, and the sweat between them. He would have felt her against him, her breasts, her belly; even her arms had been drawn round his waist.

Warden Quill came up to her. 'Sir, your mounts are saddled, equipped and waiting.'

'Thank you,' she replied. 'Warden.'

'Sir?'

'You ride in Bered's troop, yes? Good. I trust you have been informed that young Spinnock Durav will be with you.'

'Indeed, sir.'

'The commander thinks highly of him, Quill.'

The man nodded. 'I will keep an eye on him, sir.'

'Be not so obvious as to embarrass him.'

'I have already known his company at the games table, sir, and would count him a friend.'

'Oh. Of course.'

Quill smiled. 'I will be guarding his left side, sir, with Stennis on his right.'

'Very good. Thank you.'

She set off for the horses. *Now, Spinnock, I'll have my legs round you yet. As for you, Faror Hend, you have a husband in waiting, and too many crimes to cross to ever lie with your cousin. Even Calat sees the temptation in your eyes.*

There was no guessing the paths of desire. *He is young, but I will have him.*

*For a time.*

*          *          *

'I confess that I am without resolve.'

At Spinnock's words, Faror Hend turned, to see him leaning in the doorway to her cell, his arms crossed and his eyes dancing with reflected light. She shook her head. 'I have not seen that in you, cousin.'

'I envisage a life where I am like a blade of grass, flattened by the faintest breath of wind.'

'Then you will know bruises in plenty.' She studied him. 'What has taken you so, Spinnock?'

'Brave words from me, while I stood far too close to our captain.'

She looked away sharply, returning to readying her kit bag. 'There is a reason Finarra Stone is yet to find a husband.'

'I see something wayward in her eyes, it's true.'

She snorted. 'She longs for no husband, cousin. She'd rather a wife.' She looked back suddenly. 'Did you not know that?'

The surprise on his face shifted into a smile. 'Now there's a challenge.'

Faror Hend straightened, moved close to him. 'Spinnock, listen to me. She would play with you. You're not the first man she has teased. But her lust lies in the feel of soft breasts in her hands, and yielding wetness between the legs. She shies from a stubbled kiss and hungers only for velvet lips.'

'I shall scrape every whisker from my face, and deceive her in the dark.'

'You deserve better than to be used.'

'Hence the weakness of my resolve, cousin.'

'Then yield to this.' She grasped the back of his head and brought her mouth against his. She heard a grunt from him and then he pulled away. Faror moved close again and reached with her other hand between his legs, cupping the weight of him and feeling his heat through the silk.

Spinnock set his hands on her shoulders and firmly pushed her back. 'No, cousin.'

'Did you think me deaf to your invitations, Spinnock?'

He shook his head. 'I thought we but played. A game with no risk of resolution. Faror, I am sorry, but this cannot be.'

She backed away and then swung round to fix the straps of her pack. Without facing him, she said, 'Resolution is the least risk to such games, Spinnock, when in every move we fence in strategies of desire.'

'Beloved cousin, do not misunderstand me. If we were not cousins, I would have earned revile from every Tiste for stealing you from your betrothed, for making of your body a thing well used.'

She struggled to slow her breathing, cursing herself for the pounding of her heart in her chest. Every ache felt delicious and yet tortured. She could still feel his lips against her own, and her left palm remained damp with his sweat.

'What you did just now—'

'Every game turns serious, Spinnock, eventually. Now let's see your hasty retreat, cousin, and know the proof of unexpected resolve.'

'My retreat, cousin, is the very opposite. Our captain awaits you, after all.'

She twisted round to glare at him. 'In games of love, cousin, we all play to wound.'

'That is a bitter vision, Faror.'

'Is it? What greater courage than love's confession? When the duelling is done unto exhaustion, one or the other must drop their guard, and then smile at the spilling of their own blood. Next comes the question: will the one doing the wounding now step close to set tongue to that wound?'

'No, he will turn the blade upon himself, cousin, and so conjoin this crimson flow.'

'And so the game ends with the promise of scars.' She shook her head. 'Play on, then, cousin, and think not of me.'

He edged out from the doorway, his expression filled with sorrow and dismay. 'Fare you well in your journey, cousin.'

'And you.'

When he was gone she shut the door, and then sat down heavily on her cot. *The blood runs clear until every drop becomes a tear. The game is lost the moment you forget that it was ever a game. To hear the song of love is to be deafened by a chorus of fools!* Wiping at her wet cheeks, she resumed her preparations.

*       *       *

'One thing at a time,' Calat Hustain said. 'I need you here.'

Ilgast Rend grunted, and then sat down heavily in the chair behind the map table. 'I cannot understand Urusander. He should have reined in Hunn Raal – Abyss take me, he should have had the hide whipped from the dog long ago.'

'Hunn Raal's machinations would have stumbled, and then stalled,' Calat said as he paced. 'Without that damned Azathanai's interference at Yannis, this contest would have remained purely political, and so open to compromise. This war of faiths is like a weapon thrust into his hand.'

Ilgast shook his head. 'Hunn Raal is of the Issgin line. This is all down to his family's fall from glory. He yearns to be a noble and sees himself as his bloodline's champion. He will ride the wave of every concession the Legion wins, and if the foam should turn red, so be it.'

Calat nodded. 'His ambitions are well known, Lord.'

'I will keep the Wardens in a state of readiness, commander. Of course I but hold them so until your return. Then, with great relief, I will yield to you and quit this.' He looked up. 'Friend, do you think me irresponsible?'

'I cannot say, Lord. I continue to believe that the greatest threat to Kurald Galain is the Vitr. If you can glean its truths from among the Jaghut, or even the Azathanai, then we may all bless your devotion a century from now.'

Ilgast snorted. 'A century? Then I will gird myself to weather a hundred years' worth of curses until that time. Preferable, I think, to this wayward tugging I now suffer.'

'In announcing your neutrality, Lord, you perhaps offer a way out for many, highborn and common alike. I cannot imagine that every old captain of Urusander's Legion is thrilled with this pogrom. Those falling to their swords might be Deniers, but they remain Tiste. Lord, I am appalled by this turn of events.'

Ilgast considered Calat's words. He rubbed at his face. 'There is a madness, commander, that runs like a poison stream through us. It flows beneath the bedrock of our much vaunted propriety. The stone bears pressure until it cracks. Civility drowns in that vile flood, and the disingenuous thrive in the discord that follows.' He leaned back, making the chair creak with his weight. 'In my bleakest moments, I wish for the coming of a god, a thing righteous yet cool of regard. A god to reach down among us and pluck forth our most venal, self-serving kin. And then, in a realm that burns like acid through every deceit, every cynical lie, make for them all an unwelcome but most deserving home.' He closed his eyes. 'I long for a power to wash away the worst that is in us, Calat.' After a long moment he opened his eyes again, to see the commander motionless, studying him. Ilgast managed a wry smile. 'Would I fear such power in Mother Dark's hands?'

'Voice no confessions to me, Lord. I have doubts enough of my own.'

'I wonder, where are our formidable wits, commander, that we should so easily be driven into this wash of treachery by thick-skulled, obvious fools? By the malign of intent and the heartless of spirit?'

'You begin to question your neutrality, Lord?'

'I suspect its evasiveness. Still, I see before me but one path not soaked in blood. I shall travel west, into the lands of the Jaghut and the Azathanai.'

'And your Houseblades?'

'They will maintain my holdings. That and nothing more. So I have ordered.'

'Will you journey alone?'

'I will take a handful, for the company.'

Calat nodded. 'Lord, I shall endeavour to not linger too long at the Sea of Vitr. I see well the burden of this favour I have asked of you.'

'If I can, commander, I will not move from this chair until your Wardens are once more safely under your wing.'

'Trust in my officers, Lord.'

'Indeed, and if possible, I will avoid the necessity of giving a single order.'

Calat strode to the door, gathering up his weapon belt and strapping it on. He faced Ilgast Rend. 'This god you wish for, Lord. The very thought of it frightens me.'

'Why so, commander?'

'I fear that, in the name of righteousness, it would reach down and pluck us all.' Calat Hustain departed, closing the door behind him.

Ilgast stared at that barrier of rough wood for some time.

\* \* \*

'In facing the unexpected,' said Kagamandra Tulas, 'we are revealed to ourselves. I have seen this borne out among the hunting dogs I trained. Some flee. Some growl. Some attack. But I would wager, not a single beast is truly surprised by its own actions. Yet, we cannot say the same, can we? Between our bristling hide and the muscles that might quiver underneath stretches a layer of shame, and it is upon that warp that self-regard weaves its delusions.'

The wind coming down from the north was dry and cool, carrying with it dust from the harvested fields, and chaff spun in the air like a presentiment of the snows soon to arrive. Sharenas Ankhadu contemplated her companion's words, watching the wagons burdened with grain wending into Neret Sorr, although the village itself was almost lost amidst the tents of Urusander's gathering Legion.

The residents of Neret Sorr would face a hard winter, she realized. Lord Urusander was confiscating the majority of the grain. There was the promise of payment and no doubt the commander would prove generous. But one could not eat coins, and with the stores of fuel wood and dried dung diminishing by the day, neither could coin feed a hearth fire.

Yet the people of the village were too cowed to complain. Over a thousand armed soldiers now lived among them, with more arriving day and night.

She set a gloved hand against her horse's neck and waited to feel the animal's warmth seep through. 'You've not fled, friend. Nor have you growled in answer to the commander's order, and I see no chance of you ever assaulting his position.'

'And so I am frozen in place,' Kagamandra confessed. 'And still we have heard nothing from Kharkanas, yet each evening we look west and see the sun made copper by smoke. I fear for the forest, Sharenas, and all who dwell within it.'

'I am expecting Sergeant Yeld to return to us soon,' Sharenas said. 'But even without the details, we can be certain that Deniers are being hunted down and butchered.'

'Surely many have fled to the protection of the monasteries,' Kagamandra said. 'And this smoke but comes from homes set alight. Winter draws ever closer. Sharenas, will we see Tiste corpses frozen to the ground in the months to come? I am sickened by the thought.'

'With luck,' she said, 'this absurd war will be over by then. Do we not still bow to the will of Mother Dark? Lord Urusander will march soon, and you can be sure that he will see justice set upon the murderers who act in his name. By blade's edge, he will end the madness.'

'And Hunn Raal?'

She had no answer to that question. The captain's whereabouts remained unknown. Even cousin Serap could not say where Hunn Raal had gone. After a long moment, she sighed. 'He will face Urusander or he will face the ire of the highborn. Will he take responsibility for this wretched pogrom? I rather doubt it. Besides, he is not the only captain loose in the countryside.'

'It may well be,' Kagamandra conceded, 'that events have proceeded beyond his control, and that indeed the Legion has splintered, with renegade elements taking advantage of the chaos.'

'I have decided on my place in this,' said Sharenas. 'And so must you, friend.'

'No dog is so foolish as to stand in the path of a charging boar. Yet in this, the dumb brute shows more wit than me. I believe I will return to Glimmer Fate, and so bring to a close this pursuit of my betrothed.' The smile he then offered her was, she suspected, meant to be wry; instead, it was a bitter grimace. 'I will chase her down, if only to tell her that she need not fear me. That my zeal was ever honourable, and I will make my studied distance a gesture of respect. Though we clasp hands on the day of marriage, no other infliction will come by my touch.'

'Kagamandra Tulas, you have learned to savour the taste of your own blood.'

His face clouded and then he looked away. His bared hands were white on the horn of the saddle.

Returning her gaze to the wagons on the road below, and feeling the chill wind loose icy serpents beneath her clothes, Sharenas shook herself and said, 'My friend. Do look her in the eye and say the things you would say. I cannot gauge her answer beyond what I would feel if I were in her place. And what I would feel is anger and humiliation. You free her to love other men and deem this generous. But all women wish to be desired, and loved. I see your sacrifice as selfish.'

'It is the very opposite of selfish!'

'You would make a martyrdom of marriage. You would ask from your betrothed not her love but her pity. What will stand firm on such foundations? I see you both upon your knees, your backs to one another, each facing a door you long to pass through, and yet locked together by crimes of will and pride. She'll not yield to your sordid invitation, since that could only serve to confirm your own sense of worthlessness – such a choice for a woman comes after years of hard weather in an unfeeling husband's arms. The taking of lovers is a desperate search for things few would dare name. To make of this offer her wedding gift cuts to the core of her heart.'

'But I am the one who speaks out of pity! She is young. She deserves what I once had, not this broken man old enough to be her father, who would flee his ageing years! I am too frail to carry the weight of every necessary delusion in this union!'

She shook her head. 'Many a fine union has come from such disparity of age.'

'It is crass and venal.'

'You call her young and make of the word a belittlement. This hints of arrogance, Kagamandra.'

'Without the sharing of years to bind two souls—'

'Then share those to come. But at last we reach to the core of things. You yield your claim to your wife from a place of fear, a place deeply wounded and chary of sensation's return. It is no sacrifice at all, but self-indulgence. Your every wound is a trophy, with suffering worn in most resplendent regalia. But you have outstayed its season, friend, and it is threadbare. If not a wife to draw these rags from you, then who? Hear me now. If you see no courage in each woman you look upon, then you are blind and, worse, you scorn the dignity of the woman you lost years ago. Go to Faror Hend. In this much at least, your instinct is true. But meet her eye and see for yourself – she will not flinch.'

When she looked across to him, she felt a sudden fear, so pale had his visage become. Remorse cut through her. 'Oh, forgive me. I leap past all propriety. Send me on this wind with a curse and I will go without complaint. This is my flaw, and it pulls from my grasp every wisp of love. See well, sir, that my life is as forlorn as yours, and in my every word of advice I poorly hide my own bitter self.'

He said nothing for a long time, and then collected up the reins. 'It is no wonder, then, Sharenas Ankhadu, that we are such friends. We take this hill by bold storm only to be bludgeoned half senseless by truths. The wind and the grasses mock our self-importance, and the season begins to show us a cold regard. Had I known more of you, I would have silenced every offer but yours.'

Her breath caught, and she felt heat rush through her. 'I would strip the hide from you.'

'And make of it a better trophy.'

'Worn,' she whispered as she met his eyes, 'with pride.'

Then there was a moment, as if the sun had sliced through the heavy clouds, when the years were stolen from his gaunt face, and she saw the man a woman had once loved; a man from before the wars, from whom not every precious thing had been stolen away amidst violence and treachery. An instant later, it was gone and he broke her gaze.

'We will not speak this way again, Sharenas Ankhadu.'

'No,' she said. 'I imagine not.' But these words felt like water washing down cracks in stone.

'I will leave in the morning. As a highborn, it is necessary for me to relinquish my rank in the Legion.'

'It is soldiers like you and Ilgast Rend that Lord Urusander so values, Kagamandra. You stand bridging the gulf and through you he sees a path to compromise.'

'You think he will forbid me?'

'I do. That said, if you depart now, with the coming of darkness, then I will inform the commander tomorrow morning. If in anger he deems it prudent to pursue you, I will tell him that you have ridden to Kharkanas.'

'Why not leave the same time as me, Sharenas?'

'No. Too many of us cautious advisers suddenly abandoning Urusander will wound him, and the imbalance will open the breach for Hunn Raal's backers.'

'Urusander will not be tugged by fools.'

'He is old, Kagamandra. Not in flesh, but in spirit. Daily we see his indecisiveness afflict him like a bout of illness, and again and again he steps out from the command tent – and that tent in itself is an affectation, and dangerous besides, since he yields his keep to that white-skinned witch – he steps outside, and looks long upon the Legion's flag.' She paused, and then said, 'I cannot guess what thoughts take him in those moments, but they trouble me none the less.'

'It seems,' ventured Kagamandra, 'that he values Serap's presence.'

'He does. She remains the least objectionable of Hunn Raal's whores. But it is easily forgotten that she stands close to Hunn Raal, for the simple reason that she too is of the Issgin bloodline.'

Kagamandra grunted. 'Wealth to the Legion and their estate restored? Yes, I see how those two desires are now intertwined.'

'Many ambitions can share one root,' she said, nodding. She reached across to him, with a hand warmed by horseflesh, and set it firm against his shoulder. 'Give her what you dared give me this day, friend, and see how she answers.'

He nodded without meeting her eyes. 'I will.'

Sharenas let her hand fall away. A moment later, looking out past the edge of the tent rows, she rose in her stirrups. 'See that rider and the banner he bears? That is Sergeant Yeld. At last, we shall have word of the events at Kharkanas.'

'I will hear of that,' Kagamandra said.

'Do not let ill news sway you,' she said to him. 'Make your loyalty your own, Kagamandra, and direct all duty to the woman you will wed.'

He sighed. 'As you say.'

They kicked their mounts into motion, riding slow down the hillside to give time for the horses to work out any stiffness from their long stand upon the summit. The chaff rising from the stubble-filled fields swirled round them, and the dust remained high in the air, as if unwilling to settle upon the scene.

＊　　＊　　＊

The old chairs in the Vault had the look of thrones, but only one remained intact. The other was a mass of wreckage pushed to a corner and Syntara wondered at the violence unleashed upon it. She was in the habit of seating herself in the one chair that remained, settling her head back against the deerskin hide. The walls were crowded with scrolls and volumes and the close air in the room smelled of mould and dust. Servants had brought in more candles at her command and the light filled every space now, driving away shadows and gloom. Their yellow hue painted the bleached skin of her hands where they rested on the arms of the chair, until it seemed to her eyes that she had been transformed into a thing of gold.

Darkness was not the only purity in the world. Something burned inside her, blinding bright. It had frightened Urusander, had driven the man from his own keep, as if by her presence alone his loyalty to Mother Dark was under threat.

*True enough. I am indeed a threat to Mother Dark. And to all who would kneel before her. But Hunn Raal was right: it need not be that way.*

Weakness and fear had driven her from Kharkanas, and in the time since she had, on occasion, amused herself imagining a triumphant return, with light scouring the city like a purging fire. Wretched river gods would wither before her. Mother Dark would shrink back, all her secrets revealed, every flaw exposed. Darkness, after all, was a place in which to hide. But something of these desires felt old, almost rank. They were, she had begun to realize, relics of her old life in the temple.

Still . . . who had not known a childhood in which terrors moved in the dark? It was foolish to reject the truth of instinct. There were good reasons to fear what could not be seen, and to distrust those who chose to remain hidden.

The Azathanai had bequeathed Syntara a gift. Its power was growing inside her, like a man's seed in the womb. She felt full of blood, heavy in the breasts and swollen between her hips. Yet no weariness took her. She found little need for sleep and her mind felt sated, immune to the countless risks surrounding her. Urusander was yet to formally offer sanctuary.

'I am not a high priest,' he had said. 'And this is not a temple. More to the point, High Priestess, I am not Mother Dark's enemy.'

She thought back to her flight from Kharkanas. Accompanied by a dozen of her most loyal companions, bearing with them only what they could carry, she had rushed through the night, the countryside around them suddenly strange and threatening. The comforts and pleasures of the Citadel stung with bitter recollection, and she had known fury and spite in her soul, a soul still bleeding from the wounds the Azathanai's cruel words had delivered.

But against the hardships of their journey in the days that followed, thoughts of vengeance had proved a potent fuel, and she had felt herself growing in strength with each step she took, as the Citadel and its world diminished behind them.

Hunn Raal's promise of an escort never materialized, and it was her sense that the drunken fool had lost control of the situation. At night, they could see the glow of fires from the wood upon their left, and by day grey smoke hung over the forest. The Deniers had been set upon.

It was no shock to her when they came within sight of Neret Sorr and the stronghold of Vatha Urusander, and looked upon the gathering of an army surrounding the settlement, the row upon row of canvas tents, the vast corrals crowded with horses, the supply wagons and hundreds of soldiers moving about. The Legion had returned, and the alacrity with which retired soldiers arrived to resume their old lives dismissed all her cherished notions of Hunn Raal's incompetence. Her confidence stumbled then, as she watched a picket troop approach on the road.

Her followers huddled behind her, and glancing back, she saw how dishevelled and unkempt they had become. Their fine silks were stained with the dust of travel; the makeup that had once enlivened their faces was gone and what she saw now was an array of expressions drawn and frightened. During the trek she had given them little, too consumed with fear and worry over the fate awaiting her. Her companions had been, one and all, caught up in illusions of power, and now she could see how they longed for its blissful return.

But the soldiers drawing up before them bore hard visages, and the corporal commanding them gestured with one hand back up the road, and then said, 'There's too many whores to feed as it is. Go back to where you came from. You'll not find a single room in Neret Sorr, and the commander has rules forbidding your trade in our camp.'

Somehow, Syntara found the strength to simply smile. 'Refreshingly direct, corporal. It is true: we have known the pleasures of many men. I am High Priestess Syntara, and these priestesses accompanying me are under my charge. I would speak with Commander Urusander, for I have news from the Citadel.'

The young man's eyes studied her for a long moment, and then he nodded. 'There was a rumour, I now recall. I see the paleness of your face beneath that hood, High Priestess. Very well, we shall escort you to the keep.'

'Thank you, corporal. As you can see, our journey was made in haste and without the necessary amenities proper to the daughters of Mother Dark.'

'We can summon a wagon if you do not mind waiting, High Priestess.'

'Or, corporal, you and your troop can yield some room on your saddles, if the embrace of priestesses will not discomfort you too much.'

His brows lifted slightly, but he did not smile. A moment later, he edged his mount closer, kicked one foot from the stirrup, and then offered her a hand.

Syntara remained silent on the ride to the keep. She had given considerable thought to what she would say to Urusander, but in taking the measure of these common soldiers she could see that this was a troubled army, and that in turn was a reflection of those in command, and Urusander in particular. The soldiers had answered the summons, but now awaited orders, and none knew what those orders might be. Civil war exposed the flaws in a people, and though each faction would view its cause as just, the illness revealed was endemic, and so weakened everyone.

Urusander might well have recalled his soldiers in some misguided attempt to protect them. *But then, protect them from what?* Hunn Raal had unleashed renegade troops into the countryside. *From themselves, then. If I am right in this, then I understand the tensions I see here. This civil war could see Legion soldier hunting Legion soldier.*

But even that was not the end of the troubles. There could be Deniers among them. Or at the very least, sympathizers.

*And what of me? What place will I take in what is to come? Is my fate for Urusander to decide? Shall I crawl into his presence?* 'Corporal.'

The gate was directly ahead. 'High Priestess?'

'I would hope I have opportunity to redress my travelled state before seeing the commander.'

'I would expect so,' he replied, 'as he is very busy. Do not be offended, High Priestess, if your audience with him is delayed by a day or two. In the meantime, of course you will be given attendants to see to your needs.'

'Very good,' she replied. *A day or two?* She felt her face growing hot. 'I feel I need to emphasize again the urgency of the news I bring from the Citadel.'

'I will be sure to convey that, High Priestess.'

As it turned out, she was given no time at all in which to cleanse herself, as the keep's castellan, a perfunctory man named Haradegar, assumed responsibility for her at the keep's entrance and, after attaching a score of servants to her priestesses, led her into the keep for immediate audience with Lord Urusander. She assumed no tactical subterfuge in this haste; rather, it spoke to her of the commander's respect for her title, and if he was witness to the evidence of her plight, then perhaps she could make use of that.

Haradegar guided her to a chamber with shelves lining the walls, on which rested countless books and scrolls. One long table commanded the room, consuming most of the floor space. There were two well-made comfortable chairs, and one was in ruins.

After the castellan departed, she stood contemplating sitting down in the surviving chair. A moment later, Urusander arrived. 'High Priestess, I have heard of what has befallen you. But still, I must ask: what are you doing here?'

*       *       *

Syntara would not beg. In Urusander, she saw a man under siege. She well understood the ambitions of those behind him. Men like Hunn Raal dreamed of their commander standing beside Mother Dark, as husband to the goddess. Once she and he were past the first moments of awkwardness between them on that day of her arrival, she said as much to Urusander, when they stood in this very room. 'Lord, alone you have nothing to withstand her, and yet you must – but not as her enemy. Rather, present yourself as her one hope for peace. With my help, Lord, you can save Kurald Galain.'

He had moved past her then, only to turn and face her once more. 'You must know her mind, High Priestess, as much as anyone can. What fate awaits Lord Draconus?'

'Lord, she took a consort because she knows no man is her equal. Indeed, in her solitude, she seeks to protect everyone else. As it stands, any union with her will be unbalanced. This is what needs to change.'

He looked away. 'I have the Legion.'

Syntara drew back her hood and shook her head. 'Will you pour a husband's love into a darkness without end, into a realm defying your touch, refusing the blessing of your eyes? Will you give your love to an unknown?'

He cursed her questions, but not for the reasons that she might have expected. 'All this talk of marriage! Have I been consulted? Has Mother Dark? And now you speak of love?'

'Lord, forgive me. I was led to believe . . . otherwise. As you say, worship is not the same as love.'

'You have the truth of that,' he snapped.

She had studied him then, seeing a man who had unconsciously backed to one corner of the chamber, his hands restless and reaching out as if to take up a scroll on the nearest shelf, or a book, only to draw away again. She wondered where was the hero he had once been? What reasons remained for this fanatical loyalty surrounding him? Vatha Urusander was forgetting who he was, and all that had elevated him in the eyes of others was behind him now – and he well knew it. She decided that she would have to adjust her strategy, and indeed make herself more open to this man before her. 'Let us set aside notions of love, then, and speak of politics. You have announced the return of the Legion, Lord. The highborn cannot but see that as a belligerent act.'

'I am told of religious uprising against Mother Dark.'

'Do not believe the fear-mongering, Lord. The river god poses no real threat, barring how that cult clouds the way ahead.' Seeing his frown she said, 'I will explain. All this time, while you remained here in this keep, the highborn have been preparing against Lord Draconus. They oppose his growing power. When Mother Dark proclaimed the House of Purake as her First Children, the other nobles were much relieved. Even as they had each vied for that position, Lord Nimander and his three sons were one and all highborn and so confirmed the status of every Greater House. Indeed, it was thought that Lord Nimander would one day wed Mother Dark.'

Urusander was studying her, and she saw by his expression that he was unaware of the details she was telling him.

'But Nimander died, and he died badly. There was even talk that Draconus was behind it. Much as I dislike the Consort, I do not share that belief. My point is this, Lord Urusander. The highborn are ready for war. Their Houseblades but await the command. For now, they cannot act against Draconus because he has done nothing overt. Though they do not know it, he refuses the throne beside Mother Dark's – no, do not look so shocked. I was her High Priestess. She invited him and he refused her.'

'If this was to be made known to the highborn, their fear of him—'

'Would end?' Impatience and disbelief had stained her tone and she dropped her gaze. 'Forgive the interruption, Lord.'

'Why are the highborn kept from this truth?'

She shrugged. 'That Mother Dark keeps a lover is irritating enough. Should it become known that he defied her command, well, that amounts to blasphemy, does it not? Draconus is an arrogant man and I suspect this is at the core of the highborn's dislike of him. He was late to the ranks of the nobility and lacks the appropriate humility.'

Urusander's expression was incredulous. 'For this, they would go to war?'

'Lord,' she said, 'perhaps I am not as wise as Emral Lanear. Abyss knows, she would tell you as much. But I do understand this: whether political or personal, struggle is all about face. Status is longed for as a measure of others' regard, and power itself is but a weapon, to be kept close to hand when all else fails to impress.'

He surprised her with a barked laugh. 'And if I told you, High Priestess, that true justice stands in opposition to all that you have described . . .' He shook his head. 'If you see as clearly as this, then I suggest we elevate this discussion. I well grasp your warning – if the highborn stand prepared for war, it is no vast stretch to see them turning upon me and the Legion. This is absurd! I understand that Lord Draconus is not even in Kharkanas!'

'He is not, Lord. But all now hear of your troops in the forest. They are killing Deniers, and, I wager, anyone else they find. Lord, many of these Deniers live in highborn holdings. Legion soldiers invade estate lands with impunity.'

Urusander looked away, and then abruptly sat in the remaining chair. 'I have made an error,' he said. 'I should not have recalled the Legion.'

'Lord, if that recall includes the renegade companies, perhaps this can be salvaged.'

He eyed her. 'I did indeed underestimate you, High Priestess. It is I who should beg forgiveness.'

'Withhold that sentiment, Lord. There are not two factions to this religious war. There are three.'

'I don't understand.'

'I have looked well upon the Legion's banner,' she said, 'and see it as a sign. For all his foolishness, when Hunn Raal urged me to flee to you, Lord, well, I now believe some other force was speaking through him. You look upon me but do not question my transformation. Why?'

She saw his discomfort at her question. 'High Priestess, I have no understanding of the ways of sorcery. The change I see I took to mark Mother Dark's rejection of you.'

'Nothing of what you see, Lord, was by her hand. I bear the Azathanai's gift.'

'And what is the nature of this gift?'

'Lord, I wish I knew.'

'Yet you proclaim yourself to be standing in opposition to Mother Dark.'

'Perhaps, as the right hand opposes the left.'

'And the river god?'

'That god's place in all of this remains to be determined, Lord. Best await a decree from Mother Sheccanto and Father Skelenal.'

'It was my thought to send an emissary to them,' Urusander said, one hand now upon the tabletop, fingers slowly drumming. He looked up at her. 'I intend to disavow my Legion from the acts of the renegades. Indeed, I intend to outlaw them and set a bounty upon their capture.'

'It is no wonder Hunn Raal is not here.'

'You were the last to speak to him, High Priestess. What were his plans?'

'His plans? In disarray, I believe. That said, he cannot but view as threatening certain rogue elements beyond the highborn and their Houseblades. It is my thought that he has travelled to the Hust Legion, seeking overtures.'

Urusander grunted. 'Toras Redone is likely to arrest him on the spot. Even execute him.'

'Hunn Raal's courage is beyond question, Lord, and in his defence, he does believe that he acts in the best interest of Kurald Galain. He truly yearns to see you upon the throne beside Mother Dark's own.'

'I will bring him to heel, High Priestess, assuming he survives to return to me.'

There was iron in that promise. 'Lord, I have need of a place for contemplation. This transformation in me is deeper than the skin I now wear. Vanity palls. So too secular ambition. When facing my sister

High Priestess, I fear that I became her twisted reflection. There was poison in my heart, and I will not flinch from that truth.'

He rose from the chair. 'This talk of sorcery makes me uneasy. You have my keep, High Priestess. I will go now to my command tent in the Legion camp.'

'I understand that Lieutenant Serap is here. She will know more of Hunn Raal's plans.'

'She states otherwise.'

'Do you believe her?'

His gaze narrowed. 'I begin to wonder whom to believe, High Priestess. Advisers seem to breed like vermin around me, and the more there are the fewer I trust.'

She bowed. 'I will remain in the keep, Lord, and not seek you out.'

Urusander's smile was ironic, but he left without another word. It was some time before she understood, and could give words to his expression. *'Why did you not make that vow in Kharkanas a week past?'* In courtesy, he had not uttered this question, but she knew now that such courtesy was more than she deserved.

Few shadows in the room, and darkness humbled and cowering wherever it could – these details whispered like blessings through her thoughts. He gave her his keep, but said nothing of sanctuary. She wondered if enemies were seeking her, hunting her. In matters of trust, she was no different from Urusander himself.

*Perhaps this is what can bind the two of us.*

*Would that Osserc were here.* She had heard that he was a fine-looking man, possessing a wealth of appetites yet purportedly weak in spirit. A useful combination, all things considered.

Syntara had begged time and place for contemplation, and this sentiment was humble in its veracity. She still struggled to abjure the influence of old hatreds and spites, but her own thoughts, when speaking with Urusander, returned to her again and again. *Dark and Light . . . as the right hand opposes the left.*

*Urusander, I begin to see a way to draw those hands together, to clasp in union and so find strength in balance. And no, we need not speak of love, only necessity. Something I think you understand. We shall make you Father Light, whether you welcome the title or not.*

She had promised that she would not seek him out. She could hold to that promise, for now. Three religions in conflict was an untenable situation. The river god and its followers would have to be expelled, perhaps sent beyond the borders of Kurald Galain. This could be done with little or no bloodshed. It was said that Dorssan Ryl flowed south across vast, empty lands before issuing its black waters into a distant sea. Not quite empty, perhaps, but then, the Forulkan were hardly in a position to argue at a sudden invasion of refugees. The Legion had turned half their settlements into burnt-out graveyards, and had driven the rest to the edge of that distant sea.

There were ways through the times ahead that could bring to an end the violence, and if she was seen to have taken a dominant role in averting open civil war . . .

Still, the promise of light remained locked within her. Did she need sacred ground? A temple of her own, blessed in the name of . . . *of what? Light, in answer to Mother Dark? Liossan . . . who can deny the cleansing powers of revelation, when the very word points to something revealed, to the hidden exposed; and if we make of her mystery a host of banal truths, then Urusander can stand before her and be seen as her equal.*

*Cut me free, Mother Dark, and see how I take you down a notch or two. For the good of us all, of course. The good of Kurald Galain.*

Back in the Citadel, there had been little time for contemplation. But now she began to see its manifold rewards. She rose from the chair and then turned to study it. *Mother Dark sits upon the Throne of Night.*

*We shall need an answer to that.*

\* \* \*

Renarr stepped out on to the narrow balcony girdling this side of the Old Tower. She could look down on the courtyard with its scurrying figures, and beyond that to the settlement below ringed with rows of white tents.

Smoke and dust hung over Neret Sorr in thickening palls. Her home had been transformed, far beyond the details she could observe from this height. For all the crowds and canvas tents, it seemed small, paltry in its ambitions and frail in its presumptions. She remembered its streets and alleys, its crouched houses and cramped shops, and looked with a strange kind of envy upon those tiny shapes moving where she had once walked.

Modest lives marked only the succession of dreams set aside, or broken underfoot. The game of living was one of focus, an ever-narrowing horizon of what was possible and what could be achieved; but this made sharp and bright the lesser triumphs. A partner's love, a child given to the world, an object well made by a crafter's hands. Glories hid in the elegant fold of a new cloak, in the unscuffed and unworn display of new boots or moccasins; in a head of hair artfully arranged to complement clear features and vigorous health, or the paint that pretended to the same.

She remembered her own vanities as would someone who had grown past their toys of childhood, and just as the child who was no longer a child looked upon those toys with a sinking feeling that was new, that was ineffably sad, so too did she see what she had left behind, while before her was a future bereft of wonder.

These thoughts and notions settled in her now, too complicated for the world she had known, too fraught to encompass for the young woman she had once been. That woman had given her love to a man broad in his emotions, as quick to laughter as to tears – almost child-like in his rush from one extreme to the other, where wounds healed quickly and life could return to warm his eyes in an instant. He had fought against ridicule and had known blinding rage, and then had wept over one careless swing of his fist.

It would not have mattered. Bruises faded and cuts healed, and in-nocence could grow back like a scab and so seal past wounds, and if beauty was marred, then the disenchantment was temporary. But future lives had a way of vanishing before one's eyes. Possibilities died down at the roots, and before long everything above ground, once so resplendent with promise, withered and lost colour, and then the wind came to strip it bare. The path ahead of her was a place of dead trees and dead grasses, a dead river beneath listless light, with a ghost at her side who had nothing to say.

Such were the gifts of her new place in this new world. Adopted by a guilt-ridden lord, she now found herself in a tower, lifted higher than anything she had ever known before: lifted past her dreams until they sat like forgotten toys at her feet. In her mind she saw herself walking down the stairs, along the corridors with their cold, stony breath, out through the doorway and into the dust-veiled courtyard, and then beyond the gate and continuing, step by step, into the town that she once knew. She saw the old women marking her passing and how their heads tilted close together as words were whispered. She saw the new speculation in the eyes of the men, and the curiosity of children who no longer felt able to call to her in greeting. She saw the expression of wives and mothers as they were dragged back into their own past and the girls they had once been, where everything was still possible, and come the night they might hold tighter their husbands but not for reasons of love. Instead, they would need those embraces to give comfort against the losses that now crowded their thoughts.

She saw herself walking down to the taverns, where the air was charged with laughter, and if some of it sounded strained, it was still forgivable and quickly swept past. Flushed faces would turn her way, painted eyes suddenly gauging, as she moved through the crowd, and before long a man smelling of ale would press against her, and she would cling to him, smiling at his awkward jests, seeing his desires behind his guarded expressions. Before long, he would, in her imagination, turn to the innkeeper and hire a room and old Greniz would nod with a sour gleam in his eye and hold out a greasy hand. Coins would flash in the gloom and in the moment her man moved to take her through the doorway to the back rooms a woman would brush close and say, 'There's a cut, jes so ya know.' And Renarr would nod and for the briefest of moments the two women would lock gazes and pass between them the fullest understanding of this new shared world.

A world of pleasure and despair entwined, down among the dead roots. This was where her imagination took her, cold and rushing like a mountain stream, painting details she knew nothing about.

Witch Hale came out to stand beside her. 'He is gone,' she said.

Renarr nodded, if only to appease the old woman. But she had seen her father die some time before, when she had met his eyes and saw in them no feeling, and he had but studied her, detached, as if gathering details. And she had understood something then. This was how death came to the dying: from the inside out; and this was how the living took it: from the outside in.

She gathered about herself the new, rich clothing a guilt-ridden man had bestowed upon her, and then said, 'I am going down to the village.'

\* \* \*

Coming from the barracks, where she had been lounging with a half-dozen veteran sergeants before hearing the bell clang, Lieutenant Serap made her way across the compound towards the keep's front entrance. She saw that Sergeant Yeld had returned. A crowd surrounded him, but he was holding up his hands, as if to defy their questions. Haradegar had rushed inside a few moments earlier, to sound the bell that would summon Urusander back up to the keep, and thence to the Campaign Room.

Two more riders appeared from the gate and Serap glanced over to see Sharenas Ankhadu and Kagamandra Tulas. They cantered across the courtyard, forcing a path through the milling soldiers, stablers and servants, and reined in close to Yeld, who pushed free, straightening against his weariness, and saluted Sharenas.

Serap reached them, but said nothing as she followed Yeld, Sharenas and Kagamandra into the keep. Their boots rang hollow as they marched down a corridor, the walls of which bore only the bleached impressions of the tapestries that had once lined it. The sergeant looked worn, as befitted someone who had ridden through the night.

Serap had been given to understand that Captain Sharenas had sent Yeld to Kharkanas. She had assumed that the sergeant carried orders to Hunn Raal, demanding his return. *But my cousin is not in Kharkanas. What then the cause of this tension?*

Castellan Haradegar, along with the High Priestess Syntara, was awaiting them in the Campaign Room. As she had done the few other times she had seen the High Priestess, Serap found herself staring at

Syntara, half in fascination and half in revulsion. She forced herself to look away and concentrated instead on Sharenas. 'Captain, did you by chance see Commander Urusander on the road up to the keep?'

'He comes,' she replied. 'Sergeant Yeld, I trust your insistence that we make this a command meeting is justified by the news you bring.'

'It is, sir.'

'Were you able to speak with Hunn Raal?'

'No,' Yeld replied. 'Sir, it is believed he has journeyed to the Hust Legion, bearing wagons burdened with gifts to the soldiers. Presumably, sir, he seeks entreaty with Commander Toras Redone, to ensure that no hostilities arise between our legions.'

'Does he now?' Sharenas said, eyes narrowed. She then swung to Syntara. 'High Priestess, I wonder about the role you imagine for your-self at this meeting?'

'Permit me, captain, to stand as a symbol of your unease.'

Sharenas scowled. 'I doubt any of us needs one so animate, High Priestess.'

'I regret that you seem disposed to be suspicious of me, captain.'

'High Priestess, I doubt that ranks high among your list of regrets,' Sharenas retorted. 'But since you will speak of them, I would hear more.'

'Very well. Among my foremost regrets, captain, is that I do not yet know my place in this meeting, or any other. The uniform you wear announces your role no matter what the setting. To look upon you is to understand your talents in command, in warfare, and the logistics that are necessary to maintain a company of soldiers. Now, do not shy away as does Lieutenant Serap, and look upon me. What do you see? I stand here announcing a changed world, captain. If its taste is bitter, then spit me out and proclaim the end of change for all to hear. Who can say if the world will heed you?'

Sharenas stared at the High Priestess for a long moment, and then snorted. 'Forgive me, High Priestess. It was my understanding that you women of the temple talked only with your cunts.'

'You have bent an ear too often to Ilgast Rend, captain. He comes from a time when swords ruled and spoke for all. We sought to oppose and indeed usurp that domination, and offered the pleasures of love-making instead. Is it not curious that he finds us such a threat?'

'Perhaps I have indeed listened to Ilgast Rend too often,' Sharenas admitted with a faint smile. Then the smile faded. 'Alas, the age of swords has returned.'

'This regret has ascendancy in my soul, Captain Sharenas, if you would know the list complete. But then, I see before me soldiers one and all, and so anticipate an enlivening of expressions with whatever dire news your sergeant is about to deliver.'

Yeld grunted as if Syntara's words had delivered a blow to his chest. He coughed and said, 'My pardon, High Priestess, but I anticipate no joy from the tale I must tell.'

They heard the thump of boots from the corridor and a moment later the door opened and Urusander strode into the room. Whatever fires Serap had seen reignited in Urusander had dimmed beneath the burden of the Legion's rebirth. Or, perhaps more likely, it had waned beneath the fugue of confusion now afflicting the companies that had gathered in answer to his summons. He looked harried and in short temper as his flat eyes fixed on Sergeant Yeld. 'I am waiting,' he said.

'Sir, I must tell you a tale of massacre.'

Urusander's hard, angular face darkened. 'I am sickened enough, sergeant, by the reports I have already had. This murder of Deniers must cease, even if I have to lead my entire Legion into the wood.' He swung a glare on Serap that made her recoil. 'These renegades will hang.'

Yeld shifted uncomfortably. 'Sir, these victims were not Deniers. They were highborn.'

Urusander seemed to stagger. His back connected with the wall behind him. 'Speak on,' he whispered.

'Sir, forgive me this dread news. The House Enes wedding procession was attacked. Lord Jaen and his daughter were slain. Hostage Cryl Durav as well. I was told that the first to find them was Enesdia's brother, Kadaspala.'

A sound came from Urusander, but Serap could not pull her gaze from the sergeant, and she saw Yeld's face suddenly twist. 'Sir, in grief the artist gouged out his own eyes. It is said he is lost in madness. He curses all who seek to comfort him. He curses Mother Dark. He curses Lord Anomander for delaying too long in Kharkanas. Among the dead were bodies of Deniers, but Kadaspala accuses Legion soldiers – he – he points a finger at Captain Scara Bandaris's company, which he met in the wood.' Yeld abruptly stopped, and Serap saw how the poor man trembled.

No one spoke.

Then Sharenas Ankhadu whispered, 'Scara would not do this. Commander, Kadaspala has indeed gone mad. He rages at the world.'

Kagamandra slumped into a chair and sank his face into his hands.

'Still your thoughts,' said Syntara in a cold, hard voice. 'All of you, draw down hard upon the outrage and horror afflicting you. Yes, I but stumble on this new path, but I am struck. A question assails me. Lord Urusander, hear me.'

His bleak eyes fixed on her.

She took his silence as assent. 'By what laws shall we be governed? Soldiers of your Legion demand recognition. They demand compensation

582

for their sacrifices. They insist that the gifts of this world do not solely belong to the highborn. Well then' – and her uncannily pale eyes now travelled across them – 'show me this grief for the fallen peasant. For the Denier cowering under superstitious dread. A poor young girl's father has just died in this keep. From the tower I saw a funeral procession up to the town's cemetery only two days past. And yet. *And yet*. Look upon yourselves. See how you measure this latest tragedy, as a loss of greater worth. Why? Because the slain are *highborn*.'

'This attack is unseemly,' said Sharenas in a low growl. 'You berate us for the breadth of our feeling? Who weeps more for strangers?'

'I refute your defence, captain. If you will weep for one, then weep for all. Know that every stranger has kin, has loved ones. Every stranger was as trapped in their skin as we find ourselves. I have stood here. I have listened. I watched you all suddenly appear upon the top rung of grief's ladder.'

'You speak cruelly, High Priestess,' said Sharenas, 'and so pluck our open wounds. But I hear no offers of balm or healing in your words.'

'By what laws shall we be governed? This question burns me, captain. Its flames rage high, engulfing my soul. Take upon yourself the burden of the righteous, but do so with humility. Weep for us all – I assure you none here will run out of tears.'

Sharenas's hands had curled into bloodless fists at her sides. 'To what end?'

'Justice.'

Urusander's head snapped up, his eyes suddenly hard and bright.

The High Priestess straightened, as if suddenly proud of the curse that bleached her skin. 'I know of no law that proclaims the death of some to be greater cause for grief than the death of others.'

'There *is* one,' Sharenas said. 'We gauge their deeds in life, for some. For others, we measure our distance from them, and the closer they are, the deeper we grieve. When you speak of a deluge of tears, I see not a blessed ocean, High Priestess, but a bitter sea. The laws that bind us are measured by the limits of our flesh, and the capacity of our souls. What you demand would empty us—'

'Leaving what?'

'The Abyss.'

'A crowded soul, captain, is a place of shadows and gloom. Scour it clean, and nothing will remain to block the light. Hear me. I tell you, I am so afflicted. I am burned away inside. All that remains of the woman I once was is this shell you see before you, and see how even it is transformed by the Light burning in my soul.' She stepped closer to Urusander. 'Lord, do what needs to be done, to return Kurald Galain to peace. I will await you, and as proof of my power I will yield now this gift.'

Kagamandra Tulas rose suddenly, sending the chair toppling. Hands to his face, he staggered to the door, and then into the corridor. The sound of his feet as he fled was like that of a drunken man.

Sharenas snarled something Serap could not make out, and then rushed after her friend.

A moment later golden light spilled out from the High Priestess, filling the chamber. Blinded, Serap cried out.

She heard Syntara speak. 'When all your grief for the dead is washed from you, what remains? Each of you, turn now from death and face life. Grieve not for the dead but for the living. For kin and stranger both. Grieve, until you are ready to come to me.

'Come to me, and we will speak of justice.'

The light poured in, filling Serap's flesh, her bones, setting all it touched to flame. She fell to her knees, and wept like a child.

\*     \*     \*

Shuddering, Kagamandra Tulas leaned against the wall at the corridor's end. Sharenas reached him, drew him round. He resisted, but her will would not be denied and a moment later she held him in her arms. 'Damn that High Priestess,' she hissed. 'Shock weakened us and she pounced – no, I cannot guess at her ambitions. I know only to fear them. This much I have learned.'

'Stop,' he said. 'There will be war now. Don't you see that?' He pushed her away with a hard shove that sent her stumbling. 'I'll not fight. This I swear! I'll not fight!'

She stared at him from across the corridor. There were people in the main room and they had turned in alarm at this confrontation, but her eyes were for her friend and none other. 'Kagamandra, please. The highborn will do nothing. Not yet. None of them – not even Anomander. They need to summon the Hust Legion. And the Wardens. They need to make an alliance with Sheccanto and Skelenal—'

His eyes widened. 'What?'

'Listen. A rival to Mother Dark was born in the room we just left.'

'I would not listen. I stoppered my ears! I will not!'

Sharenas shook her head. 'Not Syntara, friend. She was but a mahybe, set among us Tiste by the Azathanai. There is no hope of any of us gleaning the purpose of that, unless it was to see Kurald Galain destroyed. We have seen the beginning, but cannot know the end.'

'There will be war!' His shout bounced from the walls, echoed fierce into the Great Hall.

'I am not blind, Kagamandra. But nor am I helpless, and neither are you!'

'I will not fight!'

584

The door to the Campaign Room slammed open further up the corridor and both turned. A moment later, Urusander appeared.

His skin was white as alabaster, his once-grey hair shot through with threads of gold.

'Here then,' Sharenas said in a low voice, 'comes her rival.'

Urusander strode past her and stood before Kagamandra Tulas, who stared at Urusander as if he had come face to face with a ghost, a singular apparition bearing with it a thousand losses exhumed, shaken clean, proffered like trophies. His back pushed harder against the wall when Urusander raised a hand, as if to touch him. A moment later the hand fell back.

'Old friend,' said Urusander. 'I beg you, ride to them. Tell them that I was not behind this. Tell them that I will hunt down these murderers. Tell them the Legion is at their disposal.'

But Kagamandra shook his head. 'I will not, sir. I go to find my betrothed. I will take her from Kurald Galain. As far away as we can ride. If need be, I will bind her with ropes, a gag about her mouth, a sack for a hood. Sir, leave me alone.'

There were tears on Urusander's cheeks. He stepped back, his gaze dropping. 'Forgive me,' he whispered.

'I will go,' said Sharenas.

The High Priestess was approaching, and behind her in the corridor walked Serap, Yeld, and Haradegar. With their pallid visages, they made an uncanny procession. Behind them all, white light spilled and roiled like smoke, drawing closer.

'I will go,' Sharenas said a second time, pushing herself forward. She reached out and grasped Kagamandra's sleeve, pulling him with her as she set out for the front door.

'Yes,' said Urusander behind them, 'best to flee, my friends. I cannot stop her.'

Sharenas cursed under her breath. *In this light, even justice will burn.*

*　　*　　*

*Dead?*

Ilgast Rend sat behind the desk, frozen, like a man nailed to his chair. He stared across at the dishevelled messenger with the red-rimmed eyes. Panicked thoughts flitted through him. *Send a rider to Commander Calat Hustain. Recall him. The Vitr will have to wait. We now have war.*

*But I cannot wait. The soldier in me cries out. Urusander is still weak. His companies are scattered across the realm. He hides in Neret Sorr and deems it a distant island in rough seas. I have the Wardens in readiness, and here I am like a hound-master holding a thousand leashes. I swore to do nothing, but that vow – foolish old man! That vow was made in a time of peace.*

Highborn blood had been spilled. Innocents had been slaughtered.

*Urusander, you pushed too far. But I see you in your keep, enthroned, and all the crows in your company chatter and caw until you are deafened, and the flapping wings blind you and the rush of air is sweet blessing against your face, and you think this the measure of the world.*

*Will we await your next move?*

*I think not.* He struggled to control his breathing, and cleared his throat, twice, before speaking to the messenger. 'I trust Lord Anomander has assembled his Houseblades. I trust the other Greater Houses are stirred to arms.'

'Milord,' said the messenger, 'there were slain Deniers at the scene—'

Ilgast Rend snorted and rose suddenly. 'We are to believe the rabbit showed teeth? The crassness of such deception delivers a mocking insult. No, we are not even meant to be fooled. Urusander's Legion has struck – I saw as much in Hunn Raal's eyes, when in argument he bludgeoned with threat and indignation in equal measure. He invites confusion, but does so with contempt.'

'Your orders to me, milord?'

'Rest, and then take three horses and ride to Calat Hustain in the Glimmer Fate.'

'Best I not rest, milord,' said the young man.

'You are exhausted.'

'This news is urgent. Perhaps another rider in my stead?'

'Rest. I would not have this tale become blurred beneath too many layers of varnish. Calat will hear from you what I have heard. But add this: I lead the Wardens to Neret Sorr. I intend to attack Lord Urusander while his forces remain scattered. I intend to cut out the heart of this rebellion.'

The man's face was grey, but he saluted.

'Send in my captains,' Ilgast Rend said to the man as he made to depart.

'At once, milord.'

Ilgast Rend sat once more. He settled his hands upon the flat, worn surface of the desk. *The soldier in me sees clearly. He expects us to wallow in our grief, to stand unmoving in our shock. This was calculated to make us reel in disbelief.*

He began to suspect the complicity of the Shake – Skelenal and Sheccanto could not be pleased at the resurrection of their long-dead river god. How many Deniers even recognized the religious authority of the monasteries?

*They have done nothing to prevent the slaughter of the Deniers, have they?*

The tramp of boots approached along the corridor outside the room. Ilgast Rend drew a deep breath. He folded his hands together on the desktop. To still their trembling.

*       *       *

With a third of their journey to Yan Monastery ahead of them, Finarra Stone and Faror Hend came upon the first mass of refugees. Their state shocked Faror, and she followed her captain when Finarra led her horse and second mount off the track. They reined in to watch the hundred or so broken figures shamble past.

'Where are they going, sir?'

'East, as you can well see.'

'There is nothing out there,' Faror objected. 'Except for this season's headquarters, and that is but a modest fort of bound grasses and salvaged wood.'

'Just so,' Finarra said. 'Ilgast Rend is about to face a nightmare in logistics.'

Disbelieving, Faror Hend shook her head. 'Sir, we do not have enough food. Or shelter. And the winter on the Glimmer Fate—'

'I am aware of all of that, Warden.'

'Yes sir. Your pardon.'

'Deniers, one presumes,' said Finarra, studying the wretched men and women. 'But few of them old, few of them children, and no new-born. There is something here, Warden, that is not right. Select one – that thin man who's twice looked at us – and bring him here. I will have the truth from him.'

'Yes sir.' Faror Hend dismounted and made her way to the bedraggled man her captain had singled out. He saw her coming and seemed to sag. When she gestured, he pulled away from the others and limped over on bandaged feet.

'Do not fear us,' Faror Hend said to him. 'We are Wardens and would hear what news you have to tell.'

The man squinted at her, and then shrugged.

Together they re-joined Finarra Stone.

The captain wasted little time. 'You are east of the monasteries, sir. What refuge do you people seek?'

'They sent us away,' said the man.

'Who?'

'The Shake. But first, they took our children. That was the bargain they offered. Food for us, and the promise that our young ones would be safe with them.'

'And the elderly?'

The man shook his head, and then smiled as if at a joke. 'Our mothers and fathers were of the wood and the river. They chose to remain. Now they are all dead.'

'The Wardens cannot keep you,' Finarra Stone said to him.

He shrugged again.

'They can, perhaps, protect you from bandits and . . . other enemies. But against starvation and the cold of winter, they cannot save you.'

'We have nowhere else to go.'

'Are there many more of you on this road?'

The man nodded, shifting weight from one bloodied foot to the other.

'You may go, sir,' said Finarra Stone.

They watched him hobble his way back to the ragged column. The breath hissed from the captain. 'They took the children.'

'Sir,' said Faror Hend. 'You carry word to Sheccanto and Skelenal that the Wardens are pledged to them. But if Calat Hustain knew of this – that the Mother and Father of the cult were turning away their flock, and making of children bitter coin . . .'

'We will deliver our message,' Finarra said, gathering up the reins. Then she paused and looked across to Faror. 'Forgive me, Warden, I have made of this journey a tense one, unpleasant. The waters are muddy between us, and I regret that.'

'As do I, sir.'

'But such things diminish before the plight of those we see here on this road.'

'Yes sir.'

Finarra hesitated, and then said, 'When you are done with the Hust Legion, Faror Hend, choose a place in which to wait.'

'Sir?'

'A place. Tell me of your choice before we part, and I will see to it that word will be sent to . . . to whomever you wish to know of it.'

Faror Hend held her captain's gaze. 'Sir, I will not desert the Wardens.'

'Name a place, and tell me by whom you will have it known.'

'Sir, if word must reach someone, it must be my betrothed. But I say again, I will not desert the Wardens.'

Finarra nodded. 'I understand. Nevertheless, think of a place—'

'A refuge.'

'In the season to come, Faror Hend, love will need such refuges.'

Faror studied her captain for a time, and then nodded. 'I will give it some thought, sir.'

'Very good. Now, we shall have to ride overland – I expect this road to be impassable at least as far as Yannis Monastery.'

'Could you have made such a bargain, sir?'

Finarra shot her a look. 'I have never birthed a child, Warden, so I cannot say.' Then she shook her head. 'If they see no hope ahead, and yet are offered salvation for their children . . . well, what mother and what father would not sacrifice their own lives to save those of their children?'

'The Shake well understood that, I think,' Faror said. 'Still. When I came upon one of their troops, in the wreckage of a bandit camp, it was said in passing that they had made a similar offer, only to have the mothers slit the throats of their own get.'

Finarra blinked. 'That seems a selfish act.'

'Perhaps, sir, some hold freedom higher than life itself.'

'Well enough if that life is your own. I doubt a single child welcomed the blade's kiss.'

Faror Hend fell silent, unable to argue against her captain's words. But the recollection haunted her. They rode on for a time, slowly as the ground was uneven and stony. Then she said, 'Sir, for nights afterwards, I dreamed of mothers and fathers killing their own children. But no bargains had been offered them, and no threat drew close to force their hands.'

'A disturbing dream, Warden, if there was no cause to their deeds.'

'But there was, sir, of sorts. With each child slain, I saw the slayer's wealth grow, in coin stacks, in gems and silks, and slaves at their feet. I saw them grow fat, but through windows there was the flicker of flames, drawing ever nearer.'

'Let us bend to our task here, Warden, and speak no more of ill dreams.'

When Finarra Stone pushed her mount ahead, into a pace verging on reckless, Faror Hend followed. The day's light was fading, and upon the track to their left, the stream of figures lost all colour, gave up no light, and soon were swallowed in the gloom.

# NINETEEN

T HE SOUNDS OF REVELRY FILLED THE HUST LEGION CAMP OUTSIDE THE command tent. Smiling, Hunn Raal studied the woman seated opposite him. 'It seemed a modest gesture at the time,' he said, 'but I cannot refute the blessing of this outcome.'

Toras Redone did not smile in return. Her expression remained unchanged, and this detail had begun to unnerve the captain. She held her tankard in her left hand and the jug of wine, from her private stores, in her right, resting both on her thighs. 'If you think,' she said, only slightly slurring her words, 'gifts of wine and ale to my soldiers are sufficient to win everlasting accord between our legions, captain, then your drunken ways have led you astray.'

Hunn Raal lifted his brows. 'It ever pained me, commander, that we came to view each other as rivals—'

'Your dislike of the Hust has nothing to do with rivalry. You fear our weapons and their songs of war. It is not my soldiers whom you need to ply with liquor to achieve peace between us, but perhaps such generosity applied to your own soldiers could improve matters.'

'Songs of war? Abyss below, commander, we can list the many words available to describe the uncanny cries of your weapons, but surely not the language of music.'

Her level gaze remained fixed on him. 'Indeed? What stirring symphony would you wish for war, captain? Drums to quicken the heart? A rising crescendo to mark the momentous clash of two foes meeting in combat? Sorrowful dirges to settle like ashes upon the inevitable scene of slaughter to follow? Are you a romantic, captain? Do you dream of glory and virtue, of heroism and bravery? Are we all brothers and sisters under the armour, under the skin and down among our bones which, when at last laid bare, lose all provenance?' She raised her tankard and swallowed down another mouthful. 'Is this the man who has come among us? Sodden and sentimental, yet eager to raise a hand and point an accusing finger at unbelievers?'

Hunn Raal bit back a savage retort. 'The Hust Legion proclaims itself Mother Dark's own—'

'Does Urusander resent the claim? Do you?'

He shook his head. 'Commander, there are Deniers among you.'

'What of it?'

'They do not belong to Mother Dark.'

'Don't they?'

'Of course they don't.'

She refilled her tankard – something she did after every mouthful. 'Too many things weaken your resolve, captain. Your self-doubt creates enemies and then raises them up like things of mud and straw. But whose flaws are so displayed? Many an old soldier has noted how one is measured by one's enemies. Yet, here you are, refusing to respect your foe, even as you exaggerate the threat they pose. Are you too drunk, captain, to countenance the contradiction?'

This night had begun in a contest of drinking, or so Hunn Raal had read the challenge in the commander's eyes, when she had first invited him to sit with her. In the meantime, the wagons had trundled into the encampment, and the casks were unloaded to laughing soldiers, and Toras Redone had voiced no objection to the distribution of such bounty. He struggled to steady his thoughts. 'I respect the threat they represent, commander. This is why I have come to you. Our legions must stand together, in Mother Dark's defence.'

'It is my understanding, captain, that she commands no such thing. Mother Dark does not compel anyone.' Then Toras Redone suddenly snorted. 'How could she, when the gifts of worship remain unknown? In what manner are we rewarded when we deem her a goddess? What cast this coinage of faith? The priestesses flounder in their beds and silken pillows. Mother Dark announces no laws and demands nothing from us. What kind of goddess is she, when she does not gauge her own power in terms of adherents? Worship her. Do not worship her. Either way, she remains unchanged.'

'I am a simple soldier, commander, and I admit to avoiding the confusions of religious practice. I see the world as a soldier must see it. We all wear uniforms, be they girded for war or politics, or religion.'

'Is there not room for all of us in Kurald Galain?'

'We could encompass the world, commander, and still we would fight one another.'

Toras Redone looked away, seeming to study one wall of her tent, where the silhouettes of insects made a silent audience to this exchange. 'Perhaps,' she said in a low voice, 'this is what Mother Dark is telling us. She embodies a hollowness at the core of all of our beliefs. Some would bask in what they imagine to be fulfilment, when it is in truth absence.' Her eyes slid back to Hunn Raal. 'We crowd the rim of an empty bowl, captain, and jostle for footing, blessing those who slide in while voicing our delight at those who fall off and are for ever lost. When that pleasure proves insufficient, why, we begin pushing others off, flinging them away while telling ourselves that these victims lived lives of less worth . . .' Her words trailed away, and she drank again, returning her gaze to the tent wall.

'Commander, all I seek is peace.'

She sighed and then said, 'The truth of darkness is that it hides everything and reflects nothing. We stumble in blind ignorance and swing at everyone who draws near. Do you appreciate the irony in all this, captain? In our language we voice the Abyss as a curse, but I tell you, I have knelt before Mother Dark in the Chamber of Night, and I have felt the Abyss – when she touched my brow.'

Shaken, Hunn Raal said nothing.

Toras Redone offered him a loose shrug. 'Yet she sits upon the Throne of Night, and we acknowledge her rule, such as it is. Of course,' she added, 'that throne was a gift from Lord Draconus. You would have thought – given his purported ambitions – that he would have offered up *two* thrones.'

'Commander, I have no complaint against the Consort. It is the high-born who obsess over that man's ambitions. You raise an interesting question – have you voiced it among your fellow nobles?'

Toras Redone blinked, and then shook her head. 'He swims in the bowl and so we hate him. There is nothing complicated in that enmity.'

'Do you know where he has gone, commander?'

'No.' She waved the hand that held the tankard, spilling some wine in the process. 'West.'

'Soldiers should not be the objects of resentment in times of peace,' said Hunn Raal. 'When that peace was won by our blood and sweat, well, are you not stung by this?'

'It is not resentment, captain, it is indifference. And I welcome it.'

'How can you say that? We deserve to be rewarded for the sacrifices we have made!'

'What sacrifices, captain? You are still alive. So am I. Neither of us lost limbs.'

'I speak not just for myself! I have friends who have been left crippled, blinded, or who cannot sleep through the night—'

'While others drink or smoke themselves into oblivion. Because the truths of war broke us inside, and broken we remain. Reparation, then?

For the dead, why, let us raise high bold mausoleums. For the maimed, let us entrench our pity and suckle guilt's bloated tit until we grow fat on remorse. And for the drunks like you and me, captain, why, a bounty of riches to keep our cellars well stocked, and a high seat in every tavern from which we can weave our tales of past glory. Or is it a title you wish? Very well, I proclaim you the Lord of War, and will seek for you a proper estate. In addition, I give you fields of horror to harvest nightly, and granaries filled with wretched memories, which you can daily grind to dust on this millstone you call your life.'

Hunn Raal stared at her for a long time, and then he reached into the sack he had brought into the tent with him, and drew out a jug. 'My gift to you, commander. A fine vintage I am sure you will enjoy.'

'I have my own, captain, but thank you anyway.'

'You refuse my offering?'

'Not at all.'

'Shall I refill your tankard, then?'

She shook her head. 'I am done drinking this night, captain. I must walk the pickets, lest your friends tempted the Nightwatch in their eager, if somewhat forced, generosity.'

'If they did, commander, it was well meaning.'

'Your gesture is appreciated and you have given me much to think about, captain, but my rules of conduct are explicit, and if I find even one guard with alcohol riding the breath, there will be the public lash. Discipline is a necessity, even in times of peace.'

'Indeed it is,' Hunn Raal said. 'I am impressed.'

'Are you? Good. Perhaps it will give you something to think about.'

'Commander, the Hust Legion is not our enemy.'

'Barring the Deniers in my ranks.'

'They are your concern, not mine.'

'I am relieved to hear you say that, captain. Now, feel free to use the spare cot in this tent. I doubt I will return before dawn.'

'Have you quit sleep, too, commander?'

'I save that for my staff meetings. Now, if you will excuse me.'

He rose when she did. 'It has been a fascinating evening,' he said.

Toras Redone studied him. 'You never drink as much as you pretend to, captain. Why is that?' Without awaiting an answer, she marched from the tent.

Hunn Raal stared at the tent flap, watching it settle following her departure. He sat back down. *Well, why should I be surprised? When it comes to drinking, you can't fool a drunk.* The insects had all scattered with the rustling of the canvas, but now they returned. He stared at them. *An audience with low expectations, one presumes. Better than that canny bitch of a commander.*

His gaze travelled to the jug he had given her, and then away again.

593

Sighing, he collected his cup and filled his mouth with the tart liquid. *A soldier needs no excuses to drink. You can't just walk away from dancing with death, after all, and no wall holds you up for long.*

There was a sound at the tent entrance and he looked up to see Sevegg peering in. He gestured her to enter.

'I saw her march out,' she said.

Hunn Raal nodded. 'We're leaving soon. Inform the others. Have them depart quietly and singly. Leave the wagons and animals.'

'Our horses, cousin?'

'That's "sir" to you, lieutenant.'

'Yes sir. Your pardon.'

'They remain hobbled well outside the pickets?'

'As instructed, sir.'

'Take four soldiers with you. Saddle up our mounts and then lead them to the east track. We will all rendezvous there. I want us riding before dawn.'

'Yes sir.' She saluted and left.

He looked down at the tankard in his hand, and then tilted the cup, spilling the contents to the dirt floor, and set it upside down on the centre of the commander's small map table.

*All I wanted, Toras Redone, was peace.*

∗    ∗    ∗

Captain Ivis climbed the ladder and emerged on to the parapet of the northwest tower. He came up alongside Corporal Yalad. 'Well, what is it I need to see?'

The man pointed to the ridge of hills to the west. 'Another army, sir. But this one is not passing through – see them? I'd swear they were presenting for battle.'

Ivis squinted. He could make out riders working into position along the centre hill, arraying in ranks. With the rising dust behind them, it was impossible to tell how many there were. To either side, more soldiers had dismounted and were forming up in skirmish order. 'Can you make out that banner, corporal?'

'No sir.'

Ivis rubbed at the back of his neck. His eyes felt full of sand. He'd not slept well since his journey into the wild forest – since his visit to that cursed goddess. At times, he managed to convince himself that he had but dreamed the whole ordeal, but then, he had not the imagination to conjure such horrors. What few nightmares he experienced in his life were all singular and banal in their obsessions. The loss of teeth, walking naked into a crowded hall, the maddening inability to find the stirrups on a panicked horse rushing for a cliff edge, a broken sword in the midst of battle. There were no sharpened stakes rising from a

594

glade's matted grasses, and no woman lying impaled upon them and regarding him with calm eyes.

'What should we do, sir?'

Blinking, Ivis shook himself. 'Call to arms, corporal. With luck, we'll have the time to assemble. I see nothing in the way of siege weapons.'

'No sir. We could let them circle the walls until their horses drop from exhaustion.'

Ivis turned to study the eastern sky. The pall of smoke seemed unending. He faced the unknown enemy again, watched their ragged preparations. 'No, I have had my fill with this. It is time to test our lord's heavy cavalry. Whoever they are, we'll bloody their noses and send them away, and if word races to the ears of every highborn in Kurald Galain, all the better.'

'Yes sir.'

He glanced across at the corporal and scowled. 'You're looking pallid enough to faint. Steady yourself before tackling the ladder, corporal.'

'Yes sir. I will.'

'But not if the effort takes all morning. Get moving!'

The young soldier scrambled for the trap.

Ivis returned his attention to the unknown forces arraying against them. More than half a thousand to be sure. But he saw nothing of heraldic banners among the ranks, nor any sign of company standards. The single thin flag waving was still too distant to make out, and then it was suddenly lowered, vanishing from sight.

As he watched, hearing the first barked shouts from the keep's compound at his back, he saw a troop of a dozen or so riders emerge from the ranks and canter down the hill's slope. Reaching its base, they set out, their mounts taking a low stone wall in smooth leaps, crossing through the dusty stubble of a harvested field, taking another wall and out across another field, drawing ever closer.

There was a broad ring of level, unbroken land surrounding the keep's hill, enough room for charging cavalry, and when the strangers reached the outer edge of this one rode forward and lifted the banner once more. The figure then reined in and drove the pole into the earth.

The troop wheeled round and set off back to the main force.

Ivis stared at the banner they had left behind.

*Abyss take me. They're Borderswords.*

               \*      \*      \*

Returning from the killing field, Feren's horse stumbled after clearing the last wall and coming up against the slope. She fought to right the animal and a moment later regained control. She glared across at her brother. 'Rint! We need to rest!'

He made no reply, pushing to force his mount back up the hillside.

Looking up, she studied the foremost row of Borderswords lining the crest above her. Their beasts were lathered, heads drooping, and the men and women sitting silent in their saddles were in no better shape. Anger and horror could speak in one tongue, but it was a language ignorant of reason. She had listened to its ceaseless clamouring in her skull for days and nights now, and for most of that time, there had been something of a blessing in that senseless cacophony.

The enemy had a face, and in every line, in every crease and wrinkle, it could encompass all that was wrong with the world; all that was unjust; all that was evil. Nothing could be simpler than this moment of recognition, or the relief one felt when it arrived, bright as revelation, to burn away uncertainty and doubt, to scour from the mind the sins of subtlety.

She had felt its sharp talons drag down through her mind, making wreckage of time and need, of cautious planning and preparation. This was not war, unless an entire war could be reduced to a single battle. On this day they would strike down the enemy: they would rake their own claws down that bitter visage, slicing through the bones underneath, and spilling out for all to see the mundane truth of evil. *Blood the same as our blood. Flesh the same as our flesh. The pulped ruin of brains no different from what we might splash out to a mace's blow. All disassembled and beyond repair.*

*Then we'll look on in silence, and wonder at the howling emptiness inside us. It will not last long. The horror will return, standing over spent rage.*

*Nothing goes away. It just piles up inside.*

Staggering, her horse reached the crest and she reined in the poor beast. Within her exhaustion, something cold and hard had pushed through. She could see clearly into a future too bleak to comprehend. She faced Rint again. 'At the very least wait a day! Abyss take us, the enemy is rested!' Her desperate gaze shifted to the others surrounding Rint. 'Traj! We are done in!'

'You'll not fight,' Rint told her. 'Lahanis will remain with you—'

At that, Lahanis hissed. 'I will not! See the blood still on my hands? This day I will add to it!'

'I ride at your side,' Feren told her brother. 'But we need to pause. Here and now. We need to recover our strength—'

'I am ready for this,' Traj said.

'Listen to me – Rint, Ville and Galak – we have seen those House-blades! We have watched their drills!'

'And remember how few they were!' Rint retorted, almost shouting. 'Too heavily armoured besides – we will dance circles round them! Feren – there must be eight hundred of us here! Against what? Two hundred mounted Houseblades at best?'

'Do you think we will meet their charge?' Traj demanded. 'No, we will part before it. We will sweep in from the sides, joined by the skirmishers. We will drag them down from their mounts and gut them all!'

'All very well – but let us rest first!'

'Sister,' said Rint, 'it will be noon before they ride out to meet us, assuming they have the courage to face the challenge of our banner. They know why we are here! We will await them, this I swear!'

She subsided, looking away from her brother, away from all of them. *Do I so fear righteous vengeance? No. My brother grieves. All those here grieve.*

*But this makes no sense. Has Lord Draconus lost control of his Houseblades? But then, is that so impossible? There is civil war and their lord has left them. They have chosen a side and they acted – striking us first to remove the threat from their backs; and would now face the east and south without risk of being surrounded by enemies.*

*That makes tactical sense.*

*Except for the fact that our fighters were all away, and now we are here.*

She twisted in her saddle to the young girl with the stained hands. 'Lahanis. Did you see heavily armoured Houseblades? Did you see war-horses? How many attacked?'

The girl stared at her in open distaste. 'I saw Houseblades,' she said. 'I saw the standard of House Dracons! I am not a child!'

'Activity from the gate!' someone shouted.

Feren turned with the others to see two riders emerging from the keep, picking their way down the slope. One bore the standard of Dracons.

'They accept our challenge,' Rint said, baring his teeth.

The two distant figures rode out to rein in directly in front of the Borderswords' banner. The one bearing the Dracons standard thrust it into the ground, next to the first offering. A moment later, both House-blades were riding back to the keep.

'After we have slain the Houseblades,' said Traj, 'we break into the keep. We kill everyone we find. Then we ride down to the village. We slaughter everyone and burn everything. If I could, I would see the ground salted. But I will settle for shattered bones. Curse upon the name of Draconus, by the blood of my soul.'

Feren felt a chill creeping through her, spreading out through her muscles. She reached up to touch the scar disfiguring her cheek, and felt her fingertips cold as ice.

'Everyone dismount!' Traj called out. 'Rest your horses and see to your weapons! Drink the last from your flasks and eat what's left in your saddlebags!'

'That would be leather string, Traj!' someone yelled back.

Low laughter rippled out.

Feren hunched in her saddle, studying the wiry grasses fluttering along the crest. The baby stirred in her, twice, like a thing making fists.

\*     \*     \*

Sandalath emerged from the house. Although the day was warm, the skies clear, she drew her cloak tightly about her. Her walk through the house had awakened the horror that gripped her soul, and although the bloodstains had been washed away and all other signs of the slaughter removed, the unnatural silence – the absence of familiar faces – crumbled her courage.

She had made of her room a fortress against all that lay beyond its door, but in the days and nights that followed the killings her abode became a prison, with terror pacing the corridor beyond. She feared sleep and its timeless world of nightmare visions, its panicked flights through shadows and the flapping of small, bared feet closing behind her.

It still seemed impossible that the daughters of Draconus could have, in a single night, become so transformed. She saw them now as demonic, and their faces, hovering ceaselessly in her mind's eye, made evil the soft features of youth: the large, bright eyes and rosebud lips, the flush of rounded cheeks.

Captain Ivis insisted that they had fled the keep. But he had sent trackers into the countryside and they had found no signs of their passage. At night, lying awake and shivering in her bed, Sandalath had heard strange sounds in the house, and once, very faint, the sound of whispering, as of voices behind a stone wall. She was convinced that the girls were still in the house, hiding in secret places known only to them.

There was a forbidden room . . .

She saw Captain Ivis and made her way to where he stood. Soldiers crowded the compound, silent but for the sounds their armour made as they tightened straps and closed buckles. Grooms rushed about burdened beneath saddles and the leather plates of horse armour. Ivis stood in the midst of this chaos like a man on an island, beyond the reach of frenzied waves thrashing on all sides. She drew assurance from just seeing him. He met her eyes as she drew nearer.

'Hostage, you have seen too little of the sun, but this is not the best of days.'

'What is happening?'

'We prepare for battle,' he replied.

'But – who would want to attack us?'

The man shrugged. 'It is not our way to struggle in search of enemies, hostage. Some have suggested that the invasion of the Jheleck but delayed the brooding civil war. An unpopular opinion, but so often it is the unpopular ones that prove true, while those eagerly embraced are revealed as wishful thinking. We deny for comfort, and often it takes a hand to the throat to shake us awake.' He studied her for a moment. 'I regret the risk you face in our company, hostage. Whatever may befall us, be assured that you will not be harmed.'

'What madness has so afflicted us, Captain Ivis?'

'That question is best directed at poets, hostage, not soldiers like me.' He gestured at the scene in the compound. 'I fret at the loss of our surgeon, and fear that I will not stand well in my lord's stead in this battle to come. He instructed me as to the training of these House-blades and I have done what I could in his absence, but on this day I feel very much alone.'

He looked exhausted to her eyes, but even this did not shake her confidence in him. 'His daughters,' she said, 'would not have dared do what they did, captain, if you had been home that night.'

Though she had intended her words to be assuring, she saw him flinch. He looked away, the muscles of his jaws tightening. 'I regret my foolish wanderings, hostage. Alas, it soothes nothing to promise never again.'

Sandalath stepped closer, overwhelmed by a desire to give him comfort. 'Forgive my clumsy words, captain. I meant but to show my faith in you. On this day you will prevail. I am certain of it.'

The gates had been opened and the Houseblades were mounting up and riding through them to assemble outside the keep. Corporal Yalad shouted out troop numbers, as if to impose order on the chaos, but to Sandalath's eyes it seemed no one was paying him any attention. And yet there was no confusion at the gate's narrow passage, and the flow of armed figures riding out was steady, although it seemed that that could change at any moment. She frowned. 'Captain, this seems so . . . fraught.'

He grunted. 'Everything is going smoothly, hostage, I assure you. Once we lock with the enemy in the field beyond, well, that is when all sense of order is swept away. Even there, however, I intend to hold on to control of the Houseblades for as long as I can, and with luck, if that is even a fraction longer than the enemy's commander is able to do, we will win. This is the truth of all war. The side that holds its nerve longer is the side that wins.'

'No different then, from any argument.'

He smiled at her. 'Just so, hostage. You are right to see war in this way. Each battle is an argument. Even the language is shared. We yield ground. We surrender. We retreat. In each, you can find a match to any knockdown scrap between husband and wife, or mother and daughter. And this should tell you something else.'

She nodded. 'Victory is often claimed, but defeat is never accepted.'

'It is an error to doubt your intelligence, hostage.'

'If I possess such a thing, captain, it gives little strength.' She shook herself. 'My life is measured out in lost arguments.'

'The same might be said of all of us,' Ivis replied.

'But do win today's argument, captain. And come home safe.'

When she looked up and met his eyes, she felt a rippling sensation travel through her, as if a wave of something was passing between them. It should have shocked her, but it did not, and she reached out to rest a hand against his arm.

His eyes widened slightly. 'Forgive me, hostage, but I must leave you now.'

'I shall take to the tower to watch the battle, captain.'

'The day will lift dust and so obscure the scene.'

'I will witness your victory none the less. And when Lord Draconus at last returns, I will tell him the tale of this day.'

He nodded to her and then departed, calling for his horse.

When she looked round the compound, she saw that it was almost empty, barring a dozen or so servants preparing cots along one wall and stacking strips of cloth to use as bandages. Two small kilns had been dragged out from the smithy and apprentices were stacking bricks around them, along with buckets, some containing water and others with what looked like iron rods bearing a variety of shaped ends. These were set down close to the kilns. More servants arrived with braziers, shovelling into the black-rimmed mouths of the kilns the coals and embers they contained.

Surgeon Atran should have been there, snapping out instructions and standing with her arms crossed and fury in her face at the thought of the wounded and dying soon to come. Sandalath could almost see her, just as she had almost seen Hilith in a corridor, and the keeper of records, Hidast, at his desk through the open door to his office. And her maids, showing her the welts Hilith had inflicted on them for some invented transgression. In her mind, or in some timeless corner of her mind, they still lived, still moved through the house bent on their tasks and doing all the things they were supposed to do.

She wanted them back. Even Hilith. Instead, all she had now were stones that whispered and the faint scuff of bared feet out of sight past some corner, and that chilling sensation of hidden eyes tracking her every move.

And now Captain Ivis had ridden out to join his soldiers. She saw the armourer, Setyl, with his terribly scarred face, standing near the kilns, motionless as he stared into the embers. Near the stables stood Venth, openly weeping at the thought of the horses soon to die.

Sandalath looked at the tower she had told Ivis would be her perch to witness the battle. To ascend, she would have to pass the locked door that led into a chamber she had once heard Envy call the Temple.

If the daughters remained in the keep, they were hiding in that room. She had no proof, of course. Not even Ivis had a key to that chamber, and just like her he knew not what lay behind that door.

She had been given a fighting knife after the night of the murders. It was heavy, wide-bladed and weighted at its tip. The captain had shown her how to chop with the weapon. It could be used to slice and cut as well, but these techniques involved practice, and a wrist stronger than hers. The thought of killing the Lord's daughters did not disturb her overmuch; the faith she lacked was in her own courage.

Beneath the cloak, she closed one hand about the weapon's grip, and then set out for the tower and its stairs that wound up the inside of the outer wall. There were four levels to the tower, if one included the open platform at the top. Shuttered windows were visible on all but the floor with the hidden chamber, and that one was just beneath the ladder to the platform.

Reaching the door, she was startled by a hand on her shoulder. She turned to see the horse master, his eyes still red and streaked tears on his lined cheeks. 'Master Venth, what do you wish?'

'Your pardon, hostage. But when the captain took from me the reins of his mount, he informed me that you were intent on watching from atop the tower.'

She nodded.

'He asked that I escort you there, hostage. And, if you so desire, that I keep you company.'

'Is it dangerous to be up there, horse master?'

His eyes shied away. 'Not from anyone outside the walls, hostage.'

'Then at last Captain Ivis is convinced. They are still here, aren't they?'

'Food's gone missing, hostage. Corporal Yalad shared your conviction and he has been diligent, and like you he believes that they hide in secret passages.'

'Then, Venth, I will welcome your company.'

'Permit me to lead the way, then.'

'Of course.'

*   *   *

Clearly, Envy reflected, something was wrong. Malice was rotting. They huddled under the floor of the kitchen, sharing between them a loaf of bread Spite had stolen just before dawn. They were all filthy, but the smell coming from little Malice was rank with something much worse than grime and sweat. Each time Malice opened her mouth to take another piece of bread, the stench grew worse.

'All the house guards trooped out,' said Spite. 'I was behind the hearth wall at the crack. Envy, we have the house to ourselves.'

'We can get to the hostage then. Good.'

'Not yet. She went out, too. Something is going on. I don't know what – we heard all the horses. I think they've gone to fight somewhere.'

'War? Could be. Everyone's closing in on Father. About time.'

'He's not here, though,' said Malice in a dry, cracking voice.

'Then he'll come home to ashes,' said Spite.

'I don't want to burn,' said Malice, each word spitting out crumbs of bread.

'We can use the tunnel,' Envy said, but her mind was not on the subject. She kept her gaze averted from Malice. 'We have other problems right now. Spite, you know what I mean.'

Her sister nodded, wiping at her nose. 'If they bring dogs inside, like Yalad was saying, we're in trouble. I know what to do, though, and we should do it now.'

'What are you talking about?' Malice asked.

'Don't worry about it. You thirsty, Malice? I am. Envy?'

'Parched.'

'There's no one in the kitchen. Some nice sweet summer wine – it's all I can think about. This bread is like a lump of wax in my belly.' She lifted one of her hands to study the red scar the surgeon's cutting tool had made. 'We won't heal up all the way until we get more food and drink in us. That's why we sleep all the time. We're starving.'

'I'm not hungry,' said Malice. 'I'm never hungry.'

'Then why do you eat with us?' Envy asked.

Malice shrugged. 'It's something to do.'

'Maybe it's the food inside you that's rotting.'

'I don't smell anything.'

'We do,' snapped Spite. 'But some wine should fix that.'

'All right, I'll drink some, then.'

They set out, gathering again at the end of the passage beneath the kitchen floor, where it opened out into two further tunnels. The one on the left led under the entranceway and ended up under the stables, in a room shin deep in mud soaked with horse piss, while the one on the right ran the length of the main chamber. At the junction of these passages there was a chute that reached up to behind the larder. There were no handholds and the only means of ascending this shaft was to wedge oneself against the walls, with knees drawn up. It was difficult and left scrapes and bruises, but it was the only way into the kitchen.

Envy went first, since it had turned out that she was the strongest of the three and so could reach down and help the others up. The walls had become greasy with constant use, making the climb still more treacherous, but at last she reached the ledge that marked the sliding panel at the back wall of the larder, and slid it open so that she could pull herself up and then into the room. She had to huddle since she was beneath a shelf stocked with jars. Reaching down, she let her right arm dangle. Moments later she felt Spite grasp hold of it and then use it to climb up the chute. Each yank shot pain through Envy's shoulder. Spite's harsh breathing drew closer, and then her sister was clambering through the trap. As she squeezed past Envy, she whispered, 'The oven.'

Envy grunted to acknowledge that she heard, and then reached down once more.

Malice's hands were cold. Skin and the meat beneath it slipped strangely until Envy could feel every bone, closing like talons around her arm. The stench of her sister rose up and she gagged, fighting to keep the contents of her stomach from rising into her mouth.

She felt Spite take hold of her ankles and begin dragging her out from under the shelf, and this helped Envy pull Malice after her. Moments later, all three rose to their feet in the darkness of the larder. That darkness proved no barrier to vision – one of Father's gifts, Envy assumed.

Spite crept to the door and pressed her ear against it. She released the latch and pulled the door open.

They walked out into the kitchen.

'Let's sit close to the oven to warm up,' Envy said. 'Spite, find us a jug.'

Malice accompanied Envy to the oven. The fires beneath it had just been fed, to keep the oven hot until the midday meal needed preparing. Envy suspected that this day would see no such meal; still, the habit had been adhered to and so the heat emanating from the metal door and its brick flanks was fierce and welcoming.

'I can't feel it,' said Malice, sitting down beside her.

'Do you feel cold?'

Malice shook her head. Strands of hair drifted down to the floor. 'I don't feel anything.'

Spite reappeared with a heavy earthenware jug. She came up to them, and a moment before reaching them she took the jug's handle in both hands and swung it against Malice's head.

Clay and bone shattered, spilling wine and blood out over Malice's body and the floor, and both sisters. Where the liquids splashed against the oven door there was savage hissing, and then smoke. Spite dropped the handle. 'Help me lift her!'

Envy took up a wrist and an ankle.

One side of Malice's head was flattened, although mostly near the top. Her ear was pushed in, surrounded by torn skin and cracked bones that made a pattern like the petals of a flower around that bloodied ear. The eye on that side stared up at the ceiling, leaking bloody tears.

She made a moaning sound as she was lifted from the floor, but the other eye looked directly at Envy.

'Wait!' snapped Spite, setting Malice's foot down and reaching for the oven handle. She cursed as she pulled down the door and Envy smelled scorched flesh. 'That smarts,' she said, gasping as she retrieved Malice's right ankle. 'Turn her round – head first into the oven.'

Envy could not pull her gaze from Malice's lone, staring eye. 'She'll kick.'

'So what. We can break the legs if we have to.'

Together, with Malice between them, they forced their sister into the oven, and this effort at last swept from Envy that terrible staring eye. The inside of the oven was lined with clay, and loud sizzling sounds accompanied every touch of skin, blood and hair against the rounded sides. Malice struggled, pulling at her arms, but the effort was weak. They got the upper half of their sister's body into the oven and began pushing the rest in. The legs did not kick. They were limp and heavy, the toes curling upward.

'No more bread in this one,' gasped Spite as she folded the leg she held and pushed it past the edge of the door, the knee leaving a patch of skin on the metal rim.

'They'll have to smash it into pieces and build another,' said Envy. She got the leg in on her side as well.

Spite grasped the door's handle and slammed it home.

'Feed more wood,' said Envy, sitting back. 'I want her crisp. She stank like the Abyss!'

'I wonder what we did wrong.'

'Don't know, but it tells us one thing.'

'What?'

'You and me, Spite. We should never try to kill each other. If one of us did, well, I think it's dead for keeps.'

Spite studied her for a long moment, and then went off to gather an armload of wood. 'She won't come back from this one, will she?'

'No. Of course not.'

'Because,' continued Spite, 'if she did, we'd be in real trouble.'

'Throw some wood into the oven itself, and that kindling there.'

'No. I don't want to open that door again, Envy. In case she jumps out.'

'All right. It's a good point. Just fill it up underneath, then. Lots and lots.'

'That's what I'm doing! Why not help me instead of just sitting there giving orders like some fucking queen!'

Envy giggled at the swear word and could not help but look round guiltily, if only for an instant. Then she set to collecting more wood.

In the oven, Malice burned.

Rint remembered his sister as a child, a scrawny thing with scraped knees and smears of dust on her face. It seemed she was always climbing something: trees, crags and hillsides, and she would perch high above the village, eyes scanning the horizons or looking down to watch passers-by. Her moments of fury came when it was time for Rint to find her and bring her home, for a meal, or a bath. She'd spit, scratch and bite like a wild animal, and then, when at last he had pinned her arms against her sides in a tight hug, and lifted her from the ground to stagger his way back to the house, she would moan as if death had come to take her.

He bore stoically the wounds from her thrashing about, as befitted a brother who, while younger, was still bigger, and he was always mindful of the smiles and jests of others in the village when he passed them with his sister in his arms. They had been amused, he thought, even sympathetic. He had refused to think such reactions belonged to derision, contempt or mockery. But every now and then he had caught an expression and he had wondered. Some people took pleasure in the discomfort of others: it made a balance against their own lives.

There was no reason for thinking these thoughts now, as he looked across to his sister, except for the way she was studying the Houseblades forming up below. From her perch on her horse, atop this hill, she was wearing the same expression he had seen many years past. He thought of the daughter growing inside her, and felt a deep pang in his gut. It was said the soul only came to a child in the moments after birth, when the world opened out to wide, blinking eyes, and the lungs first filled with breath and on that breath rode the soul, rushing in to claim what had been made for it. In the time before all of this, with the vessel still trapped inside the mother's body, the soul hovered near. He imagined it now: rising high above them to look down, with a girl's closed expression, a strange steadiness in the eyes, and a wall of mystery behind them.

All at once, his love for his sister almost overwhelmed him, and for an instant he felt tempted to steal her away from what was to come. Perhaps the disembodied soul of the child sensed the risk, the terrible danger awaiting them, and was crying out to him, in a voice faint as the wind that reached through him, slipping past his own hurts, his mass of wounds. Then he looked round to study his companions. Ville, silent and hunched – there had been a young man he had longed to give his heart to, but was too frightened of rejection to make his feelings known. That young man had been a potter, possessing such talent with clay that no one questioned his rejection of fighting ways, and were ever pleased at his work. He was dead now, cut down in the village.

Rint's eyes travelled past Ville and settled briefly on Galak. In the days before they had left on their mission, Galak had lost the love of yet another young woman in the village, the last in a pattern of failures. Galak had blamed only himself, as he was wont to do, although Rint could see nothing in the man to warrant such self-recrimination. He was kind and often too generous, careless with coins and his time, prone to forgetting meetings he had arranged with his mate, and hopeless at domestic tasks – but in all these things he had displayed a child-like equanimity and innocence, traits which seemed to infuriate women. As they had ridden out for House Dracons to begin their journey west, Galak had sworn off love for all time. Looking upon him now, Rint wondered if his friend regretted that vow.

He saw Traj, with his red face and belligerent expression, both permanent fixtures. Rint could not recall ever seeing the man smile, but his wife had loved him deeply, and together they had made four children. But now Traj was alone in his life, and no love surrounded him to soften his stony presence, and he sat as one exposed, suffering the weathering of a harsh world.

There were others, and each one he looked upon reminded Rint of his stoic marches through the village, with his sister trapped in his arms. The wounds could not be hidden and so must be worn as a child would wear them, struggling not to cry at the pain, or the shame, determined to show everyone else a strength well disguising its own fragility.

The sun stood high above them. Below, on the killing field beyond the plots of farmland, the heavily armoured Houseblades sat motionless on their caparisoned mounts. Some bore lances; others held long-handled axes or strangely curved swords. The round shields slung on their left arms were black and showed no crest. There were, Rint judged, more than five hundred of them.

*There are too many. All this time, while we were away, that damned captain was building his forces, preparing for war. We sat and watched them, and pretended to be unimpressed, and not once did we take heed of the portents.*

'Refuse their charge,' Traj now growled. 'We part before them. Nothing changes.'

*But everything has. We saw these warhorses. We even remarked on their impressive size. But not once did we see them arrayed in full complement. Now, even at this distance, to look upon them is to feel . . . diminished.*

'We will dance around them,' Traj continued, as if seeking to convince himself, 'striking and then withdrawing. Again and again. Those mounts are burdened. They will tire fast, as will their riders. See the grilled visors on their helms? Their vision is restricted. They'll not hear commands – the battle will roar through their skulls. They'll flounder in confusion.' He rose on his stirrups. 'Skirmishers, stay well guarded behind our advance – close only when and where we lock blades with them! Close in and kill the ones we unseat. Gut or hamstring the horses if you can. Scatter if they seek to charge or surround you.'

*An odd way to use the skirmishers, but then I see your point, Traj. They don't wield pikes, and there's not enough dismounted besides, not for a square, not even a hollow one. Their only hope is if we can make this messy.*

'It's time,' said Traj.

Rint glanced over to see his sister staring at him. Her eyes glistened and he saw once more in her face the little girl she had once been. Before things broke, before the hands trembled before all that was suddenly out of reach. *Climb a tree, sister. High above all of this. You had it right back then. I know now why you fought me so, every time I dragged you back down, every time I carried you up the street and people smiled at your temper or laughed at your wretched moans.*

*Not all of us wanted to grow up. I should have followed your lead. I should have stayed a child with you, clinging to a high branch while everyone else aged below, aged and fell so helplessly into their futures.*

Every child born sent mother and father back to their own childhoods. Like symbols of nostalgia, they were set down and watched as they made their journey away from simplicity, from the bliss of unknowing. And if, in the witnessing of this, tears came, then those tears were warm, and the sadness that joined them somehow comforted the soul, even as it reawakened old pains and old losses. To lose a child was to feel unbearable grief, as if some vital thread had been severed. Nostalgia was a bitter curse, with every memory of that journey ending in sudden loss, yielding emptiness beyond all solace.

Rint understood her now. And wished with all his heart that he didn't.

She turned away then, gathering her reins in her left hand and drawing her sword with her right. She shifted in her saddle, firming the grip of her feet in the stirrups.

*When Feren looked for that witch, her eyes lifted to the trees. And hidden up there, as my sister had known, Olar Ethil looked down with unreadable eyes. A child eager to watch.*

*Until I gave her fire.*

*Women are right to fear us. Oh, Feren . . .*

Traj gave the command, and then they were riding down the slope.

\*　　\*　　\*

Ivis watched the Borderswords begin moving down the slope. 'Yalad! Signal wedge formation!'

He remained in front of his troops, listening to them assume the new presentation. Horse hoofs thumped to make a rumble of thunder through the hard-packed ground of the killing field. Dust roiled past Ivis in thin clouds, a fortunate direction for the wind, at least to begin with. 'Centre line count right left!'

He heard voices barking the word 'right' and then 'left' in an alternating pattern down the heartline of the wedge formation. This command alone gave the Houseblades all that they needed to know for this initial engagement.

The Borderswords poured over the first stone wall, slowing up to give time to their skirmishers to do the same. Ivis saw how the foot-soldiers lagged and nodded slightly to himself. They would serve little function until all momentum was lost. Unfortunately for them, he intended no loss of momentum from battle's beginning to battle's end.

Under his breath, he cursed Lord Draconus. The man should be here, commanding this first bloodletting for his Houseblades. Instead, every order – upon which so many lives depended – would be coming from a lowly captain who had grown sick of war decades ago. *The only thing going for me is that I've seen all this before, dozens of times. And the only thing going against me is the same fucking thing.* He tightened the strap of his helm and then wheeled his mount.

The wedge was arrayed before him: a point of three elite soldiers directly opposite, the leading line swept back sharply, twenty to each side, to form the chevron.

'Houseblades! We didn't ask for this argument. We have no cause to hate our enemy. Do not fight your grief in what's to come, but set it aside with an honest vow to return to it in the days, months and years ahead. This is the soldier's burden. Now, I trust you've all pissed before mounting up – if I see a single soldier slick in the saddle it'll be the public lash!' Hearing a few laughs, he scowled. 'You think I am jesting? I have told you before but it seems you need to hear it again. In the Houseblades of Dracons, you will be told when to eat, when to drink, when to sleep, when to rise, when to shit, when to piss, when to fuck and when to kill. Now, you've done them all by our orders, except for the last, and that last has now arrived. It is time to kill.'

He rode closer a step, then two. 'I'd like to be with you for this. If our lord was here I would be, at the point of this wedge, and you all know that. But he's not, so command falls to me. Left flank, strip your shields!'

The soldiers on the left flank of the wedge rested their weapons and tore at the thin layer of dyed felt covering their shields, revealing lacquered white beneath.

'Troop sergeants and corporals, keep an eye out for flags on the keep slope! And if you can't see those, look higher, to the gate towers. At all times, you will see two flags upon each pole. Two flags on the white pole, two flags on the black pole—'

Someone's shout cut him off. 'Begging pardon, captain! But if we don't know all that already we deserve to be cut down!'

Ivis subsided, feeling foolish. 'Fine. I'm an old man and I want to dither, Abyss help us all.'

Laughter answered that comment.

'Sir! Kindly get out of the way!'

Grimacing, Ivis collected up his reins and kicked his horse into motion, swinging left and riding down that wing, his gaze fixed forward.

Voices reached out for him as he passed.

'Sir, I missed that order to fuck!'

'You lie, Shanter! You never miss an order to fuck!'

'I'll see you after, Shanter!'

'That'll take an order, Brusk, at sword's point.'

'Wait! Did I hear Shanter's taking orders?'

And then he was past, nodding to himself. He had heard it all before, a thousand flavours but ever the same taste. It broke his heart to hear such life pushing through the gathering, suffocating fugue that came in the moments before battle. Each jest, each voice raised in rough banter, shone like a gold flag in a black forest, making all that was to come that much harder to bear.

Reaching the slope, and the flag station, he reined in and swung round to face the field once more.

The Borderswords were assembling at the far side of the field. They formed up in a rough, uneven line, some readying lances and others drawing their long stabbing swords. The dust that had travelled across the field was now mostly gone, and the clear air between the two armies wavered like water in the day's heat.

This latter detail was unpleasant, as it invited dehydration and heat prostration from his heavily armoured men and women. Then again, if the battle went on too long, all was lost anyway.

'Signaller!'

'Sir!'

'Commit the advance.'

'Yes sir!'

Moments later, the wedge lurched into motion, a walk rising to a trot.

The enemy was now as committed as were his own Houseblades. With the field walls behind them, retreat was impossible. He saw them move forward.

Off to the left of both forces stood the two standards. One had loosened its grip on the soil and tilted to rest against the shaft of the other. He could not tell which was which, as dust now covered both banners. And, as the ground began to shake, when the Houseblades rose into a canter, both standards fell to the ground. Ivis frowned at that, but distant shouts from the Borderswords drew him round.

*     *     *

Sandalath watched, wide-eyed, as the two armies surged in a final rush to close. Venth was swearing under his breath at her side. He had said earlier that the enemy was an army of Borderswords, and the reason for battle was unknown.

The cantering Houseblades lifted into a charge, but as they did so the wedge formation unravelled, the centre slowing as the wings swept out, spreading wide. Opposite them, half obscured through the ever-thickening dust, the enemy line seemed to waver.

When the Houseblades reached them, the line of heavy cavalry was virtually level, the riders only three deep in ranks, and they smashed against a broad swath of the enemy forces. Sandalath gasped to see horses flung into the air, legs kicking, while in places the Bordersword riders seemed to vanish beneath the hoofs of the warhorses. The roiling dust turned pink above the line of impact. Moments later, the entire engagement disappeared into the dust, until only the clanging cacophony of fighting reached them.

She caught the flash of white shields on the left, black shields on the right, but then even those were gone. On the slope below and to her right, she could see Captain Ivis, still mounted and flanked by poles bearing signal flags – but those flags had not changed since the charge first began. She saw the same flags on angled spires set above the gate towers. There was no evidence of panic, and the signallers stood motionless at their stations.

*Is this really how it is?*

*     *     *

The wedge formation of the heavy cavalry, so inviting to the lighter mounted Borderswords, had suddenly ceased to exist, and before they could react to the lightning transformation before them, the two lines of horse-soldiers collided.

Directly in front of Rint was a Houseblade sheathed in leather plates covering chain, his visor lowered and so made into something face-less. He saw the man's lance slide up to plunge through the neck of Rint's horse, and as the Houseblade released his grip on the weapon he flung up his shield to take Rint's stabbing sword. The weapon clanged against copper riveted to wood beneath the black felt, rebounded high. His horse staggered beneath him and then pitched on to one shoulder.

Rint sought to pull free, but the animal rolled on to his right leg. Wrenching agony announced the tearing loose of his thigh bone from his hip socket. The scream that broke from him tore his throat.

610

The Houseblade had ridden past, but another came up behind him, a woman from the long hair spilling out from under the rim of her helm. Her lance drove down, punched into Rint just under his left collar bone. The heavy iron blade snapped the bone, its point pushing through to crunch into and then scrape along the underside of his shoulder blade. She tore it free as she rode past.

Rint sought to lift his sword to swing at the horse's legs.

Instead, a hoof lashed down, landing on his throat. There was an instant of impossible weight, and then it lifted clear, snapping against his jaw as it went.

He stared into the dust-filled sky overhead. Somehow, air slipped through the wreckage of his throat and filled his lungs. The pulse in the side of his neck throbbed like a fist under the skin.

*That was quick.*

Dying was within reach, but something held him back. He struggled to order his thoughts, struggled to understand what was keeping him here, lying on the ground in his own blood. He had never felt so cold, so heavy and so weak.

He tried to turn his head, to look for his sister, but nothing worked. He realized then that he could not feel his body, beyond that immense weight pressing down upon him. The sounds of fighting were falling away, or perhaps his hearing was failing.

*We are defeated. As easily as that, the Borderswords are no more. I want to die now. I want to go away.*

He squinted into the sky, and now at last saw the tree – where it had come from, how he could have missed it here on this field, were questions he could not answer, but he saw the summer wind in the branches, rushing through the dusty green leaves. And high on one branch sat his sister, young and fierce, not wanting to come down.

He would have to go up and get her, again. It was always the way and it infuriated him. But he would not show that, since he could hear people laughing, offering up suggestions.

Rint stood and began climbing. It was easy. It had always been easy, since this tree was made for climbing. He coughed in the dust, wiped again and again at his eyes, and his chest hurt as it fought for every breath. No matter. She was drawing nearer.

At last he came up beside her, and edged out along the branch. But when he looked over, to berate her for making him have to come up and get her, he saw that Feren had vanished, and in her place sat Olar Ethil.

The witch was horribly burned, her skin peeling off to reveal blistered red meat. She crouched hunched over, rocking, and the eyes she turned upon him glittered as if they still held the flames that had done this to her.

She held out to him her blackened hand. 'Fear not,' she said in a broken voice. 'It is time. I vowed to greet you on this day, Rint, and I always keep my vows.'

'No,' he said. 'It's time to go home. Supper's ready.'

'Rint of the Borderswords, Tiste-child of Night, I forgive you for what you did to me.'

He found that he was crying.

Her hand hovered, beckoning. 'It is not hard, when you understand things, this forgiveness. The word itself blesses both sides. Come to me, then.'

'Where is Feren?'

'Not far.'

'Where is her daughter?'

'Not far.'

'I want to go to them.'

'Rint, it's a big tree.'

He took that hand, felt it crumble to ash in his grip, but whatever remained was strong enough to hold on to.

*I won't fall. It's all right then.*

*I won't fall ever again.*

* * *

The sounds of battle diminished slightly, and there was boiling motion coming through the dust. Sandalath saw scores of white shields appear on one side, and then black shields on the other flank, all drawing closer, and moments later those shields numbered in the hundreds. 'Oh!' cried Sandalath. 'Is it over?'

'Can't say, hostage,' Venth admitted. 'Seemed awfully quick.' He wiped again at his eyes.

'Venth, I am sorry for the horses out there, on both sides.'

'As am I, hostage. Abyss knows, they deserve better.'

Now the flags were being changed, as the Houseblades withdrew at a slow canter. She saw some reeling in their saddles, and a few riderless horses accompanied them. The troops began re-forming, wheeling round to present an even line, while a few rode on, back towards the keep – the wounded men and women who could fight no more on this day.

The wind was lifting the dust up and past the field of battle, and she saw now the hundreds of fallen strewn all the way back to the distant stone wall. Those shapes formed humps, some seething with wounded soldiers and wounded beasts, but even between the humps no ground was clear. Sudden nausea took Sandalath and she reached out to a merlon to steady herself.

'Abyss take us,' Venth muttered. 'That was brutal. See, they chased off even the skirmishers. If not for that wall, none of them would have escaped.'

Perhaps three hundred or so riders had retreated past the wall and now milled on the nearest field of stubble. Sandalath shook her head. 'Where are the rest of them?' she asked.

'Dead and dying, hostage.'

'But . . . almost no time has passed!'

'Longer than you might think,' he said. 'But less than you'd think reasonable, I'll admit.'

'Is it over?'

'I think it might be. They've not enough to mount a second attack. I see but a score or so fallen Houseblades on that field.' He pointed to the new flags. 'The captain is recalling them all, and that higher flag is announcing a yielding of the field itself, meaning both sides can head out to recover the wounded.'

'Won't they fight each other all over again?'

'Hostage, everyone who leaves a battlefield enters a land of bogs, a swamp that sinks them to their knees. They've not the will to fight on, nor the strength neither. In exhaustion and silence, they will scour the bodies of their fallen comrades, looking for friends and kin. I will wager the captain offers his healers and cutters as soon as our own are taken care of . . . perhaps tomorrow.'

'And will the Borderswords accept them?'

He shrugged. 'I cannot say, since we know not their grievance with us.'

She studied the field, and the few figures now staggering among the dead. 'It seems such a waste, horse master.'

'War is a shout against futility, hostage, but its echo never lasts long.'

She considered his words, and shivered against their chilling touch.

'There will be wounded animals,' said Venth.

'Of course. Let us head down then.'

The horse master led the way down the ladder. Sandalath followed. As she joined him on the landing below she drew close to the locked door. A moment later she gasped. 'Venth!'

'Hostage?'

'Someone paces behind this!'

He came close. Then he shook his head. 'I hear nothing.'

'No,' she replied. 'Not now. But when I first came close – I heard footsteps. Heavy, shuffling.'

Venth hesitated, and then he reached for the latch. He tried lifting it and failed. Stepping back he shrugged. 'I am sorry, hostage. Perhaps it was your imagination. Heavy, you say? Then not the girls.'

She thought back. 'No,' she said. 'They were heavy.'

'Only Lord Draconus possesses the key to this chamber, hostage. There was dust on the latch, and this marks the only entrance – you can see as much. The room's walls here are a single layer of stone, and the chamber beneath this one has no trap in the ceiling. And no windows, of course.'

'I know, horse master. Yes, perhaps I imagined it. Mother always said I was prone to such fancies. Come, let us continue on. I have no liking for this place.'

*    *    *

Drifting back from some timeless abyss, she opened her eyes.

A Houseblade was above her, his seamed face hovering close. She saw him lift a hand and then set its palm against her forehead. It was warm but rough with calluses. She should have despised that touch, but she couldn't. Above the man, thin clouds were stretched across the sky.

'Can you hear me?' he asked. 'I am Captain Ivis. Your companions have . . . departed. They left to us their wounded. I did not imagine they would find defeat as bitter as they did, to so abandon you.' He glanced away briefly, eyes squinting, and then looked down at her again. 'You were knocked unconscious, but seem otherwise uninjured. We have gathered up a few Bordersword horses. When you feel able, we will send you back to your people. But I need to know – why did you attack us?'

The question seemed absurd, too absurd to even answer.

The captain scowled. 'What is your name?'

She contemplated refusing to answer, but there seemed to be no point in that. 'Lahanis.'

'Well, you're young. Too young for this to be your war.'

'It *was* mine!' she hissed, reaching up and pushing his hand from her brow. 'You attacked our villages, slaughtered everyone! We tracked you back – we hunted you down!'

'Lahanis, we did no such thing.' He studied her for a moment, and then cursed under his breath and turned to someone she couldn't see. 'Those Legion companies. I should have chased them off. I should have demanded to know why they camped a stone's throw from the keep.'

'We were made to take the blame for that slaughter, sir?'

'Corporal, I know you sharpened up on the night of the murders, so where does your brain go when you're in my company?'

'I wish I knew, sir.'

Ivis met Lahanis's eyes. 'Listen to me. You were deceived. If I had ridden out to parley with your commanders—'

'You would have been cut down before you got out a single word,' she said. 'We weren't interested in talking.'

'So your standard told me,' Ivis said. 'Stupid!'

She flinched at that.

'Not you,' he said. 'Lahanis, listen. Ride to your kin, to the survivors. You say you tracked us back here. Is that true, or did you backtrack?'

'We backtracked, sir. We were even hoping we'd reach the keep before you returned from the last village you burned.'

'Abyss below, who was commanding you?'

She shook her head. 'No one, really. Traj, I suppose. He shouted the loudest. Maybe Rint.'

'Rint?' Ivis suddenly straightened, looking round. 'Venth!' he shouted. 'Over here on the double!'

Lahanis struggled to sit up. She was lying on a cot in the keep's compound. There were other wounded, but with blankets swaddling them there was no way to tell if they were Borderswords or Houseblades – she recognized none of the faces she could see. The back of her skull was tender; her neck was stiff and throbbing with pain.

A third man arrived. 'Captain? I have injured horses—'

'What were the names of the Borderswords who rode with Lord Draconus?'

The man blinked. 'Sir? Well, I can't remember, to be honest.'

Hands to the sides of her head, Lahanis spoke. 'Rint, Feren, Ville and Galak. They all came back to us. They said your lord sent them home.'

'Why? When?'

Lahanis shrugged. 'Not long. I don't know why.'

Ivis stood, rubbing at the back of his neck, his gaze on the gates.

'Sir, the horses—'

'Go on, horse master. Corporal Yalad.'

'Sir?'

'Attend to Lahanis here, and select a horse for her to ride. I am going to my office to pen a missive – she doesn't leave until I return with it. Lahanis, will you at least bear my message to your kin?'

She nodded.

'Do you believe me, then?'

'I was in one of the villages,' she said. 'I saw your standards. But no soldier was armoured the way yours are, and none rode warhorses, or used those curved swords. Sir, you didn't kill us.'

For a moment it seemed that the man was about to cry. 'I have now,' he said, turning away. He walked off, his shoulders hunched, his steps uncertain.

The young corporal squatted down beside her. 'Hungry?' he asked. 'Thirsty?'

'Just get that horse,' she said.

But he did not move. 'Captain's a little . . . measured, when it comes to scribing. There is time, Bordersword. So?'

She shrugged. 'Water, then.' As he headed off she closed her eyes. *It was me they all listened to. I saw the standards. We could all read the trail. But it was me. You didn't kill us, captain. I did.*

They had disarmed her – even her eating knife was missing from its thin leather sheath. If she had such a weapon within reach, she would take her own life.

*But no. I will deliver the captain's message. Then, before my kin, I will open my throat. I will give them my name to curse.* She saw the corporal returning with a waterskin. *Hungry? Thirsty? Scratch behind the ear?* As soon as he arrived, she reached out and took the skin from him. 'Now get me that horse.'

*       *       *

Seven heavily burdened wagons, each one drawn by a brace of oxen, had begun their journey at the Hust Forge, travelling southward to the borderlands where awaited the Hust Legion encampment. Their pace was slow, stalled at times when an axle split or a wheel stripped its rim on the rough cobbles of the road.

Bearing his lord's command calling the Hust to war, Galar Baras caught up with the train half a day out from the camp. He had ridden hard and his mount was weary, and after the haunting solitude of his journey thus far he welcomed the company of drovers, wagon masters, carpenters, smiths, cooks and guards, many of whom he knew from the Forge settlement where he had been born and then raised. For all that, it was a muted welcome. News of the slaughter at the wedding hung like a pall over everyone. For many, he knew, it was not so much the sudden deaths of Lord Jaen and his daughter that sobered the crew and made conversations infrequent and hushed; rather, it was what the killings portended.

War had returned to Kurald Galain. This time, however, the enemy came not from beyond the realm's borders. Galar could not imagine the mind of a Tiste in the moments that led up to the slaying of a fellow Tiste. For himself, it was difficult to think of any other Tiste as being anything but kin. Yet now it seemed that every face, with its familiar array of traits, was but a mask, and behind some of those masks lurked an enemy, a stranger with strange thoughts.

There was nothing obvious to make simple this designation of friend or foe; not the chalky white skin and angular body of the Forulkan, nor the savage bestiality of the Jheleck. Of course, there had always been bandits and other criminals, who made a profession from preying upon their own kind, but then Galar did not understand them either. Such fools dispensed with trust, and so suffered lives of loneliness and fear. Even among their own kind, such fraternity as existed was rife with betrayal and treachery. The existence of a lifelong criminal was a pitiful one, for all the wealth they might gather, and for all the power they might come to possess.

In a world emptied of virtues, all things became vices, including wealth and even family, and each day arrived with bleaker aspect than the last.

*This war will unleash the criminal in all of us, I fear.*

As he rode in the company of this train of wagons, he could feel the future settling on everyone, thick and suffocating, under heavy skies that might never break.

This last day of the journey seemed to mock all of that, with its cerulean sky and the warm wind that came up from the south. The low hills flanking the road showed the pocks of old mines, from which rough tracks wended down; and here and there could be seen old basins excavated out centuries past, where foul water had settled and, upon drying up, left discoloured, toxic sands. Galar could see the remains of wooden structures: buildings and trestles, scaffolding and ramps, but the forests that had once cloaked these hills and the broad shallow valleys around them were long gone.

There were legacies to be found in every scene of ruination, and as much as Galar sought to grasp only those that led to triumph, even to hold these too tightly could cut him to the bone.

He rode at the head of the column, avoiding the dust. Henarald's delivery of the sword to Lord Anomander, and the blessing that had – or had not – occurred in the Chamber of Night still left Galar rattled, and he need only catch a glimpse of his hand gripping the reins, seeing the ebon hue of his skin, to be reminded of that time. In revisiting that fated day in the Citadel, he found himself shaking his head again and again: at times in wonder, but more often in disbelief. Every uttered word had seemed to blaze with fire – even those words that Galar had himself spoken had felt like incantations, or fragments plucked from some disordered, ethereal poem that all who were present somehow shared.

If this was among the gifts of standing in a god's presence, then Galar Baras at last understood the rewards of faith. In those heady words so laden with meanings; in the confessions and frustrations, the mysteries and the furies, there had been frightening power. In such moments, he realized, worlds could be changed, broken down, reshaped and twisted anew.

He could not imagine the state of Lord Anomander now, the proclaimed protector and First Son of Mother Dark, who for all his status and power had been unable to prevent the massacre. And now, it was rumoured, he had broken with his brother Andarist, and this was a breach beyond imagining only a month ago.

When Galar arrived at the encampment, he would stand before Commander Toras Redone, and voice Lord Henarald's call to war. The Hust Legion would march northward, to Kharkanas. Once there, Toras Redone would kneel before Lord Anomander and pledge the legion to his service, in the name of Mother Dark. And then, perhaps at winter's end, the weapons would unleash their voice of horror against Urusander's Legion.

Galar Baras knew the outcome of such a clash, but he wondered at how the victory would taste. *This future I see is too bitter to bear. Mother Dark, your First Son asks of you but one thing. By your word, you can command Urusander to kneel before you, and so end this war before it truly begins. Together, Urusander and Anomander can hunt down the murderers and see justice done. We can name them criminals and so keep the world we know.*

Yet a part of him wondered, in a voice venal in its clarity, if the world they all knew was in fact worth it.

*She will meet my eyes, and again I will see the truth in them. Sober or drunken, her desire overwhelms me. I yield, weakened into deceit, into betrayal. I make of vows a mockery, even as I long to utter them for myself, and find their honest answer returned to me, in this uneven woman with her uneven love. There are many fools in the world and I must count myself among them.*

Who could be righteous in this midst of failings, these seething flaws hiding behind every familiar mask? And what of this delusion, that the mind of the nefarious, the criminal, was a stranger's mind, with sensibilities alien and malign? *We are cheaters one and all. I see the proof of that in myself. Even as I long for and, indeed, demand virtues among others – in the name of reason and propriety – I am hunted by my own vices, and would elude the bite of reason and make of propriety nothing more than a public front.*

*And now I fear that I am not unusual, not cursed into some special maze of my own making. I fear that we are all the same, eager to make strangers of the worst that is in each of us, and by this stance lift up the banners of good against some foreign evil.*

*But see how they rest against one another, and by opposition alone are left to stand. This is flimsy construction indeed. And so I make masks of the worst in me and fling them upon the faces of my enemies, and would commit slaughter on all that I despise in myself. Yet, with this blood soaking the ground before me, see my flaws thrive in this fertile soil.*

Ahead, where the way sloped upward to cut through the crest line of a ridge, Galar Baras saw the picket towers flanking the road. But no guards stood on those elevated platforms. *Have they decamped? Did someone else bring the news to them? Toras Redone, will we slip past one another yet again, to ever stretch the torment of our love?* He would welcome that bitter denial, and if by surfeit alone could drown every desire, would have them never meet again.

Kicking his horse into a canter, he rode up the slope.

The banners remained on the watch towers, announcing the Legion's presence. The absence of guards marked an uncommon breach in discipline. It was possible that the commander's drinking had become terminal, ruining the morale of every soldier serving her. But even that notion rang false. What soldier of the Hust Legion did not know their commander's weakness? And did they not by every conceivable measure strive to ensure the isolation of such failing? Nor would she lose such control: by it alone she found her necessary arrogance, as was common to the cleverest drunks.

He longed to see her again, but the threshold of this meeting was troubling, and as he pushed his mount to the rise his mouth was dry and his nerves were stretched. Passing between the towers, across the level span and then to where the road began its gentle descent into the shallow valley floor, Galar Baras came within sight of the encampment. He saw the rows of tents. He saw – with vast relief – a few figures moving slowly along the avenues and tracks between the company squares.

But something was wrong. Soldiers should have been gathering to the evening meal, forming queues at the cook tents. The avenues should have been crowded. He saw the other picket stations and none were occupied. A strange stillness gripped the camp.

Urging his horse into a fast canter, Galar Baras rode down the road. He saw Toras Redone. She walked alone across the parade compound, a jug swinging loosely from one hand. A scattering of Hust soldiers stood near, but none drew close to her, even as all eyes were fixed upon her.

As he rode in between the first line of tents, Galar saw that many were still occupied – where flaps had been left open and he could see, in quick glance, the bulks of figures beneath blankets, or sprawled on cots – but no one emerged at his approach, or lifted head to his passing. *An illness has struck. Vapours from the latrine trench, a shifting of wind, or beneath the ground – a deadly flow into the wells. But then, where is the vile smell? Where are the thrashing shapes voicing dread moans?*

When he rode hard into the parade compound, he saw Toras Redone once more. If she heard his approach, she made no sign of it. Her steps were slow, wooden. The ear of the jug seemed to be tangled in the fingers of her left hand. It swung as if full of wine, and he saw that it remained stoppered.

There was a soldier nearby. Galar Baras reined in sharply. 'You there!'

The man turned, stared, and said nothing.

'What has happened? What illness is this among you? Why aren't the plague-flags flying?'

Abruptly the man laughed. 'I was on picket, sir! On the lookout for enemies!' He waved a hand. 'Our relief never showed. I almost fell asleep – but I saw them, you know. They rode out, to the east. Gathered there, and then went on. The sun was not even up, sir. Not even up.'

'Who? Who did you see riding away? Your relief? Why would they do that?'

'Like ghosts, sir. In that gloom. Like ghosts.' He laughed again, and now Galar Baras saw tears tracking down from the man's eyes. 'Corporal Ranyd came running in. He drew his sword. He should never have done that. Never, and never again.'

*His mind is unhinged.* Galar swung his mount round and rode for the commander.

She had stopped now, and stood in the centre of the compound, a ring of her soldiers facing her but keeping their distance.

He rode through that ring and reined in before her. 'Sir!'

When she looked up at him, it seemed that she struggled to recognize him.

'It's Galar,' he said, dismounting. 'Commander, I was bringing word from Lord Henarald—'

'Too late,' she said, and then lifted the jug. 'He left it. A parting gift. I did not think he could be so . . . understanding. Galar, my husband isn't here, but you are, black skin and all, and you'll have to do.' Abruptly she sat down, worked free the stopper and held the jug up. 'Join me, dear lover. I've been sober since the dawn and so it's been a long day.'

He drew nearer, and then paused and looked across to the soldiers. They watched, silent. One turned away suddenly and fell to her knees, bringing her hands up to cover her face.

'Galar,' said Toras Redone. 'Join me in this drink, will you? Let's celebrate peace.'

'Peace, sir? I bring news of war.'

'Ah, well, I fear it's over. Can you not hear how peaceful we are? No clamour, no blathering voices from fools who can't stop talking, even though they have nothing of worth to say. Have you not ever noticed that? The mouths that run too fast make dead seeds of every word, flung to barren ground in their wake, yet on they rush – and you see in their eyes a kind of desperation, I think, as they long for a gardener's touch, but no talent finds them, and never will, and surely they know it.'

'Commander, what has happened here?'

Her brows lifted. 'Oh, a night of revelry. Ale and wine, but you know how the sleep that follows gives little rest. Why is it, I wonder, that the gods of the world made of every pleasurable habit a poison? These gods, I think, have no understanding of joy. They make feeling good a thing of evil. Don't ask me to worship such miserable shits, Galar Baras. Their paradise is a desert. In such a place we must bless the sun, eschew the begging for water, and call friend the infernal heat. I see those sands, crowded with scorched remnants of souls, but at least they were pure, yes?' The smile she offered then was terrible to behold. 'Join me, sit down at my side, lover. Let us drink to peace.'

620

Uncomprehending, but feeling so bereft he was not even capable of shame or guilt each time she called him *lover*, he stepped close.

Toras Redone rocked back slightly, waving the jug. 'Come all, my friends! One last drink for the Hust Legion! Then we will be done, and we can walk into that desert and greet those sour-faced gods! We'll make of their puritanical misery a virtue, and set upon it the holiest of words! And what word might that be? Why, it is *suffering*.'

She raised the jug to drink.

Someone shouted a warning. Galar Baras drew his sword and the weapon shrieked. The blade lashed out, struck the jug. Clay shards exploded. Wine erupted like blood from a broken skull.

On all sides, the Hust weapons awoke. From every tent, from every scabbard, the swords howled.

Galar Baras staggered beneath the assault, dropping his weapon and clapping hands over his ears. But the sound was inside him, wailing through his bones, clawing through his mind. He felt himself torn free, severed from his body and flung skyward, buffeted by the cries, the ever-rising screams. Through tears, he saw wooden scabbards burst apart at the belts of the surrounding soldiers as the men and women fell or staggered, as they opened their mouths to add to the howls.

*Poison. They're all dead.*

*Toras—*

She was on her hands and knees, gouging up clumps of wine-soaked clay, pushing them into her mouth, coughing, choking – Galar saw himself spinning high above her. He saw how the first of the wagons had reached the descent, but the oxen were collapsing in their yokes, thrashing, legs kicking, and the lead wagon's front wheels cut sharply to one side, and then the wagon toppled, spilling out the wooden crates on the bed.

He saw those crates burst apart, revealing Hust Henarald's last gift to the Hust Legion – chain hauberks of the same iron, and helms and greaves and vambraces. The armour was answering the cry of the weapons in the valley below. The drovers were upon the ground, bleeding from their noses, their ears and eyes.

And still the howling built. It rent the canvas of the tents in the camp, snapped guide ropes. In the distant corrals to the west, the horses broke down the fences and fled in terror.

Galar was a battered kite in the rising storm of those terrible voices.

'*Corporal Ranyd came running in. He drew his sword. He should never have done that.*'

Abruptly, the howling stopped. Galar plunged earthward, and in the moment he struck the ground, blackness engulfed him.

'*Never, and never again.*'

621

# TWENTY

---

ENDEST SILANN LOOKED OLD, AS IF HIS YOUTH HAD BEEN TORN AWAY, revealing something aged with grief. Many times Rise Herat had seen a face stripped back by the onslaught of loss, and each time he wondered if suffering but waited under the skin, shielded by a mask donned in hope, or with that superstitious desperation that imagined a smile to be a worthy shield against the world's travails. These things, worn daily in an array of practised expressions insisting on civility, ever proved poor defenders of the soul, and to be witness to their cracking, their pathetic surrender to a barrage of emotion, was both humbling and terrible.

The young priest had come to his door like a beggar, fingers entwined on his lap and twisting ceaselessly, as if he held newborn snakes in his fists; and in his eyes there was a wretched pleading; but even this was of the kind that expected no largesse. How could one help a beggar who saw no salvation in a coin, or a meal, or a warm bed at night?

Rise had stepped back in invitation and Endest had shuffled past, moving like one afflicted by a host of mysterious ailments, proof against any medicine. He selected a chair near the fire and sat, not yet ready to speak, and studied his writhing hands. And there he remained.

After a time, the historian cleared his throat. 'I have mulled wine, priest.'

Endest shook his head. 'I close my eyes to sleep,' he said, 'and meet the same horrid dream, as if it but awaits me.'

'Ah, that sounds unpleasant. Perhaps a draught to make you sense-less would help.'

He glanced up with red-shot eyes, and then looked down again. 'I have no certainty of this world, historian. This is the dream's legacy, its curse upon my wakefulness – even now I am haunted and so in need of reassurance.'

'Set hand upon stone, priest. Feel wood's familiar grain, or the cool flank of a clay vessel. None of these things are uncertain. But if you would look to us soft creatures who move through this world, then I fear you will find us ephemeral indeed.'

Endest's hands parted and made fists on his lap, the knuckles whitening, but still he would not look up. 'Do you mock me?'

'No. I see the weight of a curse upon you, priest, as surely it is upon us all. You close your eyes and dread the waiting dream. While here I pace in my room, longing to open my eyes and so discover all this to have been a dream. So here we face one another, as if to contest wills.'

Abruptly, Endest began thumping his thighs, swinging down upon them hard with his fists, in growing ferocity.

Rise stepped closer, alarmed. 'Hear me! You are not asleep, friend!'

'How can I know?'

The cry, so filled with despair, silenced the historian.

Endest ceased punching his thighs, his head shifting as if he was looking for something on the floor, and then he spoke. 'I step into the hearth chamber. They have been arguing – terrible words, cutting like knives upon kin and loved ones. But she is not right, the woman dying on the hearthstone. I see her in the robes of a High Priestess. Of course,' he added with a weak, dry laugh, 'they are women who like to spread their legs. They do not fight, and would make of surrender a gift, even if one of little worth for its easy ubiquity.'

Rise studied the young priest, struggling to understand the scene Endest Silann was describing. Yet the historian dared not ask a question, although this prohibition seemed in itself arbitrary. The man before him had no answers.

'I walk up to her, numb, unable to stop myself. She is already wed – though how I know this I do not know – but I see her as Andarist's wife, and a High Priestess, beloved child of Mother Dark. She is not yet dead, and I kneel at her side and take her hand.' He shook his head as if refusing an unspoken objection. 'Sometimes her husband is there, sometimes not. She is badly used and dying. I watch the life leave her, and then I hear Lord Anomander. He is saying something, but none of the words make sense – I do not know if he speaks another language, or if I simply can't hear them distinctly. When I grasp her hand, I am whispering to her, but the voice is not my own – it is Mother Dark's.'

'It is but a dream,' Rise said quietly. 'Do you recall, there was a banquet, Endest, which we attended. Two years ago. It was before Lord Andarist met Enesdia – before he saw her as a woman, I mean. Scara Bandaris was there, as guest to Silchas. The captain was telling a tale of

623

when he was offered hospitality in House Enes on his way down from the north garrison. He had been amused by Lord Jaen's daughter, who walked with the airs of a High Priestess. That was the title Scara gave Enesdia, and this memory has twisted its way into your dream. Nor, Endest Silann, were you there in the time of her dying. No one was but her killers.'

The priest was nodding vigorously. 'So this world insists, and I bitterly bless its every claim to veracity, each time I awaken, each time I stumble into it. Still, what answer will you offer me, historian, when I find her blood mingled with sweat upon the palms of my hands? I have examined myself, stripped naked before a mirror, and I bear no wounds. What correction will you provide to right my senses when I walk the Hall of Portraits and see her image so perfectly painted upon the wall? High Priestess Enesdia. The label is worn, but I can make it out nevertheless.'

'There is no such portrait, priest – no, a moment. Ah, you speak of her grandmother, who was indeed a High Priestess, but before the coming of Night. Her name was Enesthila, and she served as the last High Priestess of the river god, before the cult's reformation. My friend, such is the sorcery of dreams—'

'And the blood?'

'You say that you speak in your dream, but that the voice belongs to Mother Dark. Forgive this blasphemy, but if there is blood on anyone's hands, Endest—'

'No!' The priest was on his feet. 'Have I no will left to me? We beg her for guidance! We plead with her! She has no right!'

'Forgive me, friend. I reveal only ignorance in speaking on matters of faith. Have you spoken to Cedorpul?'

Endest slumped back down in the chair. 'I went to him first. Now he flees the sight of me.'

'But . . . why?'

The young man's face twisted. 'His hands remain clean, his dreams untouched.'

'Do you imagine that he would welcome what leaves you outraged?'

'If she demanded his lifeblood he would offer her his throat, and know delight in the bounty of his gift.'

'But you are not so enamoured of sacrifice.'

'When my every prayer to her goes unanswered . . .' he glared at the historian, 'and do not dare speak to me of trials to test my faith.'

'I would not,' Rise Herat replied. 'As I said, to track down this path is for me a fast unravelling of reason. But three strides along and I am floundering, too many ends in my hands and doubtful of every knot.'

'How is it you can deny a belief in power?'

'It is my thought that without belief, there is no power.'

'What do you win with that, historian?'

Rise shrugged. 'Freedom, I suppose.'

'And what do you lose?'

'Why, everything, of course.'

The priest stared up at him, his expression unreadable.

'You are exhausted, friend. Close your eyes. I will abide.'

'And when you see the blood on my hands?'

'I will take them in my own.'

Endest's eyes filled with tears, but a moment later he closed them and set his head back against the chair's thick padding.

Rise Herat watched sleep take the young priest, and waited for the mask to crack.

*     *     *

They rode through a city subdued, where light struggled and what commerce Orfantal saw spoke in strident voices, with gestures sudden and fretful. The gloom of the alleys that led on to the main thorough-fare bled out like wounds upon the day. He was riding one of Lady Hish Tulla's horses, a placid mare with a broad back and twitching ears, her mane braided yet cut short to raise the knotted stubble into a crest. He wondered if the animal had a name. He wondered if she knew it and held it as her own, and what that name might mean to her, especially when in the company of other horses. And did she know the names given to other horses; and if she did, then what new shape had she found in her world? Was there some inkling that things were not as they had once seemed; that something foreign was now lodged in the animal's head?

He did not know why such questions haunted him. There were all kinds of helplessness, just as there were many kinds of blindness. A horse could carry on its back a hero, or a villain. The beast knew no difference and deserved no stain from the deeds of its master. A child could stumble in the wake of a father who murdered for pleasure, or a mother who murdered from fear, and yet find an entire life spent in the shadow of such knowledge. Questions could not arise without some sense of knowing, and the worst of it was, with that knowing came the realization that many of those questions could never be answered.

Directly ahead rode Gripp Galas, who had returned from the wedding that never happened at Hish Tulla's side, and the lady had been wearing armour and weapons, and there was news of deaths coming down from the north. All of this made the room where Orfantal stayed, and the house that surrounded it, seem small and woeful. Gripp and Hish Tulla had been silent and yet filled with grim news, but Orfantal had been too frightened to ask any questions, and he fled the weight of their presence.

625

But on this day they were escorting him to the Citadel, into the keeping of the Sons and Daughters of Night. He was about to meet Lord Anomander and his brothers: all the great men his mother had talked about, and if there was talk of war, then Orfantal knew that he had nothing to fear in the midst of such heroes.

Lady Hish Tulla rode up alongside Orfantal. Her expression was severe. 'You have known such hardship since leaving House Korlas, Orfantal, and I fear the unpleasantness is not yet at an end.'

Ahead of them, Gripp Galas glanced back, and then looked forward once again. They were approaching the first bridge. That brief moment of attention disturbed Orfantal, though he knew not why.

'There has been news from Abara Delack,' she continued. 'The monastery has been assaulted and burned to the ground. Alas, the violence did not end there. Orfantal, we have word that your grandmother has died, and that House Korlas is no more. I am sorry. Gripp and I disagreed on this, the telling of such terrible news, but I feared you would hear it when in the Citadel, in an instant lacking sensitivity – the place awaiting you is a buzzing wasp nest of gossip, and often words are spoken for the sole purpose of witnessing their sting.'

Orfantal hunched over in the saddle, fighting a sudden chill. 'This city,' he said, 'is so dark.'

'More so in the Citadel,' Lady Hish Tulla said. 'Such is the flavour of Mother Dark's power. At the very least, Orfantal, you will soon lose your fear of the dark, and in that absence of light you will find that you see all there is that needs seeing.'

'Will my skin turn black?'

'It will, unless you choose the ways of the Deniers, I suppose.'

'I would have the cast of Lord Anomander,' he said.

'Then Night shall find you, Orfantal.'

'At House Korlas, milady, did everyone die? I had a friend there, a boy who worked with the horses.'

She studied him, and did not immediately reply.

They rode out across the broad bridge, the clash of the hoofs on the cobbles beneath them suddenly sounding hollow. Orfantal could smell the river, rising up dank and vaguely foul. It made him think of brooding gods.

'I do not know,' Hish Tulla said. 'The fire left very few remains.'

'Well, he used to be my friend, but then that went away. I am glad Mother wasn't there, though.'

'Orfantal, grief is a difficult thing, and you have already been through a lot. Be patient with yourself. There is a substance to living, and sadness is woven through it.'

'Are you sad, milady?'

'You will find a balance. Whence comes the answer to sadness few

626

can predict, but it does come, in time, and you will learn to appreciate pleasure for the gift that it is. What you must never expect, Orfantal, is joy unending, because it does not exist. Too many strive for the unachievable, and this pursuit consumes them. They rush frantic and desperate and so reveal weakness in the face of sadness. More than weakness, in fact. It is in truth a kind of cowardice, that which espouses an evasive disposition as if it were a virtue. But this bluster is frail work.' Then she sighed. 'I am too complex, I fear, and make of advice things insubstantial.'

Orfantal shook his head. 'I am no stranger to feeling sad, milady. Tonight I will weep for Wreneck, and for the horse I killed.'

They had crossed a short span and now ascended the lesser bridge over the Citadel's moat. At Orfantal's confession, Gripp Galas reined in and turned his horse to block the way.

'That beast was on its last legs,' he said.

'You did not see its last struggles, sir,' Orfantal replied.

'True, I did not. But if you had not sacrificed your mount in the manner you did, you would not be here now.'

Orfantal nodded. 'My spirit would be free, and back on the grounds of House Korlas, and it would play in the ruins with the ghost of Wreneck, from before he decided to not like me any more. I would have a friend again, and that horse would be alive now, with a few memories of the boy it carried, a boy who was not cruel to it.'

Gripp looked down, seemed to study the cobbles for a long moment, and then he sighed and swung his mount round.

They continued on, beneath the arch of the gatehouse, watched by black-skinned Houseblades in the livery of House Purake.

Lady Hish Tulla spoke. 'Take him inside, Gripp. I will meet you later in the Grand Hall.'

'Milady?'

'Go on, Gripp. Give me a few moments, I beg you.'

The old man nodded. 'Come along, hostage, and I will see you home.'

*       *       *

Hish Tulla watched them ride across the courtyard, still fighting the sob that threatened to tear loose from deep inside her. A boy's innocent words had left her broken. The flimsy frame of her self-control, so hastily resurrected in the wake of her comforting embrace of Lord Andarist, weathering his grief on their knees at the foot of the hearthstone, had collapsed once again.

By day's end she would be leading her company of Houseblades back to her keep. With the shattering of traditions, she was no longer confident that Sukul Ankhadu was safe, although she knew enough of Castellan Rancept's talents to hope he could mitigate any possible threat, at least for the moment. But this decision strained her resolve from another direction now, one unexpected and almost unbearably precious. She thought of the man accompanying Orfantal into the Citadel, and felt once again a quickening of her breath.

She was not as old as her experience reputed, while Gripp Galas had seen a century, if not more. There would be amusement and not a little scorn behind their backs, once it became known that Lady Hish Tulla, for so long believed to be unattainable, had given her love to Lord Anomander's manservant. On better days, in times past, she would be proof against their mockery, but there was a new frailty in her now, exposed and raw.

She had believed herself settled into bitter resolution, making peace with what she imagined to be a life spent in solitude, offering up a straight line in her march through all the days and the nights to come. Even the prospect of war, detestable as it was, had voiced to her a bold welcome, if by fighting she could find reason to live, and if by righteous defence of worthy things she could give meaning to that stern march, no matter how long or how short her life's trek.

In the Citadel ahead, with its seething tumult of troubled spirits, and its host of opinions and arguments clothed in flesh and heated expressions, she would find the fate of her future. Drawing a deep, settling breath, she nudged her mount forward once again.

A groom rushed up to take her horse and she dismounted, regretting that she had elected to leave her armour behind, to await her departure from the city. But neither chain nor iron scale could serve to defend her against the ridicule to come, once her surrender became known, and bright eyes settled upon Gripp Galas, limping at her side. She imagined the disdain from her fellow highborn, and perhaps something of perturbation in her breaking with the ranks of nobility; and without doubt many would see her as fallen from the rung, divested of propriety. Among others, there would be contempt for Gripp Galas, as he would be seen as overreaching, even grasping, betraying some brazen lust for elevation. A clamour awaited them both, with the shunning by old friends and kin to make a siege of the isolation awaiting them.

Yet, for all of that, Hish Tulla vowed a refusal of such indulgences; she would weather this storm, because, at last, she was no longer alone.

With luck, Orfantal would find a new friend, even here in the Citadel, and so cease his longing for death. Still, she wondered at this stable boy, this Wreneck, and what had happened to make him turn away from Orfantal. *Oh, woman, turn sharp to observe your own thoughts, in what will come of your love for Gripp Galas. The boy voiced no pain at the death of his grandmother. You can well guess who drove the knife into that friendship.*

*Wreneck, if your spirit now haunts House Korlas, pray you find a stern regard when meeting the eyes of Nerys Drukorlat. In death you are made equal, and so, dear boy, you are at last free of her. Speak to her then, of every horror her fear inflicted, upon living and dead.*

*Tell her her grandson does not mourn her passing.*

∗     ∗     ∗

A dozen spacious rooms along the south side of the Citadel were now the demesne of Lord Anomander and his brothers. The chambers were poorly lit, and upon the walls hung the oldest of the tapestries, many dating from the founding age of Kharkanas. Time had faded the scenes to add mystery to their obscurity, and though Emral Lanear more than once leaned close in an effort to make out what she was seeing on her way to Lord Anomander's quarters, the High Priestess was left with a strange disquiet, as if the past was selfish with its secrets, and would make of the unknown something malign and threatening.

The end of beauty was never so coy. Each morning, every sign of ageing shouted its details to her unblinking regard in the mirror. She was left with no hope of fading into frayed threads, and as she walked past this succession of mocking tapestries she longed to slip into their insubstantial, colourless worlds, and so become a creature frozen and forgotten. In that world she need never reach her destination; nor open her mouth to speak. Most of all, she would be but one more figure in those pallid scenes who never had to explain themselves, to anyone.

*See how I envy the past, and long for all that it so willingly surrendered in its retreat from the present. These strident defences and pathetic justifications will fall to silence. Each breath is left half drawn. A word begun remains unfinished.* The past wore recrimination with indifference. Welcoming dissolution, it looked upon every cause with blank eyes, and cared not who stirred the dust. It was a conceit to imagine that the past spoke anything at all, not to the present, nor to the unknown future. By its very nature, it was turned away from both.

She found Lord Anomander seated in a deep, high-backed chair, legs stretched out as if he but took his leisure, unmindful of the chaos into which the world was descending. His brother, Silchas, paced along the far wall, passing in front of three floor-to-ceiling tapestries with scenes too worn to discern. The white-skinned man's expression was troubled. The glance he shot at the High Priestess was fraught.

Emral stood before Lord Anomander, although he'd yet to lift his gaze from the floor. 'First Son,' she said, 'Mother Dark will speak with you now.'

'That is kind of her,' Anomander replied.

Silchas made a sound of frustration. 'Still he sits like a thing carved from stone. Andarist is gone from us. Our brother walks the

629

burning forest, and in that infernal realm waits no salvation. But still Anomander sits, offering nothing.'

'Lord Silchas,' asked Emral, 'do you fear that Andarist will take his own life?'

'No, High Priestess. His guilt seeks no quick end. It is said ash makes fertile soil and I wager he has sown his seeds and now tends a burgeoning bounty. It will make a bitter harvest indeed, but he means to grow fat on it.'

'Everyone seeks an answer to the crimes committed,' Emral said. 'Everyone speaks of war but no army assembles.'

'We await the Hust Legion,' said Silchas, still pacing. 'In the meantime my hands are worn bloody beating against my brother's obstinacy, and with each stride I take, this room seems smaller, and with it the Citadel and indeed, all of Kharkanas. In my mind's eye, High Priestess, even Kurald Galain huddles in a shallow embrace.'

'We must find our resilience,' she replied.

Anomander grunted, and then said, 'You will search an eternity for that, High Priestess, in the smoke of darkness.' Finally he looked up at her, his eyes hooded. 'She will see me now? Does she finally offer the bones of this faith, and if so, what substance has she employed in the fashioning? Will this frame show us iron or flimsy reeds? And what of the flesh you offer in raiment, Emral Lanear? For ever soft and for ever yielding to suit the cushions and silks of your beds, but in an act stripped of love we are all diminished.'

She flinched. 'I will confess, Lord, we have made of sensation something sordid.'

'Mother Dark is free with her indulgences,' Anomander replied, carelessly waving a hand. 'Forgive me, High Priestess. In every age there comes a time when all subtlety vanishes, all veils are torn aside, and men and women will speak brazen truths. By such bold proclamations we find ourselves divided, with the span between us growing daily.'

'You describe civil war in its crux,' growled Silchas. 'It is well upon us, brother. But the time for philosophy is past; if indeed one could ever claim its worth in any time. If your clear eye hangs on every current, you become blind to the river's deadly rush. Have done with the analysis, Anomander, and draw out this ill-named but righteous sword.'

'By so doing, Silchas, I sever what remains between me and Andarist.'

'Then find him and make this right!'

'He will insist on his grief, Silchas, while I hold to vengeance. We have each made our proclamation, and see this yawning span grow between us. High Priestess, I asked for your forgiveness and I am humble in that pleading. It seems we are all trapped in indulgences for the moment. Andarist and his guilt, Silchas and his impatience, and me . . . well . . . she will see me now, you said?'

Emral studied the First Son. 'Of course you are forgiven, Lord Anomander. The very air we breathe is distraught. Yes, she will see you now.'

'I should be pleased,' Anomander said, his frowning gaze once more upon the floor beyond his boots. 'I should rise up now and with haste renew our acquaintance, and hold to the expectation of guidance from our goddess. So what holds me here, except the anticipation of yet more frustration, as she offers up the insubstantial if only to observe my floundering, and how am I to read her expression? Must I suffer again her remoteness, or will it be a look enlivened by my misery? This goddess of ours blunts my fury when she refuses to name her enemy.'

Silchas snorted. 'Name them renegades and be done with it! Leave Urusander to writhe on the gibbet of suspicion, and let us ride to take down the slayers of Jaen and Enesdia!'

'She forbids me to draw this sword in her name, Silchas.'

'Then draw it in the name of your brother!'

Anomander met his brother's eyes, brows lifting. 'In the name of my brother or in the name of his grief?'

'See the two as one, Anomander, and give it a vengeful edge.'

'The sentiments but glare at one another—'

'Only one does so, brother. Grief but weeps.'

Anomander looked away. 'That surrender I cannot afford.'

The breath hissed from Silchas. 'See the room grow smaller, and see the man who will not move. High Priestess, do report our weakness to Mother Dark. Then return to us with her answer.'

Emral shook her head. 'I cannot, Lord Silchas. She takes audience with the Azathanai, Grizzin Farl. She asks that the First Son join them.'

There was a sound from the outer room, and a moment later Gripp Galas stepped through the open doorway. He bowed before Anomander. 'Milord, forgive this interruption—'

'You are a welcome sight,' Anomander replied.

'Milord, I have with me the child Orfantal, and would present him to you.'

The First Son rose. 'This pleases me. Do bring him in, Gripp.'

The old man half turned and gestured.

Emral watched the boy edge into view, hesitating upon the threshold to the chamber.

'Orfantal,' said Anomander. 'You are most welcome. I am informed that you have made of your journey to Kharkanas an adventure worthy of a bard's song, perhaps even a poem or two. Please enter and tell us about yourself.'

When the boy's dark eyes touched briefly on Emral, she smiled in answer.

Orfantal stepped into the room. 'Thank you, milord. Of me there is little worth saying. I am told that I am ill-named. I am told that my father was a hero in the wars, who died of his wounds, but I never saw him. My grandmother is now dead, burned to ashes in House Korlas. If she had not sent me here after sending away my mother, I would have died in the fire. I see nothing in me worth a poem, and nothing in my life worth singing about. But I have longed to meet you all.'

No one spoke.

Then Silchas stepped forth and offered his hand. 'Orfantal,' he said, 'I believe there is another hostage in the Citadel. A girl, perhaps a year or two younger than you. She is often found in the company of the priests, or the court historian. Shall we go and find her? By this means I can also show you more of your new home.'

Orfantal took the man's hand. 'Thank you, milord. I heard you had white skin, but I did not think it would be as white as it is. Upon my grandfather's scabbard there is ivory, and your skin is just like that.'

'Lacking the polish, however,' Silchas said with a smile, 'though surely just as worn.' He led Orfantal back to the doorway, pausing for a final glance back at his brother. 'Anomander, do not make her wait too long.'

When they had left, Gripp Galas cleared his throat. 'My pardon, milord. The boy has yet to find somewhere to stand.'

'That is not cut out from under him, yes,' Anomander said. 'Pray he finds firm footing here, and if so, I will envy him.'

Gripp Galas hesitated, and then said, 'Milord?'

'Yes?'

'If you have no further need of me—'

'Abyss take it, friend, I see no end to my need for you.'

Emral saw the old man's eyes tighten, as if his master's words were somehow cause for pain, but he nodded and said, 'As ever, milord, I am at your disposal.'

'Prepare our horses, Gripp. We shall depart Kharkanas before the day is done.'

'Very good, milord.'

Anomander turned to Emral. 'High Priestess, I would welcome your company on my way to the Chamber of Night.'

'Of course,' she replied.

*       *       *

Orfantal felt that he had made a fool of himself. He walked with his hand swallowed up in Silchas's grip, and was already lost in the maze of corridors and hallways. At least those rushing people they came upon in their journey were quick to step aside, so none of the rough jostling that had afflicted him and Gripp Galas earlier occurred this time. He berated himself for his thoughtless words, the first he had spoken to Lord Anomander. With luck, the First Son would soon forget the introduction had ever happened.

He vowed that he would do better next time, and find the words to make Lord Anomander understand the pledge of service he intended. In time, he sought to become as necessary to the First Son as, it seemed, was Gripp Galas. It had surprised him to see the high regard that had been shown the old man, and he realized that he had been careless in his opinion of Gripp.

For all that, he reminded himself that Gripp was a murderer, cold-blooded and not above treachery. He still remembered that soldier's look on his face when the old man stabbed him in the back. In that face there had been shock, and disappointment, as if to ask the world why, with all its rules, it could do no better than this. It was a look Orfantal understood. In his games of war he had fallen to a thousand knives in the back a thousand times, and though he had never held up a mirror to gauge his expression at any of those fateful moments, he suspected that he would have looked no different from that poor soldier.

He heard the scrape of claws on the tiles behind him, and a moment later a skinny dog pushed up against his legs. Startled, he paused, and Silchas turned at the same moment.

The dog's mangled tail was wagging fiercely as the animal circled in front of Orfantal.

Silchas said, 'Well, already you've made a friend, hostage. This dog is from Lady Hish Tulla's household. For some unknown reason, it came in the company of an Azathanai.'

They continued on, with the dog now close by Orfantal's side.

'If such beasts could tell their stories,' Silchas mused, 'what do you imagine they might say?'

Orfantal thought of the horse he had killed. 'I think, milord, they would just ask us to leave them alone.'

'I see nothing of that sentiment in this animal.'

'Milord, what if what we see as happiness is in truth begging us not to hurt them?'

'A dreadful thought, Orfantal.'

The boy nodded agreement. It was a dreadful thought.

*       *       *

Lady Hish watched Gripp Galas approach. The Grand Hall was crowded with servants, with messengers bearing frantic questions and few answers, with Houseblades gathered in clumps like wolves circling an uncertain prey, and priests and priestesses passing to and fro as if desperate to find something to do. She stood near the first of the columns lining a wall, struggling to make sense of the expression on the face of the man she loved.

She spoke the moment he joined her, 'He demands yet one more task from you? Are we to be delayed then?'

'Beloved,' Gripp said, unable to meet her eyes, 'I must remain at his side. We are to ride this day. I cannot join you, not yet.'

'He has refused us?'

'I am sorry.'

'Where is he now?'

'Summoned into the presence of Mother Dark. I am to meet him at the gate, with our horses prepared.'

'I will join you in that task.'

She saw his eyes narrow slightly on her, but she was in no mood to offer explanation.

*          *          *

The First Son walked in silence, but Emral could hear the soft, muted beat of his sword's scabbard against his leg with every stride. The weapon's presence was already well known, not just in the Citadel, but in all Kharkanas, and she had heard tales twisting the truth of the sword's origins. Many now spoke as if Lord Anomander had forged the weapon with his own hands, and that the failure to give it a name was proof of the First Son's chronic indecision.

This latter argument was the conjuring of the worst of the court's inhabitants, although in nature such people were not exclusive to the Citadel. Bearing the wounds of a thousand small bites, she had once voiced this complaint to the historian and he had but nodded, and spoken of not just this time and place, but of countless others. *'It is the habit of the petty-minded to derogate the achievements and status of those who, by any measure, are their superiors. High Priestess, they are the wild dogs in the forest, ever ready for a turned back, but quick to yip and flee when the prey shows its fangs.'*

She had considered the analogy for a moment, and then had replied, *'When enough such dogs have gathered, historian, they may not flee the bearded beast, and instead show fangs of their own. In any case, any opinion on superiority is subject to challenge.'*

*'I mean not such things as titles, or wealth, or even power, when I speak of superiority, High Priestess. I refer to something more ephemeral. To find a truly superior person, follow the dogs. Or, better still, follow the blood trail. No other gauge is necessary but to observe the viciousness of the eager beasts and see for yourself the beleaguered foe.'*

Was the man at her side thus hounded? There was little doubt of that. And was there not something in the assertion that the forging of that weapon was not yet complete? Its edge was well honed to be sure, and the blade bore a fine polish. But it was not yet Anomander's own, no matter how forceful Hust Henarald's insistence that the weapon was fit for the hand of but one man.

They reached the door and Emral stepped back.

But Anomander shook his head. 'I request your presence within, High Priestess.'

'First Son, I believe it was Mother Dark's wish—'

'We will speak of faith, High Priestess. I am informed that High Priestess Syntara is now the centre of a cult that directly opposes that of Mother Dark. With her under the protection of Lord Urusander, the matter is both religious and political.'

She glanced away. 'I was not aware of this development, First Son.' A moment later she drew a deep breath and said, 'But I am not surprised. Not with respect to Syntara's ambitions. Still, Urusander's role in this confuses me.'

'You are not alone in that.'

She opened the door and together they strode into the Chamber of Night.

The darkness hid nothing. Mother Dark was seated on the throne. Facing her from a few paces away but now stepping to one side was the Azathanai, Grizzin Farl, who bowed to both Anomander and Emral, offering them a faint smile.

Lord Anomander wasted no time. 'Azathanai, I assure you that I have no unreasoning aversion to foreign advisers in this court. Still, I wonder at what of value you can offer us, since we are here to discuss the measures we must take in order to keep our realm from tearing itself apart. The legacy of the Azathanai in this matter is no less dubious than if a Jaghut stood in your place.'

'With regret, First Son,' said Grizzin Farl, 'I agree with you. Although a Jaghut might prove wiser than me and could I find one nearby to stand in these worn moccasins, why, I would give the poor creature good cause to rail at my presumption.'

'Then what keeps you here?' Anomander asked.

'By title I am known as the Protector, but this is no welcome aspect. I appear where I am most needed, yet in hope most distant. My attendance alone is a sour comment on your state of affairs, alas.'

There was a challenge to these words, but Anomander simply tilted his head, as if studying the Azathanai in a new light. 'We found you tending Kadaspala. Even then, it seems, you could have made shackles of your hands to close on his wrists, and so keep him from his terrible self-mutilation. Instead, you came too late.'

'This is so, First Son.'

'Do you stand here before us, then, to announce a threshold already crossed?'

Emral could see how Mother Dark looked between the two men, and there was, at last, alarm in her eyes.

Grizzin Farl bowed. 'You have the truth of me,' he said.

'Mother Dark,' said Anomander, 'did you understand this?'

'No,' she replied. 'It seems that I asked the wrong questions of our guest. Confusion attended me, First Son, with misleading thoughts of the last Azathanai to stand before me.'

'Of whom we know nothing,' Anomander said. 'Did this T'riss speak for the river god? Did you bargain with that rival and so win from it the sacrifice of a thousand souls?'

'You insult us both,' Mother Dark snapped. 'We bargained peace between us.'

'And what manner the currency of this exchange?'

'Nothing of substance.'

'Then, what manner this peace? Shall I describe it? The forest to the north might burn still, but the huts are surely silent. By that one might assert the blessing of peace, of a sort.'

'We did not invite death between us!'

Emral saw how the goddess trembled with her rage, but Anomander seemed unaffected. 'Grizzin Farl, what do you know of this T'riss?'

'I know of no Azathanai by that name, First Son.'

'Do you have her description?'

Grizzin Farl shrugged. 'That signifies nothing. If I so desired, I could hover before you as a bird, or perhaps a butterfly.' Then he frowned. 'But you name her born of the Vitr. Two Azathanai set out to explore the mystery of that caustic sea.' He shrugged. 'Perhaps it is one of them.'

'And the power she unveiled tells you nothing either?'

'Only that it was uncommonly careless, and so not like an Azathanai at all. There are proscriptions against such blatant interference.'

'Why?'

'It is unhealthy for any Azathanai to invite the resentment of other Azathanai.'

'And this the one named T'riss has done?'

'So it seems, First Son.'

'You are rather passive in your resentment, Grizzin Farl.'

'I am not the one imposed upon, as the Tiste do not fall under my influence.'

Emral gasped as the implications of that comment settled in her mind. She looked to Mother Dark and was stunned to see no expression of surprise in her features.

Anomander stood like a man nailed to a wall, although nothing but empty air surrounded him. All at once, Emral felt her heart wrench for the First Son. He now stared fixedly at Mother Dark. 'At last,' he said,

'I find the bitter truth to my title, Mother. A son you would have, but one swaddled and helpless, thinking only of your tit's sweet milk.'

'I cannot hasten your growth, First Son, by any other means.'

'Yet you recoil at my sour breath.'

'Only the hurtful words it carries.'

'Are you then an Azathanai, Mother, deceitfully attired in the body of a Tiste woman we once all knew?'

'I am that woman,' she replied, 'and no other.'

'Then where stands your guardian, or has it made its flesh darkness itself?'

'These questions are of no value,' Mother Dark said. 'I have summoned you, First Son, to send you to Lord Urusander. We will have the truth of his motives.' She paused and then said, 'Is this not what you wished?'

'I will indeed march on Urusander,' Anomander answered. 'With the arrival of the Hust Legion.'

'Do not wait for them,' she said. 'Ride to him now, beloved son. Meet with him.'

'To stand within reach of him, Mother, I would need to wear chains with the weight of mountains, to keep my hands from the sword at my side. But then, would it be better if I simply disarmed myself outside his command tent, knelt and offered him the back of my neck?'

'I do not believe he is in any way responsible for the murders of Lord Jaen and his daughter. Look him in the eye as he tells you the same, and together you may turn your ire upon the true slayers.'

'Renegades from the disbanded units? Or would you have me offer up the pathetic possibility of Deniers with noble blood on their hands?'

'It seems that I must do nothing but weather your scorn. Perhaps this is every mother's lament.'

Anomander turned away, 'My scorn, Mother, is not yet awakened. Indeed, you see before you a sleeping man, still lost to the night and troubling dreams. If I twitch, it but signals my helplessness. If I voice a moan, it is a sound empty of meaning. No brush of fingertips will prod me awake, and so I yearn for the knife's sharp jab. The only question that remains is: who will wield that knife?'

'If you imagine Urusander to be so treacherous,' said Mother Dark, 'then we are already lost.'

'He harbours Syntara,' said Anomander. 'A new cult rises in Neret Sorr. It faces you as a rising sun challenges the night. And so I wonder, Mother, how many gauntlets do you need thrown down?'

'Go to him, First Son.'

'There is no need,' Anomander replied. 'He prepares to march on Kharkanas. We need but await his knock on the wood of the Citadel gates.' He moved to the door. Before reaching for the latch, he glanced back at Mother Dark. 'I have listened to your counsel, Mother. But what I do now is in defence of Kharkanas.'

The door closed quietly behind the First Son. Emral thought to follow but something held her back. She remained facing Mother Dark, but could think of nothing to say.

Grizzin Farl sighed. 'My dear,' he said, 'your adopted son is a formidable man.'

'If I had another path, less painful for him, I would choose it.'

'For all of you, I would think.'

But she shook her head. 'I am prepared to bear what will come.'

'You invite a lonely existence,' Grizzin said, with sorrow in his eyes as he regarded Mother Dark.

All at once, to Emral's eyes, it seemed that Mother Dark transformed into something more solid than stone, and then just as quickly she seemed to fade, until she was almost insubstantial. 'Azathanai, with what you have told me of the events taking place to the west . . . by solitude alone can I ensure a long existence, and a role in all that is to come.' Her gaze shifted from Grizzin Farl and settled upon Emral. 'High Priestess, make of your worship an unflinching recognition of the unknown, and, indeed, the unknowable. By devotion and acceptance of mystery, the chaos that haunts us all is made calm, until the sea itself becomes a mirror content with a placid reflection.'

Emral glanced at the Azathanai, and then returned her attention to Mother Dark. 'I see no source of strength, Mother, in such surrender.'

'It opposes our nature, yes. Do you know why I did not refuse the lusts of the priestesses? In that moment of release, time itself is abandoned, and in its place even the mortal body seems as expansive as the universe. In that moment, Emral, we find utter surrender, and in that surrender a state of bliss.'

Emral shook her head. 'Until the flesh returns, with its aches and a deep heaviness inside. The bliss you describe, Mother, cannot be sustained. And if somehow it could, why, we would soon wear visages of madness, one and all.'

'It was, daughter, a flawed dispensation.'

'And now we are to embrace not flesh, but empty contemplation? I fear the void's kiss will not seem as sweet.'

Mother Dark leaned her head back, as if exhausted. 'I will,' she said in a low mutter, 'let you know.'

\*　　　\*　　　\*

Orfantal stood in the centre of the room, looking round. 'This is mine?' he asked.

Silchas nodded.

There were scrolls upon shelves, and books bearing brightly coloured illustrations. At the foot of the bed was an ancient trunk and it was filled with toy soldiers, some made from onyx and others from ivory. Upon one wall, in a horizontal rack of blackwood, rested three practice swords, a buckler and, upon a peg beside them, a boiled leather vest. On the floor beneath it was a helmet with a cage-like visor to protect the eyes. Three lanterns burned bright and the light was harsh to Orfantal's eyes, used as he was to a lone candle to fight the shadows of his room back in House Korlas.

He thought of that room again, and tried to imagine it blackened by smoke, the stone walls cracked, the bed in which he had slept nothing but a heap of ashes. Every thought of his past now came to him with a stench of burning, and the faint echo of screams.

'Are you unwell?'

Orfantal shook his head.

The dog was still with them and now, having completed its exploratory circuit of the chamber, went to lie down beside a thickly padded chair in one corner. In moments, it was fast asleep, legs twitching.

There came a knock upon the door and a moment later a round-faced young man entered, dressed in stained robes. 'Lord Silchas, I received your message. Ah, here then is young Orfantal, and already settled in. Excellent. Are you hungry? Thirsty? The first task is to show you the dining hall – not the one in the main chamber, but the lesser one where by weight of masonry alone we are not intimidated. Now then—'

'A moment,' interrupted Silchas. He turned to Orfantal. 'I will take my leave now,' he said. 'As you can see, I yield to a good keeper. You are comfortable with this?'

Orfantal nodded. 'Thank you, Lord Silchas.'

'Cedorpul,' said Silchas, 'will it be you in charge of Orfantal?'

'The historian has elected for himself that privilege, milord, and will be here shortly.'

'Oh dear,' Silchas said, smiling down at Orfantal. 'Expect an education in confusion, hostage, but one that I am sure will achieve for you admirable resilience against the eternal chaos afflicting the Citadel.'

Orfantal smiled without quite understanding what the Lord meant, and then he went to the trunk to examine the toy soldiers.

Silchas grunted behind him and said, 'I foresee an impressive knowledge of historical battles to come.'

'Glory belongs to every boy's dreams,' said Cedorpul. 'I am sure, however, that the historian will offer his share of unheeded wisdom in such matters.'

'By this we ever trek familiar paths,' said Silchas. 'Goodbye, then, Orfantal.'

'Goodbye, milord.'

After he had left, Cedorpul cleared his throat. 'Now then, the dining room. I will not be so negligent as to let you starve. Also, I expect, given the bell that just sounded, that your fellow hostage, Legyl Behust, is even now haranguing the servers.'

With a longing glance at the soldiers in the trunk, Orfantal straightened and followed Cedorpul out of the room. Moments later the dog joined them, tail wagging and tongue lolling.

Glancing down at it, Cedorpul made a disgusted sound. 'Worms. We'll have to do something about that, I think.'

*     *     *

In the absence of light and in the death of every colour, draining his imagination and the scenes it desperately conjured, Kadaspala sat alone in the room he had been given. It was not a large room. With hands groping and feet shuffling he had explored its confines, and in his mind he painted its details in shades of black and grey: the cot where he lay down at night, which creaked with his restless turning, the rope netting of its mattress stretched and sagging beneath him; the quaint writing desk with its angled surface, ink wells and footpad; the water closet with its narrow, flimsy door and the latch that rattled loose in its fittings; the long side table that ran the length of one wall, where rested jugs and goblets of copper that stung the tongue harsher than the wine filling his mouth; the wardrobe with its weathered surface. They seemed, one and all, the leavings of a past life, and he thought of this room as a tomb, artfully arrayed to honour the memory of living, but shrouded in eternal darkness, in air that tasted dead.

There were few memories of the journey down to Kharkanas. They had taken his knife, and since leaving him here, after a cadre of healers arrived to fret and sigh, his only visitors were servants coming with food and later departing with the servings barely touched. One, a young woman by her voice, had offered to bathe him, and he had laughed at that, too empty to regret the cruelty of the sound, and the fleeing pad of her feet to the door had simply made him laugh all the harder.

In a world without tears, an artist was left with nothing to do and no purpose to hold on to. Anguish was a satisfying torment to feed creative impulses, but he felt no anguish. Longing that spoke no known language offered up an endless palette, but he longed for nothing. Wonder made the brush tremble, but all wonder was dead within him. He had been betrayed by every talent sewn into his sinews, scratched into his bones, and now that he had severed the threads to vision, he shared this darkness with lifeless gods, and this room was indeed a tomb, as befitted its occupant.

He sat upon the cot, painting the air with one finger, brushing lines of black knotted with touches of grey to give shape to the creaking of the ropes under him. There was little talent in perfect rendition. Setting banal reality upon a board or canvas made sordid the modest virtue of craft; as if perfect brush-strokes and obsessive detail could exist as something beyond technical prowess, and could in fact announce profundity. He knew otherwise and it was this contempt that sat like swirling ripples marking the surface of his dissolution, turgid but hinting of life.

In the world he had left behind, an artist needed to tie contempt down and make the bindings tight, and take damp cloth to where it bled through. To let it loose was to attack both artist and audience, and he had neither the strength nor the will for such a thing: even the sentiment left him exhausted.

He had descended into madness, there in the chamber of the house his memory dared not revisit. He was not yet certain that it had departed. Blindness made a mystery of everything just out of reach. He had decided to wait, and upon the only canvas left to him paint sounds upon the ephemeral walls of this crypt: the creaks and faint echoes; the muted slap from people passing by the door, those footsteps so urgent and so pathetic; the dull repetition of his own breath and the sullen thump of his heart; the languid surge and ebb of the blood in his veins.

All in shades of black and grey, upon the insubstantial but exquisitely absolute walls of his blindness.

Once he was done, perfectly rendering this chamber, he would reach outside, to wander the corridors, recording everything. *There is a new history coming, my friends. History as seen by a blind man. I will find Rise Herat, who gives us his delicious version as told by a man who says nothing. I will find Gallan, who sings unheard and walks unseen by any. Together, we will set out to find our audience, who heeds us not. And by this, we perfect the world and raise for posterity every grand monument to stupidity.*

*I see towers and spires. I see bold bridges and the palaces of the privileged. I see forests where the highborn hunt, and where poachers are hanged by their necks beneath trees. I see jewels and stacked coins inside guarded fortresses and upon the walls stand earnest orators, crying down the paucity of all. I see their lies catch up to them, in flames and vengeance. I see a future laden with ash and soot-coated pools, and gibbets groaning. And all that I see, I will paint.*

*And all the historian would not say, keeps him mute.*

*And the weeping poet will walk away, to hide his absence of tears.*

*And everything ends.*

He heard himself laugh, a low cackling sound, and quickly etched its wavy, juddering lines with his finger. The streaks hung there in the darkness, slowly fading as the echoes dwindled.

*The blind man paints history. The voiceless historian mimes the tale. The poet dispenses with music, dancing in discord. There is no rhythm to these brush-strokes. There is no beginning and no end to this tale. There is no beauty in the song.*

*And this is how it is.*

*My friends, this is how it is.*

*       *       *

At the Citadel gate Hish Tulla and Gripp Galas found three of Anomander's officers awaiting their lord. Kellaras, Dathenar and Prazek were girded as for battle, and as Gripp went to collect Anomander's horse from the stables Hish Tulla waited a few paces away from the Houseblades.

There was no conversation under way. Of the three, only Kellaras bore the ebon hues that were a legacy of his time in the Chamber of Night, and it seemed that this had made a tension among the three, as if loyalty itself was perhaps no thicker than skin.

Gripp returned with Anomander's mount and his own. 'Both had been left saddled,' he said to her in explanation.

'Distress is a flavour,' Hish said, 'that none welcome but none can avoid.'

At her comment, Dathenar grunted in amusement. 'Wail for the world's end, milady, when even the grooms lose sleep.' He gestured grandly. 'Observe our befuddled state in this courtyard, and imagine the same throughout Kurald Galain. I have had many thoughts on civil war in the times leading to this, but not once did I imagine it so shrouded in confusion.'

'It is the failure of certainty that has you reaching for the sword at your side,' Hish replied. 'We all strike out from a place of fear.'

Before Dathenar could answer, Lord Anomander appeared in the doorway of the Citadel and strode towards them, unconsciously cleaving a path through the disordered ranks in the compound. Arriving, he reached for the reins of his horse.

'Captains,' he said, addressing his Houseblades, 'ride now, south to the Hust Legion. Accompany it on its march to Kharkanas. Request of Commander Toras Redone to make encampment upon the north side of the city, and see to the Legion's provisioning.'

Hish watched as the three men mounted up. They departed without another word.

'Now, Gripp—'

'I wish a word with you,' Hish cut in.

Anomander hesitated, and then sighed. 'Very well. I intend no rudeness, Lady Hish, but I seek to find Andarist, and so cannot measure the length of my absence from Kharkanas. This invites impatience.'

'And the fear of being alone, too, it seems, Lord Anomander.'

He frowned.

'Gripp spoke to you of his desire to be with me, and you refused him. I have never asked anything from you, Lord Anomander, until this moment. Here I stand, pleading. Has he not done enough for you? Has he not given enough of his life in your service?'

Gripp stepped towards her, his face wretched. 'My love—'

But both Anomander and Hish held up a staying hand.

'Lady Hish,' said the First Son, 'Gripp Galas made no such request of me.'

Hish swung on Gripp. 'Is this true? Did you fail in this one request of your master?'

'Forgive me,' the man said, bowing his head. 'My lord said that his need for me was pressing.'

'I did,' Anomander said. 'But I see now they were careless words. Lady Hish, your pardon. That you are brought to this, by my insensitivity, shames me. You ask for dispensation, but I ask that you withdraw your request.'

Hish stared, struck speechless.

Then Anomander turned to Gripp Galas. 'Old friend, long have you served me, with valour and with honour. As my most trusted servant I have set my weight upon you, and not once heard from you a word of complaint. You have dressed my wounds on the field of battle. You have mended the damage of my clumsy youth. Did you truly believe that now, on this fraught day, I would once more draw tight this leash? We are all weakened by distress, and indeed it seems every tender emotion lies exposed and trembling to a forest of knives. Gripp Galas, old friend, your service to me ends here and it ends now. You have won the heart of a woman who in all things is nothing less than breathtaking. If love needs permission, I give it. If your future with Lady Hish can be served by any sacrifice within my ability, I give it.' He set his gaze upon Hish Tulla. 'Nothing need be asked and nothing need be surrendered by you, my lady. On this, of all days, I will see love made right.' He swung into the saddle. 'Go well, my friends. We are done here.'

As he rode out through the gate, Gripp Galas stared after his ex-master. He reached out one hand to his side, groping.

Hish stepped close and clasped that hand, and then felt some of his weight as he seemed to sag.

'You damned fool,' she said in a low voice. 'I thought you knew him.'

*　　*　　*

The forest had broken down in this place. It left skeletal trees rising from marsh grasses, and rotting logs blanketed in moss. Black water surrounded every hummock and the smaller islands were made from tufts of grass and reeds. The air smelled of decay and insects swarmed. They were camped upon the verge of this sunken land, brought up in

643

their flight from the south. A dozen fires smouldered, green grasses fed into the flames to fill the air with smoke and so drive back the biting insects. Narad sat near one of them, eyes watering.

They had been criminals marching in file, and he was the last of that line, the last to despoil this miserable congress of civility. The proclamation of his ugliness was smoke-stained, fly-bitten and filthy, and he felt at home in this place, barring the company he kept.

Others had joined them. From the west had come a company commanded by Captain Hallyd Bahann, and with him was a beautiful woman named Tathe Lorat and her daughter, Sheltatha Lore. Their soldiers brought tales of slaughter at a monastery and the pillaging of Abara Delack. And now, riding up from the south, another troop approached and with their sighting the squads around Narad stirred, collecting their weapons and donning their helms. At last, he heard, their captain had arrived.

There were many kinds of curiosity, Narad realized as he stood with the others and fixed his gaze on the riders. To see a face behind a name, if that name was wreathed in tales of heroism, was a clean kind of curiosity. But the face of a monster invited its own fascination, perhaps in the shock of recognition, since every face could be seen in one; or, more to the point, from that one face, it took little imagination to find one's own. Narad did not know which lure made him strain to see Captain Scara Bandaris, but he knew that a transformation awaited the man.

Since their flight from the slaughter at the wedding site, Narad had begun, with quick glances, to set upon the features of the soldiers around him the semblance of corpses. In his mind he looked upon his companions as if they were lying on the ground, all life gone, with faces frozen in death. Perhaps it was only a game, or perhaps it was a promise, or even a prayer. He wanted them all dead. He wanted to gaze down on the once-laughing eyes and see the look of men and women who no longer had anything to laugh about. He wanted to see the jest of fate, and would show each face he saw a smile they would never answer, and could never challenge.

At the head of his troop, Captain Scara Bandaris rode up, harshly reining in his lathered horse. Narad squinted up at the man's face, eager to set that lifeless mask upon it.

Instead, he saw nothing but blinding rage.

'By whose command?'

The soldiers who had begun gathering close to greet their captain suddenly recoiled.

Something bright, like a fire, ignited in Narad.

Scara Bandaris dismounted. He strode directly towards Sergeant Radas. 'Who is your commanding officer, sergeant? Tell me!'

'You are, sir.'

'And what orders did I leave you with?'

'We were to await you in the forest. But sir, Lieutenant Infayen Menand brought us orders from Captain Hunn Raal.'

Scara's face displayed incredulity. 'Hunn Raal ordered the Legion to murder Lord Jaen and his daughter? To take the lives of highborn gathered to celebrate a wedding? Hunn Raal ordered you to unleash your soldiers on Enesdia? To rape her and leave her to die on the hearthstone? The hearthstone that was a gift from Lord Anomander to his brother? May I see these orders, sergeant? May I see for myself the sigil of Hunn Raal?'

Radas had gone white. 'Sir, Lieutenant Infayen, who bore the word of Captain Hunn Raal, assumed command. I am a soldier of Urusander's Legion. I follow the orders of my superiors.'

'Where is Infayen now?'

'East, sir, to join Commander Urusander.'

Captain Hallyd Bahann approached, Tathe Lorat at his side and trailing behind them an old man with but one leg, who struggled as the sodden ground made uncertain purchase for his crutch. Narad had looked upon Hallyd before, and had found it easy to imagine his visage made lifeless, all arrogance stripped away. It had been a delicious vision. Hallyd Bahann was a bully and the proof of that was in his bearing and his swollen features. He was a man who would look his best when dead.

'Scara, old friend, welcome,' said Hallyd. 'There have been miscalculations, I think. We are agreed on that, you and me. The challenge before us now is to mitigate the damage to our cause.'

Scara was studying the man with level eyes. 'Our cause indeed, Hallyd,' he said in a suddenly calm voice. 'Do remind us, Hallyd, of that cause. I find myself in need of this noble list uttered aloud. Be logical in your assembly, and lift us all once more into the realms of virtue. But pray, old friend, begin at the bottom, there in the blood between a dead woman's legs.'

Hallyd's smile vanished.

Without awaiting a reply, Scara continued. 'Will you not carry us higher then, ignoring the stains as best you can, to a hostage slain defending that woman, cut down not in honourable contest, but as a wild dog staked to the ground? Then to an old man, a father and hero of the wars against the Forulkan, who died on the threshold of his son-in-law's house?' He spoke loudly, with weight, and that voice carried through the camp, pushed harsh against the silent soldiers. 'But wait. Let us add a new rung in this righteous climb to our cause. A maid, one arm severed and then cut down. A *maid*, venal benefactor of the inequity we so despise. And the Houseblades, barely armed, who laid for our cause a carpet of split flesh and matted grasses.' He raised his arms, like an orator set aflame with outrage. 'But here anew we see more signs of Hunn Raal's certain path to justice! The burnt corpses of Deniers in the forest! Why, those old wax witches grew fat at our expense, did they not? And the children showed improper pomp in the cut of their rags. Do speak to us, Hallyd Bahann, of our pure purpose. Tell me how a choice of faiths divides the realm we have sworn to defend, and do name your reasons for the side you set us on. Write your list in the columns of smoke behind me and stretch it across the heavens—'

'Cease your tirade!' snarled Tathe Lorat. 'There will only be justice for Urusander's Legion when we stand unopposed. We needed to strike first, Scara, and in a manner to divide our enemies that remain.'

He turned on her a sneer. 'Divide? Did anyone truly believe that scattering a few corpses of Deniers among the slain would win a false trail? Lord Jaen was a master with the blade, but even he could not match Cryl Durav. That man slain by Deniers? He fell to multiple thrusts, killed by trained soldiers who knew how to fight a blademaster. Do you all take Lord Anomander for a fool?'

'He is but one man,' said Hallyd Bahann, who had made use of the momentary inattention to regain his bluster. 'The plan was ill-conceived, but we all know how propriety is surrendered in the midst of bloodlust, Scara. It was regrettable, but there will be other crimes committed before this is done, by both sides, and you are a fool if you think otherwise.'

'Oh, I am a fool to be sure,' Scara replied. He returned to his horse and swung into the saddle. 'I am done with this,' he said. Twisting in his seat, he looked upon those soldiers who had accompanied him from Kharkanas. 'Stay here and fight with your comrades, if you will. I yield command and reject my commission in Urusander's Legion.'

Tathe Lorat laughed. 'Flee back to Sedis Hold, then, and take what-ever cowards would ride with you. Did I not warn you, Scara, against your friendship with Anomander's brother? Be sure that white-skinned freak is upon your trail now, with vengeance in his heart.' She shook her head. 'Stand aside, will you? That choice no longer exists, Scara. Not for anyone, and especially not for you.'

Narad saw a few of his companions gathering their gear, clearly intent on joining their now outlawed captain. He hesitated, and then began collecting his own kit.

Tathe Lorat then went on, raising her voice. 'And should Silchas Ruin not find you, then one day Urusander's Legion will. That I promise, and you all know what Commander Urusander does to deserters.'

More than half of the soldiers readying their gear stopped then, and Narad saw many setting their packs back down.

Scara Bandaris led his troop away from the camp, riding west to return to the river road. A thin line of additional soldiers fell in behind it. Narad was among them, and he saw, just ahead, Corporal Bursa. Sergeant Radas had remained behind, but he still had her face in his memory. It was dead, and never again would those lips twist, or make the shape of words. Never again would she say *'Still hanging limp, Waft?'* and never again would she rant on in the smoke and fire about all the wrongs done to her and her comrades in the Legion.

It was a dead face he saw, there in his mind, and when he drew back, to hover over her as would a gleeful ghost, he saw how she was sprawled on the stones, her legs spread wide, and blood pooling down there.

The vision should have made him recoil, but instead he felt nothing. *Not by my hand, sergeant.*

Scara Bandaris's words in the camp reverberated through him still. Their scorn comforted him. Their indignation carried the echoes of rightful condemnation, and if Narad himself stung to the lash, well, did he not deserve it?

A short time later, the captain drew up and he and his fellow riders waited for the newcomers. The road was at their backs, the river just beyond.

Scara said, 'We will rest here for a time. But not as long as I'd like. It may be best if you simply scattered, finding for yourself remote places in which to hide. I will wait in Sedis Hold, and if Silchas Ruin finds me, I will not fight him. I will, in truth, bow to one knee and await his sword upon my neck. By these words I have given you, I trust that you understand that it will not be safe for any of you, should you remain in my company.'

At that, a number of riders swung round to retrace their route.

The scene felt sordid, pathetic.

Then the captain's eyes fell upon Narad and the man frowned. 'You I do not know.'

'This then,' said Narad, 'is my only reason for hope.'

Corporal Bursa cleared his throat. 'We collected him up in the forest, sir.'

'You vouch for him, corporal?'

Narad felt his spirits plummet. He felt once more that woman lying under him, and heard the laughter making a ring around his clumsy motions, and how it rained down like stinging sleet.

Bursa said, 'He obeyed orders, sir, and was accepted as one of us.'

'Very well,' said Scara Bandaris, his gaze shifting away. 'The ascent to Sedis Gate is a long climb, and any who approach will be seen from half a day away, thus giving all of you time to flee into the north, on the Jheleck Trail. I am content to meet my fate alone.'

647

A soldier spoke. 'We would ride with you, sir.'

'Until Sedis Hold?'

'Yes sir.'

Scara Bandaris offered them all a wry, bitter smile. 'Fools delight in company, my friends.'

*    *    *

*'High Priestess, make of your worship an unflinching recognition of the unknown, and indeed, the unknowable. By devotion and acceptance of mystery, the chaos that haunts us all is made calm, until the sea itself becomes a mirror content with a placid reflection.'*

As the words of her goddess they marked scant scripture, and Emral Lanear felt lost as she sat in her private chamber. She had sent the priestesses away, and was alone with her blurred reflection, sitting so motionless in the mirror. As befitted any adherent, she had pledged her devotion in the frail hope of gifts in return, and while this notion, so crassly expressed, laid bare the one-sided bargaining that was faith, she was no longer in any mood for dissembling. All that was indistinct and imprecise could well remain in the mirror, where every smudge was a blessing, and she would leave it at that.

Still, this face she saw before her was no placid reflection.

There was no end to the irony, if what Anomander had said about Syntara was true. Youthful beauty could bear the revelation of light, while its ageing loss welcomed the darkness; and so these two High Priestesses were indeed well positioned, and if Emral knew bitterness at finding which side she inhabited, there was nothing to be done for it. At least the darkness was eternal in its disguising gifts. In the centuries to come, Syntara might well come to curse what her light revealed.

But now they stood opposite one another, poised to attend a clash neither side could truly win. *In the death of one, the meaning of the other is lost. Shall I add this truth to our modest scripture? Perhaps as a note upon the margin, less elegantly inscribed, a thing made in haste, or perhaps regret.*

If holy words could not offer up an answer to despair, then what good were they? If the truths so revealed did not invite restitution, then their utterance was no more than a curse. *And if the restitution is found not in the mortal realm, then we are invited to inaction, and indifference. Will you promise to a soul a reward buried in supposition? Are we to reach throughout our lives but never touch? Are we to dream and to hope, but never know?*

*'High Priestess, make of your worship an unflinching recognition of the unknown, and indeed, the unknowable.'*

Such devotion promised no reward. It made every stance abject and solitary. Revelation proclaimed a vacuum, where faith was doomed to flounder. *Then again, perhaps she intends by her prescription just such a revelation: that while we are light inside, there is nothing but darkness upon the outside.*

*Syntara, we face one another as enemies. But I wonder if even that is a profane conceit.*

Frowning, she drew out her writing materials. It was time, she decided, for overtures.

The sound of rushing feet and then a rapid knocking upon the door startled her. She rose and adjusted her robes. 'Enter.'

To her surprise, it was not a priestess who appeared, but the historian, Rise Herat.

'High Priestess, I beg you, accompany me.'

'Where?'

'To the courtyard,' he replied. 'A conjuration is under way.'

'A what?'

'Please,' he said. 'Emral, there is darkness there, impenetrable darkness, and . . .' he hesitated, 'High Priestess, this darkness *bleeds*.'

*     *     *

As they strode towards the front doors, Emral could hear faint screams, through which cut shouts as some sought to quell the panic in the courtyard. 'Historian,' she said, 'this may well be Mother Dark's sorcery, and so nothing anyone need fear.'

'Your arrival and subsequent comportment might well invite that thought, High Priestess,' Rise replied, 'which is why I sought you out.'

'But you do not believe it belongs to Mother Dark, do you?'

He glanced at her, his lined face pale. 'As I arrived at your door, I admit, I longed for a calming response from you at the news I delivered.'

'But in its absence?'

He shook his head.

They arrived outside. Figures had retreated from the manifestation, which dominated the centre of the courtyard, and from the entrance to the Citadel the gates themselves were no longer visible, blighted by the immense darkness. The stain filled the air, black and roiling, with tendrils spilling down to writhe like tentacles upon the cobbles. As Emral stared, she saw it grow larger, bleeding out to hide the gate's towers, and the platforms where stood transfixed Houseblades.

The clamour of voices had begun to die away, and Emral's outwardly calm appearance seemed to seal the silence.

The emanation itself made no sound, but cold drifted out from it – the same cold as was found in the Chamber of Night. Emral stared, wondering if indeed Mother Dark had begun this conjuration. But for what purpose?

In that moment, when doubts crowded her, a mounted figure rode

649

out from the darkness, arriving at a canter. The huge, armoured man drew hard on the reins of his warhorse, and sparks danced out from the beast's hoofs. He halted directly before Emral Lanear and Rise Herat.

She struggled to breathe for a moment. The emanation was fast dwindling behind the rider.

At her side, the historian bowed. 'Consort,' he said, 'welcome back.'

Lord Draconus dismounted. Cold drifted from his shoulders, and there was frost glistening on his riding boots, and his armour. He drew off his gauntlets. 'High Priestess,' he said, 'I need you.'

'Consort?'

He gestured to the building behind her. 'She knows I have returned. I promised her a gift, and for that, you must attend me.'

'In what manner?' she asked.

'As the First Daughter of Night.'

'I hold no such title.'

He approached. 'You do now,' he said, moving past her and entering the Citadel. Emral followed, trailed by Rise Herat.

Lord Draconus strode into the Grand Hall, and halted in the centre of the vast chamber. 'Clear the hall!' he commanded.

The quiet, brooding man Emral had known before now stood as if transformed. The power around him was palpable. His heavy gaze found her. 'High Priestess, seek the emptiness within you. Surrender the will of your eyes to Mother Dark, so that she may witness my gift.'

'Consort, I know not how to do that.'

'Only because you have never tried. Look well upon me now, and within your soul, kick open the door of faith.'

All at once, Emral felt a presence flow into her body, shifting as if finding itself in ill-fitting flesh, and as she looked upon Lord Draconus there was a sudden surge of discordant emotions. She felt Mother Dark's pleasure at seeing her lover again, and her relief, and in the midst of that, there was profound trepidation. Emral struggled to give herself over to her goddess, so that Mother Dark might speak through her, but something defied her efforts. She felt Mother Dark's desire to address Draconus, blunt and heavy as a fist, pounding upon some inner door – a door that remained locked – and as her goddess pushed against it from one side, so too Emral pulled against it from the other. Their efforts failed, leaving to Mother Dark only the vision of her Consort.

He had thrown off his cloak now, and there was something in his hands, cupped like a precious flower, but all that Emral – and Mother Dark – could see was what looked like a fragment of forest floor, a flattened layer of humus. Draconus looked into Emral Lanear's eyes, and then spoke. 'Beloved, in this gift, I offer you the consecration of this Citadel, and so make of it a temple in truth. You have embraced the Night, yet hold but a modest fragment of its power.' He paused, and then said, 'There is a war of forces here, waged in the stone walls, the stone floor. It seems my return was timely indeed. By this gift, all challenge is banished from this place. I give to you, and to all the Children of Night, this Terondai.'

With these words, he let fall the object in his hands.

It landed softly, like folded parchment, and for a moment sat motionless upon the tiled floor. And then it began to unfold, sending out angled projections upon the surface of the tiles, and these projections were black as onyx, and the pattern they formed seemed to sink into the worn marble, indelibly staining it.

Emral felt a growing horror within her, coming from Mother Dark.

The pattern continued to unfold, spreading across the entire floor. It bore twenty-eight arms, like the points of a black star. In the centre was a multi-angled circle. Draconus stood within it. The expression on his face was one of pride, yet there was something fragile in his eyes. 'Beloved,' he said, 'from the lands of the Azathanai, I returned to you upon the Road of Night. I rode through the realm of Darkness.' He gestured to the pattern, which now spanned the entire chamber. 'You need reach no longer, beloved. I have brought Night here and offer you, once more, its perfect embrace. It is a gift borne on love. By what other means do we consecrate?'

Emral could feel her goddess, a presence recoiling in fear.

'Beloved,' said Draconus, 'I give you the Gate of Kurald Galain.'

The pattern ignited. Darkness blossomed.

And the goddess fled.

*     *     *

In the Chamber of Night, Grizzin Farl stood before Mother Dark, watching as she grew ever more insubstantial. The unfolding of Night was fast encompassing the Citadel, pouring out from the Terondai to take every room, spreading like blight down every corridor. It swallowed the light from lamps, candles and lanterns. It stole the brightness from flames and embers in every hearth.

He felt it when the darkness spilled out past the walls of the Citadel, rushed like a flood across the courtyard. When it flowed down to the surface of the river, Grizzin winced at the shock that trembled through the water, and he heard in his mind the wretched howl of the river god as the darkness broke the barrier and rushed down into the depths. That howl became a death-cry, and then it was gone. And the river flowed with Night.

The darkness spread rapidly through all of Kharkanas.

'You wondered at my presence here,' he said to the goddess seated on her throne. 'You wondered at my role. I could not let you speak. The silence needed . . . protecting. Forgive me.' He then raised a hand towards her. 'You will recover,' he said. 'You will find the strength to resist its pull. That strength will come from worship, and from love. But most of all, it will come from the balance that awaits us all. Alas, the achievement of such balance, so long overdue, will be difficult.'

'What balance?' she asked, her voice left hoarse by the denials she had screamed, the helpless cries against what her lover was doing; against what he had done.

'All forces are arrayed in opposition, Mother Dark. It is this tension that weaves the threads of existence. Even the Abyss stands, and exists, in answer to something – to us. To you, me, and every other sentient creature upon this and every other realm. Will I speak of gods, then, and their dominion over lesser beings? I will not. Such hierarchy signifies little. We must all stand upon this side of the Abyss, and make what we can of words and dreams, of desires and ambitions. The gods are only elevated in the boldness of their arguments.'

'The river god is slain.' She brought her hands up to cover her face.

'An argument lost,' Grizzin Farl replied. 'And yes, I do grieve.'

Behind her hands she asked, 'What will come of the Deniers?'

'I cannot say, Mother. Perhaps they will walk the shore, in eternal longing for the world they have lost.'

Mother Dark visibly trembled, and then slowly lowered her hands. They stole out along the arms of the throne to grip the elegantly curved ends. She drew a deep breath. 'And now?'

'Lord Draconus brought to you his gift, his power. He is the first Azathanai to have done this solely for those who dwell in his domain.' Grizzin Farl hesitated, and then said, 'I did not know that your children were ignorant of your Consort's true nature.'

Her eyes went flat. 'Mothers have secrets.'

After a long moment, he nodded. 'Do not blame Draconus. All that comes was begun by another Azathanai.' Then he shook his head. 'My apologies. I dissemble. We all have had a hand in this. The one you name T'riss, who walked into, and then out of, the Sea of Vitr. My own children . . . but most of all, this belongs to K'rul, who answered worship with generosity. Who, assailed by prayers written in spilled blood, gave answer to them. But the power he surrendered was not intended only for those who worshipped him. He has given it freely, to everyone. By this, new sorceries are born, Mother Dark. By this, the forces in opposition are given names, and aspects. They are given realms of influence. A storm awaits us all, Mother Dark. To save you . . . to save your children who worship you, Draconus has done only what was necessary. The Gate of Kurald Galain now belongs to you, and over Night you now have dominion.'

'And my lover will just step aside?' There was venom in that question.

652

'The giving of gifts is a fraught enterprise, Mother Dark. I am sure I was not alone in warning him. Stem this tide of fury in your heart, I beg you. He has done what he has done out of love.'

'As did this K'rul, too, surely.'

Grizzin Farl nodded.

'And what has it cost him, Azathanai?'

'The tale of that is not yet complete, Mother.'

'Then the blood still flows.'

Grizzin Farl started, and then he sighed. 'A most apt description.'

'He comes to me now. Will you remain to witness our reunion?'

'Mother Dark, I fear there is nothing left here to protect.'

Her gesture of dismissal was perfunctory. Grizzin Farl bowed, and then strode from the Chamber of Night.

Outside the chamber he paused in the corridor. *I forgot to warn her. With the birth of one gate, there will be others.*

*      *      *

Their horses labouring in the acidic air, Spinnock Durav and his commander rode down to the shores of the Sea of Vitr. They had heard a thunderous reverberation, as of the air itself splitting open, and hastily saddling their mounts they had left the camp among the boulders well above the shoreline, and ridden out to discover the source of that terrible sound.

For three days, Spinnock and the others in the troop had explored the strand, moving among scores of dead and dying monstrosities, no two alike. If born of the Vitr, each had been nurtured on foul milk, and the sea in which they found their home had set upon them with frenzied hunger. The creatures crawled free of the silver waters torn apart, bleeding, their flanks hanging loose, bones exposed and many ruptured by unbearable pressures. Even then, they took a long time to die.

The horror of these births assailed the Wardens. There was no sense to be made of this failed invasion, and for all the violence borne in the arrival of the demons, nothing but pity could attend their death throes. As Calat Hustain had observed only the day before, any entity, beast or otherwise, could not but lash out in the midst of such agony.

They knew well to keep their distance, and the veracity of Finarra Stone's report was evinced time and again, when creatures little more than exploded carcasses somehow found the strength to thrash and fight on, seeking to drag themselves out from the Vitr.

This horror was a weight upon the Wardens, and Spinnock Durav felt a dulling of the pleasures he took in life. Each morning he awoke enervated, feeling helpless, and dreading the next journey down to the shoreline.

As the thunderclap seemed to shiver on through the caustic air, they rode clear of the final boulders above the strand, and could see at last the source of that event.

A wall of fire hovered in the air above the Sea of Vitr, as if a new sun had been born. Yet it was not so bright as to blind them. The flames writhing about its edge seemed to erupt, flying outward in strands and threads, like molten gold escaping the edge of a spinning wheel. These fires vanished like sparks, and none curved in flight or arced downward to the surface of the silver sea.

The emanation was stationary, hovering in the sky. It was difficult to determine its size, but the reflection it cast upon the sea was immense.

The troop reined in on the strand, forming a row. Their horses trembled under them, and glancing to his right and left Spinnock was struck by the audacity of this conceit: that he and his fellow Wardens – that the Tiste of Kurald Galain and even Mother Dark – could somehow stand firm against such forces of nature.

A sudden conviction took hold in him: this sea would never be defeated. It would continue to grow, devouring land as it did behemoths, poisoning the air, stealing the life from all that it touched. Sorcery would fail against it, and will alone proved frail defiance.

'There are shapes within it!' one of the Wardens cried.

Spinnock looked back up at the blazing conjuration.

The air cracked anew, with a force that staggered the horses and flung men and women from their saddles. Spinnock managed to remain mounted, fighting to keep his balance. A rush of sweet wind rushed out, lashing across the surface of the Vitr, revealing at last something of the distance out from the shoreline of this raging sun. The power of that gale, as it poured out from the emanation, lifted waves upon the sea.

It seemed that Spinnock was the first to comprehend the portent of that. 'We must flee!' he shouted. 'Commander! We must retreat!'

He saw Calat Hustain, who had also managed to remain on his horse, swing round to stare at him, and then the commander began shouting. 'Withdraw! Hurry!'

The horses that had unseated their riders had already fled the onslaught. Those Wardens now on foot were quickly gathered up by their comrades. The beasts were shrilling in terror, and the surface of the strand itself was shivering.

A third eruption sounded.

Spinnock glanced back.

*Abyss take me. Abyss take us all!*

Dragons emerged from the emanation, wings outstretched, their tails scything the air in their wake. One after another, Eleint were rushing out to lift on the air, like birds freed from a cage. Faintly, through the howling wind, came their piercing cries.

Upon the sea, a succession of monumental waves advanced towards the shore.

There was no need for further exhortations from Calat Hustain. The troop rode up from the strand in frantic retreat. Even the boulders did not seem proof to what was coming.

Plunging into the rotted tumble of crags and rock, Spinnock left his mount to find its own way. A massive shadow swept over him and he looked up to see the belly and translucent wings of a dragon sailing above them. The Eleint's long neck curled and the head came into view, almost upside down as the creature flew on, and Spinnock saw how its eyes seemed to blaze as they looked down on him. Then that wedge-shaped head tilted, as the beast scanned the other riders who were just breaking clear of the boulders and beginning to cross the dead ground, towards the black grasses of Glimmer Fate.

The dragon's talons spread wide, and then closed again.

Moments later, with savage beats of its wings, the creature lifted higher into the sky. One of its companions swung close and then, as the first dragon's jaws snapped the air in warning, away again.

A rider came alongside Spinnock, and he saw that it was Sergeant Bered. He shot Spinnock a wide-eyed look. 'Nine!' he shouted.

'What?'

'Nine of them! And then it closed!'

Spinnock twisted round, but at that moment his horse reached the high grasses and plunged into the mouth of the nearest trail. The tall, razor-edged stalks whipped and slashed at him. Spinnock was forced to drop his visor and keep his head down as his mount galloped deeper into the Fate.

The ground shook to a succession of concussions, and the wind redoubled, flattening the grasses on all sides.

Glancing back, he saw the first and largest of the waves pounding over the boulders, knocking many aside as if they were but pebbles.

The silver walls rushed across the dead ground, and struck the edge of the grasses.

A flash lit the air, blinding him. He heard shouts and then screams, and then his horse was tumbling, and he was spinning through the air, landing hard on the flattened mat of the grasses. Skidding, feeling countless blades slicing through his leather armour as if they were sharp iron, Spinnock kept his forearms against his face. He rolled and came to a stop.

He was facing the way he had come, and he stared in disbelief.

The Vitr thrashed against an invisible wall, delineated by the edge of Glimmer Fate, and there the silver water climbed and lunged, only to be flung back. Wave after wave hammered against this unseen barrier, and each spent its power in raging futility. In moments the sea began its foaming, churning retreat.

Spinnock sat up, surprised that no bones had broken. But he was slick with blood. He saw his horse stagger upright a dozen paces away, to stand trembling and streaming red from its wounds. On either side other Wardens were appearing, stumbling over the flattened grasses. He saw Calat Hustain, cradling an arm that was clearly broken between shoulder and elbow, his face cut open as if by talons.

Dazed, Spinnock looked skyward. He saw a distant spot, far to the south now, marking the last dragon visible in the sky.

*Nine. He counted nine.*

*       *       *

Hearing a horse upon the road behind him, Endest Silann moved to the shallow ditch to let the rider past. He drew his cloak tighter about him and pulled up the hood to send a veil of shadow over his eyes. Three days past, he had awakened alone in the historian's room to find his hands bound with bandages, to take up the blood that had wept from them.

There had been a faint sense of betrayal in this, given Rise Herat's promise to abide, but upon leaving the chamber and finding himself in a corridor crowded with half-panicked denizens, and learning of the frightening manifestation of darkness in the courtyard, Endest pushed away his disappointment.

The Consort's dramatic return had reverberated throughout the Citadel, and it seemed that the conjurations of that day were far from done. He had felt Night's awakening, and then had fled, like a child, the flood of darkness that took first the Citadel, and then all of Kharkanas.

Carrying nothing, he had set out upon the river road, sleeping in whatever remaining hovels he could find amidst the grim wreckage of the pogrom. He saw no one for long stretches at a time, and those he did come upon shied from his attention. Nor was he inclined to accost any of them, hungry as he was. They had the furtiveness of wild dogs and looked half starved themselves. It was difficult to comprehend how quickly Kurald Galain had surrendered to dissolution. Time and again, as he walked, he had felt tears streaming down his cheeks.

The bandages still wrapped about his hands had become filthy, freshly soaked through with blood each night, drying black in the course of the day. But he now walked clear of the sorcerous darkness, and still as the forest was, with its burnt stretches and scorched clearings, he had found a kind of exhausted peace in his solitude. The river upon his left marked a current that he felt himself pushing against on this road. He had begun this journey knowing nothing of his destination, but he had realized that that ignorance had been a conceit.

There was but one place for him now, and he was drawing ever closer to it.

The rider came up from behind and Endest heard the animal's pace slowing, until the stranger appeared alongside him. Endest desired no conversation and cared nothing for the rider's identity, but when the newcomer spoke it was in a voice that the priest knew well.

'If we are to adopt the habit of pilgrimage, surely you are walking the wrong way.'

Endest halted and faced the man. He bowed. 'Milord, I cannot say if this path belongs to the goddess. But it seems that I am indeed on pilgrimage, though until you spoke I knew it not.'

'You are weathered by your journey, priest,' said Lord Anomander.

'If I fast, milord, it is not by choice.'

'I'll not impede your journey,' Anomander said. He reached down and drew out from a saddle bag a leather satchel, which he threw over to Endest. 'Break your fast, priest. You can do so while you walk.'

'Thank you, milord.' In the satchel, there was some bread, cheese and dried meat. Endest partook of this modest offering with trembling fingers.

It seemed Anomander was content, for the moment, to keep pace with Endest. 'I have scoured this forest,' he said, 'and have found nothing to salve my conscience. No birdsong finds me, and not even the small animals spared by our indifference remain to rustle the leaves at night.'

'The meek of the realm, milord, have but one recourse to all manner of threat, and that is to flee.'

Anomander grunted, and then said, 'I'd not thought to include the forest animals, or the birds for that matter, as subjects of the realm. It is not as if we can command them.'

'But their small lives, milord, tremble atop our altars none the less. If we do not command with the snare and the arrow, then we speak eloquently enough with fire and smoke.'

'Will you lift back your hood, priest, so that I may see you?'

'Forgive me, milord, but I beg your indulgence. I do not know if penance awaits me, but this journey is a difficult one, and I would not share it for fear of selfish motives.'

'You choose, then, to walk alone, and to remain unknown.' Lord Anomander sighed. 'I envy your privilege, priest. Do you know your destination?'

'I believe I do, milord.'

'Upon this road?'

'Just off it.'

Something changed in the First Son's voice then, as he said, 'And not far, priest?'

'Not far, milord.'

'If I made a spiral of my search,' said Anomander, 'I now close upon a place where I believe it ends. I think, priest, that we will attend the same altar. Will you make of it a shrine?'

Endest started at the notion. He fumbled to close the satchel, and then made his way over to Anomander to hand the leather bag back. 'Such a thing had not occurred to me, milord.'

'Your hands are wounded?'

'No more than my soul, milord.'

'You are young. An acolyte?'

'Yes.' Bowing his thanks for the food, Endest returned to the side of the road.

They continued on in silence for a time. Ahead, the track leading to the estate of Andarist appeared, flanked by burnt grasses and the skeletal remnant of a fire-scorched tree.

'I do not think,' said Anomander, 'that I would welcome a consecration in that place, acolyte, even could you give it. Which you cannot. The only holy object in the ruin before us is an Azathanai hearthstone, and I fear to come upon it now, and see it broken.'

'Broken, milord?'

'I also fear,' Anomander continued, 'that my brother is not there, when I can think of no other refuge he might seek. I was told he chose the wilderness for his grief, and can think of no greater wilderness than the house where his love died.'

Endest hesitated, and then drew a deep breath. They were but a dozen paces from the track. 'Lord Anomander,' he said, halting but keeping his head down. 'Mother Dark has blessed her.'

'Her? Who?'

'The maiden, Enesdia of House Enes, milord. In the eyes of our goddess, that child is now a High Priestess.'

Anomander's voice was suddenly hard as iron. 'She has blessed a corpse?'

'Milord, may I ask, where were her remains buried?'

'Beneath the stones of the floor, priest, upon the threshold to the house. My brother insisted and would have torn those stones from the ground with his bare hands, if we had not restrained him. Regrettably, there was some haste in that excavation. Her father lies beneath the ground at the entrance, and at his side is the body of the hostage, Cryl Durav. The Houseblades lie encircling the house. Priest, Mother Dark has never made claim to the souls of the dead.'

'I cannot say, milord, that she does so now.'

'What has brought you here?'

'Visions,' Endest said. 'Dreams.' He then lifted his hands. 'I – I bear her blood.'

To utter those words was to unleash the torment within Endest, and with a cry he fell to his knees. Anguish rushed through him in waves black as midnight, and he heard his own voice emerging, broken and torn.

And then Lord Anomander was beside him, kneeling to draw an arm around him. When he spoke it seemed that it was not to the priest. 'Why does she do this? How many wounds will she make us carry? I'll not have it. Mother, if you would so share your guilt, look only to me. I will take it upon myself, and know it as familiar company. Instead, you make all your children carry the burden of your legacy.' He barked a harsh laugh. 'And what a wretched family we are.'

Then he was helping Endest to his feet. 'Give me your weight, priest. We take these last steps together, then. Set hands upon the blank stones that mark her grave, and leave the stain of her blood. High Priestess she will be. Mother knows, she was used as one.'

The bitterness of those last words reached through to Endest, and perversely he took from it strength and renewed fortitude.

Together and on foot, lord and priest made their way up the track.

Through blurred eyes, Endest saw the half-ring of low mounds of freshly turned earth. He saw the front of the house, its doorway still bereft of a door. He saw the larger mound that marked the barrows of Lord Jaen and Cryl Durav. He had seen it all before, in his dreams. They drew closer, neither speaking.

Blood flowed anew from Endest's hands, dripping steadily now as they came to the entrance to the house.

Lord Anomander paused. 'Someone waits within.'

The stones of the floor just within the entrance were tilted, uneven now, and stained here and there with dirt, many of them in the patterns of handprints. Seeing this, Endest halted once more. 'In my dreams,' he said, 'she is still dying.'

'I fear the truth of that is in us all, priest,' said Anomander. Then he moved past and stepped within. 'Andarist? I come to set aside vengeance—'

But the figure that rose from its seat upon the hearthstone, in the heavy gloom of the unlit chamber, was not Andarist. This man was huge, with fur upon his shoulders.

Endest stood, watching, the blood from his hands dripping down on to the stones of Enesdia's grave, and Lord Anomander strode forward to stand before the stranger.

'The hearthstone?' the First Son asked.

'Beleaguered,' the man replied in a deep voice. 'Trust is strained, and the stains of blood cannot be washed from all that has befallen this place.'

Lord Anomander seemed at a loss. 'Then . . . why have you come?'

'We are bound, First Son. I have been awaiting you.'

'Why?'

'To defend my gift.'

'Defend? From me? I will not breach this trust – for all that Andarist now denies me. I will find him. I will make this right.'

'I fear you cannot, Anomander. But I know this: you will try.'

'Then stand here, Azathanai, until the death of the last day! Defend this mockery of blessing so perfectly shaped by your hands!'

'We are bound,' the Azathanai said again, unperturbed by Anomander's outburst. 'In your journey now, you will find me at your side.'

'I wish it not.'

The huge figure shrugged. 'Already we share something.'

Anomander shook his head. 'You are no friend, Caladan Brood. Nor will you ever be. I cannot even be certain that your gift was not the curse at the heart of all that has happened here.'

'Nor can I, Anomander. Another thing we share.'

The First Son set a hand upon his sword's grip.

But the Azathanai shook his head. 'This is not the time, Anomander, to draw that weapon in this place. I see behind you a priest. I see in his hands the power of Mother Dark, and the blood she now bleeds, and so the bargain of faith is made.'

'I do not understand—'

'Lord Anomander, she has now the power of an Azathanai. This power is born of blood, and in the birth of a god, or goddess, it is that entity that must first surrender it. And you who are to be her children, you will surrender your own in answer. And by this, Darkness is forged.'

But Anomander backed away. 'I made no such bargain,' he said.

'Faith cares nothing for bargains, First Son.'

'She has left me nothing!'

'She has left you alone. Make of your freedom what you will, Anomander. Do with it what you must.'

'I would end this civil war!'

'Then end it.' Caladan Brood stepped forward. 'If you ask, Lord Anomander, I will show you how.'

Anomander visibly hesitated. He glanced back at Endest, but the priest quickly looked down, and saw the grave stones crimson beneath him. He felt suddenly weak and sank down to his knees, sliding upon the tilted cairn.

He then heard, as if from a great distance, Lord Anomander speaking. 'Caladan, if I ask this of you, that you show me how . . . will there be peace?'

And the Azathanai answered, 'There will be peace.'

*　　*　　*

Arathan stood at the window of the highest tower next to the one named the Tower of Hate. The morning sun's light swept in around him, filled him with heat.

Behind him, he heard Korya sit up on the bed. 'What is it?' she asked.

'I am sorry,' he said, 'to have so disturbed your sleep.'

She grunted. 'This is a first, Arathan. A young man rushing into my chambers without even a scratch at the door, but does he take note of my naked self? He does not. Instead, he rushes to the window and there he stands.'

He glanced back at her.

'What lies beyond?' she asked. 'The view is nothing but a vast plain and the hovels of fallen towers. Look at us,' she added, rising from the bed with the blankets wrapped about her slim form, 'we dwell in a wasteland with miserable Jaghut for company, and on all sides the view is bleak. Do you not even find me attractive?'

He studied her. 'I find you very attractive,' he said. 'But I do not trust you. Please, that was not meant to offend.'

'Really? You have a lot to learn.'

He turned back to the window.

'What so fascinates you with that view?' she asked.

'When Gothos woke me this morning, it was with mysterious words.'

'Nothing new there, surely?'

Arathan shrugged. 'The mystery is answered.'

He heard her move across the room, and then she came up alongside him. Looking out upon the plain, she gasped.

After a long moment, she said, 'What did the Lord of Hate say to you, Arathan?'

'"He is such a fool I fear my heart will burst."'

'Just that?'

Arathan nodded.

'Haut tells me . . . there is a gate now.'

'A way into the realm of the dead, yes. Hood means to take it.'

'To wage his impossible war.' Then she sighed. 'Oh, Arathan, how can the heart not break at seeing this?'

They stood side by side, looking down upon a plain where thousands had gathered, in answer to Hood's call. *No, not thousands. Tens of thousands. Jaghut, Thel Akai, Dog-Runners . . . lost souls, grieving souls, one and all. And still more come.*

*Oh, Hood, did you know? Could you have even imagined such an answer?*

'And Gothos said nothing more?'

Arathan shook his head. *But when I found him again, seated in his chair, I saw that he wept. Children come easy to tears. But the tears of an old man are different. They can break a child's world like no other thing can. And this morning, I am a child again.* 'No,' he replied. 'Nothing.'

*　　*　　*

*I did not walk among them, Fisher kel Tath. Would that I had. He raised a banner of grief, and this detail waves my intent, but Lord Anomander, at this juncture, was not ready to see it. They were too far away. They were caught in their own lives. Too much and too fierce the necessities hounding them.*

*But think on this. Beneath such a banner, there is no end to those drawn to it, not from the weight of failure, but from the curse of surviving. Against death itself, the only legion who make of it an enemy belongs to the living.*

*Behold this army. It is doomed.*

*Still, even a blind man, in this moment, could not but see the shine in your eyes, my friend. You blaze with the poet's heat, as you imagine this assembly, so silent and so determined, so hopeless and so . . . brilliant.*

*Let us rest for now in this tale.*

*Time enough, I say, for two old men to weep.*

# ABOUT THE AUTHOR

Archaeologist and anthropologist **Steven Erikson**'s debut fantasy, *Gardens of the Moon*, was shortlisted for the World Fantasy Award and introduced readers to his bestselling ten-book sequence 'The Malazan Book of the Fallen', which has been hailed as one of the finest works of fantasy of our time. Steve lived in the UK for a number of years – most recently in Cornwall – before returning to Canada in the summer of 2012. To find out more, visit **www.malazanempire.com** and **www.stevenerikson.com**.